DAZZLING PRAISE FOR LAURIE R. KING'S

THE GAME

"AS DRY, SPARKLING AND DELIGHTFUL AS GOOD CHAMPAGNE." —*Washington Times*

"Of the many fine writers currently adding to the canon of stories about [Holmes], the nimblest is Laurie R. King....SPLENDID FUN, perhaps the rippingest of all of Russell's ripping tales." —*Seattle Times*

"Excellent...King cleverly uses her own erudition to set up the action...[and she] never forgets the true spirit of Arthur Conan Doyle....*The Game* distills the essence of the decline of the British Raj into one EXTREMELY EXCITING volume." —*Chicago Tribune*

"Vibrant local color, described by Russell in the droll tongue of a woman with the wit to realize that, while she may be dirty and tired and in constant danger, she is having the time of her life!" —*New York Times Book Review*

"A good mystery seriously spiked with adventure...KING'S TALENT FOR HISTORICAL RESEARCH SHINES EXTRAORDINARILY BRIGHT....A feast fit for a raja, *The Game* is an engrossing tale told by a master storyteller." —*Santa Cruz Sentinel*

"A ROUSING adventure story made credible by the sheer force of its characters' personalities and the sharply realized details of their surroundings. Good historical fiction is as close as we'll ever get to time travel, and historical fiction doesn't get any better than this. Nor do literary pastiches, which, at their best, like this one, take on a life of their own." —*Denver Post*

"Witty…The charm of the book…derives from King's skill at description—HER INDIA IS AS ALIVE AS E. M. FORSTER'S OR GEORGE MACDONALD FRASER'S." —*San Jose Mercury News*

"Imaginative…DAZZLING. Lush, colorful and utterly compelling, this is a superbly wrought novel of suspense that evokes its period with enviable panache. FOUR STARS OUT OF FOUR STARS." —*Detroit Free Press*

"A creative, unique, and thoroughly believable series…A briskly paced story that is steeped in history, literature and an original take on well-known characters…A tightly woven, action-packed plot…A fresh continuing of a character who has transcended generations."
—*Fort Lauderdale Sun-Sentinel*

"May well be the best King has yet devised for her strong-willed heroine…the sights, smells and ideas of India make interesting, evocative reading….ALL READERS WILL APPRECIATE THE GRACE AND INTELLIGENCE OF KING'S WRITING IN THIS EXOTIC MASALA OF A BOOK."
—*Publishers Weekly* (starred review)

"A wondrously taut mystery, ticking away like a malevolent clock...Fabulous reading, breathless excitement, and the myriad pleasures of watching great minds at work." —*Booklist* (starred review)

"DELIGHTFUL...King's intense descriptions will make readers feel as if they, too, are on a vital mission in India. Riveting from start to finish." —*Library Journal*

"The descriptions of the country and the lifestyle of the maharaja alone make this worth the read. King's entire Mary Russell series IS A TREAT." —*Daily American*

"When it comes to compelling and erudite suspense, leavened with character, humor and insight, King is among the very best writers working today."
—*Grand Rapids Press*

"Reading Laurie King is much like eating dark chocolate. The writing is RICH AND FULL, AND FULL OF SURPRISES. The characters come alive, as does the country of India....Very polished and entertaining." —*Deadly Pleasures*

"Political intrigue, exotic settings and historical fact add intriguing layers to the mystery at the heart of the book."
—*Monterey County Herald*

"RICH IN MAGIC, MYSTERY AND INTRIGUE, *The Game* is A TANTALIZINGLY CLEVER STORY." —Bookreporter.com

"The mystery…broadens and deepens as the tension rises until all WWI seems to come under indictment….Most accomplished." —*Kirkus Reviews*

"All the classic ingredients embellished with King's unique twists." —*Booknews* from The Poisoned Pen

"Exquisite…The accretion of detail mesmerizes….Russell really shines here." —*Upfront*

"King once again creates intriguing and believable characters….Formidable…compelling and well-written." —*Library Journal*

"A wonderfully involved book…thoroughly entertaining." —*Mystery Lovers Bookshop News*

"A rich, multi-textured tale that is as much a historical mystery as it is a parable of the human condition…A must for Holmes fans." —*Midwest Book Review*

"A fine mystery." —*Booked and Printed*

"In this latest installment of the series featuring Mary Russell and Sherlock Holmes, King has written the consummate English country house mystery. This is Laurie King writing at her considerable best, which means this is definitely one of the finest crime novels of this, or any, year." —Dean James, *Murder by the Book*, Houston, TX

"King created the perfect partner for fiction's greatest detective. This isn't second-rate Conan Doyle; it's first-rate Laurie King." —*Grand Rapids Press*

O JERUSALEM

"*O Jerusalem* returns to the fascinating, shadowy, psychological terrain of [Holmes and Russell's] courtship....[King has] stepped onto the sacred literary preserve of Sir Arthur Conan Doyle, poached Holmes, and brilliantly brought him to life again....*O Jerusalem* is a standout." —*Washington Post Book World*

"[Mary Russell is] a worthy foil for the great, if sometimes insufferably arrogant, Sherlock Holmes....A robust, intelligent adventure story." —*Cleveland Plain Dealer*

"Inspired...King puts us into each scene so quickly and completely that her narrative flow never falters."
—*Chicago Tribune*

"King's considerable talent makes history virtually leap off the page....Readers can't lose." —*Booklist*

"King's impeccable research combines with her colorful, fully drawn characters to make this another memorable addition to a strong series."
—*Ellery Queen Mystery Magazine*

"The portrait of the region and of Jerusalem is irresistible....Part spy story, part murder mystery...and part thriller moving to an explosive climax."
—*Booknews* from The Poisoned Pen

"Vivid...a satisfying and dramatic conclusion."
—*Library Journal*

"All the ingenuity of Holmes' creator, and [with] a layer of political sophistication that Arthur Conan Doyle might have fought shy of. A sterling addition to the Holmes library that really deserves a place on any crime lover's shelves." —*Crime Time*

THE MOOR

"There's no resisting the appeal of King's thrillingly moody scenes of Dartmoor and her lovely evocations of its legends." —*New York Times Book Review*

"Erudite, fascinating...by all odds the most successful re-creation of the famous inhabitant of 221B Baker Street ever attempted." —*Houston Chronicle*

"King has the tone, mood, and voice precisely right....Very good—as satisfying at this time of year as a truly rich fruitcake." —*Boston Globe*

A LETTER OF MARY

"A lively adventure in the very best of intellectual company." —*New York Times Book Review*

"The great marvel of King's series is that she's managed to preserve the integrity of Holmes's character and yet somehow conjure up a woman astute, edgy and compelling enough to be the partner of his mind as well as his heart....Superb."
—*Washington Post Book World*

"Suspenseful...Laurie R. King takes on England and literature's most famous detective with masterful aplomb. I loved it." —Elizabeth George

"An intellectual puzzler, full of bright red herrings and dazzling asides." —*Chicago Tribune*

A MONSTROUS REGIMENT OF WOMEN

"As audacious as it is entertaining and moving." —*Chicago Tribune*

"Beguiling…tantalizing." —*Boston Globe*

"One of the year's best…Enormously appealing…Rich in atmosphere and a plot that will keep the reader breathing hard." —*Mostly Murder*

THE BEEKEEPER'S APPRENTICE

Editor's Choice of 1994, *Drood Review of Mystery*

"Wonderful: an intelligently and imaginatively crafted novel that's also great fun." —*Drood Review of Mystery*

"Rousing…riveting…suspenseful." —*Chicago Sun-Times*

"Remarkably beguiling." —*Boston Globe*

"Worthy and welcome, with the power to charm the most grizzled Baker Street Irregular." —*New York Daily News*

The Novels of Laurie R. King

A DARKER PLACE

FOLLY

KEEPING WATCH

Mary Russell Mysteries

THE BEEKEEPER'S APPRENTICE

A MONSTROUS REGIMENT OF WOMEN

A LETTER OF MARY

THE MOOR

O JERUSALEM

JUSTICE HALL

THE GAME

and coming soon in hardcover
LOCKED ROOMS

Kate Martinelli Mysteries

A GRAVE TALENT

TO PLAY THE FOOL

WITH CHILD

NIGHT WORK

THE
GAME

*A Mary Russell
Novel*

Laurie R. King

THE GAME
A Bantam Book

PUBLISHING HISTORY
Bantam hardcover edition published March 2004
Bantam mass market edition / March 2005

Published by
Bantam Dell
A Division of Random House, Inc.
New York, New York

Library of Congress Catalog Card Number: 2003055684

ISBN 0-553-58338-7

Printed in the United States of America
Published simultaneously in Canada
OPM   10   9   8   7   6   5   4

For the librarians everywhere,
who spend their lives in battle against the forces of darkness

The Game

Illustrated map by Laura Hartman Maestro ©2009

RUSSIAN EMPIRE

Wild Boar

AFGHANISTAN

N.W. FRONTIER PROV.

KASHMIR AND JAMMU

IRAN

BALUCHISTAN

PUNJAB

Simla

Indus

PUNJAB STATES

Delhi

UNITED

N

PROVIN

Arabian Sea

SIND

RAJPUTANA

WESTERN

INDIA

GWALIOR

CENTRAL

INDI

Bombay
(Port)

CENTRAL PROVINCES

BERAR

EASTERN STATES

DECCAN STATES

HYDERABAD

British Colonial India

Gôa
(Port)

Indian Princely States

Provinces directly administered by Britain

MYSORE

MADRAS STATES

MADRAS

(Fr.)

(Fr.)

(Fr.)

CEYLON

to Russian R.R.
200 miles

Pass
9400

The Forts

Khanpur City

Khanpur

Hijarkot

CHINA

Langur Monkeys

BET

BHUTAN

Bramaputra

Ganges

BIHAR

BENGAL

MANIPUR

TRIPURA
E.ST.

(Fr.)

Calcutta

STATES

BURMA

Bay of
Bengal

2 miles to
airfield,
(past polo
fields and
elephant pens)

Stables

ZOO

Old
Fort

New
Fort

5 miles
to
Khanpur
City

SIAM

Gulf
of
Siam

cheetah

THE
GAME

Preface

It was a dramatic setting for a human sacrifice, give my murderer credit. He had drawn together the entire populace, crones to infants, in a dusty space between buildings that in England would be the village green, and all were agog at the sight. A circle of freshly lit torches cracked and flared in the slight evening breeze, their dashing light rendering the mud houses in stark contrast of pale wall and blackest shadow. The bowl of the sky I was forced to gaze up at was moonless, the stars—far, far from the electrical intrusions of civilisation—pinpricks in the velvet expanse. The evening air was rich with odours—the oily reek of the rag torches in counterpoint to the dusky cow-dung cook-fires and the curry and garlic that permeated the audience, along with the not unpleasant smell of unsoaped bodies and the savour of dust which had been dampened for the show.

I lay, bound with chains, on what could only be called an altar, waist-height to the man who held the gleaming knife. My sacrifice was to be the climax of the evening's events, and he had worked the crowd into a near frenzy, playing on their rustic gullibility as on a fine instrument. It had been a long night, but it seemed that things were drawing to a finish.

The knife was equally theatrical, thirteen inches of flashing steel, wielded with artistry in order to catch the torchlight. For nearly twenty minutes it had flickered and dipped over my supine body, brushing my skin like a lover, leaving behind thin threads of scarlet as it lifted; my eyes ached with following it about. Still, I couldn't very well shut them; the mind wishes to see death descend, however futile the struggle.

But it would not be long now. I did not understand most of the words so dramatically pelting the crowd, but I knew they had something to do with evil spirits and the cleansing effects of bloodshed. I watched the motions of the knife closely, saw the slight change in how it rested in my attacker's hand, the shift from loose showmanship to the grip of intent. It paused, and the man's voice with it, so that all the village heard was the sough and sigh of the torches, the cry of a baby from a nearby hut, and the bark of a pi-dog in the field. The blade now pointed directly down at my heart, its needle point rock-steady as the doubled fist held its hilt without hesitation.

I saw the twitch of the muscles in his arms, and struggled against the chains, in futility. The knife flashed down, and I grimaced and turned away, my eyes tight closed.

This was going to hurt.

Chapter One

Travel broadens, they say. My personal experience has been that, in the short term at any rate, it merely flattens, aiming its steam-roller of deadlines and details straight at one's daily life, leaving a person flat and gasping at its passage.

On the first of January, 1924, I was enjoying a peaceful New Year's evening with my partner and husband, Sherlock Holmes, in our snug stone house on the Sussex Downs, blissfully unaware that scarcely forty hours later I would be sprinting desperately for a train across a snow-covered railway siding. But on the first day of the new year, I was at peace and I was at home, with a full stomach, a tipsy head, and—most pleasant of all—warm feet. No fewer than three bottles of wine stood on the sideboard, in various stages of depletion. Holmes had just taken a connoisseur's sip of the last to appear in our glasses, a dusty port twice as old as I. He sighed in satisfaction and stretched his slippers out to the fire.

"It is good to find that the French vineyards are

recovering from the War," he noted, although of the three wines, only the champagne had gone into its bottle since 1918.

I agreed, rather absently I will admit. As I took a swallow of the glorious liquid, it occurred to me that some part of the back of my mind was braced for a ring of the telephone or a furious pounding on the door. The visceral mistrust of leisure was perhaps understandable: Twice in the past six months the outside world had crashed in on us; indeed, we had been similarly seated before the fire one evening a scant two months earlier when an investigation literally fell into our arms, in the form of an old friend with a bloodied head. It was not yet midnight, and I had no faith in our stout oaken door to keep out surprises of the kind Holmes tended to attract.

However, pleasantly enough, no pounding fist came to trouble our companionship or, later, our slumber, and we rose early the next morning, fortified ourselves with one of Mrs Hudson's hearty breakfasts (this one even more elaborate than usual, to make up for her being cheated of preparing the dinner for this, my twenty-fourth birthday), and bundled into our warmest clothes for the sleet-drenched trip to London. We rode the train in silence, taken up with our thoughts and with the newspapers, both as cheerless as the landscape outside the windows. Foot-and-mouth disease, the rising Seine, and doomsayers with apocalyptic predictions on both sides of the Atlantic, set off by the recent Labour victory.

Grimmer yet was the real reason for our visit to the great city. We had no end of business there, of course, from a long-delayed appointment with the bank manager to calling on a noble family in order to follow up on our most recently concluded investigation, but in truth, we were there to see Holmes' brother Mycroft, whose health was giving, as the euphemism goes, cause for concern.

He was home from hospital already, although the doctors had strongly advised against it, and embarked on his own programme of therapy. I personally wouldn't have thought a near-starvation diet of meat and red wine combined with long hours of vigorous calisthenics would be the best thing for a shaky heart, but not even Holmes' arguments made much of an inroad on Mycroft's determination. We had maintained a closer contact with him than usual over the past week and a half, none of us voicing the thought that each visit could well be our last. We hurried through the day's business, I listening with half an ear to the urgent recitation of calamity that trembled over the head of my American possessions, thinking only that, affection for my father or not, the time had come to rid myself of his once-cherished properties across the sea. I kept glancing at my wrist-watch, until finally with a sigh my solicitor threw up metaphorical hands, gave me the papers that required my signature, and allowed me to escape.

When we arrived at Mycroft's door, however, I had to admit that his self-prescribed fitness régime did not seem to be doing him any harm. He was up and around, and if he opened the door in his slippers and dressing-gown, he moved without hesitation and had colour in his face. There was also nearly a stone less of him than there had been on Christmas Day, which made his jowls flaccid and his eyes more hooded than usual.

"Many happy returns of the day, Mary," he said, and to Holmes, "I believe you'll find a corkscrew on the tray, if you'd be so kind." After toasts came the inevitable discussion of the impending disaster that the new Labour government was certain to bring in. Predictions were rife that the institution of marriage was sure to be done away with, that rubles would replace the pound sterling, the Boy Scouts and the monarchy would be abolished, the House of Lords sold for housing flats—everything short of plagues and rains of frogs. There were strong rumours that the Prime Minister would refuse to step down to Labour's minority vote, thus igniting a constitutional crisis if not outright revolution; the newspapers that morning had mentioned the concern of America, politeness thinly concealing Washington's growing alarm. When I said something of the sort, Mycroft nodded.

"Yes, the Americans are becoming increasingly nervous about the Reds. They seem to envision a Socialist state that stretches from London to Peking, and don't know whether to be more worried about the Bolsheviks succeeding, or about the chaos that will follow if they fail."

When we had exhausted the various topics, we sat down to a meal only marginally less sumptuous than one of Mycroft's usual, accompanied by what passed for small talk and polite conversation in the Holmes household, in this case an interesting development in forensic science from America and a nice murder that was baffling the authorities. Dessert was a small decorated cake, which none of us ate.

The pouring of coffee, offer of brandy, and fingering of cigars indicated that the meal was finished, business could be resumed. The talk circled back through the Labour victory and the huge problems facing a minority government, before Mycroft took a last, ritual mouthful from his cup, put it onto the table, and asked, "Have you been following the news from Russia?"

My head snapped up as if he'd hauled back on my reins—which in a way, he had: I knew him far too well to think his question innocent. "No!" I said sharply, before things could edge one syllable further down that slippery slope. "I absolutely refuse to go to Moscow in January."

He made a show of shifting feebly in his chair, letting out a quiet sigh of infirmity before he looked up. "I said nothing about Moscow."

"Siberia, then. Some place either deadly or freezing, or both."

He abandoned the attempt at innocence. "I would go myself," he tried, but at my disbelieving snort and Holmes' raised eyebrow, he dropped that as well. All the world knew that Mycroft Holmes went nowhere outside his tightly worked circle if he could possibly avoid it: Dr Watson had once referred to Mycroft's unexpected appearance in their Baker Street flat as akin to finding a tram-car running down a country lane.

It did, however, answer a question that had been in the back of my mind ever since the general election, namely, how would the radical change in government affect Mycroft? Mycroft's rôle in the outgoing Tory government was as undefined as it was enormous; it seemed he intended to simply ignore the shuffling of office-holders all around him.

"What has happened, Mycroft?" Holmes asked, drawing my attention back to the until-now overlooked fact that, if Mycroft, in his condition, had been consulted on a matter by whichever government, it had to have struck someone as serious indeed.

By way of answer, the big man reached inside the

folds of his voluminous silken dressing-gown and pulled out a flat, oilskin-wrapped packet about three inches square. He put it onto the linen cloth and pushed it across the table in our direction. "This came into my hands ten hours ago."

Holmes retrieved the grimy object, turned it over, and began to pick apart the careful tucks. The oilskin had clearly been folded in on itself for some time, but parted easily, revealing a smaller object, a leather packet long permeated by sweat, age, and what appeared to be blood. This seemed to have been sewn shut at least two or three times in its life. The most recent black threads had been cut fairly recently, to judge by their looseness; no doubt that explained the easy parting of the oilskin cover. Holmes continued unfolding the leather.

Inside lay three much-folded documents, so old the edges were worn soft, their outside segments stained dark by long contact with the leather. I screwed up my face in anticipation of catastrophe as Holmes began to unfold the first one, but the seams did not actually part, not completely at any rate. He eased the page open, placing a clean tea-spoon at its head and an un-used knife at its foot to keep it flat, and slid it over for me to examine as he set to work on the second.

The stained document before me seemed to be a sol-dier's clearance certificate, and although the name, along with most of the words, was almost completely obscured by time and salt, it looked to belong to a K-something O'Meara, or O'Mara. The date was un-readable, and could as easily have been the 1700s as the past century—assuming they issued clearance certifi-cates in the 1700s. I turned without much hope to the second document. This was on parchment, and al-though it appeared even older than the first and had been refolded no less than four times into different shapes, it had been in the center position inside the leather pouch, and was not as badly stained. It concerned the same soldier, whose last name now appeared to be O'Hara, and represented his original enlistment. I could feel Mycroft's eyes on me, but I was no more enlightened than I had been by the certificate representing this unknown Irishman's departure from Her Majesty's service.

Holmes had the third document unfolded, using the care he might have given a first-century papyrus. He made no attempt to weigh down the edges of this one, merely let the soft, crude paper rest where it would lest it dissolve into a heap of jigsaw squares along the scored folds. I craned my head to see the words; Holmes, however, just glanced at the pages, seeming to lose interest as soon as he had freed them. He sat aside and let me look to my heart's content.

This was a birth certificate, for a child born in some place called Ferozepore in the year 1875. His father's name clarified the difficulties of the K-something from the other forms: Kimball.

I looked up, hoping for an explanation, only to find both sets of grey Holmes eyes locked expectantly onto me. How long, I wondered, before I stopped feeling like some slow student facing her disappointed headmistress? "I'm sorry," I began, and then I paused, my mind catching at last on a faint sense of familiarity: Kimball. And O'Hara. Add to that a town that could only be in India. . . . No; oh, no—the book was just a children's adventure tale. "I'm sorry," I repeated, only where before it had connoted apology, this time it was tinged with outrage. "This doesn't have anything to do with *Kim*, does it? The Kipling book?"

"You've read it?" Mycroft asked.

"Of course I've read it."

"Good, that saves some explaining. I believe this to be his amulet case."

"He's real, then? Kipling's boy?"

"As real as I am," said Sherlock Holmes. "And yes, this is his amulet. I recognise it."

"You *know* him?" I don't know why this revelation startled me as if he'd claimed to have met a hippogryph; heavens, half the world considered *Holmes* fictional. But startle me it did.

"I knew him, long ago. We spent the better part of a year in each other's company."

"When?"

He smiled to himself. "While I was dead."

I knew my husband and partner was not referring to some spiritualist experience of a previous lifetime. "When I was dead" was his whimsical term for the period beginning in the spring of 1891, when he disappeared at Switzerland's Reichenbach Falls, and for three years wandered the globe, returning to London only when a mysterious murder called him back to the land of the living. Knowing that Mycroft had preserved his Baker Street rooms for him during those three years, and knowing what Mycroft was, I had no doubt that at least a portion of that time, Holmes had been about the Queen's business. Still, I had never heard the details.

I was not to hear them now, either. Holmes had already turned to his brother, and was asking, "How did these come to you?"

"Through the hands of a certain captain who has an interest in both worlds."

"Not Creighton?"

"The man who currently holds the same position that Creighton did then, fellow by the name of Nesbit."

"And the story that accompanied them?"

"So tenuous as to be nonexistent. An Afghan trader brings a rumour that a light-skinned native man is being held by a hill raja. Six months later, a camel caravan modifies the story, that the man was being held but took ill and died, asking that these, his last effects, be returned to his people. We did trace the amulet's arrival to such a caravan, but no man could say who had carried it south, or whence it came."

Holmes nodded, but said only, "I find it difficult to imagine that particular individual being held against his will."

I broke in, with a request I did not think unreasonable, particularly as we seemed to be on the edge of being dragged into a case involving Kimball O'Hara. "I'd appreciate a little background information, just a few details about what you were doing when you knew the boy."

Holmes glanced sideways at his brother, assessing his condition, then suggested, "Perhaps it would be best if we saved the tale for a later time."

I started to protest, then decided that Mycroft's colour was indeed not peak, and brought my curiosity under control, allowing them to continue.

Mycroft answered, "As you say, it takes some doing to imagine O'Hara in custody for more than a few days. He was—how did you put it to me? 'Wily as a mongoose, slippery as a cobra, more deadly than either.' "

"If not in custody, then what?"

"The Bear is awakening."

" 'The Bear,' " I said. "You mean Russia? But I thought our relations with them had settled down—don't we even have a trade agreement now with the Bolsheviks?"

"Oh, yes, they've played on our attachment to India by accepting industrial supplies in exchange for little more than a verbal guarantee that they would cease their intrigue in the sub-continent. But then last May, Curzon had to threaten to withdraw trade unless they took their agents out. And, oh the surprise, they have not."

"And you imagine the Bolsheviks might have laid hands on O'Hara," Holmes asked, sounding dubious, "or got him in their sights, where the Tsar's agents could not?"

"Not precisely," Mycroft replied.

Holmes frowned. "A native agent, then, who worked his way inside O'Hara's guard?" He seemed only a shade less doubtful about this possibility, but still Mycroft shook his head.

"Sherlock, I am not convinced the man is dead."

"What, then? Not dead, not held, then—No," Holmes said sharply as Mycroft's meaning fell into place. "Kimball O'Hara would never side with the Russians against the Crown. Never."

"Perhaps not side with them, necessarily, but use them? As a tool for India herself? The move towards self-rule—Gandhi's *swaraj*—has adherents on all levels throughout the sub-continent, and between their systematic obstructionism and the actions of outright revolutionaries, the country is a powder-keg. One more atrocity like Dyer's and the entire country will rise up, battering its own way between the British and the Bolsheviks. Neither of whom has much affection for Mr Gandhi. But even lacking outright revolt, the educated classes are pressing strongly for a voice in their own affairs. And the boy was always more native than white in his sensibilities."

"Sensibilities, yes, but not in his loyalties. He would not turn coat against His Majesty."

"Then perhaps he is truly imprisoned. Or dead."

Holmes did not answer. Instead, he took up the much-folded papers from the table, holding them to the light, one by one, for a long and close study. He found no marks, no pinpricks, nothing to indicate a secret message to the outside world. He even turned the leather case outside-in, as if the stitches of closure might have been embroidered into a code, but there was nothing. And as I knew that Mycroft would have given the objects the same scrutiny, I did not bother doing the same: If neither Holmes brother had found a hidden message, it was unlikely that I should do so.

"Has Kipling been questioned?" Holmes asked.

"The last he heard of O'Hara was in 1916. A letter of condolence arrived some months after Kipling's son was killed."

"Who was O'Hara's contact within the Survey?"

"O'Hara hasn't worked with the Ethnological Survey for nearly three years, but at the time it was Nesbit, and before that, Apfield. You knew him, I think?"

"We met," Holmes said, not apparently enchanted with the memory. He turned to me to explain. "The Survey of India is responsible for producing accurate maps of the country, but it is also the home of the Ethnological department, wherein lies Intelligence. Under cover of survey and census, the British government assembles the subtler kinds of information concerning secret conversations and illicit trade among the border states. When I was there, Colonel Creighton headed the Survey. A good man." He finished packing the documents into their leather amulet case and slid the object back across the table to Mycroft. "You need me to go?"

"I don't want to ask," Mycroft said, which was answer enough.

"We're off to India, then?" I said. Ah well; we'd had a pleasant holiday for nearly an entire week. And at least it wasn't Russia: India was the tropics, which meant that my chilblains, begun in Dartmoor in October and not improved by two months in an underheated Berkshire country house broken by a cross-Atlantic trip for a missing ducal relative, might have a chance to heal. Still, I thought of the newspaper headlines I had read on the train, "Hindu-Moslem Bitterness—Riot in Calcutta Suburb," and suppressed a sigh. "Do we have time to pack a bag?"

"I shouldn't think so," Holmes said absently.

"Holmes!" I protested, but to my surprise, Mycroft came down on my side.

"The Special Express leaves Victoria at one-forty tomorrow afternoon. The P. & O. steamer meets it in Marseilles at midnight Friday. Plenty of time."

Not precisely what I would term *plenty of time*, but better than taking off for the East in the clothes I stood up in. Which request, frankly, wouldn't have surprised me.

We were even allowed to finish our coffee before having to race for a cab.

The late train for Eastbourne was standing at the platform when we reached Victoria, but for some reason it proved unusually popular, with the result that we did not have a compartment to ourselves. This meant that the tale of Kimball O'Hara had to wait until after the car had deposited us at our door, and we had retrieved our trunks from the attic, and we had begun to pack them. Mrs Hudson, although we insisted we could manage, wrenched the clothes from our hands and took out her copious supply of tissue-paper. I admitted defeat and, leaving her bemoaning the lack of time to repair and tidy the summer-weight garments retrieved from the back of the cupboards, I followed Holmes down the hall-way and into the laboratory, where I cornered him.

"Very well, Holmes, you may proceed."

"About young O'Hara? Yes, an intriguing lad. You know his history, you said?"

"Born in India to Irish parents; mother died early; father drank himself to death, leaving Kim in the charge of a native nurse, who let him run wild so that he grew up in the bazaar."

"Save that it was opium that killed O'Hara, not alcohol, the rest is correct."

"As I remember it, when the boy was twelve or thirteen he finally came to the attention of the authorities, particularly the man who was in charge of the spy network operating along the Northwest Frontier. That was Creighton. He sent the boy to school for a while to learn his letters and numbers, before reclaiming him for the Intelligence service. Kim and some other agents foiled a Russian plot, something about treason among a group of hill rajas, and that's where the book ends."

"It was immediately after that tale's conclusion that I met him. He was only seventeen, but already a full operative of the Survey. He had befriended an old Tibetan lama, and was returning him to his home when our paths coincided, and I joined them."

"You mean you actually got to Tibet? I assumed that was one of Conan Doyle's romanticisms. Wasn't Tibet closed to outsiders until Younghusband's expedition in, what was it, 1904?"

"That set off in the final weeks of 1903, and yes, all that time Tibet was closed tighter than a miser's purse-string," he said with satisfaction. "Which is why I needed to accompany the lama."

"And you wanted to go to Tibet because . . . ?"

"Mycroft, of course."

"Of course," I muttered.

"This was 1892, when the Russian threat was at its height. The Tsar wanted India, the Viceroy wanted to know which pass the Cossacks would come pouring through, and I happened to be on hand. As was young Kimball O'Hara. I had joined with a group of explorers, calling myself Sigerson, and made a lot of careful notes and maps. O'Hara came to our camp one black night, begging food for his lama, this grubby dark-skinned lad with eyes that saw everything. As he was leaving, he allowed his shirt to fall open and reveal a certain charm around his neck which, combined with an exchange of phrases, told me that he, too, was engaged in the 'Great Game' of border espionage. He crept back to my tent at midnight and we had a long talk, and ended up travelling together for a time. Most of what we did is no doubt still under lock and key in some ministry office, but after the Bolshevik revolution, I had assumed that the need for guarding India's passes had faded. However, it would seem that in Mycroft's eyes, The Game persists, albeit against different players."

He made to leave the room, but I had to protest, for his tale had been in no way adequate.

"But what was he like?" I persisted.

By way of answer, Holmes paused with his hand in a trouser pocket, then drew it out and dashed the contents onto the table nearest the door. A handful of small, disparate objects danced and rolled and threatened to fall to the floor, but no sooner had they come to a rest than he scooped them up again, and turned a questioning eyebrow on me.

We hadn't done this particular exercise in a long time, but I had sufficient experience with Holmes' ways to know what his action signified.

"You wish me to play Kim's game?" I asked.

"The boy himself called it the 'Jewel Game,' but yes."

It was a test of one's perception, first of seeing, then of committing to memory. I was tired, and I couldn't see what this had to do with my question, but obediently I began to recite.

"Three mismatched collar studs; a nubbin of India rubber; two paper-clips, one of them Italian; the cigar-band from Mycroft's cigar; a gold pen nib; the button that came off your shirt two weeks ago that you couldn't find, so that Mrs Hudson replaced all the shirt's buttons at a go; the stub end of a boot-lace; a seed-head from last summer's *nigella*; a penny, a halfpenny, and a farthing; two pebbles, one black and the other white; a tooth from a comb; and one inch of pencil."

He smiled then, and headed back into the bedroom. "You and O'Hara will find you have much in common, I think." When I protested that he hadn't answered me, he put up his hand. "We shall have many days of leisure in which to recount fond tales of derring-do, Russell. But not tonight—we have much to do before we catch that train. And, Russ?" I looked up to find him outlined in the doorway, a pair of patent-leather shoes in his hand, his face as grim as his voice. "Make certain to pack adequate ammunition for your revolver."

Chapter Two

We rose from our brief rest to a world of white, and the news that the trains to London were badly delayed. Nonetheless, we had my farm manager Patrick put the horses into harness and take us to the Eastbourne station, where we found that indeed, the London trains were not expected to reach Victoria until late in the afternoon. I glanced at my hastily packed bags and tried not to look too cheerful.

"That does it, Holmes. We shall have to wait until next week."

"Nonsense. Off you go, Patrick, before you end up in a drift over your head."

I shrugged at my old friend, who touched the brim of his cloth cap and picked up the reins. Holmes had already turned to the station master, a lugubrious individual long acquainted with this particular passenger's idiosyncrasies, and, I thought, secretly entertained by them. Very secretly. "Are the telephone lines still up?"

"Not to London, Mr Holmes."

What about the telegraph?"

'Oh, aye, we're sure to get a message through by me route or another."

The two went off, heads together. I looked at the trunks, gathering snowdrifts to themselves, and took myself inside out of the cold.

A couple of hours later something intruded upon my attention: a pair of shoes gleaming at me over the top of the book I'd snatched from Holmes' shelves on the way out the door. I blinked and straightened my bent spine to look up into my husband's face. His grey eyes were dancing with amusement.

"What is it?" I asked.

"Russell, I am constantly filled with admiration at your ability to immerse yourself in the task at hand."

I closed *The Riches of Mohenjo-Daro* and rose, in some confusion, only noticing when I was upright that the trunks had been brought in and arranged at my side, long enough ago that the snow had not only melted but dried as well. What was more, a tea tray someone had set by my other side bore a half-empty cup and a half-eaten biscuit. I could taste the biscuit in my mouth, but I had no recollection whatsoever of having consumed either.

"Glad I amuse you, Holmes. What have you arranged? An aeroplane journey to Marseilles? A submarine boat to run us to Port Said?"

"Nothing so exotic. The delay is due less to the quantity of snow than it is to something on the tracks the other side of Lewes. All other trains, though slow, are still getting through. Mycroft has arranged for the Express to wait for us in Kent."

I looked at him with astonishment. "I should have

thought a submarine boat easier to arrange than delay of a train."

"The Empire is but a plaything to the whims Mycroft Holmes," he commented, glancing around f● a porter.

"The Empire, yes, but the Calais Express?"

"So it would appear, even with the Labour Party bearing down on the horizon."

Not that the catching of it was a simple thing. It meant boarding an east-bound train, one of those locals that pauses at every cattle shed and churchyard, and which cowers in a siding every few miles that an express may thunder past in majesty. Not that anything much was thundering that day; I began to suspect that even Mycroft's best-laid plans might leave us stranded in the middle of Kent.

Still, I had a book.

Either through mechanical problems or through some deep-seated class resentment of the driver (he'd probably cast his ballot for the incoming Socialists), our train stopped well short of the assigned station. This expression of class solidarity (if that is what it was) became somewhat derailed itself when Holmes summoned many strong men to haul our possessions over the slippery ground, to the puzzlement of the local's passengers and the huge indignation of those on the Express. Class warfare at its most basic. Holmes did, however, tip the men handsomely.

The instant we had spilled into the waiting train it shuddered and loosed its bonds to steam furiously off for Dover. I understand that mention was even made in the next day's *Times* of a puzzling stop in the wilds of Kent for a hasty on-load of essential governmental equipment. Mycroft's decrees were powerful indeed.

The entire trip to Marseilles carried on as it had begun, rushed and uncomfortable. And dreary—it was on that train that we read of the death of the Reverend Sabine Baring-Gould, an old friend of Holmes' whose problems on Dartmoor had occupied our early autumn. Then the Channel crossing was rough, so rough that I spent the entire time braving the sleet-slick deck rather than succumb to sea-sickness, reaching Calais with nose, hands, and toes not far from frost-bite. Paris was flooded, its higher ground packed with refugees and their bags, the train crowded and all the first-class sleepers occupied by fleeing residents. We spent Friday with an aged Italian priest and his even more aged and garrulous sister, both of whom exuded clouds of garlic. The rain and snow persisted, slowing the journey so much that I began to doubt that we would actually arrive before the steamer had departed, but in the end, the boat, too, was held (for the train as a whole, not merely for the two of us), and when we reached the docks, our possessions were hastily labelled and carried on, divided between cabin and hold. We scurried up the ice-slick gangway in the company of a handful of other train passengers, slipping almost apologetically onboard the sleeping boat, witnessed only by P. & O. officials and, I thought, one or two other sets of eyes in the higher decks, their presence felt but unseen in the darkness.

Once in our cabin (this, at any rate, had no priest in residence) I crept into bed, praying that exhaustion would take my body into sleep before the pitch and toss of the boat asserted itself. To my relief, such was the case: The steam-roller of the past fifty-four hours rumbled over my recumbent body, and my last memory was of Holmes wrestling open the small port-hole, letting in a wash of frigid air scented with salt, and nary a hint of garlic.

I woke a long time later to a more subdued sea, a pallid attempt at sunshine, and the *ting* of a spoon against china. When I reached for the bed-side clock, my hand knocked against the water carafe; after a moment Holmes came through the doorway with a cup of tea in each hand. He set one on the table, and sat down on the other bed with his own. It was, I saw, nearly noon.

The tea had the bitter edge of a pot that has sat for a while, but it was still hot, which told me that Holmes, too, had slept late, and was only on his second cup. I slurped in appreciation, grateful that the bed wasn't tossing beneath me. When the cup was empty, I threaded my glasses over my ears so I could see my partner.

"I suppose I shall be spending the next two weeks being force-fed some language or other?" I asked.

"Hindustani is the common tongue of the north, used by all traders. You won't find it difficult."

"Before we begin, I want to know more about this O'Hara person."

"Not a 'person,' a young gentleman, despite his history and lineage. A *sahib*."

"But he was only a lad when you knew him."

"Even then."

"That was, what, thirty years ago? Why hasn't he made a name for himself in that time?"

"A man does not play The Game successfully for thirty years and more if he catches the eye of any but his superiors."

"O'Hara has been a spy for the Crown for all that time?"

"O'Hara has been many things, but yes, he has been there when he was needed."

"Tell me about—"

"Breakfast first, and a lesson in Hindi. Then I shall tell you old and happy, far-off things and battles long ago."

He reinforced his edict by standing up and walking into the adjoining room.

I finished my tea, dawdled over my morning rituals, and joined him moments after our mid-day breakfast came through the door. As I came in, he looked up from the fragrant plate and said, "*Begumji, hazri khaege?*" Lessons had begun.

At first my mind tried to slide the new language sideways into its niche for Arabic, a tongue I had learnt under similar circumstances five years earlier, but by the end of the afternoon, it had grudgingly begun to compile a separate store-house of nouns and verbs in a niche labelled Hindi. With concentrated (that is, around-the-clock) effort, the rudimentaries of most languages can be grasped in a week or two, with childish phrases and a continual "Pardon me?" giving way to slow, stilted fluency a week later. By the end of four weeks, under Holmes' tutelage, I had no doubt that my bruised brain would be dreaming in its ... it went without saying, my accent ... negligible. By the time we landed in Bombay, I would be able to pass for a genial idiot; another fortnight, and I would merely sound stupid.

However, it seemed that Hindustani was not the only subject Holmes had in mind. When our plates were clean and I had satisfactorily recited the nouns and articles for all the objects on the tray, he swept the leavings to one side and laid a pair of tea-spoons and a linen napkin onto the table between us, and began a demonstration of sleight-of-hand.

Under the command of those long, thin, infinitely clever fingers, the silver came alive. It vanished and reappeared in unlikely places; it multiplied, shrank, changed shape, became near liquid, and finally sat quietly where it had begun. I knew his tricks—basic conjuring was a skill I'd begun to learn early in our relationship—but my young fingers had been no match for his. Still, I'd spent one summer conjuring with coins so, although the spoons were more difficult to palm and vanish, my grip was accustomed to the motions. Now I picked up one of the spoons and performed a few of his moves back to him, albeit more slowly and clumsily, and leaving out the multiplication trick since he had stashed the other spoons somewhere about his person. He looked on critically, grunted his approval, and produced the spare silver from an inner pocket.

I had been many things as first the apprentice, then the partner of Sherlock Holmes: gipsy fortune-teller in Wales, personal secretary to a misogynist colonel, Bed Arab wandering the Palestinian desert, workig the matron, and Sweet Young Thing. Now to India, where I supposed I migh a harem or take up a positi lepers. Or perform co

"We're to be hindu magicians?" I asked.

As Dr Johnson said, 'All wonder is the effect of novelty on ignorance.' And as fire-breathing bears the hazards of flaming beards or self-poisoning with phosphorus or brimstone, and the more spectacular conjuring depends on equipment too hefty for easy transport, we shall concentrate on prestidigitation."

"But why?"

He settled back and steepled his fingers for a lecture; I poured myself another cup of coffee.

"We in the West have developed the unfortunate habit of training and arming insurgents, then dropping them when they become inconvenient. As a result, there is a certain lack of long-term trust on the part of the native inhabitants, even those who declare themselves our stout friends. And as a part of that lack of trust, we cannot always be certain that our 'friends' are telling us all they know. The Northwest Frontier of India has known spies for so many generations, even the least sophisticated of communities suspects any outsider of nefarious purposes. One of the perpetual dilemmas for the man wishing to come and go freely along the border territories has always been finding an acceptable disguise to justify his presence, so that he is not thrown into gaol, or summarily shot. Some players of the Great Game go as *hakim*s, with patent cures for fever and eye infections to supplement rudimentary medical skills; others bluster their way as hunters, collecting heads and skins openly as they surreptitiously map an area. I've known wandering antiquarians, big-game hunters, and itinerant *durzi*s—tailors—but each depends on specific skills. One wouldn't care to be a *durzi* if one could not handle a needle, for example. O'Hara was note-perfect as a holy man, due to his long wandering in the company of a Tibetan lama. But for the man—or woman—with the necessary skills, one of the best disguises is that of a travelling entertainer. Native peoples expect a magician both to be itinerant and to behave in a mysterious fashion. And as long as there are no inconvenient coincidences, no village bullocks die or floods come to wash out the crops, the people are happy to accept most witchery as benign. I want you to practise your movements until you can do them backwards in your sleep."

I could see already that we wouldn't be spending much of the voyage up on deck, open to curious ears and eyes.

Too, this would clearly not be a visit among the exotic comforts of India. From the sounds of it, we'd be lucky to sleep under a roof.

Worst of all, this talk of "frontier" made my heart sink and my chilblains tingle: It did not sound as if the warm, frangipani-scented south was to be our destination.

It was not until tea-time that Holmes broke off the lessons, when my tongue and my fingers were both about to stutter to a halt. We went up to the salon for tea, and the genial drink coupled with the fresh Mediterranean air soothed me as if I'd been granted an afternoon nap. Afterwards, we bundled up and strolled the decks, where at last Holmes began the story of his meeting with the young Kim O'Hara—in Hindi alternating with English translations, a broken narrative rendered yet more difficult to follow by the necessity of switching to something innocuous whenever another set of ears came near. It was a method of discourse with which, by that time, I had some familiarity: I had known the man at my side for just under nine years, been his partner for five, his wife for three.

"It was in the spring of 1891 that I encountered Professor Moriarty at the Reichenbach Falls, an encounter from which only I walked away. Watson, as you know, thought I had met my death there, and made haste to inform the rest of the world. I was indeed dead to the world for three long years. When I finally returned to London, I told Watson that my absence had been due to the ongoing investigation of the Moriarty gang, but in truth, my heart had grown weary of the game. When I set off for my meeting with Moriarty, I anticipated that our final confrontation might well cost my life. To find myself still standing on the edge of the Falls while Moriarty was swallowed by its turbulence—it was as if the sky had opened up and a shiny Christmas parcel had been lowered into my waiting hands. All it required was for me to tug at its ribbons.

"The temptation was enormous. I had by that time been working out of Baker Street for ten very solid years, and although many of the cases were of interest, a few of them even challenging, I had reached a point at which the future stretched long and dull ahead of me. I was, remember, a young man, scarcely thirty, and the thought of returning to the choking fogs and hum-drum crime of London was suddenly intolerable. I stood with the Falls at my feet and gazed down the path leading back to Watson and duty, then up at the steep cliff that was my other option, and my hands reached for the cliff.

"Once at the top, setting my face to the East, I paused. In fact, I sat among the bushes and stones for so long, I saw Watson reappear in a panic on the path below me. I saw the poor fellow find the note I had left there, saw him . . . He wept, Russell; my loyal friend broke down and wept, and it was all I could do not to stand and hail him. But I was silent, not because I wished to cause him sorrow, not even because I had a thought-out plan of action. No, it was merely that I had been given the priceless gift of choice, and could not bring myself to throw it away.

"I made my surreptitious way back to London, and to Mycroft's door. My brother was surprised to see me, and I venture to say pleased, but he was not in the least astonished—we are enough alike, we two, to distrust a death without laying our thumbs on the corpse's pulse. And as it turned out, my very public demise had come at an opportune time for his purposes.

"What do you know of the conflict along India's northern frontier?" he asked me.

"I know that war in one form or another has gone on for most of the last century, until the Bolshevik revolution five years ago. The Tsar wanted to extend the Russian borders across the mountains into Afghanistan and ultimately India, while we kept him out by a show of force and holding close watch on the passes. In the meantime, both sides have been mistrusted, manipulated, and often murdered by the countries in the middle; the Afghans particularly have made the trapping of outsiders a national sport.

"In 1891," Holmes resumed, "Kim O'Hara was seventeen years old and fresh from school when he was dropped straight into the thick of The Game. A pair of 'hunters' came out of the hills carrying, along with their rifles, trophies, and a collection of well-hidden survey equipment, secret messages from the Tsar to some hill rajas entertaining treasonous thoughts. O'Hara was at the time in the company of his lama, and used his rôle as the man's *chela,* or disciple, to conceal his government work. The job was hard and nearly killed him, but he succeeded in capturing the relevant letter, and was rewarded by being turned loose for a time. His lama was dying and wished to breathe his last in Tibet—and the boy's superiors knew full well that if they attempted to keep him from his duties as a disciple, he would simply slip the reins and vanish."

"Tibet."

"Yes. A country all too aware of its vulnerability and

its desirability, and therefore closed with grim determination against the eyes of all foreigners, a place with the habit of executing anyone even suspected of secret doings, a place where no Westerner had ever set foot. Unfortunately, just four months earlier, a Survey agent had gone missing from a mission into the reaches of Tibet, and it was feared that he had been taken captive, and was being questioned, under fairly drastic means—certain pieces of inside information had come to public knowledge. It was feared that any agent known to this man was in danger of exposure."

"So Mycroft suggested sending in someone whom the man could not have known," I supplied. "You."

"Correct again. The timing was coincidental—my own unlooked-for availability and their sudden and urgent need for a competent stranger. And although by the time I reached India, O'Hara and his lama had left the plains, I managed to join a Scandinavian expedition into the mountains whose path would coincide with theirs."

"Wheels within wheels."

"Quite an appropriate image, Russell. The Tibetans often pray by means of a wheel spun on the end of a stick, its body filled with written prayers. With prayers, or with any other piece of writing a man might wish to carry with him. A map, say, or the copy of a private letter."

"So you persuaded a couple of Tibetan monks to take on a Norwegian explorer?"

"They were, as I mentioned, begging for their meal by the side of the road, as is customary for religious individuals in the East. I was in the habit of concealing a roll in the breast of my coat, for just such an eventuality, and slid inside it a wadded-up note suggesting that a 'son of the charm' might find a friend in the tent with the orange door. The boy came to me after his lama was asleep that night, bristling with suspicion, fingering in a most un-monk-like fashion the revolver he wore inside his shirt lest I prove an enemy—or worse, a colleague set on dragging him back to his responsibilities.

"I gave him food—the boy ate meat as if he was starving, which he may well have been—and tobacco, and we sat on our heels in the dark and talked. He was the most remarkable blend of hard and soft, cunning and naïve, schoolboy one moment, petty criminal the next. He was a prodigy, who'd played a similar Game in the streets before he'd even heard of Crown or Tsar—if Creighton had sat at a drawing-board to design the very tool for bearing the Survey's eyes and ears, he couldn't have come up with anything better than Kimball O'Hara. His only weakness was a distaste for lying to his friends, and even then, he would practice deceit joyously when it was part of The Game.

"In the end I managed to convince the lad that, far from wishing to pull him out of the mountains, I would urge him to go as far and as wide as he could with his lama—my sole request being that he take me with him. Two purposes had I: The more immediate was to find word of Creighton's missing agent, but beyond that, I had been asked, if it came into my purview, to whisper into the Dalai Lama's ear that, despite the alarming actions of certain importunate missionaries, England was in fact more interested in treaty than takeover. That we had no wish to rule Tibet, merely wished Tibet's assurance that they would not side with Russia and allow The Bear to use their land to stockpile troops and matériel for an invasion of India.

"At that time, I had no real thought that I would be

allowed within shooting distance of the Dalai Lama, much less close enough to converse. That possibility came much later.

"The boy didn't want me. He was afraid I'd give them away, and bring some impossible-to-predict form of wrath down on his lama. However, he was greatly tempted, seeing that supporting my assignment might go some way towards obviating his rebellion against his Survey masters. O'Hara would freely have given his life for the lama, but it troubled him greatly to give up his future. In the end, the benefits outweighed the risk, and he agreed to take me with them.

"Because the old lama was growing feeble, he and the boy moved more slowly than our well-equipped expedition. So I remained a Norwegian for some weeks, and acquitted myself well enough to receive mention in the world press before the Scandinavians pulled back to the foothills in front of the snows. I went with them, then slipped away and doubled back to join O'Hara.

"Somehow or other he'd managed to assemble another set of monk's clothing for me, complete with prayer-beads and the sort of tam-o'-shanter cap they wore."

I paused in our peregrination of the foredeck to study Holmes, trying to picture him in the colourful fittings of a Tibetan monk. I could not.

"We wintered just below a pass, taking shelter in a monastery of like-minded individuals until the snows retreated in the spring."

"That must have felt like a long winter," I commented. If he'd fled England because he hungered for action, months in a snow-bound monastery must have been hugely frustrating.

But to my surprise, he leant forward to rest his elbows

against the ship's rail, a half-smile coming onto his narrow mouth as memories took his gaze to the horizon. "In some ways, yes. Certainly it didn't take long to run out of objects to play the Jewel Game with. But those two, the young white boy raised as a street urchin and the ancient Buddhist scholar, made for the most extraordinary company I've ever encountered, Russell. The one bursting with youth and beauty, the other a sea of wrinkles, the one a guttersnipe and petty thief, the other a revered head of a monastery—but when they met, the old man laid a potter's hands on the boy, and re-formed him in his image. The bond between them was so powerful, and so completely unlikely, it made one begin to believe in the doctrine of reincarnation. It was the only way to explain it, that they'd known each other many times over the ages."

I stared; the strange thing was, I couldn't tell if he was jesting.

He felt my gaze, and although he did not meet it, he straightened and went on more briskly. "In any event, the winter did grant me sufficient leisure to become word-perfect as a red-hat monk. I spent many hours teaching the boy certain skills he might need, if he chose to return to the road of the Intelligence agent, and in exchange he coached me until I could recite the lama's prayers better than he could, could expound on texts and write simple charms. And long hours out-of-doors in that high altitude rendered my skin as dark as those around me. When the pass cleared, I could probably have strolled into Lhasa without them.

"But Lhasa was where the lama was bound, and Lhasa was where his *chela*, and now their companion, would take him.

"We crossed over into Tibet in late March, reciting

our rosaries all the way. The snows were so high, I would have chosen to wait another fortnight, but the lama was impatient—for a man who had attained enlightenment, he could be remarkably susceptible to his desires—and O'Hara thought himself strong enough for both. In the end, I had the old man on my back for a number of very rough miles—and at fifteen thousand feet, that can be rough indeed. But we half-staggered, half-rolled down the other side, tipped our hats to the startled border guards and said a blessing on their unborn sons, and went our way.

"And there we were, inside Tibet, two British *sahib*s in a place where, had they known, the countryside would have swarmed up like an anthill and exterminated us, or at the very least thrown us out on our ears. But because the lama was known and loved, and because he vouched for his *chela* and the companion who had joined them some months before, no man questioned us, no official barred our way.

"I spent the rest of that summer and autumn there, during which time I succeeded in locating our captured agent—who was not actually within Tibet, but gaoled in a neighbouring kingdom—as well as planting amiable suggestions in certain important ears. I even managed two audiences with the Dalai Lama himself, who was much of an age with Kim, and although he hadn't young O'Hara's advantages in the wide world, he was nonetheless remarkably sensitive to nuance and willing to question his advisors' assumptions about the British threat.

"In the end, young O'Hara left his lama long enough to help me break the agent free from his prison and to secret him into hiding near the border. I tried to convince the lad to come with me back to India, but he stood firm.

He was utterly devoted to his lama, and he had given his word: He would not leave until the old man was finished with his *chela*'s services. Neither of us thought that would be past mid-winter, but I had no choice but to leave, and return the prisoner to his home. We parted there, on the road fifty miles from Lhasa, and never saw each other again."

The wistfulness in Holmes' voice, his faraway gaze over the water, the fact that he had neglected to inter-ject the running Hindi translation for the past five min-utes, all gave me the odd, sure sensation that a part of him regretted that he had not remained behind, deep in Tibet with the boy and his lama. It was a peculiar feel-ing, finding this entirely unsuspected stream flowing within a man I believed I knew so well.

And, as I could not then admit, not even to myself, the knowledge brought with it a faint trickle of jealousy of the apprentice Holmes had taught so assiduously, and come to admire so warmly, nearly a decade before I was born.

Chapter Three

Before the Port Said light grew on the horizon, our new shipboard community was well on its way to becoming an ephemeral village. In many ways, it was a duplicate of the society we had left behind: the aristocracy of First Class on the upper decks, the peasantry of enlisted men, clerks, and their families under our feet, with the true labouring classes either tidily concealed beneath P. & O. uniforms or else thoroughly hidden away in the bowels of the ship. Rigid social custom swayed not a millimetre in the dining rooms: One never spoke to a neighbour at table if one had not been introduced, and since there were few mutual acquaintances to proffer the necessary introductions, conversation was largely nonexistent. Holmes and I attended few of the dining room meals.

Other areas of the boat were less severely bound by the strictures of human intercourse. In the exercise room, for example, it proved difficult to maintain a dignified formality with the woman at the next stationary bicycle when both of you were sweating and panting and furiously going nowhere. And because of the limited population in our floating village, group events such as card games, mah-jongg, or table tennis tended to require a certain loosening of rules in order to maintain a pool of players, which broke the ice sufficiently to permit one to nod to one's fellow player when one came upon him or her perambulating the deck the following morning.

However, as I used the ship's gym rarely and played neither mah-jongg nor table tennis, I was permitted, in the brief periods of free time permitted me by my taskmaster, to remain firmly sheltered with my books. I had finished with the archaeology of Mohenjo-Daro and was sitting bundled on a sheltered deck chair with a translation of the massive and hugely complicated Hindu epic called *The Mahabharata*, when an unexpected voice intruded.

"So, what are *you* going as?"

I blinked up at the voice, which had come from a slim girl of perhaps seventeen who was dressed in an ever-so-slightly garish fur coat, a pleated skirt, a cloche hat over her bobbed hair, and a long beaded necklace. She was standing near the railing, trying to set alight the long cigarette she'd fitted into an even longer ivory holder; the wind was not giving her much joy with it.

"I beg your pardon?" I asked. I couldn't think what she was talking about, nor did I think we had met.

She seemed unaware of the repressive overtones in my question, unduly taken up with the problem of getting the match to meet the tobacco before the wind blew it out. I thought she had not been smoking long. Come to think of it, her presence on such an inhospitable and deserted bit of deck might not be unrelated to her inexperience: hiding from a disapproving parent, no doubt. "The fancy-dress ball," she explained, and then bent over the match to shelter it, nearly setting her fur coat on fire in the process. At last—success. With an air of accomplishment she let the wind snatch away the spent match, placed the ivory mouthpiece to her lips with two elegant fingers, sucked in a lungful of smoke, and promptly collapsed in a gagging, retching fit of coughs that left her teary-eyed and weak-kneed. I sat with my finger between the pages, watching to see that she didn't stagger over the railings, but the fit subsided without my assistance. She hiccoughed once, swabbed her eyes, and tottered over to collapse onto the empty deck chair next to me, glaring accusingly at the cigarette that burnt serenely in its holder.

"Next time just hold the smoke in your mouth," I suggested, "instead of pulling it all the way into your lungs."

"Whew!" she exclaimed. "I mean to say, I've smoked before, of course, but I guess the wind . . ."

"Quite," I said, and opened my book again.

"So, what *are* you going as?"

"Sorry? Oh, the fancy-dress ball. I didn't realise they had one." I might have done, had I stopped to consider the matter. Shipping lines invented all sorts of ways to keep their passengers from succumbing to the throes of boredom, and encouraging wealthy men and women to make utter fools of themselves was a popular ploy, not the least because it ate up hours and hours in the preparations. "I shouldn't think I'll be going."

"Oh, but you have to!" she said, sounding so disappointed I had to wonder again if we didn't know each other. But before I could ask, I noticed her burning tobacco sinking forgotten, dangerously close to her coat.

"Er, watch the end," I urged her.

"Oh! Gosh," she exclaimed, patting furiously at the smoldering fur and plucking the still-burning cigarette out of the holder, tossing it into the wind, which I hoped might be strong enough to carry the ember clear of the unsuspecting passengers below. "Maybe I'm not cut out for smoking."

It was on the end of my tongue to reassure her to never mind, she'd pick it up with practice, but I kept the thought to myself. Why should I encourage the maintenance of a filthy habit?

"Mama wants me to dress as a Kewpie doll, but I was thinking of being an Indian dancing girl—you know, scarfs and bangles."

A certain degree of negotiation was clearly in store for the girl and her mother. Who was she, anyway?

As if I had voiced the question aloud, she thrust the ivory holder into her pocket and stuck out her hand. "Sorry, I'm being rude. I'm Sybil Goodheart. Everyone calls me Sunny."

"Mary Russell," I offered in return.

"And of course, you're just joking about not going to the ball. I'm so bad, I never can tell when someone's pulling my leg. What are you going as?"

I gave up; the child was too persistent for me. "Perhaps I'll just wear my pyjamas and go as the downstairs neighbour, come to complain."

She clapped her hand across her mouth and giggled, blushing slightly, perhaps at the idea of a proper lady coming in her nightwear. For a Flapper, she was easily shocked.

"You're an American," I said. If the accent hadn't told me, the brashness would have.

"From Chicago. You ever been there?"

"I passed through once, when I was young."

"It's *got* to be the world's stinkiest city," she declared. "What're you going to India for?"

"Er, my husband and I have business there." Impossible to give the deflating retort a proper Englishwoman would have wielded at the importunity of the question; poor Sunny would have gone behind the clouds.

"Is that nifty old—er, older man your husband?" she asked in astonishment. "I mean to say, Mama and I noticed him earlier when you were on the deck."

"That is my husband, yes," I told her. And if she delivered a third rudeness, I would smack her. Verbally, of course. "And you, why are you going out?"

"I'm a little late for the 'fishing fleet,' aren't I?" she said with a most disarming grin. "Actually, we had meant to come out in October, but Mama had a message from the spirits saying it was inauspicious, so we waited, which in the end was fantabulous, because I got to meet Ivor Novello at a party in London."

" 'The spirits,' " I repeated carefully.

Sunny inclined her head towards me and confided, "Hokum, isn't it? But Mama has had some powerful experiences in her time, and who's to argue? That is to say, I did argue at the time, because who wants to come all the way here and have to skedaddle away after a few weeks as soon as the weather gets hot? But Mama chose her time, and we will at least have a month to sight-see before we go to see her Teacher."

There was no mistaking the capital letter on the noun. Knowing I was going to regret it, I asked her which teacher that was.

"His name's Kumaraswami Shivananda, have you heard of him? No, most people haven't. Mama met him when he was on a lecture tour through the States, and came to Chicago. He's absatively keen for an old man—has to be at least forty, but has those dark eyes that seem to look right through you. Anyhoo, he channels the spirits, especially one he calls The Vizier, who was something big in ancient Egypt. The Vizier sent Kumaraswami on his world tour, to gather pupils and then teach them all about enlightenment through the body. Ever so much nicer than all those skinny, unhealthy-looking characters who tell you to renounce all sensation, don't you think?"

"Is, er, Kumaraswami Indian, then, or Egyptian?"

"Oh, no, he's from Pittsburgh. But The Vizier spoke to him one day in a séance and told him to change his name and go to India, so that was that."

Keeping my face straight was a struggle, but I agreed solemnly that enlightenment through the body did sound far nicer than some of the ascetic disciplines I had heard of. Sunny smiled, not knowing what I was talking about, but happy to have found what she took to be a kindred spirit.

"Have you ever been to a séance?" she asked.

"I, er, I know people who have."

"They're bunk, really, but tons of laughs. Everyone sitting so serious and then the channeller begins making all these squeals and groans, and you have to sit there fighting not to giggle."

At least I shouldn't have to warn the child not to be too gullible, I reflected, somewhat relieved.

"Come meet Mama and Tom?" she urged, jumping to her feet as if there could be no doubt that I would instantly agree.

"I should be getting back to w—" I started, but she pleaded.

"Oh, just for a jiffy! They're right below us waiting

for tea, it would be ever so nice to show Mama I've made a friend so that when I want to go off and flirt with those tasty young officers she won't worry."

Who was I to shackle a free spirit such as Sunny Goodheart? And if she had originally intended to join the "fishing fleet" of eligible young women travelling to India to hook a husband, she would need all the help she could get to make up for three months of lost time. "I'd love to meet your mother," I said, causing her to give a little jump of pleasure before she seized my hand and led me down the deck towards the stairs. It was impossible not to smile at the creature; despite her dress and her cultivated worldly airs, she struck one as little more than a child.

Mama, on the other hand, was formidable, and I vowed not to venture into the heavy waters of theology with a woman possessed of that determined jaw. I offered her my hand, did not bother to correct Sunny's introduction of me as "Mrs Russell," and then shook the hand of the tall young man who had been seated at Mrs Goodheart's side. He had placed a bookmark in his collection of the works of Marx (an English translation) before unfolding himself from the deck chair, a process rather like that of a standing camel or an unfolding crane. He was at least three inches over six feet, taller even than Holmes, and thin to the point of emaciation. One might think he'd been ill, except his colour was good and his movements, although languid, showed no discomfort.

"And this is Tom," Sunny told me. "My brother. He finished at Harvard last June and has been taking the Tour in Europe. He decided to include India, since Mama wanted to go. Tommy's a Communist," she appended proudly.

Personally, I couldn't see much to be proud of, either in the political stance or in the young man himself. Tom Goodheart's features were pleasing enough, and he appeared to have some wiry muscle under his European-tailored jacket, but even seated, he looked down his nose at one—not openly, but behind an expression so bland, one immediately suspected it of being a mask. I decided that he was a member of the supercilious generation—no doubt he fancied himself an artist or a philosopher, or both—and the attitude as much as the clothes the three wore told me that Communist or no, money did not go wanting in the Goodheart family. The swami from Pittsburgh, I decided, was on to a good thing.

"How do you do?" I said, and before Sunny could drag up a chair (and it would be she who dragged it, not her brother) I glanced at my wrist and began to apologise. "I'm terribly sorry, I just remembered that I promised my husband I'd meet him a few minutes ago, it went right out of my head. Lovely to meet you, I look forward to seeing more of you all on the voyage."

And made my escape.

~ ❧ ~

But in the end, there would be no escaping Mrs Goodheart. The following afternoon, the rapidly filling pouches of my brain threatening to burst and spill out all the verb forms and adjectives I had ruthlessly crammed inside, Holmes and I took a turn around the deck. It was, I found, very pleasant indeed, with a degree more warmth in the winter sun. As we strolled arm in arm, dodging nannies pushing perambulators and the marching khaki-shorts brigade, I was doubly grateful that our haste had forced us to bypass the inevitably heaving Bay of Biscay and pick up the boat in the relative calm of the Mediterranean. Had we boarded in Southampton, I should only now be recovering from sea-sickness.

Then I heard a voice from a shaded corner, and the biliousness threatened to return.

"Mrs Russell, how good to see you. Won't you introduce us to your husband?"

Two-thirds of the Goodheart family, mother and son. I opened my mouth to correct the American matriarch, but despite her opening volley, she did not wait for introductions, merely thrust her many-ringed hand at Holmes and said, "Mr Russell, glad you could join us. We were just talking about you, wondering if you were going to hide out in your cabin the entire trip."

"Actually," I began, but this time Holmes broke in, taking a brisk step forward to grasp the woman's hand.

"Mrs Goodheart, is it?" he said. "And this must be your son. Afternoon, young man, I hope you're enjoying your voyage?"

Amused, I let my correction die unborn: It seemed that Holmes was to be "Mr Russell" for a time.

Mrs Goodheart ordered her son to find another chair; to my surprise, Holmes did not object. Instead, he settled into the deck chair at her side as if a leisurely contemplation of the sea in the company of a bossy American spiritualist was just the thing for a Sunday afternoon. Bemused, I subsided into the vacant chair on Mrs Goodheart's other side and waited to see what Holmes was up to.

"Where is Sunny?" I asked the mother.

"She said she was going to try her hand at shovel-board. I would have stayed to watch, but I found the sun rather warm for my delicate complexion. She'll be here in a while,

I'm sure. And you, Mrs Russell—have you found some shipboard entertainment?"

Stuffing my head with Hindi verb forms and hurling tea-spoons back and forth at my husband, I thought, but said merely, "I'm not much of one for games, Mrs Goodheart."

"Sunny will change that," she said, with a somewhat alarming confidence. "Thomas my dear, tell the Russells what you've been doing in Europe."

The languid young Marxist settled into the chair he had caused to be brought, and launched into a recitation of the Paris literary salons visited, the avant-garde artists met, the underworldly haunts flirted with, the firebrand politicians-in-exile drunk with. He had even met Lenin—well, not met, precisely, but they had been at a function in Moscow at the same time early the previous autumn, and had friends in common.

"And tell them about your maharaja," Mrs Goodheart said, oozing with complacency.

"Oh, you mean Jimmy?" he said, magnificently casual. "Fellow I met last year—at the same party Lenin stopped by, in fact—turns out he's a maharaja. Never know it by looking at the man, he's as common as you or me" (Sherlock Holmes did not even blink at being dubbed "common") "and interested in everything. We got to talking about the States, he wanted to know if I'd ever seen a herd of buffalo—he called them bison, turns out they already have a kind of buffalo there in India, very different animal, could get confusing. I had to tell him I'd personally only seen them in a zoo, but that I had a pal who lived out in the Plains and he had one he kept as a pet. Well, Jimmy—his name's Jumalpandra, but that's a bit of a mouthful—he got so excited, nothing would do but for me to cable my friend immediately and ask where Jimmy could get a few bison for himself.

"Turns out the fellow's got a reputation as a sporting maharaja, travelled the world taking all sorts of big game, but he's getting tired of the local varieties, the buffalos and tigers and such. So he's started his own zoo, been buying up breeding stock of game animals from around the globe—lions from Africa, emus from Australia, panthers from South America. That's why he was in Russia, to arrange for some wild boar to juice up the local variety. Any rate, he'd heard somewhere that bison were great sport. And as luck would have it, a friend of my pal could get his hands on three cows and a bull."

Mrs Goodheart broke in. "And since Thomas here arranged it, the maharaja's invited us to come and spend some time with him. In his kingdom," she added, lest we think they were to be shelved in some Bombay hotel. "Khanpur is its name."

A mild expression that might have been annoyance flitted across Tom Goodheart's face, irritation at having the climax of his story snatched away, but before he could respond, a hugely contrasting swirl of pink and white merriment came dashing up the deck to confront us.

"Oh! Mrs Russell, how super! Have you ever played shovel-board? On a boat? You shove the little puck down the deck and it's going perfectly and then the boat tilts a little and—oops! There goes your nice straight shot, so then you try to compensate on the next turn and the deck tilts the other way and there goes your shot to the other side. Oh, it's ever so funny!"

"Sunny, this is Mr Russell," her mother told her.

"Oh!" the girl squeaked. "So pleased to meet you.

Your wife is such a darling, and such a sense of humour!"

"Oh yes," Holmes agreed gravely. "Quite the joker is my wife."

The girl turned to me again. "They're going to have an egg race next. Wouldn't you like to come and join?"

There was very little I would enjoy less than a shipboard egg race, but since one of those lesser pleasures was the idea of remaining within reach of Sunny's mother and brother, I made haste to stand before we could be assigned some other task. "I won't participate, but I shall come and cheer you on."

Holmes would have to manufacture his own escape.

The old-fashioned egg race was every bit as fatuous as I had expected, the girls shrieking and giggling and bouncing on their toes for the benefit of the onlooking officers. One side of the deck had been roped off for the games, but the participants were somewhat thinner on the ground—or rather, on the boards—than they would have been during the autumn migration. Still, the girls made up for it in self-conscious enthusiasm during the first two heats of the P. & O.'s quaint idea of fun. After those, however, the paucity of numbers brought about a defiant change of house rules, and the relays became co-educational. The baritone voices were accompanied by a shift in the merriment to something resembling true competition, and if the men looked even more ridiculous than the women had in racing down the deck with spoon and teetering egg, everyone had a splendid time, and there was plenty of opportunity for jovial banter and a certain degree of innocent physical contact.

The change in noise, however, attracted the parental authorities of those girls young enough to view the game merely as pleasurable exercise linked with mild flirtation instead of early negotiations in the serious economic business of matrimony. Repressive suggestions were made, Mrs Goodheart decreeing that Sunny looked quite flushed and a rest might be in order before it came time to dress for dinner, and the egg-race orgy died a natural death. The young men straightened their collars and went back to their corners; the young women recalled their sophistication and lounged off for a cigarette, illicit or open, depending on the smoker's age. Holmes and I seized the opportunity for retreat.

We made for the less occupied reaches of the deck, up where smuts drifted from the steamer stacks and the vibration from the engines far below bounced one's feet on the boards. I had a coin in my hand, to practice flipping it across my knuckles. My fingers were remembering the drill and becoming more supple, the motions more nearly automatic.

"Why on earth did you wish to speak with those people, Holmes?"

"That is 'Mr Russell' to you."

"Holmes."

"I merely wished to examine the phenomenon of a wealthy and educated young American who embraces the cant of the Bolsheviks. I have some familiarity with his British counterpart, but I was interested to see if there were regional differences."

"And were there?"

"None of import. The aristocracy amuses itself in many ways, among which is the pretence of being a commoner. You will note, however, that rarely is the claim accompanied by a renunciation of status or wealth."

"I suppose it's a harmless enough flirtation. Better than yanking a variety of exotic animals from their homes and shipping them halfway around the globe in order to shoot them."

"Having granted them a long and prolific life before their demise," he pointed out mildly. "And by comparison with the extreme behaviour of some of the native princes, the attitude of young Goodheart's maharaja seems fairly tame. The boredom of the aristocracy reaches new highs amongst India's hereditary rulers, and the lengths to which some of them go to escape it—well, let us say merely that ancient Rome might learn a few things about depravity."

I might have explored that interesting topic, but a sudden thought made me glance apprehensively at the dancing boards under my feet. "You don't suppose those beasts of his are in the hold of this ship, do you?"

"This is a P. & O. liner, Russell. They don't even permit lap dogs."

That was a relief. I had seen bison, and did not like to imagine what an irritated one could do to a ship's hold.

We took our evening meal in our rooms, as well as breakfast on Monday, and by making immediately for the more insalubrious portions of the decks during the middle of the day, we avoided the Goodhearts until Sunny caught us strolling down the stairs at tea-time, her brother ambling along behind her.

"Oh! Mrs Russell, I've missed you so. I hope you haven't been ill, I was looking for you at lunch. Hello, Mr Russell."

"We've just been elsewhere," I told her; Holmes murmured something vaguely apologetic and pulled a vanishing act. "Did you need something?"

"Oh, yes, I just wanted to ask if you were thinking of going ashore at Port Said tomorrow. Tommy and I are skipping off to see Cairo and the pyramids by moonlight, although Mama says it's too strenuous a jaunt for her. The purser says we'll rejoin the ship in Suez, he absolutely promises. Please, won't you come?"

Moonlight? I thought. The moon would be but a tiny sliver, handsome enough in the desert sky but short-lived and less illuminating than a candle. Little point in saying anything to this young lady, however—the shipping line might not permit lap dogs, but Sunny was doing her best to make up for their absence, endearing herself to all and polishing off whatever odd scraps were put on her plate. I stifled an impulse to snap the order to *Sit*!

"No, thank you, Sunny. I may go ashore in Aden, but not here." I had not yet seen the pyramids, but I did not wish to do so for the first time on a rushed day-trip in the company of a shipload of tourists. Call me a snob, but I prefer to take in the world's grand sights when I can at least hear myself think. Not that I was killjoy enough to say so aloud.

Her round little face fell in disappointment. "I'm so sorry. Tommy was looking forward to it."

Tommy, I thought, cared not a whit if I came, although at the memory of the fellow's bland and disinterested mask, I experienced a vague stir of disquiet. Before I could pursue the thought, Sunny perked up again. "Well, maybe you'll join Mama? There's a group going ashore to buy pith helmets and such, sounds ever so fun."

I rather doubted that, and could only imagine the

sort of solar topees on offer at a shop catering to lady tourists fresh from England. Holmes would go ashore in Port Said to send a telegram to Mycroft; I'd ask him to buy me a sun-hat while he was there. "No, I'll wait, thanks. You have a good time. And, Sunny? Please call me Mary."

Her face blossomed again, simple soul, and she chattered for a while about maharajas and camels before bouncing off to consider the proper wardrobe for pyramid-visiting. I smiled at her retreating back: It would not be long before the one-woman fishing fleet was reeling in a whole school of handsome young officers on her line.

Chapter Four

After Port Said, the Suez Canal sucked us in. As the shadows grew long we drifted down its narrow length, exchanging impassive gazes with the goats, camels, and robed humans that inhabited its sandy banks. I sat on the upper deck with a couple of the oranges we had picked up in Port Said, reading the tattered copy of *Kim* I had discovered in the ship's library, rediscovering the pleasures of a classic tale with unexpected depths. The story sparkled as I remembered it, the orphan boy free to attach himself to Afghan horse-trader and wandering holy man alike, learning the Jewel Game from the enigmatic Lurgan Sahib, meeting the Babu with his clumsy surface concealing his deep committed competence. I sighed when I finished it, and dutifully returned it to the shelves between Chesterton and Wodehouse. I perused the library's other offerings, but its contents proved considerably less informative than the armload of books I had raided from Holmes' shelves, and I went back to them.

I was slowly putting together a picture of India in my mind, the size and immense variety in land and people, its hugely complicated caste system, based originally on the distinction between Brahmin/priest, Kshatriya/warrior, Vaisya/artisan, and Sudra/menial. The lowest of these was called "Untouchable," but in truth, it sounded as if no one was allowed to touch anyone else, for fear the other might be of a lower caste and hence ritually unclean. And since the original four castes had splintered into thousands—as well as having Buddhists, Moslems, Sikhs, Christians, and a hundred others thrown into the mix—I thought the population must spend most of its energy sorting out where it stood on the ladder.

I read for hours, absorbing India's long history of conquest and re-conquest, from Alexander to Victoria; the Moghul influence on the country, long and ongoing; the East India Company's rule so violently cut short by the 1857 Mutiny; the subsequent authority of the British government, ruling directly those portions of the country not under the command of their native rulers. The Empire in 1924: a bit worn around the edges, perhaps, but still strong.

The night was desert-cool and brilliant, and Holmes and I settled beneath the crisp crescent of moon and sat until long after midnight, wrapped in our thoughts and memories. The next day the canal spat us out into the Red Sea, and the younger Goodhearts rejoined us, transformed into old Egypt hands by nineteen hours inland, clothed in a variety of peculiar garments including topees (they no longer used the outsider's term "pith helmet") of a shape unknown outside the *souks* of Cairo, constructed of some vegetable matter (pith, one presumes) that sagged as the weather warmed.

Which it did as we continued south. Cabin trunks

went down to the hold in exchange for those marked "Wanted on Voyage," and the shipboard community traded its English hats for rigid solar topees, casting off a few of its inhibitions along with the woollens. Wanton conversation broke out all over the ship, as formerly aloof ladies unbent so far as to offer comments on the weather and rigid-spined gentlemen exchanged opinions on cricket and horse-racing. The men's dark serge suits changed to pale drill or linen (or, for the hopelessly flamboyant merchants known as *box-wallah*s, tussore silk) and male dinner-wear began to take on variations of the tropics, with white jackets or trousers but, oddly, never both. Women's arms appeared even during the day-time, and some of the more daring members played short-skirted games of tennis on the top deck in the early mornings, until all the balls had vanished into the sea, after which they changed to the more controllable badminton. Decks sprouted awnings, making it more difficult to find a patch of sun, and beds were made up there at night—men on one side, of course, ladies on the other. The exercise equipment in the stifling shipboard gym went unused after mid-morning, and vigorous deck games were replaced by the more sedate shovel-board and quoits. Holmes and I spent the mornings in our rooms, palming coins, renewing our juggling skills, repeating and refining common phrases in my new tongue, until we were driven out by the mid-day heat. In the open, even in our less attractive chosen corners, magic tricks were set aside in favour of bilingual conversation and the relief of books. I was still working my way through *The Mahabharata* when a familiar shape plopped down beside me where I sat in the shade of a large crate.

"There you are!" Sunny exclaimed. "What on earth are you reading?"

I showed her the book, half irritated at the interruption, but also glad for it. An unrelieved diet of Holmes, Hindi, and Hindu mythology surely couldn't be good for one.

"Good heavens, look at those names!" she said. "I can't even pronounce half of them. What is this, anyway?"

"The great Indian Hindu epic, the battle between their great gods and demons, the founding of the people."

"I think I'd rather read one of Mama's Ethel Dells," she said, handing it back to me.

"At this point, I think I might as well."

She sat for a rare moment of stillness, studying the distant shore. "Isn't the Suez Canal just the superest thing? Tommy says it saves weeks and weeks of sailing all around Africa, with storms and all. You English were so clever to have built it."

It was slightly startling to be given personal credit for the project, and I felt an obligation to set her—and Tommy—straight. "Actually, the canal was here long before England was even a country. Ramses the Second was the first Egyptian to begin it, although it wasn't completed until the days of Darius, about twenty-four hundred years ago. Not that it's been open all that time. The silt blocks it, and a couple of times it was deliberately filled in for defence purposes, but we can hardly be given credit for thinking of the thing. Anyone who looked at a rudimentary map would be tempted to get out the shovels."

"Well!" she exclaimed. "I never. And Tommy said . . . But aren't you clever, to know these things? I should have gone to school, university I mean, but somehow it just never seemed to come up."

"It's not too late."

"I suppose," she said dubiously, but we both knew she never would. She spent perhaps thirty seconds mourning her lack of education, then held out one arm alongside mine, which was growing darker by the day. (For, whatever our disguises might be in the weeks ahead, I doubted that pale-skinned English lady would be one of them.)

"When Mama notices how brown you're going, don't be surprised if she has ten fits. Whenever she finds me sitting in the sun, she gives me a lecture about wrinkles until I put on my topee."

"Topees make me feel as if I'm speaking inside a bucket," I said.

She giggled. "Does your mother nag you, too, or does that stop as soon as you're married?"

"My mother's dead," I told her.

Her expressive face crumpled. "Oh, I am so sorry. How stupid of me, I didn't—"

I interrupted before she burst into tears. "Don't worry, it's been a very long time. So tell me, have you decided to be a Kewpie doll or a harem dancer?"

The fancy-dress ball was to be the following night, and the ship quivered with the thrill of anticipation, the ship's tailors working round the clock, sworn to secrecy. Holmes and I planned on taking advantage of the evening's empty cabins to begin juggling clubs. Wooden belaying pins when dropped make quite a noise.

My distraction worked. Sunny clapped her hands and leant towards me as if there might be spies lurking on the other side of the crate to ask, "Have you ever been to the cabarets in Berlin?"

I reared back to stare at the child, speechless. A Berlin

night-club was not a thing I'd have thought Sunny's mother would have allowed her daughter within a mile of.

"Er, yes."

"Well, I haven't seen one" (Thank goodness for small mercies, I thought.) "but Tommy told me about one girl who dances on stage with a big snake. And that made me think about the snake charmers in India, and, voilà!"

"Where are you going to get a snake?" I asked. Did snakes perhaps not come under the P. & O.'s pet-exclusion clause?

"Not a real snake, silly!" Sunny's eyes danced. "I'm having the *durzi* make up a snake for me—*durzi*'s what they call tailors in India—and I'll wear it around my shoulders. And I have a dress that matches its skin. Won't that be fun?"

I thought that it might be more fun than she was prepared for, considering the number of young men on board. "It sounds . . . exotic. But, Sunny? Perhaps you shouldn't mention Berlin in relation to the costume. Those night-clubs might be considered somewhat . . . risqué for a girl your age."

"Okay. But what do you think of the snake idea?"

"I think you'll have every young man on the ship slithering along the decks after you," I said.

She giggled.

However, later that evening as we were dressing for dinner, Holmes astonished me as well. He chose a moment of weakness on my part, as he was brushing my long hair.

"Russell, I think it might be a good idea to go to this costume ball."

"*Holmes!*" I jerked away from his hands to look up at him. "Are you feverish?"

"Russell, I did not say that *I* intended to go."

"Oh no. If I have to go, so do you." I took the hair-brush from him and turned to the looking-glass. "But why on earth should either of us wish to dress up with a room of drunken first-class passengers wearing bizarre clothing?"

"Thomas Goodheart."

Holmes had continued to cultivate the young man's acquaintance—I cannot call it a friendship, precisely—and the two spent a part of every day either lounging on the deck or in the depths of the all-male enclave of the smoking room, playing billiards, whist, or occasionally poker. My husband's uncharacteristic sociability with the supercilious young American might have puzzled me had I not overheard some of their conversations, and known that, more often than not, the Communist Party and the politics of India were the chief topics of Holmes' casual enquiries. Still, to Mr Goodheart I was clearly beyond the pale. Educated, free-thinking women were not his cup of tea, and he made no attempt at concealing that fact.

"Is Goodheart going? I shouldn't have thought his convictions would permit him the frivolity of a fancy-dress ball."

"His mother assures me that he will be attending."

To observe the enemy, or to convert the bourgeoisie to earnest Bolshevism? "But why should his presence or absence at a fancy-dress ball be of the least interest to you?"

"I have found the lad peculiarly . . . self-contained. Remarkably so—I've seldom seen a man who gives away as little as this one. I believe he knows more than he tells."

I considered the statement for a moment, but failed

to make a connexion. "Sorry, Holmes, what does self-containment have to do with fancy dress?"

"A costume ball is all about masks and the freedom they confer on the wearers. I wish to see what the fellow looks like when he imagines himself concealed." Seeing that I had my hair wrapped into place, he handed me a pin.

"Ah," I said. "You wish to get him drunk and see what he lets slip."

"Sometimes the old methods are the best," Holmes said, although he looked somewhat abashed at the admission.

"You think Goodheart is some kind of a villain?"

"I think it possible, although it is far from clear whether his particular brand of villainy need concern us. Still, it is the sort of thing Mycroft likes to hear about, to pass on to his fellows. Assuming," he muttered, "anyone in the incoming government will be interested in stray Bolsheviks."

"Oh, very well, I shall go if you wish. But I don't know what sort of costume we might pull together at this late date—all the Cleopatra masks and chimney-sweeper's coats are sure to have been taken. And I do not think it at all appropriate to dress as Lady Godiva," I said, picking up an extra and unnecessary hair-pin and jamming it in for emphasis.

"I have an idea," he said.

"Yes," I said, stifling a sigh. "I was afraid you might."

A sari is not a carefree sort of garment. To a person accustomed to clothing that remains where it was put, the lack of any fastening more secure than gravity is, to say the least, disconcerting. A sari, I found when Holmes presented me with the thing, was little more than a remarkably skimpy blouse and an enormous length of impossibly slippery silk, which is arranged into intricate folds and tucked into what amounts to little more than a piece of string around one's waist, after which the loose end (hah! It is all loose end.) is drawn gracefully up across one's chest and over the opposite shoulder, where it then spends the entire evening yearning to slither to the floor, taking the rest of the garment with it. If the wearer were to suck in her stomach, many, many yards of silk would collapse into a lovely pool on the floor around her near-naked legs. And this was before I added the gossamer silk shawl over my head and shoulders.

The fourth time I tried the thing, standing before the glass afraid to breathe, I scowled at the reflection of Holmes behind me. "You had this planned back in Port Said and didn't warn me."

"Not planned, precisely. I merely thought it best to have the costumes, just in case."

Holmes' fancy dress, hanging in the wardrobe, looked by comparison a thing of Chanel-like comfort. He was attending as an Indian nobleman, with snug white trousers underneath a gold brocade jacket trimmed with chips of topaz. At the moment he was trying on the snowy white turban or *puggaree* (whose intricate folds, unlike those of the sari, had come pre-arranged on a hatmaker's dummy). At its front was a spray of peacock feathers, which he eyed critically in the glass.

"Are you going to wear your emeralds?" he said suddenly.

Trying to avoid motion, I looked back at my reflection. The sari slid from my shoulder, and I snatched at it to avert the unwinding process, but too late. Half the tucks came crooked, and I cursed under my breath.

"I'll trade you my necklace for your emerald stick-pin," I told him grimly.

Ah, success! With the sari's end secured to the under-blouse with Holmes' tie pin, the danger of instant nudity retreated considerably. Then during the afternoon I hunted down the purser and, by dint of offering an enormous bribe, found a stray maid willing to come with a needle and thread to sew me into the folds and tucks.

And in truth, the emerald necklace looked magnificent nestled among the peacock feathers on the *puggaree*.

When the maid had scurried away with her needle and her payment, I sat down to arrange my hair. Indian women tend to wear theirs gathered into a heavy knot at the base of their necks, which was not a style I found easy to arrange without assistance. As I was struggling to contain my own hair, which was sufficiently long but lacked the malleability of black hair, Holmes came in. I glanced in the glass, and had to smile.

"You look regal, Holmes."

He walked over to where I sat, and wordlessly removed the brush from my hand.

Where Holmes learnt to arrange a woman's hair I never knew—never wished to ask—but he was remarkably proficient at it. It was, however, never easy to stifle the sensations caused by his strong hands in my hair, the palm smoothing the strands after the brush had passed through, the clever fingers working their way from one side to the other, gathering the heavy length in a controlling grip, tugging and smoothing and shaping. In this instance, lest something begin that put all our preparations to naught, I shut my eyes and thought of England, horrible and cold under the snow, wet and miserable and filled with political turmoil. His long fingers smoothed and twisted, sending delicious tingles down my spine, and cold England faded. But in a few minutes my hair was sleekly gathered in a secure but comfortable knot, and Holmes' hands drew away, after a brief grasp on my shoulders and the salute of a kiss where the heavy bun now lay against my neck. I pushed away a shiver and reached firmly for my ear-rings, then draped the breath-fine silk scarf across my shoulders and slid my hand through the arm of my nobleman.

Dignity, I remembered as we drew near the ballroom, was not a necessary component of a dress ball. The ducal version we had attended just the month before had been bigger than this one, and more elaborate, but the passengers made up for numbers and style in sheer high spirits. I balked just inside the entrance, and Holmes spoke into my ear.

"I believe we shall both require a quantity of champagne to get through this. Wait here."

Obedience occasionally has its place, particularly when it allows one's husband to press through to the nearest tray-bearing waiter. Holmes took many admiring looks, from women for the most part, and amused me by appearing oblivious of all. He returned with two glasses of the fizzy stuff, which we lifted to each other, then poured down our throats.

One problem with fancy dress comes when one wishes to find a particular person whose disguise one does not know. I was quite certain that Sunny Goodheart was not yet here, since there was no sign of a snake, nor of the snake-dance line of males that was sure to follow as soon as she passed through the room. And although her brother's height should have made him instantly recognisable, a number of tall hats and *puggarees* protruded above the heads, concealing their wearers' stature. Holmes and I waited, drinking our wine, turning down dance offers from individuals of both sexes and (apparently) neither.

Then a ripple ran through the room, and I turned, already smiling, to see the snake charmer. And my suspicions were correct, it was an extraordinary costume, which on a less naïve and charming individual would have been instantly engulfed in a travelling rug and ushered briskly outside. As it was, Sunny looked like a child dressed in a harem outfit, her wriggles for fun, not seduction, her innocence shining out under the sinuous creature that lay across her shoulders. The dress was not quite as form-fitting as the snake's skin, but was not far off. What saved it were the multiple layers of scarf she wore over it, gauzy and shifting. The effect was that of a snake shedding its old and lacy·skin for the bright, snug new one beneath. I tipped my head to the man at my side and murmured, "If they're aiming her at their maharaja, all they have to do is make sure there's a fancy-dress ball."

"Pardon?" asked a strange voice.

Startled, I glanced up at the person beside me, whose ears were somewhat higher than those of my husband, and who might therefore have missed my hugely impertinent words. It was Thomas Goodheart, but to my enormous consternation, it was also Sherlock Holmes—not he of the Sussex cottage but the figure of stage and, recently, screen, complete with deerstalker, absurdly large calabash pipe, and tweed cloak.

I gaped at the figure, my mind working furiously to understand the meaning of his costume. Tom Goodheart, in the meantime, allowed his glance to trail down my own length of silk. "You would look at home in Jimmy's palace, Mrs Russell. Very, um, authentic."

"I, er, thank you. You too. That is to say, not in the palace." *You're babbling, Russell,* I said to myself. *Stop it.* "Your sister's costume is extraordinary."

"Isn't it just? I can't imagine what my mother had in mind, allowing that. Still, it's not as bad as it was before she added the scarfs and scrubbed off her rouge."

"She's a great girl," I said.

"Yes, she's all right. She's very fond of you."

What is it about the subtle signs between men and women? The words themselves were completely innocent and his eyes remained on my face, but some tiny pause before the word "fond," some slight emphasis of voice or intensity of gaze, made it abundantly clear that Thomas was talking neither about his sister nor about mere fondness. For the first time, I became conscious of a streak of iron beneath the waffle, and caught a glimpse of someone older and considerably more determined under the rich boy's bland features.

And then he was looking out over the crowd, and Holmes was there with another glass of champagne, and the sensation was gone completely. Thomas Goodheart was merely the superior older brother of a kittenish girl who had befriended me, a young man patiently enduring a rather boring party for the sake of his family.

But I did not think I had imagined the glimpse of iron, nor the meaning behind his words.

And I began to speculate whether the likes of a Berlin cabaret might not be considered downright wholesome by Mr Goodheart, if perhaps the lessons in depravity Holmes had mentioned might not apply to certain American aristocrats among the rajas.

Villain, I would now believe. But also, I had to agree, what sort?

Without realising I had done so, I found myself drawn slightly away from the stagey Holmes until my arm pressed against that of the maharaja's ornate coat. Holmes glanced at me, surprised at my uncharacteristic demonstrativeness, then frowned slightly at whatever remnant of discomfort he glimpsed on my face. But it was gone in an instant, and I stood away and raised my glass in a toast to the festive gathering. Goodheart drained his glass, as did Holmes and I. I do not know about Holmes', but this particular drink was nothing more intoxicating than ginger beer.

And so it continued throughout the evening, with every other glass he put into my hand containing sweet nothingness. Tommy, however, continued to down his bubbly wine, with the predictable results when the strength of that substance is underestimated. The young man became increasingly intoxicated, and although Holmes appeared to match him in consumption and in effects, I knew my husband well enough to see it for an act.

Goodheart's drunkenness was not an act, although the slipping of his controls was not wild and overt. No, it came out in two ways, one of which he had already shown me, and which Holmes soon witnessed for himself. Holmes was enough of a professional to control his rage, and was also sure enough of his wife and partner's strength and self-respect that he did not feel the need to protect her by a simian pounding of chest, or of Goodheart's face. But it was an effort for him to stand by with smiling incomprehension and good will as Goodheart made one suggestive remark after another in my direction, and I was glad for his sake when the young man's intoxication ripened and bore fruit in the form of a hobbyhorse.

"These people, they haven't a clue," he declared, sweeping his glass at the room. Holmes plucked it from his hand and substituted a miraculously full one, and Goodheart slurped it with a scowl. "They haven't a damned clue. Pardon my French, Mary." I had not given him permission to use my first name, but I was hardly going to object now.

"That's true," Holmes agreed emphatically, then drew his eyebrows together in exaggerated confusion. "What about?"

"The world," Goodheart explained, pausing to belch lightly. Fortunately, he did not stop with the generalisation, but went on. "Look at them, prancing about like a bunch of aristo . . . , 'rishtocrats with the mob pounding on the gates. Like France, don't you know? Haven't a clue that there's a mob out there."

"With guillotines," Holmes encouraged.

The tweed deerstalker wagged enthusiastically. "Right, you are so right." His diction was sliding, the dental sounds long turned to mush, the "s" sounds now "sh." Soon the labials would become difficult; in another half hour, he'd collapse with his head on the table.

"But look what's happened in England," Holmes urged. "The Red Flag is practically flying over Parliament."

Goodheart's eyes tried to track, with limited success. "Right," he said, although he sounded somewhat dubious, as if unsure why Holmes had introduced politics into the discussion.

"Isn't that a good thing? To have a Labour victory?"

"Of course," he said, more stoutly now. "But they

think it's the end, when it's only the beginnin'." It sounded like a quote pulled from memory, and served to confuse him for a moment. Then he rallied, raised his glass, and shouted, "By s'prise, where it hurts!"

But the effort was too much—either that, or some vestige of self-preservation ordered him to be silent; in either case the effect was the same. He let his glass fall to the floor and slapped his palm across his mouth in the gesture of a child hushing itself, or in the more likely identical motion of a man whose stomach is on the verge of rebellion. I took a hasty step back while Holmes seized the man's free arm and hustled him speedily out of the doors and to the railing, where the deerstalker caught the wind and sailed off into the night.

A gentleman in the P. & O. uniform came to tidy away the broken glass, and another appeared to help Holmes lead Goodheart away. So much for *in vino veritas*.

I traded my glass of sweet nothing on a table for one of the real thing from the first passing waiter, and went outside for air and thought. After a while a snake-dance of celebrants came shuffling out the door, Sunny Goodheart at their lead laughing gloriously at her long tail of admirers.

I put down my empty glass and went to bed.

Chapter Five

⌘

The following day we came to Aden and the mouth of the Red Sea, where the ship would pause for a few hours to take on coal. This would be our last land until Bombay, and Holmes and I were among the few walking wounded of the night before who waited to go ashore. The hills around the town seemed covered with tiny windmills, spinning in the hot wind, and the instant the ship dropped anchor, the sea around us filled with small canoe-type boats paddled by young boys, calling for the passengers to drop coins for them to dive after. From where I stood at the rail, the water looked so murky, thanks to the steamer's huge screws, that I couldn't imagine the boys seeing anything smaller than a gold guinea flashing past, but clearly the exercise was worth their while, or they wouldn't have risked the sharks.

Heat settled over us as the launch approached the town, making me glad for once of the topee's shade. We passed through the canoes and the dhows to tie up at the pier and be ceremoniously handed off; the solid ground felt oddly unforgiving beneath my feet, which in the eight days since leaving Marseilles had grown accustomed to the rise and fall of the decking. The air smelt intense, marvellously complex with the odours of dust and spice and animals, and only occasional whiffs of burnt fuel.

Our first stop was the post office, where we retrieved a handful of letters, including one from Mrs Hudson and two from my solicitors in London. A quick glance through them showed that there was nothing of any great urgency, although I did send off a telegram to the legal people to say that I'd got their letters and would write at leisure. We then slid the post into our pockets and turned into the bazaar.

Aden rides the border between several worlds, all of them represented in her marketplace. Skin tones from ebony to ivory, a thousand shapes of head covering, dialects to keep a linguist in ecstasy for a lifetime. Three dusty Bedu slipped down the streets behind a pair of British soldiers; a dark-skinned Jew displayed his copper pots to an African Moslem headed home from Mecca; four British tars with their distinctive rolling gait haggled with a Christian shopkeeper over the price of a small carpet; a pair of Parsee women, wrapped in loveliness and followed by a pair of watchful men, fingered lengths of brilliant silk; a British captain strolled with his lady, his eyes on her and not the pick-pocket trailing close behind.

All that in the first fifty feet, before Holmes ducked inside a gap between shops. However, I was ready for it, and made haste to follow him.

The noisome passageway was clotted with filth, its air stifling, the darkness such that one was tempted to feel for the walls—but for the knowledge that one really didn't want to touch what was on those walls. I took half a dozen steps and stopped, waiting for my eyes to adjust before I found myself stepping into a coal cellar.

Then a door opened and the end of the passageway grew light, and I picked my way through unexamined shapes in that direction.

The room at the end was considerably tidier than its approach. It was a small space with a high ceiling, light but shaded from the direct sun hitting the courtyard outside its latticed windows. As soon as the door closed, the room's fragrance of jasmine-flower and musk reasserted itself; it even seemed cooler in here, although it was probably an illusion brought about by judicious use of blues and greens in the hangings, and the pale wood of the walls and chairs. Just as, I noticed, it seemed larger than it was, since all the furniture was somewhat smaller than normal.

A light and lightly accented voice interrupted my survey. "You like my house, Miss Russell?"

I whirled, unaware that there had been anyone in the room. I had to look around for the owner of the voice, then look down, to find a tiny figure scarcely four feet tall, nearly hairless but wizened with wrinkles, seated in a nest of silk cushions beside a burbling hookah.

"It's very attractive," I replied. "How do you know me?"

He giggled, a sound I normally mistrust in a man but which seemed natural in him. "We have, shall I say, mutual friends. And you, Mr Holmes. I had not thought to lay eyes on you again this side of Paradise."

"Good of you to imagine I might be headed in that direction, Solly. Russell, this is Suleiman Lal. Suleiman is the uncrowned king of Aden, and this room is the junction-box through which all the power of the Red Sea is dispersed. The state of the hall-way outside is his little jest."

"I imagine it also keeps away stray tourists," I said drily.

"Precisely," said the small man, and took a draw at his pipe. "You have come for your mail, I think?"

"To see if there was any," Holmes replied.

"In the cigar box on the second shelf," said Lal. Holmes stepped over to the diminutive shelves and drew out the wooden box, thumbing open its lid and taking out the pieces of paper therein. They were not mail, but telegraph flimsies. "Please, do read them," the small man urged. "You may wish to send a reply. And while you do so, we shall take tea."

With that, a narrow door behind Lal opened silently and a very dark-skinned man of normal height padded in with an ornate brassware tray set with the makings of an Oriental tea. Lal laid his pipe aside and shifted forward to pour from the tall pot into the handleless porcelain cups, and as the odour of mint filled the room, I was transported back to Palestine. Yes, this was already sweetened, and I slurped at the scalding, syrupy mint essence with pleasure.

Holmes read the telegrams and handed them to me. Both were from Mycroft. They read:

YOUR PRINCE INDEED OF QUESTIONABLE
VIRTUE
MAKING ENQUIRIES RE AMERICAN
MYCROFT

Followed two days later by:
TGH ACTIVE POLITICALLY AT UNIVERSITY NO
CHARGES BUT MOTHERS GURU ARRESTED
TWICE SPIRITUALIST FRAUD NO CONVICTIONS
TGH SEEN IN COMPANY OF MOSCOW SECURITY

SUGGEST YOU MENTION TO FRIEND IN DELHI
MYCROFT

"TGH" was doubtless Thomas Goodheart; his "political" activity at Harvard (to Mycroft, "political"
would be synonymous with "subversive") and his proximity to "security" in Russia went some way to justify
Holmes' interest in the man. Goodheart might be nothing more than Holmes' shipboard hobby, but I agreed
that whomever we were seeing in Delhi should be informed of our chance meeting.

I handed the flimsies back to Holmes, who stretched
his arm over to Lal's hubble-bubble to uncover its burning coal, using it to set the telegrams alight. He allowed
them to burn out in an ash-tray, then thoughtfully
tamped the ashy curls into black dust with his finger.

"There will be no reply," he told Lal, who nodded.

"I was told your brother was unwell."

"Is there any place you have no ears?" Holmes asked,
sounding amused.

Lal thought for a moment. "Within the American
White House I am currently friendless, but no doubt
someone will come to my aid before long." And with
that revelation his smile changed from a thing of easy
humour to a hint of what lay behind it, a knowledge of
the world's wickednesses and the sheer joy of possession. Suddenly his giggle was not so child-like and endearing.

Holmes continued to sip his tea, but I found the
stuff too sweet, cloying along my throat, so that I had
to force the last swallow down for the sake of politeness. The two men chatted of names I did not know
while I hid my impatience to be gone; hid, too, my

growing suspicion that there were things behind the airy silken drapes that I did not wish to see.

At long last, Holmes put down his empty cup and rose.

"You will not stay to lunch?" Lal asked, not really expecting that we would.

"We have purchases to make before the ship leaves, but thank you."

Lal nodded, that curious sideways gesture of the Oriental, and his eyes slid to mine.

"Miss Russell, I am not, perhaps, on the side of God as you would see it, but I assure you, I am not on the other side, either. I am glad to have met you, my dear."

He inclined his head, the equivalent of an offered hand, a gesture I returned. Then we left, through a door into the courtyard instead of the filthy alley, and came out on the next street over under the eye of a very large and well-armed Turk. I glanced around to be sure there was no one listening, and said in a low voice, "Holmes, do you trust that man?"

"Solly collects information, he does not sell it. He is utterly safe as a conduit because he is completely impartial, and would as willingly have given us our messages and served us tea if we were sworn enemies of the British Crown. Every side uses Lal because they know he will not sell them out. And no side tries to lay hands on his secrets because if they did, hell would pour down on them—secrets have a way of accumulating, and he lets it be known that his untimely death would loose them. Now, tell me what sort of silk you would like to practise your scarf act with."

We submerged ourselves again in the *souk*, making small purchases such as any English visitors might, as well as two or three items that Holmes appeared to have ordered beforehand, no doubt through his diminutive friend with the conjoined Moslem-Hindu names.

One of these purchases was at a jeweller's shop, and we were standing at the man's small counter examining a cunningly linked trio of bangles and conversing with the shopkeeper in Arabic when Holmes abruptly shifted his position so that the bangles disappeared into his sleeve. He continued the motion by reaching out to pluck a ring from a nearby display, saying in a loud English voice, "My dear, isn't this very like the ring your sister lost last year?"

As I had no sister and Holmes would no more address me as "my dear" than he would embrace me in public, it took no great subtlety of thought to know that he had spotted an intruder in the doorway. And sure enough, when I had taken the spectacularly ugly piece and turned with it to the lighter portion of the shop, there stood a familiar figure, ill concealed by his topee and dark sun-glasses. I looked up, surprised, and let an expression of recognition cross my face.

"Mr Goodheart, so you decided to come ashore after all! What do you think of this ring?"

He pulled the dark glasses from his bloodshot eyes and came fully into the shop, giving the ring I held out the merest glance. He seemed more interested in what we had been looking at earlier, but the bangles had vanished, and the shopkeeper was as phlegmatic as Holmes.

"I should think it would turn one's finger green in a day," Tommy Goodheart told me, looking more than a little green himself. "Say, you haven't come across my mother anywhere in this madhouse, have you? I was looking at some carpets and turned around and she was gone."

"I haven't seen her, no."

"Maybe you could ask this fellow for me," he said to Holmes. "Since you seem to speak the lingo."

So, he'd been listening outside long enough to hear the exchange. I didn't look at Holmes while he asked the man behind the counter if he'd seen a large American woman in a flowered dress (all Mrs Goodheart's dresses were flowered) looking lost. The man regretted that he had not seen such a person that day.

Holmes translated the man's reply, then told him that we would take the ring, please. I was glad to see the jeweller pick up the unspoken message, that the bangles Holmes had made away with were not to be mentioned, but would now be paid for; he made no protest, and reacted not in the least to a payment vastly greater than the price of the trinket for my "sister." He merely wrapped the ring, thanked us profusely, and turned to the young man and asked him in English if he wouldn't like to look at some pretty necklaces for his girlfriend.

"I don't have a girlfriend," Thomas snapped. "And if I did I wouldn't buy her rubbish at those prices. You really should've got him to come down," he said to Holmes, following us out into the street. He winced at the brightness and put his sun-glasses back on.

"Oh, that's my fault," I told Goodheart. "I hate haggling over a pittance, it always seems so rude. And these people have so little, compared to us."

I was interested to hear the committed Communist sniff in disgust at my willingness to share the wealth.

"Where'd you learn to speak the language?" he demanded, as if Holmes had revealed some distasteful habit.

"Oh, it's one of those things a person picks up," Holmes answered blandly. "I lived in Cairo for a time."

"That's right—the reason you didn't care to take the train down to see the pyramids. You two heading for the sights here? The tanks are supposed to be quite something."

"Not just now," Holmes said. "We've a bit more exploring down here to do. In fact," he added as if at a sudden thought, "we might just have a meal, something good and spicy. Have you ever eaten mutton *pilau*, Goodheart? The Arab style of mutton is memorable. A trifle greasy, perhaps, and the eyeballs take some getting used to, lying half buried amidst the rice—"

Goodheart flushed a most peculiar shade of puce, swallowed convulsively, and turned away, waving his hand in wordless farewell that attempted nonchalance.

"Enjoy yourself," I called. We turned into the nearest arm of the bazaar, and in a dozen steps had lost young Goodheart in the crowd.

I laughed aloud. "Holmes, that was pure cruelty, the detail of the eyeballs."

"The young puppy deserved it, forcing me to guzzle all that bad champagne and giving so little in return. I've a head-ache myself, you know."

"Holmes, if we weren't in an Arab country, I'd take your arm."

"If we weren't in an Arab country, Russell, I should allow it."

We wandered, amicable if apart, through the ethnic potpourri for an hour or so, buying the odd item of foodstuff or decoration, dried figs and a double handful of almonds, *kohl* for the eyes and an ornate pair of embroidered slippers for Mrs Hudson, shopping more for the delight of the purchase than the thing itself, for the pleasure of fingering and sniffing and haggling in a variety of tongues. The sun continued to beat through

the awnings, but slowly it shifted angle, until with reluctance Holmes drew out his pocket-watch to confirm
the time. He snapped it shut, and I had just stepped
around a small child to reverse direction when a rattling noise from over our heads was joined by a single
cry of alarm from the far end of the narrow street. Without an instant's pause, Holmes lunged, scooping up the
child with one hand and tackling me with his other
shoulder, shooting us through the adjacent doorway at
top speed. We three tumbled headfirst into the shop,
sweeping before us a group of robed matrons and landing with a stunning crash and clatter that shook the
walls. I felt for a brief instant that we must have dived
into a shop of pots and pans, such was the racket, but I
quickly perceived that not all the softness underneath
me was human, and that the boom and clatter had
come from outside of the door, not all about us.

I sat up, only half aware of Holmes, who was full of
ornate apologies to the ladies and desperate attempts
to soothe the terrified child before it could loose its reaction. The horrendous din outside slid away into
diminuendo, then trailed off with a couple of clangs.
For a moment, the world seemed a place of remarkable
stillness. But only for a moment, until the child's
breath caught in its throat and it filled the air with a
roar as terrifying as the crash itself. As if at a signal, a
tumult of voices joined the chorus, soprano fury within
the door and excited horror without. I dusted myself
off and went to see what had so nearly come down
upon our heads.

It was difficult to tell at first just what had happened, since the awning of the shop—it sold carpets,
which explained the softness of our landing—had been
crushed and ripped, and was being further demolished

by a crew of eager rescuers. The men seemed somewhat disappointed at the absence of corpses, or even blood-shed (other than one of the outraged matrons, who had broken one of her glass bangles and nicked her arm on it), but the shopkeeper's assistant, miraculously pre-served by the chance of having been leaning against the wall, was first terrified, then ecstatic at the wails of the infant. He snatched up the child, startling up a new round of screeches, and patted him all over, unable to believe him whole. In familiar arms, the child's sounds gave way to hiccoughing cries, and his tears and those of his father mingled down the man's shirt-front.

When eventually the awning had been ripped from the front of the shop and we could step tentatively out onto the paving stones, it became immediately appar-ent how lucky we had been. Holmes' quick reflexes had saved us from certain maiming, if not death outright, for the object that fell where we had been standing was probably three hundredweight of metal and wood.

"What is it?" I asked Holmes.

"I fear to ask," he said, sounding more disgusted than troubled. I glanced over and saw that he was look-ing, not at the tangle of pipes and boards, but at his hands, smeared with some dark and noxious substance. He bent to appropriate a corner of the dusty awning cloth, scrubbing at his fingers.

"I meant the thing that fell."

He ran his eyes over the object that had so nearly ended the eminent career of Sherlock Holmes, then lifted his gaze upwards, as half the people around us were doing. One dusty beam still clung to the rough mud-brick wall some twenty-five feet above, with a clear line of holes and dirt showing where the rest of the thing had been. A glance down the street showed a number of similar makeshift balconies, bits of wood and metal tacked onto the walls high above street level, all of them strung with drying laundry, decorated with petrol tins overflowing with flowers and herbs, furnished with cushions and rugs, and stacked high with various household goods not wanted inside. This one had linked to its apartment by way of a flimsy door, now opening onto thin air. And as we gazed upwards the door did open; the face of a horrified woman looked straight out, then down at us. She gaped down at the crowded street before belatedly realising that there were strangers looking back at her; she whipped her headscarf across her face, gave us one last white-eyed look, and slammed the door, dislodging a few more scraps of timber and dust.

Holmes waded through the wreckage, searching for the end pieces of the balcony. I joined him, our search somewhat hindered by the determination of the carpet-seller to keep people away from his now-vulnerable wares. I found Holmes fingering a pair of iron bolts, both of them old, one bent into a sharp angle, the other sheared off. Neither showed any sign of a saw's teeth.

"We must examine the wall above," he told me, and raised his voice in Arabic to ask how we might gain access to the above apartment. This took forever, first to brush off the teary gratitude of the young assistant whose son we had preserved and then to find a person who could show us the relevant corkscrew stairway. And once at the top, we were halted by the custom of the land, when Holmes would have gone within an apartment housing women alone.

In the end, I suggested instead that I might be allowed to venture within. The shopkeeper's wife had by that time appeared from their nearby house and followed us up the stairs to deliver her thanks. As soon as she understood what we were about, she added her voice to mine, begging that they grant the request of this thrice-blessed if baffling foreigner. The women within knew perhaps six words of Arabic—I wasn't even certain what their native language was—but they gave in. With a wide smile and many appreciative noises over the squalling, snot-nosed, *kohl*-eyed infant one of them clutched, I crossed the two rooms to the door that now gave out onto the bazaar.

Stretched out on the floor with my head and shoulders extending into thin air, I failed to spot any obvious saw-marks, merely holes in the walls where bolts had once stood. I ignored the fearful noises of the women behind me, the heftiest of whom had thrown herself across my ankles lest I fly into space, and I shaded my eyes to squint at the building on the opposite side of the street. Something odd there: a gash in the wall beneath a window, fairly fresh. I made to stand, found I couldn't move, and had to plead with the woman on my legs to allow me upright, which took a while. Before I left the apartment, I looked around for some heavy piece of furniture, finding a sort of divan that weighed nearly as much as I did, which I wrestled across the room to block the rickety door. Then, exchanging mutually incomprehensible pleasantries with the gabbling women and thanking them for the various sticky foodstuffs they thrust into my hand, I finally rejoined Holmes on the landing outside.

"Can we get into the apartment on the opposite side of the street?" I asked him. "There looks to be a fresh bash on the wall there." I looked around me for some place to deposit the sweetmeats, which were oozing over my palm.

Holmes looked at the collection of unlikely shapes and colours. "What is that?"

"By the feel of it, mostly honey."

He peeled one from my palm and popped it in his mouth, pausing briefly to consider it. "Sage flower," my beekeeper husband pronounced. "And something else. Rather piquant."

"Holmes, we haven't time to hunt down the source of the pollen in those ladies' honey," I said firmly.

He pulled out his watch, nodded in agreement, and turned for the rickety stairs. "You're quite right, the ship's siren went a few minutes ago. We risk missing the launch if we delay too long."

I hadn't heard the siren. "Can't we send someone to have the ship held for us?"

"I shouldn't like to chance it. The P. & O. lines pride themselves on keeping to the rules. Perhaps fifteen minutes."

But fifteen minutes proved too little time to find the owner of the empty apartment across the street. There was indeed a bash in the wall, and the boards that had created it—a balcony railing and four or five carved supports—were lying by themselves at the very base of that wall, across the alley from the bulk of the débris. There was no convenient length of rope or chain attached to the middle of the railing, and the marks were too myriad to be certain, but it did look as if something had torn a fresh groove into the wood in the centre of the fallen railing. It was the sort of mark that might result if a person standing at a window were to toss a hooked line at an already unsteady structure across a gap of some fifteen feet, then give it a mighty pull. On the other hand, it was also the sort of mark that might come from hanging almost anything from that same railing, and the gouge in the wall could be days old. Without a look at the room to see if the window-frame bore the marks of a rope or if the opposite wall showed where a pulley had been mounted to make one man's strength sufficient, without even a ladder to examine the wall more closely, there could be no certainty.

In any case, the ship's siren sounded again, impatiently, declaring its intention to leave without us. We grabbed up our few purchases, which had been preserved and guarded by the carpet-seller (grandfather to the half-naked child), accepted a small rolled carpet thrust into Holmes' hands as a token of gratitude, and trotted away.

The launch was idling at the pier, held there almost bodily by our friend the carpet-seller's son-in-law. The child in his arms seemed remarkably pleased to see us, considering the fright we'd caused it, and the man himself was nearly in tears again by the time we'd been pulled on board the boat and out of his grasp. We waved patiently as the boat pulled away, then turned to deliver our apologies to our huffy companions.

Thomas Goodheart was there, and his mother. Both watched us from behind dark glasses, their faces in the shade of their topees. I gave a surreptitious glance at his hands as I sat, but they were no more red than the rest of him; certainly they bore no signs of rope-burn.

Mrs Goodheart spoke first. "My, you two look like you've been in a riot. What on earth have you been up to?"

I looked down at my filthy skirt and torn blouse, glanced sideways at the state of Holmes' pale suit, and looked up with a rueful smile. "Being a tourist in places such as this, it's an arduous business, isn't it?"

Chapter Six

Aden's gulf opened into the Arabian Sea, and for days, the watery expanse in all directions was broken only by the passing of the occasional ship and the island of Socotra, well to the south two days out of Aden. The life of our floating village went on, the aristocrats of the high decks intruded on regularly by voices rising from the lower, now that the heat had driven the population out-of-doors at all hours, with dancing on the decks long into the night, under the glare of arc lights. For some days, the taps had run with phosphorescence, adding an exotic touch to one's toilette, bathing in cool blue flame. Holmes befriended a lascar in the depths, I approached the final scenes of *The Mahabharata*, Sunny received three marriage proposals, and her brother remained as he had been before, supercilious and aloof as he read his Marxist tracts. Certainly he gave no sign of having tried and failed to murder us in the Aden bazaar. He did not even make reference to his drunken indiscretions on the night of the fancy-dress ball, except once when he approached me to beg my pardon if he had said anything he shouldn't while in his cups. Something about the apology made me suspect that it was delivered at his mother's command, but I told him merely that he had done nothing to offend, and that I was sorry champagne gave him a head-ache.

On the Thursday evening, precisely two weeks after we had struggled with our bags through a snow-clotted Kentish railway station, we stood in the ship's bow and watched a cloud of flying-fish flicking and splashing magically from the indigo-tinted water. The sun's setting turned the sky to a thousand shades of glory, and gave us the sensation of cool. I breathed in, and for the first time in many days the air bore an indefinable promise of solid land, far-distant traces of smoke and dust and vegetation that the olfactory organs can only perceive when they have been long without. We went to bed surrounded by nothing but the heave and swell of open sea, and woke in the morning with the Western Ghats rising blue-grey into the haze of the horizon. As the brutal sun travelled overhead, the land drew us ever nearer, until by the afternoon passengers crowded the rails to see the city of Bombay approach.

When we were close enough to pick out the peculiar architecture of the yacht club, my heart began to quail: Land was a solid, pulsating, cacophonous, and even from this distance, malodorous wall of people, and the water was not much less heavily populated, by boats of all shapes and sizes. Perhaps we could just wait on board for a few hours, or days, until they all went away. But we were being met, it seemed, by shipping agents who would nurse us and our luggage through customs, and here, as elsewhere, company pride would undoubtedly demand that each man fight to ensure that his client be early through the process. I shook my head and went down to my suffocating cabin to assemble my last-minute things, to be startled five minutes later when the great engines fell silent.

We were, as I'd anticipated, claimed instantly by a round and obsequious brown-faced man in a tropical suit, accompanied by a pair of uniformed *chuprassis*. He introduced himself as Mr Cook and apologised five times in the first quarter hour for this "unseasonable" great heat which his great city was inflicting on ourselves, since at this time of year we might have justifiably anticipated a more gentle climate, a temperature more suited to our English selves, a less trying degree of mercury. After the fifth such synonymous phrase I wished him violently struck mute, but I was too flattened by the "unseasonable tropical humidity" to do so myself.

He herded us off the ship in the shade of a wide umbrella, following in the wake of four scarlet elbows that jabbed a path through the riot of colour and motion, a confusion of tongues raised at never less than a shout, with the ferocious sun beating down on us all. The Goodhearts were ahead of us, their umbrellas larger, their crowds kept at bay by rifle-bearing guards in trim red turbans with a white device at the forehead. The three Goodhearts wore garlands of brilliant marigolds around their necks, and were under the supervision of dignified individuals with nothing of our Mr Cook's air of commercial traveller. Their maharaja, it seemed, was already smoothing the path of his bison-providing guests; as some heavy foot came down upon my shoe, I could not suppress a twist of envy for the truly blessed.

But, I reminded myself, if Mycroft had thought it sensible for us to stand out from the other passengers, he, too, would have arranged for a noble's escort—with a marching band and caparisoned elephants, if the fancy had struck him. This way was hellish, but unavoidable.

Had I been in charge of this adventure, I might also have given us a few days in Bombay to get our bearings before we were shut inside a rattling train car for twenty-four hours, for the northwards journey to Delhi. That idea, however, had died a quick death at the sight of the crowds all along the waterfront: If the remainder of the city was anything like this portion of it, a stay here would not be a restful thing.

However, it appeared that there was a problem with our onward journey. My luggage was incomplete.

"What do you mean, 'incomplete'?" I asked Mr Cook, for whom I had developed an instant and completely unreasonable dislike. He was so polite, I longed to kick his shins.

"I mean, *memsahib*, that my list says that you, Miss Russell, are the possessor of two small trunks: one from your cabin, the other from the hold, which was sent down to the hold when the ship reached Port Said, and yet there is but the one which was in your cabin. I have had this trunk placed into the baggage car of the train, along with the two trunks of Mr Holmes, but alas, I lack the requisite companion from the hold of the ship."

"What's happened to the other one?"

"We are endeavouring to determine that, *memsahib*."

"Oh Lord, they've lost half my things," I groaned, then was nearly knocked down by a large woman clutching a carpet bag to her chest so tightly that it might have held her virtue. Holmes caught my arm to save me from falling amongst the feet. The shipping agent did not notice, so caught up was he in my accusation.

The round head shook vigorously. "*Memsahib*, the P. & O. does not lose trunks from the hold."

"Then where is it?"

"We are endeavouring to—"

"Yes, I know," I snapped. "Is there some place we can sit out of this heat?"

"I could, if you wish, have you taken to your train. I will, of course, remain here until the matter is made straight."

More likely he would wait until our backs were turned and make off home, I thought sourly, preparing to dig in my heels. But Holmes, to my surprise, agreed. "I can't see that our presence or absence will make the trunk appear any more rapidly. Mr Cook can be trusted to see the matter through. If necessary we can replace most of what you'll need in Delhi."

The small man practically melted in obsequity. "Oah, yes, sir, I will not sleep until I see the trunk of this good lady. I will personally see that it is delivered by hand to you in Delhi. I will not fail you," he vowed, then rather spoilt it by adding as an afterthought, "if the trunk is on board the boat."

I did not see where else it could be, but I bit back the remark, reminding myself that I had the clothing I had worn on the ship; I would not go naked.

Although, with my clothes already clinging against my skin as if I'd run several brisk laps through a steamroom, nakedness was not altogether unattractive. Indeed, the very idea of woollens was repugnant. I should miss my revolver, yes, but we had Holmes' gun, and his box of magic equipment. If ever I needed something warmer than sheer lawn, I would buy it.

We oozed onto the train, our compartment dim and shuttered against the sun. I headed for the nearest sofa, tripped over a shallow tin tray that someone had abandoned smack in the middle of the floor, and sprawled onto the heat-sticky leather cushions. "Who the hell left that thing there?" I grumbled, neither expecting nor receiving an answer. I wrenched off my topee, threw it across the room in petulance, and lay back, grateful at least that the floor was not tossing underfoot. Yet. After a time, I dashed the damp tendrils of hair from my forehead and told Holmes grimly, "This compartment is far too big for two persons. If our companions are the Goodhearts, I'm warning you now, I shall walk to Delhi."

"I believe you'll find that Mycroft has exerted his authority to grant us solitude."

"God, I hope so."

At my tone, Holmes turned to look at me. I shut my eyes so I couldn't see his raised eyebrow.

"It occurs to me," he said, "that I have neglected to warn you against one of the dangers of life in India."

I jerked upright, expecting a cobra or a scorpion, but he was shaking his head.

"India has a most unsettling effect on Europeans in general—which collective noun, by the way, embraces residents of England, America, and half of Russia as well. This is a land that gives one little of what is expected or desired, but an abundance of what proves later to have been needed. The process proves hugely disorientating, with the result that even the most stable of individuals rather go to pieces. One tends," he concluded in a sorrowful voice, "to shout at people."

"Holmes, I do not shout."

"That is true. Nonetheless."

I stared at him, wondering what on earth he meant. His words seemed to indicate a personal experience with that state of mind, but—Holmes, red-faced and furious? I could not begin to envision it. And I certainly was not in the habit of shouting at anyone, particularly strangers. I might let fly with a barbed and carefully chosen remark if need be, but shout?

"Don't be ridiculous," I told him, my voice low and reasonable, and subsided back onto the sofa.

While Holmes prowled the car, investigating its fittings, I lay motionless, wincing at the crashing, yells, and bustle outside, hoping that it would not intrude on us. After several minutes the voice of Mr Cook came from the entrance door, and before I could growl at him that we wanted no more news of disasters, Holmes called for him to enter. He did so, accompanied by the uniformed *chuprassis* carrying our cabin bags, the small carpet given us by the Aden carpet-seller, and a pair of closed-topped wicker baskets. Behind them came a sun-blackened man with a brief and grubby *lunghi* around his loins and a scrap of turban on his head. He staggered under the weight of an enormous block of ice, which he dropped with a crash into the offending tin tray, then vanished instantly. The two *chuprassis* paused at the door, and Mr Cook bowed nearly in half.

"This is for your comfort, in this most unseasonable heat, which truly I do not believe will continue to grip you as you journey to the north. If, however, it does, and if you wish the ice replenished, you need merely ask and it will be provided at the subsequent station. And although this train has a dining car, or you may wish to have a request for tea or a meal telegraphed ahead, I thought perhaps a little refreshment would not go amiss." He gestured at the wicker baskets, and my unreasonable animosity against him retreated a small step.

"Thank you, Mr Cook." I hoped I did not sound too begrudging. "That was very thoughtful. And I hope the hunt for my missing trunk does not prove too difficult for you."

"I will not sleep until it is found," he declared again stoutly.

"I shouldn't want you to lose sleep over the matter," I assured him, visited by a sudden image of the poor man fretting himself to an early grave, haunted by the *memsahib*'s lost baggage. "There was nothing irreplaceable in the trunk." Except for the gun, to which I was attached, but if it was gone, so be it.

"Oah, that is so very good of you to say," he whimpered, his accent suddenly going south. "I render the deepest apologies of my company and myself, and promise to hunt the solution to its bitter end."

Holmes got to his feet and thanked the man out the door, shutting it firmly behind him. He then rummaged through the wicker basket, coming up with a vacuum flask of tea and a bottle of fizzy lemonade, proffering them wordlessly to me.

"If you can chip off a piece of ice from that block, I'll have the lemonade," I told him.

He shook his head. "No ice, the water won't have been boiled first. Have the tea, and the lemonade later." He poured me a cup, then hacked away at the block with his pen-knife until he had carved a depression in the top deep enough to hold the bottle. By the time the train shuddered into life, my bare toes resting against the block of ice were chilled, and the lemonade going down my throat was cold.

Bliss.

And, I told myself with satisfaction, Holmes was quite wrong: I hadn't shouted at anyone.

✦

Nor did I shout at any of the irritations of the train journey. Not when Sunny Goodheart, comfortably ensconced in the maharaja's private cars, discovered that we were in the same train and trotted forward to join us at one of the stops. Since the cars were without linking doors, we could not be rid of her until the next station—and then, when I had all but pushed her bodily out onto the platform, to my horror the door came open just as the train was about to pull out, and Sunny tumbled back in, brother in tow, and we had to sit through fifty miles of Thomas' fatuousness. I was, I will admit, somewhat short of temper with the railway employee who delivered our noontime meal, when the lamb curry I had requested turned out to be greasy tinned ham: It seemed to me that in a country with more major religions than it had states, it shouldn't prove so difficult to explain that my religion forbade the eating of pork. The man seemed to think that "English" was a religion characterised by a love of tinned ham, warm claret, and suet-rich steamed puddings. In the end, I ate the mashed potatoes that had been meticulously arranged into the shape of a swan, picked at the grey boiled peas, and polished off both servings of stewed fruit.

And I held back my disgust at the pair of flies in the bottom of the milk jug the next morning, and my indignation at the oddities of the door latch that, while letting in all the world at all times, half the time prevented those of us inside the compartment from getting out, and my near-claustrophobic repugnance for the human tide that closed over the train at every station, the rapping knuckles and calls offering wares: flowers and shoes, hot snacks and cold water, handkerchiefs and melons, *chai*, toothache paste, oranges, and kittens. And those were just the words I understood. After a while I took to sitting in the middle of the car with my eyes on a page and my ears plugged, reading aloud to myself. But I did not shout, not even at the utter confusion of the Delhi station, where an iota of forethought would have prevented what was clearly a customary spectacle enacted countless times each day, as one trainload of passengers fought to emerge in the midst of another complete trainload, they battling in turn with an equal determination to board.

It wasn't until I discovered the state of my shoes the following morning, following a good night's rest in a quiet hotel room, that I lost control. The unassuming brown shoes I had left out to be cleaned the night before had been turned to a peculiarly mottled shade of dried blood. They were, granted, marvelously shiny, but the leather beneath the gloss looked as if the cow had died of leprosy.

The hotel manager himself was standing before me, straight-spined but tilted slightly back from the gale of my fury, before I remembered what Holmes had said about shouting. I stopped dead, panting a little. The ruination of a pair of shoes was a small matter, hardly cause for such a reaction, yet my cheeks burned with fury, my throat ached with long constriction. I looked around for Holmes, found him seated with his spine to me, bent over the morning paper, and I turned back to the manager. He braced himself. I drew a slow breath through my nostrils, let it out, and smiled.

"I am sorry, I don't know what's got into me," I told him in a low and pleasant voice. "Perhaps you might recommend where I could find a shoe-shop in the area?"

Wary, unwilling to relax his guard, the man minutely settled his lapels and suggested, "*Memsahib*, I would be honoured if you were to permit me to arrange for a man to bring to your room a selection for your approval. And of course the hotel will make a gift of them, by way of a small apology."

I felt very small myself. When he had made his escape, I went to sit near Holmes.

"Very well, you were right. Why did I do that?"

"I don't know, but every so-called European does. Do you wish to wait until you have your new shoes before we go out?"

"Oh, no. I'll just pretend that leprous shoes are the latest French fashion."

I could only hope that they would remind me not to lose control again. Perhaps it only happened once, and then one had it out of one's system.

If only they weren't all so friendly and agreeable as they drove a person mad.

And the beggars—my God! I had met beggars in Palestine, but nothing like these. Of course, there I had worn the dress of the natives, but here, in European clothing, the instant we set foot outside the hotel we were magnets for every diseased amputee, wild-eyed woman, and sore-riddled child in the vicinity. Unfortunately, the note that had been waiting for us on our arrival the night before had neglected to say anything about transport being provided, so Holmes had asked for a cab. What awaited us was powered by four legs rather than a piston engine, but we did not hesitate to leap in and urge the driver to be off. The *tonga*'s relative height and speed would afford us a degree of insulation from the beggars' attentions.

Delhi, the Moghul capital that was currently in the process of being remade as a modern one, nonetheless more closely resembled Bombay than it did London. The streets through which we trotted looked as though someone had just that instant overturned an anthill—or rather, as if a light covering of earth had been swept away from a corpse writhing with maggots. Furious, pulsating activity, occasional wafts of nauseous stench, unlikely colours. And blood, in seemingly endless quantities, spattering the recess in which a blind beggar perched, forming a great scarlet fan on a whitewashed building past which a pair of oblivious officers strolled, reaching up a mud-brick wall towards the sleeping figure along its top (at any rate, I trusted he was merely sleeping). I was just turning to say something to my companion when a rickshaw puller hawked and spat out a gobbet of the same red colour that decorated every upright surface, at which point I realised that the substance was of a lesser consistency and not quite the crimson of fresh blood. This had to be betel, the mildly narcotic chew of the tropics. The marks were still revolting, but considerably less alarming.

We left the main thoroughfare and rose into an area both newer and cleaner, with fewer pedestrians and the occasional motorcar. We went half a mile without seeing a beggar. The high walls were iced with hunks of broken glass, each gate attended by a man with a rifle. The guards wore a variety of regional clothing and their turbans could have stocked a milliner's shop, but each face held an identical look of suspicion as we clip-clopped past.

The gate before which our *tonga* stopped was no

higher than its neighbours', the guard no more nobly clad, but where some of the others had given the distinct impression that their guns were empty and for show, the stout Sikh here left one with no doubt that he would not hesitate to shoot down even a *sahib*, if it proved necessary. He watched us climb down from the horse cart, his only response a brief twist of the head (his eyes never left us) and an even briefer phrase grunted over his shoulder in the direction of the gate.

Before Holmes could dig into his pocket for the note we had received, the stout gate swung open. Inside it stood a slimmer, younger Sikh in beautifully laundered *salwaar* trousers and long, frock-like *kameez*, who bowed his snug sky-blue turban in greeting.

"You will please walk with me?" he suggested.

Chapter Seven

The garden within the gates was a place of Asiatic loveliness, a Paradise of birds and flowering trees, decorated by an old *mali* and his young assistant wielding watering cans, and a pale, cud-chewing bullock placidly waiting to be attached to the lawn mower. Brilliant potted flowers—rose, hibiscus, bougainvillea—marched the length of the drive, and near the house a fountain splashed and glittered. The rush and stink of the town was cut off as if by an invisible wall, and I felt my skin relax against my already-damp dress.

The bungalow was worthy of its grounds, simple and white, its verandah set with rattan chairs and tables, the entrance hall-way an expanse of linen-covered walls and gleaming dark flooring of teak or mahogany. The servant's soft sandals made slight noise as we crossed to a doorway. He stood back to let us enter, said, "I will bring tea," and left us.

The room was a light, open space looking out onto the garden. Its simple furniture was a far cry from the

Victorian stuffiness, mounted animal heads, and heavy draperies that I had expected from a Raj household. The house's silence seemed another carefully chosen furnishing of the room, its texture broken only by a rhythmic creak of machinery out-of-doors and the rise and fall of a voice from somewhere deeper in the house. It was a one-sided conversation—over the telephone, I decided, since it paused, resumed, and paused again. Tea was brought and poured, the servant departed without a sound, and I carried my cup over to examine the objects on the wall.

Near the door was a collection of framed photographs, groups of men with horses and dead animals such as one sees in the social pages of *The Times*. One photograph, placed centrally among the others, showed three men on horseback: at the left side a dark-haired Englishman, and on the right a smaller man with a bandaged arm, whose face was half hidden by the shadow of his topee but whose blond moustache said he was European as well. Between them sat a darker-skinned man, hatless, aiming his black eyes at the shutter as if he owned it, with an expression beyond pride—more an amused patience with the antics of underlings. Out of focus on the ground before them were two mounds resembling small furry whales, with a scattering of dogs and turbanned beaters behind. At the bottom of the photograph were written the words "Kadir Cup, 1922." Beside the photograph was one of identical size and frame, showing only the blond man and the native, except in this one, the darker face was tense about the jaw, as if a furious argument had broken off moments before. The black eyes flashed at the camera, the hand holding the reins was clenched tight. This one said "Kadir Cup, 1923."

The other photographs were of similar occasions, several showing the blond man, although in most of them his face was at least half obscured by hat or hand. Beside one of them hung a plaited horsehair thong with a single claw nearly as long as my hand, which I thought might be from the tiger shown dead in the picture. Mounted above this shrine to the masculine arts were two spears, or rather, one long spear and the remains of a second, consisting of a broken head and about eighteen inches of shaft. The viciously sharp iron heads on each were stained, probably with dried blood.

I moved on to the more customary art-work on the next wall, and found it pleasingly light, almost feminine in its sensibilities. Half a dozen watercolour sketches of the Indian countryside alternated with ink drawings, crisp black lines on the white paper showing simple scenes of village life—a woman with a large jug balanced on her head, a man and bullock ploughing, a child and dog squatting beside each other to stare down a hole. The drawings especially were striking; I thought they would not look out of place among a display of Japanese art. I took another sip of my tea, which could have been chosen to set off the room, its clean, slightly smokey aroma blending with the room's faint odours of lemon and cardamom.

And, suddenly, of horse. I had not noticed the distant conversation cease, nor heard anyone approach, but between one breath and another there was a third person in the room, the compact, blond-haired man of the photographs, moving to greet the equally startled Holmes.

"Thank you for coming. I see Hari has brought you tea. Did he give you the Indian or the China?"

"The Indian," Holmes answered, "and very nice indeed."

"Good. With Hari, one can never be sure. I am very pleased to meet you, Mr Holmes. We did, in fact, encounter each other long ago, when you visited my father's camp in Himachel Pradesh, but you won't have remembered. I was seven; my last tour with him before I went home to school."

Holmes held the man's hand for a moment as he studied the man's features, and then his mouth twitched in a brief smile. "He was a district officer and you were in short trousers. A boy with a thousand questions about . . . turquoise and rubies, wasn't it?"

Our host's face opened in a grin. "I should have known you would forget nothing. And you must be . . . Miss Russell, I'm told you prefer? I'm Geoffrey Nesbit."

His hand was cool and strong, and I thought, as he turned to face me fully, that Holmes' act of memory was less impressive than inevitable: Even as a child, this would have been a difficult person to forget.

Nesbit was one of the most beautiful men I have ever laid eyes on, the thin scar running down his jaw line merely serving to emphasise his looks. Neat, blond, and sun-burnt, he was not the kind who usually stirs me to admiration, but his green eyes shone with intelligence and humour, and he watched with the quiet attentiveness of a cat, missing nothing. Like a cat, too, he appeared ageless, although the skin beside his eyes and down his throat testified to an age near forty. He reminded me eerily of T. E. Lawrence, another small, tow-headed, and youthful man who looked at the world out of the corners of his eyes, as if in constant dialogue with an amusing inner voice.

Nesbit was dressed in an odd combination of garments, jodhpur trousers beneath a long muslin *kameez*, and if the aura of horse he carried with him explained the trousers, he had certainly changed his footwear upon returning from his morning gallop. Unless he was in the habit of riding in soft leather slippers, in the style of an American Indian. Certainly in the photographs the man wore ordinary riding boots.

He poured himself a cup of tea, taking it black with sugar, and urged us back into our chairs, sitting down on the other side of the low, intricately carved table. He settled into a third, legs stretched out, ankles crossed.

"How is your brother?" he asked Holmes.

"Improving. I had a telegram yesterday night, he sounded himself."

"I am glad. The world would be a lesser place without Mycroft Holmes. And a great deal less secure."

Which observation declared, as surely as an exchange of Kipling's whispered code-phrases, that this man knew well that Mycroft Holmes, who described himself as an "accountant" in the Empire's bureaucracy, kept ledgers recording transactions considerably more subtle than pounds and pence. The suspicion was confirmed with his next words.

"When we have drunk our tea, we shall take a turn through the garden." His raised eyebrow asked if we understood; Holmes' curt nod and my reply answered him.

"We should love to see your garden," I told him. And, clearly, to talk about those things the walls were not to hear. It was difficult to press one's ear to a key-hole when the speakers were surrounded by open space. And the sad fact was, there were some things with which servants were not to be trusted.

So we drank our tea and passed a pleasant quarter of an hour hearing Nesbit's suggestions about what to see during our stay in the country. He particularly urged us north, even though the weather would still be cool, and suggested one or two of the hill rajas who might show us an entertaining time.

"Do you shoot, either of you?"

I suppressed a wince: The last shooting party I'd joined had nearly ended in tragedy for the duke who was our host and friend.

"Some," Holmes replied. "Russell here is a crack shot."

"Of course, it's pretty tame compared to some sports—even going after tiger from the back of an elephant pales once you've tried pig sticking. Or tiger sticking, although that's harder to come by. You ever ridden after boar, Mr Holmes?"

"Er, no, I'm afraid not."

"Is that what the Kadir Cup is about?" I asked, adding, "I noticed the photographs."

"Yes, that's it. Held annually, near Meerut, just north of here. Pig sticking is the unofficial sport of British India. Great fun. Though not, I fear, for the ladies." He smiled at the thought. I smiled back, automatically plotting how I might go about learning to stick pigs— until I caught myself short. I didn't even like fox-hunting, much less what sounded like a rout fit for overgrown adolescent boys, scrambling cross-country after a herd of panicking swine. Still, it brought up the obvious question.

"With what does one stick the pig?"

In answer he nodded towards the weaponry on the wall. "That's the spear I took the Cup with last year."

"The broken one?"

"Er, no. That one's there to remind me to be humble." He threw us a boyish grin. "Big job, that. No, the broken one's from the '22 Cup. The first day, I'd flushed a big 'un, run it across the fields a mile or more, right at its heels when it jinked back in a flash and came for my horse. Which very sensibly shied, dumping me top over teakettle. Somehow I landed on my own spear and took a great hunk out of my arm. Nearly the end of my career."

"So, what, did you shoot the creature? Or did it run off?"

"Good Lord, no," Nesbit said, affronted. "One doesn't carry a gun when pig sticking. And once a pig's decided to fight, it generally doesn't quit until one or the other of you stops moving. No, one of the other fellows took the beast. And the Cup as well. Native chap—maharaja in fact, though nothing like what you think of at the title. That's him in the photo. He nearly had the Cup from me last year, he's that good. 'Course he should be good, he has enough practice going after any kind of game you can mention. African lion, giraffe—you name it."

Sports; maharaja; exotic animals: The unlikely conjunction rang some bells in my mind, but Holmes got the question out first.

"What is the name of this maharaja?"

"They call him Jimmy. Rum chap, a bit, but a great sportsman. He's the ruler of a border state named—"

"Khanpur."

Nesbit's eyes locked onto Holmes over the top of his cup. Then, calmly, he took the last swallow, placed the cup and saucer on the tray, and stood. "Shall we go and look at the garden?"

"Looking at the garden" seemed to be a common ritual in the Nesbit establishment. At any rate, the ground was clear for a circle of thirty yards around the two benches he led us to, benches located in the shade of a tree which had recently been thinned so its inner structure could hide no person, benches facing in opposite directions to cover all approaches. A low fountain played nearby, obscuring our voices.

"You seem to have an interest in the maharaja of Khanpur," he said as soon as we were seated.

"Not directly, but the name has come to our attention."

It took a while, the story. Thomas Goodheart and the bison-collecting maharaja who had been at a Moscow gathering attended by Lenin. The defiant words of the drunken Goodheart, and his odd choice of fancy dress, preceded the odder decision to enter Aden with a debilitating hang-over on the day a balcony fell. To say nothing of the interesting coincidence that Khanpur was one of the kingdoms along the northern borders insulating British India from her long-time Russian threat. Holmes even mentioned my missing trunk, although by this time neither of us thought that was due to anything more sinister than inefficiency, or at the most a garden-variety thievery.

Nesbit listened without comment, but with such intensity that I thought he might well be able to recite Holmes' words verbatim afterwards. At the end, he sat forward with his elbows on his knees, his eyes not seeing the playing fountain while his mind explored the information. Eventually, he sat upright.

"If Goodheart is a known Communist, we probably needn't worry, although I'll pass his name on to the political johnnies. As for Khanpur, the state has always been staunchly loyal to the Crown. During the Mutiny, a handful of sepoys fleeing north attempted to pass through the kingdom, carrying with them two English captives, a mother and her young daughter. The then raja, Jimmy's grandfather, allowed them entrance, but then set up an ambush on the road that passes through two halves of his hill fort. Dumped a thousand gallons of lamp-oil down the hill and set it alight. Killed them all, including the woman, unfortunately, but the child lived and was returned home. By way of recognition of their service, all the Khanpur tribute is remitted annually. And the raja's rank was raised to maharaja. Khanpur has a seventeen-gun salute, which is big for its size—the girl's family was important."

"The Mutiny was a long time ago."

"The Mutiny was yesterday, as far as every white man in the country is concerned. But it is true, that was the grandfather, and much can change in sixty-seven years. I shall bring this to the attention of my superiors."

His eyes came back into focus. "Now, as to the reason why you are here. Kimball O'Hara. Mr Holmes, you knew O'Hara, did you not." It was not a question.

"When he was a boy."

"By all accounts, the man he became was there from the beginning."

"The lad was remarkably well suited to The Game," Holmes agreed.

"Which makes it all the more troubling that he has vanished."

"How long has it been since he was last heard from?"

"Just short of three years."

"Three—" Holmes caught himself. "We were told that he had not worked for the Survey in that time, but I had the impression his actual disappearance was considerably more recent than that."

"It's only in the past months that we've become aware of it. But once we cast back to look for his tracks, the last sure sighting we could come up with was in August of '21."

"Where was that?"

"In the hills above Simla. He stopped the night with an old acquaintance, and told her that he was going back to Tibet for a time, although he intended a detour to Lahore first to visit a friend."

"But the friend in Lahore never saw him?"

"We could uncover no one in Lahore who had seen him. In fact, we couldn't even find anyone there who would admit to being O'Hara's friend."

"And the amulet?"

"Ah. That arrived ten weeks ago. By post." The dry answer forestalled any exclamations, for clearly the surprise of such an unadorned delivery had sent waves through the department, leaving a thousand questions in its wake. Holmes ventured one of those.

"Posted where?"

"In Delhi. Handed in at an hotel by a French tourist, a lady here to paint botanical watercolours. She was given it by a middle-aged Parsi who guided her through the gardens in Bombay, requesting that favour in return."

"Extraordinary. I don't suppose you still have the paper it came wrapped in?"

"Of course. It's in my safe, if you'd like to see it."

"Very much."

I broke in with a question. "Pardon me if I ask things I either should not, or which I ought to know already, but was Mr O'Hara still on what you might call 'active duty'?"

"Not really. After the War, with the Bolsheviks apparently having their hands full in Russia, we had all begun to think we might relax our guard and turn to other concerns. Since O'Hara's expertise is that of the borders and Tibet, he sat at a desk for a year, possibly a bit more, then in late 1920 asked for a holiday. He was forty-five and had not taken one since returning from Tibet when he was nineteen, so one could scarcely object. But when we needed him this past autumn and went looking, we couldn't find him."

"You say you needed him. The Russians are back?" Holmes asked.

"If not yet, then soon. You know that Labour will grant the Bolsheviks formal recognition?"

"It is to be expected."

"A mistake. MacDonald has his head in the clouds if he imagines The Bear will turn cuddly simply because they share a theoretical conviction. Belief was, The Game was finished with the Anglo-Russian convention seventeen years ago. But then the Reds came in and tore up all the treaties and back we went. Lenin—or whoever's in charge while he's ill—is buying time to sniff out our weak places, and will very soon be nudging through the passes like the Tsar before him. Our enemy may have changed his hat, but the Bolsheviks want a Communist East as much as the Tsar did, you can count on it. They won't settle for the Congress Party—as far as they're concerned, Gandhi's worse than we are, a religious reactionary. And since the Bolsheviks will assuredly look to Tibet as a potential point of entry just as the Tsar before them did, we need O'Hara back on the force. True, Tibet has been receiving our own overtures of late—our giving the Dalai Lama shelter in 1910 saw to that—but whether the Russians or the Chinese get to Lhasa first, we're going to need Tibet, and they us. We're sending a political officer out this summer, but that's all bells and whistles. We need someone who can see outside the diplomatic circle, and O'Hara knows the ground as a tongue knows its teeth." He paused, to watch a pair of small black-headed birds dive at the fountain, and gave an almost imperceptible sigh.

"Still, that is not the main consideration here. What it boils down to is, O'Hara's one of ours, and we want to know where he is."

"And, perhaps, to know if he actually is still 'yours'?"

Nesbit stood abruptly, taking three quick steps to bend over a fairly unexceptional flower. When he spoke, his voice was even but taut. "I refuse to believe that O'Hara has turned coat. I worked with the man. He is the King's man to his bones."

I waited for Holmes to agree, but he said nothing. Clearly, he had been rethinking the question since his vehement declaration in Mycroft's rooms three weeks before. It sounded to me as if he was no longer quite so certain of Mr O'Hara's bone-deep loyalties.

Holmes allowed the silence to hold for a while. Nesbit prowled up and down, gravel crunching under his soft shoes, until Holmes spoke.

"How many other agents have you lost in recent years?"

"That depends on what you mean by 'lost.'"

"Any of the word's definitions will do," Holmes said irritably.

"Sorry," Nesbit said, coming back to his bench. "I don't mean to evade your question. It is merely that the answer is difficult to give. In the sense that we've 'lost' O'Hara, there have been four others in the past thirty months. In England, or if they were Army, that number would be alarming. But here, it's commonplace to go months, even years without hearing from one of our 'pundits,' as the native agents are called—it's often just not possible for a man to report in. And frankly, I expect that one or two of those missing simply decided that their period of service was over and slipped quietly back to their families. I am aware of three other such who informed us openly of their retirement from The Game. All of whom, I have confirmed, are healthy and home, thank you very much. It is more than possible that the four missing agents have done the same, merely neglecting to tell us—which would be a typically Indian way to do things, by the way. Indians hate to disappoint a person to his face, and often say yes to something they know they can't provide. I shouldn't have expected the attitude from O'Hara, but it's not beyond the imagination. We've made enquiries for him in all the obvious places, including his old lama's home monastery. He's either not there, or won't respond."

"And what about the other sense of 'lost'?" Holmes pressed.

Nesbit's green eyes wandered across to the playing fountain. "Three. All in the last nine months. John Forbes, Mohammed Talibi, and a new man—just a boy—Rupert Bartholomew. All good men. All dead."

"How?"

"One shot, one knifed, one strangled." He paused, and then gave us the worst. "All tortured first, beaten and burnt."

It was suddenly all too clear why Mycroft had sent us.

"You have a traitor in the ranks," Holmes said.

The handsome face grew still, as if movement might bring a return of pain. After a moment, he nodded, once.

"I no longer know whom I can trust. Even Hari, who has been with me for twelve years, even him . . ." Nesbit broke off, to dig a silver case from a pocket and light a cigarette, pinching the match between his fingers and tucking it back into the case. "I begin to understand how the officers must have felt during the Mutiny. Their own men, men they'd fought beside, marched with, trusted with their lives—with the lives of their wives and children, for God's sake—turning on them, slaughtering them. And five years ago, I saw Jallianwala Bagh, the morning after. I saw the results of Dyer's order to fire on the demonstrators. Sixteen hundred and fifty rounds and nearly every one of them hit civilian flesh—men, women, and little children heaped against the walls where they'd tried to get away from the machine-gun fire. I'll never outlive the nightmares, never. Hundreds dead, thousands bleeding, and every white man in India wondering when the country would rise up and kill us in our beds, rid themselves of us once and for all.

"And who could blame them? We collect their taxes and we give them nothing but the bottom of our boot. You heard of Dyer's 'crawling order'? Where he set guards to make certain no native could walk past the spot where an Englishwoman had been attacked, but had to crawl—even the natives who'd rescued her? God help us, with such officers. There are days when, if I heard that someone in a position to undermine the Survey from within had chosen to do so, I couldn't altogether bring myself to condemn him."

"Yet you don't believe O'Hara capable?"

"No. Not him."

"Even though since he was a child his white blood has warred against his love and loyalty to the country that nurtured him?"

"Even so. He would not deceive his friends in that way."

"O'Hara is quite capable of practising deceit, when it comes to playing The Game."

"No."

Holmes looked at the younger man and gave a small shake of his head, but said merely, "I'll need all the details on the three men found dead, and on those missing."

"I've included a précis in the O'Hara file I have for you. I prepared it myself; no one has seen it."

"That's as well."

Nesbit crushed his cigarette out under his heel, then said abruptly, "I am having doubts as to the wisdom of this venture."

"That is understandable, but we shall take the file nonetheless."

"I should not have allowed you to come here, openly to my home. What if you were seen, and followed?"

"Who knows we are here?" Holmes asked.

"You and Miss Russell? By name? No more than four men within the Survey, all of them high ranks. But still . . ."

Holmes smiled happily and reached over to clap the man on his shoulder. "I shouldn't worry. By tomorrow, your two English visitors will have ceased to exist."

The smaller man looked taken aback, then forced a grin. "And I'm supposed to find that reassuring?"

With that, the more clandestine portion of our interview was at an end. Nesbit led us inside to his study, where he opened the safe and took out a flat oilskin envelope and a japanned-tin box, laying both on his desk. The tin contained a crumpled and torn paper wrapping with an address in the government offices. Holmes laid the paper out on the desk and set to with the magnifying lens he carried always, but in the end, it told him little more than it had Nesbit: that some tidy person—a man, to judge by the printing—had parcelled up O'Hara's amulet and sent it to Captain Nesbit, but as the address was entirely in capital letters, it had little personality.

"I couldn't say if that was . . . our man's writing," Nesbit told us, his voice low and avoiding names, "but I'd lay money that it was a St Xavier's boy who wrote it— the way he's made the numerals is fairly distinctive. I went to the school myself for two years," he explained. "Not at the same time, of course, but these numbers look like what I might do, were I attempting to conceal my hand."

Holmes bent again over the paper, and when he stiffened at some characteristic invisible to me, standing at his shoulder, Nesbit said, "The sand, yes. Unfortunately, there's nothing to set it apart—it might have come from anywhere in the country."

"In London," Holmes muttered, "I could say for a surety that a mite of soil had come from one spot or another, but in this vast land, there are ten thousand places where such grains might have come from."

"Such as from another parcel," I pointed out, unnecessarily. Holmes laid the paper back in the tin and took up the twine, turning his lens on its knots. But as they were not tied in a manner known only to Bolivian merchant sailors or a small tribe of gipsies from northern Persia, and since the fibres bore no traces of raw opium, gold dust, or a face-powder sold only in one exclusive shop in Paris, the string told him no more than the paper it had covered. Nesbit seemed mildly disappointed, but unsurprised. He put the box back into his safe, pulling out a lumpy envelope in return. Bringing it to the desk, he fished from it a pair of small silver lockets strung on copper-wire chains and handed us each one.

Holmes smiled, as if he'd seen an old friend, and thumbed the surface of his with familiarity. I held mine up to the light. It was a rude piece of jewellery, with touches of black enamel in the silver and an almost invisible latch on one side, which opened to reveal a small twist of soft rice paper around a hard centre. I unfurled this cautiously, set aside the tiny chip of turquoise it contained, and examined the paper. It had been stamped with an inscription, its ink bleeding into the fibres; the script was unknown to me.

"What does the writing say?" I asked Nesbit.

"It's a standard Buddhist benediction, for protection on the road. The usefulness of the charm lies in catching the eye of another who holds one. And since such objects can be stolen, the phrase that accompanies it is paramount." He told us the phrase, in Hindi, and had us repeat it twice so he could be sure we had the proper and essential emphasis on the fourth word.

Holmes dropped his over his neck, working it inside his collar, then murmured, "The three men found dead and tortured. Were they, too, 'Sons of the Charm'?"

"They were. And yes, the charms each wore are missing."

I thought to myself that it might be time to replace this style of charm with something less widely circulated, but at least we were forewarned. Holmes slid the oilskin document case into his inner pocket, and stood up.

We shook Nesbit's hand, and he locked the safe and walked us to the door. We paused on the verandah, listening to the sound of an approaching motor. As it pulled up before the house, Nesbit turned his head slightly and said, "It might be best to commit as much of the file as possible to memory, and burn the rest. I've also given you three methods of reaching me in an emergency. If there's anything at all I can do, any time . . ."

"We shall be in touch," Holmes told him. Hari stepped out of the motorcar to hold its door for us, then climbed behind the wheel and drove us back into the city.

Chapter Eight

Somewhat to my surprise, we did not instantly pack our bags and dash from the hotel into hiding, taking refuge in some Oriental equivalent of Holmes' London bolt-holes. Rather, he poured the contents of the leather case out onto the floor and set about reading them.

"I thought you and Nesbit agreed that we might be in some danger here," I said, with what I considered admirable patience.

He looked up with a frown at the distraction. "Oh, no more than usual. We shall be away before any rifles can sight down on our necks."

"Good to hear," I muttered, and picked up a page from the file.

Nesbit had made no attempt at presenting a coherent narrative of Kimball O'Hara's life and work; he'd merely copied specific documents pertaining to the man's last year or two of active field service in the Survey, before he had vanished from the Simla road.

The ongoing problem of independent border king-doms had been O'Hara's main concern, as indeed it had been the concern of his superiors since the days of the East India Company: One minor king who defied British rule and surreptitiously opened his state to the enemy could spell disaster for British India. And in the past, hereditary rulers of the native states had not all demonstrated an unswerving sense of loyalty when it came to bribes and blandishments. Moslem nawabs and Hindu rajas, squelched into their borders first by the Company and later the Crown, had spent their entire lives with nothing to do but squabble over rank and invent ways to spend their money. The idea of an hereditary prince joining sides with the Communists was, of course, absurd on the surface, but that by no means ruled out the possibility, no more than it had for that American aristocrat, Thomas Goodheart.

O'Hara's last report, three tightly written pages reproduced in photograph that we might recognise the handwriting if we happened upon it again, concerned a number of apparently unrelated but nonetheless provocative events and overheard statements concerning two of the principalities along the northern border. A seller of horses commenting on the sudden interest in his wares by the raja of Singhal's men; an itinerant fakir bemoaning the treatment he had received in Khanpur's main city, where before his begging had been welcomed; a huge order for raw cotton, enough to clothe all of Khanpur's subjects in one go; and a dozen other incidents.

Cotton, I reflected idly, was also an essential element in the manufacture of high explosives.

When I had absorbed the contents of the letter, I turned to the writing itself. The distinctive running script was indeed similar to that of his copyist, Nesbit, although whether or not the printed numerals of the parcel reflected the same school's training I was not prepared to say. In either case, behind the anonymous precision of the script could be seen evidence of a remarkably self-contained and self-assured hand. There was a touch of egotism in his capital *E*s and obstinacy in his lowercase *B*s, but those were balanced by the humour in his *S*s and *I*s and the simplicity of his capitals in general. All in all, the hand that had written this document was ruled by precision, toughness, and a high degree of imagination, and I found myself thinking that, if "Kim" had indeed sided against the British government, he might well have had good reason.

I caught myself up short. That kind of romantic nonsense would get us nowhere. In any event, we had to find the man before we could lay judgement upon his actions, and I could not see that the documents provided us with any clear direction.

"What do you think, Holmes?" Generally, venturing such a vague query resulted only in a burst of scorn, suggesting as it did that I was at a complete loss to know where I stood; but sometimes, and particularly if Holmes was as wrapped up in his thoughts as he appeared to be now, a vague probe merely loosed his tongue. To my relief, so it proved.

"Simla first, I believe. Three years makes for a glacier-cold trail, but he has always been a memorable character, and cautious enquiry might uncover a trace from his passing."

"From what you told Nesbit, we will not be openly taking the train as Sherlock Holmes and wife."

"I shouldn't think that a good idea, no. And as we shall have to assume that we have attracted notice, it would be pushing our luck to board the train as two stray Europeans."

I sighed to myself, and told him, "Well, whatever disguise you come up with, kindly make sure that the shoes aren't too crippling."

He paused to gaze up into mid-air. "Yes. Odd, that your trunk has not come to light."

"You think its disappearance may be related? But that would mean that someone knew we would be on board that ship before we left Marseilles."

"Not necessarily. It could have been diverted with the first rush of coolies in Bombay."

"In either case, what would anyone want with my trunk?"

"The Baskerville case began with a missing boot," he mused. "The same question occurred then. Perhaps they wished to compile evidence. Or wanted to steal your revolver. Which reminds me, we shall have to get you another one."

"Perhaps they wished to be sure I had only one pair of shoes, and then arranged for the ruination of those, that they might pick me out of a crowd," I said. I intended to be facetious, but Holmes took my suggestion at face value.

"True. It's the one garment you might find time-consuming to replace." My feet are large for a woman's shoe, yet narrow for a man's, and that morning the hotel manager's shoe-seller had come up with nothing wearable. I should, I supposed, have to have a pair made, but bespoke footwear did indeed take longer to make than clothing.

"Are you serious?" I asked, but he merely grunted, and returned his attention to the document in his hand.

We took lunch in the hotel dining room—sitting well away from windows, I noticed. Afterwards, Holmes folded his table napkin and got to his feet.

"Russell, I should appreciate it if you were to stay in our rooms this afternoon while I make the necessary purchases for our disguises."

"Why?"

"Because as an Englishwoman, you would stand out in the bazaars more than I do."

"Very well," I said, surprising him. "But if you haven't returned by six o'clock, I shall walk out of the hotel's front doors and come looking for you."

He believed me.

I went back upstairs to our first-floor rooms, locking the door behind me. I was never entirely comfortable when Holmes took off like that—which was odd, considering how often it happened. But that afternoon I wandered the rooms, unable to settle to the work at hand, picking up objects and putting them down again. At one point I came across the small lumpy envelope Nesbit had given us, containing the amulets. Holmes, I noticed, had taken his already. I took the other, fastening it around my neck, and went to the looking-glass to inspect it.

The silver charm looked like the sort of thing a tourist might buy, or a poor Indian. It was the kind of decoration sold at any of a thousand shops in the city, crudely worked but not unattractive. I rather liked it, in fact, and although I hadn't intended actually to wear the thing, changed my mind. Its secret-society overtones, which I found somewhere between quaint and silly, nonetheless held a sneaking kind of reassurance. I clasped my hand around it, then laughed at my fancy and got out my books.

I spent the afternoon immersed in Hindi grammar, deciphering the written letters and trying to make sense of the vocabulary. When my mind began to stutter, I rested it by conjuring coins from mid-air and practising the hand movements of deception, then relaxed with the headlines on that day's *Pioneer*. Halfway through the afternoon, the hotel's shoe-seller came with another selection of footwear, but I dismissed him—gently—after I had examined his ideas of footwear suitable for European ladies.

When he had left, I rang for a cool drink and a map of the country. With commendable promptness I received a pitcher of some sweet, mango-flavoured drink (with no ice) and a crisply folded map of India, which I spread out onto the floor. I sipped and studied and passed the afternoon without too much dwelling on the possibility of snipers' cross-hairs following my husband's back, but I will admit that my heart rose when I heard his key enter the lock.

"Thirty years," were his words of greeting. "Thirty-two years since I was here, during which time the city has gone from Moghul backwater to capital city, and still the same shopkeepers cling to their corners."

"You had success," I noted.

"Indeed."

"And yet your hands bear no parcels."

"Certainly not. To walk out the door of this particular hotel in native garb would be noteworthy. Better to slip away as ourselves, and drop those identities behind us in the bazaar."

"You found a bolt-hole?"

"One might call it that," he prevaricated, and refused to tell me more. Which meant, I was sure, that the place in which we would transform ourselves would be filthy beyond belief.

"When shall we set off?"

"The cook tells me that the night watchman comes in just before midnight, and invariably visits the kitchen for a few minutes upon arrival. An ideal time to make our departure through the back."

I rose briskly and walked out of the room.

"Russell, where are you going?"

"Holmes, I intend to bathe, long and deep. Knowing you, it will be my last opportunity for some days."

It was, as it turned out, an optimistic judgement.

We dined downstairs, Holmes on roast meat that was billed as beef and I on a dish largely rice, with bits of dried fish. We lingered over the meal, and even allowed our waiter to serve us with apple tart, which proved delicious once it had been dug free from the thick clots of Mrs Bird's Custard. Coffee and a brandy for Holmes, and we retired up the stairs as if to our beds.

Instead, we prepared for our departure from India's European community. Between the contents of my luggage that had survived our voyage and a judicious plundering of Holmes' possessions, I put together a costume that would pass for an Englishman's in the dark. My hair, as always, was a problem in disguise, and topees were simply Not Worn after sunset; in recognition of this Holmes had brought back with him from the bazaar a cloth cap not too unlike those worn in England by lower-class labourers and upper-class bloods.

We settled to our studies, planning on a couple of hours' work before our midnight departure. But just past ten-thirty, a time when the floors vibrated with the motion of our neighbours and the hum of guests going past in the corridor was at a peak, a shudder of alarm ran through the building, a shout and a pounding on doors, one after another, working its way rapidly towards us.

We were on our feet in an instant, Holmes hurling objects into his half-packed travel case, me thrusting Nesbit's papers into an inner pocket and stuffing my bound hair up under the cloth cap. When he saw that I was ready, he tucked the box of magician's equipment under his arm and cracked open the heavy door, and then finally the cries of an Indian voice came clear:

"Fire! Oah, *sahib*s must leave in a hurry, we have a fire! No, *memsahib,* there is no time to gather your items, please oh please to hurry, *memsahib.*" More voices came, the lilting pleas of accented servants and the sharp tones of alarmed guests. Holmes and I looked at each other.

"Do you smell smoke?" he asked me.

I moved to the doorway and breathed in the air. "Maybe—yes, I'm afraid I do."

I stepped out into the hallway, causing a frightened servant to dodge around me and urge the *sahib*s to "go down please to the lobby right quick" before he continued on to the next room. But Holmes laid his hand on my elbow, and instead of joining the excited guests scurrying towards the central stairs, we ducked against the traffic in the direction of the servants' stairs. And—clearly Holmes had made a fairly thorough reconnaissance earlier in the day—once within the stairwell, we turned up instead of down.

With many twists and turns through the servants' passages, we eventually came out at the side entrance of the hotel, where we stepped over the hastily abandoned bags of some late arrival and trotted down the dim alley, past the guest stables and garage until we came out on the next major thoroughfare. We slowed to a stroll among the night traffic, its pedestrians as yet unaware of the nearby alarms, and after a few minutes hailed a rickshaw. The puller did not comment on Holmes' destination, which proved to be a brightly lit palace of the senses such as one found in any city of size. It catered to Europeans, although I glimpsed a pair of brown faces in the party of men going through the door, and the music that rolled out with the opening of the doors seemed a peculiar amalgam of West and East. The tune rendered by the weird and wailing native instruments was that of a popular song I remembered my father crooning, "A Bird in a Gilded Cage," although I doubted that he would recognise it without help.

I was just as glad, however, that our path did not take us into the place, but around it. Holmes had clearly laid out this escape, and walked without hesitation down the side street and through a gateway into a yard lit only by a feeble oil lamp. He opened a door, taking my hand to guide me inside, and shut it behind him. I waited in the blackness as his bag hit the ground and his fingers sorted through the contents of his pocket before coming out with a rattling match-box. The box rasped open and with a scrape, light flared. He stepped across to where a handful of fresh candles lay on a tea chest, set the match to one, and dribbled a puddle of wax onto the chest to hold it upright.

We were in what I would have called a cellar, had we not entered it from street level. It was a dank and rustling space about fifteen feet square, with neither windows nor stairs, although the door appeared stout enough. Two walls were heaped with anonymous crates and barrels, on top of which lay a number of string-wrapped, dust-free parcels. The fruit of Holmes' shopping expedition, I had no doubt.

He wedged a chip of brick under the edge of the door to discourage intruders, and took out his folding knife to slice through the twine of one parcel, tossing its contents in my direction. Most of the garments landed on the dirt floor—thus, I supposed, adding to the verisimilitude of my appearance. From another parcel he took a bottle about five inches in height, containing a thick, dark liquid. This he did not toss, but placed with a scrap of soft cloth on the top of one of the barrels. I removed most of my upper garments, uncorked the bottle, and set about turning myself into a Eurasian.

Without a mirror or adequate light, the walnut-based skin dye was a somewhat haphazard affair, and would need attention the next morning in order to pass close inspection. But for now, by night and heavily clothed, our faces and hands would give the necessary impression. When the dyestuff had worked its way into our pores, Holmes prised the top from one of the barrels, and we washed our skin in the water it contained.

Baggy *salwaar* trousers of coarse white cotton, knee-length *kameez* and padded waistcoats over, floppy turbans wrapping our heads and woollen shawls around our shoulders: We would disappear into a crowd. My once-handsome shoes went into the bag Holmes had found to replace the dignified leather case, and I pulled on a pair of toe-cutting native sandals. We looked more like a pair of enthusiastic guests at a costume party than we did two residents of the great sub-continent, but it would do for the moment. Holmes blew out the candle, and we slipped away into the city.

Chapter Nine

For two days, we camped in a tiny room in the back of a spice-seller's in a small bazaar to the south of Delhi. The warring fragrances were a mixed blessing, becoming at times so powerful as to make one dizzy, but even when sealed up for the night they succeeded in overriding the less appealing odours of our surroundings.

I should say, rather, that I camped there, for Holmes spent the entire first day scavenging through the city for what we should need; on the second day, he abandoned the shack well before dawn, leaving me with a jug of a particularly disgusting and considerably more permanent skin dye. He was away until the afternoon, and returned to find me black of hair and brown of skin, to say nothing of bored to tears. He rapped on the sheet of metal that was the door, and I removed the prop to let him in.

I had to admit, Holmes dressed down better than I did. Apart from being far too tall, he was every inch a native labourer, and even his height he could disguise by rearranging his spine to drop a full six inches. He set a frayed flour sack onto the dirt floor and dropped to his heels by my side, pulling a dripping leaf-wrapped parcel from his breast and laying a slab of fried *puri* on top. I eagerly peeled back the leaf and mashed the rice and lentils into manageable little balls, a technique I had perfected in Palestine.

"Did you get everything you needed?" I asked around a mouthful.

Holmes chuckled. "Nesbit nearly rode me down. It would appear that beggars are not welcome along the British rides, and he sits a high-strung horse. But yes, his sources are better than my own, and even if the wrong person hears of his purchases, little will be thought of it—the man is forever acquiring odd objects for his own purposes."

Most of what Holmes required for the next stage in our campaign he had found in the bazaars, but it would appear that revolvers were not generally available on the open market, and to ingratiate himself into the underworld of Delhi in pursuit of firearms would have taken time. So he had set off that morning with the intention of asking Nesbit for one, and had clearly returned successful. I swallowed the last of the rice, scrubbed the inside of the banana leaf with the stub of bread, and pulled the flour sack over to see what he had found.

I raised my eyebrow at the revolver. It was a pretty thing—almost ridiculously pretty, with mother-of-pearl inlay on the grip and a curlicue of flowers up the barrel. Was this Nesbit's idea of a lady's gun, or his idea of a joke? Remembering the quiet amusement in his eyes, I thought it might be both.

"He assures me it is more authoritative than it appears," Holmes said, answering my dubious look. "And it takes .450 bullets, which are readily available. I should think it all right."

I balanced it in my hand, feeling its weight—it was indeed more substantial than it looked. When I cracked it to look at the chambers, I found its mechanism smooth, the surfaces well cared for, so I shrugged and laid it by my side: I have no objection to decoration, if it does not interfere with function.

Further in the sack I uncovered a change of raiment—and, more important, a change in identity. This was the garb of a Moslem, instead of the Hindu clothes I wore now, subtly different to English eyes but a clear statement to natives. The itinerant trader in northern India is more often a Mussalman than a Hindu, and that identity possessed the singular advantage that I was already able to recite all the important prayers and a good portion of the Koran in near-flawless Arabic. As Moslems moving through a mixed countryside, we would be both apart and identifiable, an ideal compromise. Best of all, Holmes had included a more satisfactory pair of native boots of some soft, thick leather. I pulled them on and stretched my toes in pleasure. I wouldn't have put it past my husband and partner to indulge his occasionally twisted sense of humour by presenting me with an all-over *chador* in which to stumble the roads, but it seemed I was to be allowed my oft-assumed identity as a young male, younger brother to the identity Holmes was now assuming, although his was unrelieved black, for some reason, and he wore a Moslem cap instead of a turban like mine.

As I bound my hair tightly to my head and prepared to wrap the ten yards of light cloth over it, I mused aloud, "How long do you suppose it will be before a woman in these parts of the world won't have to disguise herself as a man to be allowed some degree of freedom?"

"I can't see the Pankhursts making much head-way in this country," Holmes said absently.

"No, you're right. Perhaps by the time this generation's grandchildren are grown, freedom will have grown as well."

"I shouldn't hold my breath, Russell. Here, you'll need to change the shape of that *puggaree*."

My hands had automatically shaped the thing as if I were moving among Bedu Arabs, but Holmes tweaked it from my head and unrolled it with a snap of his wrist before demonstrating on himself. He went through the motions twice, then handed the cloth back to me and watched as I attempted to copy his motions. His had looked as if he'd worn the garment his entire life, while mine felt as if a faint breeze would send it trailing to the dust, but I told myself that the sensation would pass, and tried to move naturally while I put my new belongings into some kind of order.

"You'll be pleased to know we have a donkey awaiting us, Russell," Holmes said cheerfully.

"Oh Lord, not again!"

"It was mules last time."

"And they were bad enough."

"Better than carrying everything ourselves."

"You can be in charge of the beast."

"That would be most inappropriate," he said, and curse it, he was right. If I was to be the younger partner on the road—apprentice, servant, son, what have you— then the four-legged member of our troupe would have to be my responsibility. As well as the cooking pot. Cursing under my breath, I thrust my spare garments into the cloth bag and tied my turban once again. This time it felt more secure, which improved my temper somewhat. It was never easy, partnering a man with as much experience as Holmes had—I truly detest the sensation of incompetence.

We spent the night hours practising with the equipment Holmes had conjured out of the bazaar. A set of linking rings, larger relatives of the linked silver bracelets he had bought in Aden, appeared welded in place, awaiting only the magician's touch before the metal miraculously gave way and allowed the rings to part. A long knife that collapsed into itself at the press of a button; a light frame with a pneumatic pump to lift me in levitation; a small laboratory of lethal chemicals whose reactions would give clouds or sparks or other useful effects. And, when we were ready for it, torches wrapped for flaming, for the ever-impressive juggling of fire.

In the hour before dawn, when only the *chowkidar*s were awake at their posts, we shouldered our cloth bags and in silence left the spice-seller's shop. The air was still fresh, without the dust raised by a quarter of a million tramping feet, the stars still dimly visible before fifty thousand cook-fires threw their pall over the heavens. Holmes made his way as one who was intimate with the place, ducking past *godown*s and crossing over deserted boulevards, until the smell of livestock rose up around us and we entered a sort of livestock market, horses in one area, large pale bullocks in the other. Magnificently oblivious of the dung heaps, Holmes strode forward to a shed with a tight-shut door. He banged the side of his fist against the shed's side, but answer came there none. He drew back his hand to hammer again, when a voice piped up from behind us, speaking Hindi.

"If you are wanting the horse-seller Ram Bachadur, he has gone away to see his mother."

It was a child, a small person of perhaps nine or ten in Hindu dress, perched atop the low stable wall eating peanuts. Even in the half-light of early dawn it was clear that there was something curious about him, some slightly Mongolian angle to his features, so that one expected him to be slow, his natural development retarded by nature. It took but one brief exchange to begin to question the assumption.

"Do you know where he has gone?" Holmes asked, his arm still raised.

"But of course I know; how else would I have agreed to await your coming?" the boy retorted, the scorn in his voice perfectly modulated to place us a step below him. He spat a shell on the ground by way of punctuation.

Holmes lowered his hand, his head tipped to one side as he, too, re-evaluated the urchin. "Are we to take delivery of the donkey and cart from you, Young Prince?"

The boy slid down from the wall and sauntered around towards the pens. "Not the same animal you had agreed upon, oah no," he answered, the last two words an English interjection before returning to the vernacular. "That creature was good only for feeding the vultures, and moreover had the trick of breaking its hobbles on the first or second night out and trotting home to its stable. I succeeded in loosing its rope during the night and exchanging it for its sister, who is an 'altogether more satisfactory beast.'" Again, the final phrase was in ornately accented English, which might have been disquieting except that I had the clear idea that it was merely his way of demonstrating what a man of the world he was.

We followed our unlikely guide past some stinking pens that were full to bursting with horseflesh, to one that was deserted but for one lone donkey, dozing in a corner. The boy climbed up on the gate and gave a little *chirrup* sound with his teeth, and the creature's ears flapped, its head coming up and all four feet planting themselves on the ground. It then hesitated, seeing three of us, before sidling around to greet the boy, who reached out and scratched its skull; even in the dim light, I clearly saw the cloud of scurf and dust the motion raised. However, I could also see that the animal appeared well fed and alert.

"And the cart?" Holmes asked.

The boy swung his legs over the gate and dropped into the pen, splashing through the half-liquid and entirely noxious ground to the far corner of the pen, where he stuck his toes into invisible niches and clambered over the wall like a monkey. A minute later he reappeared around the outside of the pen, heaving at a miniature cart that contained a child-sized armload of hay. He stopped in front of us, let the traces drop, and gestured proudly at the light little vehicle. It had probably started life as a cart for the entertainment of small English children, and although its paint was long gone and the high sides had seen rough use, the solid craftsmanship held, and the repairs to its two big wheels and leather straps were neat. The boy stood looking up at Holmes, taking no notice of the muck to his knees; I wondered again about his mental acuity.

Holmes surveyed the object solemnly, and nodded.

Instantly, the child shot back over the gate to leap

onto the animal's scrofulous back, nudging it forward with heels and knees. I opened the gate to let it out, and in a moment the beast was standing amiably between the cart shafts while the boy strapped it in. After some adjustments to the girth, the boy slapped the animal's shoulder in satisfaction and stood away. "You are to pay me what is owed," he said.

"Oho," Holmes retorted, "and when it comes to light that the horse-seller merely sleeps, and you have delivered to my hands a stolen donkey and cart, what then do I tell the police who come to arrest me?"

The boy's indignation was profound, and well polished. "Sir, never would I do such a thing! You came to buy a donkey, here is your donkey, and I am here to collect for the horse-seller. You have paid him one-half, and all the cost of the cart, and one day's food. You may pay me the remainder."

"That much at least he knows correctly," Holmes said to me, then to the boy, "But you will have to tell me exactly what is owed, before I believe you."

The child hesitated, caught on dilemma's horns. If he quoted the amount Holmes clearly had in mind, then we might believe his veracity; if, however, he followed his gut instincts and demanded more—which is the only way to do business in India—then he risked losing all. He sighed, and rolled his eyes to express his disgust for the whole affair.

"Twenty-three rupees," he admitted. Holmes raised his eyebrows and inclined his head slightly in a nod before turning his attention at last to the beast herself, looking to see if the trick lay with the substitution. But she looked sound beneath the filth, and if she was willing to respond to the blandishments of an urchin, no doubt her affections, or at least her attention, could be

bought by owners willing to ply her with plentiful food
and the occasional application of a brush to her sides.
Holmes reached for his money-pouch, and thumbed
the coins into the child's hand.

The boy accepted the coins with the gravity of a bank
manager, bound them up into a rag, and then scam-
pered over the shed and pulled himself up its outside
wall, diving headfirst through a small, high window. A
minute later he re-emerged, the coin-rag replaced in his
hand by a horse-brush and a small sack of grain. His
grin told us without words that these were not part of
Holmes' original bargain, but a *baksheesh* he had appro-
priated from the horse-dealer's store. He tossed both
sack and brush into the cart beside the armload of hay,
gathered up the donkey's lead, and looked between us
expectantly. "Where do we go?"

"Oh no," Holmes said firmly. "I required a donkey,
not a donkey-master. We travel alone."

"But if you do not take me, I shall be beaten and starve,"
the child whined, pitifully. Holmes merely laughed.

"I cannot imagine one such as you starving," he said.
"Give me the lead."

"Then I shall follow you on the road," the boy declared. He sounded determined, alarmingly so; Holmes
eyed him curiously.

"Why would you do so?"

"Because I had my horoscope cast two days past, and
I was told that my path lay with two strangers dressed
as Mussalmani."

I was not certain that I had caught the subtle oddity
in his phrasing—not "two Moslems" but "two men
dressed as Moslems"—but Holmes' reaction made it
clear that I had heard it correctly. He went very still, his

grey eyes probing the child like a pair of scalpels. The boy squirmed, and changed his words.

"I cannot help it, that is what I was told. That there would be two Mussalmani come to buy a donkey, unlike any men I knew from the bazaar. That is all, oah yes."

Holmes did not believe in the retraction any more than I did. He raised his eyes to mine, consulting; I could only shrug. I did not doubt that the child would follow us, and keeping him close at hand made controlling him, and finding out what he was up to, more likely.

Besides, I was more than happy to have someone else in charge of pack animals and drudgery.

Holmes cast his gaze down at the servant we had just acquired. "And how much will it cost me to have you look after this beast and serve our needs?"

"Oah, next to nothing," the boy chirped in English, elaborating somewhat more believably, "Five rupees every week."

Holmes burst into laughter at the effrontery, causing the donkey to snort and tug at the rope. The boy controlled her without a struggle, and said, "Very well then, you will give me my food and drink and whatever small money you think I am worthy of. You see, I am trusting you gentlemen not to torment and tease a homeless orphan."

Boy and man gazed at each other for a time. Then Holmes said, "What is your name?"

The urchin wriggled with satisfaction, taking this as it was clearly meant, an acceptance of his proposal. "I am Bindra."

"Well, Bindraji," Holmes said, adding a mock honorific, "we are in your hands."

The deed settled, we dropped our bags into the cart;

the boy, after enquiring again as to which road we wished to be on, tugged the donkey into motion and led his small caravan out onto the road.

"Why do I get the idea that the child is going to take us wherever he thinks we should go?" I asked Holmes in a low voice.

"A most determined infant," he agreed.

"It's going to be very difficult, not to give ourselves away in front of him."

"Hm," Holmes commented, unconvinced. "I should say that his wits tend more towards the cunning than the analytical."

I thought privately that the child would have to be remarkably obtuse to spend much time in our company without noticing that one of the "gentlemen" had some very odd habits when it came to private matters, but I said nothing. If the boy's presence became difficult, we could always drive him away.

Or, we could try.

We turned north, the sun rising on our faces as we walked the road with a million other inhabitants. We were making for Simla, the government's summer capital and year-round home of the Ethnological Survey of India. Holmes had debated heading south first in order to shake off any possible enemies from our tail, but he had decided that disguise and the sheer number of people on the road ought to be enough, so north it was, with the sun to our right.

Five miles outside of the city we paused to take tea at a roadside café that seemed to double as a motorcar repair shop, hung about with rubber belts and tyre tubes. Holmes wandered away to talk with the mechanics, and when we had finished with our refreshment I was not surprised to find him directing our steps around the back of the garage. There we received the rest of our possessions for the road, left there by Nesbit: a tent of some light but tightly woven fabric with a silken sheen, a pair of sleeping rolls, pots, pans, and paraffin lamp.

Everything a travelling magic show might require.

We kept close eyes on our new assistant, but although he darted to the side from time to time, picking up the odd twig or discarded object, he made no attempt to flee with our possessions. He appeared to have a jackdaw's love of shiny objects, nearly coming to grief under the feet of a gaily caparisoned elephant when he spotted a silver button about to be trampled into the dust. He darted forward, under the animal's very belly, and out the other side with his fist raised in triumph; the button he polished on his shirt-front, and hung on a piece of twine from the donkey's harness.

Being caught up in his own affairs, the boy spent most of his time well ahead of us, which meant that I could continue my language lessons without attracting his questions. In another day or two, I thought, I might even venture the odd phrase in the boy's direction.

Or perhaps three. I was already beginning to suspect that young Bindra was neither as innocent nor as feeble-minded as he appeared.

Chapter Ten

I had been in India for nearly a week, but only that morning, on foot and beneath the hot blue sky, did I begin to see the country. From the train I had witnessed a dream-like sequence: canals and hamlets; elephants bearing massive loads and camels hitched to wagons; a dead cow in a field, decorated with vultures; a man in homespun *dhoti* and purple socks wobbling on a shiny new bicycle; an Englishman in khaki shorts solemnly jumping rope on his verandah; a peacock atop a crumbling wall, feathers spread wide in a blaze of shimmering iridescence before his dull and disinterested lady; train stations without number, each packed like sardine-tins with veiled women hugging bundles and *kohl*-eyed babies, men draped with a thousand goods for sale, cows stealing from the food-sellers, policemen pontificating, and scabby dogs picking up the edges. Just before dusk I had seen a red-eyed *sadhu* seated cross-legged at a roadside shrine, his forehead smeared with the three white lines of the holy man, his thin body clad only in beads and the scrap of cloth around his loins. At first light the following morning I had seen a group of men in a river, brushing their teeth and washing their heads, while farther out from the bank three elephants were being bathed. From behind the dirty windows I had watched the passing of a dusty and unreal landscape, as if I were being transported through an art gallery.

Now, I had stepped into the painting, which mixed Breughel's activity with Persia's colours, with just a touch of Bosch horrors.

Women dressed in crimson and apple-green and yellow ochre swayed with loads balanced on their heads, one hand steadying the brass pot or the straw basket, the other holding one end of their scarf up, lest strange eyes see what they shouldn't. Men in cheap suits and men in filthy *lunghi*s scurried or lounged, chewing betel or smoking thin brown *bidi*s. Naked children tumbled in the gutters while pale hump-backed cows roamed freely through the markets, snatching greens where they might.

And when we were finally clear of the city, when the tree-lined road stretched out before us through fields of cauliflower and onions, sugar cane and chilis, the air began to smell of something other than dust and diesel. The acrid odour from a brilliant field of flowering mustard blended with the soft sweet incense wafting from the doors of a small whitewashed temple. The stink of putrefaction slunk over from a heap of scrap-draped bones, too leathery even for vultures, then the next moment the nostrils tingled with pepper and turmeric from a spice-seller's, and rejoiced with the rich rosewater smells from the sweetmeat stand. Wet dust around a well; drying clothing from a long hedge; the ripe dung of an elephant; hot-burning coal and overheated metal from a blacksmith's; urine and feces; opium from an upstairs window; sweet-cooking wheat chapatis from below.

We were on the Grand Trunk Road, that river of humanity flowing fifteen hundred miles across northern India from the swampy heat of Calcutta to the thin, dry air of the Khyber Pass, linking the Bay of Bengal with Afghanistan, passing the lands of conquest: Darius and Alexander, Timur and Babur, slaughtering and conquering and looting; the plains of Kurukshestra where the Aryans first took root; the battlefields of *The Mahabharata* and of the Indian Mutiny three millennia later; the place where Babur killed fifteen thousand and brought the Moghul empire to Delhi, where Afghans killed Mahrattas, and where Persians killed Moghuls (twenty thousand in two hours, the historians say) then walked on to strip Delhi of its gold, its Peacock Throne, and its Koh-i-noor diamond. Holy places and bloodshed lay all around me, while in the fore, Bindra gnawed on a length of sugar cane and skipped beside the placid donkey.

To begin with, all was dust and turmoil, even at an hour when the dew was still damp on the canvas. With the distinct sensation of becoming a twig tossed into a fast-moving stream, I gave myself over to the current, needing only to keep the boy's head in sight, and to keep from stepping under the feet of an ill-tempered camel along the slower edges or the wheels of a hurtling lorry in the swift-flowing centre. It was exhilarating, it was exhausting, and it served as nothing else to set me firmly into this foreign land. We paused for lunch at a roadside tea shop, an open-fronted shack with a roof half thatch, half waving tile, beside a spreading mango tree under which the café owner had arrayed his ranks of the ubiquitous wood-framed *charpoy* beds, the piece of furniture that is dining table, chaise longue, and business centre in one. As I took up my position on the sagging ropes, I felt almost at home in my foreign raiment, as if my skin had changed.

Certainly my tongue had. Without much pause for thought, I told the boy to bring us some *samosa*s, pointing with my chin at the seller across the way. We ate our greasy snack from the clean leaf-plates as the road swept past, watching the traffic as if we were a Thames-side picnic party on a summer's Saturday afternoon. At the end, we tossed our earthenware cups onto the pile of such, and continued on our way.

We came that night to a caravanserai that Holmes said had been there since the days of the emperor Akbar, where men and animals from all the reaches of the land came together for the night to shelter behind the crumbling Moghul walls. Bindra took some annas from Holmes and came back with an armload of feed for the donkey, then requested a greater sum and went off again. I eased myself down onto my pack, feeling all the muscles that I had not worked for months. My skin, toughened though it was from the sea journey, tingled with sunburn, and my feet had rubbed raw in three or four spots. I was very happy to sit quietly. I would have been happier to lie down and sleep, but it was still broad daylight, so I compromised by closing my tired eyes and paying attention to my other senses.

The cooking fires here smelt like nowhere else. Not coal or wood, nor Irish peat, nor even the varied substances used in Palestine. Here, cow dung mixed with straw was slapped onto the walls in dinner-plate–sized mounds to dry, then peeled off, heaped into baskets, and hawked to travellers in the caravanserai. The musky smoke rose around me, blended with the odours of fresher droppings, horse sweat, unwashed clothing, and the spices that went into the evening meals. Some-one was cooking chapatis, the delicious smell of wheat flour waking my salivary glands and making me aware of a sharp interest in dinner.

I was just stirring to ask Holmes if he thought we had seen the last of Bindra and our rupees when the boy sauntered up, laden with sacks and twine-wrapped scraps of paper, onions and carrots sticking out of his pockets. He caught up one of the pots and filled it at the communal pump, then dropped to his heels before the fire that we had made (he had gathered a surprising quantity of sticks in his apparently aimless scrounging during the day) and set about constructing dinner. A generous pinch of mustard seed popped and spattered into melted *ghee,* followed by a sliced onion, half of a somewhat tired cauliflower, and pinches of turmeric, pepper, cumin. And as that mixture was cooking, he took a pair of bowls and placed them between his feet, then pulled over the heavy little canvas sack he'd come back with, rolled down the top, and plunged in a grubby hand. Without taking his eyes off the bustle and activity of our various neighbours, Bindra began to sort the contents. I watched his quick little fingers for a few minutes, then curiosity got the better of me and I went over to see what he had in the sack.

It held a mixture of rice and pulses—an inadvertent mixture, it would seem, because Bindra was separating it back into its component parts. And he did so at an amaz-ing speed, flicking the rice into one bowl and the pulses into the other, dropping any stray pebbles to the ground. I looked at him, looked back at his hands, and couldn't believe the mechanical speed and precision of his motions: Watching closely, I could see no rice grains join the lentils, no pulses among the rice. The boy pretended to ignore me, but if anything, his hands speeded up.

I took a handful from the bag, to try it myself. With fierce concentration, I could tell one tiny grain from the other after rubbing them for some seconds between finger and thumb. Without benefit of vision, it would take me hours, days to work my way through the two or three pounds his sack contained. He was halfway through it already.

I went to sit next to Holmes, and whispered in English what I had seen. He raised his voice and asked the boy, "Bindra, tell us why you have bought these sweepings from the market?"

"Not sweepings! I do not eat unclean food from off the ground. This is merely the work of a clumsy seller of grain, who allowed one to spill into the other. And he is lazy as well, for rather than going to the labour of sorting, he would rather sell it for next to nothing."

"And have I paid the full cost of the dhal and the rice, or next to nothing?" Holmes asked drily.

"Not full, no!" the boy declared, filled with righteous indignation. But under Holmes' gaze, he faltered, and made a show of checking the water to see if it was boiling yet. "I divide the cost of the two, that you may thus pay me for my labours of sorting. Since," he pointed out darkly, "you have not agreed on a wage for my other hours."

Holmes chuckled. "You speak fairly, Bindraji. Next time buy the lentils and the rice already separated, and spend your hours at some other work. I shall grant you one rupee each week. And more, when you prove your worth."

The boy nodded, satisfied for the moment. When the sack was empty he tipped the bowl of lentils into the fried onion and the rice into the water. He scooped up half a dozen round chapatis that he had bought in the market and laid them on top of the pot lids to warm.

"We seem to have found a most capable servant," Holmes murmured.

"That dinner does smell good."

"It is, however, provocative to reflect that the trick with the rice and lentils is commonly used to teach sensitivity to the fingertips of apprentice pick-pockets."

As our meal cooked the caravanserai had been filling up, so that when we looked up from our empty bowls, we found ourselves between a group of Rajputs on their way to the races in Calcutta and a family of Sikhs going home to the Punjab. The Sikhs were four men and a boy of about twelve, all of them handsome and proud.

The men settled their livestock and sent one of their number off to buy a meal. Bindra swilled out our pots beneath the pump, then squatted next to the donkey and smoked one of the noxious Indian cigarettes called *bidi*s before getting out the purloined horse-brush and applying it to the sides of the appreciative donkey. Holmes took out a shiny coin and began to fiddle with it until he caught the Sikh boy's eyes; he then sharply stretched out his right hand, palm down and fingers outstretched, but the coin, instead of dropping to the ground, vanished. More slowly, he extended his other hand, turned the hand palm up, and there sat the coin. Simple tricks, playing on the shininess of the silver in the firelight, and ignoring the sensation he was causing when the boy tugged at the sleeve of his uncle and pointed at the flicker and dash of silver in the stranger's hands.

When Holmes appeared to lose the coin, patting all over his garments for it and searching the ground around his feet in alarm, the Sikh family began to do the same—until Holmes looked up, seeming to notice them for the first time. He rose upright, marched across the four paces that separated our two encampments, and shot his hand out to snatch the coin from the brief head-covering of the startled boy.

Holmes held the coin out to the lad, pinched between finger and thumb, but when the boy reached out for it, the coin was gone.

The older men laughed, appreciating the trick, and the boy ducked his head in confusion. But when Holmes moved into his marginally more advanced routines, the adults' superior smiles faltered, and soon gave way to expressions of frank amazement very like that worn by the boy. And when the magician pulled from his cap a distinctive bridle decoration, which none of them had noticed him steal from their mare a full hour before, there was a general "Oah" of astonishment and much fondling of beards as they discussed the magician's authority.

Holmes threw me a half-wink, and turned to his bedding roll.

I lay long and listened to the sounds of the Indian night, the murmur of voices and the bullfrog groans of hookahs slowly dying away, leaving only snores, coughs, the bubbling grumble of the camels, the coo of doves, and the distant yammer of jackals to break the great stillness.

I had anticipated enormous problems, living in such public circumstances as a male. It is one thing to adopt the guise in a desert place such as Palestine, when one may see a handful of others in the course of an entire morning, but here, there would be no such privacy. Very fortunately, I have been blessed with a strong bladder, and found that by timing my visits to the fields to the dusk hours, and by making use of the privacy afforded by the tent, my uncharacteristic physiognomy went unnoted. Either that, or my neighbours were too polite to comment.

At first light, with the coughs and throat-clearing rising around us like the sounds of a hospital mustard-gas ward, we beat the frost from our tent and continued on our way. The dawn turned the sky to a yellow-pink at the east, a deep rose to the west, with all the world between made up of insubstantial pink-grey silhouettes, treetops and temples and distant buildings called into being from the drifts of rosy mist, disconnected from any objects that might have roots and foundations, mere islands of dark solidity in a glowing pink sea.

And then the light grew stronger, and the silhouettes took on depth, and soon the sun lumbered huge and orange over the horizon, pulling free of the obscuring mist and dust and smoke. India's great age and crowdedness and solidity re-established itself, sucking the frost and freshness and youth from the air. The land grew colour and dimension, the spectacular mountains on the horizon retreated into the haze, and a small troupe of wandering magicians left the hurly-burly of the Grand Trunk Road to set off across the Indian countryside.

Of all the possible disguises an English spy might choose, doctor or antiquarian or big-game hunter, ours was one of the more idiosyncratic. For one thing, we were on foot, our pace confined to what our legs would permit, our possessions in a cart so small it looked more a joke than a useful form of transport. To have it pulled by a donkey rather than a bullock, or even a mule, added to the disarming unlikeliness of the entourage, and with Bindra to cook our decidedly non-English meals and barter for staples and fuel added the final touch of verisimilitude. We were foreign, certainly, but nothing about us said "British." That was, after all, the point of the exercise.

It is something over one hundred and fifty miles between Delhi and Simla. We could have made it there in a forced march—indeed, we might have saved ourselves a great deal of trouble and taken the train, or even hired a motorcar—but at this point in our expedition, the need was greatest to perfect our act, that when we got into the hills, we might be word-perfect. Moving at donkey rate, pausing each day to set up camp and do our performance, we covered at most twenty miles a day.

But in that time I learned to levitate under Holmes' hand and to swallow a sword without gagging, and we even began to juggle flaming brands between ourselves. When he first saw our conjuring and magic, Bindra was apprehensive, but once he had witnessed the similar reaction of the rustics, he immediately took on the garments of sophistication and scorned to gape, other than secretly. I think he understood that what we did were tricks, not actual necromancy; on the other hand, I do not know that to his mind, there would be much difference between cleverness and supernatural powers.

By the third day on the road, however, he clearly decided to throw himself into the act. On the morning of that day, we passed through a small town, too large for our purposes but convenient for the purchase of supplies. So when the boy turned to Holmes and demanded some money, I figured it was because he'd spotted some *brinjal* or eggs that he thought we needed, or some of his horrid little *bidi*s. Holmes fished out a rupee, but Bindra left his hand out and said, "Five."

"Five rupees?" Holmes asked. "But why?"

"You will see."

Holmes thought about it, and after a moment the remaining coins fell out of the sky, bouncing off the boy's head. Bindra gathered them from the dust without remark and trotted back the way we had come. Holmes and I continued on our way, for by this time the donkey was nearly as willing to go with us as it was with the boy.

Outside of town, we joined a flock of goats for a time, then found ourselves following a veritable mountain of rustling greenery down the road. When it turned off into a field, we paused to watch a group of men scramble up to loose the huge load of sugar cane from the elephant's back, leading the animal to one side where it stood patiently, swinging one hind foot while it picked over an offering of the cane it had borne. This was a *gur* factory, the cane fed through a hand-run crusher so that its grey juice ran into a series of vats set over a fire. All four vats were already boiling furiously, great clouds of intoxicating steam billowing into the cool air. Holmes bargained for half a dozen fist-sized lumps of molasses-rich *gur* sugar, still warm, which melted under our tongues as we continued on our way.

It was, I thought, both like our wandering time in Palestine and yet very different. Most of the difference lay in the population density, I decided: In Palestine we might walk all day and see but a handful of other nomads, whereas here, we were rarely out of sight of farmers working their fields, holy men tending their roadside shrines, a caravan of camels wending their way from the hills, or women swaying back from the wells with heavy brass pots of water balanced on their heads. Every piece of flat ground was being planted or harvested, every stream was inhabited, if not by young boys and their bullocks, then by the local laundry service, the *dhobi*s slapping their garments on the wet rock, draping the clothing on the bushes to dry, laughing and calling to us without inhibition.

We were well out of town when Bindra came trotting up, but instead of aubergines and oranges he carried an armful of small tin pots, which he arranged carefully inside the jolting cart. And then, instead of taking his place at the head of the donkey, he hopped inside to perch on the canvas-wrapped shapes. Taking out a small stiff-bristled object resembling a tooth-brush for an iron-gummed giant, he dangled over the side of the cart and started scrubbing away at the shabby wood. Bemused, Holmes and I exchanged glances, then moved forward to avoid the flying specks of old paint and dried muck. The boy had, over the past couple of days, succeeded in burnishing the donkey's coat until it shone; now, it appeared, the cart was to be brought up to snuff as well.

It took him hours to scour the cart down to clean wood. But rather than stop there, he turned to his little tin pots, prised the top from the largest, and pulled another, softer brush from inside his clothing. Dangling over the front of the cart like a monkey from a branch, completely oblivious of his two companions who were all but walking backwards down the road to watch him, he dipped his brush into the pot, stuck out his tongue in concentration, and drew a line of deep, rich blue along the edge of the much-abused wood. This was so interesting, we resumed our position behind the cart in order to watch his progress. The donkey seemed happy to walk without guidance, its long ears swivelling from time to time as it listened to the boy's encouragement and conversation.

The boy, too, looked healthier, I thought. Certainly he kept cleaner than he had in the livestock-seller's pens. Holmes had bought him a change of raiment, child-sized pyjama-trousers and buffalo-hide sandals underneath the European-style shirt Bindra had chosen. He went bareheaded, either because of his age or his inclination, and generally bare-footed unless the track was particularly rough, but since he and Holmes had come out of the clothing shop, I had not once seen him without the colourful vest decorated with small chips of mirrored glass held in place with circles of embroidery floss. The shiny specks caught the sun as he dangled on the cart, his brush transforming the entire thing to the colour of the Indian sky an hour after the sun had set, and I had to smile.

"A curious child," I commented to Holmes. (A distinct advantage of male dress here was that it permitted me to walk closer to Holmes than I could have as a woman, thus allowing us conversations we might not otherwise have had.)

"He has his pride," my companion answered, and I saw what he meant: Bindra's vision of our troupe's dignity did not include a bashed-about wagon.

"What did Kipling call his Kim? 'Little friend of all the world'?"

"Yes; being all the world's friend, O'Hara ultimately belonged to no-one. In that respect, the phrase applies to young Bindra. Kim, however, formed his own family as time went on, binding himself to the chosen few irrevocably and utterly. I am not certain that this child has that capacity."

"He seems to have formed an affection for us—certainly for you."

"But can you see him hesitating for a moment to drop us if something better came along?"

I could not. The jackdaw-boy, with his fascination for shiny knick-knacks and decorations, was probably just taken by the oddity that we represented, and perhaps by the challenge. "Do you think he'll try to steal us blind when he goes?" I had been keeping all my valuables on my person, not where he could find them on the cart.

"Oddly enough, I do not. He seems to have a set of standards he holds himself to. If he leaves, he may well help himself to some of our possessions, but only by way of compensation for what wages he considers earned but unpaid. Not more."

With this reminder of the curious Oriental concept of ethics, back my thoughts circled to the enigma of Kim. "And do you think O'Hara might not have done the same? Was the Survey part of the world with which he was casual friends, or was it family, to which he bound himself irrevocably?"

Holmes sucked his teeth, a peculiar habit he had never demonstrated before coming here—a part of his current persona, no doubt. "That's the essential question, is it not? I had the impression that O'Hara would lay his life down for Creighton's organisation, but it is, I suppose, possible that his mind differentiated between Creighton and the Survey. That when Creighton went, the ties of brotherhood lapsed, and O'Hara merely stayed on for a while out of good manners."

"The same good manners Nesbit was talking about,

that drive an Indian to tell you yes when he knows the answer is no."

"Precisely."

"Which means that if O'Hara has joined the other side—whichever side that might be—it isn't so much treason as a resumption of deeper loyalties."

"Yes."

"I can't see that helps much."

"No."

⁂

By dusk, we had a mostly blue donkey cart, and Bindra went about preparing the meal with a hum of satisfaction between his teeth. And while Holmes and I were occupied with the evening's performance, the donkey-boy laid claim to our paraffin lamp to continue his work. I looked down the road at the bright glow of the light, and saw him dusting off the wheels preparatory to painting them, squinting over the smoke from his *bidi*. Later I saw that he had begun to sketch some other design along the upper edge of the cart with a charred twig. Before Holmes forcibly reclaimed the lamp and shut it down for the night, the boy had laid a precise border of yellow Indian *swastik*s along all the edges, and begun a large, all-seeing magic eye on the front panel, to precede us down the road. The next day he found frustrating, as the painting of the sun and moon he wanted on the side panels was not made any easier by the jostle of the cart, and eventually he gave up, sulking when Holmes would not stop the night at a pleasant village reached at two in the afternoon.

However, the enforced delay proved beneficial. The night before, I had been replacing the small mirrored juggling balls back into their protective bag, under the watchful eye of the young artist, when the method of their manufacture attracted my closer attention. The balls were made of some sort of plaster into which, while it was soft, many small pieces of mirrored glass had been set. Holmes had chosen them carefully, lest they have protruding edges that shred our fingers, and the plaster nestled closely against each segment.

If damp plaster could hold glass, other things could as well, I thought, and began watching for a shop that sold manufactured goods. These were rare in rural India, but late that day we passed a shop with tins of marmalade and boxes of Mrs Bird's Custard stacked in its door, jammed in between a carpenter's piled high with half-sawed tree trunks, wooden ploughs, and half-finished furniture, and a lacquer-goods manufacturer draped with toys, utensils, and decorative *charpoy*s. I ducked inside, made my purchases, and was out before Bindra noticed. That evening after dinner, I handed him the parcel.

He undid the twine, taking care with the knots, and unfolded the newspaper from the broken pieces of a looking-glass. It was enough to cover about a square foot, although it was in eight or ten pieces.

"If you press small pieces into the wet paint," I told him, having checked my vocabulary with Holmes earlier, "I believe they will stick."

He turned the shiny treasure over and over in his hands, relishing the potential. Then he picked up the other object, a dented, palm-sized metal case missing most of its original enamel which, due to the wear, had not cost me much more than the broken glass had. I waited for him to find and manipulate the side latch, then said, "This is the looking-glass of an English lady. The cover protects it from breakage."

I might have given him solid gold. He peered into it, looked at me over it, and went back to the contemplation of his own eye. I stood up to get ready for the performance, and as I pulled open the tent flap, I heard a small voice say, "I thank you."

"It is nothing," I told him.

That night the cart's sides grew stars, the mirrored glass broken down further with infinite care, rock against rock, each splinter treasured. And despite the proliferation of sharp edges, the boy didn't so much as scratch himself in the process.

Under the morning sun, our progress was glorious.

Chapter Eleven

The next day began like the others. The dust rose and the villages passed—variations on mud walls, communal well, and fields—while we left behind the early-morning murmur of grindstones and walked to the music of the bells on grazing cattle, the melodious dirge of camel-drawn Persian wheels, and the chorus of cooing doves. Halfway through the morning we bought bowls of yogurt-like *lhassi* from a veiled woman and crumbled some of the *gur* over it, taking our refreshment in the fine-speckled shade of a *neem* tree while Holmes traded news with the farmer who came to see who we were. As the sun slanted and softened into the smoke of the horizon, we began to look for a village of the right size and, preferably, state of affluence, to appreciate our labours with an offering of food and perhaps a few annas—not a town, just a centre of fifteen to thirty mud houses around the inevitable small stone temple. Up to that time, when we had spotted a promising candidate along the road or across some fields,

Bindra and I would wait with the donkey while Holmes went ahead to consult with the village headman. On our first day out of the caravanserai, this had been quickly done, and permission granted to make camp just outside the village walls. The next day, Holmes had been gone for two hours, since the man he sought was working in his fields and had to be tracked down. Today, Bindra took charge.

I thought at first the scamp had tired of us and decided to steal away—with all our possessions. Holmes and I had been deep in conversation when I looked up and realised the boy and animal were nowhere to be seen.

"Hell!" I exclaimed, in English. "The brat's gone."

Holmes examined the dusty track ahead of us, which was devoid of the familiar shapes. He said nothing, but picked up his pace. After half a mile or so we came to a field occupied by an old man clearing his channel from the nearby canal.

"Ho, my father," Holmes called. "Have you seen a small boy and a blue donkey cart come this way?"

The elderly man straightened his back, with difficulty, and shaded his eyes against the sun. "An imp with a quick tongue?"

"That is he."

"He asked after the *mukhiya,* seeking permission to bring to the village a *jadoo-wallah* with a wonder show." He sounded rather dubious; despite the sparkling cart, Holmes and I looked far from wondrous or magical in our dust-caked clothing.

"Oah," Holmes said with a sideways shake of his head. "He is a good lad, if too quick with his elders. I hope you will join us for the show, father."

"We have not so many entertainments passing through

our village that we turn our backs like city dwellers," the old man said with a chuckle, and resumed his chopping with renewed vigour.

When we neared the village, a collection of mud walls like any other, we spied young Bindra squatting in the shade of an enormous *peepul* tree, laying out twigs and branches for a fire, the donkey already freed of its load and chewing at a handful of leaves, the noisy little mynas already gathered in attendance. The lad looked sideways at us as we came up, his small body swelled with complacency.

"And to think you would have cast me aside back in Delhi," he told us smugly. "I shall be earning my salary, I think."

"If you can find some *puri*s to go with the curry, I shall increase your salary to two rupees a week."

The boy snorted in a ritual of derision, but he scrambled up eagerly enough and trotted off to the collection of walls that formed the village centre. And with that, Bindra's responsibilities expanded to include arrangements for our night's lodging.

On this, our fifth night on the road, negotiations had been swiftly concluded, and dinner was being arranged. Holmes and I bathed our faces and beat the dust from our clothing, then set about erecting the small tent, a necessary shelter in so many ways, concealing us (and particularly me) from curious eyes and allowing us to practice our conjuring in solitude. Bindra returned before the last peg was hammered in, bearing a laden tray. As before, he helped himself from the communal dish and took his bowl to one side, while we unclean types finished it off, after which the boy took the tray and bowls back to their owner. Holmes sat with his pipe while I enjoyed the dusk and the sounds of the fruit-bats that roosted overhead, going out for the evening while their human neighbours came in. Three small children peered at us from the entrance to their courtyard, giggling, until the woman of the house came to shoo them inside; she, too, peeked at us, her scarf securely over her face, before she disappeared with a swirl of garments.

The men came in from the fields, most with rough-handled hoes resting on their shoulders, a few driving dark buffalos and pale bullocks before them into the lanes, where the animals stayed, ruminating and urinating outside the houses while their masters ate the evening meal. India's quick dusk settled into night, voices rose and fell from behind the mud walls, and we sat in the open beneath the paraffin lamp, that the villagers might see our every move and be assured there was nothing to fear: This land believes in the evil eye of strangers, and would come after us with sticks and fire if they thought us a threat to their crops and cows. The cooking aromas faded, replaced by the occasional whiff of the men's pipes. When the cattle in the lanes began to be brought inside the walls, Holmes got to his feet, took up the three torches he had prepared from oil-soaked rags wrapped tightly around the end of a staff, and strolled out from under the shelter of the tree.

I followed, silent as always. I played the enigmatic one, never answering if a child called to us, rarely acknowledging a gift. I was also the one to warm the audience up, as soon as Holmes had snared their attention.

He began by planting the torches, forming an equilateral triangle with two straddling the road and one on the side away from the town. He worked methodically and with a touch of drama, as if the placing of the three staffs was a sacrament. Within seconds of his stepping onto the road, the village was hushed, every eye upon us from behind gate and walls.

When Holmes was satisfied with the position of the cold torches, he went to stand in the precise centre, extending his right arm to point his finger at the torch to his right, ten feet away. After a moment, during which he chanted some phrase continually under his breath, it burst into flame, and the darkness filled with exclamations. He did the same with the second, and the third—although his timing was slightly off and the two lit nearly simultaneously, the combustive reactions of chemicals under those circumstances being difficult to control with precision.

Then he retired, leaving the stage to me.

Luckily for me, the demands of our rural entertainments were on a fairly basic level. Indeed, putting on too slick a show would only alarm the simple folk, and cause any of the more knowledgeable residents to ask themselves why we were here rather than in some city or raja's town where we might actually earn some rupees. Rudimentary and clumsy, and clearly tricks rather than the more sinister magic.

I juggled. Not very well, and taking full advantage of the humour in the odd fumble, I juggled, looking puzzled as the balls turned into apples, then potatoes, and exclaimed and nearly dropped them when they began to sparkle and shine with the shards of mirror embedded in the bright plaster. Then one at a time, the five mirror-balls transformed themselves into small golden birds, which one by one flew away, leaving me with four balls, then three, until I tossed one lonely, sparkling ball from one hand to the other. Finally, it, too, flew off. I stood gazing into the darkness after it, bereft, when all of a sudden the sky began to rain down apples and potatoes and mirror-balls, causing me to stumble and trip in confusion and in the end duck down under cover of my arms. The rain of objects slowed, and ceased, and I cautiously peeped out from under my hands—at which one final potato dropped down on my turban. I sat down abruptly on the ground, and the entire village roared with laughter at my misfortune.

A good start.

Still seated on the ground, I reached into my pocket and pulled out a cap, a simple Moslem cap such as Holmes wore. I peered inside and took from it an egg, which I held up to look at, and to allow the village to look at, before placing it on the ground in front of my tucked-in legs. I looked back into the cap, and drew out a flower, then a mouse (which ran, fortunately, away from my cloth-covered legs) and a small sparkling ring and a clay cup full of tea, which I drank thirstily and set down. I gazed again into the cap (which measured, of course, no more than the circumference of a head and four or five inches tall), then reached into it. This time my hand went in, and kept going. In a moment my fore-arm was buried in the shallow headgear while I frowned, deep in thought, over the heads of the vil-lagers (all of whom had by now emerged from behind their walls, even the women). I felt farther into the cap, up to my elbow and beyond, scowling ferociously now. A boy of about seven started to giggle, and it spread through the audience. My upper body contorted with effort, my arm almost entirely consumed by the inade-quate scrap of cloth—and then triumph! I jerked as my hand (which had travelled unseen up my other sleeve as far as my rib cage, through a well-concealed slit in the cap) seized some elusive object hidden impossibly deep inside, and began to draw it out. Arm, elbow, forearm, wrist, then—slowly, slowly—two fingers, delicately pinched around a scrap of bright orange, clear in the flashing torchlight. I tugged gently; the scrap grew, and I pulled and it grew some more, inches and feet of silk until I was hauling yards of the brilliant stuff out onto my lap. I swam in it—a sari length is a lot of silk—and beat it away from my face, drowning in orange, until with a sharp jerk the last of the fabric snapped into the air. I worked to gather it, armloads of orange with a sparkle of silver along the border, climbing awkwardly to my feet with the unwieldy burden bursting from my grasp in all directions. And then I bent to look at the ground, and freed one hand to pat at my clothing, and looked in increasing desperation at the ground all around, but the cap was gone.

Putting on my face a look of Harold Lloyd sadness, and crumpling the stubbornly escaping ends of silk back into the wadded armload, I carried it over to the audience and handed it to the first person who did not draw back from me, a boy of about seventeen. He took it, half reluctant, half pleased, and I heard a gasp from the darkness behind him where his family stood—probably a young wife, who I hoped would know what to do with all those yards of orange sari fabric. Saris were a costume of the south and of the cities, but it was hard to create humorous drama by pulling the legs and sleeves of a *salwaar kameez* out of a cap.

With the villagers warmed up, I retired to the sidelines while Holmes came forward to claim the light. His portion of the act was more dramatic, closer to the heart of the magic arts, and demanded a fine understanding of the sensibilities of the audience. If he went too far, drew too heavily on the *mysterium* of awe, the rustic folk would retreat, might even turn on us, fearing that we brought true darkness into their midst. Holmes had to read them at every instant, keeping them on the edge of discomfort and mystification without allowing them to slide into open fear, convincing them of his power, but only over the inessentials, transforming a mouse into a sparrow; setting fire to an inert glass of *lhassi*; and separating and re-joining two sets of clashing rings, one of silver bangles, the other big and brass; and setting into motion the dancing figures in a cloud of perfumed smoke, projected from the phantasmagoric lantern he had brought from home. As a climax, he drew me from the shadows, passed his hand over my face to put me into a trance, and then levitated my senseless form some feet above the earth.

Very basic stuff, dependent on quick hands, firm distraction, and simple equipment sold in magic shops the world around (or, in our case, made to specification by Delhi metalworkers). We garnered a handful of coins and a lot of wary glances, and moved on in the dawn when the buffalos were back ruminating in the lanes and the grindstones had begun to sing, with the snow-topped Himalayas little more than faint pink ghosts riding high above the horizon. The menfolk interrupted their morning ablutions to watch us leave, while the women pulled their curious babes back inside the gates of their humble compounds, just in case.

During the days of our partnership (or, as he no doubt viewed it, of his management of this road show) Bindra had grown ever more cocky. He was, after all, a city boy among farmers—he kept himself aloof from the village children, occasionally deigning to answer them while he worked on the cart by the light of the lamp, and it occasionally seemed to me that his moon face was older than those of the others his size. He did not understand how our tricks were done, but by this time he was convinced that they were tricks, and that was enough to make him superior to the gullible. On this, our sixth morning on the road, he got the donkey started, then hesitated, and turned to me.

"Teach me to draw a coin from an ear," he commanded.

"You have not the purity of spirit," I said blithely.

He was not impressed. "I do not believe it is the spirit that does the act. It is a trick of the hands, and I wish to learn it."

"I cannot teach it," I told him, and that was the end of it for the moment. I did not imagine the boy would let it drop, however; nor did I imagine the way in which he would force me into teaching him.

With the morning sun behind us and Bindra and the cart far enough ahead to give the dust time to settle, he discovered a new game. My first inkling of it was when the road ahead of me exploded into a flare of light, painful and completely blinding.

"Damn!" I cried, and raised my hand to block it— only it had stopped. I blinked furiously, and when I could see the road again, it was as before, with the boy and the glittering cart. At first I thought one of the looking-glass stars had caught the light, although they seemed too small for that. Then I noticed the boy's hands, holding the folding ladies' looking-glass up before his face.

"Bindra!" I shouted. "*Khabadar! Shaitan ka batcha!*"

He turned around to walk backwards, shrugging his shoulders at me, all innocence.

A few minutes later it happened again. Deliberate, the little brat, I knew. The kid needed something to keep his hands busy—oh.

"He really is something," I muttered to Holmes, and trotted ahead to dig the cloth practise balls from the cart.

I took out the red one, showed the boy how to toss it, then told him to practise the motion until he could do it for fifty paces down the road with his eyes shut.

"Er, do you know how to count to fifty?" I asked him. He glared at me and snatched the ball.

That took care of him for the rest of the morning: no more blinding flashes. The red shape would appear rhythmically over his head for a while as he walked alongside the placid donkey, then he would drop it, run after it, and start again. He improved rapidly, and kept the ball going for longer and longer. I could tell when he began to experiment with closing his eyes, because he tended to veer slowly away from the donkey's side, the ball slapping between his hands as he headed for the fields to the side, or came closer and closer to the animal's sharp little hooves as the beast followed a turn in the road and her barefoot master did not.

Most entertaining—although I was glad we were no longer on the crowded Grand Trunk Road. The boy would surely be crushed in the first mile.

In the meantime, Holmes and I conversed, almost exclusively in Hindustani now. My brain had grown calluses with the heavy use, and I no longer found the exercise exhausting.

"How old do you think Bindra is?" I said to Holmes in the vernacular tongue.

"He is of the hill people, and they are small. I think him older than he appears."

"I thought he might be—he was watching one of the girls in that last village, and she had to be at least thirteen. Are hill people round of face, like him? From his features, I thought at first he was mentally retarded."

"Oh, that he is not."

"He really should be in school, then."

"You may find he has been, at some time in his past. I saw him reading a notice on a wall the other day."

"Then what on earth was he doing shovelling muck for a horse-dealer?"

But Holmes could not answer that, any more than I.

Chapter Twelve

Over the week of our sojourn, the radiant and majestic line of snow-covered peaks had grown from a line of white teeth to a wall of jagged peaks stretching so wide there was nothing else in their half of the world, towering so high they ate the sky itself. Step by step we had been drawn into their icy embrace, until finally on Wednesday we reached the town of Kalka, huddled at their very feet.

We found rooms for the night, and arranged to leave the donkey and our heavier belongings with the innkeeper while we took the train to Simla. The man swore that no one would so much as lay a finger on anything, and guaranteed it by taking only a small payment, leaving the larger part until we returned. Holmes then went off to make arrangements with an ironmonger and carpenter for some conversions to the cart itself, which negotiations took the better part of the afternoon. We had intended to leave Bindra with our possessions, but the boy, unimpressed by the town, would have none of it, and in the end, it was easier to allow him to come than to keep arguing. At least he did not insist on a space in our room that night, making do with a *charpoy* in the stables. I saw him at dusk, sitting cross-legged, tossing the red and green balls up and down.

The boy was waiting for us when we came down in the morning, no doubt fearful we would sneak out and leave him behind. Still, I could not quite understand why a trip into the mountains with us was preferable to a warm, quiet holiday in the stables. So when we were standing on the platform waiting for the train that would climb with us to Simla, I asked him.

"Why do you keep following us?"

"Because you are so very interesting," he retorted. "And I learn many things—see?" That morning he had demanded that I give him the yellow ball, and he now stood, tossing the three spheres up and catching them in a smooth rhythm, talking nonchalantly all the while. Soon he would be better than I.

"You're going to wear them out," I said.

"When do I throw the mirror-balls? And when do I throw with you?"

"The mirror-balls when you can keep these in the air for two hundred paces without dropping them. And as a partner when you can keep five up." It would be far more expertise than he'd need to hold up his end of a two-person team, but it condemned the urchin to solitary labours for a few more days while I accustomed myself to the idea of a three-person partnership. "Bindra, can you read and write?"

"Oah yes. I write my name," he asserted, but he began to concentrate closely on the trio of coloured balls he was tossing and catching with smooth competence.

"Why are you not in school?"

"I told you, I learn things from you."

"You should be in school."

He did not bother to answer. I tried another tack. "How old are you, Bindra?"

"Maybe twenty?" But before I could react, he changed it to "Or eleven? I think more than eight, I can remember eight."

"Where are you from? Where is your family?"

"I have no family."

"You're an orphan?"

"I have an auntie in Calcutta. I was with her, oh, two or three years I think, before she sold me to the horse-dealer."

"*Sold* you?"

"Oah yes," he said nonchalantly. "I was happy to go. His hand was lighter than hers."

"There's no slavery in India."

The brief look he shot me was eloquent. It occurred to me that I'd just given myself away definitively: He'd long overlooked my chronic oddities of speech and habit, but only a foreigner could assert that slavery did not exist in a place where clearly it did. I tried to regain my standing.

"Truly, Bindra, under the white man's law, slavery is not allowed. Your aunt could not sell you, although she told you she could."

"Oah, I know that. But I am a child. If I stand up and say, 'I am not to be sold,' what then? I am turned out to live on the street and go hungry. I did not mind. And ho! It has meant that I found you and the magician. I eat good food and breathe clean air. And now I am going to ride a train."

Every boy's dream, in this country as in others: to

run away and join the circus. "Yes, well. We must talk more about a school for you. Because one day you will be a man, and need the skills you can only learn in school. Unless you wish to be a farmer in a village," I added, knowing his disdain for the man with the hoe.

"I shall be a magician," he said, adding slyly, "when you have taught me to pick the coin out of the air."

I laughed and reached out to clap him on the back, and stopped with my hand an inch from his shoulder. To most Hindus, I as a Moslem was horribly unclean, and making contact with them would be deeply offensive, requiring lengthy purification. "What is your caste, Bindra?"

"Oah, I have no caste."

"No caste? What do you mean, all India has some kind of caste."

"No. I am a Kee-ristian." It took a moment for my ears to translate the word from Hindi. The boy was a Christian? Good Lord, I thought; were we dealing with another Kim here, an abandoned European? The boy went on, oblivious. "Some Kee-ristians came into our village when I was quite small—this was before I went to Calcutta to live with my auntie. They wore long dresses, the women always, the men on some days, and one such day they made a great ceremony under the trees and dipped water on our heads and told us that in Jesu there was neither Brahmin nor Kshatriya, no Sudra or foreigner. Some of the village were angry, and in the end they drove those Kee-ristian men away with sticks and paid the priests great sums to return them to their proper place. I had no money to pay the priests, but although I did not ask to have my caste taken from me, truly, I have found that to have no caste is altogether a good thing, for now I can eat what I like, sleep where I please. I will have to pay a priest to restore me when I wish to marry, of course—who but the lowest Sudra would take a casteless man into his house? But that is a long time away."

I could only gaze at him, open-mouthed, and follow him into the little carriage when the train pulled in a few minutes later.

Holmes had told me that the narrow-gauge train would climb six thousand feet, in sixty miles, taking six hours or more to do so. We should need our heavy coats at the end of it. The sites of my chilblains tingled in anticipation, as I found that our third-class car was heated only by the body warmth of its occupants. Bindra seemed not to notice, so rapt was he with wonder at the passing scenery. Then the train entered a tunnel, and he scrambled away from the window in surprise.

"Have you ever been on a train before?" I asked him.

"Oah yes, many times," he said, although his unconcealed excitement declared that he was lying through his teeth. Still, he had plenty of practise on that run to become used to passing hills and the darkness of tunnels: Holmes thought there were a hundred or more, although I would have believed it if he'd said a thousand.

Simla was the year-round headquarters of the British Indian Army and with it the Survey of India, both its open and its hidden faces. The government as a whole moved up here, bag and baggage, as soon as the temperature climbed in the plains. From March to November this small Olympus ruled all the land from the Red Sea to the hills of Burma—what Gandhi a few years earlier had scornfully called "government from the five hundredth floor"—and it bustled with life, bursting with political and social intrigue, ringing with the voices of

English children and their *ayah*s, vibrating with the conversations of their mothers about the latest scandal or shortage or piece of amateur dramatics. Today, however, was the last day of January, and we found the hill-town bitter cold, largely shuttered, and nearly bereft of an English presence.

Hotel rooms for our kind, however, were plentiful, and we had our choice of locations, sizes, and services. We hiked into the native bazaar that lay below the town's European centre, a tumbling hotch-potch of buildings that climbed onto one another's backs and looked over one another's shoulders, with the street entrance of one shop giving out onto a rooftop exit at the rear. We took a suite of rooms in a native-style hotel that did not look too poisonous, with a mat near the kitchen for Bindra. I indulged in my first true bath since the night of the hotel fire, eleven days before, although I had to renew my skin and hair dye at the end of it. And if the meal we were served was a bastard imitation of English-style mutton curry, the beds we were given were soft, the sheets thin with wear but fairly clean.

I settled under the thick cotton coverlets with a sigh of contentment. My hair was still damp, but I was warm, and the solid walls were a reassurance after canvas. Holmes shed his shoes and crawled into the shelter beside me.

"I found myself looking for the shop of Lurgan Sahib, as we came through the bazaar," I told him. The mysterious Lurgan, who introduced young Kim to the Jewel Game and taught him many arcane arts, had disappeared from Simla some years before.

"The building itself is still there, though much changed."

"What its walls could tell." I lay looking at the play of firelight on the ceiling for a minute. "Holmes, do you think Bindra could be one of Nesbit's? An agent of sorts?"

"An Irregular? One does have to wonder, but somehow I doubt it. The boy does not seem interested enough in us. I've never caught him trying to overhear a conversation, have you?"

"No. Or go through our things. He's pretty much a force unto himself."

"Of course, he could simply be remarkably subtle with it."

"At his age?"

"True. Even a prodigy such as young O'Hara concealed his interest by pretending to an alternative preoccupation, not by showing no interest at all."

This was rather too complex for my drowsy state; after a minute, I let it go, and murmured instead, "Do you think we'll find him?"

"O'Hara? If he's there, and if he wishes to be found, yes."

"And what shall we do then?"

I felt Holmes' fingers on my hair, following the shape of my long night-time plait, before he answered. "We will bring him back. And if he does not wish to come, I shall look him in the eye and ask him why."

❧

It snowed during the night, two inches of dry flakes that rose up around our boots and blew like spring blossoms. Bindra took one look at it and dug in his heels like a startled mule.

"Oah, that does not look at all good."

"It's just snow," I told him. "Frozen rain."

"I know snow, thank you," he retorted with some force. "I will be staying inside today. When you return, I shall be able to keep the blue ball in the air."

I rather doubted he'd convince the cook to allow him to juggle in her warm kitchen, but I wasn't about to argue. I buttoned my heavy skin-lined coat and scurried to catch Holmes up.

The boots of the plains people were not adequate for walking on the cobbles of a hill-side town covered in snow, and I was glad when we stopped at the corner of two roads that fed into the Mall. I stared up at the town, astonished. With the snow, it looked more like Switzerland than sub-continent, all peaked chalet roofs and carved frontispieces.

"Holmes, this place is extraordinary."

"No English!" he chided, then added, "You ought to see it in the summer. It looks as if you'd plucked up the inhabitants of a Tibetan town and set them down in Surrey."

Holmes pulled the mirrored balls from about his person and set to juggling them; I left my hands deep in my coat pockets.

"What are we doing here, Holmes?"

"Waiting to attract attention. Even in the busy summer we could not risk going openly into the Survey offices. We must wait until someone comes to see what we are about."

"Shouldn't we go a little closer?" I asked. We were still among the ramshackle buildings of the native bazaar, before the road widened into the sloping plaza.

"If we did, we'd risk being thrown out, even in the winter season. No native is permitted there except on business."

I sighed, drew my hands from their warm nests, and prepared to catch whatever he might throw me.

There is a nearly hypnotic rhythm to a session of juggling, where the world narrows down to the other's hands, when sight and sound merge into an almost psychic anticipation of one's partner's moves. It would have been a pleasurable interlude, had the temperature been on the melting side of freezing, since we had no audience to speak of. The occasional passer-by paused for thirty seconds before the cold urged him on, and two infants of five or six squatted in the drifted snow for far too long, their teeth chattering and their brown skin going an alarming shade of blue before an older sister appeared to chase them inside. My own fingers were turning white, rather than blue, and I did not know how much longer they would respond to their brain's instructions to open and close.

We had been working the corner for nearly forty minutes before Holmes straightened marginally; when I shot a glance up the Mall, I saw a man, strolling unconcernedly, glancing into shop windows. He went inside one, coming out a few minutes later with a rolled newspaper under his arm. He greeted a man walking briskly up the hill, tipped his hat at a pair of well-wrapped ladies getting into a two-horse *tonga,* and took a very long time to descend the length of Simla's social centre. Finally he paused to watch our increasingly clumsy game of catch.

It was none other than Geoffrey Nesbit. He ran his eyes over Holmes, identifying him, before studying me. I thought there was a little smile resting along the corner of his mouth, although I kept my eyes on Holmes' hands.

"That is quite clever," he said in Hindi. Somehow, I didn't think he was talking entirely about the juggling.

"Thank you, *sahib*," Holmes replied, in the same tongue.

"In fact, I think I might be able to steer you towards a bit of work. Children's parties and the like."

"Oh, sir, we can do many tricks."

The smaller man stifled a laugh, and said merely, "I don't doubt that."

"And we go where we are told," I added. The fluency of my phrase snapped his attention back onto me. He opened his mouth, but I was not to hear his words, for behind his shoulder, coming from the warren of side-streets that lay beneath the Mall, three figures were approaching. One brief glance, and I caught and placed the balls, one-two-three-four-five, on the trampled snow between my feet before turning my back on Holmes and saying in a low voice, "I'll see you later." I took three rapid steps and ducked into the next alleyway.

I trusted that Holmes was safely concealed under dye and clothing, but my spectacles, which I tended to leave off only when comparative blindness was preferable to the needs of disguise, would be a dead giveaway when it came to the Goodhearts. What the hell were they doing in Simla? I paused just around the building with my ear bent to listen.

Mrs Goodheart's distinctive voice rang stridently through the streets, bouncing off the brick and stone buildings. ". . . not get me into one of those *jampani* machines again, I thought we'd end up at the bottom of the hill. And here I thought we were coming to the tropics! If I'd wanted snow I'd have stayed in Chicago. Really, Thomas, couldn't we have gone to your maharaja directly? There's nothing at all to see in this town."

"Mother, I thought the Teacher's message said that hard experiences took one on the road to enlightenment." The young man sounded a bit snappish.

"And what would you know about that? Sunny, watch you don't get too close to that beggar."

Holmes obligingly started up the whine for *bakshish,* although he was hardly dressed for the part, and beggars rarely juggled mirrored balls. I could only hope the Goodhearts did not find it peculiar for a white man to be carrying on a conversation with a beggar. However, Mrs Goodheart's next words reassured me, for they were spoken in a politer tone than she had used for her son.

"Pardon me, sir, but I wonder if you can recommend a place to get a cup of tea that won't poison us?"

"Poison you?" Nesbit asked, his voice nicely puzzled.

"You know what I mean. My son informs me that at this altitude it is necessary to boil water for considerably longer than in the lowlands, and I can't get the waiter at the hotel to understand it. That may be fine for local constitutions, but I fear that ours won't survive. My daughter is too delicate to risk it."

I smiled at Mrs Goodheart's unsubtle nudge of her daughter in the direction of this apparently eligible male. Sunny's constitution was about as delicate as a tornado.

"Certainly, I'd be more than happy to show you a dependable tea shop. Perhaps you would be my guests?"

Pressed back into a doorway, I peered cautiously at their retreating backs, Mrs Goodheart's arm through her son's, which more or less forced Nesbit to offer Sunny his. At the place where the road opened out, young Goodheart turned to look back. I was in shadow and therefore invisible, but I could only hope that Holmes had continued with his act in their absence.

One sharp glance over his shoulder, and then Nesbit was ushering them through a gaily painted doorway, a cloud of lovely warm steamy air billowing into the frigid outside world at their passage.

I went back to Holmes, and was glad to find him still seated and juggling, turned slightly downhill now. I hunkered onto my heels at his side.

"Thomas Goodheart looked back at you before they went into the tea shop," I told him.

"Did he now?"

"What do you suppose they're doing up here?"

"They must have diverted on the way to Khanpur. I can't see them going the land route through Simla, even if the pass is still open."

"Mrs Goodheart doesn't seem too pleased to be here."

"Perhaps Nesbit will find out why they've come here rather than visit Jaipur or any of the usual places. Thanks to your quick eyes, I had just enough time to tell him who it was."

"I do wish there were some way to disguise spectacles," I grumbled. It was a complaint I had made before.

"We shall have to see about getting you a pair of those on-the-eye lenses the Germans are working on," he said thoughtfully, and I shuddered; the very thought of wearing paper-thin slivers of curved glass pressed up against my corneas made me queasy.

"Thanks, but I prefer to walk into things," I said. "How will we get back into touch with Nesbit?"

"Look in the cup."

Among the small coins in the tin mug Holmes had set out lay a twist of fine paper. I reached for it, then paused. If I tried to pick it up, it might well be lost to my clumsiness.

"Perhaps we might go back to the hotel for a while?" I pleaded. "My fingers are numb to the elbow."

We were greeted at the hostelry door by young Bindra, who crowed "Look! Look!" and set four balls into the air. Holmes patted his head by way of approval, I told him "Good job" around my chattering teeth, and we requested much hot tea and made for the nearest fireplace.

The note Nesbit had dropped into Holmes' cup bore the words "Viceregal Lodge, 10:00 P.M." I hoped the formal venue did not indicate that we were to dress, but decided that the hour was not that of a dinner invitation. It scarcely mattered: I had nothing suitable to wear anyway.

Chapter Thirteen

At nine-thirty of a winter's evening in the Himalayan foothills, few pedestrians picked their way over the ice-slick roads. Those who did were so thoroughly bundled that only the breathy clouds rising from their swathed heads showed that they were animate. The thin air here smelled of wood smoke instead of dung fires, and the sharp green aroma of deodar was intoxicating.

I had decided, given time to think over the matter, that considering the time of year, the Viceroy himself was not likely to be in residence, and so it proved. The ornate stone fortress two miles from the Mall, which even in the moonless black resembled a Scottish castle, had lights in few of its windows, and those behind drawn curtains. We were not even required to decide which door to approach, since as we drew near, a shadow detached itself from a tree and intercepted us, speaking the single English word "Come."

We went around the back and entered Viceregal

Lodge through a scullery, empty but warm, and followed our guide up a narrow and uncarpeted stairway to an upper room, warm and well lit, with armchairs, sofas, and low tables gathered in front of a great stone fireplace. Our guide closed the door behind us, and we all three peeled, unwrapped, and tugged ourselves free from the multiplicity of coats and shawls we wore.

Once free of his wrappings, our guide proved to be, not the *chowkidar,* but Geoffrey Nesbit. He heaped logs onto the coals in the grate, then pulled open a capacious and well-stocked cupboard. "Brandy? G and T?"

It was peculiarly exotic, to be seated on a high-backed sofa with the taste of brandy on the tongue, speaking English. There was a sort of echo in the first minutes of speech, almost as if my mind was translating the words into themselves.

"Have you had a successful week?" he asked.

"A valuable one," Holmes replied.

Nesbit nodded as if he understood the value in a week on the road, but I thought he had not really heard the reply. My suspicion was confirmed when he said abruptly, "I don't know how much you have heard of the world's news while you were travelling here."

"Not a great deal. There was a rumour that Lenin is dead—although it came to us as 'the king of Russia.' "

"No rumour. He died the day you left Delhi, or the day before, it is far from certain. It appears the country will be governed by a triumvirate, never a good omen for stability."

"But our own Parliament, that transfer of power has gone ahead?"

"The Americans are voluminously unhappy and the Russians grimly inclined to gloat, but yes, Mr Baldwin stepped down in the end, and Ramsay MacDonald has been confirmed. The new Secretary of State for India is Lord Olivier."

"The governor of Jamaica? But he's not Labour."

"A number of the new cabinet aren't. Critics are saying it's because there aren't enough competent Socialists to fill the ranks, although I'd say it's more an attempt at mollifying the opposition. Still, there might have been considerably less alarm about a minority government had the Socialists not celebrated their victory by publicly singing both 'The Marseillaise' and 'The Red Flag.' The Bolsheviks will be invited to discuss the treaties and claims they tore up when they came into power. I can only pray Olivier has the sense to hold firm on India." He put his glass to his mouth, discovered that he'd already drained it, and leant forward to replenish it with brandy and a very small dash of soda. "And Gandhi's health is deteriorating. The man goes on a hunger-strike, then we get blamed when he becomes ill. Bombay may be forced to suspend his sentence so he doesn't die in custody—the last thing we need is to create a martyr for the *swaraj* cause." He tipped the glass down his throat, although I wouldn't have thought him a heavy drinker.

As if he'd heard my thought, he slapped the glass down on the table and sat back. "Now, you wanted to know about the maharaja of Khanpur. I'm probably not the man to ask for an objective view."

"You like the man," Holmes noted.

"I'd even call him a friend, although our paths don't cross that often, and then usually at events. But I've been a guest in his home any number of times over the years, and have found him not only a staunch supporter of Britain, but a fine sportsman as well, which to my mind counts for a lot."

"Pig sticking," I said, not intending to say the words aloud. But I did, and Nesbit heard the amusement, even distaste in my voice. Before he could do more than bristle, Holmes drew out his clay pipe, sure indication of a lecture.

"Russell, I don't know that you are clearly picturing just what this particular sport entails," he said sternly. I permitted Nesbit to refill my glass, as this was clearly going to take a while—although given the topic, I couldn't see why. "The British pig is an indolent creature of unsanitary and occasionally comic habits, who most of the time is no more dangerous than a milch cow or draught horse. A wild Asian boar, on the other hand, is as much as three hundred pounds of furious muscle directed by a sly and malevolent brain and armed with four curved razors as much as eight inches long, any of which is capable of slicing through a horse's leg, or a man's—few other blood sports give the quarry such an equal opportunity for victory. The whimsical name of the sport aside, pig sticking demands strength, endurance, and a degree of horsemanship far beyond what one sees on, for example, a fox hunt. Pig sticking, or to use the slightly more dignified term employed in Bengal, hog hunting, embodies the warrior virtues of both cultures, East and West. It reduces a soldier's training to its essence: iron nerves, an acute sensitivity to the enemy, the ability to commit to an instantaneous response, and an overpowering determination to win—precisely those qualities one requires in battle or to quell a riot. Saying that a man is a pig-sticker does not mean merely that he is proficient at relieving the countryside of a pest; it says that the man is possessed of singular ability and self-control, even wisdom. In the context of India, pig sticking is the game of games."

Nesbit, twice possessor of the Kadir Cup, looked abashed at this implied tribute, but it was as well Holmes said it. If nothing else, it clarified Nesbit's attitude towards his sporting friend "Jimmy," although to my mind, the male's passion for games often led him to become frivolous towards those things requiring serious thought, and to be serious about the essentially frivolous. But this was hardly the place for philosophical debate.

"I understand," I said. "You will pardon me, Captain Nesbit, if as a Jew and a woman who lives on a farm, I don't take pigs seriously. But I shall endeavour to keep in mind the sharp edge of the tusks rather than the comical twist of the tail."

Nesbit studied his glass, trying to retrieve the conversation's thread before Holmes had diverted us into sport. "Yes, well, the maharaja of Khanpur. He is as near to what the Americans might call a 'self-made man' as an hereditary ruler can get. You no doubt realise that the hundreds of native states within India have huge differences. One state has a population of less than two hundred in under an acre; on the other hand, Kashmir occupies an area larger than France, while Hyderabad possesses an income greater than most of the European countries. Some are one step from feudal barbarism, in their society and their economy, others well on their way to becoming industrial powers; it's entirely up to each state's prince. The British Resident may suggest and recommend, but he rarely asserts any authority. It's the price we pay for their loyalty—the princes saved us in the Mutiny. Indeed, one might even say that they made the Empire possible. They are still essential to British rule, a guarantee that if the tide turns against us again, we have a bulwark against the waves. If you will pardon the flight of fancy," he added.

"The princes are, to put it bluntly, above the law of British India. Short of declaring war or entering into independent diplomatic relations, they are free to do as they like, to spend their time and their fortunes gambling in Monte Carlo or hunting tigers or filling their days with dancing girls. Only if they become too wildly erratic, or too political, do we step in. But their sins have to be pretty extreme."

I kept my face expressionless, but all in all, it sounded as if British India had managed to preserve and encourage all that was bad about an hereditary aristocracy, buying the princes off by averting eyes from their misdemeanors while heaping them with ritual displays of power—the big shooting parties, the nine- or seventeen- or twenty-one-gun salutes—in hopes that they might not notice their essential impotence.

"A generation ago," Nesbit was saying, "a man in my position might argue that the British would remain a part of India always; now, only the most self-deluding *burra-sahib* would claim that. This country is set on the road to independence, a journey we have the responsibility of assisting and guiding. And as we prepare to step aside, two competitors are jostling to move into the vacuum of power: the Congress Party, which is largely Hindu, and the Moslem League. I'm sure you are fully aware of the deep and abiding mistrust and simmering violence that exists between Hindu and Moslem here. The two religions are essentially incompatible: Moslem views Hindu as a worshipper of idols, Hindu condemns Moslem as unclean cow-killer. And that isn't even beginning to touch the other parties, the Communists on the one side and the *swaraj*ists on the other, who hate and mistrust each other. In order to reach a common ground between the Congress Party and the League, there are many who believe that the princes will come into their own, as a sort of House of Lords with real power, providing continuity between a colonial past and a more democratic future.

"And that is where your maharaja comes in, Mr Holmes. His father died when the boy was small, four or five—poison was suspected, but never proved, although half a dozen servants and two of his wives were put to death over it. Having had a look at the file, I should say it was more likely to have been some treatment for the syphilis he picked up in southern France—the man had an unfortunate fondness for the rougher side of life.

"The old man, Jimmy's grandfather, was one of the feudal types, interested only in harem and toys—quite literally: He had one of the most extraordinary collections of mechanical oddities in the world, and seems to have had some fairly rum practices behind the walls of his palace. In fact, at the time he died, despite his service during the Mutiny, an investigation had begun into some of his less savoury practises. I mean to say, we're happy to allow a proved friend of the Crown a certain amount of leeway when it comes to governing the country his family have ruled for centuries, but one can only turn a blind eye on depravity and despoilment for so long, and buying small children for..." Nesbit stopped to study his hands pinkly for a moment. "For purposes best suited to the harem, goes too far. In any event, his age caught him up before the government could step in, and he died in his bed at the age of eighty-four, his only son long dead and his eldest grandson Jimmy just eleven.

"Remarkably enough, Jimmy seems to have avoided inheriting his father and grandfather's worst excesses. He likes his toys, true, although with him it's motorcars and aeroplanes—he's got one of the sub-continent's highest air fields. But the worst of the debauchery passed him by, and by some miracle he seems to have found some brains and backbone as well. He went away to university—America, funnily enough, rather than Oxford or Cambridge—then played in Europe, Africa, and South America for eight or nine years, developing his taste for big game. And then he turned his eyes on his home, and brought some ideas with him. In the fourteen years he's been back, the kingdom has gone through enormous changes. Khanpur's already got one of the best programmes of sanitation in the country, and Jimmy regularly sends boys out to school in England and America.

"He has two wives and a dozen or so concubines, eight or nine children, which are fairly conservative numbers for a man in his position. He's sending his heir to school in England, and spends a certain amount of the state monies on improvements for the people— schools, water, sanitation. His heaviest personal expenditures, if the word 'personal' has any meaning in a princely state, have been on his zoo, used also for the breeding of exotic game animals, and on the restoration of what they call 'The Forts,' five miles outside of the city—actually two halves of the old Moghul palace, called Old Fort and New Fort, since there's two or three centuries between them. Jimmy maintains the Palace proper in the city, where his womenfolk live, but he seems to prefer The Forts. Certainly whenever I've visited Khanpur, that's where he's been. It's closer to the hunting.

"He's made friends of most of the high-ranking political officers, and always invites visiting dignitaries for a shoot—generally the kind that ends up with a football-field covered with birds, although from time to time he'll take the truly honoured on a tiger-hunt, with elephants and the lot. He has friends in high places, and a genius for combining European sensibilities with traditional Indian warrior virtues. He's a Kshatriya, if that means anything to you."

We nodded; the warrior caste was theoretically a step under the priestly Brahminical elite, but in practice they wielded the greater political and economic power, and were twice-born as the Brahmins were.

"So you are saying that the maharaja of Khanpur is beyond reproach?" Holmes asked.

"Well, no. I am telling you that to all appearances, he is a high-ranking aristocrat, loyal to the Crown, stable, and forward-looking. What, indeed, I have always regarded him."

" 'To all appearances,' " Holmes repeated. "And beneath the appearances?"

"Understand, I have not seen the man since last year's Kadir Cup in March. And I will say that at the time, he struck me as being uncharacteristically short-tempered. Nothing extreme, you understand, just general impatience. He clubbed a beater with the weighted butt of a short spear, knocked him out briefly."

Beating a servant unconscious was evidently not considered "extreme" behaviour on the part of a pig-sticker, I noted.

"Further enquiries this past ten days have come up with some disturbing facts. Our Resident in Khanpur took ill four months ago and hasn't yet returned from England, which makes communication from within the state considerably less efficient than usual. Khanpur has recently instigated a relatively aggressive border patrol, which is frankly unusual in a native state—although border guards are by no means forbidden under the treaty, it would have been brought to our attention had the Resident been there. One of the neighbouring states has issued a complaint that its nawab's daughter is missing, stolen into Khanpur, although from the girl's reputation, they'll probably find her in Bombay with a lover. And there have been a number of unsubstantiated complaints concerning the ill-treatment of his people— a young man who made speeches in Khanpur city has vanished, and bazaar rumour has it he's been fed to the maharaja's pet lions, which is slightly absurd. Another whisper concerns a concubine killed in a fit of pique, which is a rumour I hear at least twice a year from all over the country, that when investigated has proved true once, to my memory. And a rumour of a train from Moscow carrying three dismantled German aeroplanes, which went missing at the end of the train line. These are, of course, all things which the Resident would have investigated, if he'd been there. But added to the maharaja's visit to Moscow, when we had only known of his being in Europe, and compounded by his invitation to a young man with known Bolshevik contacts and sympathies, then, yes, it is time we had a closer look inside the state."

I had been involved with this life long enough to hear unspoken messages behind a monologue; I waited for the man to work around to what he wanted of us.

Holmes, too, was clearly impatient to hear the man's proposal, and urged him onward with the dry observation, "To say nothing of the matter of three dead agents, tortured and robbed of their charms, all found dead within twenty miles of the Khanpur border."

Nesbit grunted unhappily. "You came to this country to look for Kimball O'Hara," he said, then stopped again to reach for the brandy decanter and pour himself a couple of undiluted inches. I was starting to feel positively apprehensive about this. Whatever his point was, he clearly did not expect us to like it much. "On the voyage out, this other matter came to your attention, and you brought it to me."

Holmes had had enough. "Come, man, get it off your chest. Are you saying you wish us to go to Khanpur for you?"

"Yes," Nesbit said, sounding relieved. "But it's not just—here, let me show you what I'm getting at." He abandoned his drink and went to a low, deep cabinet on the wall, opening one of its shallow drawers and pulling out two maps. He cleared the glasses from the table and smoothed the first page out before us, a map of all India, its long triangle heavily marked with irregular blue shapes that covered nearly all of the north and a great deal of the centre: the princely states.

I blinked in surprise. "I hadn't quite realised how much of the country is in private hands."

"A third of the land, a quarter of the people. Native states hold some of the richest agricultural land, diamond mines, key passes into Afghanistan and Tibet." His finger tapped a place heavily marked by topographical lines, orientating us to the whole. "Here's Simla. There's Delhi," he added, touching his finger to the city three inches south, then dragging it up in the opposite direction. "The Afghan border here; Tibet; Kashmir up here, and just below it, looking deceptively small and out-of-the-way, lies Khanpur." When we had absorbed its setting, he plucked the other map from the floor and allowed it to settle over the first.

Where the first map had been a product of some government printing agency, a cooperative effort with more detail than personality, this page was a work of art, a depiction of the northernmost knob of the Indian nation, lettered by a hand both neat and familiar. I bent over it to be sure.

"Yes," Nesbit said, "this is O'Hara's work. It took him five years walking every hill and track, counting those steps on his Tibetan prayer-beads, recording what he had seen and done each night on the back of a sheet inside his prayer wheel. I had the privilege of accompanying him once, and I've never seen a man more single-minded at the task. One year, O'Hara spent an entire hot season as a *punkah-wallah,* pulling the fan in a wealthy merchant's house, his ear to the wall listening to everything said inside. When we worked together, I'd see him interrupted time and again by locals wishing a blessing or a piece of news, or wanting to give him food or shelter, and each time he would turn aside and talk yet somehow keep track of his count, never losing track once. Brilliant man. And beyond being simply a surveyor, he seemed to know just where to ask the questions, precisely how to find the key people, however unlikely they might be. He was . . . It is difficult to explain, other than saying he took joy in his work. The hill folk saw that joy and interpreted it as holiness. He went everywhere as a monk, and was apparently never doubted, even when he was young. He wasn't like any monk I ever met, but somehow when he put on that red hat, you believed him completely. It was something in the eyes."

Suddenly, Nesbit caught himself, and his handsome

face flushed. "Sorry, I'm not used to strong drink at these altitudes."

"I do know what you mean about O'Hara," Holmes reassured him. "Did you ever meet the old Pathan horse-dealer?"

"Mahbub Ali? Of course."

"He told me that the boy was a steel whip, although he gave far too freely of the truth. He said the lad could bend and contort into all sorts of shapes, but he always returned to himself, and he would only be broken when forced to break his word. Mahbub intended that as a criticism, I believe."

"No doubt. In any event, this map is the work of O'Hara's hand, and accurate down to the last stream and serai. And if you study it for a bit, you will begin to see the strategic potential of the kingdom of Khanpur."

I had been studying it, while the two men exchanged their eulogies of the lost Survey agent, and could well see what he meant. The state was a long, narrow strip, mountains in the north giving way to a broad central plateau, where the capital city straddled a river. Four or five miles north of the city was a dark square marked "The Forts"; far beyond it, at the state's northern tip, a pair of reversed brackets marked a pass, beside which was written "9400 feet." Khanpur city was perhaps sixty miles from its southern neighbour and the city of Hijarkot, where the railway ended, but a scant fifteen from the country's eastern boundaries; the square marking The Forts was even nearer the border, perhaps six or eight miles. Beyond the country's eastern boundaries an uneven square marked a British encampment, but my eyes strayed to the strategic, relatively low pass at the northern end. The brackets were less than two hundred miles from the southernmost point of the

Russian railway system: by aeroplane, perhaps two or three hours.

As if he had seen the direction of my gaze, Nesbit said, "That pass was actually a fairly late discovery, not on the maps at all until the late eighties. There used to be a lake there, with sheer mountain sides, until the big Kashmir earthquake of 1875. It brought an enormous flood down the valley, hundreds killed, but it wasn't until three years later that a Scottish botanist wandered up there looking for new flowers and before he knew it, found himself in Afghanistan."

"And suddenly Khanpur is of strategic importance," I remarked. "Captain Nesbit, it's been a long day and Holmes and I have spent far too much time on the road already. Why are we here?"

"Um, yes," he hesitated, and finally decided to meet bluntness with bluntness. "You came here to search for O'Hara, inadvertently bringing me this conundrum of the American Thomas Goodheart. I do not know if the two cases are at all related—as I told you in Delhi, it is more than likely that O'Hara is living in a hill village somewhere, growing rice and raising a family. But I do know that Khanpur and its maharaja have suddenly become an urgent concern. Let me ask you this: Do you believe that Goodheart's costume on the boat, dressing as a stage Sherlock Holmes, was a coincidence, or a deliberate statement?"

The question was odd, but the intent was clear. Holmes answered him. "If you are asking, does Thomas Goodheart know who I am, I can only say that if he does, he's a better actor than he is a political analyst. I am constitutionally opposed to the idea of coincidence, but I spent the better part of two weeks in his company, and he never let his mask slip."

"So you would say that he does not regard you, or Miss Russell here, as the enemy?"

"Apart from our unwillingness to commit to the Socialist cause, no."

"Very well. You two are in a unique position, one that would take a Survey agent months to duplicate. I re-alise that you have spent the last weeks in perfecting your travelling-magician disguise, but I would like to ask you to drop that disguise and take up your friend-ship with the Goodheart family."

"No," Holmes said flatly.

"What friendship?" I said simultaneously.

"Acquaintance, then," Nesbit said, choosing my ob-jection as the less intractable. "I believe you more than capable of ingratiating yourselves into their lives to the extent that they would invite you to accompany them to Khanpur. The girl seemed particularly fond of you, Miss Russell. She mentioned you this morning, with no prompting on my part, I should add."

"Fine," Holmes said. "Russell will change back into an Englishwoman and observe the palace from within. Bindra and I will take the more circuitous route, and we shall meet in Khanpur."

This time it was Nesbit and I who spoke at the same instant.

"I don't think—" he began.

"Look at me!" I demanded. "I'm dark as a native—I even blacked my eyelashes, for pity's sake. And my arms have burn scars all over them from the cursed fire-toss."

"—that it's a good idea for you to . . . Fire-toss?"

"The dye will come off, Russell."

"Yes, along with most of my skin."

"Suffering for the sake of enlightenment, Russell?"

"And who is Bindra?" Nesbit asked, to no effect.

"I never asked for enlightenment. Apart from which, it's my skin that needs enlightening, not my soul."

Nesbit finally decided to return to his original objection, and inserted firmly into our bickering, "I don't know that it's the best idea for the two of you to divide up. It might not be entirely safe."

"Holmes," I said, distracted by his remark, "have we *ever* had a case in which you and I did not go our separate ways at one point or another?"

He paused to reflect. "I believe we spent most of the Colonel Barker spy investigation in each other's company."

"A minor investigation, nine years ago," I said. "No, Captain Nesbit, we generally work separately at some point in an investigation."

"But this is India, and I shouldn't like to think of a woman—"

I froze the words on his tongue with a gaze as flat and icy as the Simla Skating Club rink. Holmes threaded his fingers together over his stomach and studied the ceiling. Nesbit cleared his throat and tried again.

"I am sure you are remarkably competent, Miss Russell, but were anything to happen to you—"

"Captain Nesbit, what sort of demonstration would satisfy you?"

Holmes murmured *sotto voce*, "Swords, or pistols at dawn?" but Nesbit did not hear him.

"I do not require—"

"Oh, I think you do," I said, and in the blink of an eye the slim little knife I wore in my boot whipped past him and thunked into the bad painting on the wall, parting Nesbit's hair in its passing. He whirled around, stared at the slip of the throwing handle where it quivered between the eyebrows of the man in the portrait, then turned to look at Holmes for explanation. Holmes was now studying his fingernails.

Nesbit glanced at me, stood up, and went to look at the knife. After a minute, he pulled it out, rubbed at the canvas as if to heal the scar, and brought my blade over to lay it beside my glass on the table. I returned it to its boot-top sheath, and we looked at each other.

"Very well," he said. "I stand corrected."

"I still don't want to go with the Goodhearts," I told him.

Holmes spoke up. "I think you should."

"Oh God, Holmes. Why don't *you* go with Sunny and her mama? I'll stay behind and teach Bindra the fire-toss."

"Who the deuce is this Bindra chap?" Nesbit demanded.

"Our general factotum," I told him.

"Sorcerer's apprentice," Holmes amplified. "No, if one or the other of us needs go with the Goodhearts, it should be you. Even if it was not Goodheart who tried to kill me, he would be more closely guarded around me than he would be with you. If," he added, "you can refrain from demonstrating your extreme competence with him as well."

I thought about it. If O'Hara had been killed or was being held prisoner inside Khanpur, evidence would be somewhere within the palace. And having one set of ears inside, the other in the town outside the walls, I had to admit, greatly increased our chances of hearing something. I should much rather be with Holmes than with the Goodhearts, but my own preferences could not be of primary consideration here. And it need only be for a few days, before I rejoined Holmes.

I looked down at my arms, trying not to think too closely about the coming ordeal. "What can we do about my colour?" I asked. "And I shall have to have something other than homespun *salwaar kameez* to wear."

"I brought with me the things you left at the hotel," Nesbit told me. "And I have the necessary bleaching materials for your skin and hair."

"Very sure of yourself, weren't you?" I said, but he was not about to repeat his mistake.

"Merely relying upon your professionalism, Miss Russell." His boyish grin was irresistible.

Chapter Fourteen

I stayed on that night at the Viceregal Lodge after Holmes left, having been given a room considerably more luxurious than our hotel in the native bazaar. In the end, however, I spent little time in the room itself, and many hours in the marble bath-room, scraping some of the brown from my face and hands and turning my black hair back into a substance the colour and, alas, texture of straw. Dawn found me damp, raw, jaundice-skinned and red-eyed from the combination of chemical fumes and lack of sleep. And because Nesbit and I agreed that the fewer people who witnessed this transformation the better, I saw no servants until one brought me a breakfast tray at seven o'clock. He was followed shortly by Nesbit, who apologised for the early hour, and ushered in a pair of the staff carrying not only my things from Simla but the bags I had abandoned in Delhi.

"I see the hotel didn't burn to the ground," I commented. "Coffee?"

"Thank you. And no, it was but a smokey collection of oil-soaked rags in a cellar stairway."

"The alarm was the thing."

"If we assume that the fire was deliberately set and aimed at you two, yes. However, even if it was not an accident, that same stunt has been pulled at two other hotels in the past year. An hotel emptied of fleeing foreigners makes rich grounds for a burglar."

I handed him his coffee without comment.

"The Goodhearts plan to leave for Khanpur today," he said, but when I set down my cup with alacrity he added, "however, I fear they will find that their porters are infected with the current intransigent attitude of the Indian working classes, and are holding out for more pay."

"You talked the workers into going out on strike?" A gambit Mycroft would be proud to claim.

"Not precisely. But one of my agents filled their ears with sedition. And, incidentally, their bellies with strong drink."

"Leaving them too hung-over to work." He was good; his humble smile told me that he knew it.

"They should be fully restored to the maharaja's services by Monday."

"That gives me two days in which to ingratiate myself. Should be plenty. Thank you."

"I have also arranged for a *durzi* to come here and provide you with two or three new garments for your time in the palace, and a shoemaker waits downstairs to measure your feet."

My toes cringed in anticipation of the native craft, but there was always the leprous footwear, and a pair of formal slippers in my bags if I needed those. He drained his cup, preparing to leave, but first I had a question.

"What did you mean yesterday, that O'Hara counted his steps on Tibetan prayer-beads?"

"Oh, yes. It's a thing the 'pundits' do, when surveying. The standard Tibetan prayer-beads hold 108 beads, along with two subsidiary strings of five each. If one removes eight, the rosary appears the same, but an even hundred becomes quite useful for survey purposes: One bead for each hundred steps, ten thousand steps to a circuit; with the side-beads a man can survey a small country. Assuming the length of his steps is unchanging."

"I see." I tried to imagine keeping track of steps while carrying on a conversation, and maintaining perfect distance on each stride; I failed.

When Nesbit left, he took with him the débris from the enlightenment of skin and hair so as not to provide fodder for below-the-stairs gossip. As I struggled to bring my straw-like mane under control, I made a mental note to purchase some sort of oil in the town to keep the strands from snapping off entirely. A short session with the white-bearded *durzi*, choosing samples and lending him some of my clothes to copy, and a shorter session with the shoemaker, then I was off to town.

I reminded myself to use the front door of the Lodge, where I nodded briefly to the regal *chuprassi* who held it for me, and was about to take to the road when I noticed the motorcar, its driver holding its door. *You're English again, Russell*, I reminded myself, and climbed inside.

Nesbit and I had sketched out a plan to bring me back into the Goodheart circle, beginning with a chance meeting at the tea shop where he had taken the family the day before. As soon as he heard of their distressing abandonment by their porters, he would extend a breakfast invitation to the family matron, who would no more leave Sunny behind than she would walk the two miles to Viceregal Lodge. And indeed, when I happened to wander through the Gothic doors of that particular tea shop across from the band-stand, Mrs Goodheart and her Flapper daughter were seated opposite the eligible young British officer, all smiling merrily over their coffee cups. The other patrons of the shop watched Sunny from the corners of their eyes, as much, I thought, for the gaiety of her person as the extremity of her wardrobe. Mrs Goodheart's smile faded somewhat when I came to their table with my exclamations of surprise, but then she remembered that I was safely married, and invited me to join them.

"My, Mary, haven't you gone dark!"

You don't know the half of it, I thought, and accepted the invitation to coffee with some remark about the strength of the sun at these altitudes.

It was Sunny who asked the question. "Where is your husband this morning?"

"Oh, nothing would do but that he had to go off and climb some mountain or another, can you believe that? So vexing, he's simply abandoned me here at the end of the world. No offence meant, Captain Nesbit."

"None taken; I agree there is not much to occupy a young woman in Simla at this time of year."

"Come with us," Sunny piped up. I forbore to look at my wrist-watch, but out of the corner of my eye I saw Nesbit pull his own watch from his pocket and note the time; I had to agree, even for me thirty seconds was something of a record for the manipulation of innocent victims. I beamed at dear, fresh, pretty, boring little Sunny.

"Oh, I couldn't do that. What do you call it, 'crashing' your party?"

"Oh baloney. Mama, tell her she has to come along. Tommy's friend would think it was posalutely nifty."

I blinked, but the phrase seemed to indicate affirmation, and although I couldn't imagine having the temerity to invite myself to a maharaja's house party, that is precisely what I seemed to be doing. I put on my most lost and wistful expression to say, "Well, it *would* be perfectly lovely. What do you think, Mrs Goodheart?"

Had I been an unmarried woman, she'd have abandoned me in the snow without a gram of compunction, but a matronly companion for her daughter might have its advantages. By providing contrast to the child's looks and sparkle, if nothing else. "It does seem a bit forward of us, but . . . I know, I will ask Thomas to cable his friend, and see if we might bring another guest. Seeing as how we're stuck here for the day, anyway."

Sunny clapped her hands and I said, "That is very generous of you, Mrs Goodheart," and to the disappointment of both women Nesbit took his leave, pleading the demands of work. Mrs Goodheart eyed the heaps of snow with no enthusiasm and declared her intention of returning to the hotel, but I suggested that Sunny might enjoy a walk through the town. The older woman hesitated, then concluded that I was capable of guarding her baby girl from harm in broad daylight, and agreed.

We began at the skating rink, hiring skates and edging out onto the uneven ice. It had been so long since I had been on blades, I clung to the rail like a child, but to

Chicago's daughter ice was a lifelong companion, and she sailed merrily back and forth, her cheeks pink as a china doll's, her teasing laughter ringing across the trees. My ankles were watery when we turned in our hired skates, and we paused to drink a cup of sweet tea sold by the establishment.

I used the moment of leisure to question my young companion. "It was a lovely surprise to see you," I told her. "But I can't really imagine what you're doing here."

The innocent did not hesitate to answer. "I know, Simla's not much compared to Jaipur or something. But Tommy wanted to see it, and the maharaja isn't at home until tomorrow. We had thought to go to Khanpur today, or at least go back down today and head for Khanpur tomorrow—what a *fantastic* train ride, isn't it? All those tunnels? But then today the coolies wouldn't work, so we're here for longer. I'm glad; it gives us a chance to see something of each other. Have you finished? It's pretty chilly, sitting here."

We returned our cups, and Sunny tucked her arm into mine as if we'd been friends for years.

"I have to say, it's absolutely *fantabulous* of you to have found something that I can do better than you. I'll bet you planned it out."

"What on earth do you mean?"

"Oh, Mary, you can do just *everything*. You *know* everything, you'll talk to anyone, you do all these things that just give me the heebie-jeebies, sometimes I feel about six years old around you. But I am *so* glad you're coming with us to see Tommy's maharaja—a genuine *maharaja*, for gosh sake! I just know that when I stand there in front of him my lips will just freeze up, but with you there it'll make it easier, sort of following your lead."

I looked down at her fur-covered head, astounded. Although why should I be? Elaborate fronts were often constructed to conceal doubts and insecurities. I laughed, and said, "Just think, you'll probably be the first Flapper to reach Khanpur."

"What a nifty title for a book—*The First Flapper in Khanpur*. When I write my memoirs, I'll thank you for the name. Where are we going now?"

"Shall we take a look at the native bazaar?" There would be no chance of stumbling across Holmes; he and Bindra would be long gone, on the first train out of Simla to retrieve the travelling show and make for Khanpur, questioning people about O'Hara all the way.

"Oh, that would be fun! I wanted to go into those shops yesterday when we walked through with Mama, but she took one look at them and said they were too dirty and that we'd probably get robbed."

"I should think they look worse from the outside than they are."

"And do you know, it was funny to see you come into the tea shop this morning? We'd just been talking about you yesterday."

"Oh yes?" I asked, warily.

"Yes, Tommy swore he'd seen a native that looked just like your husband, there in the bazaar, can you imagine? I mean, anyone less like an Indian than him, I can't picture, and he was squatting down at the side of the road like they do, trying to beg some money off Captain Nesbit."

"It's not likely to have been my husband," I assured her mildly, squelching the alarm I felt at Goodheart's unexpected perceptiveness, but she burst out laughing at the thought.

"Of course not, silly, it's just that Tommy was reminded of him, and so we were talking about you a little, telling Captain Nesbit about the voyage out, that's all. Say, do you think we could find a sari in this bazaar? That one you wore on the ship was posatively dreamy."

"We'd be more likely to find a sheepskin coat than a silk sari, but we can look."

We found many things, from a dozen bright, rattly bangles for Sunny's wrist to an embroidered cap for Tommy's head, including two sari-lengths of silk for the girl, one bright green with a silver border, the other saffron-yellow with a heavy stripe of darker orange, along with their under-skirts and blouses. Next door lay a shop with a dusty display of necklaces in the window, a place dark and mysterious enough to have belonged to *Kim*'s Lurgan Sahib; with a squeal, Sunny dived inside.

The shopkeeper was no teacher of spies, but we did make him a happy man. Something about his wares, which were rough to the point of primitive, appealed to the girl from Chicago. And I had to admit, she had a remarkable eye for the unlikely treasure, uncovering a shimmering breastplate of opals set in native gold that added five years and a lifetime of sophistication to her face. I was fingering a heavy necklace made of amber beads when she snatched it from my hand, turned me bodily about, and propelled me over to the only clean surface in the shop, a looking-glass. Standing behind me and craning to see around my shoulders, she pushed the silver amulet-charm I wore under my collar and fastened the amber around my neck in its place, chatting all the while.

"I don't know why you wear that funny old thing, it's nowhere near as nice as some of the pieces you wore on the boat. There, that's better," she said, and exclaimed, "Oh, Mary, amber is so tasty on you!"

"Don't be ridiculous, Sunny," I said, reaching behind my neck for the clasp.

She slapped at my hands and urged me at the glass. "I mean it, Mary. Look!"

I looked, and saw a pale-haired, scrubbed-looking woman transformed by a wealth of Baroque colour riding her collar-bones. The uneven stones of the necklace, graduated in size from cherry-pit at the top to a baby's fist at the centre, were the deep and cloudy orange of good amber, with tantalising slices of shimmering clear stone twisted through them. It looked like nothing I would wear; that, in truth, was a great part of its appeal. Nonetheless, I reached up to unfasten the clasp, and handed it to the man. Sunny, however, grabbed it first and dropped it beside the bangles, the opals, and the other pieces under whose spell she'd fallen.

"We'll take all of these," she told him.

"We'll take none of them," I corrected her, and when she began to sputter in indignation, I turned to the man and started the age-old bargaining rituals of the East.

In the end, I beat the price down so that the girl had the amber for nothing and saved a third of his original price on the opals. Pleased, she gathered up the heavy orange beads and pressed them into my hands. I protested, and tried to give them back to her, but when she started to look hurt, I thanked her, and subsided.

While she was making arrangements for the delivery and payment, I opened my fingers and gazed at the necklace. A gift from a rich girl to a new friend she imagines to be comparatively poor, although she is not. A rich girl whose brother is the subject of that friend's suspicions, a girl whose brother may have tried to kill the friend and her husband. A rich girl who was even now being used, with cold calculation, by her friend.

Amber, when warm, gives out a faint aroma, the odour of slow time. I put the spilling double-handful up to my face, and inhaled its trace of musk, laced with the tang of betrayal. Sunny Goodheart gave me the necklace because it looked pretty on me; I accepted the gift because it would remind me of consequences.

We took lunch at one of the restaurants facing the Mall, and afterwards walked up for a look at the shivering monkeys on Jakko before I led her back to their hotel. There we found that Thomas had sent a telegram to Khanpur, and had already received a reply: Yes, I should be welcome to join the party. I told Sunny I would have my bags brought to their hotel first thing on Monday morning, trusting that the porters would have settled down from their insurrection and would be willing to take to the road, and before anyone could ask where I was staying, I invented an almost-missed appointment and hurried away.

My steps dawdled through the shambling lower bazaar, however, my fingers playing with the warm beads in my pocket as my mind went over and over the episode in the shop. It was the thing I liked least, in all the requirements of this odd investigative life which I had entered when I became the partner of Sherlock Holmes: the need to use and manipulate the innocent.

At times, the means by which we reached our end left a most unpleasant taste in my mouth.

❦

I spent all of Sunday wandering the mountains above Simla, ostensibly asking questions about Kimball O'Hara, but in fact merely enjoying the glimpse of a new world. I hiked the lanes past native dwellings stacked on top of each other, around furniture shops and blacksmiths spilling out into the road, dodging mountain people with huge tangles of firewood or anonymous bundles across their shoulders, balanced on their heads, or worn in long *kirta* baskets slung between their shoulders. Craftsmen sawed and hammered, infants tumbled, and schoolboys played a Himalayan version of cricket. A mountain of immense deodar logs had been built outside of the town, and on its peak sat a lone monkey, looking very cold. I was more of a stranger in this remarkable land than the simian was, and I prized every moment of the experience. Particularly when, once away from the centre of the town, the beggars became thin on the ground, and I could look the residents in the eye without fearing the outstretched hand.

I found no word whatsoever of O'Hara, and got back to Viceregal Lodge when the sun was low against the western hills, footsore, light-headed from the long exertion at that altitude, and yearning for many cups of hot tea. The tea was provided within moments, and as the man was leaving, he said, "Madam, the *durzi* and the shoemaker are at your convenience. When you wish to see them, please ring."

I had forgotten all about them, and frankly was not looking forward to the interviews, since I did not expect that anything they had produced would be wearable in any but a last resort. But obediently, when I had drunk my tea and scrubbed away the worst of the day's dust, I rang the bell and prepared my words of polite thanks.

But the *durzi* was a magician. Open-mouthed, I looked over the wares he spread out on the chairs of the anteroom. Two of the blouses appeared identical to one I had given him for copying, but three others, while cut to the same size, had clever details of cuff and front that the original had not. The four skirts he proffered were similar variations on a given theme, and my thanks and praise had no element of polite sham. And then, with a curious air of humble pride, he had his assistant produce the last garments.

"Nesbit *sahib* requested that I make this as well," the old man told me. "He said, 'If the lady does not wish it, that is of no matter, but it is best she have the choice.'"

What he spread out on the stuffed sofa was a classic *salwaar kameez,* only far, far more formal than anything I'd seen on the streets. Voluminous trousers, gathered at the ankle into stiff, embroidered cuffs, matched the knee-length tunic, which was worked with intertwined patterns of beaded embroidery along the neck and down the buttoned placket, as well as following the two long seams that ran up the front and down the back. With the shirt and trousers came a breathtaking Kashmiri shawl woven of whisper-fine wool and heavily embroidered with silken arabesques, so beautiful my rough hands could not keep from caressing it. The old *durzi*'s eyes warmed at my response and he told me it was his wife's work, then demonstrated how it was worn. The ensemble was even more stunning than the sari Holmes had bought in Port Said, and every bit as graceful, with the inestimable advantage of leaving its wearer able to walk, sit, and even stretch out her arm for something without the risk of sudden nudity.

I embarrassed him with my praise. And when he had left and the shoemaker come to show me what he had done, I vowed to appoint Geoffrey Nesbit my permanent lady's maid. Three offerings, all as comfortable as an old pair of moccasins; one formal pumps, one sturdy oiled leather hiking boots, the other a close facsimile of my leprous shoes, only in a deep and delicious shade of brown. He had even brought a small leather handbag that matched the black pumps.

Riches.

I spent the evening trying on and gloating over my new wardrobe, and slipped between my lavender-scented sheets with a smile on my face, while Holmes, bundled against the cold, lay somewhere on the road west of Kalka.

First thing on Monday morning, the Goodhearts and most of the hotel staff were gathered in the forecourt of the grandest hotel in Simla, overseeing the loading of enormous quantities of luggage from door to *tonga*s. Why hadn't they left the bulk of their things in Delhi, or shipped them ahead to await their side-trip? But I didn't ask, merely offered to take one or two of the trunks in my *tonga* and meet them at the railway station. I ended up with three, along with four hat-boxes and a rolled carpet.

Similar activities at the Simla station made me glad that one of my trunks had vanished into the Red Sea, and by the time we had gone through the same rituals in Kalka, shifting to the larger-gauge train (Mrs Goodheart wouldn't hear of allowing the porters to do it unsupervised—one would swear she had the Kohinoor amongst her bags), then twice in Umballa, from train to hotel in the evening then back again the following morning, I was thoroughly sick of every trunk, bag, and hat-box in the collection, and tempted to stand up with the small bag holding my new clothes, comb, and tooth-brush, forswearing the burdens of civilisation.

But the maharaja's own saloon coach had been sent

down for our use, and an appropriately princely train car it was, all sumptuous glitter and spotless carpets, overhead fans and electric lights, its staff in spotless white and wearing the red turban with white device I had seen on the docks in Bombay. The car had its own baggage compartment, which meant that once we had picked our way past the Umballa platform's sleeping bodies, which eerily resembled corpses sheeted for burial, we were not required to oversee the shifting of anything more complex than a tea cup for the rest of the day. I settled into my armchair with a sable-lined travelling rug over my knees, and prepared to be pampered. Mrs Goodheart, having spent the past twenty-four hours labouring heroically to maintain Yankee order in the face of Oriental chaos, collapsed onto a softly upholstered sofa, where she allowed Sunny to prop up her feet and slip off her shoes under cover of her own fur rug. After a spate of fussing, dabbing wrists and forehead with cool scented waters, and downing a mighty slug of purely medicinal brandy, she retreated into sleep, her snores rising and falling with the beat of the train over the tracks.

Sunny came to sit near me at the window, giving me an apologetic smile.

"Your mother is finding India a challenge," I observed.

"She's not used to letting other people do things for her."

I lowered my voice so that her brother, seated at the other end of the car with a book, might not hear us. "I'd have thought your brother could help a little more."

"He's pretty preoccupied," she replied, which was both an agreement and an excuse.

"By what?"

"Oh, it's something to do with the maharaja. I don't really know, but Tommy's hoping to get the maharaja interested in one of his pet projects. His backing, you know?"

"Ah. A business venture."

"Not really. I think it's something to do with setting up a school in the States. But like I said, I don't really know. Just that Tommy's got a lot of hopes hanging on it."

Not altogether a social visit, then. I wondered if the maharaja was aware of that.

We sat at the window, chatting idly, with the mountains looking over our shoulders as the musical names unfolded beneath us: Sirhind, Ludhiana, Jullunder, Amritsar. At this last, with a lot of jolting, the prince's car separated from those continuing on to Lahore and points west, leaving us for a while on an empty siding (empty of trains, that is: there appeared to be a small village living on the tracks) before we could join with a north-bound train. Batala, Gurdaspur, Pathankot, up into the mountains again, the people along the snow-speckled rails again showing the rounder features of the mountain folk. Flat roofs gave way to peaked, sandals to boots, bullock carts to loads carried on the back in long *kirta* baskets. The snow-laden mountains drew near, the trees grew in height, the windows radiated cold.

A luncheon was brought to us, and Mrs Goodheart woke and put on her shoes, Tommy laid aside his tracts, and we ate the uninspired cutlets and two veg, Mrs Goodheart sighing, Tommy distracted, and me thinking wistfully of Bindra's curries and the large, greasy, chewy *puris* we had used to scoop them up.

"Miss Russell." I blinked and looked across at

Tommy Goodheart. "That is right, isn't it? You prefer Miss?"

"Generally, yes."

Mrs Goodheart raised her head sharply. "I thought you were married?"

"I am, I just—"

"A lot of married women keep their names, Mother," Sunny explained.

"But—"

Her son ignored her confusion. "Your husband and I spent a lot of time together, but I'm afraid that you and I never had much of a conversation. You're English?"

"I live in England and my mother was English, but my father was American. From San Francisco."

Mrs Goodheart said doubtfully, "I don't know any Russells from San Francisco."

"His family was from Boston originally," I admitted, and saw the woman's eyes go bright.

"The Boston Russells? Well, well. I wonder if I ever met your father? I went to any number of parties there, when I was young."

"I doubt it," I said firmly. "His parents moved out to California when he was very small. So yes, I regard myself as English. Proudly so, particularly at the present."

As I hoped, Goodheart took the bait of distraction. "Are you referring to the Labour Party's victory?"

"Yes. Extraordinary, isn't it? I've heard it called a bloodless revolution."

He was launched: For the first time, he betrayed a degree of animation, and the rest of the meal was dominated by his questions about the English working classes (about whom I knew little, other than farm labourers and London cabbies) and whether or not I had met MacDonald or a dozen other men, most of whom, indeed, I had never heard of. Then one name caught my ear.

"Yes, I believe I've met him," I said. "At a fancy-dress party in a Berkshire country house, just before Christmas. He was dressed, let's see—oh yes. He was in a very chilly costume, that of a pyramid builder, complete with red-paint whip marks on his back." And a very unsuitable costume it had been, too, for the man was pudgy and his back showed acne beneath the paint.

"Strange place to find him."

"He was probably experimenting with subversion from within," I told him, keeping my face completely straight.

"I suppose. Odd, that your husband didn't seem all that interested in politics."

"Well," I said, "he's on the conservative side. I wouldn't call him a reactionary, exactly . . ." This was by no means the first time I'd had to deny Holmes in the course of a case. And as before, no cock crew.

Goodheart's face was, as always, remarkably difficult to read, but I thought his interest was piqued. If so, it would be understandable: A woman abandoned—even temporarily—by her considerably older husband, who then expresses an interest in radical politics, might be worth cultivating. I still couldn't tell if he knew who Holmes actually was, but if this young man had indeed tried to murder us in Aden, separating myself from Holmes in his mind might stop him from pulling another balcony down on my head in Khanpur. Mrs Goodheart, however, was not pleased at what she perceived as the intimacy of our glance. She fixed me with a sour gaze, and demanded that Thomas search out a deck of cards. I subsided and went back to my window.

At long last, the train slowed, and sighed, and came

to a stop. Noses pressed against the windows (all except the proud Thomas, who nonetheless watched with great interest), we waited to see what manner of royal vehicle would come for us. Sunny was hoping for camels and elephants, although I thought a Lagonda or Rolls-Royce more likely—and less crippling, considering we were still more than fifty miles from Khanpur city.

What came for us was an aeroplane.

Chapter Fifteen

We heard it first, above the shouts of the coolies and the dying huff and hiss of steam from the engine, a rising and directionless mechanical presence among the wooded peaks. We peered and craned our necks, Thomas Goodheart no less than the lowliest of coolies, and then suddenly the noise had a source as a wide pair of brightly painted red-and-white wings shot from behind a hill and swept in our direction.

It dropped so low above the train station, I could see the distinctive corrugation of its siding—although even its elegant shape identified it as a product of the German Junkers company, building passenger aeroplanes now that potential war-planes were forbidden to them. This one wagged its long wings over our heads in passing. It flew on south for a minute or so before rising sharply into a high turn, then dropping down to come back at us. Children went scurrying—not, as I thought, in terror, but to slap and shove a pair of cows from a stretch of nearby road. As soon as the beasts had been encouraged from the track, the aeroplane aimed itself at the roadway, touched down lightly, and taxied up in our direction, coming to a halt before the nearest telegraph lines a quarter of a mile away. Its propeller coughed to a halt, and in a minute a man kicked open its door and jumped from its wing to the ground.

Thomas Goodheart's reaction made me look at the approaching figure more closely. The young American straightened and started down the road, walking more briskly than I had seen him move before. When they came together, the pilot grabbed Goodheart's hand and pumped it, slapped his arm, and continued towards us. The coolies and *tonga* drivers paused in their work, the railway workers turned to watch; this could only be the maharaja of Khanpur, come to greet his guests.

He bent over Mrs Goodheart's hand, not quite kissing it. "Mrs Goodheart, thank you for gracing my home with your visit. I feel as if I know you already, Tommy's spoken of you with such affection. And you are the sister, Sybil. Welcome, Miss Goodheart." He took Sunny's outstretched hand before turning to me. "And Mrs Russell, you, too, are welcome. Any friend of Tommy's— I'm glad he felt free to ask you."

Not that Thomas Goodheart had done anything more than bow to his mother's pressure, but I wouldn't mention that, not to a man with eyes as filled with speculation as his. I merely thanked him, laid my fingers briefly within his hard hand that bore the distinctive callus of reins, and pulled away.

His Highness was not what I might have expected in a maharaja, and further removed still from the folksiness of a "Jimmy." A small man, shorter even than Nesbit (and, I thought, irritated at being forced to look up into my face), the maharaja resembled an Oxford undergraduate—the athlete rather than the aesthete, with fashionably bagged trousers, a white knit pull-over, and an astrakhan cap pulled over black hair. His lower lip was full, a faint intimation of the family habit of debauchery, and his dark eyes were lazy with the same self-assurance I had seen in the photograph on Nesbit's wall, speaking of a bone-deep aristocracy that relegated the House of Windsor to the status of shopkeepers: This was the most important man in his particular world, and he assumed those around him agreed. There was nothing in his manner or his dress (apart from the cap) that spoke of India, certainly nothing in his lack of concern about castely impurities that permitted him to take the hands of strange women, nothing other than a faint dip and rise in his accent and the old-penny colour of his skin.

Mrs Goodheart looked confused; Sunny, on the other hand, was bedazzled. I couldn't help speculating about Mrs Goodheart's opinions on inter-racial marriages.

The aeroplane would hold the four of us and our smaller bags, with the maharaja at the controls. We would leave behind a small mountain of Goodheart possessions and my solitary trunk, guarded by a uniformed *chuprassi* until the plane came back for them.

We settled into the padded seats, Thomas beside the maharaja, with Mrs Goodheart on one side and Sunny and I on the other. The noise made speech impossible, which was just as well. Mrs Goodheart turned pale as the plane roared and bounced and then leapt skyward. Her knuckles remained white the entire way as her hands clenched the arms of her chair, holding her from falling to the ground below; once when the air dropped away beneath us, I feared she was going to faint. Sunny did not notice, but spent the entire forty-five minutes in the air with her head craned and turning, to see the hills, the glimpse of road, the brilliant white peaks that seemed at arm's reach, the occasional pocket of lake. Goodheart seemed even less concerned, moving easily into his seat and paying more attention to the actions of our highly capable pilot than to our height, our movements, or the scenery. Thomas Goodheart, I thought, had flown before.

After forty minutes, we flew over a town, a hillside collation of tile roofs near a white river, then continued on for a few minutes before we dropped lower, skimmed the tops of some trees (Mrs Goodheart moaned and squeezed her eyes shut), and then set down smooth as cream on a wide, long, tarmac runway, taxiing along it to a wide shed, in front of which waited two motorcars and several men. The landing strip even had lights marking its sides, I noticed. Near the hangar at the southern end were tied down a small fleet of aeroplanes, six in all, ranging from a battered RAF fighter plane to an enormous three-engined thing with wings that must have stretched nearly a hundred feet. It looked as if it had just come from the factory, and was still sheathed in gleaming metal, not yet having received the red-and-white paint that covered the others. Its sides, I saw as we flashed past it on the landing strip, were corrugated like the one we were in, the same distinctive duralumin siding of the Junkers corporation. The bigger version probably had a flight range of seven or eight hundred miles; a person would be well inside Russia before having to refuel.

We slowed and made our turn, little more than halfway up the long macadam strip. The northern end of the runway rotated slowly past my window, affording me clear view of the five substantial warehouses or *godown*s facing one another across the tarmac.

For a maharaja's plaything, the air strip was a serious affair.

For someone storing goods best kept out of the British eye, those *godown*s were ideally placed. I itched to see inside at least one of them, but all five doors were shut tight, and appeared locked. I craned my head against the window-glass until they had disappeared behind us, then subsided into my seat like a good guest, waiting to disembark at the formal southern end of the field.

The engine died and the propeller kicked to a halt, leaving our ears ringing furiously in the silence. "Welcome to Khanpur," our pilot announced, and opened the door with a flourish.

Mrs Goodheart needed assistance across the wing and down the folding steps. On the ground, she gulped wordlessly at the cold air and allowed her son to settle her into the seat of the waiting sedan car, grateful beyond words to enter a vehicle that was not about to leave the earth behind. Sunny, when she reached the ground, turned a circle, hands clapped together, oohing at the setting. Goodheart, filled with cool insouciance, gave a glance to the high circle of white mountains before turning his attention to our host.

I waited, intending to thank the maharaja, but he was moving off with Goodheart in the direction of the sleek little racing car, while we ladies were placed in the roomier, more sedate Rolls. The two men got into the small car and tore away at high speed without a backwards glance. Our bags were placed in the back of the Rolls, and the driver, wearing a uniform of red and silver, his red-and-white turban microscopically perfect, got in and turned us in the great man's wake. As we left, one of the men sitting next to the building tossed his cigarette to the ground and sauntered over to the plane, his skin and features European, his very posture proclaiming him an RAF man.

I looked back to see him climb into the plane, and I wondered what a one-time fighter pilot thought of fetching baggage for a maharaja.

The Forts, two miles south of the air field and five miles north of Khanpur city, were aptly named, a pair of high fortified walls crowning a pair of sharp hills bisected by the north-south road. The two halves Nesbit had called Old Fort and New Fort were clearly from different eras, that on the east an early Pathan hill fortification with walls ancient enough to appear fragile, whereas the larger, western, and well-maintained New Fort was pure Moghul, its small, tower-flanked gate reached by a narrow road that climbed from the hillock's southern end to its eastern, every inch of it nicely exposed for the purposes of defence. Round towers surmounted by flanged caps like German helmets jutted out from the red, age-streaked stone walls every hundred feet or so, each one large enough to shelter a dozen archers. The big sedan car passed through the dividing chasm, turned sharply right to climb the narrow drive, and finally eased through the gate, where raw patches betrayed the passage of many incautious drivers.

With the name of the place and its master's passion for hunting, I had expected it to be a cross between a hill fort and an all-male hunting lodge, with a veneer of comfort over a utilitarian base. Instead, we drove into an earthly Paradise.

As the mountains encircled Khanpur itself, so high, warm-red walls, built for military purpose, now gave shelter to a garden, several acres of closely planned and maintained lawn, flower, and tree. Its centre was half an acre of lotus pond with playing fountain and water birds; a trio of tame gazelles in jewelled harnesses tip-toed across the close-trimmed lawn sloping up from the water; bright birds sang in the trees that rose half as high as the three-storey walls. In places the pillars of the ground-floor arcade were overgrown with a riot of crimson bougainvillea that reached the open-air passage-ways of the second and even third levels.

The great building inside which we stood followed the outline of the hill, forming a skewed circle but for the flat eastern side, which contained the gates and faced the Old Fort across the road; late-afternoon sun-light glittered off fresh gilding around the east wing's deep-set windows. Before us to the north, a wide terrace spilled flowers from pots the size of a man, and the arcade behind it gleamed with mosaics of lapis-blue and gold. To my left, the western wing was more or less obscured by trees, and a glance behind me at the south walls gave the only indication that the conversion of The Forts was not yet complete, for flaking paint and stained stone peeped from between branches of bamboo as thick as my forearm.

There was no sign of the maharaja, although his motorcar stood open-doored on the gravel drive. In his place, we were met by a man as grand as the uniform he wore, its snug trousers spotless white, the heavy silk brocade of his tunic dropping past his knees, the ends of his greying moustaches trained flawlessly upwards. To one side stood two men with leashed cheetahs, the cats' collars flashing with rubies; both animals eyed the delicate gazelles with feline interest, the very ends of their tails twitching, twitching. Up on the terrace, half a dozen musicians had begun to play the moment we came through the gates. Behind these ceremonial figures, a platoon of lesser *chuprassi*s stood waiting to retrieve us and our bags, to show us to our rooms, to draw us scented baths and tea trays and finally to take up positions outside of our doors, awaiting our least wishes. I was given a suite of two rooms with its own small bathroom, the bath's square-footage more than compensated for by the ornateness of its walls: It had enough mirror and gilt to send Bindra into a thousand ecstasies. I, on the other hand, was overjoyed to find that it had running water, both hot and cold. Someone in Khanpur's past had been remarkably progressive when it came to the comfort of guests; I couldn't imagine what it must have cost to install nineteenth-century plumbing in a sixteenth-century building.

When I had been shown the glories of the water closet and had illustrated for me the geyser controls over my bath and the resultant spouts of furiously hot water, the two men who had accompanied me to my rooms left me in peace, one of them pausing only to adjust, with ostentatious ceremony, the ornately worked album resting on the writing table beneath the window. When they had left, I went to see what the album's significance might be, and found it to contain a magnificently calligraphed document with the day's date at the top.

5 February 1924

Welcome, friend, to Khanpur.
While the riches of Khanpur are many, the demands on its guests should be few. For however long you may grace us with your presence, please feel completely at home here, free to participate in our many activities, or free to remain in

your quarters in quiet meditation, or with a book from our library. Bells will be rung at the following times, but if you wish not to join us at table, please, merely turn your name-plate outside your door to face inwards, and we shall know not to make a setting for you.

And again, if there is anything we might do to serve you, you need only ask.

There followed a list of times, most of them for meals—tea, I saw, was being served now on the upper terrace, wherever that might be; the next bell that came would indicate drinks, followed an hour later by dinner, which was followed by the notation "Dress: Casual." I turned the page and found a description of the palace, with the interesting sights in the vicinity and suggestions of places to go in the town, all written in an ornate English that had me smiling.

There was even a map.

It was an odd document, I thought, one more suited to an hotel than to a private estate, and it said a great deal about the mind of the man behind it. Clearly, the maharaja was accustomed to entertaining large numbers of guests with highly disparate interests, and found it more convenient to present each with this cool, almost commercial document rather than convey the information in some more personal manner.

Well, it suited me nicely. I left my name-tag facing outwards, and took myself to the marble-and-gold bath to explore the intricacies of the Victorian hot water system.

The bell that rang the summons for the programme's drinks-before-dinner event was no gong, but a small, silvery voice that approached, paused outside of my door, and continued on to the next guest. I finished arranging my hair, thrust my revolver into hiding beneath the feather bed, and checked the palace plan in the album. Map-reading proved unnecessary, for a uniformed *chuprassi* was squatting patiently in the hallway outside; he stood instantly to guide me to the room where the guests were gathering.

I stopped dead, brought up short as much by the intense beauty of the room as by the crowd it held; there had to be thirty people in the room already, drinks and cigarettes in their hands, the inevitable empty talk of the cocktail party on their tongues. Three flighty German girls nearby chattered madly about the lakebirds they had seen, two American men debated the relative merits of two makes of shotgun, a mixed trio of Italians seemed to be trying to sell a race-horse to another American—and that was the mixture within earshot. Only a handful of the guests appeared Indian, and none of those wore traditional dress. I was glad I hadn't put on the lovely garment the Simla *durzi* had made for me—I'd have been as out of place as a caparisoned camel.

Sunny stood across the room, her face flushed with excitement and, I thought, with the drink she held. She spotted me an instant later and began to wave furiously, so that half the people in the room turned in amusement to watch me come in.

"Ooh," she burst out, "isn't this just the superest thing? Isn't my brother just the darlingest?"

I looked up and around the jewel-box of a room, its walls and ceiling of creamy white marble inlaid with semi-precious stones, predominantly jade and lapis lazuli with spots of coral. The upper level was obscured by carved marble screens, designed for the use of the women in purdah, I supposed, and the colours made it feel as if one stood in a tropical sea, blue-green waters sparkling with the bright colours of the fish. "It certainly is impressive. What are you drinking?"

"It's something called a White Lady," she said, peering doubtfully into the glass. On the boat, I'd never seen her permitted drink stronger than a single glass of wine.

"Perhaps you should stick to the lemonade," I suggested. "If you take it in a champagne glass, nobody'll know."

She giggled, and I decided it was probably too late to worry about her sobriety. "Where is your mother?"

"Feeling a bit under the weather," she confided. "Mama went on a barn-storming ride once at a fair and the aeroplane landed sort of hard. Well, crashed, really. So she's not too keen on them anymore."

"That's understandable. Thank you," I said to the uniformed entity who appeared at my side with a tray of champagne and gin fizzes. I took the wine. "Your brother, though—he seemed more experienced."

"Oh yes, Tommy's flown a lot." Sunny giggled at nothing much, then leant forward to whisper, "Have you talked with His Highness yet?"

"No, I've been in my rooms."

"Neither have I. Isn't he dreamy?"

"He seemed very nice," I agreed somewhat noncommittally; actually, I thought his brisk abandonment of his lady guests at the air field, and his absence at our arrival in The Forts, rather unusual.

"Do you know, are all these people house-guests, too?"

"I haven't a clue. There are rather a lot, aren't there?"

"I'll never keep them straight," she moaned, although having seen her in action on the boat, I thought they'd be eating out of her hand by evening's end.

She turned to the young man at her side, while my eyes strayed to the gathering. They were a remarkably attractive collection of individuals, the majority of them male, most of them between the ages of twenty-five and thirty-five, although a handful had grey heads. Now that I was actually among them, I saw that there were a greater number of Indians than I had originally thought: I had moved among the country's rural inhabitants for too long for my eyes immediately to interpret as Indians the man in Oxford bags and tennis sweater, or the young woman with crisply shingled hair and knee-length skirt who was smoking a cigarette in a long enamelled holder. Such was the young lady Sunny was now talking with, and to whom she introduced me, more or less.

"Mary, this is my new friend, she's from the Punjab." Sunny sounded infinitely happy that she could bring us together.

I held out my hand. "Mary Russell. How do you do?"

"Gayatri Kaur, call me Gay." Her perfect upper-class English drawl was betrayed only by the faintest lilt of accent.

"What part of the Punjab?" I asked politely. Why on earth had I come here to make inane conversation that I'd never have put up with in England? Damn Geoffrey Nesbit, anyway.

"Farathkot, along the southern border of Patiala state. You know it?"

"Unfortunately, I've only seen the western portions of Uttar Pradesh. And Simla, of course, that's where I stumbled on Sunny here."

"If you have nothing to do, let me know. My uncle's the raja, he'd be happy to put you up for a while."

"Oh, well, thank you."

"He adores Englishwomen. Nothing improper, you understand—none of his wives are English, not even his concubines—he just enjoys their company. A dear, really."

"I'm sure," I murmured, and drained my wine and looked around: When faced with Sikh Flappers, I felt a sudden need for a full glass.

My search for strong drink was interrupted by a ripple that travelled through the room, set off by the arrival of our host. Perversely, the "Dress: Casual" notice had passed him by, for he was resplendent in a gold brocade *achkhan* coat, high of neck and snugly buttoned to the waist with amethysts, its tunic skirts flaring to the knees of his white trouser-leggings. He didn't look like an undergraduate now, not even one in fancy dress—no European could wear that exquisitely wrapped white turban with such aplomb, no mere scholar would possess those dark and captivating eyes.

In a word, dreamy.

The room surged gently towards him, leaving me with Gay Kaur beneath an archway. I asked her where she had gone to school, and listened with half an ear while I watched the maharaja work his way through the guests, shaking hands, gracing one after another with his flashing smile, laughing aloud at a remark made by Thomas Goodheart. The prince had a habit of speaking to taller men with his head slightly turned away, I saw, which forced the other to bend to his height. He also seemed to disconcert some of the people, particularly those most eager to put themselves close to him, and I watched him fix those seductive eyes on Sunny, take her eager hand, and lean close to whisper something into her ear. He turned away to the next person just as Sunny stepped back sharply, looking badly startled. What on earth had he said to her?

Just then his eyes scanned the wide room to where Gay and I stood, and the frown on my face seemed to catch his attention—either that or my height and the straw-coloured hair piled on my head. He shook off his admirers and stalked across the floor to us. His dark eyes were on me the whole way, unreadable in a face arranged for polite greeting, but once in front of me he continued on for another step and seized my companion's face in both his hands to kiss her full on the mouth, taking his eyes from me only at the last instant. A shock ran through the room, but it was nothing to Gay's reaction. She dropped her glass and her cigarette to push against his shoulders, squirming back from the embrace that went on for about three seconds too long for friendly greeting. I had just reached the reluctant decision to intervene when he let her go, laughing heartily. Gay's face darkened with fury as she bent to snatch cigarette and holder from the floor.

"Jimmy, you're such a bastard," she hissed, jabbing the end of the cigarette back into the ivory, all of us ignoring the servant's quick gathering-up of glass from around our feet.

"Cousin, aren't you glad to see me?" he asked, and without waiting for her answer, turned at last to me. Fortunately with his hand, not his lips.

I hesitated. Had I not been here for a purpose, I would have turned my back on the maharaja of Khanpur, but the impulse ran up against the thought of explaining to Geoffrey Nesbit why I had departed the state so hastily. I looked at his outstretched hand just long enough to make my feelings clear, then without enthusiasm allowed him my fingers.

"Mrs Russell, I trust you found your rooms to your satisfaction?" His grin was boyish, his eyes danced with amusement, but there was something altogether too calculating behind the charm.

"It's Miss Russell," I corrected him coolly, "and yes, Your Highness, they're quite nice, thank you."

"Ah. Tommy told me you were married," he said, his voice rising to a question.

"I am." Let him figure it out. The element of puzzle allowed the calculation to edge further into his expression, and then it was gone, and his firm and welcoming handshake was over. "Very well: Miss Russell, welcome to Khanpur."

"Thank you."

"Do you ride?" he asked, as at a sudden thought.

"I do."

"Some of us are going out in the morning," he said. "If you don't object to blood sport. You too, Gay. You used to be one for the spear." I could not tell if I was imagining the air of double-entendre to his last comment, but Gay seemed in no doubt. She put up her chin and gave him a regal glare.

"I've grown up some since then, Jimmy. I'm a little more choosy about my sport."

He laughed, and said to me, "Seven o'clock if you like, Miss Russell, just ring for a riding outfit."

And then he was gone back to his other guests, leaving me wondering at the peculiar tremors that followed in his wake.

Gay was working to get the knocked-off end of her cigarette alight, her hands not altogether steady. I watched her, thinking that it would take a good deal to shake an aristocrat like this from her self-confidence.

"He's your cousin?" I asked.

She finally had the thing going, and drew deeply on it, closing her eyes briefly against the smoke. "Distant cousin, of a sort. My mother's mother was married to Jimmy's father's sister's brother-in-law."

"And people say the European monarchy is confusing."

She did not seem to register my remark. "We went to school together for a couple of months, when my parents got the emancipation bug and decided I should go with my brothers, and the school took a while to figure how to get rid of me. And later Jimmy came home with my brothers a couple of holidays." She shot a dark look across the hall to where he stood, his back to us. "If that girl is your friend, her mother should be told not to leave the child alone with him."

"I'll keep an eye on her," I promised.

"It's just that he's . . . persuasive."

"I see."

Gay glanced down at the end of her holder, where the stub was nearly burnt out, and plucked it out with her long fingernails, allowing it to fall onto the ornate tiles. "Suddenly I'm not hungry. I think I'll go back to my rooms. Have a nice ride in the morning."

Shortly thereafter we were ushered in to dinner. "Casual dress" extended to the procession, as well, which was more of a general drift in the direction of a doorway than an arm-in-arm procession. But the place we were taken belied any informality.

This had been, I thought, New Fort's *durbar* hall, where traditionally the king met with visiting dignitaries whom he wished not only to entertain, but to intimidate. The Fort's was immense, and if the adjoining room had felt like an underwater grotto, this was like standing inside the world's largest emerald. Flashes of green and blue quivered in the air, the mosaic so lush the hand wanted to brush the walls, the tongue to taste it. Where the stone was not inlaid, it was covered either with gold leaf or high mirrors, tossing back the colours and the light of two dozen elephant-sized crystal chandeliers that hung from a golden ceiling forty feet above our heads. The floors were thick with silken carpets, and an orchestra, half hidden behind the inlaid marble purdah screens of the upper level, began a Mozart concerto as we rinsed our hands in rose-scented water poured from long-necked silver jars.

The meal itself was extreme, a bizarrely overdone ordeal-by-food, the kind of meal forced on unwelcome courtiers for the bitter amusement of bored kings. Dish after dish, each richer than the last, European alternating with Indian to the benefit of neither, all ornately arranged on the heavy gold plates, half of them giving offence to one guest or another—beef appeared twice, in this Hindu land, and slips of prosciutto ham so the Moslems (or in my case, Jew) wouldn't feel neglected. Lobster flaked with silver leaf and whole grilled songbird served on platters made of their brilliant feathers, saffron-infused snakes' eggs and curried peacocks' tongues, roast kid stuffed with raisins and pistachios, and a score of other dishes beat upon our senses. Whatever wasn't swimming in honey or *ghee* was drenched with cream, and long before the final courses, all my neighbours had been reduced to picking at their plates, and most of them looked somewhat green, particularly when the dizzying odour of sandalwood wafted in clouds from the upper levels.

When at long last the final glistening blancmange

had passed from our plates and the music that had accompanied the banquet ceased, we staggered from our places like so many pardoned criminals, only to have the announcement come that there would be dancing on the terrace. The man at my side, an English popular novelist, groaned, and muttered something about the maharaja having given up sleep. Sunny, the peacock tongues clearly wreaking havoc with her sense of well-being, tried to summon her customary enthusiasm.

"It might be nice, to work off some of that food," she said gamely.

I suspected that the maharaja's rather sadistic sense of humour would not permit a gentle glide across the floor, and indeed, the band instantly set off on one of the more vigorous modern dance-steps. I shook my head.

"Perhaps we'd best go and see how your mother is," I suggested in a firm voice. The relief with which Sunny seized on this escape would have been funny, if the very idea of laughter hadn't been so physically repugnant.

We found a servant to lead us to the Goodheart rooms, where Sunny did not argue overmuch with her mother's prescription of early bed. I, too, escaped the dance terrace, despite the opportunity for asking questions of half-stunned individuals ripe for indiscretion. With the amount of sleep my distended abdomen would be allowing me this night, the seven o'clock ride would come all too soon.

Chapter Sixteen

A set of riding clothes awaited me in the morning, although all I took from the laden tray that accompanied them was a single cup of tea. I moistened my long, mistreated hair with some almond oil that I had bought in the Simla market and bound the plaits closely to my head. The jodhpur trousers I had asked for fit well, and the boots, although somewhat loose around the calves, were long enough not to cramp my toes. I stretched my arms and shoulders against the shirt and jacket, finding the fit just loose enough for free movement, and put on the gloves (snug but long enough) but left the spurs where they lay. I then picked up the hat sent for the purpose, a sort of fabric-wrapped topee, and presented myself to the waiting *chuprassi*.

The servant led me into the gardens, where more servants and a motorcar stood waiting.

"How far is it to the stables?" I asked. I'd seen the map and didn't think it far. "Can't we walk?"

"Certainly, *memsahib*." The man closed the motorcar door obediently. "It takes fifteen minutes only."

We went out of the gate and into the morning sun, where I stopped to raise my face to the welcome warmth. Directly across from me, separated by the chasm of cliffs and road, were the gates of the Old Fort. The doors themselves stood open, although there was no sign of life there. Weeds sprouted from the walls, and from potholes in the narrow track climbing from the road.

The drive that circled New Fort's hill, on the other hand, was surfaced with closely fitting paving stones. At the bottom, where the drive turned back on itself to join the main road, my red-*puggaree*d guide went right, following a wide path that circled the hill. Halfway around, I was startled by a sudden jungle shrieking and the sight of dozens of monkeys of various shapes and sizes, leaping frantically around inside an enormous cage. The servant glanced at me with mingled apology and reassurance, and I went on, even when the roar of a lion came up nearly under my feet. The zoo, I realised: I wasn't about to be fed to the carnivores.

A lake appeared in the distance, decorated with white birds; beyond it stretched a great field punctuated with large grey shapes. I squinted, then smiled in delight as they became moving creatures: elephants, thirty or more of them, their attention centred around bright heaps of greenery. There were even babies among the herd, indistinct, but magical even from afar.

Belatedly, I realised that my guide had stopped to wait for me, and I hurried to catch him up. As the path continued, rooftops came into view: a lot of rooftops, long low buildings arranged around six immense courtyards. This could only be the maharaja's stables, but the complex was lavish, larger than any race-track facilities I'd seen.

"How many horses does the maharaja own?" I asked my guide.

"I believe His Highness pleasures in two hundred and twenty-five, although I am not completely certain as to the numbers. Does *memsahib* wish me to make precise enquiries?"

"No," I assured him weakly. "That's fine."

We walked down a wide stairway and through a magnificent archway into the yard farthest from the lake. There we found nine horses saddled, five of them claimed already by their riders, all men. The maharaja saw me approaching and dropped his conversation with a young Indian Army officer named Simon Greaves, whom I had met the night before, to come and meet me.

"Miss Russell, how good you could join us."

"I wouldn't have missed it for the world," I told him easily.

"I didn't ask what kind of a rider you were, so you'll have to let me know if you'd like something less flighty."

He had gestured to one of the servants, who tugged the reins of a glossy chestnut gelding and led him over, carrying an ornate little stool in his free hand. The horse was the tallest animal there, although I thought it scarcely fifteen and a half hands, with muscle in its hindquarters that suggested it could jump anything I might care to point it at. I ran my hands down its legs and along its back, pleased that it didn't twitch or move away.

"Does it have any bad habits?" I asked the *syce*, who looked at his master before answering me.

"Oah, no, *memsahib*, his manners are good. His mouth is hard, but he will not run under a branch or drop a shoulder to have you off, oah no."

The affection with which the old man patted the animal's neck more than the words reassured me that my host wasn't out to amuse himself at the expense of my bones. I let the beast snuffle my hand, and checked the girths before using the stool to boost myself to the saddle. The maharaja watched me as I took the reins and got the feel of the gelding's mouth, which did indeed require a firm hand. Then he went over to a beautiful pure-white Arab stallion and mounted up. He and Captain Greaves had spurs on their boots, but none of the others did.

The four strangers were introduced as a polo-playing cousin of the captain's from Kent, on a world tour, an American recently retired from the Army, and a pair of Bombay industrialists. As we exchanged greetings, I had to wonder if such iconoclastic relationships were common amongst India's nobility. Khanpur's prince seemed determined to deny his orthodoxy on all kinds of levels, from the consumption of alcohol and meat to the company of foreign women and businessmen— mere *box-wallah*s were almost as below the salt here as manual workers.

The men went on with their various conversations as the *syce* and I made adjustments to the stirrups, and after a few minutes the motorcar from the Fort drove into the yard and gave forth our two missing riders—the Goodhearts, brother and sister. Although he was taller than I, Thomas was given the marginally shorter twin of the chestnut I was on, while Sunny was mounted on a placid mare little larger than a pony that probably wouldn't have jumped a branch if it was lying flat on the ground, but then again probably wouldn't spook and dump its rider. With all the saddles full and our host in the lead, we continued around the New Fort hill until we met the main road again.

Before I turned my mount's head north, I glanced up at the hillside of the eastern Old Fort across the road. There, with the morning sun streaming through the gap, I could see the marks of fire, clear on the stones of the cliff face, where the mutineers and their hostage had been set to flame by the old maharaja in 1857.

We jogged along for nearly an hour, past the polo grounds and the elephant pens with their Brobdingnagian stables, then skirting the air field, which showed no sign of life this morning, not even around that tantalising cluster of *godowns* at the northern end. My cheeks tingled with the brisk air, and I did not need the sight of the surrounding peaks to be reminded of Khanpur's altitude. An eagle rode the breeze above our heads, the air rang with the pleasing sounds of bridle and hoof, and I listened with half an ear to the conversations wafting to and fro. Thomas Goodheart was even less responsive than usual, being either hung-over or just uninterested in scenery and small-talk, or both. Two of the others began to grumble interestingly about their losses the previous night at cards, speculating on just how it was the maharaja had been cheating, but revelations were cut short by their belated awareness of an audience, and they talked about the Delhi races instead. Sunny commented on every form of wildlife we passed, and half the domesticated stock, topics that did not distract me much from my own appreciation of the day. Once past the air field, we entered a land of cane and corn. Men working their fields paused to honour our passing. A whiff of *gur* came to me from a nearby factory, followed by the rhythmic creaks of a water wheel whose design was older than India herself. I mused over the range of technology represented in such a short space, from Persian wheel to modern air design, and made a mental note to talk about it with Holmes when I next saw him.

Whenever that might be.

Four or five miles past the air field, at a spot on the road marked by a small wayside shrine, we turned into an area of *terai*, open scrubland dotted by trees. Half a dozen *shikaris*—hunt attendants—squatted near a smokey little fire, standing up as we came into sight. One of them walked out into the road, waving his arms in some unintelligible signal directed, not at us, but at another figure on a nearby hilltop. Signals exchanged, he then came forward to speak with the prince, who, after a few minutes' consultation, wheeled his Arab and joined us.

"The beaters have found pig, they're driving the sounder—the herd—towards us up the next hill. I would suggest that you ladies rest here, or if you'd like to continue on to the tank—the lake—you'll find tea set up there."

"You're going pig sticking?" I asked.

"We are." Was that a challenge in his eyes, or did I imagine it? I had no real desire to murder pigs with a sharpened stick; on the other hand, what was I here for if not to work myself close to the maharaja? If that weedy Flapper cousin of his could stick pigs, so could I.

"Do you mind if I join you? It sounds great fun."

"Mary!" objected Sunny.

"Not you," I hastened to add. "It doesn't look to me like your horse would be much use on rough ground." Unlike my mount, whose pricked ears indicated that he knew precisely what was over that hill, and knew what he was supposed to do about it. *Just don't let me fall off with a pig staring me in the face,* I prayed, and committed myself. My host seemed pleased, although his male companions looked as if they'd bitten into a bad apple.

The *shikari*s came up carrying an armload of wicked-looking spears and handed us each one. Mine had a bamboo shaft two feet taller than I was, strong and flexible and packed with lead in the butt, the tip mounted with a slim steel head the length of a child's hand, sharp as a well-honed razor and with grooves running down both sides. I held the spear in my hand, feeling its heft and balance, trying to visualise how far a person could lean out of the saddle at a gallop without tumbling off, and trying to imagine how much practise it would take to be able to harpoon a pig in full flight. In truth, the shaft did not seem nearly long enough to me: If even half of what Holmes had told me about wild boar was correct, the farther from the pig, the better.

As I held the weapon, a *shikari* noticed my awkwardness and took pity on me. "You have not done this before, I think, *memsahib?* Very well. You are left-handed? Then the spear is held thus," he began, shifting my fingers around the long bamboo shaft. "And you must ride with the point well forward, always. When the boar breaks from cover—and only a boar, no female pigs— you pursue it, fast fast. Hold yourself twenty, thirty feet in back, and when the beast begins to tire, speed up and aim just behind its shoulder blade." He eyed the uncertain waver of my spear-head and modified his instructions. "Or you can jab where you wish—first blood is considered an honour, and the animal will weaken and die," he explained.

"But *memsahib,* you must watch for a flare of the eye

or the chewing of its tusks, for that tells you that he is about to turn and come for you. This is called 'jinking,' and it is very dangerous, you must watch for that at every instant. If by great bad fortune you lose your spear" (I thought all in all this was highly likely) "you must not dismount to retrieve it unless you can be completely and absolutely certain that the pig is gone." The *shikari* stood watching me try to find the spear's balance and to work out a way of carrying the thing so it didn't slice the gelding's legs to ribbons; with an almost imperceptible sigh and shrug of his shoulders, he went back to his work.

The maharaja divided us into pairs, which I supposed was to lessen the severity of a collision or a stray spear. I thought he would put me with another inexperienced rider and thus dismiss the incompetents from his mind, but to my surprise he chose me for his partner. After the first flush of pleasure, it occurred to me that he was all but guaranteeing that he have the day to himself. I firmed my grip on the shaft, and determined at least to remain in the saddle.

We made our way down the road towards some hills. As we rode, I began to get a feel for the spear's movements; I could even see the reason for allowing the pig so close: Were the shaft any longer, it would be impossible to manoeuvre it with any precision at all. In the end, I decided it must be like jousting; given the chance, I'd simply count on the horse to run me over the pig, bracing the spear like an eight-foot-long skewer.

With my eyes closed, praying fervently.

As the road cleared the top of the hill, we left it to set out into an open plain, several miles of rough *terai* with patches of waist-high sugar cane, dotted by thickets of weedy trees and some rocky outcrops. We distributed

ourselves, pair by pair, in a long string of riders, and
there we stood, listening to the beaters working their
way down, half a mile or more away. They sounded very
different from the beaters used to drive game birds in
England, but their purpose was the same, raising just
enough noise to make their target edgy, representing in
their numbers enough of a threat to encourage the animals to move away, not to panic—or in the case of pigs,
turn and attack. It was a lovely morning, clear and still
cool, and the horse beneath me was promising, needing
little attention from its rider to avoid obstacles, responding easily to my suggestions. I relaxed, and decided that, in spite of the vicious weapon in my hand,
the true purpose of pig sticking was the same as that of
fox-hunting, namely, an excuse for a pleasant day's vigorous exercise in the open. And, no doubt, for the
sumptuous hunt lunch that would await us at the tank.
I fingered the silver charm I wore for reassurance, and
wondered where Holmes was.

Then without warning, two things happened simultaneously: When the first of the beaters came into sight,
I was astonished to see, not simply men on foot, but
with them mounted elephants, ears waving and trunks
up. And no sooner had I focussed on those amazing
and glorious beasts, when the corner of my eye caught a
number of fast dark objects shooting out of a patch of
thick green cane to rocket across the grassland at an angle from me, aiming for a thick stand of trees a mile or
so away. Without pausing to consult me, my horse
gathered its hindquarters and lunged after the pigs
with the other riders stretched out, right and left, the
white Arab in the fore. In three seconds flat we were
pounding at a full gallop across dry grassland while the
smaller members of the herd, sows and piglets, started

peeling away from our path, ducking under bushes and doubling back for safety, leaving three, then two, and finally a solitary black creature that flew along the ground on its stumpy legs, an angular, hairy slab of muscle and bone that showed no sign of lagging. I did not know where the others were, but the white Arab was in front and fifty yards to my left, its rider up in his stirrups, his spear as steady as if it were mounted to a track. My own weapon bounced and wove with each beat of the body beneath me, giving all too vivid illustration to Nesbit's casual remark about ending up with a spear through his arm.

I wouldn't have imagined that a pig would be fast, but this one maintained its distance from both horses for half a mile. The trees were fast approaching, but either the pig was tiring or the horses had their stride, because my mount was coming up on the pig's right side. Afterwards, I decided the experienced bay had done it deliberately, cutting the boar off from the trees while the white Arab fell away on our left. The pig veered reluctantly away from the trees, then farther away, until it was headed into open ground.

And then it jinked.

Such light-hearted and adolescent words the sport used, my mind threw at me in its last instant of clarity for some time. Sticking, jinking, pig—all those short vowels lent it such a jaunty air.

What happened in fact was that, thirty feet ahead of me, the boar turned with the ease of a swallow in flight and aimed itself at the Arab's white belly. Our quarry had no intention of being driven out into open ground, and anything in its way would be ripped apart, it was as simple as that—except that it was not simple, the jink was a feint. The maharaja's spear was already down and waiting, but the charge at the white belly stopped as swiftly as it had begun, and the animal whirled on its hooves in the clap of a hand and shot straight at me.

In an instant, my fear of embarrassing myself and letting down the women's side vanished completely, gulped up by a flood of pure mortal terror. The pig looked the size of a bear, with murderous little eyes over a cluster of curved razors; I half expected the thing to leap into the air and rip out my throat. Thank God the horse at least knew what it was doing. While my arm froze and the spear bobbled up and down like a broomstick balanced across a clothes-line, the big bay gathered its muscles, paused for a moment—only later did it occur to me that the horse was waiting for me to stick the thing, had I been either so inclined or so able—and then vaulted hugely forward out of the boar's way. As we rose, the spear-head dipped to bounce ineffectually off the pig's rock-like shoulder, a tap that jarred my shoulder down to my boots.

I came within a hair of dropping my stick as the horse flew forward, tucking its feet miraculously clear of the searching tusks and coming back to earth at a dead run. It took just half a dozen strides and then, with absolutely no instruction from me, dug in its front hooves. Spear and topee flew over the horse's ears, nearly followed by rider as I clung hard to mane and saddle, losing one stirrup as the horse hauled itself around to face the boar again.

Which meant that I looked back over my gelding's neck just in time to see a textbook illustration of how a pig is stuck. With its right side now clear, the animal was sprinting for the trees, the maharaja riding hard to catch it first. Ten feet from safety the spear—so steady it resembled the javelin of a bronze athlete—slid into the tough hide. The beast tumbled and regained its feet, the horse veered and came about, and spear met pig in mid-stride, the point slipping effortlessly into the fold where the thick neck began. The boar hesitated, then collapsed slowly and was still.

"Jesus Christ!" I said, loud in the silence. I was trembling all over, but the maharaja's breathing was only slightly quickened, and both horses seemed more interested in the grass than in the bloody object on the ground. I half-fell out of the saddle and went in search of my dropped headgear and weapon, clinging to the reins as support, feeling as if I'd narrowly missed a fall from a high rooftop, shaking but gloriously alive. I located the spear by tripping over it, picked my topee from a bush and clapped it onto my head, and walked somewhat drunkenly back to where the maharaja sat, still on horse-back, waiting as some of his men approached at a fast trot.

"You accounted well for yourself, Miss Russell," he said.

I squinted at him in disbelief. "I didn't get us killed, if that's what you mean."

"Not at all. In fact—" He held out his hand, gesturing for my spear. I thrust it out and he snatched at the wavering shaft before I could disembowel him, then ran his thumb up the steel groove, showing me the thick red ooze he'd pulled from it. "First blood to you, Miss Russell. Congratulations."

I took back my weapon to examine the evidence, then went to look at the animal itself, expecting a small nick where my spear had bounced off. Instead, there was a rip in his flesh the size of my hand. My shoulder still tingled with the impact.

The servants came up then. They gave the maharaja

a cloth to clean his hand, gave me a glass of ice-cold lemon drink to clear my throat, and handed us each a fresh spear.

The day, it seemed, was far from over.

I tucked in my shirt, bathed my face, and settled my hair back under my topee. The *syce* with the decorated stool held my horse's reins and tucked the spear under his arm, positioning the stool near the stirrup for me. I looked from dead pig to complacent horse to clean spear and back again, then pushed my spectacles up onto my nose and climbed into the saddle.

My first-timer's luck did not give me a second pig that morning, although by morning's end I had to admit that it was indeed a sport rather than a means of disposing of pests, with its own demands, skill, and even artistry. Rather like a high-speed variety of bull-fighting, with the horse and rider themselves taking the place of the cape.

With the sun directly overhead, the riders began to gather, handing the servants their spears and talking with varying degrees of excitement. Captain Greaves, his polo-playing cousin, and our host were old hands with the spear, and had taken five pigs between them, but only one of the others, the partner of Thomas Goodheart, had landed a blow. In his case the pig had run off with the spear trailing behind him; the beaters were tracking the wounded animal through the scrub.

The morning's exercise had put paid to the evening's excesses—I was famished, and hoped that our gathering together marked an impending meal. And so it proved. We rode a mile back to the lakeside that we had passed earlier, to find that in the hours since we had last seen the grassy field that stretched down to the water, a transformation had occurred. Half a hundred guests, attended by an equal number of servants, lounged about on cushions and brocaded divans that had been arranged around a silken tent the size of a minor dormitory, from whose open sides came tantalising odours and a glimpse of linen-draped tables. The two cheetahs, still wearing their ruby collars, crouched with their attendants; golden cages filled with songbirds had been hung from the trees. More usefully, a cart carrying a tank of warm water and scented soap had been set up at the back of the tent, along with mirror, face flannels, and all the comforts of a bath short of the actual tub. I scrubbed my hands, wound my hair back into place, and was claimed instantly by a servant as I stepped out of the enclosure.

Inside the tent, I accepted a glass of champagne and my attendant conjured up a silver tray with flatware and an empty plate, and moved along the tables at my elbow, arranging my choices on the luminous bone china. To my relief, the meal was considerably less oppressive than that of the night before, a buffet composed of English sandwiches, soups hot and cold, and several kinds of curry. My plate and tray filled to excess, I shook my head at the offer of more and walked over to where the Goodhearts sat, their padded stools and divans shaded by the wide branches of a tree and protected from the ground by layers of priceless Oriental carpets. My attendant arranged cushions and fiddled with the silver tray, unfolding a pair of supports that raised it a few inches from the ground. He draped my table napkin over my lap, positioned the table-tray in front of me, and retreated, lingering nearby to fill my glass and fetch additional temptations.

The tank—what I would call a lake—covered several acres, and had been in existence long enough that large trees lined its borders. Reeds stretched out into the water, sheltering a wide variety of birds, from tiny green things no larger than a butterfly to slow-moving storks. A princely barge shaped like a swan lay moored to one side, simply begging to be taken seriously, although it looked like a rich man's jest.

To be a prince in British India must, I reflected, be an uneasy thing. The knowledge that, but for this foreign power, one would be fully a king had to cause some degree of frustration, some sense that despite the riches and the honours, despite being (as Nesbit had put it) "above British law," one's life was essentially composed of empty ritual. A proud man like the maharaja of Khanpur surely had to chafe at his enforced impotence, and a certain resentment against the Crown could be understood. I could also begin to see the importance of a thing like pig sticking: Where war is forbidden, sport becomes the substitute, wherein a man's conduct determines his worth, and a silver trophy represents a battle won.

It was, I decided as I speared the last delicate asparagus, a small miracle that more of India's princes did not assuage their boredom and frustration by descending into feudal ruthlessness.

I permitted the servant to clear my plate and take the tray, turning down his offer of more wine, a third ice, a sliver of chocolate . . . , and stretched out my legs into the sun, deliberately putting dark thoughts from my mind. From where I sat I could see elephants on the other side of the water, languidly reaching for leaves. Closer to, half a dozen peahens pecked their way along the base of some shrubs, oblivious to the full display of their ever-hopeful male. After a couple of minutes, they were startled by the cry of a parrot, and the colourful feathers folded away as the flock slipped into the bushes.

The noisy parrot was not a wild creature, but harbinger of our luncheon amusement. I personally would have been happy to sit and watch Nature's entertainments, but the great enemy, Boredom, was to be given no chance of a toehold in this place. Three young men trotted up with brilliant green parrots on their shoulders, and proceeded to put on a show. The birds rode miniature bicycles across diminutive tight-ropes, loaded and shot Lilliputian cannon, counted out the answers to elementary mathematical problems by dipping their heads, and in conclusion lay flat on their feathered bellies in salute to the maharaja. The parrot-trainers were followed by a troupe of gymnasts and contortionists, children who tied themselves into knots and threw one another into the air. The third act, a voluptuous young woman who played tunes on a sea of water-filled crystal goblets, lacked the ability to sustain interest, and the warm afternoon combined with the wine made us an inattentive audience. She left after a third tune, and a gramophone was brought out and wound. Sunny gave a little sigh of happiness, and her brother stirred and sat up.

"So, Jimmy," Goodheart called. "Who took the morning's first blood?"

"Miss Russell did, although she permitted me to finish the beast off."

A startled silence fell, before Sunny squealed and clapped her hands. "Oh, Mary, how super! Have you ever done this before?"

"We don't have all that many wild boar in southern

England," I pointed out. "I shouldn't think the domesticated variety make for quite the same challenge."

"You ought to introduce them," Goodheart suggested. "Get into training for a world cup of pig sticking."

The man had been making a joke, but the maharaja's voice cut in, an edge to his words that overrode all conversation. "The British do not need to train for sticking pig. They simply arrange the rules to their satisfaction."

The green field and its tent and rugs froze into an awkward silence, until our host shrugged to indicate that he had only been making a joke, and then rose to consult with the *shikaris* gathered on the far side of the tent. Mrs Goodheart made some kind of enquiring sound at her son.

"Don't worry about it, Mother," he reassured her. "Jimmy's just a little touchy about having lost the Kadir Cup last year, some kind of technicality. Don't much understand it myself; I s'pose I shouldn't have said anything."

After a while, Sunny went down to dabble in the water, and I stretched out on the silken carpet with my legs in the sun and my topee over my face, half listening to the conversations around me. The gramophone played, a few guests danced laughingly on the manicured grass, and I was nearly asleep when I heard my name, said loudly as if not for the first time. I pulled the topee from my face and sat up, looking into the dark unreadable eyes of the maharaja.

"I'm terribly sorry, Your Highness," I said. "What was that?"

"The beaters have located the wounded pig," he said. "I don't like to leave it. Would you care to come?"

I was speechless. Six men at his disposal, two of

whom were old hands, and he was asking me, a woman, and dangerously inexperienced at that.

One of the old hands had the same thought. "I've finished here, Jimmy," Captain Greaves interposed. "I'll go with you."

"Thank you, Simon, but Miss Russell and I shall have no problem."

"From what Goodheart said, it's a big 'un, I'm happy to—"

"No." It was said in a flat voice, no anger, but it laid another uncomfortable silence over the gathering, which I hastened to break.

"Certainly, I'm glad to be of help. Shall we go now?"

The servants had brought fresh horses with them. The maharaja had another Arab, a white gelding otherwise identical to the stallion, while I was given an ill-tempered little mare whose ears went back when I approached and who tried to shy against the reins the *syce* held. I checked her girths with care, since this was the kind of beast who holds her breath to keep the saddle from being secured, but I found them snugly secured. I glanced at the man holding her for me, and saw the humour in his eyes: Yes, she'd tried the trick on him.

"Thank you," I told him, and mounted briskly.

Once I was in the saddle, the worst of the mare's temper subsided, and she responded to my directions without much hesitation. We followed the road back to the tree, where the *shikaris* still waited, and took the spears they offered us. My host conferred with them, in a language that was not Hindi, then led me into the fields, in the opposite direction from that in which we had gone the first time.

I had hoped to use the opportunity to question the prince, but quickly realised that this was not going to be possible, not until we had dispatched the wounded pig. The maharaja was completely focussed on the task at hand, and once we had caught the beaters up, his undergraduate style dropped away completely. He studied the splintered spear-shaft one of them had retrieved and listened intently to their information, his eyes searching the landscape as if he might see the pig through the thick brush. North of us stretched scrubland, but to the south, a thick stand of trees rose up, following some kind of a stream-bed. At last he grunted, and turned to me.

"They've tracked him as far as that split tree, you see? There's a *nullah* down there—a stream-bed—and heavy brush. He's already ripped open the leg of one bearer; they're not too keen on going in after him. And if he gets as far as those trees, he's lost."

"I hope the man's all right?"

The maharaja looked at me as if I'd spoken in a half-understood language that he had to translate internally, then replied, "Yes, he's sure to be. But you do understand that once we get in there, your mare won't have any clear ground where she can escape? You have to have your stick ready at every moment."

"But if I can't see the boar, how do I know where to point the spear?" I asked, reasonably, I thought.

"Your horse will know. And you'll feel him."

Oh, this is just grand, Russell, I berated myself. *You're about to have one of your host's animals ripped apart underneath you, because you couldn't pass the opportunity to prove yourself. Clever.*

We rode into the two-acre thicket from two angles, me at four o'clock and the maharaja at seven, pressing towards the top, where at least twenty beaters stood, banging on rocks and trees, staring nervously at the ground between us and them. I suddenly noticed that the men were armed only with long sticks, not spears, and of course none of them were mounted. I hoped for their sakes they were fleet-footed, and could climb trees like monkeys.

A partridge exploded from the tree in front of me, nearly stopping my heart and making me laugh nervously. I was perspiring heavily, as was the mare. Contrary to the maharaja's claim, she didn't seem to think there was anything in here at all, and the only thing I felt was growing nerves.

Then, between one step and another, her ears swung forward. I made a faint whistle between my teeth to catch my companion's attention, and nodded at the direction the mare was watching, more or less straight ahead. Jimmy studied the land, then gestured for me to circle more to the right, that we might trap the animal between us. I urged the mare to the side and began to circle in on the offending scrap of shrubbery.

Fifty feet, forty, and at thirty-five I began to understand what he had said about feeling the animal. It was as if the boar gave off waves of heat, or just fury; it wouldn't have surprised me if the bush burst into flames. My mount began to twitch, picking her way delicately, and the beaters a hundred yards away kept up their drumming on the ground.

This time I saw the blood first, a splash of shocking red against the dusty vegetation as a black shape the size of a small water buffalo shot out of his hiding-place like a launched shell, the broken-off spear protruding from his left haunch, bouncing with every move as he aimed his rage at the gelding's white gut. The maharaja was ready for him, but the horse was not, and it shifted a fraction, taking the readied spear a degree or two off aim. The pig hit the spear hard, but instead of sinking into his vitals, the sharp head sliced across the shoulder blade and then stuck.

I had an unclear idea of pig physiology, but by the looks of it, a spear in that position was not going to prove immediately fatal. Nor did it seem all that securely planted, I noticed in alarm. As if to illustrate the matter, the pig began to push, grunting in fury, while the man on the horse tried to change the angle to one that might bite in more deeply. The pig pushed hard and the horse gave way, until they were circling around and around in the bush, held apart by a slim length of wood.

I put my heels into the mare's side, trying to get close enough to use my spear without getting in the way of the partners, but I couldn't, not while mounted. Without thinking, I kicked my feet from the stirrups and dropped to the ground.

The prince caught sight of me out of the corner of his eye and shouted something, and there was a sudden increase of noise from the beaters, but I could see that there would be an opening after the white hindquarters next passed, and I readied myself to dash forward.

But I didn't know pigs. I didn't realise that the animal would see me as well, didn't foresee that the distraction of two enemies would make him back away, yanking the spear from its resting place. Didn't realise that once the beast was free, it would come for me. But that is precisely what it did: a quick reverse scurry and the maharaja's spear was swinging free while the blood-drenched creature got its legs under it and ran again—this time at me. Instinct alone lowered the point of my spear—anything to keep that furious bristling face away from my soft skin, to keep those wicked tusks at a distance, to postpone the inevitable for a moment.

The spear took him straight in the chest, and it was like slamming into a train. I flew backwards, clinging to the spear with every ounce of self-protection in my being, scarcely aware of sitting down hard onto the rocky ground. The universe narrowed down to this tiny space, my entire being focussed on the fact of my straining muscles pushing one way and the huge, stinking, primeval Fury shoving the other, two opposing forces separated only by a thin and sharply arching bamboo stalk, its fibres audibly creaking with strain. The boar was so close I could count its long, feminine eyelashes, so near I memorised the smear of dried blood on its lower right tusk and the scars on its snout, knew the shape of the pebbles crunching beneath its hooves. The creature's breath was hot and intimate on my face, and we stared into each other's eyes while its legs thrust towards me, its tusks yearning for my vitals with an urge so all-consuming that it overpowered any awareness of the steel blade driving ever more deeply into its chest. It grunted and strained, then suddenly my vision went pink as the breath blowing across my face went bloody, and through the red mist on my spectacles I saw the boar give a last convulsive push. The spear snapped, his legs buckled, and he came to rest with his upper tusk pressing against the leather of my outstretched boots, his back legs still twitching with effort. And then he died.

At some time in the past minute—hour?—the maharaja had come down from his horse, and was standing at my shoulder with his spear at the ready. But he had held off using it, and now he allowed its point to rest on the ground.

"Again, congratulations, Miss Russell," he said.

I stared up at my host, trying to make sense of his words. I lay sprawled at the prince's feet, filthy, scraped, and sore, my hair in my face and my topee nowhere to be seen. After a moment I shifted my gaze to the impaled animal against my boots, and the world abruptly rushed back in, tumbling about me in all its size and complexity. I felt like whooping with exhilaration.

By God, pig sticking was indeed a game of games.

The maharaja helped me to my feet and said in a mild voice, "It's not generally recommended that an amateur attempt spearing a pig on foot."

"Yes, I can see why," I told him. "But your horse wouldn't stand still."

"The pig would have bled to death soon enough. But I have to say, I'm glad to have been witness to that manoeuvre."

The beaters came up then, exclaiming and, it seemed to me, abjectly apologetic, even terrified, although I was not sure if it was over the danger to me, or to their master. I was not even certain why they were apologising. Did we imagine they ought to have battered the vicious creature to death with their blunt sticks? One of them gave me a pristine linen cloth with which to clean my bloody face and spectacles; another brought the mare, holding her firmly; a third knelt that I might use his knee to step up. I needed the help, despite the mare's lack of stature, and on the way back to the road I was glad, too, that I was not riding the hard-mouthed gelding. I felt weak as an infant.

Pig sticking, it seemed, was over for the day, although the cheetahs were being readied for coursing, and three large enclosed bullock-drawn carts rattled and jerked with the motion of whatever the cats' prey was to be. I apologised, and told my host I preferred to return to The Forts, thank you. Taking my leave, and with a pair of mounted servants at my back, I rode—slowly, slowly—back to the castle and crept upstairs to submit my bruises and bashes to the ministrations of my hot-water geyser.

Chapter Seventeen

I was greatly tempted to remain chin-deep in hot water until midnight, but after an hour I forced myself to leave the comforting porcelain nest. As I dried myself with the thick towel, I discovered a number of sensitive patches, and moved over to look at my exterior in the glass. Oh, my.

A long gouge across my collar-bone recalled where a branch had snapped into me, and the butt of the spear had left an angry swelling the area of a man's hand where it had braced against the hollow of my left shoulder. There was a smaller welt on the outside of my right arm that I couldn't remember incurring, and several interesting bruises (as well as a general tenderness) where my backside had met the hard earth. I pulled on long sleeves, and with difficulty got my hair into place.

The day's hand-lettered itinerary said that tea would be served, again on the terrace. With longing glances at the soft bed, I left my rooms: The rest of the party would be away until dinner, and I badly wanted another conversation with my host's distant cousin before his return.

To my disappointment, Gay Kaur was not there. Nor was Sunny, although her mother was, stolid and flowered and looking restored to herself as she lectured an older Indian gentleman about the Spirit World and her Teacher (one could hear the capital letters). Giving her wide berth, I settled with my cup near a conversational cluster made up of four men and two women whom I had seen previously but not actually met. I nodded a greeting, but did not interrupt.

Their topic was politics. One of the men was a Moslem, who had things to say about Jinnah's suitability as a Prime Minister, but inevitably Gandhi and his Congress Party dominated the talk. It became increasingly heated, so much so that I thought it was about to become out of control until one of the women rose to her feet. She was a small woman, but she dominated the gathering with ease.

"I shall ask that you two be tossed into the fountain if you can't keep your heads," she said. "I propose a change of topic. You're Miss Russell, aren't you?" she asked, turning to me. "I'm Faith Hopkins. This is my friend, Lyn Fford, and these argumentative gentlemen are Harry Koehler, Trevor Wilson, Vikram Reddy, and Taran Singh."

Hands were shaken, and my chair incorporated more fully into their group. No less than four of the names had rung bells in my mind: those of the two women, Wilson's, and Koehler's, although of these, only the face of Koehler the American seemed familiar as well.

I started with Trevor Wilson, fairly sure of myself there. "The writer, aren't you?" He was a novelist, best-selling in the years immediately after the War. Even I had read one of his books, and I read very little fiction.

"I used to be."

"But it couldn't be that long since you've published, could it?"

"Nineteen months and counting. I'm the maharaja's secretary. It doesn't leave me much time for my own work."

Wilson sounded grim, and I began to say something vaguely encouraging, realised that pretty much any statement I produced would sound patronising, and turned instead to the man whose face tweaked my memory. "Mr Koehler, isn't it? I believe we've met somewhere, although I can't at the moment remember when it was."

He turned rather pale and gazed into his tea cup as if it might suddenly hold a shot of something harder. "Oh no, no, I don't think so. I'd have remembered meeting you."

I searched his features for clues, but couldn't retrieve anything more than the vague sense of having seen him in person, across some busy and crowded room. A train station, perhaps? It would come to me, I thought, then went back to the first woman. "I don't believe we've met before," I told her, "but your name is familiar."

She laughed. "Not surprising. Lyn and I were all over the headlines a year or so back."

"The newspapers, yes. Something about the Archbishop of Canterbury, wasn't it?"

"He eventually became involved, yes."

The other woman, Lyn, took pity on me. "Faith and I tried to marry. We registered with our parish church, banns were posted, and it wasn't until we showed up on the day that the priest figured out that Lyn wasn't a man."

"If you'd been wearing the morning suit I got you, we'd have managed it," Faith said with a rueful shake of the head, which launched them on a story in two voices, a narrative of ecclesiastical derring-do and upper-class humour. It sounded like an oft-told tale, but none the less amusing for its worn edges, and I remembered some of the details as she went along. The two were artists, of a sort—one a sculptor of huge ugly bronze masses, the other the creator of bizarre canvases thick with *objets trouvés*. I thought they had moved to Paris, after which they had not been heard of again.

By common consent, our conversation skirted the topic of politics. Reddy, it turned out, was a playwright who had produced two critically acclaimed plays, the second of which had spent some months on Broadway in New York, before being hired to come here and produce something for the maharaja. He had been here for two years, with nothing to show for it but a lot of paper and a fading presence on Broadway. I didn't find out who Taran Singh was, aside from being an opponent of Jinnah's Moslem League, before the sporting contingent arrived, fresh from their horses and smelling of sweat and gunpowder.

I excused myself to go and change for dinner, but I did not go directly to my rooms. Rather, I walked, deep in thought, through the dusk-washed gardens. The mild exercise helped loose my muscles, and the distraction loosed my mind as well, because as I bent to smell a flower I abruptly remembered where I'd seen the face of Harry Koehler.

It was a trial. I'd been there by coincidence, meeting Holmes for dinner (he in a frivolous mood, with a gardenia in his lapel—Ah! The memory had been freed by aroma), and as we left the court-room where he'd been watching a trial, we'd got caught up in the press of people leaving the next room. At their centre had been Koehler, testifying for the defence in a case involving the sex-lives of aristocrats and the embezzlement of a great deal of money. Holmes had pointed him out to me, with the dry comment that the man was one of the best-paid witnesses in London.

So what was he doing in Khanpur?

I stirred myself from my thoughts and was picking my way through the dark garden towards the lighted walls of the palace when the darkness nearby suddenly moved. "Who is there?" I asked sharply.

In response, a flame snapped into being, settling at the end of a cigarette being held by Gay Kaur. "Oh, Miss Kaur, you startled me."

"Sorry, I was just enjoying the garden. Care for a smoke?"

"Thanks, no, never got the habit." I felt for the edge of the bench her flame had illuminated, and eased down beside her.

"I hear you made a great success at the pigs," she said.

"Purely by accident. And I'm black-and-blue all over."

"Yes, it's a fairly ferocious sort of entertainment."

"Your cousin is very good at it."

"People like us have to be good at something."

There are a number of ways to approach a statement like that, but in the end, I decided to let it lie, and come in at an angle, trusting to the darkness to encourage confession. "The maharaja seems to have a variety of friends. I mean to say, men with single-minded passions often surround themselves with people of similar interests. But here I've met a novelist, a playwright, two avant-garde artists, and of course the Goodhearts."

"Jimmy's pets."

"Pardon me?"

"Jimmy likes to collect interesting people. Animals, too, of course—he'll probably show you his zoo tomorrow, although he prefers to take people there under a full moon—but he's forever bringing home some odd character from his travels and giving him a job. Usually something the person is most unsuited for. I suppose it's more amusing that way."

"I don't think I understand," I said, although I was beginning to catch a glimmer.

Gay drew in from her cigarette, the sudden flare of light showing her pensive face, then let out a cloud of fragrant smoke. "We're spoilt children, all of us, and it can be difficult for someone in Jimmy's position to think of ways to fill the day. Unless one is taken with administering roads projects and building schools, there's basically nothing to do. My own father drank himself to death at the age of thirty-one, there's another uncle who reached the age of forty and locked himself up in his palace to become what you might call a connoisseur of perversion. Jimmy himself spent a few years gambling in Monaco, then he turned to racing cars, and of course you've seen his aeroplanes. I think he found danger boring after a time, if that isn't a contradiction in terms, because he threw it all over and came home. He spent a couple of years setting up elaborate practical jokes on people, and getting a reputation for sorcery—the servants are still convinced he can walk through solid walls—and then got tired of those games as well. That's when he began to restore The Forts, and a couple of years later he started the zoo. So far that's kept him busy. I suppose African lions and Australian birds make for a more satisfying collection than Moghul miniatures or Japanese armour, or even motorcars and fast planes."

"Are you saying that your cousin, what? Collects human oddities?"

She snorted delicately. "Those you've met, they're nothing, they're practically normal. He had a two-headed child for a while, although I think she died last year, and he found a pair of albino dancers in Berlin who can't venture into the daylight. And you won't have seen his village of imported dwarfs—it amuses him to put the smallest people he can find in charge of the lions and giraffes. The village headman is three feet tall, and used to be with Barnum and Bailey. Not that the circus was sorry to be rid of him—he's got the foulest mouth of any creature I've ever heard. Jimmy thinks he's hilarious. Or he used to; I think he's beginning to find it all a bit tedious. He's showing signs of looking around for something new.

"Oh, is that the bell already? Hell, I've got to dress." She tweaked the end of her cigarette out of its holder and tossed it into the shrubbery, tracing an arc through the night, then left without saying good-bye.

Up in my rooms, I was faced with a problem. Evening wear generally exposes a fair bit of the arms and shoulders, and I did not think I had face-powder enough to conceal my dramatic bruises. However, fortune and Geoffrey Nesbit's Simla tailor had provided me with an alternative to evening dress. I tied the trouser cord around my waist and slid the cool silk *kameez* over my head, draping the gauzy *dupatta* loosely across my shoulders and hair. I looked approvingly at my reflection, then noticed the silver charm, a discordant note in the elegance. I dropped it under the garment's high neck, then after a moment's thought, I fetched the amber necklace from my jewellery box and fastened it around my neck.

I studied my reflection in the heavy cheval-glass: much better. Bruises decently covered, exotically festive, and I couldn't help it if I looked like a candidate for the maharaja's harem. Perhaps I should paint a vermilion mark on my forehead, to remind everyone that I was already married. I laughed to myself at the fancy, and let the shawl fall away from my hair to rest on my shoulders.

To my surprise, the maharaja claimed me as his dinner companion, so that I was seated at his right hand. A second surprise came with the meal itself, which for the first time was of strictly Oriental fare, and almost Spartan by comparison with that of the previous night. Mutton *pilau* (without an eyeball in view) and *brinjal* curry, tangy curds, spoonfuls of hot red, cool green, and sweet-and-sour brown relishes, and many unidentifiable small dishes offered all the contrasts of salty and sweet, soft and crisp, and even cold with a tangy sweet-sour frozen sherbet, with piles of buttery stuffed *paratha* bread to chew on. A few of the guests ate with their fingers, most with fork and knife, and the general atmosphere was one of calm satisfaction.

During the meal, our host offered genial conversation. The cheetah coursing had gone well, the injured beater would recover (I thought the maharaja had made enquiries especially for me), and a bag of six pigs made for a decent morning's work. Particularly our last, which he said was the biggest he'd seen that year, thirty-five inches at the shoulder and nearly two hundred fifty pounds.

"Good heavens," I said. "No wonder I'm sore."

"I shall send my masseuse," he said. "I ought to have done so immediately, how thoughtless of me."

"Oh no, a hot bath set it aright," I assured him, and hastened to insert some general question about his zoo, which he was happy to answer, and we were off.

The maharaja was skilled at the art of dinner conversation, when it suited his fancy. Before long I found myself telling him about Oxford degrees and the education of women, and he asked some intelligent questions, and seemed even to think about what I had to say, unusual enough in an Englishman. Perhaps his boredom with danger and side-show curiosities was driving him to, how had Miss Kaur put it? "Administering roads projects and building schools" in order to assuage his ennui.

We were still on the topic when the final plates were cleared. Our host gestured for the glasses to be filled again, and as that was being done, he said to me, "We shall talk further about this, Miss Russell. It is time the women of my country were taught more than forming chapatis and making *ghee*."

Then he rose with his glass held high and declared, "I should like to propose a toast. To Miss Mary Russell, the most beautiful Oxford bluestocking ever to take both first blood and a kill in the entire history of Khanpur."

I blushed furiously at the unexpectedness of it, and accepted the applause from my companions. Then I stood and raised my own glass to say, "And to our host, as deft with words as he is with his spear." I then sat down hastily.

When the meal was over, the musicians who had been playing softly in the background filed out, leaving their violins and flutes on their chairs. It appeared as if

we were to follow them, the maharaja leading us to a
room I had not been in before, somewhat smaller than
the *durbar* hall he used for dining, but none the less ornate. Its floor was strewn with carpets, rich maroons
and indigo colours that gleamed with silk, across which
had been scattered cushions and couches, and the walls
were alive with frescoes of hunts and life in palaces. The
wall nearest me showed an elephant with a tiger climbing up its side, the men on the huge beast's back fighting the cat off with spears. In the background, a pair of
English soldiers in red coat were riding furiously away,
one of them having lost his stirrups so that he was
about to tumble off his horse. My eyes followed the
paintings to the far end of the room, where the painted
musicians were echoed by their living counterparts, setting up on a low stage. Now, instead of the familiar im-
plements of chamber music, they were wielding drums
and woodwinds and stringed instruments of peculiar
construction and more peculiar sound. After a minute
or two I decided that they were merely tuning up, not
playing some spectacularly atonal piece of music.

The maharaja led me over to a floor cushion next to
Sunny Goodheart, who greeted me as a long-lost friend
in a desert wasteland. "Mary, oh, how completely great
to see you. Oh, you're wearing the necklace, how sweet!
Tell me, was it thrilling, to spear that great beast? Are
you going to have its head mounted for your wall?"

"No," I said. "Thank you." I had absolutely no wish
to keep the nightmare object as a souvenir—and I could
just imagine what Mrs Hudson would say if I walked
into the house with that tucked under my arm.

"Oh, but you should," she urged.

"It would be quite impressive," the maharaja said.
"Generally speaking, the tusks go to the man who took

first blood off a beast, but in this case you've earned them."

"If you want the head for your wall back in Chicago, Sunny, it's all yours. Unless the maharaja has other plans for it."

"Call me Jimmy, please," he told me. "And although the unique circumstances of this particular animal make it tempting, I think I have about as many boars' heads as the walls will take. Let me know if you change your mind, Miss Russell. Now, will you be comfortable here? Yes? Then enjoy your evening."

Sunny watched the maharaja's retreat to what appeared to be the men's side of the room. A jungle of hubble-bubbles rose up there, the graceful bodies wound around with their flexible tubes that held the mouthpieces, although the women's quarters had a pair of them as well, for those who cared to indulge. Gay Kaur, I noticed, had claimed a place near one of the instruments, as had the two Parisian artists Faith and Lyn.

"Mr Wilson told me it was dangerous to go after a wounded pig." Sunny's face was screwed up in worry.

"I'd have to agree."

"The word he used was 'foolish.' "

I couldn't argue with that, but if the child was waiting for some promise that I wouldn't do it again, she would not get one. After a minute, she sighed and moved on.

"Mary, what are those things?" she asked.

I followed the direction of her eyes, back to the jungle of burbling tubes. "Those are hubble-bubbles. *Hookah*s, they call them."

"Oh, yes! The caterpillar in *Alice* smokes one!"

"Er, right."

She lowered her voice, and her gaze. "Tell me . . . is it drugs?"

"Sometimes. Often it's just another way to smoke tobacco." I thought, all in all, that most of these in the room held nothing more intoxicating than pipe tobacco, although as the evening went on I did catch the occasional whiff of something stronger. "Sunny, are you enjoying your stay in Khanpur?"

"Oh yes," she replied, although her tone was not one of unrelieved ecstasy.

"What's the matter?"

"Nothing, really. Mama's wanting to go, and I have to say, although this has been just the most fantastic thing ever, it's also a little, well, strange."

The entertainments were a bit too grown-up for her, I thought; I could only hope that what was to come did not shock her bone-deep innocence further.

But in the end, the gyrations of the *nautch* girls were more athletic than erotic, and the three impossibly flexible Chinese contortionists who came onto the floor afterwards gave no reason to cover the child's eyes. Sunny imbibed more champagne than she would have if her mother had been watching, but the fizzy wine brought no more harm than high spirits and the promise of a head-ache on the morrow, so I did not interfere. She laughed at the antics of the swirling-skirted women with the heavy *kohl* on their eyes and the chorus of bells on their ankles, sat up astonished at the three slim figures tying themselves into knots, and clapped like a child half her age when a boy with a black-and-white monkey came to do tricks. Then the *nautch* girls returned, to the somewhat raucous approval from the other side of the room.

Sunny glanced over at the burst of male laughter, old

enough to know what they were reacting to, too inexperienced to know precisely why. Suddenly, I had to know the answer to a question.

"Sunny, what did the maharaja say to you that first night, that embarrassed you?"

It embarrassed her still, as a flush beyond that of wine crept down her neck. "It was just a silly joke. The kind of thing Daddy says to my girlfriends when he's had too much to drink."

"What was it?"

"Just a comment on my skin. Something about, he wondered if it was as soft all the way down."

I glanced involuntarily over at where the maharaja was reclining, the mouthpiece of a hookah in his hand, his head bent to hear something Harry Koehler was saying.

"How much longer are you stopping here?" I asked her.

"I think Mama needs to go in a couple of days. Kumaraswami is expecting her by the end of the week. Tommy wants to stay on, but I'll go with her. I don't like to think of her travelling by herself," she added virtuously, although I thought she would be glad to see the last of this place, with its uncomfortable nuances and scarcely comprehended activities.

I had to agree with Gay Kaur, that Khanpur was no place for the child. And when the evening's entertainment came to an end, I made certain that Sunny did not give in to her temptation to linger with the adults, by standing myself and patting down a yawn.

"Time for us girls to get some beauty sleep," I told her.

She looked around the beautiful room as the noise

level rose sharply, the guests chattering as noisily as a flock of bright birds in a palm tree.

"Maybe in a bit," she said. Her eyes swept over the exotic crowd, but then her anticipation faded, and she took a little step back.

I looked to see what had caused her to shy away—the maharaja himself, his eyes on us, working his way through the crowd. When he reached us, I found that I was between him and the girl, although I couldn't say whether she had moved to seek shelter, or I to provide it.

"I hope you'll join us, we have any number of games set up in the hall. Billiards, darts, cards."

"We were just saying that we felt tired, but thank you."

His eyes smiled at Sunny past my shoulder. "I hope you enjoyed today," he said.

"Oh yes," she said, a polite child again. "Very much, thank you."

"Tomorrow you must see my zoo. And you, Miss Russell. Have I made a convert of you to the art of pig sticking?"

"It was extraordinary," I admitted. All evening—in the bath, sipping my wine, watching the twirling dancers—I had found myself reliving that moment when, on the ground with the pig's tusk touching my boot, the world had come rushing back in on me. I met his gaze and said, "I've never felt anything quite like it."

His eyes held mine, and a look of—what? understanding? memory?—came into them. "The exhilaration of survival." He said it so softly I didn't think it was meant for me to hear. It was as if I had reminded him of something long forgotten.

And then he blinked, and the moment passed. "So I take it to mean that you will join us again."

"I don't know about that," I told him. "I should

think the sensation becomes less astonishing with repetition. It may be a thing that should be done once, and treasured for its uniqueness."

I wished him a good night, and steered Sunny through the crowd of guests and servants to the door. She paused to look back in, half wistful, and we both saw the maharaja watching us.

On the stairway, she said to me, "He doesn't seem entirely happy."

"The maharaja? No, he doesn't, does he?"

"But you'd think, with all this . . ." She gestured at the stones, the garden beyond, the world created for this one man's pleasure.

I didn't answer. I thought the maharaja had, in fact, looked at me with envy. And how else, if a man had arranged his entire life with the goal of excitement? He had conquered every danger he had set himself against—racing cars, aeroplanes, casino tables, dangerous game animals fought with sparse weapons; what thrills were there left to seek?

Chapter Eighteen

The morning found me aching from scalp to soles, and I nearly asked the *chuprassi* who brought the tea tray to fetch me strong drink, or a nice dose of morphia. But then I noticed the thick white envelope tucked under the saucer, which proved to be a note written by the same elegant hand that produced the daily schedule:

His Highness will see you at nine o'clock for a tour of Khanpur zoo. Please meet him in the toy room.

Under those circumstances, intoxication did not seem a good idea, so I waved the servant away and tottered into the bath-room to switch on the geyser. At least with a gentle walking tour of the maharaja's zoo, I might avoid too much sitting on my black-and-blue posterior.

The bath loosened me enough to dress and take a

gentle turn through the gardens, where the combination of motion and crisp, fresh air had me moving almost normally as I turned for the dining room. Half a dozen of my fellow guests were there, distributed among three tables. I waved to Faith and Lyn but chose a seat near the novelist Trevor Wilson, whose presence in Khanpur interested me. I eased myself onto the chair, murmured a greeting, and opened his discarded copy of the previous day's *Pioneer*. When he'd had a few minutes to become accustomed to my presence, I pushed the paper away as if weary of the world's problems.

"Mr Wilson, pardon me, but you've been here for quite a while, I believe you said? It's just that I was thinking of taking a walk into the city this afternoon, and wondered if there was anything you could suggest that I see there?"

"I'm not much of one for sight-seeing," he answered, then proceeded to list for me a dozen sights that should not be missed, encompassing as he did so a fairly comprehensive history of Khanpur. I kept my gaze on him as he spoke, nodding and exclaiming occasionally to keep him going. We spoke of Moghul ruins and inheritance rights for a while as I slowly worked the conversation around to what I was really interested in.

"So, how long have you actually been here?"

"Eighteen months, more or less."

"I imagine you'll have enough material for half a dozen books, by the time you leave."

He couldn't hide a wince, although whether at the idea of leaving or of writing, I couldn't be certain. "Oh, exotic adventure stories aren't exactly my bailiwick." The book of his that I had read comprised two hundred pages of hallucination, internal monologue, and sexual reminiscences on the part of a young man who lay in hospital after having been sent down from Cambridge, joined the Communist Party, and been knocked unconscious by a police baton during a violent march in Trafalgar Square.

"No," I said, "of course not. But your writing seems to be concerned with people and their struggle for"—I nearly said *integrity,* but changed it at the last moment—"independence. It occurred to me that the context of an Indian 'native state' would give a writer of your calibre considerable scope. The political world in microcosm."

He stared at me, either because he hadn't thought of such a topic, or because he hadn't thought anyone else would. Finally he pulled himself together enough to say, "Microcosm, yes."

"I mean to say, the maharaja seems a benevolent enough dictator, but still, one has to ask oneself about the people living under him. Take the poor coolies yesterday, one of them was rather badly hurt by a boar, and all because we—"

But Trevor Wilson was not listening. His gaze had gone inward, and he abruptly stood and dropped his table napkin on his plate. He took two steps away before his manners recalled him enough to turn back and say, "Excuse me, Miss, er . . ." Then he was gone, leaving me staring open-mouthed at his retreating back. So much for my idea of picking the brain of the maharaja's secretary for his master's inner thoughts.

Faith and Lyn had finished their meal, and paused by my table on their way to the terrace. "More pigs today?" Faith asked, a sparkle in her eye.

I laughed. "I don't think I could even look at a horse for another couple of days. His Highness is showing me the zoo this morning, but I thought maybe this afternoon I might walk into the city and have a look at the bazaar."

"Would you like some company?"

"I'd love it. Shall I send word, when I've returned from admiring the bison and orangutans?"

"That would be fine."

"I won't be joining you," Lyn said. "I have a date with a novel."

Not, I noted, with a piece of sculpture. I finished my coffee, glancing through a copy of *The Times* that was only three days old. A few minutes before nine o'clock, I presented myself to the *chuprassi* outside my door for guidance to the "toy room."

We set off as if going to the main block with the *durbar* hall and ball-room, but continued on to the western wing, mostly hidden from the gardens by large trees. Its shaded arcade was chilly, the marble floor damp enough to require caution in places. The electrical lights that brightened the guest quarters, it appeared, had not extended here, and a faint odour of lamp-oil betrayed the means of illumination.

We travelled for nearly ten minutes around the great inner garden and down the twisting passages before the *chuprassi* stopped at a door that had been painted a startling blue. He held it open, then closed it behind me; I was alone.

"Hallo?" I said. There was no answer, although the back of my neck prickled, as if I were being watched. The room's only light came from a shaft of sun through a high window; it shone onto more purdah screens—they seemed to be a feature of the Fort architecture, although this maharaja's ladies lived in town. By the dim reflected light, I peered around me, trying to make out the room's contents. That it contained a great deal was immediately clear, but it seemed more the clutter of a storage room than a used living space, and I looked in vain for an electric switch to throw light on the matter.

"Toy room," the note had said. And hadn't Nesbit's brief biography of the family mentioned that the previous ruler, the current maharaja's grandfather, was an enthusiastic collector of mechanical oddities? With that hint, my eyes began to adjust to the gloom and pick out its contents.

The first figure to come into focus appeared to explain the sensation of being watched: a full-sized suit of armour, parked at the other side of the door. So strong had the feeling been that, half embarrassed, I flipped up the visor to be certain, but there was no face behind it, only cobwebs.

The overall texture to my left proved to be an entire wall of open shelves, laden from floor to the ceiling fifteen feet above with metal wind-up toys of all makes, conditions, and vintages. White-painted Indian cows and German birds in nests, tigers and horse-drawn carriages, clowns and Victorian gentlemen. A lady in the dress of the nineties sat at an elaborately painted tea table, one hand frozen halfway between table and lip—although on closer examination the hand held, not a tea cup, but a cigarette: shocking. Next to this iconoclastic figure, a roughly clad and bearded man awaited a turn of the key to resume his chopping of firewood. And here was one that brought back my childhood with a thump—a tin boy on a pennyfarthing bicycle, identical (if in better condition) to my father's childhood toy, given to me when I was five. Life in a myriad of forms, all with keys in their backs or on the shelves beside them, all frozen and awaiting the animation of tension on their mainsprings.

When I returned the pennyfarthing boy to his place, I was surprised to feel dust on my fingers, although the air smelt faintly of machine oil. The room was maintained, but not tidied.

My eyes had adjusted sufficiently to trust myself not to bump into something, so I pressed on into the room. Scattered across the floor, looking as if they had been unloaded there rather than arranged, were display cases, some of which contained larger machines such as those in fun fairs near the sea. As I threaded my way across the room I saw at least six fortune-tellers, two of them old gipsy women, the others turbanned swamis, all set to different coinages. In two machines, the customer's coin seemed to produce nothing more thrilling than a circuit of a train through a painted landscape, with a duck-laced pond here, a mountain tunnel there. No doubt the whistle blew several times during the circuit.

Behind the smaller display cases rose four enormous constructions of mahogany and plate glass, their contents more diorama than mechanism. At first the figures within appeared to be dolls about six inches in height, but on closer examination, underneath their costumes they proved to be specimens of taxidermy art. Most of the creatures were furry, blunt-faced rodents with no tails to speak of and short ears—a variety of guinea pig, perhaps. One case held perhaps thirty of the things, posed on their hind legs and dressed for a formal ball, half of them in white tie, the others wearing silk or velvet, with diamonds on their hairy throats and diminutive champagne glasses clasped in their upraised paws. The second case represented, I assumed, a box at the Ascot races: A dozen of the creatures clutched tiny binoculars and wore elaborate spring hats. The third was a night-club, with dancers on a stage, their furry bodies graced with strips of costume and feathers perkily jutting from their heads. The fourth case held eight infant piglets, of the pale domesticated kind, gathered in a Victorian conservatory around a laden tea table; something about their attitudes made it seem a cruel parody of society at the time—English society, that is.

As elaborate pieces of humour, they were most emphatically not to my taste. I thought it more than a little perverse, in fact, to raise a hundred small creatures just for the purpose of being transformed into facsimile human beings.

Along the back wall of the room a trace of gravel on the floor gave further evidence of the paucity of attentive servants in this place. (And as for their master, I thought, where was the maharaja, anyway? I'd been well after nine o'clock getting here, thanks to the unexpected distance between my rooms and this place.) Farther along, nearly in the corner, I came across the collection's more, well, esoteric contraptions. The first startled me by appearing to be a man; this, on closer examination, proved to be what he was, a life-sized wax-work Englishman in the uniform of the Crimean War, complete with musket. I supposed he fired it when animated. He had been placed, possibly by accident, as if to stand guard over a cluster of glass-cased boxes, although these had neither gipsies nor swamis, and one glance made me glad I did not have the requisite tokens for putting them in motion. The women had skin that was uniformly pink and pearly, the men ranged from white to a darker shade of English pink, and all of them were comprehensively nude. I shook my head and turned to retrace my steps to the door, and nearly shrieked at the silent and unpainted figure ten feet away.

"Heavens!" I said, my heart pounding. "Your Highness, I'm sorry, I didn't hear you come in."

"My grandfather's collection. And I do wish you'd call me Jimmy."

"They're . . . extraordinary."

"Do you want to see them work?"

"Oh no," I said, more hastily than I had intended.

He laughed. "Not those, no. He was a dirty old man, my grandfather. Here, let me show you one I rather like."

He slipped through a part of the room I hadn't got to yet, ending up not far from the door. Before him stood a particularly magnificent carved wooden plinth about waist height, on which stood a foot-tall mechanical contraption and a perfect little celadon bowl holding half a dozen old-fashioned coins. The maharaja took one of them and pushed it through a slot on the wooden base.

With a creak that I at first thought was the protest of disuse, the machine began to move. But it was not a creak, it was a mechanical simulation of a roar, because the creature was a tiger. Its tail wagged and its legs began to carry it forward to where a man in red uniform lay. It stopped—a marvelously complex piece of clockwork, this, considering its obvious great age—and bent to the man, seizing him in its great jaws. The man kicked, the tiger's tail wagged, the geriatric roaring went on.

The maharaja was watching me watch his tiger, and

although it was too dim in there to be sure, I thought the man smiled.

"This is magnificent," I told him, my voice rather louder than it needed be. "I've seen something of the sort, in London."

"Tipoo's Tiger, in your Victoria and Albert Museum. A smaller, less sophisticated version. My grandfather saw it, liked it, and had this made. Two years after the Mutiny, in fact."

That took me aback. A man who had made a clear gesture of loyalty to the British, and had been lavishly rewarded for his brutal but effective actions, less than two years later commissions a piece showing a British soldier chewed to bits by an Indian tiger.

"Did your grandfather show this to many of his English visitors?" I asked.

The man at my side laughed, pleased that I had understood the underlying jest. "Not many, no. Come, it is too nice a day to be closed in this stuffy room."

Stuffy, I thought as I followed him out the door, it was not. Uncanny, perhaps. Even macabre.

The sun was a welcome antidote.

Four others waited for us in the gardens, watching as a servant scattered food over the lotus pond to bring a school of exotic white and golden carp to the surface. It was not until I saw my fellow guests that it struck me how odd the means of my retrieval had been. Why have me go first to the room of mechanical toys, when the others had clearly been told to gather near the pond? And beyond that, why had a servant not fetched me back here, instead of the prince himself? I could only assume that my host had wanted me to see his grandfather's machines, and me alone; and moreover, he had wanted to see my reaction to them.

I did not know what this meant. Perhaps, I told myself, it was just that he'd wanted to keep Sunny Goodheart's innocent eyes from the erotic devices and the small furry creatures, for Sunny was one of those at the pond. Or maybe it was something about me that promoted me above the others. As an honorary member of the pig-sticking fraternity, were my sensibilities hardened beyond those of most women? I decided to prod, gently.

"Your Highness, why—"

"Please, call me Jimmy."

"Jimmy, then. Why not display the machines more openly? It's an extraordinary collection."

He continued walking, until I thought he was not going to answer. Then, just out of earshot of the others, he said, "I am a public figure. I like to keep some things to myself, and a few chosen friends."

Then the others were with us: Sunny, her brother, the Kentish polo-player (whose name was, I thought, Robbins), and a tall, silent woman I had seen but hadn't realised was his wife. We walked across the courtyard to the gate, where we were joined by three merry salukis, and a pair of armed guards fell in behind us. The dogs raced ahead down the road that circled New Fort, their plumed tails adding a touch of gaiety, although the maharaja ignored their antics entirely. At the base of the hill we continued around, as I had done the first day, although instead of going on to the stables, the salukis flashed down a tree-lined set of steps leading to the left, in the direction of a growing chorus of jungle noises. In moments, a great uproar was heard from the tall monkey-house.

"The monkeys don't seem to care for the dogs," I noted.

"Oh, they don't mind them so much. But the dogs signal my arrival, which always causes excitement."

Then the steps gave way to a pathway of crisp, white gravel, and we were in the Khanpur zoological gardens.

It was, indeed, a zoo, with cages and paths, but considerable aesthetic attention had been paid, and the areas behind the bars resembled landscape rather than merely concrete and iron boxes to hold the specimens. The lions watched us from a little piece of Africa, a cunningly constructed rock wall with ledges and caves wrapped around by heavy bars; on the other side of their enclosure half a dozen varieties of African herbivore ran free, zebras and wildebeests and even, hiding in a far corner, a pair of wan-looking giraffes. The monkey-cage was the height of a three-storey building, and although the trees inside had long since been stripped to dead trunk, a natural-looking waterfall welled up from a pile of rocks in the centre of the cage, and the tall trees outside of the cage provided shelter to the inhabitants.

Sunny was nearly speechless with pleasure, exclaiming over the glimpse of a baby monkey and clapping her hands together at the lemurs, who looked disgruntled at being prodded from their rest by a servant.

The most startling thing, at first glance, was the collection of servants tending the animals. They bore the skin tones and facial characteristics of peoples from across the world—Asia, Africa, Scandinavia—but not one of them was taller than four feet: These were the inhabitants of the dwarf village Gay Kaur had referred to. And sure enough, between the cages and the sprawling plain filled with African wildlife lay a pseudo-African village whose proportions were at first disconcerting, the height of its grass huts and the size of its residents making it appear farther away than reason permitted.

I thought it somewhat tasteless to house this particular group of servants alongside the zoo they tended, as if they were a part of it, but I supposed it was no stranger than the archaic European fashion of importing Nubian boys as decorative pages and footmen. Certainly, the small people seemed pleased enough with their lot, bustling officiously along the white paths and giving brisk orders to *chuprassi*s twice their size. I tore my eyes from the shrunken village and joined the others at the lion cage.

I often think that caged predators are kept alive by their deep inner fantasies of ripping apart the two-legged creatures outside their bars. It would explain their habit of watching our movements from beneath half-lowered eyelids, as if tempting us to venture too near. These, no less than their brothers in Regent's Park, seemed to be salivating at the proximity of their small attendants, and I had no doubt that they would be even happier to make a fuller meal should, say, a royal personage stray close. The maharaja, however, kept his distance, although he did take us into the building behind the cage so that we could look through thick, smeary windows at the great dun carnivores lying in the shade two feet away. I could practically feel the heat rising off them; when one of the females stretched luxuriously and her claws scraped on the stone floor, more than one of us shivered.

The dogs were snuffling in the bushes behind the building, but the maharaja called them sharply back, and indeed, this white path ended at the door to the lion building. Instead, we retraced our steps into the central area, past the cages of hippopotamus and wart hog, finally going into a low stone building with pens behind it. The inside was light and, despite the smell of animals, well kept. The maharaja led us over to a small, glass-fronted cage built at chest height into one wall; I, being taller than most of them, had no problem in seeing what he was doing.

The cage contained a single slim, short-haired creature resembling a cross between a cat and a ferret, with clever hand-like paws and a wise-looking face. More of the creatures could be seen in the open-air pen attached to the outside of the building, many perched upright on their hind legs, watching their trapped comrade through the intervening glass with worried expressions. They were clearly perturbed, making quick forays in and out of their burrows, sitting up, chattering to one another. But the one inside was nearly frantic, for the maharaja had inserted his arm into the cage through a small trap-door, on his hand a glove-like puppet the shape and colour of a dove.

"You see?" he was saying. "They have an instinctive fear of birds, even harmless ones such as this. I have been trying to overcome this instinct by invariably feeding them with a hand concealed inside a dove, but time and again they panic, and need to be hungry to the brink of starvation in order to overcome their fear of a thing with wings."

As he lectured, he glanced at Sunny, whose reflection in the glass showed her face twisted with an agitation nearly as great as that of the animals imprisoned outside.

"Oh, don't tease it!" she pleaded. "The poor thing, it's—"

Her interruption had caused the maharaja's attention to shift, with the result that his hand dipped inside the cage. The small creature, wild with the terror of this perceived attack, leapt to defend itself. In a tan blur, the thin body flew up and attached itself to the dove, biting down furiously. With a bellow of pain, our host shook his hand hard. Puppet and creature slapped into the side of the cage, and the animal lay there, stunned, unable to defend itself from the bare, blood-smeared hand that snatched it up by the scruff of the neck and hauled it from the cage.

The creatures outside had vanished, the holes in the ground looking empty and bereft.

The maharaja held up the creature, studying its faint struggles. And then he snapped its neck.

Sunny fled outside, Thomas and Mrs Robbins moving to comfort her while Mr Robbins protested. "I say, was that really necessary?"

But the maharaja's eyes followed Sunny, as they had been on Sunny since the moment he drew the creature from its cage. He had done it deliberately, I realised incredulously, just as he had showed me the Englishman-eating tiger and the obscene mechanicals. He had forced the captive to bite his hand precisely in order to demonstrate cruelty to this girl, little more than a child, who thought him "dreamy" and romantic.

Tossing the limp body into the cage, he strode out into the sunlight in pursuit of the girl and her comforters. There he apologised, he explained, he charmed, until poor Sunny found herself agreeing reluctantly that an animal that bit couldn't be permitted to live, too confused by the varying faces of our host to remember that he himself had tormented the poor creature into attacking. He was most solicitous the rest of the tour, allowing her to feed a baby elephant, giving her and Mrs Robbins wide hats so they might walk through the aviary with its flashing tumble of colours and screeches, and finally making her the present of a sleek infant mongoose, an endearing slip of a creature that snuffled into the girl's neck and hands before curling up in her pocket to sleep.

By the time we retraced our steps around the Fort and through the gates, even Sunny's protective older brother appeared to have forgotten, or forgiven, the dull crack of the spine within the maharaja's fingers.

After the morning's unsettling events, I was tempted to remain in my rooms, thinking. However, the idea of a long walk, and of being free of The Forts for several hours, was too appealing, so with the sun high in the sky, Faith and I swung out happily from the gates. I paused to lean over the waist-high stone wall that separated the upper section of the drive from the precipitous hill. There was, I noticed, a vestigial sort of path leading straight down to the main road, duplicated on the other side by an almost imperceptible smooth line leading up the other side to the gate of the eastern fort. Worn by guards too hurried to follow the winding road, I thought; certainly no threat to the security of New Fort itself.

When we had doubled back to the main road, a movement behind us caused me to look back.

"Hell," I said. "There's someone coming after us."

Faith glanced over her shoulder and kept walking. "Just one of the guards. Don't worry about him."

"But I don't want a guard."

"You don't have a choice. If you're Jimmy's guest, he has you looked after."

The man, red-turbanned and uniformed, complete

with a sidearm in a belt-holster, had stopped dead when I came to a halt and looked back at him. When I reluctantly started up again, he followed at the same distance.

"Maybe we'll lose him in the bazaar," I told Faith.

"You'd better hope for his sake we don't," she answered.

"The maharaja takes guarding his guests seriously, then?"

"Oh, yes."

"All right. I wouldn't want the fellow to lose his job."

"Or his head," she added. She was joking, of course. I turned my back on the man, physically and mentally, and determined to enjoy the outing.

Snow-capped peaks lay on three sides of the valley that was Khanpur, brisk contrast to the near-tropical crops that grew alongside the road, the sugar cane and new-planted melons. Men worked the fields, women swayed beneath loads of copper water-jugs and cloth-wrapped bundles, children wielding cane switches urged goats and cattle from the cultivated land, and Faith and I strode along talking, our armed escort an unvarying two hundred yards to the rear.

Faith had been here for a little more than three months, she and Lyn having met the maharaja in Paris the previous September. He had seen Lyn's work at a gallery and showed up one day at their door, toured their studio, and commissioned them to do some projects for him in Khanpur. The only problem was, once they got here, one hindrance after another had fallen across their path. The maharaja had not been here when they arrived; then he'd returned, but been too busy to consult with them. And when he'd finally been able to bend his attention to their projects, it turned out that what he had in mind was some sort of collaboration between what they were accustomed to doing and a traditional Indian style. And Faith had to admit, learning Indian techniques of painting and sculpture was fascinating, and no doubt valuable for the future, and the maharaja was extremely generous with his hospitality and advance payments for works not even begun. She shouldn't complain, and she wasn't, exactly, but she could wish she didn't get the feeling that she and Lyn would sink up to their knees here and grow old eating lotus and sleeping beneath silk bedsheets.

Listening to her, I wondered if all native princes were surrounded with as many hangers-on as Khanpur's seemed to be, stray novelists and feckless wanderers caught in the honey-trap of palace life. Thank goodness, I said to myself, I should soon be on my way.

The capital of Khanpur was a walled and dusty town of perhaps six thousand souls, fields nearly to its gates, blessedly free of the stench of human waste—as Geoffrey Nesbit had said, the country was noted for the advanced state of its sanitation. The buildings were the usual jumble of Moghul masterpieces and tacked-on petrol-tin shanties, but the dogs wandering its crowded streets had a modicum of flesh over their ribs, and few of the children were completely naked.

As two Englishwomen, we were the immediate target of every salesman in the town, and offers for carpets and jewellery came fast and heavy. The beggars more or less left us alone, perhaps because of the red-turbanned figure who, once inside the gates, had moved up until he was close to our heels. We did our best to ignore his presence. Faith led me to the Palace proper, where the maharaja's womenfolk lived—his two wives, dozen concubines, and eight or nine children, according to Nesbit. We could see little but high walls and, in glimpses through the iron gate, trees and the occasional patch of brilliant white marble, so we kept moving through the upper city, into ever-narrower alleys, more or less following our noses until we came to the bazaar itself.

Because Khanpur was well away from the tourist routes, the bazaar offered little beyond the wants of its inhabitants, its luxury goods running more along the lines of astrakhan caps and golden brocades than carvings of Shiva and mass-produced bronze Ganeshas. Faith paused at a silk merchant's to finger a length of iridescent green fabric; my attention was caught by an ash-smeared holy man seated nearby: I myself had only been in Khanpur little more than forty-eight hours, and it was unreasonable to expect Holmes this soon; still, I examined him closely.

"I loved the garment you wore yesterday night," Faith said, as oblivious of the shopkeeper's lively attentions as she was of my inattention. "I was thinking of having one made for Lyn. What do you think of this colour?"

"Sorry?" The near-naked *sadhu* had a matted beard and wore his hair gathered into a snake's nest atop his head; he sat motionless on a scrap of what had once been a leopard skin, a brass begging bowl next to one of his folded knees: No, it was not Holmes in disguise. I turned back to Faith, retrieving her words from the back of my mind. "That colour would be beautiful. And the maroon over there would do wonders for you."

In the end, she bought lengths of both, arranging that they be sent to New Fort. "Jimmy has a tailor who can sew pretty much whatever a person wants," she told me. "I've seen him produce an evening gown from a pencil sketch."

We bought a bangle here, a handful of dried mulberries there, following the curving streets down towards the river, Faith talking while I studied every passing veiled woman over five and a half feet tall, but again, none of them were Holmes. Eventually the buildings fell away, revealing an open square of pavement with a few weedy trees. A shrine occupied one corner, its deity unidentifiable under the heaps of wilting marigolds and the smears of blood-red dye; in the opposite corner a silent circle of men stared down at a cow, which lay panting in a manner that did not bode well. I was wondering what city-dwelling Hindus did with cows that died, whether they just stood back and let the vultures in or if they found someone to drag it away, when my speculations were interrupted by Faith.

"Oh, look," she said. "A magician. Shall we go see?"

I looked: dramatic black garments, shiny fat donkey, a magnificently painted and mirrored little wagon that had once pulled English children, a great eye now gracing its front.

Sherlock Holmes had arrived in Khanpur.

Chapter Nineteen

Holmes was just coming to the end of the prelimi-
nary part of the act, the flashy tricks and joking
patter designed to capture an audience. He drew glittering balls from the air, made others vanish from sight,
and caused one to burst into flame, its ashes floating upwards on the breeze. Young Bindra was nowhere in
sight, and Holmes' face looked tired to gauntness beneath the dye.

When he had brought together a sufficient number,
he turned to the mind-reading portion. Faith's Hindi
was limited to "How much is it?" and "Get away from
me," but the magician's gestures and the reaction of his
impromptu partners was entertainment enough. After
he had astonished by perceiving a number of unknow-
able things about five or six of the men (the process of
deductive reasoning working as well in this setting as it
did in London), he caused a deck of playing cards to appear, and proceeded to guess which was in a person's
hand (as if Sherlock Holmes would stoop to guessing!).

In the smaller villages, he had used coins, but in a large town, playing cards would be common enough to be used for the trick. Again, Faith could not understand what either he or his partners were saying, but there was no mistaking their declarations of astonishment.

When the man in the black garments had magically transformed the entire deck into black aces, then flung it into the air to float down as fifty-two ebony feathers, he came around with a small bronze bowl. Faith and I dropped silver rupees on top of the annas; I held the grey eyes for a moment, warning him not to speak. But he had already seen the armed guard, and he merely *salaam*ed us and passed on.

We left him there and headed back into the bazaar. At the narrowest spot, when Faith stopped to take a closer look at a necklace she had been fingering earlier, I spoke into her ear.

"I just want to check something—I'll meet you at the main gates in ten minutes," and before she could object, I ducked my head down so our escort couldn't see me, stepped behind a water-seller, and scurried away. At the next corner, I craned to see, but Faith was talking to the shopkeeper about the necklace, and the guard had not yet realised that I was no longer with her.

Holmes was seated on the ground in the shade of the wagon, counting his money, when I slid in beside him. He'd changed his Moslem cap for a black *puggaree,* tied elaborately with its starched end sticking up, and the thin moustache he'd grown since we parted in Simla added a rakish touch to his exoticism.

"Greetings, *memsahib*," he told me.

"Holmes, you certainly got here quickly. Where's Bindra?"

"It would seem that the same Delhi astrologer who

instructed the boy to go with the two Mussalman gentlemen also warned him against entering Khanpur. Our young apprentice remained at the border, swearing to all the gods that he would wait there for me."

"Wait there! So you've been doing all the work yourself, the donkey and everything?" The magician shrugged, and I muttered, "I'll take off my shoe and give the brat *thapad*."

"What do you make of the maharaja?" he asked, and he was right, we had time only for urgent business.

"Holmes, he's . . . I don't know, he's an enigma. It may simply be the circumstances of his upbringing, but he's thoughtful one minute and horribly cruel the next. An honest sportsman who apparently cheats at cards, a man who surrounds himself with artists and then keeps them from working, who is hugely generous with his hospitality but won't let his guests out without watch-dogs. I have to get back," I added, "before mine panics. And there's a strange assortment of people at The Forts. He hired a best-selling novelist for a secretary; has two lesbian artists so avant-garde they make Epstein look staid, whom he's commissioned to do works better done by an Indian; there are a couple of criminal types doing heaven knows what—remember the man Harry Koehler? He's lived here for a year. The odd Communist like Thomas Goodheart. And me, whom he's trying to convince to take on a project involving the education of Khanpur women. 'Pets' for his amusement, his cousin calls them. And a collection of individuals poached from side-shows, dwarfs and albinos. The dwarfs live down at the zoo, which I saw this morning. His treatment of the animals there is . . . troubling."

"Cruelty?" he asked, coming alert. He knew, better

than I, that a man who mistreats dumb beasts is apt to do the same to his human subjects. And I would have told him all about the zoo, if we hadn't been so short of time. I'm sure I would have told him, if it wasn't that I needed to think about it myself first. And if I didn't know that if I described the maharaja's act of cruelty, Holmes would become very nervous and would try to convince me that I shouldn't return to The Forts. One thing I did not need at the moment was a nervous husband.

"Nothing extreme. It's more that he's experimenting to see if he can reshape their natures."

"The lion lying down with the lamb?"

"No, more along the lines of convincing the lamb to become a lion."

He thought about this for a moment, then to my relief, pushed it away for future consideration. "No sign of O'Hara?"

"If he's here, he's in the Old Fort. Have you seen the way The Forts are laid out?"

"I have."

"The western half is where all the guests live, there's a huge courtyard garden, the maharaja's quarters. But the eastern part isn't deserted—one occasionally sees guards on the walls. If the maharaja had a dungeon, it would probably be there, where the guests wouldn't stumble on it."

"Is there any way you can get in?"

"New Fort is locked up at night, although a circumspect individual might come and go. I don't know about the other side, but it, too, looks the sort of place that might be invaded by one or two."

"How much longer do you wish to stay?"

"Honestly, I can't see that I'm going to uncover

much more than I have. Another day or two, perhaps? And, if you can arrange it, a telegram recalling me to the outside world might be helpful. My host seems reluctant to permit his guests to leave."

"Very well. If I'm not here, I'll be half a mile down the Hijarkot road, there's a caravanserai there. You'd better go or your watch-dog will come looking for you."

I threaded my fingers through his, and we sat for a moment, eye to eye and hands joined, before I separated myself from his presence to dart from the shade of the wagon and into the nearest alleyway. I reached the city gates before Faith; our sweating guard was greatly relieved to see me. We strolled demurely back to the palace, and allowed ourselves to be shut in again.

∽⟨7⟩∽

The telegram came the following morning, Friday, and said merely, MARY RUSSELL PRESENCE REQUIRED MONDAY MORNING DELHI. It was brought while I was at breakfast; I took it from the golden salver and opened it publicly, arranging a look of intense irritation on my face before wadding the flimsy and dropping it beside my fork. I left it there when I went to watch the morning's entertainment, which proved to be a doubles tennis-match between dwarfs. Some of the guests seemed to think it uproariously funny, although I found that once my eyes had adjusted to the diminutive size of the players, it was just another amateur game. Perhaps the afternoon's ostrich race would be more amusing, I thought, and closed my eyes in the sun.

My doze was interrupted by a cleared throat, and I opened my eyes to find a *chuprassi* clutching a note. It read,

Miss Russell, would you join me in the gun-room.

Its signature was the letter K, with a stamp that I thought might be the crest of Khanpur. I stood up and said, "Could you tell me how to find the gun-room?"

The *chuprassi* conducted me to New Fort's east wing, where the maharaja's private quarters lay. We entered through a brightly gilded archway just to the left of the gates, and within half a dozen steps, my jaw dropped. I had grown accustomed to the grand opulence of the central wing, but the corridor we walked down, the rooms whose open doors we passed, were another thing altogether. Here were unlocked display cabinets of exquisite miniatures, ivory and gold, beside paintings that any museum in Europe would covet. In one room, I saw Louis XIV furniture, clearly in daily use; in another room stood a display of trophies and photographs, including the one for the 1922 Kadir Cup that I had seen in Nesbit's house. I tried not to gawp as we walked past, but my head swivelled unceasingly.

It was a revelation. These paintings, those trophies, had been placed here for the sole pleasure of one man, not as a way of impressing his guests—these fragile carpets took no concern of the wear of many feet, and the rooms had been arranged for his privacy and comfort, not for the appreciation of groups. The maharaja clearly enjoyed—even gloated over—his possessions, but he kept the true treasures to himself.

At the very end of the long corridor, the *chuprassi* opened a door and bowed me through; once inside, I stopped dead.

I do not know what was more disconcerting, the completely muffled sound in the room or its dim light, but one's immediate response on entering the room was a frisson of alertness up the spine. Perhaps it was some trace aroma of the predator all around that made one go still, not even breathing, until the only motion to defy the room's smothering atmosphere was the hair creeping upright on one's skin. In any case, it wasn't until one's eyes became used to the light that the sensation of entering a lair became strong. And perhaps a full minute had to pass before the eyes told one why.

The walls, floor to ceiling, were covered in tiger fur. Black and orange stripes, running first in this direction, then that, fitted together like a jigsaw puzzle, seamless but for a faint rectangular shape in the back wall. In the upper corners of the room, clustered and snarling, were mounted the heads.

I shuddered in reaction, and someone chuckled, the sound damped and muffled.

I whirled, and there was the maharaja, sitting in a chair of unrelieved black. Panther, my mind informed me; and the fluffy black-and-gold rug on which his boots were resting was made of the tails of the tigers on the wall. I swallowed convulsively, whether to repress fear or visceral disgust, I was not sure.

The maharaja rose from his panther-skin chair and walked over to a table that appeared made of grey-painted wood, and on closer look proved to have a texture. It was covered in elephant hide, I realised, and somehow that final outrage tipped me over the edge, and I was suddenly icy calm.

"I have something for you," he said. "Since you did not wish the boar's head for your wall, I had this small souvenir made, a memento of your first pig-hunt."

I looked apprehensively at the velvet-covered box he was holding out to me, and kept my hands at my sides. "That's really not necessary."

So he opened it himself and turned it for me to see.

Since Wednesday's hunt, he had somehow contrived to have all four tusks of the boar removed and handed over to a goldsmith for mounting. The object before me had a central shaft as long as a hand, made of heavy, deep-red gold that had been intricately worked with a design I recognised from the stamp on the note that had brought me here, the crest of Khanpur. From the gleaming metal protruded the tusks, the shorter pair curving up from the bottom, the longer upper tusks rising from the shaft above them to curl together, nearly forming a circle above the gold. The tusks themselves had not been touched, aside from their removal, and looked as they had when they came to rest on the ground near my foot: the ivory as yellowed as a smoker's teeth, the tip of the upper left one snapped off and worn blunt, even the dried spatter of blood that had been burned into my memory when the beast had been struggling to eviscerate me. The art of the goldsmith had been linked to these brutal tools for digging and killing, man's most intricate craftsmanship used to set off all the nicks, grime, and blood that Nature had provided.

It was quite the ugliest thing I had ever seen in my life.

Beyond its mere appearance, the ornament was repugnant on any number of levels: aesthetically, yes, but also emotionally, in its attempt to create beauty from what was essentially a grisly extermination; theologically, in its glorification of the uncleanest of animals; even politically, that in a poor land, so much gold should be used for a frivolity. The maharaja of Khanpur held the box out to me, willing me to take it. I did so, reluctantly, then laid it immediately upon the elephant-hide table.

Satisfied, he went around the desk and sat down behind it, gesturing me to the chair on the other side. Since this appeared to be merely wood, not bison's leg-bones or stiffened cobras, I sat down in it. He crossed his legs and said, "I wanted to have a further conversation with you about your proposal for women's education."

I had made no such proposal, but there seemed little point in arguing with him. Instead, I said, "Yes, I'm sorry about that, but it appears as if I'll have to abandon it for the moment. I've been called back to Delhi. I'll need to leave tomorrow."

His eyes narrowed, but I could see that the news came as no surprise. Indeed, I should have been amazed if it had.

"Oh, Miss Russell—Mary—you must stay. We're going after tiger on Sunday, you can't possibly miss that." The firmness in his voice left no room for contradiction, yet contradict I did.

"That is a disappointment," I replied, although it was all I could do to keep from looking at the walls and asking him if enough damage had not been done to the state's feline population. "But my husband is expecting me, and truth to tell, he's quite capable of sending someone after me if I don't show up. You'll just have to take the tiger for me."

"But you did promise to look at the schools here," he said, which again I most emphatically had not. He kept his voice even, reasonable, although it seemed something of an effort. The maharaja was not accustomed to being crossed.

"Yes, I suppose I did. Perhaps I can return, when

we're finished in Delhi. It's just, well, my husband can't do this particular piece of business without my presence."

His eyes darkened, and he rose to come around the desk, standing over me in a clear attempt to force me into obedience. Another woman might have been cowed, but another woman was not Mary Russell; another woman had not spent nine years in the company of Sherlock Holmes. I set myself against the waves of domination and anger coming from him, bracing to repulse him if he decided to hit me. He managed to keep control, though, and merely said in a rather strangled voice, "I'm afraid the aeroplane is not available until the end of the week."

"What a pity. Well, perhaps I can find a motor to take me to Hijarkot." From the sudden, hot anger in his face, a free car anywhere in the country would be no more forthcoming than the aeroplane. I stood up, forcing him to retreat a step. "In any case, I thank you for your hospitality. I've had a most interesting time here, and appreciate it hugely."

His voice stopped me at the door, saying my name. I looked back; he had the velvet box in his hand.

"There is an interesting fact about pigs," he observed, his voice gone silky soft. "The killing tusks are not the prominent upper ones, but the smaller, more hidden pair beneath."

I looked from his expressionless face to the box, and in the end I took the thing, walking back across the tiger-lined lair to do so. I took it because to refuse would have forced the issue of my rebellion into the open, with unforeseen consequences. Perhaps I took it because the smell of predator was strong in my nostrils, and I was afraid. I am not sure precisely why I allowed my fingers to close around the box containing that freakish object, but of one thing I was absolutely certain: I would not hold on to it any longer than I had to.

I closed the gun-room door, and stood for a moment in the hall-way, breathing hard, feeling the dampness on my palms and scalp, unable to say why I felt as if I had just put a door between me and a live tiger.

I had two visitors during the afternoon. First came Faith, whose gentle knock I missed at first, busy as I was with folding away my clothes. When it came a second time, I realised what it was and went to open the door.

"Hallo," I said, "do come in. Why is it one's things never seem to go back into the same space they originally occupied?"

"Mary, please don't go," she said without preamble, sounding upset.

I sat down beside my pile of folded blouses. "Faith, I've been away for a week. I have a life to return to."

She laughed, a sound with little humour in it. "Yes, don't we all?"

"Faith," I asked slowly, "are you being kept here . . . against your will?" It sounded too melodramatic for words, especially considering the woman I was talking to, and she reacted as I might have done.

"Don't be ridiculous. Although I suppose you could say—Oh, it's too complicated to explain! No," she asserted, suddenly firm. "Nobody's being kept against their will. This is the twentieth century, not some feudal state. But Jimmy's touchy sometimes, and one thing he hates is to think his generosity is unappreciated. You're an honoured guest, and for you to just shake his hand and take off, well, it seems gauche to him."

"Faith, I have business to attend to."

"Can't it wait?"

"The repercussions would be considerable."

"They will be here, too."

"Such as what?" I demanded, suddenly a little touchy myself. "Will he put the rest of you in chains? Torture a few coolies in a fit of pique? Come after me with a pig spear? What repercussions are we describing, precisely?"

But she either couldn't or wouldn't say what he might do, and left shortly afterwards, glum at her inability to convince me to stay within the golden bars. Then an hour later, while I was sitting with a book in the shade of the garden, Gay found me, and asked me to stay as well.

I closed the book with a snap. "Gay, this concerted effort to keep me here is becoming a bit worrying. What is going on here?"

"Nothing at all, it's only that Jimmy had plans for Sunday and is very disappointed to find them slipping away. He's fond of you."

"Fond or not, most people would be glad enough to see the back of an uninvited guest. I don't wish to overstay my welcome."

"But you're here, and you interest him, and he'd like you to stay for a few days longer."

I leant forward to look the woman in the eye. "Gay, I'm not one of Jimmy's pets. I need to leave." And so saying, I stood up and left the garden.

But before I was quite out of earshot, I thought I heard her say, "Good luck."

Chapter Twenty

Dinner was a tense affair, ill attended and again composed of great numbers of greasy and overcooked dishes. Our host drank heavily, although it did not affect him other than making him ever more morose, and Faith and Gay on either side of him worked hard at keeping him distracted. I made empty conversation with the people on either side of me while I pushed the food back and forth on my plate, until over the seventh or seventeenth course, I overheard Faith telling him about the magician we'd seen in the town.

". . . so tall and mysterious looking, all in black with this incongruously cute little donkey standing in the background. He did the usual things, pulling coins out of the air and changing mice into sparrows, but then he called people from the audience to read their minds. I couldn't understand most of what they were saying, of course, but they seemed mighty impressed."

For the first time all evening, the maharaja's eyes rose from his glass as he snarled, "If you couldn't understand what they were saying, how do you know what he was doing?"

Faith hesitated at the accusation, then rallied. "One could tell from the sequence of events. The magician would invite the audience to ask him something, and then one of them would come forward and he would talk for a few minutes and then hold his hand up in front of the other's face with his eyes closed, and sort of hum for a bit and then he'd say something and everyone would sort of ooh and aah. Then he took a deck of cards and had the person choose one and tell him which it was he had in his hand. That sort of thing."

"Not an astrologer?"

"I don't . . . He didn't have any charts or anything."

"What else could he do?"

Juggle fire, pull coins from the turbans of Sikh boys, levitate his assistant, I thought.

"He made a stone hang in mid-air above his hand. And he took a turban from the head of one of the audience and cut it in half, then restored it." From her tone of voice, Faith assumed these were tricks, although she couldn't have said how. The maharaja, however, took them at face value.

"This magician, he is in the town?"

"He was yesterday."

Abruptly, he stood up, his chair saved from crashing to the floor by the servant at his back. "We will go to see this man."

"What, now?" Faith said.

"Why not? Gay, Thomas, you come with us."

"May I come, too?" Sunny asked. "I adore magicians."

"But of course," the maharaja declared, and swept out of the room, servants and guests alike scurrying to catch him up. The rest of us stood or sat where we had been abandoned, looking at one another quizzically. Mrs Goodheart was the first to move, folding her table napkin and rising ponderously to declare, "I believe I've had enough dinner. I'll wish you all good night."

The spell broken, men hastily swallowed the contents of their glasses and rose to allow the ladies to depart. Most of them would make for the billiards room, along with a number of the women, but I followed Mrs Goodheart up the stairs. My light went out early, and silence fell.

I did not hear when the servant came, turning his key in the well-oiled lock and padding on bare feet across stone and carpet to glance briefly through the bedroom door at my sleeping figure, then padding back out to the corridor to sabotage my door lock and make my rooms a prison. I did not hear the maharaja and his gold-plated Hispano-Suiza filled with high-spirited guests drive back through the gates, bashing the stones of the narrow opening and spewing gravel across the carefully swept lawn. I did not hear the maharaja ask his servant if the deed had been done, nor did I see the two of them go to make ready quarters for me in a quieter portion of The Forts.

I did, on the other hand, hear the motorcar fly past me on its passage back from town, when the violent drop of one fast-spinning tyre into a pot-hole resulted in shouts and shrieks of laughter.

I witnessed none of these events within New Fort for the simple reason that I was not there. I left my rooms less than five minutes after entering them, having stopped there only long enough to pull on black trousers and a long dark pull-over. I wrapped a dressing-gown over the clothes and handed a note to the servant who lurked at my door, asking him to take it to Sunny Goodheart. When he had gone, I dropped the gown and grabbed my soft Simla boots, pausing only to dip my hands into the lamp's soot and wipe it across my face. Then I slipped unseen down the stairs and into the dark gardens. With my boots on my feet and a handful of tiny pebbles in my pocket, I took up a position near the gates, crouching there for a few moments until the guards went to investigate the rattle of tiny stones in the shadows. I eased out of the gates and over the waist-high stone wall onto the rocky hillside. Easing down the faint, near-vertical path that I felt more than saw, inching on all fours from rock to shrub, the back of my neck crawled with awareness of the mysterious eastern half of the fortress, looming behind me in the darkness. As I moved with infinite care down the slippery slope, I fancied I could hear the ghostly echoes of screaming Mutineers, trapped and burning sixty-seven years before.

I reached the road at last, leg muscles quivering, two fingers ripped and bleeding from a rock, but undiscovered. I gazed south, where lay the town of Khanpur, then turned resolutely north. This was the first time that I'd been out unobserved, and I was not about to waste the opportunity. I strode briskly north, towards those beguiling *godowns* that had been calling to me since I had first laid eyes on them from the window of the maharaja's aeroplane.

Little more than an hour later, I was hunkered behind the lip of a drainage ditch halfway between The Forts and Khanpur city while the maharaja's laden Hispano-Suiza flew raucously past. I rose to watch the great head-lamps illuminate the stone drive, its driver blithely unaware that the disapproving eye of the Crown was about to turn upon his little kingdom. I watched the car stagger its way through the gates, then turned, finally, towards Holmes.

The city gates were shut for the night, so I went on to the *serai* south of town, and there in the dying firelight I found the outlines of a familiar mirrored wagon. As I laid my hand on the flap of the tent, a faint slipping noise came from within, and I stopped to say, "It is I." When I heard the blade slide back into its sheath, I continued in.

"I had word that men were seeking me in the town," said Holmes in Hindi, to explain his haste in drawing steel.

"The maharaja and his friends, in search of entertainment."

"Ah. And you?"

"The time has come for Mary Russell to return to her husband."

"And time for her to disappear as well, do I take it?"

"It would be best. The maharaja dislikes . . ." I did not know the Hindi word, so I used the English. ". . . ingratitude."

"Interesting. Fortunately, I have a good supply of walnut dye."

"Holmes, it is best if we depart the city. Its prince might think to look again tomorrow, and it would be easier if he were to find you gone."

"And O'Hara?"

"I have a few ideas on that," I said. "However, it's complicated, and I think we should get on with doing my skin. Oh, but Holmes, remember when Nesbit made mention of a report that the maharaja had been buying large quantities of cotton? I found it."

Say one thing for Holmes: He always appreciated the little gifts I brought him, and this no less than any. He even permitted me to tell the story properly: creeping past the inhabited buildings at the air field and to the silent *godowns*; the makeshift pick-locks I had fashioned from hair-pins; the discovery of no fewer than three of the big triple-engined Junkers planes, awaiting assembly; a disconcerting number of machine-guns and light artillery; and (best for last) the biggest *godown* with its store of cotton bales, floor to ceiling, and neatly arranged beside them, drums of the other materials one would need for making explosives.

Oh yes; Nesbit was going to love this.

The more, perhaps, if we could find him Kimball O'Hara as well.

We slipped away from the *serai* during the night, again disguised as a pair of itinerant Moslem magicians, and headed west into the broad plateau that formed the centre of the state, a rich source of pulse and cane, wheat and vegetables. I had been, I thought, remarkably patient; no more.

"Holmes, it is your turn. What happened after you left Simla?"

"Remarkably little," he replied. "Quite odd, really."

"As a narrative, Holmes, the statement is by no means sufficient."

"No? I suppose not. Very well. Bindra and I left the hotel early. I had decided that the train out of Simla being unlikely to provide a rich source of information concerning that itinerant monk O'Hara, we should walk out of the hills."

"Walk? That must have taken days—what was Bindra's reaction to that?"

"He was not pleased. I did offer to provide him with a ticket back to Kalka, but for some reason the boy decided he would rather stay with me. So we walked, and caught rides on bullock-carts and *tonga*s, and stopped regularly to thaw ourselves out in wayside hostelries, drinking tea with the locals and gossiping about this and that."

"Monks, particularly," I suggested.

"By all means, especially considering the way a certain scoundrel of a red-hat Buddhist monk had just made off with my purse and train ticket, leaving me to trudge through the snow and survive on cups of tea bought with the few coins that remained in my pocket."

"And did any of them recall another such monk, oh, say about three years before?"

"Surprisingly few. And both of those who did—the sweeper of one inn and the cook in another—remembered him as going uphill, towards Simla, not away."

"So he took the train out," I said, disappointed.

"Or went overland to the north. In the summer months, the passes there would be reasonable, for a man who loves the hills at any rate. One thing did come to light: A band of *dacoits*—robbers—was working in the area north of Simla during that time."

"Do you think—?"

"I think it highly unlikely that Kimball O'Hara was the victim of casual dacoitry."

Still, it gave me thought, as I walked along. A while later, another question came to mind.

"What did Bindra make of your tale of woe?" I asked.

"The boy seemed unsurprised. In fact, he tended to embellish my stories rather more than was necessary."

And that, too, was thought-provoking. The child was shrewder than he appeared and without doubt unscrupulous, but I could not bring myself to picture him as a spy planted in our midst, by Nesbit or anyone else. For one thing, the child was too young for that sort of sustained purpose of mind: Holmes had habitually used youthful Irregulars in his Baker Street days, but only for specific and limited missions.

But if the child was not there under orders, why did he stay? And more to the point, why did he not question the oddities of Holmes' behaviour?

The mysteries kept me occupied all that day, but they remained mysteries.

We set up that night in a village of perhaps ninety souls, earning a handful of copper for our pains, but with the coins supplemented by a generosity of food and fodder. The village got a bargain, because in my absence Holmes had cobbled together the equipment for a new act which, together with the levitation frame, my bottomless Moslem cap, and the conversions to the blue cart effected by blacksmith and carpenter back in Kalka, was spectacular enough to make even the least superstitious folk uneasy.

Not until we were in our bed-rolls that night could we speak freely, murmuring into each other's ears in English, the sound inaudible from outside the walls of the tent. Holmes had been thinking about what I had said.

"You say Old Fort appears deserted, but is not," he said.

"There are no lights, but when one watches with care, one sees the occasional splash of lamp and gleam of a sentry's gun atop the walls. And twice, a guard's careless cigarette."

"What of its gates?"

"They are generally open. I presume they're guarded, although if the men are anything like those on the main gates, it should be no great task to get past them. You wish to see inside Old Fort?"

"Why else should we be here?" he asked.

Why else, indeed? "I merely thought that perhaps we ought to send word to Nesbit first, in case something happens."

"Report or no, Nesbit knows where we are. Our disappearance alone would tell him all he need know."

Slim comfort.

We moved on the next day, our path a wide circle leading back to The Forts. Here the ground was less fertile, with fewer people working the fields. We strolled the dusty road, the unnaturally amiable donkey following along behind, and as we went I tried to describe the maharaja and his coterie.

"He is, as Nesbit said, a fine sportsman. Having ridden after pig myself now, I understand Nesbit's praise of the man. Of course, he's completely insensible to damage inflicted on horses or coolies, but he does play the game by the rules, and was unwilling to leave a wounded boar to die in the bushes."

"Which may merely be because, were the boar to recover, it would be both ill tempered and experienced when it came to men."

"True, and it wouldn't do to have a berserker pig come after, say, a visiting Prince of Wales."

"But you already told me that the hearty sportsman is not the only side to his personality."

"His cousin said it: He collects grotesques. In his zoo, but also the people living under his—ach, the sun is so hot today," I broke off to say, as a farmer reclining in the shade of a tree stirred and sat up at our approach. Holmes asked the man about the next village, and learned that it was tiny but that a few miles farther on was a larger village, with two wells and many clay-brick houses. We thanked him, shared a *bidi* with him, and returned to the road.

"You were saying, Russell?"

"His pet grotesques. He collects them, but I would have to say, he also creates them. In the zoo, he plays God with animals, seeing how far he can drive them before they go mad. And in the palace, he does a similar thing with his 'guests,' finding their weaknesses and twisting his blade in an inch at a time. It's a game to him, baiting and teasing his hangers-on, undermining their skills, seeing if he can drive them nuts." Then I told him about the zoo, the casual extermination of the thin creature and my impression that he was using the act deliberately to disturb Sunny Goodheart. And, for the sake of completeness but feeling somewhat embarrassed, I went on to describe the toy room, its taxidermied inhabitants, and my profound distaste for that as well.

Holmes walked for a while, staring sightless at the bright wagon, deep in thought. I was braced for his disapproval, that I had not told him this part of it earlier, when I first saw him in Khanpur city. I had my refutations all in a line: that simply failing to reappear in The Forts would have stirred up all kinds of uproar, that not being a small furry animal nor a servant, I was hardly in any danger, and so on. But he just kept walking, and eventually sighed to himself, as if he'd gone through all my arguments in his head and had to admit my position. Sometimes, the speed of Holmes' wit could be disconcerting.

"An unbalanced man" was, in the end, all he said.

"But you, Holmes, you've been in Khanpur nearly as long as I have. What impression of the prince have you got from his subjects?"

"The people are extremely wary of their ruler. They acknowledge that he has improved their lot in any number of ways, appreciate that their sons are learning to read and that their villages have clean water, but they accept these things with the caution that an experienced fox will use in retrieving bait from a trap. And twice I have heard rumours of men vanished into the night."

"Men, not women?"

"Strong, middle-aged men."

"Not the sort of target one would expect for perversions."

"No. And as evidence, it would be dismissed by the most forgiving of judges. Men disappear for any number of reasons, in Khanpur as in London.

"So tell me, Russell, having spent five days in his company: If the maharaja of Khanpur did lay hands on Kimball O'Hara three years ago, would he have killed him or kept him?"

"Kept him," I answered instantly, then thought about it. "Assuming he knew who the man was. And unless O'Hara drove him to murder."

"For what purpose?"

What Holmes was asking me to do might to the uninitiated sound like guesswork, but was in fact a form of reasoning that extended the path of known data into the regions of the unknown. Unfortunately, this sort of reasoning worked best with the motivations and goals of career criminals and other simple people; the maharaja of Khanpur was not a simple man.

"I can envision two reasons, although they would not be exclusive. One is, for lack of a better term, political: The maharaja knows O'Hara is in fact a spy, and he wishes to extract from him all possible information about the workings of the British Intelligence system. Although after three years, I can't imagine there would be much he had not got out of the man."

"You see political power as the maharaja's goal?"

I found myself fiddling with the silver-and-enamel charm around my neck. "Nesbit indicated something of the sort, that a native prince might be a compromise between the Congress Party and the Moslem League."

"Even if he does not come into power through the ballot box."

"You think the maharaja is setting up a revolution of his own? He could hardly expect to take over the country as a whole."

"Even a small blow at the right place might be enough to shatter the British hold on the country, given the current political climate."

" 'By surprise, where it hurts,' " I murmured. Goodheart's drunken cry at the costume ball had stayed with me.

"Precisely. And the provocative elements in this drama are mounting."

"His friendship with a self-avowed Communist who, according to his sister, has considerable experience with aeroplanes—perhaps to the extent of piloting them himself," I said. "The capture—possible capture," I corrected myself before he could, "—of one of the lead spies of the occupying power."

"His superior air field, with stockpiled arms and explosives," Holmes added. "Its proximity to the border. A trip to Moscow; three British spies found dead in the vicinity of Khanpur."

"The remarkable number and variety of guests who come through this rather remote kingdom."

"The maharaja of Khanpur as a Lenin of the

sub-continent?" Holmes mused. "We are reasoning in advance of our data, but it is an hypothesis worthy of consideration. What was your other reason?"

"My other—? Oh yes, for keeping O'Hara in custody. Because the maharaja wants to gloat over him. Not openly, but secretly—what was it he said to me? 'I like to keep some things to myself.' His private rooms show it, that the things that are really important to him he guards close to his chest. And," I said more slowly, trying to envision the complete picture, "maybe he even regards it as a sport, trying to get inside the man and twist him."

Holmes did not respond, and I glanced to see his reaction. His face was stoney, his eyes far away.

"Holmes, I've heard a great deal about Kimball O'Hara, from you and from Nesbit, and I suppose you could say from Kipling's story before that. So, what *is* O'Hara's weakness? How would the maharaja turn him?"

We had covered half a mile before Holmes answered me. "O'Hara's greatest weakness, when I knew him, was his unwillingness to lie. Oh, he was superb at playing The Game, turning the truth until it went outside-in, creating stories for himself—those small deceits of history and character that are part of a good disguise. But when it came to direct questions, and particularly when dealing with a person who knew him, telling a lie was almost physically painful for the lad. He had an almost superstitious aversion to breaking his word."

I thought about this the remainder of the afternoon, asking myself how a person might use a man's honesty against him. Offhand, I couldn't come up with anything terribly likely, but I had no doubt that, if it were possible, the maharaja of Khanpur would be the man to do it.

Well before dusk we came to the village the farmer

had described to us, a small but prosperous collection of walls and trees, fields stretching out in all directions. I waited with the donkey and cart, surrounded by the excited twitter of the village children, while Holmes came to an agreement with the headman. We set up camp beneath the assigned tree, then hobbled the donkey and gave it food.

Dusk settled in; the men came in from their labours; the odours of dung fire and spices rose up in the soft air. I missed Bindra, more than I would have thought, and hoped the urchin had found safe haven on the other side of the border—and then I caught myself and chuckled aloud. That boy would survive in a pit of angry cobras.

The sky shed the sun's light, giving way to half a moon, and Holmes and I readied ourselves for the evening performance.

❦

It was a dramatic setting for a human sacrifice, give my murderer credit. He had drawn together the entire populace, crones to infants, in a dusty space between buildings that in England would be the village green, and all were agog at the sight. A circle of freshly lit torches cracked and flared in the slight evening breeze, their dashing light rendering the mud houses in stark contrast of pale wall and blackest shadow. The bowl of the sky I was forced to gaze up at was moonless, the stars—far, far from the electrical intrusions of civilisation—pinpricks in the velvet expanse. The evening air was rich with odours—the oily reek of the rag torches in counterpoint to the dusky cow-dung cook-fires and the curry and garlic that permeated the audience, along with the not unpleasant smell of unsoaped bodies and the savour of dust which had been dampened for the show.

I lay, bound with chains, on what could only be called an altar, waist-height to the man who held the gleaming knife. My sacrifice was to be the climax of the evening's events, and he had worked the crowd into a near frenzy, playing on their rustic gullibility as on a fine instrument. It had been a long night, but it seemed that things were drawing to a finish.

The knife was equally theatrical, thirteen inches of flashing steel, wielded with artistry in order to catch the torchlight. For nearly twenty minutes it had flickered and dipped over my supine body, brushing my skin like a lover, leaving behind thin threads of scarlet as it lifted; my eyes ached with following it about. Still, I couldn't very well shut them; the mind wishes to see death descend, however futile the struggle.

But it would not be long now. I did not understand most of the words so dramatically pelting the crowd, but I knew they had something to do with evil spirits and the cleansing effects of bloodshed. I watched the motions of the knife closely, saw the slight change in how it rested in my attacker's hand, the shift from loose showmanship to the grip of intent. It paused, and the man's voice with it, so that all the village heard was the sough and sigh of the torches, the cry of a baby from a nearby hut, and the bark of a pi-dog in the field. The blade now pointed directly down at my heart, its needle point rock-steady as the doubled fist held its hilt without hesitation.

I saw the twitch of the muscles in his arms, and struggled against the chains, in futility. The knife flashed down, and I grimaced and turned away, my eyes tight closed.

This was going to hurt.

But as the knife began its downward descent, as the mechanical device now built into the bottom of the up-turned cart clicked open and gave way, as the lit pyrotechnic sputtered in my ear, my eyes flew open again, for in that brief instant, a stray splash of light had illuminated a pair of figures at the back of the crowd. But I was too late: By the time my eyes came open again to seek them out, the trick knife had collapsed against my body and I was dropping to the rocky ground beneath the cart, artificial blood flying all over and the flash blinding everyone but Holmes. Cursing furiously under my breath, I shook free of the chains, fighting to turn over in the restricted space without overturning the cart and giving myself away, while Holmes raised his voice above the sudden clamour that the flash always stimulated, telling the villagers that the sacrifice had been taken up by the gods. I pressed my bare eye to the side of the cart where a small crack let in the torchlight, searching for the figures.

Even without my spectacles, the turbans caught my eye: red and high, with a gleaming white device over the forehead; and beside them, a smaller, bareheaded man, his features indistinct—but I didn't need to see them.

The maharaja of Khanpur had caught us up.

There were more guards, I saw, closing in on our rustic stage as the villagers faded quickly back behind the protection of their walls. I lay helpless, waiting for strong hands to lift the cart and drag me away. But to my surprise, the maharaja seemed more interested in Holmes than in me.

"How did you do that?" he asked, speaking Hindi.

"Oah, my lord, it is the Arts," Holmes replied.

"It is trickery."

"My lord, no trickery. I am a follower of the Prophet, but my skill is in the hands of Vishnu and Shiv."

"I wish to see it again."

"I will happily come to your court and—"

"Good," the maharaja said, and turned away. I let out the first breath in what seemed like several minutes, but too soon. The prince's hand came up in command, and through my thin crack I saw figures in red *puggarees* closing in on the cart—or rather, on the cart's owner. Holmes had only time enough to bend over where I lay and speak what sounded like an incantation, but which was actually a command, in German: "Stay there, then go for aid."

There was a scuffle and Holmes' querulous voice demanding explanation, followed a minute later by the sound of a motorcar starting up. Then, awfully, silence.

Chapter Twenty-One

I crawled out from beneath the shiny wagon, rubbing unconsciously at my wrists and at the bruise on my hip that came with every fall through the trap-door. What the hell was I supposed to do now? I asked myself. We'd avoided the maharaja because we feared he might recognise me; we hadn't even considered that he might go to the effort of hunting down a magician to add to his collection, however temporarily.

I pulled my spectacles from my pocket, but clarity of vision had little effect on clarity of thought. Holmes had said, "go for aid," which meant that he didn't think I should wait around for him to be returned. "Aid" could only mean Geoffrey Nesbit, but even if the man was at home in Delhi, it could take him days to get here. And I couldn't see that walking openly into a telegraphist's to send a message would be the most sensible action: Clearly, the maharaja had ears throughout his country, or he'd never have found the magician Faith had seen in Khanpur city.

Think, Russell!

I had, it seemed, three choices. I could wait here; I could go after Holmes by myself; or I could ask Nesbit for help. And if I forced myself to overlook the alarming method by which the prince had laid hands on the magician—not an easy thing to do, to ignore my body's nearly overwhelming impulse to race down the road in the wake of the car—I had to admit that Holmes was very probably in no great danger. Yes, he had been abducted in an alarmingly similar fashion once before, and yes, that time the results had been nearly catastrophic, but I had no reason (no rational reason) to feel that anything of the sort was going to happen here. Potential Lenin or no, there was no indication that the maharaja was arresting Holmes for a spy; his words had said merely that the prince of Khanpur wanted to see a magician do his tricks. Annoyed he might be by having to search for the magician, and granted, he was in the habit of "inviting" his guests to stay on, and on, but once my heart had ceased to pump in buckets of adrenaline, my mind's voice could be heard, saying that it would not be much harder to retrieve Holmes in four or five days than it would be if I stormed the palace tonight.

And—my brain at last beginning to function with clarity—it was quite possible that Holmes might find traces of Kimball O'Hara where I had failed. Particularly if, as I thought possible, the spy was quartered in Old Fort rather than among the European guests.

Still, I did not think that sitting in this mud-walled village would help anyone, so I wiped away the artificial blood from the "slashes" on my arms and legs, doused the guttering flares, and went to look for the headman.

It took some doing to convince the man that I was

neither dead nor spirit. In the end, the solidity of the rupees I put in his hand decided the matter. He would guard the wagon and feed the donkey, and although he had no horse himself to sell me, he could send for a man who did.

By midnight, I was jogging north out of the village on a sturdy pony that had a bone-jarring gait but loads of stamina. I took the first road that came in from the right, and pressed on for half an hour before the moonlight failed entirely and the horse let me know that it was blind. I hobbled the creature and curled up in a blanket for a short time, rising and setting off again as soon as the road became visible.

We travelled all day, passing Khanpur city with the end of my *puggaree* drawn across my face against the dust, without spectacles most of the time, trusting to my anonymity and the pony's sureness of foot. In the afternoon I began to watch the telegraph lines that dipped and rose on poles beside the main road to Hijarkot, but I found no telegraph office until the road gave birth to a caravanserai, its air already heavy with a dozen smokey cook-fires, clusters of men sitting around eating, coughing heartily, and spitting red splashes into the dust. I might have gone another hour or two before dark, and certainly would have continued had I wished merely for sleep, but instead I hired a string *charpoy* from the same establishment that stabled my pony, and bought a large plate of rice and dhal so hot it brought tears to my eyes. The smoke rose and then died away in the serai, the horses and camels complained and quieted, the lights were turned out in the telegraph office, and eventually the *charpoy*s around me subsided into a night-time chorus of snores and mumbles.

I lay without moving, to all appearances asleep; in fact, my brain whirred, dredging up images of Holmes in chains, or tortured, or fed to the lions, one pointless speculation after another. I dragged my thoughts from him and placed them instead on Kimball O'Hara, this phantom of the Survey who had brought us thousands of miles and occupied us for weeks now, a world-famous Irish-Indian lad who was also an unknown middle-aged Intelligence agent, a born trickster who found it painful to lie, a man who might be dead, or farming in Tibet, or sleeping on the next *charpoy*. Or who might be in chains, or tortured, or fed to the lions, or . . . I wrenched my mind from these futile images, and decided I'd waited long enough.

I had chosen my bed at the far reaches of the free-air dormitory, so it was an easy matter to slip from my bed-roll and, avoiding the watchman (who like all *chowki-dar*s spent the night warning villains off with his coughs), circle around to the stout mud-brick building that held the telegraph office. At its door, I pulled back the lining of my spectacles case to reveal a set of pick-locks, and bent over the door's lock. It was the work of no time before I was inside among the silent equip-ment, grateful that the Khanpur line was not busy enough to require manning around the clock.

Wishing I had a torch, or even an old-fashioned dark-lantern, to supplement the sparse illumination that came through the barred window, I felt my way past chairs and tables until at last my fingers encoun-tered the familiar shape. I was taking a risk, and not only that of some curious and sharp-eared passer-by. If the agent in Hijarkot thought it curious that this rural outpost should be sending a message at this time of night—and in English, as I couldn't trust my Hindi spelling; if he made enquiries instead of just sending it on; if the maharaja got news of it . . . Well, in for a penny, I thought, and began to tap out the Morse address.

I made it back to my snoring neighbours, and managed to doze away for a while myself, in between listening nervously for the approach of constabulary footsteps and royal motorcars, but hard hands did not seize me, and the disgruntled pony and I were on our way before the sun.

The next caravanserai, the last before the border, came in the middle of the afternoon, but I bypassed its dubious charms, hoping to make Hijarkot that same day. However, we ran out of light well short of the border, and rather than press forward and off a cliff, I fed and hobbled my footsore companion and curled up at its side, continuing on with daylight.

Unfortunately, this made me an uncharacteristically early border-crosser, hours ahead of those who had stopped the night in the serai, and when dealing with officialdom, one ought never appear out of the ordinary. It is difficult to remain amiable and apologetic when every muscle in one's body is straining towards action, but to allow shortness of temper only invited reciprocity on the part of the men with the red turbans, and I had to get across that border. So I smiled and repeated my story about an aged grandmother's urgent summons to her bed-side, and allowed the pony to eat the chrysanthemums growing near the guard-house door.

Finally the two border guards got tired of me and waved me through. I kept the smile plastered on my face as I rode on, although it felt more of a grimace by the time I entered the outskirts of Hijarkot. I watched for the boy Bindra, thinking that he might be sitting by the side of the road, but he was not there, and although I would have expected his absence would be a relief, in fact it was just one more vexation to rub at my raw nerves. When a uniformed British officer appeared on his shiny big horse in front of me, angled to cut me off, I felt like pulling my knife on him.

"Miss Russell?" the officer said.

The unexpectedness of that name in this place made me startle the pony into a panic, jibbing around in the street until I could get it under control and facing the officer again.

"Good Lord, Captain Nesbit! How on earth did you get here so quickly?"

"I was in Delhi, rather than Simla, so I didn't have to waste half a day in getting down from the hills. Come, let us get off the street."

We rode out of the city to a nondescript villa in the middle of broad fields of pulse and corn. A *syce* took the two horses, and Nesbit led me to a room furnished with a narrow bed, some prints of English landscapes, and a door leading to a bath-room.

"You'd probably like to bath," he said. "If you need clothes, there are things in the drawers. When you're finished, the breakfast room is down the hall to your left. I'll be there."

As the stinking, travel-grey garments on my back were the only clothing I had with me, I pawed through the drawers in gratitude, coming up with an odd assortment of English and native garments that smelt deliciously of sun and the iron. I scrubbed, rinsed, and towelled vigorously until my skin was nearly its normal colour, pulled on the trousers and shirt I had found, and bound my damp hair in a turban-cloth. There was even a tooth-brush, which I had neglected to bring from the mirrored wagon and had missed terribly.

Nesbit was sitting at a table with coffee and a sheaf of official-looking papers, which he cleared away so I could take a seat in the sun that poured through the window. Plates appeared mere moments later, softly poached eggs, toast, kippers, and tomatoes. I devoured every crumb, and helped myself to more of the toast and jam, while Nesbit ate more sparingly and talked of politics and news from home.

When I was replete, he gathered his papers and we went down the hall to a study, where he closed the door and pulled two chairs close together.

I told him everything, beginning with the arrival of the aeroplane on the road outside the train station and ending with my breaking into the telegraph office. He interrupted only when my narrative passed over some detail, commented mostly with nods and raised eyebrows, although my description of the *godown*s and what I had seen there brought him briefly to his feet. When I had come to an end, he gazed out the window for a bit and then asked me for further details on the maharaja's other guests; after that, he pulled out maps and asked me precisely where one thing or another had taken place.

In all, it took the rest of the morning. After lunch, he excused himself, saying that business required him elsewhere.

"Are you going to report what I've told you?" I asked him.

"I shall have to write a report, certainly. But I shan't send it, not just yet. The contents of those *godown*s will prove explosive in more ways than the one." He smiled. "Get some rest. I'll be back for tea."

With that domestic parting, he left. I chose a book from the shelves and carried it onto the veranda, although I was certain that I would not be able to concentrate on anything other than my agitation over Holmes. However, I woke three hours later to Nesbit's boots on the boards and the gentle ting and clatter of a tea tray.

He sat down, waited for the *khansama* to go out of earshot, and said, "I've made arrangements for the both of us to be invited to The Forts."

"How could I—" I started to ask, but he was still talking.

"I'm a regular guest there, or I used to be. Once or twice a year I would send Jimmy a telegram to say I had a few free days and suggest we ride after a few pigs. And every so often I'd bring a guest, so it would appear commonplace if I were to bring a friend. That's what I've done. The only question is, you're good at dressing the part of an Indian man; how are you at English men?"

I considered the possibilities, then suggested, "Someone relatively new to the country, who is coming to Khanpur primarily to look for his missing sister, Mary Russell? His twin sister, shall we say, as they look so much alike."

"That would do nicely. Would a brother fit with the story you gave in Khanpur?"

I hadn't really given much of a story in Khanpur, merely fact with some of the details left out. "I never told anyone I had a brother, but I never told anyone I didn't, either."

"Then that should be all right."

"I do a marvellous Oxford undergraduate."

"It'll have to be an officer, I'm afraid."

"Why? Couldn't it be a trader or an accountant or something? Or a student on a world tour?"

"Any of those would be unusual to find in my company, from the maharaja's point of view. An officer wouldn't fraternise with a *box-wallah*." The faint scorn in Nesbit's voice echoed the general attitude towards tradesmen I had found since boarding the liner in Marseilles.

"Becoming an officer will take a lot of coaching." It would take a week's practice to deceive a general, although perhaps only twenty-four hours for civilians.

"We have nineteen hours. Jimmy's sending the aeroplane for us at noon tomorrow."

I set down my cup smartly. "Then we'd best get to work."

At precisely mid-day on Friday, the throb of the maharaja's aeroplane grew in the hot air over Hijarkot, and soon the sleek red-and-white Junkers I had ridden before lowered itself onto the cleared road half a mile from Nesbit's villa. The pilot was the RAF man I had glimpsed in the Khanpur air strip; he gave Nesbit the handshake of acquaintances, received my introduction, and climbed back behind the controls. The ground I had so laboriously travelled earlier that week unreeled beneath us, and in well under an hour we set down on the Khanpur air field.

I wore civilian clothes, as befitted an officer on holiday, but I had spent most of the previous twelve hours enclosed in the uniform of the Indian Army, and my body retained its awareness of the shape and responsibility of it. I stepped out of the plane with the posture of a young Captain, so absolutely sure of his position in the world that he need not assert it. I thanked the pilot, waited while the coolies put our things in the motorcar, and joined my friend Nesbit in the back.

The road was unchanged; The Forts loomed as before, sliced in two by the shade-filled death trap of 1857. As the motor climbed the narrow road up the western side, my eyes were on the silent half of the palace, wondering if Holmes was there, wondering if he had heard the aeroplane go overhead and known that I had returned.

The maharaja was not present to greet us, having taken a party out into the hills after a panther that had mauled a villager the previous day. We were greeted by the major-domo, whose tongue stuttered briefly into silence when he saw my familiar female features in their new, male setting, but he was too experienced at dealing with his master's varied acquaintances to betray more than a moment's bemusement before pulling himself back into the rôle of professional dispenser of honours. And we were given honours beyond those that Mary Russell had received—Nesbit's quarters comprised three spacious rooms complete with balconies overlooking the inner gardens, while mine down the corridor were not much smaller. The pig-sticking fraternity, it seemed, was of higher rank than stray Americans brought in for amusement.

When we had overseen the stowing of gear in the wardrobes and splashed the dust of the journey from our faces (and I, in the glass, checked that the adhesive was secure on my slim and excellently crafted blond moustache), Nesbit, with the familiarity of the regular guest, took me on a tour of The Forts, showing me all the nooks and corners that I had not even glimpsed as Mary Russell. Naturally, he included the zoo, a mustsee for a first-time visitor to Khanpur, and again I wandered the white gravel paths, greeting the orangutans and lions, admiring the ostriches and crocodiles. We continued our circumnavigation of New Fort, through the stables and back to the main road, where we turned south, strolling between the two halves and looking up at the eastern half of the fortress.

"You've never been inside that?" I asked Nesbit in a quiet voice.

"No, although this past week I tracked down an eighteenth-century description of it, written by a Frenchman. It wasn't terribly detailed—he was more concerned with the inlay and gilding in the *durbar* hall—but it seems to be laid out along the lines of a keep built around an inner courtyard. He says there are windows within, but as you've seen, none on the exterior walls."

"A ready-made prison."

"Or simply a place so inhospitable it isn't worth keeping up."

"Holmes has to be somewhere."

"There are acres of possibilities in the New Fort alone."

That was true, I had to admit, although it made my heart sink to consider the task of sneaking through the fortress's endless and well-attended corridors in search of one itinerant magician.

We emerged into the sunshine again, and as if our reappearance had been a signal, there came a shout from behind us. Turning, we saw a body of horses trailing down the road from the north. Even at a distance, the heaviness of their stance and movements spoke clearly of having been ridden hard; nonetheless, the distinctive Arab at their head was kicked into a trot, then a canter, and in a moment the maharaja's voice rang out from the depths of the defile.

"Nesbit! So glad you could come, we've been holding the pigs for you—I got news of a giant among beasts up where you lost the horse last year. Rumour has it that the thing measures thirty-eight inches, not that the peasants know anything, but still."

He had been shouting happily all the way down the pass, and the moment he came into the sunlight he allowed the horse to slow. It came to a halt within half a dozen paces, so tired was it, but its rider seemed unaware of its distress, merely dropped to the ground to greet his fellow enthusiast.

"Had any good rides lately?" he asked, pumping my companion's hand.

"Been saving it for the Cup," Nesbit replied, slipping into the easy banter of old companions, revealing nothing of the strain he had to feel at suspecting this long-trusted comrade capable of acts ranging from kidnapping to treason.

"I'll take it from you again this year, I can feel it. And this is—*achha!*"

His astonishment was so great, his English fled. He peered under the brim of my topee, his eyes telling him that he was looking at the young woman who had escaped his hospitality the week before, his brain insisting that this was someone else. The shadow from my topee obscured the upper half of my face; the wax I had stuck along my back teeth made my face squarer and more masculine; the thickened eyebrows, steel-rimmed spectacles I wore (hastily manufactured in Hijarkot), and a moustache said: man. Blessedly, the marks from the pig-hunt had faded, and the bruised fingernails on my left hand, ripped on my downhill climb from the gate, had been done since he'd seen me last.

"Martin Russell," Nesbit offered, into the silence.

I thrust out my hand, its palm roughened overnight with sand, and greeted the maharaja with an officer's drawl pitched lower than my usual voice. "Even if I didn't know she'd been here, Your Highness, I'd have guessed from your reaction that you've met my sister."

The vigorous shake of my hand loosed the prince's voice. "The resemblance is truly extraordinary."

"Yes, Sebastian and Viola, I know. They say Shakespeare got it wrong, that identical twins have to be, well, identical. But as you can see, it sometimes happens that a brother and a sister come pretty close to being cut from the same mold. We're even both short-sighted and left-handed. However, I assure you that I'm half an inch taller, have a better sense of humour, a superior seat in the saddle, and can beat her at darts any day of the week. I'm also not nearly half the trouble she can be. I don't suppose she's still here? Her husband's having the devil of a time finding her; he's peppering me with telegrams, sending me chasing all over the country."

The dark face was busy re-evaluating the person in front of him, trying to shape me into this new form. I left an amiable look on my face, and prayed that my moustache would stay in place.

"No," he said at last. "She left here a week ago precisely. Vanished during the night, taking a few articles and leaving a note to ask that we forward the rest of her things to an hotel in Delhi. Which I believe we did."

"Oh, you did, all right. That's what set a burr under the old man's tail, Mary's bags showing up without her. Not that it's the first time she's pulled a disappearing act. Last time it was Mexico; she spent the better part of a month with the wife of Pancho Villa, or girlfriend or sister, some damned thing. 'She only does it to annoy, because she knows it teases.' Nesbit invited me here more to escape the telegrams than because I thought she'd be here. You have any luck with your panther?"

"Panther? Oh, yes. We got him, although we had to use a gun to do it, unfortunately. He came for me out of some rocks, and I was ready for him but he had one taste of the spear and decided he didn't like it much. He turned tail, swiped a chunk out of one of the beaters, then took to a tree and wouldn't come down. We'd have set fire to it to bring him out, but the field was too dry, it would have burnt the village with it." During the telling, his attention had shifted from me to Nesbit, the one who might appreciate the tale. I was glad to see the shift, because it indicated a degree of acceptance that, unlikely as it seemed, Martin Russell might be who he appeared.

I didn't ask after the wounded beater. Mary would; Martin wouldn't.

The others began to catch us up, their horses plodding and stained with sweat, and we went through the same shock of introductions with the four of them who had met Mary. With the maharaja's acceptance, however, the lead was down for them to follow, and I slipped into the rôle of visiting male friend without great difficulty. One of the young women, a newly arrived friend of the novelist Trevor Wilson, even batted her eyelashes at me.

We met for drinks on the terrace, with the sun slanting low over the rooftops behind us and the talk circling about the panther, its ferocity and speed, the bravery of the men approaching it with nothing but sharp sticks. At one point the animal itself was paraded through on a sort of decorated stretcher for our approval. Its sleek hide had been sponged to remove the gore, but I thought that, while the pair of gashes in its shoulders should prove easy for a taxidermist to stitch into invisibility, the great hole in its chest might prove more of a problem, particularly if, as the maharaja clearly did, one regarded a bullet as somewhat shameful.

Perhaps damaged skins were set aside to upholster more furniture.

The sun retreated up the walls, and a thousand small oil lamps were lit for our festivities, tiny earthenware saucers with floating wicks that added an incongruous touch of romance and tradition to the evening. A passing servant asked if I would like another gin and tonic, but I turned down his offer, knowing that we would shortly be off to our rooms to dress for dinner.

However, the maharaja had a surprise up his sleeve. With a flourish, not of trumpets but of his arm, he raised his voice and called us to attention.

"Ladies and gentlemen, I have for you a small entertainment, a performance for your amusement and your mystification."

That was all the warning I had before the tall, black-clad figure of my husband was escorted in from an un-lit corner. Holmes had kept his own clothes, I saw, although he wore a Moslem cap instead of the starched turban, and his boots had been replaced by soft native shoes (which meant, damn it, that the knife and pick-locks in his heels were no longer a part of his equipment). I saw with relief that he had not been mistreated—his motions with the mirrored balls were fluid, his posture dignified, the broken English of his patter word-perfect. Whatever the maharaja was doing with him, Holmes seemed happy enough to go along with it for the moment.

He ran through most of the one-man stunts, and if the audience was vastly more sophisticated than the rustic villagers he normally performed for, even the English guests were caught up in the mystery of where objects went when they left his hands, and why they might reappear in unlikely places.

After twenty minutes, the mirrored juggling balls sparkling into nothingness for the last time, he bowed first to the maharaja, then to us, and made as if to leave. But the maharaja would have none of it; he called various people forward to examine the innocent hands of the magician, to pat his sleeves and marvel at the absence of hidden pockets (Holmes was a surprisingly competent tailor, when the need arose). Nesbit and I hung back, but we did not go unnoticed.

"Come," our host called. Nesbit stepped forward and I reluctantly followed. The prince held up the magician's hand as if this were the foot of a horse to be examined for stones, and he patted Holmes' wrists, which showed nothing but brown skin—not nearly brown enough, I saw in alarm; dyestuffs are not readily available inside gaol. Holmes stood impassively under the handling, his eyes meeting mine but giving no sign of recognition—clearly, he had studied the crowd on the terrace from his dark corner and seen me talking with Nesbit.

And then the maharaja said to me, "Do remove your topee, Captain Russell; you'll be able to see better." Holmes tensed, his hand making a fist, his eyes darting to the guards as he prepared to fling himself to my protection.

But a topee is not a turban, and I had been my

teacher's pupil before I became my husband's wife, learning to my bones that half a disguise is none at all. I lifted my topee, smoothed my regulation officer's hair-cut with my other hand, and bent forward obediently to witness the lack of tricks up the magician's sleeve.

The moment my short-cropped, pomade-sleek, un-questionably masculine hair passed beneath his nose was the closest I've ever seen Holmes to fainting dead away.

Chapter Twenty-Two

The magician was led back into the palace, either escorted or under guard, according to the eyes that watched him go. The rest of us drifted away to dress for dinner. My clothing had been ironed and either folded away or hung in the spacious wardrobe, and the safety razor and shaving mug I had borrowed from Nesbit were laid out in the bath-room, ready to lend the verisimilitude of smooth cheeks to my appearance. I launched into the laborious process of donning a man's formal attire, fumbling with the studs and cursing under my breath at the tie, working for just the correct touch of insouciance. The indicators of quality in a human male are more subtle than those of the female, hence all the more essential to hit it right. Hair combed but not plastered; shoes of the highest quality and shined to a mirror gloss, but clearly not new; fingernails clean but not pampered. When the knock came on my door, I presented myself with all the nervousness of a débutante at her Court presentation.

Nesbit ran his eyes over me, coming up with approval and a trace of amusement, which made me glad, that he was beginning to get past his dislike of the clandestine impetus for our invasion of Khanpur. He did not care for spying on his friend, but he would do so at the top of his bent.

"Shall we go?"

"I didn't hear the bell."

"Time for a drink before," he suggested, and Martin Russell followed him agreeably down to the billiards room.

The atmosphere of the palace had shifted in my absence, although I could not lay my finger on the how or why. Mrs Goodheart had left, off to Bombay to see her "Teacher," taking Sunny with her; that accounted for some of the change. And although Gay Kaur was there, her hands trembling as she lit a cigarette, I saw neither Faith nor Lyn, who had seemed to me steadying forces in the maharaja's ménage.

For one thing, we seemed to be heavily weighted to the masculine now, the three flighty German girls gone, a couple of visiting wives returned to their homes. The feminine exodus had left behind eight rather hard-looking females who would only by the furthest stretches of chivalry be termed "ladies," two of whom I thought I recognised from the *nautch* dancers, as well as four diminutive Japanese girls, two peculiar-looking albino women, and three of the maharaja's female dwarfs, all of them wearing heavy make-up and scanty dress.

We didn't actually make it as far as the billiards room, not with drinks being served on the terrace. We were standing with our glasses in our hands and a couple of flirtatious women in our faces when Thomas

Goodheart came onto the terrace, spotted me, and stopped dead. I carefully took no notice of him, bending instead to listen to the witticism of the painted lady, but he certainly took notice of my every action. After a few minutes he brought his drink over to where Nesbit and I stood.

"Hello, Captain Nesbit," Goodheart said, although he was watching me as he spoke. "I didn't know you were coming to Khanpur."

"Good evening, old chap," Nesbit said, pumping the American's hand in greeting. "And I didn't realise you were still here. I don't see your charming sister. Or your mother."

"No, they've gone to meet Mama's friend. I stayed on to . . . I don't believe we've met," he said, although he didn't sound at all sure of it.

"Captain Martin Russell, old friend of mine," Nesbit told him. We shook, and I arranged a somewhat tired smile on my face.

"From your reaction I take it that you, too, have met my twin sister. Whatever she did, I probably don't want to know."

Nesbit's ease and my hearty masculinity completed what the haircut and false moustache began, and Goodheart, like the others before him, began tentatively to accept this peculiar coincidence. I felt various eyes on me during the evening, but my mask did not slip, and by the evening's end, I was Captain Russell, not Miss.

After dinner we were again entertained by *nautch* girls, and although they were the same dancers who had entertained us the other night, their performance tonight was a rather different thing from that wholesome version. When the dozen figures came into the *durbar* hall, whirling and clashing and gyrating seductively, I could not help glancing to see what Geoffrey Nesbit made of it. He seemed much taken aback, so much so that he looked over at me and then quickly away, his face going blank, if slightly pink about neck and ears. Clearly, this was not a form of entertainment commonly offered on his past visits.

I kept my place, grateful that I was not on the outside and thus a target of one of the sinuous women, and it was with huge relief that I saw them leave: It would have been exceedingly awkward had the evening degenerated into a whole-scale orgy then and there. When the group rose to adjourn in the direction of billiards or cards or the smaller-scale orgy that no doubt was scheduled for elsewhere, I made my excuses and headed for the doors.

Unfortunately, Nesbit was not with me. The maharaja had claimed him early, kept him by his side, and looked to be intent on keeping him now. I met his eyes across the room as I left, an exchange that said without words that he had no idea when he might join me. I sat for a while in the fresh air of the garden, making a display of smoking a cigarette through, then went upstairs to my quarters to wait for Nesbit. As I passed, I offered a cigarette to the *chuprassi* positioned outside our rooms, who took it with gratitude. Inside, I changed my formal wear for something dark and tough and suited to climbing cliffs. Then I waited.

I waited a very long time.

When Nesbit came, there was no missing it. Scuffles, loud grumbles, and a stifled burst of laughter preceded him down the corridor; his door slammed back, and a minute later a crash came, followed by more hilarity. I pulled pyjama bottoms and a smoking jacket over my clothes and went into the hall-way. Three servants were backing out of Nesbit's door, looking amused until they spotted me and went obsequious again.

"Is the old man all right?" I asked the one assigned to squat at our door.

"Oah yes, he has merely taken much drink."

"Thanks for getting him here in one piece," I said, and absently distributed cigarettes to all four, then let myself into Nesbit's room, closing the door behind me.

The man's drunkenness was not an act, not entirely. I thought at first it was, expected him to put it aside and go rational, but he was too far gone for that. Not that the rational portion was entirely overwhelmed. He was sitting on the edge of his bed, shoeless and wearing neither tie nor coat, when I came in. He raised his wavering head.

"Ah, Russell. My ol' fren' Martin Russell. Have to ask you to help me into the johnny, that's a good man." He raised his arm, asking for my support, and I went to his side to haul him upright. My shoulder kept him from falling, and we made the cloakroom without mishap. "Tha's fine, you jus' leave me here for a minute."

From the bedroom I listened to the sounds of gagging and retching. When the splash of the flush toilet had run its course, I took him a glass of water and helped him back to the bed. He dropped heavily down, his hands clutching his skull to keep the world from whirling.

"Sorry," he said, slurring the sounds. "Sorry. He wouldn't let me stop, and there's only so much whisky you can spill on the floor. God, this is bad." I saw his face change, and hurriedly shoved the shaving-bowl into his hands. A second glass of water was sipped more slowly, and stayed down. "Never seen him like this. Madman," Nesbit muttered.

I took the description as hyperbole, and waited impatiently for him to tell me what we were going to do next. All plans of making a reconnaissance of the Old Fort had clearly shot out the window; by the time Nesbit was sober enough to walk, it would be light.

"Saw the magician again," he said.

I straightened sharply. "Where?"

"In the . . . Where were we?" he said to himself. "The gun-room."

"That horrible fur-lined room? Why?"

"Jimmy wanted to see his tricks. Clever man."

"I know," I said. "Did you say anything, accidentally?"

"No." He spoke firmly, with absolute assurance, and I thought that this might be one drunk who retained a thin edge of control.

"Did he give you anything?"

"Who?" He raised his head, struggling to focus on my face. "Jimmy?"

"No, Hol—the magician," I said, although we were speaking quietly.

The green eyes narrowed exaggeratedly in thought, and Nesbit started to pat his pockets, then looked around for some place to put the glass. I took it, and watched him search pockets with clumsy fingers until impatience got the better of me, and I dipped my own into breast and coat pockets until I encountered the tiny twist of paper, no bigger than an apple seed.

"Got it," I told him. He blinked owlishly at the object, and I resigned myself to the fact that there would be no more help or even sense got out of the man tonight. Holmes' skin dye would have to last another day. I pulled back the bedclothes and patted the pillow. "You go to sleep. I'll see you in the morning."

"Got things to do," he declared, and prepared to rally his body's mutinous forces to his side.

"Nesbit," I said in a firm voice. "Geoffrey, there's not a thing either of us can do tonight. Sleep it off. We'll talk in the morning."

He focussed on my face, inches from his, and then his eyes went soft, and after a minute he sagged sideways into the pillow and went limp. I pulled the bedclothes up to his shoulders and crossed the room, but at the door I heard his voice.

"Pig sticking. In the morning. Early."

Damnation.

Outside, I gave the servant a third cigarette and told him, "Nesbit *sahib* will need aspirin and strong coffee when he wakes. And someone to help him shave," I added.

"Yes, *sahib*," the man said merrily. "Aspirin and coffee we have much of."

I'll bet, I said to myself.

In my room, with a chair braced under the door's handle, I eased open the tiny wad of thin paper Holmes had secreted in Nesbit's pocket:

First floor, southeast wing. Keys in the desk box. Bring rope, morphia, needle.

I was accustomed to odd shopping lists from Holmes, but this gave me a moment's pause. Rope I could probably find, but the rest? As I traded my dark clothes for nightwear and climbed into bed, my mind was taken up with ways in which I might casually ask the servants for a drug addict's gear.

Nesbit looked like death in the morning. The aspirin and coffee might have got him dressed and on the horse, but only time would restore the colour to his face and the flexibility to his posture. Still, he was there, and mounted, albeit looking decidedly queasy. His greeting to me was a brief nod; his answer to the maharaja's hearty greeting not much more effusive. The prince laughed and clapped his guest on the shoulders.

"You're getting soft, Nesbit," he declared. "Not holding up the British side."

"The day's not over yet, Jimmy," Nesbit answered, but the maharaja only laughed the louder. I realised with a shock that this drinking partner was still half drunk; how the hell could he manage the intellectually tricky and physically demanding business of going after pig? And I was none the happier when he chose Nesbit and myself as his partners for the run.

We rode five miles northwest, past the air field to where the servants were waiting. During that time, Nesbit pulled himself together, his seat improving with every minute, his green eyes taking on the gleam of challenge. It was a relief, to think that we weren't all going to be hopeless at the task ahead.

The maharaja, on the other hand, became increasingly peculiar. His high spirits seemed to twist as we went along, climbing and turning hard, his remarks to his guests taking on an edge of spite, even cruelty, his hand on the reins causing his lovely white Arab to fret and sidestep nervously. When we reached the servants, it had worked itself into a sweat despite the coolness of the morning, and the lead *shikari* eyed his master and the Arab's sweaty neck with equal apprehension.

The attitude was quickly justified, when the first spear handed the maharaja proved to have some flaw in its polish; petulance became fury and the razor-sharp head flashed down, missing the servant's foot by a hairbreadth, and that only because the man had jumped back. The substitute spear proved more satisfactory. I exchanged a long look with Nesbit, and accepted a weapon of my own.

Riding behind our host, I murmured to the blond man, "What the hell is wrong with him? He acts like he's taken some kind of drug."

"Possibly. I've never seen him quite like this. Watch your back." But before I could ask how exactly I was to do that, given the already hazardous setting of a pig-hunt, the man ahead of us turned to shout us forward, and we kicked our mounts to obey.

The day passed in a confusion of fury and high apprehension, until I felt as if I were dancing over a bed of planted swords with a partner courting suicide. We flushed three pigs, each one increasingly vicious, stronger than the last, ever more clever. It was as if Nature itself was being fed by its prince's wild force, his manic laughter and cutting barbs driving his guests and servants on, welding us all into a kind of wild hunt, a pack out for blood. It was, I thought in a brief clear moment, only a matter of time before we turned on one of our own. Nesbit's emerald eyes glittered and I found skills I could not have imagined, coaxing the horse into the turns of an acrobat, balancing the awkward spear like an extension of my arm.

It was with the fourth pig that it all came crashing down on us. It was an old and wily creature, still enormously broad across the shoulders but with one of its upper tusks broken down, and it came out of its thicket as ill-tempered as the prince himself. It ran and jinked and I dropped back so the two men didn't ride me over, only to find the creature halting dead and reversing straight for me. Nesbit and the maharaja had ridden well past it by the time they could pull up, and the tusks were closing in, too fast.

What followed was the most furiously incomprehensible dance yet, the boar in the middle, all three of us jabbing and ducking away and coming back to its charges, waiting for an opening, the boar too experienced to allow us one. Around and around we went, the pig a welter of blood from a dozen minor wounds, not giving an inch, missing fetlocks and bellies by a breath, bolting and feinting and furious.

And then the maharaja came off his horse. I was looking straight at him when he did it, or I shouldn't have believed it: I saw him toss his spear to one side and kick free of the stirrups, dropping to the ground, completely defenceless and grinning like a schoolboy. The boar was facing Nesbit at that moment, but the animal heard the sound behind it and started to whirl about. Without thinking, I shouted some nonsense sounds and kicked my horse forward, waving the spear over my head. The horse quite sensibly refused to take more than a couple of steps, but that was sufficient to attract the boar's attention and turn it back to face me. It lowered its head to charge, but before it could find traction, its hind legs were jerked up from the ground, both of them, by the maharaja.

Incredulously, I watched the boar twist and scrabble to free itself, snorting and screaming its outrage, but the small man's strength somehow held it up, and then Nesbit's spear took it in the side, and it dropped, dead before it hit the earth.

My spear-head slumped to the ground as I fought for breath, but Nesbit had dropped off his horse and was standing over the dead pig, panting and shaking his head at his friend, who had collapsed to the ground behind the pig, still grinning.

"Jimmy," Nesbit managed to gasp out. "What the hell was that about?"

"I haven't done that since I was a boy," the maharaja said when he'd got his breath. "Didn't know if I still could."

"Christ! I wish you'd warned me."

"Where would the fun in that be?"

Nesbit stared, then gave a bark of laughter and thrust out his hand. Our host took it, allowing himself to be pulled upright, and they stood shoulder to shoulder admiring the dead animal until the appalled servants had brought the horses back. Both men mounted, and the maharaja surveyed the scene.

"I can't imagine we'll improve on that kill. Shall we let the day stand?"

I tried not to show how abjectly grateful I was.

❦

Nesbit and I lagged behind the others on the ride back, and I told him about Holmes' note. To my surprise he nodded at the list of requests.

"Not a problem. How much rope does he mean?"

I started to tell him that I thought it would be for tying prisoners, but hesitated. In that case, wouldn't Holmes have specified "twine"? The more I thought about it, the more likely it seemed. He had, after all, had some time to consider the contents of the note. "I shouldn't think all that much. He says he's being held on the first floor."

"But if we need to come off the roof?"

"You're right. Where are we going to get that much strong rope?"

"Again, not a problem, unless Jimmy's had the lumber-room cleared out. He had a team of mountain-climbers here a few years ago, bought the equipment for learning, I shouldn't think he's used it since. And the morphia? How much of that does he require, do you suppose?"

Of that I felt more certain. "If it had been for more than three or four people, he'd have specified. Is that also in the lumber-room?"

"Morphia I carry with me." He caught my look, and smiled. "And skin dye, which I shall bring as well. One simply never knows what emergency may come up."

My spirits rose somewhat; we might yet pull this off.

They dipped again at dinner, when our host stormed in, after keeping us all waiting for half an hour, back in the strange, unsettled state of the morning, if not worse. Nesbit worked hard to keep him entertained and on a straight track, although it was quite a job, made no easier by the grim determination with which the maharaja drank and the black looks he shot at the Englishman. My heart sank when the prince abruptly dismissed most of the hangers-on and told Nesbit to come with him to the gun-room. But Nesbit demurred.

"Look, old man," Nesbit said pleasantly, "another night like the last one, and I won't be fit for the Cup next month, far less whatever you've got planned for to-morrow. Thanks, but I'm for bed." He drained his glass and stood up; the prince's dark eyes narrowed, and I braced for an eruption.

But it did not come. Instead, the maharaja seemed to have been distracted by something in what Nesbit said;

he sat back in his chair, smiling as at a private joke. "The Kadir Cup, yes. Britain's honour at stake, and it will be arranged that India will lose yet again. But tomorrow, on India's ground? Yes, Nesbit, let's see what you do with my entertainment tomorrow."

He waved a hand of dismissal, and we left, but as we went out of the door I suddenly understood the traditional method of bowing oneself out of the royal presence: It was not out of respect, but for reluctance of presenting one's back to the throne.

In the hall-way, I murmured to the man beside me, "I don't know that I cared much for the sound of that."

"It had the distinct ring of a gauntlet thrown, did it not? Wouldn't be the first time, you know. Still, if he offers a round of tiger sticking, I really shouldn't volunteer if I were you."

I thought he was joking, until I looked at his face. My God, *tiger* sticking?

In compensation for the disturbances of the night before, New Fort quieted quickly. I left my lights burning until half past eleven, and then wandered out, again wearing a dressing-gown over dark clothing, and stood on the outside walkway, smoking a cigarette. As was my habit, I offered one to the squatting servant, holding the match to him without thinking, then strolled away to gaze over the courtyard garden, comprised of mysterious shapes in the moonlight.

It took less than ten minutes for this particular cigarette to have its effect on the man. The moment I heard him slither to the side, I walked back and propped him upright, then went to Nesbit's door and put my head inside. He was there waiting, his clothes black, face half-hidden by a dark scarf. We slid through the silent hallways like wraiths, and he knew precisely where he was going.

In half an hour, we were looking up at the walls of the older fort, black against the moonlit sky. I settled the decorative revolver in the back of my belt, and prepared to storm Khanpur's castle.

Chapter Twenty-Three

The moon rode blessedly near full in a cloudless sky, which made the task of approach far easier. Of course, had anyone been watching for us, it would have simplified their job as well, but they did not seem to be doing so, and we slunk up the road in the shadow of the wall, gaining the gates without an alarm being raised.

The entrance to Old Fort was a mirror image of the other, but less well-kept-up. The paving stones were uneven underfoot, and where the western fort smelt of sandalwood and flowers, even from its gate, here the air was heavy with must and decay. The slovenliness extended to the guards as well. In the courtyard two men had made a fire, and sat warming themselves as they ate something from tin bowls; one of them had his back to us.

I put my mouth to Nesbit's ear, and breathed a question. "Just the two?"

I felt him nod, and followed him as he crept into the gateway, our sleeves brushing the massive wooden doors that I had never seen closed, keeping to the side of the passage lest we be outlined against the moon-bright sky behind us. He stopped where the passage opened into the inner courtyard, then slowly leant forward to peep around the corner; over his shoulder I could see the two men, who were arguing loudly over something in the local language. Nesbit reached back to touch my arm in warning, then stepped out, moving lightly around the wall to the arcades that began twenty feet from the gates. My heart leapt into my throat, but I followed, even though it was impossible that neither guard would spot us—we were in the open, less than fifty feet from them.

Yet they didn't. They kept arguing, kept eating, and then we were behind the first column, my pulse racing furiously. My God, this Englishman was madder than the maharaja!

He led me along the arcade that circled the open yard, a smaller version of the New Fort's, although the only resemblance to a garden here was one lone tree growing against the walk directly across from the gates, which even in the thin light looked half dead. When we had circled two-thirds of the complex, Nesbit began to feel for a door. We were nearly to the gates again when he found one; the latch lifted easily, the door's creaks were minor, and he stepped within. After a moment he put his head back out to breathe the word "Stairs." The door shut, and as soon as the arguing voices had faded, I exploded at a whisper.

"What on earth were you thinking? God knows why they didn't spot us!"

"The one was looking away, the other'd been staring into the fire. The only way they would have noticed us was if we shone a torch at them."

And so saying, he gave the torch in his hand a brief

flash, illuminating a run of worn stone steps. I touched the revolver, for the hundredth time that night, and crept on his heels up the concave surfaces, pausing at the top; the hall-way to the left glowed faintly, as at a tiny candle. As we came up on it the light proved to come from an oil lamp set in a wall niche. Another lamp burned thirty feet along; halfway between the two and facing them was a ramshackle table, on which sat an equally bashed-about tin box.

Unfortunately, the guard sitting behind the table looked remarkably strong and healthy, and far from slumbering at his post, he studied the walls, bored for something to do.

I nearly jumped out of my skin when a loud Hindi voice rang down the stones, and even Nesbit jerked. "Oh my brother," it called. "I hunger for your wife's good curry." My husband's voice, sounding strong and sure; I felt a thickness take over my throat. Not that I had been worried about Holmes, not really. But my body had been.

The bored guard raised his head to reply at the door nearest the first lamp, "Quiet, old man. It is too early."

"And yesterday night and the night before, did I eat before our master called me to work my magic before him? I did not. He called me and I laboured, and pleased him, yet when I returned, cold and hungry, I found your good wife's food gone cold and her chapatis dry to leather. It is not a great thing to ask, my brother, that you set my dinner before me now. It is there, to be sure—I can smell it rising from the air below."

I doubted he could smell anything but the mustiness of The Fort, but his suggestion got the guard thinking, and in a minute he stood up and put his face to the small barred window. "Very well, old man. I shall bring your food now, and you shall show me the trick with the coin."

"It is agreed, my brother. I shall show you all manner of wonders, if my strength permits."

The guard chuckled at the feeble bribery, and marched down the hallway, to my relief in the opposite direction. When he came to the second wall-lamp, he paused to glance briefly through the small barred window set into its door, but his look seemed a gesture of no great interest, merely habit. His feet scuffed down the hall; the moment he cleared the first curve, I was dashing for the tin box with the key.

The door opened, and there was Holmes, black clad, bareheaded. I threw myself at him. And my undemonstrative husband, disregarding our audience, responded with a reassuring vigour, his arms circling mine, muscles drawing tight as if he intended never to let me move away, his right hand pressing my head to his shoulder, fingers moving against my skull.

"I'm sorry we took so long," I babbled. "It took me days to get out of the country, and then we couldn't get here yesterday night, and I was afraid that tonight, too . . . But how did you know to send the guard away?"

"The lamps shift when one of the lower doors goes open. I thought this a likely time for it to be you. Did you bring what I asked?"

Reluctantly, I stood away, although my hand lingered near his, and his grey eyes studied my face as if it had been months, a smile playing across his mouth. "We did, but we won't need them, now that the guard's gone."

"And the key?"

"It's—" But the key was not in the cell door, and

when I looked for Nesbit, I found him at the other
door, drawing it open, standing back.

His face was alight with the intensity of his pleasure,
and he thrust out his hand with only a degree less enthusiasm than I had embraced Holmes. The prisoner of
the second cell emerged into the dim light, his hand
preceding him out of the door.

"Captain Nesbit," said a low voice, its English lightly
accented. "I am so very pleased to see you."

"Mr O'Hara." That was all, but he might as well have
dropped onto his knee and said the words "My Lord."
All the love and respect of a student for his tutor welled
into Nesbit's voice, relief and affection and just a hint
of amusement, that they should find themselves in this
place.

The hand-clasp ended, and the man turned to us, curiosity enlivening the pale face—I had altogether forgotten that Kipling's lad was not a native, that both
parents had been Irish. He was a clean-shaven, black-
haired Irishman going grey at the temples; kept from
sunlight for nearly three years, his skin had faded to a
sickly shade of yellow. But the dark eyes danced as they
sought out Holmes, and as he came up, he stopped to
place both hands together and bow over them. Holmes
returned the gesture, then grinned widely and grasped
the smaller man's shoulders.

"By God, Mr O'Hara, it's good to lay eyes on you."

"And you, my brother Holmes. The Compassionate
One has smiled upon you, it appears." And with that,
the Irishman's gaze slid to one side, and took me in,
and if anything the grin widened. He moved over to
look up into my face, and I studied with interest this
phantom we had been following for all these long
weeks.

He was dressed as a monk, in dark red robes that left his arms uncovered, and now that I was standing in front of him I could see that his facial hair was not shaved, but had been laboriously kept plucked. Aside from that tiny detail, his features could have been those of a fellow passenger on a London bus. The face before me was remarkably unlined, so that he appeared younger than his forty-seven years, the dark wells of his eyes calm, peculiarly open and unguarded. He did not look, I thought, like a man long held prisoner. His eyes reminded me of something or someone, although before I could hunt down what or who that was, his light, amused voice addressed me.

"And you, appearances to the contrary, can only be Miss Russell."

I suddenly remembered how I looked, and abruptly understood both his laughter and Holmes' fingers exploring my scalp—in the extremity of the moment, I had forgotten that I was Martin Russell, not his sister. But this middle-aged Irishman saw what the maharaja had not, and accepted the disguise for what it was.

He continued, "I am grateful to God that I have lived to see this day. I call your husband brother now, but in days gone by he was my mother and my father, and I rejoice that my eyes can see the woman who pleases him."

I was so confused, all I could do was look at him. And even more confused when he turned and walked back to the door of his cell. "But now you must be on your way, before Sanji returns with the supper."

Both Nesbit and I started to protest, but Holmes took over. "Russell, there's no time for discussion. The guard takes at a minimum fourteen minutes to get to the kitchen and back, and we cannot count on this being one of those times he stops to gossip. Listen to me. Did you bring the drug?"

"Here," I said, fishing it from my pocket, along with the small vial of skin dye Nesbit's kit had provided. The purloined climbing rope was best left around Nesbit's waist until we needed it.

As Holmes secreted the bottles and needle away, he said, "The one thing you must understand, and accept, is that Mr O'Hara has given his word that he will not make any attempt at escaping Khanpur."

"That's ridiculous—" I started to say, but Holmes cut me off sharply.

"We have no time, Russell. O'Hara has given his word. Absolutely. If you want him out of here, you shall have to carry him."

"What, we drug him and carry him down the stairs?"

The man standing in the doorway of the adjoining cell spoke up. "Drugging shall not be necessary. My vow merely said that I should not attempt escape; there was nothing whatsoever about resisting abduction. If you choose to remove me from this place, so be it. I shall not take one voluntary step towards the border to assist you; however, neither shall I raise my voice in protest."

"This is lunacy," I said.

"Nonetheless," O'Hara said placidly, folding his hands and standing patiently just inside the door to his cell.

"You can't mean it."

"I'm afraid he does," Holmes said.

"Nesbit, do something," I said. "Order him."

"Would it help if I ordered you?" Nesbit asked the recalcitrant prisoner.

"Not in the least," O'Hara said cheerfully.

"How much do you weigh?" he asked, then said, "Oh, never mind."

"I hope to God you haven't taken a vow, too, Holmes," I grumbled.

"No. However, in any case I shall not be going with you, not tonight."

I felt like screaming. "For God's sake, why?"

"Because in eight minutes Sanji will be back with my food, and if he finds me missing, he will raise the others and you will not make it to the gates."

"All right, then, we'll use the drug to keep him quiet."

"And in twenty minutes," Holmes added, as if I had not spoken, "according to the custom we have established over the past days, six guards will arrive to escort me to the maharaja's presence for a midnight entertainment. If I am not here, the alarm will be raised, after which they may think to look into the neighbouring cell and find that empty as well, and a hue and cry will be raised, and we will all be caught within a mile of the gates. If, however, I remain here, and perform my act, and return to my cell until morning, no one will look next door until O'Hara's breakfast tray goes unclaimed. That will give you six hours to make the border, an easy matter even though you shall have to carry him every step of the way. You can return for me at another time, or wait for the maharaja to tire of my paltry tricks and turn me loose, which I estimate will happen in another two or three days. You have six minutes."

"Holmes, don't be ridiculous. I'm not leaving you hostage."

"Russell, understand this: I am not a hostage. O'Hara is political, I am mild entertainment. A world of difference. The maharaja only put me under key in the first place because I slipped away from him in the city, and he was irked. That was a week ago. If the magician vanished overnight, they might send word out for him, but if he was not to be found, no one would bother further—unless he took O'Hara with him. But if they find O'Hara missing and the so-called magician still locked inside, what harm will come? They will question me as to what I heard in the night, and I will tell them I heard men speaking, and men moving, and then my dinner came. Yes, the other prisoner disappeared, but what of it? I did not know him, I have never spoken to him, so far as they know. The Morse tappings through our wall were things unheard ten feet away. Five minutes."

"Stop it!"

He relented, so far as he could, stepping forward to take my head in his hands. "Russell, once, once only, I was taken and suffered for it. Please, my dear wife, believe me, this is not the same situation. If you want O'Hara free, you and Nesbit must take him and leave me. I will drug Sanji tomorrow night and slip away—one man, alone and unencumbered. If I have not shown up in Hijarkot inside the week, come back. Please, believe me: I shall be safe. After all, as a last resort I need only stand up and declare myself an English citizen to be made invulnerable."

I turned, reluctantly, to consult with Nesbit.

The blond head nodded. "It's true. A public declaration like that, Jimmy'd be furious, but I can't imagine he'd dare take it further."

A weight far greater than that of Kimball O'Hara settled over me. I turned back to Holmes and hissed, "If you're wrong, I shall be extremely angry with you." Then I kissed him hard on the lips, more threat than affection, and let him step back into his cell.

Before the door shut on him, he stuck his head back, his hand on the slim line of hair on his upper lip. "However, Russ? I think that, all in all, given the choice, I prefer you with the hair and without the moustache."

Suddenly the light in the hall-way shifted as the oil flames ducked and fluttered: A lower door had opened. Aware of Nesbit apologetically slinging O'Hara across his shoulders, I made haste to lock Holmes' door, then that of the other cell, before dropping the keys back into the tin box and scurrying away on Nesbit's heels.

Our nice, smooth rescue operation had turned into something out of a Gilbert and Sullivan operetta, thanks to two hugely reluctant prisoners. Why could nothing in this damnable country be simple?

❦

We had to use the distraction of small stones to make our escape through the gates, but both guards behaved as the first set had, and went to investigate the rattles, allowing us ample time to gain the road outside. Carrying our burden, however, we could not take a short-cut down the hillside, but were forced to keep to the paved surface, and made the main road seconds before the sound of marching feet rang out from the New Fort gates high above us. Six guards started down the hill to fetch the magician for his midnight rendezvous with the maharaja. We huddled behind a heap of stones and waited for them to cross the road and go through the gates of the Old Fort; as he had promised, our reluctant escapee made not a sound. When the guards had disappeared, Nesbit resumed his burden and staggered off across the moonlit landscape.

A mile later, we stopped to let Nesbit tip his burden to the ground and drop down beside him. O'Hara watched the younger man wheeze and rub his legs, a sympathetic look on his face, the beads of his rosary slipping regularly through his fingers. Damn him, anyway.

"How many beads on your rosary?" I asked the monk; my voice revealed my great displeasure with the entire episode.

He turned on me a beatific smile. "One hundred eight. My days of counting paces are over; now I count prayers."

Stifling a groan, Nesbit stood again and prepared to take up his burden.

"Wait," I said.

"I'll take him another stretch, then you can try."

"No."

"We can't delay, we're too close to The Forts."

"It's only five miles to the border," I noted.

"And three—"

"Three more to the British encampment, yes. But once we get to the border, couldn't we send Mr O'Hara on under his own power?" I turned to our unhelpful burden, the monk sitting patiently and untroubled. "Wouldn't that be within the scope of your vow?"

"Oah yes," he replied happily. "Once outside the borders of Khanpur, I will have already—however unwillingly—effected my escape. The vow would thus be broken, well and truly; I could come and go wherever I pleased."

I felt another pulse of rage at the absurdity of this escapade, arguing Jesuitical minutiae with an Irish Buddhist spy while Holmes performed conjuring tricks before a mad maharaja—and then I pushed the emotion down: No time for it now.

"I'd like to propose a change of plan," I said grimly.

"I think it might be a very good idea if you and I, Nesbit, were inside The Forts when the sun comes up."

Nesbit was no longer too winded to argue, but I spoke over his automatic objections.

"I know, the original plan was for us four to make for the border and abandon Khanpur. But thanks to Mr O'Hara here, we are only three. It's less than five miles to the border, and not yet one o'clock. Eleven miles forced march there and back, you and I could be in our beds before daylight."

Nesbit's quick brain considered my words, saw their truth, and picked out the glaring problem. "We can't manage the pace carrying him."

"No," I agreed. So I pulled the fancy revolver out of my belt, cocked it, and lowered it until its gleaming barrel pointed directly between Kimball O'Hara's arched eyebrows. "He's going to walk."

A great silence fell sharply. A pi-dog barked in the distance, a peahen screamed, and I became aware that only one of us was breathing evenly. Then Nesbit gave an uncertain laugh.

"I don't believe that's going to work."

I allowed some of my anger to surface, which was not difficult. "My husband chose to remain in the hands of a powerful and mentally unstable man in order to buy time to get Mr O'Hara free. I, however, have no particular affection for your retired spy, and I have no intention of abandoning Holmes under those circumstances. Mr O'Hara's unwillingness to carry his own weight delays me and puts my husband into even greater danger. You honestly think I won't pull this trigger?"

In any performance, the key is convincing oneself first, and at that moment, with my fury and frustration welling close to the surface, I could well imagine my finger tightening. My performance certainly convinced Nesbit, whose breath froze completely in his throat; in the end, Kimball O'Hara, too, allowed himself to believe I meant it. He stood, brushed down his clothing, turned his back, and started walking: east towards the border. I eased the hammer down and took a much-needed lungful of air of my own before pushing past the stunned-looking captain.

I kept the gun on O'Hara's back all the way to the borders of Khanpur, so it could not be argued that he was escaping of his own volition.

And footsore, famished, and exhausted, we made it back to New Fort a good forty minutes before dawn, to find our drugged *chuprassi* still snoring gently in his corner.

Before we parted, Nesbit caught my elbow and spoke into my ear. "Would you have shot O'Hara?"

I looked at the man's features, haggard with fatigue but beautiful still, and I saw only Holmes' face as the door locked him in. The false moustache shifted on my upper lip as I smiled. "If he'd refused? I honestly don't know."

I fell exhausted into bed, half dressed, my legs still twitching with the rhythm of the long miles of jog-trot. But as the first wave of sleep came to carry me away, it brought with it a troubling piece of flotsam.

On first seeing O'Hara, I had been struck by the peculiarly open and unshuttered quality of his eyes; now I recalled where I had seen eyes like those before. They had been in the face of a man Holmes had hunted down in the south of France, a man who preyed on gullible women, to whom he appeared an innocent, friendly, open. Up to the moment his hands closed around their throats.

Chapter Twenty-Four

The horrendous clamour of a laden tea tray came through my door what seemed like minutes after I had shut my eyes. I squinted at the white-clad servant from my tumble of pillows, hating him with a deep passion. Him, I would have shot. Joyously.

"His Highness says, the horses will be ready in one hour," he informed me, and left before I could find my pretty revolver.

I peeled my moustache from the pillow sourly, and went to assemble Martin Russell from the dregs left behind by the night.

After some thought, I thrust the revolver into an inner pocket, just in case.

Afterwards, thinking back, I realised that I had gone six nights with little sleep, my last uninterrupted rest having been the night before Holmes was abducted. Three nights on the road to Hijarkot, a night with

Nesbit preparing to be Martin Russell, and two much-broken nights in Khanpur had left me far from sharp-witted.

Thus it was that I went down the stairs in a fog, walked to the breakfast room and automatically chose foodstuffs from the buffet, wanting only to lean up against a post and go to sleep. It wasn't until I saw Gay Kaur's face that I woke up, fast.

"Good Lord, Miss Kaur! What happened?"

The brown face smiled crookedly beneath the swollen lip and the sticking-plaster on her cheekbone. "You sound so like your sister," she said, and gingerly sipped from her cup of tea.

I pulled myself together. *Martin; you're Martin,* I recited fiercely, lowering my voice, resuming my formality, and surreptitiously straightening my spine for its absent uniform. "It's been the cause of more than one confusing telephone conversation," I told her. "Seriously, that looks rather nasty. How did you do that?"

"I got in the way of an angry beast," she said. "Not the first time. I must learn to be more careful."

The contusions showed no sign of claw, hoof, or tooth; I could not help speculating that the beast had two legs. She changed the subject.

"I understand that you and Captain Nesbit are to be singularly honoured today."

"Yes? How is that?"

"You didn't know? Jimmy's taking the two of you out with him, no one else."

"I was only told that the horses were being brought out. Pig again?" I thought it slightly out of the ordinary for the maharaja to repeat his sporting activities that soon. Perhaps Nesbit's presence, and their shared passion, made shooting or cheetah-coursing less appealing.

But Miss Kaur shrugged nervously and said, "I really don't know. It sounded rather as if he'd got something special arranged."

With that I recalled the maharaja's final words to us the previous evening, long hours before. What had it been? Something about the Kadir Cup, and how Britain's honour will demand that India lose—yes, and it had been followed by the thrown-gauntlet statement, "Let us see what you do with my entertainment tomorrow."

If we were going ahead with the maharaja's plans, then it would seem that he had not yet received news of a prisoner's escape. I ate my eggs without tasting them, trying to envision the details of the cells. Would breakfast have been handed the prisoner, or simply shoved beneath the door? Yes, I decided, the door to Holmes' cell had certainly been far enough off the stones to allow for a tray to be slid beneath. In which case, O'Hara's absence might well go undiscovered until the guard went to retrieve the breakfast utensils.

It seemed likely that our day would end abruptly at noon.

Permitting us to creep silently off to our beds.

Slightly cheered by the possibility, and marginally restored by food and coffee, I smoothed my freshly glued moustache and went to face the day's "entertainment," my mind not so much forgetting Gay Kaur's bruised face, as putting it aside.

I walked through the gardens and down the road to the stables, nodding at the guards, seeing no one else, which was slightly unusual. The animals in the zoo seemed restless, the monkeys' chatter on seeing a human pass louder than usual, their leaps and swings on the high perches nearly frantic. The great African lion loosed its coughing roar every half minute or so, although as I went by its cage, I could see nothing out of the ordinary through the trees. Then at the stables, I found five horses saddled: the white Arab stallion, two bays, and the two nearly matched chestnut geldings that Thomas Goodheart and I had been given the first day. I greeted the *syce*; he responded with a sickly grin and would neither answer nor meet my eyes.

My skin began to prickle with uneasiness.

Minutes passed, and the gabble of monkeys heralded the approach of Geoffrey Nesbit, his perfect features looking older in the morning sun.

"Jimmy's not here yet?" he asked.

"Not yet," I told him, keeping my voice cheerful in the proximity of servants. "I was just going to have a smoke and watch the birds."

We strolled around the stables to the rise overlooking the great tank, and settled on a half-wall in view of the swans and exotic fowl. A snowy egret picked its way through the reeds, perusing the water, and my companion held a match to the end of my cigarette. I filled my lungs with as much appreciation as act.

"If I'm not careful," I said, "I'm going to find myself liking these things."

Nesbit was not interested in my bad habits. "Have you any idea what's going on?"

"None. But the maharaja's cousin has a badly bruised face, and the *syce* won't talk to me. Something's wrong. You think he's discovered O'Hara missing?"

"I went to borrow a stamp from Trevor Wilson. He told me that Jimmy had a letter yesterday, from Delhi. No one seems to know what was in it."

"If it came yesterday, it could explain his evil temper yesterday night."

"And if he then found O'Hara gone . . ."

I was suddenly glad for the weight of the revolver against my leg.

"How will that change things?" I asked him.

"Impossible to say. However, if he decides to make another all-nighter of it with me, I don't think we ought to wait. You play ill. An attack of malaria should do it, you can start looking flushed over dinner and excuse yourself. As soon as it's dark, make your way over to Old Fort and wait for them to bring Holmes out. The two of you should be able to overcome the guards—I can give you another vial of morphia, if you like, so they stay unconscious for a while, although I haven't another syringe."

I stared out over the lake, the forgotten tobacco burning down towards my fingers as I pushed the various parts of the puzzle about in my mind. Would Holmes use the syringe and drug his guard as soon as darkness fell, or would he wait until after the maharaja's midnight matinée? He had no way of knowing that, with the current turmoil, the call might never come. In which case, how long after midnight would he wait, before having to risk the dawn? No, better if I ventured again into the prison fortress and brought him out. Nesbit would simply have to watch his own back.

My tobacco had burnt itself out; Nesbit ground his out under his boot and said, "It's possible he's forgotten—oop. Spoke too soon."

The clamour from the monkey-cage rose as they spotted someone coming down the path. We stood to see, over the roofs of the stable; in a moment I could make out three men, the first bareheaded, the two taller figures behind him topped with red *puggarees*. The monkeys screamed and bounced around their trees wildly, the men came down the path, and then the three stopped, directly adjacent to the high, noisy cage.

The maharaja seemed to be speaking to his two guards, although at this distance, I could not even make out the gestures, just that they had stopped and were facing each other. Then the smaller man flung his right arm out at the monkey-cage, and one of the guards seemed to move slightly back, the sun briefly glinting off the barrel of the rifle he carried. I saw his free hand, too, raise up in a weak gesture, and then the maharaja stepped forward, snatched the long gun, and brought it down, butt first, in the guard's face. The red *puggaree* staggered back; the maharaja brought the rifle to his shoulder and pivoted ninety degrees towards the cage. The barrel spat flame, and the sound of a shot rolled across the landscape, startling the lake birds into sudden flight. A dark shape dropped from its high perch, and the other monkeys went crazy. A second shot flashed and sounded; with the third, terror sent the creatures cowering into the corners, silent at last. The maharaja flung the gun back at its owner and continued on down the hill.

"Christ Jesus," Nesbit murmured into the shocked air. The three men disappeared behind some trees, and Nesbit set off for the stables at a run.

The stable-hands were furiously tightening girths and polishing saddles, their faces pale and taut, when their lord and master swept into the yard with the two armed guards on his heels, one with blood streaming from his smashed nose, the other gripping his gun with white knuckles. The maharaja marched straight over to the white stallion; the *syce* ran for the mounting block, but he was too slow, and received a kick from the spurred boots for his delay.

Up in the saddle, kerbing the stallion with hard hands, our host glared down at us, his face terrible in scorn and rage. "My ancestors ruled this land when yours were squatting in grass huts picking for lice," he shouted. "My father and grandfather made treaties with the British Crown, and we have remained loyal to those treaties. And now your government thinks it can summon me—*me*, the king of Khanpur—to stand before them like a schoolboy answering for his petty crimes. They threaten me—*threaten*! With what? Next they will be sending men to spy upon me. I swear, before that happens I will disembowel their stinking *sudra* of a Viceroy and leave him for the vultures."

I was more than prepared to dive for cover, but my companion was made of the stuff that had built an Empire. Nesbit stood his ground as the horse jittered and turned under its enraged rider, and even took a step forward into range of those spurred boots, looking up at his friend.

"Jimmy," he said, and, "Your Highness. What has happened? I don't understand. Tell me what has happened."

"A letter! From London, telling me—not asking, *telling*!—that I am to report to Delhi immediately to answer questions concerning some damnable woman. What woman, I ask? Who am I to care if my neighbour has lost one of his daughters?"

It suddenly became a lot clearer: The complaint of the neighbouring nawab had percolated upwards, and hit the sensitive place of England's new régime. I cursed under my breath, and knew Nesbit would curse too. The timing could not have been worse for a display of the Socialists' determination to treat all its citizens near and far with an equal hand.

"Jimmy, it's the new government, you know?" Nesbit said in soothing tones. "New boys, they mean well, but they haven't a clue as to how things are done, and are stumbling around stepping on toes right and left. Look, I'll go back to Delhi immediately and straighten it out. Honestly, think no more about it. I'll talk to the CinC—he knows me, he knows you've been a loyal friend to Britain, he'll hear me out."

The prince hauled himself back from the edge, but his now-stifled rage sharpened into a look of calculation, even cruelty, and he interrupted Nesbit's ongoing explanation of the delicacies inherent in a change of governments.

"This is an insult to my very blood. You have been my friend, Nesbit, but you are first and foremost one of them. And your friend here." The look he gave me was enough to curl my toes. "I invite his sister to share at my table and my sport, and the woman gets it into her head that she must leave, and walks away from my hospitality without even an as-you-please. I long thought the English had some sense of honour, or at least manners. I find now you have neither. You people imagine that you rule here in Khanpur. I tell you, Nesbit: You do not." He spat out the three words like bullets. "*I* rule Khanpur; I and I alone. I invited you here; I am prepared to disinvite you. But before you go, you will take today with you, and—by God!—it will give your English government something to think about. Mount and come, both of you."

He whirled the stallion on its haunches and kicked it into a gallop, its hooves sliding dangerously over the stones of the yard. Nesbit and I climbed more reluctantly into our saddles and followed at a more sedate gait; as we left the yard, the two armed guards were shouting at the *syces* to bring up their two bays.

"What do you suppose he has in mind?" I asked Nesbit as we trotted along the dusty road. "Panthers? His pet African lions?"

"I suppose we should be glad he didn't just have his men tie us up between two elephants."

He looked glum, but the thought of that sort of punishment made the breakfast go queasy in my stomach. "You don't think . . ."

"That he's going to do us in? No, I don't think he's that mad. Besides which, he seems to have in mind more of a demonstration. Or a contest—yes, that may be it."

"Whatever it is, for God's sake let him win."

"I'll do my best. But I shouldn't think that doing so openly would be a good idea. Having a rival deliberately throw a game could well be the match that lit the charge."

I could see that, and I reflected, not for the first time, that those who had decreed that British boys grow up playing demanding games had a lot to answer for.

"Perhaps it's time just to tell him who we are."

Nesbit screwed up his face and shook his head, more in doubt than in disagreement. "We may have to. But I'd rather keep that as a last resort. That, too, might be the spark that drives him to violence, to think that a friend was now spying on him—you heard what he said about spies. The other princes would probably feel much the same—a lot of uncomfortable questions would be asked if they thought they might be the object of surreptitious surveillance. No, none of them would like it one bit."

We rode for an hour, into the open land where we had ridden after pig on the first day. My exhaustion retreated with the exercise, the clean air clearing my head, the horse's eager energy proving contagious. I had no wish to pit myself against some deadly animal while armed with nothing but a sharp stick, but if the maharaja was determined to do so in order to prove Khanpur's superiority over the effete Brits, so be it. I had a gun that would give pause to anything smaller than an elephant, and a horse under me that could outrun most predators.

All in all, although I was not pleased with how the day was turning out, it could have been worse. The maharaja might, as Nesbit said, have thrown us into the cell next to Holmes', or had us executed outright. Or he could have come up with some kind of competition that would have proved instantly disastrous for Martin Russell, such as wrestling or employing the more primitive skills of the *nautch* girls. With any luck, he would merely rub our noses in our inferiority and throw us out of the kingdom, leaving us no worse off than we had been yesterday night. Yes, there remained the problem of retrieving Holmes, but as Holmes himself had said, he need only stand up and publicly declare himself an eccentric English magician, and the maharaja would have no choice but to allow him to leave.

With any luck.

Again the *shikaris* waited beneath their tree, spears in their hands, but this time with apprehension in their straight spines and the sideways glances they cast at the man on the white horse. The dry grassland rustled beneath a light morning breeze; the fields of sugar cane and barley glowed green and lush in the bright light;

the stand of trees from which the herd of pigs had been driven stood on the rise, unchanged. The single new element in the drama was a solid-sided farm cart, roofed and with a door in the back, bolted securely shut. The thought passed through my mind that the bullock drawing it was a remarkably phlegmatic animal, considering that it stood dozing less than a dozen feet from whatever wild beast the cart contained, but I did not really think about it further. I was too busy feeling relieved that, whatever our prey was to be, it could be no taller than a man, and light enough to be pulled by a single bullock.

At a signal from their prince, one of the servants walked over to the cart. To my astonishment, he did not climb up to work the bolt from the safety of the roof, but simply reached out for it. His hands weren't even nervous, the fool. I lifted my spear, and readied for the charge.

What came out instead was a tall man, clothed in black from boots to turban, unfolding himself from the cart's dark interior to open ground, tugging his starched black *puggaree* down to shade his eyes from the sudden glare, showing no iota of surprise at seeing two of us who should have been gone.

Holmes.

Chapter Twenty-Five

"What the bloody hell kind of a joke is this?" Geoffrey Nesbit demanded, allowing his spearhead to drop.

"Not a joke. This man is my prisoner. He was seen in front of any number of witnesses to slay his assistant, one week ago. He has been condemned to death. We are his executioners."

Suddenly, breathing became difficult.

"If he committed murder, where's the body?" Nesbit challenged him.

"I assume the villagers disposed of it."

I found my voice. "It was merely a trick."

"No trick. It was murder."

I had had as much of this charade as I was willing to take. "All right, this is ridiculous—" I started, but Nesbit's hand on my sleeve stopped me. I turned to hiss at him, "Geoffrey, this has gone far enough. The border is less than five miles off. Thank the man for his kind hospitality and let's go."

He didn't answer, just looked over my shoulder until I shifted in my saddle to follow his gaze. The *shikaris* under the tree had been joined by the two guards, both of whom had their rifles at the ready, aimed at us.

"Yes," came the maharaja's voice. "You see the problem. I am fully within my rights to execute my prisoner in whichever way I like. A pig spear is, I grant you, less usual than shooting or hanging, but can be as fast as either. And if my two English guests choose to interfere, my two guards may—inadvertently, tragically—interpret my commands to mean the death of the meddlers. Particularly if they refuse to lay down the revolvers both carry. Alas, how sad."

"You would never get away with shooting us," Nesbit told him, outraged.

"No, probably not. But can you see the maharaja of Khanpur condemned and hanged? I think not. The greatest punishment would be for me to abdicate in favour of my son, and live out my days in Monte Carlo or Nairobi. But," he said, his fanatic eyes lit from within, "the English would never forget Khanpur. Never."

My God, he was dead serious. I looked to Holmes, completely at a loss, but Nesbit distracted me, putting his head near mine that we might not be overheard.

"We have little choice," he said.

"You don't honestly think he'd go through with it?"

"Jimmy, on his own, would probably come to his senses before it was too late. But those guards have the determination of men under orders. They'd bring us down before he could speak up."

Nesbit was a captain in the Indian Army; one thing he knew was the habits of soldiers. "So what do you suggest?"

"We can do nothing here, where we'd be a pair of

ducks on the lake, awaiting the gun. Out in the field, however, anything can happen."

"Nesbit, you swore that man would set Holmes free if only we declare our citizenship. Let's do that and be done with this farce."

"I said, if we publicly declare his identity. What public have we here?" His green eyes drilled into mine; I tore my gaze away, looked at the two guards with their motionless rifles, looked at the maharaja with his triumphant smile, then at Holmes, standing with his hands tied together, saying nothing. His attitude brought home to me how very far from England we were. One grows accustomed to being the citizen of no mean country; to find oneself in the hands of a person to whom that signifies nothing is humbling. And frightening.

"He's mad."

"I fear so."

"And your only suggestion is that we take to the field and improvise?" We both heard my unvoiced scorn: *This is the best an Army captain can come up with? This is the flower of British Intelligence, heir to Kimball O'Hara and Colonel Creighton?*

On the other hand, I was the student and partner of Sherlock Holmes, sister-in-law to the renowned Mycroft, and I had nothing in my repertoire, either.

"We could hope to get close enough to Jimmy to take him hostage—they'd not shoot if one of us had a spear to his throat. Barring that, we can attempt to manoeuvre ourselves beyond the range of the rifles and into the cover of those trees, then make a run for it."

"We'd never make it, not without our guns."

"I don't know that we have an abundance of

choices," he said grimly. And thinking it over, I had to agree. He saw it in my face, and turned to the prince.

"That's not exactly fair play, Jimmy. You've got the guns, we've got sticks, and even when we've finished with this blighter you can have your men shoot us down."

"I will not. Indeed, why would I? Once you have executed this condemned murderer for me, why need I bother further with the British?"

Nesbit looked at me for confirmation, and I wavered in an agony of indecision. The maharaja was beyond a doubt insane, but it appeared to be a more or less linear madness, with the goal of shaking the Englishman to his boots and re-establishing the autonomy and honour of Khanpur's rulers. Monomania, rather than outright psychosis. If we did manage to thwart his plans and make our escape, God only knew what outlet his wrath would take. But once outside the borders, the Army encampment was a matter of hours away, and the wholesale rescue of the maharaja's remaining "guests" would be their concern.

It was to be a game, then, with deadly results if we did not play it according to its inventor's rules. Three of us, three of them, with two rifles on the opposing side. With deep foreboding, but not seeing much choice, I pulled the fancy revolver from my pocket and handed it to the *shikari* sent to us for the purpose; Nesbit gave over his gun as well. We were given pig spears in exchange, of a different design than the one I'd used before. This one was more than a foot shorter, with a smaller blade and weighted at the butt. Nesbit took his as if there was nothing unusual in the shape, but the maharaja's was the long style. A servant carried another long spear with him when he cut Holmes' bonds; to my surprise, he handed the weapon to Holmes.

Holmes hefted it, silently eyeing the man on the white horse, who showed him his teeth and said in Hindi, "Yes, you wish to use it, magician, I can see. And you will have your chance—if you succeed in killing these other two first. This is a fair game, you see? Your spear is long, theirs short. They have horses, you have your feet, along with whatever magic you can find here on this hillside. You claim to read minds, so here is your opportunity. One man at a time; I give you to the count of one hundred before the green-eyed man comes after you. If you live, next will come the man with the eyeglasses, and after that, me. Nesbit, here is your chance at first blood in the first-ever Khanpur Cup." And he laughed.

Nesbit and I looked at each other, but I had no idea how we might get out of this impossible dilemma, and clearly neither did Nesbit. I automatically turned to consult with Holmes, and found him making off rapidly in the direction of the first trees, his jaunty cocked turban waving sharply with every step—he was wearing the boots he'd brought with him, I noticed, not the soft shoes; the maharaja must have decided that decent footwear was more sporting. Which meant that Holmes had a small knife available to him as well as the long spear, along with a set of pick-locks—although I couldn't see what difference either would make.

I straightened my back and shrugged mentally, more as a means of ridding my mind of dread than an expression of confusion. Something would come up, I told myself. Holmes would see to it. He always did.

The dark trotting figure surprised a flock of birds into flight, their sudden rise giving him not a moment's pause. He skirted a stand of waist-high shrubs, dipped into a hollow, then followed the line of the hill, closer now but still terribly far from the trees where the pigs had sheltered that first day, a mixed stand of about an acre. The maharaja's lips moved as he counted the seconds off under his breath, then said aloud, "Fifty." As if he'd heard, Holmes speeded to a lope. Nesbit's hands tightened on the reins, causing his horse to champ and fret. I glanced over at the two armed guards; they had lowered their rifles to rest across their saddles, but they were watching closely.

How good were they with those guns? I speculated. If Holmes made the trees, if Nesbit met him there, perhaps . . .

I nudged my horse over until I was knee-to-knee with the Survey man. "Look, Nesbit, chivalry be damned, and uncomfortable questions can be dealt with. The maharaja won't kill me once he sees I'm a woman. You two make for the border and I'll strip to my under-shirt, take off the moustache, simply tell him I'm Mary Russell and not her brother. He'll be angry, but he's a Kshatriya—he might slap a woman, but anything more than that would go against his warrior's ethic. If he doesn't have me dumped immediately over the border, you can have the Viceroy send a delegation to fetch me. The only thing we lose that way is my pride, and a few days." His set jaw told me what he thought of that idea. "For God's sake, man," I urged, "use your head! If I go, the guards—"

"Ninety," the maharaja interrupted. "Ready, Nesbit?"

In answer, the blond man kneed his horse away from my side and loosed the reins. His horse, somewhat puzzled at the lack of any pigs in this pig-hunt, obediently pricked its ears, and I cursed.

"Nesbit, you fool," I hissed, but then, "One hundred!" and the man was off, straight as a loosed arrow, his posture sure, every inch of him an officer on the hunt, his game—

I froze, ice beginning to flood my veins—and then caught myself: *Don't be ridiculous, Russell. Of course Nesbit knows that's Holmes. He said as much when* . . .

But as I went over our exchange in my mind, I could not lay my hands on any scrap of conversation that proved Nesbit had connected the maharaja's pet magician with the Holmes he had seen in gaol.

I gave myself a smart mental slap. *Don't be a vaporous female, Russell!* How could Nesbit not know? For heaven's sake, the man wasn't blind. And he wasn't stupid enough to be fooled by the turban (*the black turban that shaded Holmes' face as he got down from the cart, the turban he hadn't worn before in Nesbit's sight* . . .) or by the boots or the renewed dye on the prisoner's skin. Nesbit was a professional. Certainly he'd known who the magician was the night we arrived. Hadn't he? We didn't speak Holmes' name, of course, for fear of listening ears, but still. . . .

But dear God, the man looked determined on that horse, galloping full-tilt towards the running figure, looking for all the world a man making the best of an unpleasant but necessary task. I gathered my reins to take off after them, but the maharaja's voice stopped me.

"Captain Russell, I am gratified by your eagerness, but you will please wait until one or the other of them is down." With the reminder, I could feel the guards behind me, knew they had raised their guns in preparation. I loosed my grip on the spear I had unconsciously lifted, and stared across the *terai* at the fast-closing figures, burning with fear and with the painful irony of the entire situation: If the man on the white Arab had known who his magician was, known he had Sherlock

Holmes in his collection, he would have been more eager to hide him than to hunt him.

I nearly whooped when I saw Holmes leap into the trees, bare yards in front of the rider, who reined back hard before his mount pelted headlong into trunk and branch. The horse half-reared at the harsh hand on its reins, and Nesbit began to circle, looking for a more congenial way in. He might have followed on foot, but it looked as if he wished to preserve the advantage of height in the face of his prey's longer spear. He trotted south thirty or forty yards, then turned back and cantered past the place where Holmes had disappeared.

Thick, dark forest began in earnest two miles away, rising up to the endless snow-capped mountains that sheltered Kashmir and, beyond it, Tibet. Unfortunately, this stand before us was in no way connected with the greater forest—had it been, the prisoner would never have been allowed anywhere near it. Still, Holmes could use it as the pigs had, as shelter and weapon against the hunter. It's the hidden tusks that kill, the maharaja himself had said.

Abruptly, a herd of pigs launched itself out of the stand fifty feet or so from Nesbit. My horse jerked in response, eager to get on with the business of the day, but I kept him in line, murmuring for him to wait, that he'd get his turn to run in just a while. The sudden flushing of game loosed a chatter among the men behind me, but it quickly died away as realisation of the nature of the prey returned to them. None of them would risk speaking out against their master, I thought, but I noted their fear, and beneath it their disapproval, as something that might be used.

Nesbit had reached the northern end of the trees and slowed to circle around. We could still see him, his light coat and the colour of the horse flitting behind the trees. The guards did not care for his vanishing from their sights. One of them said something in the local tongue, but the maharaja's sharp reply evidently told them not to move. And indeed, while I was there, they did not need to; I knew better than they did that Captain Geoffrey Nesbit would not ride away and leave me.

Now, however, Nesbit was not visible. Two minutes went by, three, and the same guard spoke again, to no reply. Four minutes, and the Arab stallion arched his neck in reaction to the hand of his rider, but before the prince could send his guard to see what was happening amongst the trees, Nesbit burst from the thickest section of growth, on foot and racing in our direction. He took perhaps ten steps out from the tree line, then flung his hands up in the air and collapsed forward onto the ground. Even without the maharaja's binoculars, I could see the short, weighted spear sticking out from between his shoulder blades, see, too, the brilliant red stain that spread across the back of his coat. He lay still.

Immediately, the maharaja shouted a string of commands that had his guards hastening into action, although they did not go anywhere near Nesbit. Rather, they were after his horse. They reappeared a few minutes later, the gelding trotting behind them; the maharaja relaxed, and mused aloud.

"So. It appears that our magician throws the javelin as well as conjuring coins and mice. And he still has his own weapon. I suggest you watch yourself, Captain Russell." His manner said the opposite, that he would like nothing better than to see me sprawled on top of Nesbit, leaving the field free for him. Still, he was not about to trust to the magician's skills. He shouted at the other guard to go to the southern end of the copse, where his weapon would ensure that I remained in play until either I or the magician was out of the game.

I gripped the shaft of my short spear and kicked my gelding forward towards the trees.

My path took me twenty feet from where Nesbit lay. I glanced involuntarily at the spear haft that protruded from the back of his blood-soaked jacket, but I did not stop; there seemed little point. Instead, I continued south, towards the guard, sitting with his rifle across his saddle. From where he waited, he could watch both sides of what I now saw was an overgrown *nullah* or stream-bed, a long, rock-strewn dip in the earth that resulted in a trickle of water at its southern end. His horse lipped at some green shoots that followed the water-course; I passed between guard and trees, ignoring both.

Halfway up the eastern side, Holmes' face peered out at me from between two trees. I said nothing, did nothing to let the guard know what I had seen, but Holmes grinned at me before slipping back into the undergrowth. As I rounded the northern end of the trees, he used the momentary distraction of my reappearance to make his move.

His black figure darted out from the trees to where Geoffrey Nesbit lay. The guard immediately raised his rifle and fired a shot, which missed his target wildly but ricocheted alarmingly ten feet from my horse's nose. I shouted in fury, hauling back on the reins to force my gelding into a rear, but only when the maharaja added his voice to the protest did the guard lower his gun and kick his own horse into a run instead.

He was too late. Holmes had grabbed Nesbit's ankles and dragged the limp body face-first at high speed across fifteen feet of ground and up the rocks into the shelter of the trees. Nesbit's arms stretched out after him, muscles slack, head bouncing back and forth wincingly across the rough ground. A dozen steps and they were gone. The guard galloped up, pressing his bay close to the wall of green.

"I say," I shouted at him. "Unless you want a spear through you, I'd suggest you move back."

His English was quite good, and he moved away briskly. After a minute, seeing that there was nothing he could do now to keep the magician from retrieving the spear that had killed the English captain, he looked to his master for instructions, then rode back to his position at the southern end.

I made a great show of peering this way and that into the growth before circling back north and turning down the far side of the copse. The guard shifted a few yards to the east so he could keep track of me, but came no farther, wanting to remain within sight of his maharaja. I rode to the spot where Holmes had shown himself to me, then dismounted, looping the reins over a dead branch and patting the damp chestnut neck. The horse bent to lip at the grass; I hefted my spear up to shoulder level for effect, then stepped into the trees and the dappled half-light.

In a clearing near the creek, I found Nesbit sitting hale and hearty, bathing the blood from a scraped cheek while Holmes unthreaded the doctored spear from the resurrected man's coat. I saw that its blade had been thrust through a flat piece of wood then bent sideways to lock it down, after which the spear's butt end had been threaded through a slit in the garment and bound up against the victim's spine with a length of black turban fabric. The blood was explained by the carcase of a young pig that lay on the rocks, the spearing of which no doubt explained the sudden exodus of the rest of the herd.

"A masterly bit of illusion, Holmes," I said. He nodded his acknowledgement, gave my cropped scalp and blond moustache a pained glance, then concentrated again on the work in hand. "Now, if you can just conjure up one of our host's aeroplanes, we'll be well out of here."

"I couldn't even manage to hang on to Nesbit's horse," he said apologetically.

"You did well to lay hands on me," Nesbit objected.

"Don't worry," I told him. "Self-criticism is my husband's way of patting himself on the back."

"Nonetheless," Holmes went on, deigning to take note of my psychological insight, "we're three riders with one horse, and a border at least six miles away."

"Have to do something about that, won't we?" I said. The situation ought to have filled me with alarm, but instead I felt irrationally cheerful. "What's our arsenal?"

"One long spear, one short, another short one with a ruined head. You have your knife, Russell?" he asked with a glance at the borrowed riding boots.

"Of course. Nesbit?"

"No. Well, a pen-knife, that's all."

"Still, there are plenty of rocks. You take my spear," I told him. "You're better with it than I am. Shall we go?"

The puzzled Army captain put on his ruined coat and followed us through the green to the eastern border. My absence had brought the guard, who was stirring his horse into a trot. In a minute he would be behind the trees, invisible to the maharaja and the other guard. I scooped up a pocketful of round rocks and yanked down several branches of fresh new leaves.

When the guard was fifty feet away, I stepped unconcernedly out from the trees, my arms full of greenery, and carried it over to drop at the chestnut's feet. As he lowered his head to explore it, I took out Martin Russell's cigarette case and picked one out, setting it between my lips.

"Why do you stop?" the guard demanded. His rifle was in his hands, but pointing still at the ground between us.

I flicked my lighter and got the tobacco going before telling him, "Go and see." I slid the lighter back into my pocket, and as he turned to peer into the trees, I pulled out a pair of rocks and let fly.

The damnable *puggaree* he wore gave little chance of knocking him cleanly out, but my rocks were heavy and fast, and at the third blow between his shoulders the startled bay shied and dumped him. I went after the horse as Holmes and Nesbit swarmed out to overcome the guard.

I couldn't have caught the animal if he'd run, if the guard had got off a shot and truly frightened him. As it was, he slowed to a halt forty feet away and watched me walking more or less in his direction, but at a safe angle away from him. I strolled, dreading the sudden appearance of the second guard, murmuring idly at the creature until the ears twitched forward. Gently, doing nothing to alarm his equine sensibilities, I drifted closer, tempting him with greenery, until I had my hand on his bridle.

The moment my hands touched the reins, Holmes kicked the other horse into a run, Nesbit behind him on the wide haunches with the fallen guard's rifle. I threw myself into the saddle, drove my heels hard into the horse's sides, and flew on their heels across the grassland in the direction of the Khanpur border.

But the guards were superbly trained, or the maharaja cautious. Less than twenty strides into our gallop, the first shot came. I felt as much as heard the bullet cut through the air, saw a puff of dirt rise up on the other side of Holmes and Nesbit, and looked back over my right shoulder to see the second guard as he rounded the southern tree line. The crack of the gun reached us, and Nesbit, ahead and to my left, twisted around, trying to bring his stolen rifle up as he clung to the bare horse with his legs. Unfortunately, I was directly between the two weapons.

I wrenched the reins to the left so I was heading back towards the trees, desperate to clear Nesbit's line of fire. After a quarter of a mile, I twitched them back to the right, and was in a line with the other horse when out of the corner of my eye I saw a white flash, beating its way flat-out around the northern end of the trees.

Four horses, five riders, their trajectories coming together at a point where an arm of forest stretched out into the grassland of the *terai*. The maharaja's Arab was ideally suited for this race, deft on its feet over the rough ground and filled with stamina, whereas stamina was just what the doubly-laden gelding in front of me was running short of. My stolen bay might, possibly, have outrun the smaller Arab, but the chestnut under Holmes and Nesbit was already showing the first signs of foundering. From the south, the guard's sturdy bay would reach the point last of all, but it would all be over before then.

Nesbit was the first to move in the sacrificial stakes. He and Holmes seemed to be shouting at each other, but before the magician could act, his tow-headed passenger flung himself off the horse, hitting the ground hard and rolling. He came up on one knee and turned his rifle at the guard, magnificently—if suicidally—oblivious of the bullets spitting dirt around him. One shot slapped at his leg the instant his rifle fired, jerking his aim to a miss. The guard continued roaring down on him from the south, the maharaja from the north, and I in the middle. Nesbit's trouser leg reddened, and then he rose to a stand, took careful aim, and fired again. I saw the guard's bay stagger; the man himself kicked free of the stirrups and rolled clear before the animal went down. Kneeling now, half concealed by the wounded beast, the guard aimed at the still-standing Nesbit.

And then something odd happened. Before he could fire, the man seemed to flinch, then duck. He raised his hand as if to shade his face, and seemed to glow briefly in the bright mid-day sun. Then Nesbit's gun went off, and the guard fell backwards.

There was no time to consider the meaning of the man's peculiar gesture; the maharaja was fast closing in on Nesbit, his long spear in deadly position, the Arab's ears forward: only one thing to do. I hammered my heels down, pulling the thin knife from the top of my boot; the broken, bloodied spear on Nesbit's wall in Delhi flashed through my mind. *Nearly the end of my career.*

The prince saw me shift direction and responded instantaneously. His spear swung up to the place where I would be when my horse collided with the Arab, eight feet of steel-tipped bamboo against my own five inches of blade. There would be no throwing the knife underhanded and behind me—all I could do was try to avoid his blade, shoving it forward and crashing into the shaft or jumping at him the instant before it impaled me. I slipped my boots free from the stirrups and braced for the impact, cringing from the approaching razor.

And then the world flared in a soundless explosion, blinding me for precious moments before moving on. Frantically I blinked, but in that instant the two horses came together, the maharaja's spear sliding between my body and the bay's mane as my knee smashed into the prince's. Without thought, I clamped my right hand onto the bamboo shaft and stabbed out with my left; before the horses leapt apart, I heard the man gasp.

The two horses veered away from each other the moment the pressure on their reins permitted, but I couldn't understand what had happened. My dazzled vision confirmed that I had the spear in my right hand and a blood-smeared knife in my left, but where had the silent explosion come from, a flash like the sudden burst of a—a looking-glass! I'd suffered that blinding flash before.

Bindra.

The white stallion was pounding off north nearly as fast as it had come, its rider's left hand clapped over a bleeding right biceps. Holmes was circling back at a gallop, Nesbit was bending to examine his leg, and I brought the bay to a halt and stood in the stirrups to search every bump and shrub, but not until the boy repeated the mirror trick did I find him. Bindra saw me, and rose from his hiding place half a mile away, the ladies' compact in his hand, grinning hugely.

But that was not the end of the surprises. A few hundred yards beyond the boy, a light-skinned man in monastic robes stepped out of the beginnings of the forest, carrying in his hand some dark shape that could have been a short spear, but which I thought was a rifle. After a minute, he swung it up to rest across his shoulder, which I took as confirmation. And soon he was close enough to recognise: Kimball O'Hara.

All our chicks come home to roost.

Nesbit finished strapping his belt around his thigh and accepted Holmes' arm to pull himself onto the gelding. But Bindra paid us no mind. Instead, he turned and flew across the ground towards the man with the rifle, leaping into O'Hara's arms so that the monk staggered back. The sound of their laughter reached us through the still, hot air, and I kicked my mount into a canter until I was even with Nesbit.

"Who the hell is that boy, anyway?" I demanded, but the handsome, somewhat battered face just grinned at me. "Did *you* arrange for him to be at the horse-seller's? Is the brat one of yours?"

"Oh no, not mine. I didn't even know for certain that he existed, although I had my suspicions. No, I'd say the boy belongs to what one might term an earlier régime of Intelligence."

As we approached, O'Hara's free hand rested on the boy's shoulder; our close-mouthed donkey-boy grinning and chattering in a manner I'd not have imagined of him. We came closer, until I saw the same exact grin displayed on the man's face; with a flash like that of the brat's mirror, I knew what I was seeing, wondered only that I hadn't seen it before.

The urchin donkey-boy could only be Kimball O'Hara's son.

Chapter Twenty-Six

We had no time to spend on explanations or even greetings, not with the maharaja's stallion skimming across the ground in pursuit of reinforcements. O'Hara paused only long enough to look at Nesbit's leg, then whirled and set off at a fast trot, his robes dancing around him and the rifle over his shoulder, the boy on his heels.

"Wait!" I called. "We can double up on the horses." But O'Hara never looked back.

So Holmes and I rode my fresher horse, putting Nesbit up on the chestnut; once we had the wounded man in safety, I could always come back with both horses to fetch O'Hara and the child.

We left them far behind across the *terai*. Once among the trees, however, we began to climb, dismounting every half mile or so to lead the horses around some precipice or across the slick stones of a quick-running stream. When we felt quite certain not only that we were well free of the Khanpur border but that we would see the maharaja's men should they pursue us onto government land, we brought Nesbit down from his horse to see to his bleeding. Holmes loosed the belt tourniquet and ripped open the fabric to explore the bloody wound with delicate fingers.

Nesbit, white-faced but in control, said, "The bullet will need to be cut out. But it's doing no harm for the present. It'll keep."

Holmes nodded, but replaced the too-snug belt tourniquet with lengths torn from the remains of his *puggaree*. I was about to suggest that I take the two animals back for the others while Nesbit rested, when Bindra's chatter floated up the hill. We put Nesbit on one horse and the boy on the other, and hiked over hill and ice-girt stream until we were above the snow-line. Soon we came to a path, much trampled by booted men and heavy bullock-drawn carts.

The encampment lay to the north, but Nesbit said, "There's a *dak* bungalow a mile and a half to the south."

"I think we should go on to the encampment," I said. "That leg needs a surgeon."

"All it needs is to have the bullet dug out; even the boy could manage that."

"It is right under the skin," Holmes agreed.

"Going to the encampment would necessarily bring the Army into our actions," O'Hara pointed out in a mild voice. "Have we decided to do that?"

I looked at the others and sighed. "All right. But just overnight. And if there's any sign of fever, I'm going for a doctor myself."

We turned south and soon came to the promised *dak* bungalow, one of the network of travellers' rests scattered across India for the use of European officials. It was a low stone building with two more ramshackle

structures behind it, one for horses, the other for resident and visiting servants. Bindra led the horses away
towards the one, while from the other scurried a startled pair of men, astonished at our unheralded approach and unaccustomed anyway to parties on the
road at this time of year. The inside of the bungalow
would have benefitted from a broom and scrub-brush,
but the plaster had been whitewashed within the last
year, and the place was too cold to smell of anything
but damp.

The men were even more taken aback by our scant
baggage, which consisted of two rifles and a cloth bag
belonging to Bindra, and that contained nothing but a
blanket, some very old chapatis, a handful of dried apri-
cots, and his mirror. With ceremony, the older of the
two servants carried the grubby object before us into
the bungalow, laid it onto a rough-hewn table, and
turned to the business of making a fire, shaving slivers
of dry cedar from a log with the heavy knife that had
been left on the hearth for the purpose.

Camp chairs were quickly brought, sheets for the
two iron beds promised and bed-rolls for those condemned to the floor, but the first things Holmes demanded were a honed razor and a pot of well-boiled
water. I sat before the fire and pointedly turned my
back to the operation behind me. Clothing rustled,
Holmes and O'Hara consulted briefly, and then the patient was wheezing a forced breath from his lungs as
the razor bit in. In no more than thirty seconds came
the dull *tink* of a metal slug sinking to the bottom of an
enamelled dish-pan.

Tea was brought and drunk with gratitude, and the
khansama brought a hastily killed and curried chicken
to our table. We five ate enough for a dozen civilised

persons, and sprawled afterwards before the fire with tobacco in various forms—all but myself and, I noticed with private amusement, Bindra, whose eyes followed the cigarette given by Nesbit to O'Hara, but who did not then pull out one of the foul little *bidi*s I felt sure he had about his person. Instead, the boy took out the five coloured balls, and with the supreme nonchalance that does nothing to conceal great pride, he juggled. His father watched, making noises of appreciation and awe, his chest swelling along with that of his son. Holmes scraped out a disreputable pipe that one of the servants had found for him, and filled it with black leaf. A contented silence fell on our unlikely little band.

When Nesbit reached the end of his cigarette, he tossed it into the flames and glanced at where O'Hara sat, comfortably cross-legged on the floor. Bindra pocketed the balls and curled before his long-lost father, small head cradled by the man's robes, the young face gazing at the low flames, eyes slowly closing in the warmth. O'Hara's left hand rested on the tousled hair, his right played unceasingly with the beads of his rosary; he looked as content as the child.

Nesbit broke the silence, keeping his voice low. "Why did you not tell me about the boy?"

O'Hara smiled. "Because you would have wanted him. I was given over to Creighton's hands when I was thirteen; plenty soon enough."

"But the child has been living unsheltered for three years. Surely having him come to us would have been better than wherever he's been."

"Two years and three months, since we were separated. He has been among friends." O'Hara's fingers told the rosary, over and over, while the wood fire crackled and the boy's breathing deepened.

"But how on earth did he find us?" I wanted to know.

The monk smiled down at his sleeping son. "Until twelve weeks ago, he was with his mother's brother, in the mountains. When I succeeded in getting the amulet out, it passed through the hands of a man who knew where to find the boy. He told the lad I was safe, and then my son got it into his mind to watch Nesbit, that he might participate in his father's rescue. You two came; he followed Holmes as he came and went, talking to Nesbit, purchasing many interesting things, and finally going to the horse-seller's; when you arrived there to take possession of the donkey and the cart, Ram Bachadur himself lay sleeping, thanks to some drugged *pilau* he had eaten."

"Who was the man that helped you?" Nesbit demanded.

The calm eyes looked back. "A friend."

"He was one of us, wasn't he? Within the Survey?"

"That is possible."

"What he's done could be called treason."

"Or brotherhood."

"There is some man performing treason, from within the walls of the Survey. Men have died because of him. Men who were our brothers: Forbes, Mohammed Talibi, and a new boy, Bartholomew."

O'Hara's fingers paused on his rosary, his head dipped as the names registered with him, but when he spoke again, his voice left no room for doubt. "I grieve for their deaths, Nesbit, but it was not he who put the knife to their throats."

Nesbit scowled at the man on the floor; still he had little choice at the moment but to put aside the question of the traitor in the Survey ranks, and go on. "But how did you end up in that prison in the first place?"

"Pride," O'Hara answered promptly. "Pride is a sweetmeat, to be savoured in small pieces; it makes for a poor feast. I know that you received my letter telling of the fakir's ill treatment and the order of cotton—my friend Holmes here told me as much during one of our long Morse code conversations through the stones. But the means of my uncovering the thread, of picking it free from the surrounding design and following it to the source, I did not tell of that. I was clever," he said, making it sound like a character flaw. "When I was good at The Game, there was none better; this time, two years and more ago, it happened I had my son with me, a son any man might be happy to claim, and I wanted him to witness his father's cleverness and skill. The Wheel of Life turns hard and fast, and my pride rode its top but for a moment, before it spun down to crush me underneath."

He saw Nesbit's impatience with the metaphor, and relented. "I went more deeply into suspect territory than I ought, and asked questions more pointed, and became more visible than any player of The Game dare do. I became, in short, a rank amateur, showing off for my son. His mother had died of the cholera when he was six, and he lived with his Tibetan grandparents for the three years after that. I thought the time had come to take him by my side, and as this was to be my last such expedition, I saw no harm in showing him some of the rules of our Game."

He sighed, and shook his head. "My Holy One spent long hours expounding on the Wheel that is life, trying to re-form me from the imp I was. In the Wheel that holds the essence of Tibetan Buddhism, the hub is formed of the conjoined animals whose individual natures are ignorance, anger, and lust. Taken together, the hub of Illusion is pride.

"Yes, Nesbit, I see you wish fact and not philosophy. Very well. The boy and I went into Khanpur itself, selling copper pots. Which might have been innocent enough, but why then should a seller of pots take himself north out of the town for six or seven miles, to a place where there is no village, only a fort? Why should a seller of copperware be so interested in the maharaja's air field, he ventures into the very buildings where the aeroplanes are stored? In my eagerness to come up with a prize for my last round in The Game, I chose to forget the danger of my opponent.

"I would have been executed forthwith, I think, but for the presence of the boy, which puzzled the men who took me, and puzzled their master when we were brought before him. Had they let him go, I would have gone to my death with a degree of equanimity—after all, when one has cheated The Great Illusion as many times as I have, it is hardly sporting to complain when it catches one up. But they held the boy, and they were preparing to use him to open me up.

"So I offered to give them what they wanted, without having to go to the effort and delay of torture, if only they would let him go free. And moreover, I told the maharaja, I would offer him a great prize, one he would never get from me by the brand or the rack, as soon as I had seen the child cross the Khanpur border. I promised him that it would be worth it, and he looked into my eyes, and he decided to gamble that I was giving him the truth.

"I sent the boy to my friends, extracting from him first the promise that he must never enter Khanpur again without my word, and watched him go down the road and through the guard's post. As soon as he had passed, I turned to my captor and told him who I was. That I was not only an agent of the British Intelligence service, but that I was also the boy known to the world through the writings of Rudyard Kipling."

"And you gave him your word that you wouldn't try to escape under your own power," Nesbit concluded. "Thus condemning me to a case of severe back-strain."

"I did make a considerable effort not to grow fat inside the prison," O'Hara countered. "Since I thought it possible that such a scenario might come about."

"Possible, my foot," his superior officer said with a grin. "You planned for it. That's why you worded your vow the way you did. You knew someone would come after you sooner or later, and had to trust that they would be able to haul you off."

"Or drive me at gunpoint," O'Hara said, shooting a grin of his own in my direction. "Yes, I admit it: another tit-bit of pride, to sweeten the tongue."

"The sweetness of the plan must have faded considerably, after two years in a cell."

"Not at all. I knew my son was safe, and I knew he would arrange things as needed, with the assistance of my . . . friends. Once I had the amulet away, I knew it was literally only a matter of time."

By way of response, Holmes reached forward to knock out his pipe against the stones of the fireplace, then pulled the heavy knife out of the cedar kindling-block and drove its point into the side of his boot-heel. Reluctantly, the heel parted, and Holmes picked from the base of it the small oilskin-wrapped amulet that had set us on our play of The Game long weeks before. He tossed it over to O'Hara, who dropped the rosary in order to catch it. He cupped the object in his right palm, his face going soft with affection.

"One of the guards had a small son he loved, who fell ill," O'Hara told us. "I cured the boy where the physicians could not, and in gratitude, the man passed my amulet on to a friend in Hijarkot, who would give it to a relative in a camel caravan, and so on. I was glad to hear that it survived." He slipped it into his robes, and his hand resumed the beads. His left hand had not moved from the boy's dark head.

"And now, Mr O'Hara," Nesbit said, his voice taking on the edge of a superior officer. "Do you have a report to give me?"

With that demand, tension took hold of the dank stone room. It all came down to this: a report demanded and given. From the beginning, his friends had sworn to O'Hara's loyalty, but his being locked in the maharaja's gaol did nothing to obviate the doubts. He could as easily have been working for India as for Britain.

But the imp Kim looked out of the middle-aged eyes, as if he knew what we were thinking.

"Oah, of course I have a report," he said. "I have ears, the guards have tongues, their master enjoys teasing his prisoners, and the hours are long for purposes of analysis. Do you wish my report now?"

"The gist of it will do."

"The maharaja of Khanpur plots rebellion, but of a twisted and most secretive kind. He is using The Russian Bear to supply himself with guns and ammunition, which he will pass on to the most radical of firebrands he can find—the makings of tons of explosives, guns fresh from Germany. When he is ready, he will then secretly open his borders to the Bolshevik troops.

But he has no intention of handing them India. Instead, he plans to allow them in just so far, and then raise the alarm. When the British respond, in force, after the Russians are extended into his land, he will shut the door behind The Bear's back. The Bolsheviks will be trapped between Khanpur and the Indian Army, where they will be crushed entirely. For the second time, a maharaja of Khanpur will become an heroic defender of the Crown, and his reward this time, for saving British India from The Bear, will be vast.

"His reward, in fact, will be India itself."

"The Lenin of the sub-continent," I interjected softly.

"You might say that," O'Hara agreed. "Or a native Viceroy."

"Native prince, hereditary ruler," Holmes mused. "The blood of the Moghuls in his veins, a thousand years of experience in his hands. A compromise between Congress and the Moslem League, certainly, but a shining opportunity as well, for India and England. Gandhi and Jinnah wouldn't have a chance."

"The English would seize upon Khanpur's maharaja with vast relief, that with a man of his stature in charge, they could now withdraw with honour."

"Leaving the country in the hands of a murderer and a madman," I pointed out.

"Which is why we cannot allow his plot to ripen even one week further." It was O'Hara who spoke, which surprised me.

"Wouldn't continuing to involve yourself in Survey business be furthering the actions of the Wheel of Life?" I asked him.

"One attains merit through action as well as by refraining from action," he answered piously. "The innocent must be given the opportunity to attain self-knowledge, which the unfettered actions of the wicked would prevent.

"To say nothing of the fact," he added, "that it should be jolly fun."

Our startled laughter woke Bindra for a moment. He kneaded his eyes with his fists, located his father, and settled again, nuzzling into the robed lap with a sigh of contentment.

"If I understand you aright," Nesbit said, ignoring my digression, "you would suggest that action be taken that does not bring the Army into this? Since," he noted, his green eyes beginning to dance, "it was you who suggested that we might not wish to approach the encampment at this time."

"Oah, Nesbit, truly you are a man after my own heart."

"What do you propose?"

"Well," the Irish Buddhist said, "you were willing to carry me on your shoulders from The Forts to the borders of Khanpur, until Miss Russell drew her gun." Holmes stirred, and I realised, belatedly, that he knew nothing of the events of the previous midnight. "But as that demand was not made upon your back and sinews, perhaps, given a few days for your leg to heal, you would not mind carrying the considerably lesser weight of the maharaja?"

"Kidnap him?" The quirking of Nesbit's mouth showed his love of the idea, although the hesitation in his eyes said he was thinking, too, of the report he would have to make to his superiors. Particularly if the plan went awry.

"Invite him outside to Delhi, for conversations," O'Hara suggested.

Holmes took his pipe out of his mouth to point out gently, "He is in a heavily guarded fortress."

"There is at least one concealed entrance," O'Hara said. "When he came to the Old Fort in the night, he did not always come smelling of the outside world, but of stones and dampness."

Holmes nodded. "I thought as much, the first time he came to my cell. But if a passageway links the Old Fort with the New, that would still require passing a number of guards. Unless it also has an opening to the outside."

I sat up as if brushed by a raw wire. "The zoo!" The three men looked at me. "When the maharaja showed us the zoo, I noticed a small pathway going around the back of the lion pen, past the entrance used by the zookeepers. The big path was marked heavily by bits of spilt food and the drag of equipment, but beyond it was the sort of footpath worn by a single set of feet, walking it with regularity. His dogs knew it as well—when they would have gone down it, he called them back. Sharply."

"That could be anything," Nesbit objected.

"I think not. The lion pen itself is built right up against the hill of the Fort, firmly into its westernmost side. And just before going to the zoo, I was in a room in New Fort located on the heights of that same side. The toy room, he calls it. Have you seen it?" I asked Nesbit.

"Years ago, and briefly. But you're right, it is on the western spur of the New Fort."

"It has a hidden door. I noticed the wear on the floor there, where the marble is grey with soil and scattered particles of gravel. The servants do not clean in the toy room very often. And in fact," I said as another piece of the puzzle came to me, "the maharaja has the reputation of sorcery—of being able to appear and disappear unexpectedly. No doubt this is partly explained by the number of purdah screens throughout the Fort, which would conceal a small elephant, but there may be a network of hidden passages as well. And you'd expect one to the outside, such as down to the zoo.

"Too," I said before they could object, "there may be a similar hidden passage in that horrid fur-lined gunroom of his. A room which is near the gates on the east side, a location which would be very convenient for crossing under the road to the Old Fort in the night. A passageway smelling of stones and dampness."

Silence again fell in the room, but it was an electric silence of intense speculation rather than repose. Even the boy was awake—or had given up the pretence of sleep—and had drawn himself up at his father's side.

"Provocative," Holmes said at last, and proceeded to repack his borrowed pipe with the Indian black leaf.

"You're certain?" Nesbit demanded.

"Of soil and wear on the floor near two blank walls? Yes. That those doors lead to the zoo and the Old Fort? Of course I cannot be sure."

"Even if we find a door out of the zoo, we could wander underneath the Fort for hours," he fretted.

"Oah, Nesbit," O'Hara said gently, "you English are so unhappy with uncertainty."

"And you Indians are so deucedly eager to embrace it."

The two men grinned at each other in easy understanding.

"However," Nesbit said, struggling to get to his feet. "Tomorrow I ride to the encampment, to arrange a proper show of support once we get the gentleman across his border."

We spread ourselves around the main room, Nesbit and myself on the narrow iron-framed beds, the others on the floor. Bindra turned down the paraffin lamp and padded back to his sleeping roll in front of the low-burning fire. We lay, silent with our thoughts, Nesbit's bed creaking and complaining as he sought to find a comfortable position for his leg, but at last even he fell still.

But it was O'Hara who had the last word, voicing a thought that was going through my own mind, and I think Holmes' as well.

"In the morning, when we are fresh, I should like to propose that the expedition into Khanpur be done posthaste." Nesbit's bed squealed in preface to his reaction, but the Irishman on the floor cut him off by saying, "I do not propose this tonight; but in the morning, we need to talk about it."

Nesbit subsided, positively radiating distrust and suspicion. One by one, we slept.

All but O'Hara. Whenever I woke during the night, I could see him sitting before the dying embers, breathing the words to the prayer *Om mane padme om,* over and over again, his long rosary beads clicking softly as outside, light snowflakes whispered against the window-glass.

Chapter Twenty-Seven

In the morning, Nesbit's green eyes glittered with fever, although he swore that it was nothing, that he was capable of riding, that he would carry the maharaja on his back if it came to that. Holmes and O'Hara glanced at each other over the wounded man's head, and said nothing, not then. But after we had eaten the eggs and bacon the servants cooked for us, both men drifted away outside where they stood, Holmes trying to get his pipe alight, O'Hara again fingering his rosary, their breath swirling into clouds in the heatless morning sun. I gave them five minutes, then walked out onto the fresh snow after them, my unprotected scalp tightening with the cold.

I saw no reason not to come to the point. "I'll not be left behind to play nursemaid."

O'Hara's hands stopped their motion as he gave me a look of surprise, but Holmes merely smiled into his troublesome pipe.

"You want to go today," I continued. "I agree: If the

maharaja was angry enough to shoot his pet monkeys yesterday, then today, after having all of us escape him at one time, he'll be insane with rage. I'm glad Sunny is out of things, but the others are too vulnerable. We can't wait until Nesbit is fit, but I refuse to stay with him. Leave Bindra here."

"Unfortunately, I have given my word that the boy will not be left behind again," O'Hara told me.

"As you wish, although I don't believe I'd take a son of mine into that hornets' nest. When do we go?"

"It is better that you stay here," O'Hara said. Holmes took an involuntary step back.

"And why is that?" I began, then stopped. "No, don't bother, I don't need to ask. What do women need to do in order to be taken as equals? Become Prime Minister? For heaven's sake, just pretend I'm 'Martin' if it makes you any happier, but let's have no more words about leaving Miss Russell out of anything. Besides, you need me. I'm the only one who's been to the toy room."

"You can draw us a map."

"Inaccurate. And you'd need to use a torch or matches, either of which would be seen from the room's high window. I can walk it in the dark."

O'Hara's dark eyes travelled to consult Holmes, who nodded and said, "She has a certain skill at the Jewel Game."

O'Hara studied me, as if such a talent would show on the surface, then said abruptly, "You went into the stables yesterday night."

"Yes," I replied, wondering if he was accusing me of something. "I wanted to see that the horses had been looked after."

O'Hara had something else in mind. "We will cover

your eyes, and you will walk through the stables by way of demonstration."

It seemed to me a rather silly exercise, but we were, after all, embarked on a game here, and perhaps my accepting the challenge would move things ahead more rapidly.

And so it proved. From the moment O'Hara snugged the linen dish-cloth around my head to the time we slipped across the Khanpur border was a matter of half a day.

We left with a rucksack Bindra had found somewhere, provisioned with food, water, and candles; two knives and an ancient revolver Holmes had got from the *khansama*; the rope and morphia, which Holmes had hidden about his person ever since the night in the gaol; and several small but vital pieces of inside information possessed by Nesbit. Only when we had extracted the facts did we reveal to the man that we were leaving him behind. He was not pleased; we had to chain his wrist to the iron bed to keep him from joining us.

His curses, however, followed us far down the snowy road.

Nor was Bindra happy to be left outside of the Khanpur border with the horses, but the boy had to admit, when pressed by a father employing all the logic of Socrates, that bearing the weight of an abducted maharaja would be beyond his abilities, and that someone needed to watch the beasts. We built a makeshift shelter for them below the snow-line, in an area of deep brush and woods far from the track, where Bindra could keep the animals quiet: The weightiness of that responsibility calmed him. At least we hadn't left him back at the *dak* bungalow, making sure that Nesbit did not get free.

Just before dark we reached the end of the forest, east and slightly to the south of The Forts, more or less where Nesbit and I had left O'Hara after the gaol-break. The moon rose with the darkness; when it was well clear of the mountains behind us, we slipped from the trees into the cultivated edges of the rough *terai*.

At ten o'clock, with an enormous, bright moon full in the sky, we crossed the main road without having disturbed anything more than pi-dogs and a few night birds. On the other side, the land was more heavily used, but in India even farmers tend to live inside village walls. We gave those wide berth, keeping to fields and paths and moving cautiously; we saw no person.

Well before midnight, the smells of the zoo came to us across the frigid air. A rooster crowed, some big animal—one of the lions, perhaps?—coughed irritably, nocturnal habits lying uneasy beneath the daylight régime of its keepers. Another half mile, and we were at the walls surrounding the village of dwarfs. There we paused for whispered consultation.

"The fence here seems to be nothing but thorn brush," I noted.

"Too noisy to move," Holmes countered. "We go around."

The tangle of dry thorn eventually gave way to high, strong wire fencing that kept the maharaja's giraffes from straying into the sugar cane. We had brought rudimentary burglary tools with us, but it proved unnecessary here, as the fence was not topped by barbed wire. We climbed up and dropped into the pen, keeping near the fence as it pushed deeper into the zoo, then at the far side climbed out again. The white gravel paths glimmered in the light from over our heads, giving us direction, although we did not walk on the gravel for fear of the betraying crunch.

The lions' pen would have been easy for a blind person to locate, stinking of carnivore, the faint splash of water from the hillside spring the only noise in the great stillness. Our boots made no sound on the winter-soft grass, our clothing gave less rustle than the breeze in the leaves. We drew near the high, gleaming bars, the trees and rock wall behind them a dapple of light and dark.

Then a lion roared from what seemed ten feet away, and I nearly screamed in response. We froze, and my heart coursed and leapt in my chest, making me dizzy; the night seemed to pulse and fade. There came the sound of a large body shifting, the pad of enormous feet, and a second roar. We remained motionless. Would a night watchman come to investigate? Did the roar of lions mean the same as the bark of a dog? Or was the animal merely calling into the night, in hopes that his voice might be heard by another?

After an interminable time, which was probably only six or eight minutes, the animal grunted to itself and padded across the ground. Then it dropped with a breathy grunt and quieted.

I began to breathe again. After a minute, one of the men touched my arm, and we crept forward, cautious as mice in a cattery.

At the end of the lion cage, the greenery closed in so it became impossible to avoid the gravel, but when I gingerly set my foot onto its pale surface, I found that here it had not been refreshed as recently as in the centre of the zoo, and the stones in this damp place had sunk into the ground. We passed the door to the keeper's building behind the cage where the food and cleaning equipment was stored, and where the white gravel came to an end.

But as I had remembered, there was an unnatural space between the bushes and the building where the salukis had bounded as at a familiar way, and the ground under our feet bore the unmistakable imprint of traffic. Working by feel alone, unable to see anything but the glow of the sky above, I patted my way along the walls until I came to the place where baked-mud wall merged with the naked rock of the hillside.

There we found the door. Unevenly shaped to suit the rough wall, too low for even a short man to pass while standing, and narrow enough to require slipping through sideways.

And locked.

Holmes eased past me to deal with that little problem, and when his pick-locks had done their work, we all breathed a sigh of relief to find the door unbarred. A battering-ram would not have suited our purposes at all.

We slipped inside, into a tight space that smelt of must and stone and the dampness of ages. Holmes closed the door behind him, and I lit a candle. We stood in a hollow perhaps five feet square and seven feet tall, rough-hewn from the rock. I had expected one passage, but we found two, both just wide enough for a man's shoulders and tall enough for Holmes to walk without being forced to duck. We took the one to the left, which began by heading north, but soon doubled back south, then north again. We were, I decided, cork-screwing upwards in the hill below New Fort, the floor of the passageway ever rising beneath our feet. Twice we came to junctions, and after debate, we took care to mark our choice with small pebbles. After the second junction, we went for five minutes or so before Holmes and I stopped almost simultaneously, sensing the way diverging from where we wanted to be. Returning to the junction, we shifted the pebbles and went on, ever climbing, until the passage came to an end at a door as broad as the outside one had been narrow.

This door, however, had no lock, merely an expanse of uneven, time-darkened wood. I pushed against it, then dug my fingernails into one of the cross-pieces and pulled, but the heavy thing did not budge. Without a word, I stepped back far enough to allow Holmes to pass, and handed him the candle.

He ran the light back and forth over the surface, looking more for signs of wear than for a trigger, but found nothing. Not until he began to search the surrounding rock did he give a grunt of triumph. Shifting the low-burning stub to his left hand, he reached up with his right forefinger to press something hidden by a rough place in the stone. There was a faint click, and the flame danced wildly and snuffed out in the sudden current of air from around the concealed door.

Holmes pressed back against the rock to allow me passage. I laid my hand against the wooden surface, which despite its weight gave way with the silent ease of oiled hinges, and felt forward with the toe of my boot for the high marble trim that had run around the toy-room floor. It was there, and moreover, the air smelt of dust and machine oil. I stepped inside, listening for motion or the sound of stifled breathing, until I was satisfied that we were alone.

I turned back to the invisible door, and breathed, "It's clear. Could you do something to the lock so—"

"It's done," Holmes whispered back. The last thing we needed, should this mad mission actually succeed, would be hunting for another trick switch with an ab-ducted maharaja on our hands.

The two men slipped into the toy room beside me, and I pushed the door shut, more or less. As I turned into the room, two hands came to rest on my shoulders, Holmes' familiar long fingers gripping my left, O'Hara's on my right. Now was the time to make good on my foolish assertion to Kimball O'Hara that I could find my way through a black room I had visited only once.

I bent my head and allowed my mind's eye to sum-mon a view of the room as it had been. The door; the high shelves of mechanical dolls and animals to its left; the scattered arrangement of glass-enclosed mecha-nisms across the floor—not in a haphazard pattern, not once one knew that there was a doorway hidden behind them. The Englishman-eating tiger was over *there,* the erotic toys *back there.* Which meant that we need only circle the piggies' tea party and dodge the pair of fortune-telling gipsies, and we would be at the room's entrance.

I led the way forward—slowly and with my hands stretched out to be sure, since I was not all that supremely confident. But we reached the door without noise or mishap, and I felt a surge of pride as I laid my hand upon the doorknob.

The corridor stretched out in both directions, lit by oil lamps every thirty feet or so. The nearest one was smoking and guttering, a black stain on the ceiling showing that it had not been properly trimmed. We closed the door quietly and turned south, away from the *durbar* hall and the billiards room, where late guests and their attendant servants might still be up.

The southernmost quarter of the New Fort, hidden

from view behind a thick stand of timber bamboo, had not yet known the hand of the maharaja's renovators. Behind the greenery, the plaster was chipped, the paint long peeled away, the stone floor of the arcade worn and gritty underfoot. But not uninhabited—these were the servants' quarters, with faint cooking odours wafting in from the open corridors. We slipped from one darkness to the next, freezing into imitations of the stone pillars around us when two tired-looking *chuprassis* scurried from the Fort's central courtyard and slipped between two columns into the south wing.

I stood pressed up against the greasy stones and looked through the bamboo at the guest centre above the *durbar* hall and dining rooms. It had to be nearly one o'clock, but all the lights were still burning, the band played, the sounds of merriment spilled over the lotus pond and trimmed bushes. I thought the merriment sounded more than a little forced, but perhaps that was imagination. Certainly the sound was drunken. What state could the maharaja be in? Thwarted at every turn, his captives escaped, first Mary and then Martin tweaking their Russellian noses at his compulsory hospitality. No wonder the servants looked edgy.

For the first time, it occurred to me that the man might be too overwrought to enter his rooms at all. Our loose plan called for abducting the maharaja as soon as we found him alone, and either taking him away immediately or, if it was too near dawn, finding an abandoned corner of this vast place and keeping him drugged until night fell.

It was, frankly, a terrible plan. It was no plan at all. But it was marginally preferable to watching a regiment march across the borders and force a madman into open battle, and the three of us were all old hands at making do with whatever opportunities that presented themselves.

And in the event we did not succeed, the servants at the *dak* bungalow had been given a letter for the commander at the encampment. It would be taken to him if we did not return by dawn Wednesday, some thirty hours hence.

The two *chuprassis* came back out of the crumbling corridor, carrying what appeared to be a canvas stretcher. The object seemed weighty with implications, and my eyes followed it all the way across the gardens and up the steps into the hall. Holmes had to tug my sleeve to get me moving again.

The maharaja's private quarters lay adjacent to the main gates at New Fort's easternmost limits. The so-called "gun-room" with its fur walls was to the north of the gates, and according to Nesbit, the prince's bedroom and private suites were immediately to the south of the gates, reached by a corridor that linked both halves of the wing on the top level. We planned to reach his quarters from the rear, by means of a little-used servants' stairway at New Fort's most southeastern corner, which Nesbit had seen but never tried to enter. He thought it might be passable.

It was, but only just. I think, looking back, it was probably the thought of that stairway that kept Nesbit from fighting harder about being tied to the bed. His wounded leg would never have got him up it.

But it did mean that, once we had shinnied up the abandoned stones and pulled ourselves over the gaps, we were in a place no one would have expected to find us. I had gone first, as the lightest and most agile, and now I folded the rope the others had used to traverse the final gap while we discussed what came next.

"It sounds to me as if the maharaja is having a pretty determined party," I said, in little more than a murmur.

"Which merely means that the Fort will sleep late in the morning," Holmes replied, his voice deliberately soothing. "Are you ready, O'Hara?"

"Oah yes," he said. "May the Compassionate One be watching over us all."

We stole north along the corridor towards the lighted section, there to reconnoitre. On the other side of a bend in the corridor, restoration had taken place: The carving around the doors gleamed; intricate carpets lay on the polished marble; brightly coloured frescoes graced the fresh plaster walls. There were even electrical lights in this section, as if a line had been drawn between the twentieth century and the seventeenth. O'Hara walked down the hall-way, opened a door, and disappeared from sight. We settled ourselves for a long wait.

This portion of the evening's sortie had caused us the most vigorous argument. The maharaja was rarely alone for more than a few minutes while he was awake. Therefore, our best opportunity for laying hands on the man, short of a pitched battle with his guards, was to take him asleep, or at least alone in his rooms. And if he was not alone, at least the numbers would be few, and presumably any woman he took to his bed would not be armed.

But we couldn't all three hide in a wardrobe or under his bed. And in the end, O'Hara's talents, and the fact that he was smaller than either of us, gave him the job. He had the morphia, he could move as silently as a ghost, and heaven knew he had as much patience as might be required. So Holmes and I watched him go, and adjusted the revolvers in our belts, before settling ourselves to wait beyond the reach of the lights. As we waited, my hand kept creeping to my near-naked scalp, exploring the loss, and the freedom.

It is always at least mildly astonishing when plans actually work out, and I was indeed mildly astonished when, an hour later, the maharaja actually appeared, accompanied by two stoney-faced guards and a giggling German girl. The guards took up positions on either side of the door; after a few minutes, however, they looked at each other, and in unspoken accord retreated to the head of the main stairway, standing with their backs to the lit corridor.

I tried not to grin at the picture of O'Hara, silently reciting his rosary and trying to close his ears to the noisy events that had forced the guards' retreat. It seemed forever before the shrieks of the girl's laughter faded, and longer before the thuds and sense of movement died away, but in truth, less than an hour after we had come up the derelict stairway, the door nearest us eased open and the girl slipped out. Five minutes later it opened again, and Kimball O'Hara looked out at us.

We were on our feet in an instant. Holmes held up two fingers to warn him of the guards, then put one finger to his lips before gesturing that he should come. O'Hara stepped back inside for a few seconds, then reappeared with a weight slung across his shoulders, pausing to glance down the corridor at the two distant backs. He emerged fully, pulled the door shut, and in a few silent steps was with us.

The maharaja, wrapped in a dark red dressing-gown, stank of alcohol, but his sleep was that of drugs as well. He stayed limp as we slung him down the pit of the stairs; he remained lifeless across O'Hara's shoulders through the shadows of the ground-floor arcade. The festivities on the other side of the gardens seemed to have died rapidly away once the maharaja was gone; half the lights had been extinguished, and the only voices I could hear were the querulous calls of the overworked servants. Still, we kept to the deepest shadows, and made the western wing without raising an alarm.

We shifted our unconscious burden from O'Hara's back to that of Holmes, and I led the way through mostly unlit passages to that off which the toy room opened. Nearly half the oil lamps had burnt out, including the one nearest the blue door itself. In near darkness, I reached for the doorknob, when the smoothly working mechanism of abduction suddenly hit a rough patch that sent it through the roof.

"Hey," said a familiar voice. "What's going on here?"

O'Hara stepped in front of Holmes as if he might conceal a six-foot-tall man with an insensible maharaja on his shoulders, and I reached for my gun, only to freeze when the figure down the hall-way stepped under a lamp, a large Colt revolver in his hand.

Thomas Goodheart.

Chapter Twenty-Eight

The tableau held for six long breaths, seven, and then all hell broke loose. Another figure appeared beside Goodheart, dressed in the uniform of a *chuprassi* with a scarlet turban and an outraged voice.

"What is this thing?" the newcomer demanded in the lilting accents of the Indian, looking from us to him. "You have found *dacoit*s stealing the master's treasures, oah, sir—"

But to my utter confusion, Goodheart raised his revolver and pointed it, not at us, but at the red *puggaree*. The servant choked off his words in confusion and stared at Goodheart, as flabbergasted as I.

Tommy started to gesture with his gun, saying "You'll have to come—" when the man broke, turning on his heel to sprint for the outside door. Without a moment's hesitation, the American shot him.

Instantly, he turned and said urgently, "You two come fetch him, then stay in that room until I join you." And without a word of explanation he fled up the passageway and burst outside into the courtyard gardens.

O'Hara and I looked at each other, then he kicked open the toy room door for Holmes and we ran to gather up the *chuprassi*. The servant had died instantly, shot through the heart. We took him, shoulders and feet, and scurried back to dump him inside the blue door.

"What the hell was that about?" I demanded of Holmes, but he could not enlighten me. I looked down at the dead man, but he, too, could tell me nothing apart from the obvious: that Goodheart had shot him, and not us.

"I think you two should get into the tunnel," I said.

"I will wait here," O'Hara said, but I was already shaking my head.

"You're stronger than I am," I told him. "Easier for you and Holmes to carry the maharaja five miles than Holmes and I."

I did not wait for the men to agree, merely ripped the red turban from the dead man's head and hurried back to where he had fallen, thinking that I might remove the worst of the stains from floor and wall, thus delay a full-scale search of this specific area. I shook out the tightly wrapped fabric and was just kneeling down to scrub at the stains when more gunfire cracked the stillness, followed by shouting voices. Or rather, a shouting voice.

I pinched out the oil lamp over my head, then ventured down the corridor to the nearest window onto the courtyard gardens. There I saw a puzzling sight: Thomas Goodheart, swaying like a foundering sailboat, seemed to be arguing with a pair of *chuprassis*.

"These god-damned bats!" he roared. "They drive a

man insane with their infernal chatter. All night, in and out, get in the rooms and try and roost in your hair! I'm going to shoot every one of the accursed monsters."

Quieter voices could be heard, apparently pleading for reason; the servants continually glanced over their shoulders at the dark rooms above.

"I won't give it to you, damn you both!" the American raged. "I tell you the bats are—what's that?"

More rapid conversation, much patting of hands in an attempt to reassure, and Goodheart swayed again, then suddenly relinquished his gun. The relief of the two servants was palpable and immediate, and the one with the gun took a step away from this obstreperous guest. The hand of the other hovered near Goodheart's elbow, urging him back in the direction of the guest quarters, and he succeeded for a time. But when they reached the shadowy edges of the gardens, Goodheart shook the hand off. I heard him shouting again, something about leaving a man alone to have a quiet smoke.

Both servants immediately retreated. Goodheart slumped into a bench, his legs alone visible by the light of a lamp on the nearby terrace; then came the flare of a lighter, followed by the unsteady waver of a cigarette. His voice said something else, quieter now but still threatening, and both of the servants went away across the terrace into the hall.

I was not particularly surprised when, before I had reached the end of my muslin turban and the bloodstain was faded and nearly colourless, the man appeared at the far end of the passageway, moving without the slightest sign of drink, and without a cigarette. I stood up, bundling the last end of the sticky fabric into itself.

"Captain Russell?" he asked dubiously, peering into my face.

"And his sister as well," I said. After all, I was armed, he was no longer; I could afford to experiment with honesty.

"Thought that might be the case. Where are the others?"

"In the toy room."

"Where's that? And once you're there, how do you think you're going to get out of here? That was the maharaja you had, wasn't it?"

But I was not about to give him the secret passageway, not yet.

"Look, who are you?" I demanded.

"You know who I am. Shouldn't we get out of this hall-way?"

He did have a point. I led him to the toy room, pulled a candle from my pocket and lit it, sheltering it with my hand while I bent to feel the *chuprassi*'s pulse. Yes: dead. Goodheart knelt beside me at the man's side, tentatively pushing on one shoulder to reveal the face and the bloody chest. After a minute he stood up, unnecessarily wiping his hands on his evening jacket.

"He's dead."

"Yes."

"I've never . . . I didn't intend to kill him. But he had to be stopped."

"Why?"

That distracted him from staring at his victim. He stared at me instead. I hoped Holmes and O'Hara could hear all this.

"Oh God. Don't tell me you're kidnapping Jimmy for *ransom*?"

"What other reason might you imagine?"

He heard in my voice not an answer, but a test question. He nodded slowly, and looked around him into the darkness, clearly searching for my accomplices. "I think it's very possible we're both working toward the same goal."

"And what might that be?"

"Jimmy's clearly . . . unbalanced. But I wouldn't guess it's easy to arrest a native prince openly on his own ground."

I let the words stand, and waited, cocking my head at the darkness. Goodheart waited, too, although he could not know for what. In seconds, I had my partners' answer.

"Bring him," said Holmes' voice.

Once inside the hidden passage, we let the door click shut. I made cursory introductions. "Thomas Goodheart, Mr O'Hara, and you know my husband."

Hands were shaken, and Goodheart said, "Mr Holmes, not Mr Russell. The purser told me, the day after the fancy-dress ball."

"So the costume was an accident?" Holmes asked.

"Er, not entirely. I'd heard one of the passengers, a lady from Savannah, talking about Sherlock Holmes. At the time I just thought she meant that you looked like Sherlock Holmes, not that you were him. I hadn't meant any disrespect."

"I shouldn't worry, young man. A lady from Savannah, you say? I don't remember meeting her."

"Yes, odd that. She must have left the ship at Aden; I didn't see her again."

"Holmes, can we leave this for later?" I suggested.

"Indeed," he said, although the puzzle remained in his voice.

It proved impossible to shoulder our still-limp burden down the narrow passageway, but with one each at his head and feet and the spare two lighting the way with candles, we transported him through the belly of the hill, sweating and cursing, and no doubt bruising him all over. But the maharaja didn't complain, not in his condition, and the necessarily slow rate of progress made it possible for me to repeat my question to Goodheart, at the fore of the procession. This time I received an answer.

"So, who are you?"

"Tommy Goodheart, travelling through India with his somewhat dotty mother."

"But something else as well."

"Yes. You see, when I was at Harvard, one of my friends had an uncle who is high in the War Department. Military Intelligence. He told me that I had such a superb poker face, I mustn't waste it. And so I played along with him, went to a couple of Red meetings, even got myself arrested once—what a lark. Then when I graduated, and he found out I was going to be travelling in Europe, he called me in and gave me a serious talk.

"Our government believes that the Soviet Union is a spent force, militarily. We've been helping them rebuild their factories, giving them food, in the hopes that they might stay where they are. I mean to say, one only has to look at a map to be a bit nervous about the Reds, don't you think? There's a considerable acreage there.

"So he sort of suggested that if I went in that direction, I might just keep my eyes open. Nothing formal, you know? The U. S. of A. as a whole doesn't have much of an interest in Intelligence—we seem to think it's what the Brits would call 'unsporting.'

"But when I got to Russia, I found the factories looked just fine, and there are an awful lot of healthy-looking soldiers. And then I've been told that the Soviets are buying guns and planes from the Germans. A whole lot of planes.

"I'd guess this uncle of my friend's feels even more jittery after the last few months, what with your new government and all. Too many comrades make an outsider feel a mite uncomfortable. Although truth to tell, I haven't been in touch with him since I left Europe, so I'm sort of playing it all by ear, here."

"A one-man Intelligence operation," Holmes commented from his position at the maharaja's shoulders. He did not, however, sound disbelieving, and I had to agree with him: It made a certain amount of sense that the young man was independent, rather than under the control of some organised group.

"Did you arrange for that balcony to fall on us in Aden?" I asked Goodheart.

"Balcony? Is that what happened to you? Good Lord, no."

I listened carefully, and could not hear a lie, but as I was at the rear, I could not see his face. His poker face. "What about the hotel fire in Delhi?"

"Ah. Well, there wasn't really a fire. That is, there was, but it sort of . . . got out of hand."

"And my missing trunk, off the boat?"

"Well, yes, I am terribly sorry about that. I tried to work some way to have it returned to you, but then you disappeared from the hotel. I only arranged to have it mislaid for a while. It seemed to me that searching your luggage would be one way of finding out if you were Russian spies."

At that, all three of us stopped dead to stare at his

back. At our sudden silence, he turned and saw our expressions. "Really!" he protested. "I'd been told that the most dangerous Bolsheviks were those that didn't look like the enemy. And I couldn't see the two of you travelling to India for any of the usual reasons, you just didn't fit in. So I thought, maybe . . ." His voice died away in the tunnel.

Then O'Hara began to laugh. It started with a snort, then merged into giggles, and in a minute he had dropped his half of our prisoner and collapsed into uncontrolled merriment. Holmes, too, was grinning widely, and despite the vast inconvenience this man's amateur sleuthing had caused me, even I had to grin. O'Hara giggled, repeating to himself, "Bolshevik spies! Sherlock Holmes a Russian spy!"

Goodheart looked vastly embarrassed. "It's . . . I know. It was stupid of me, and I'd better give up this spy business before I do something really dangerous. So anyway, when I saw you with Jimmy, I figured you must know what you were doing, and I'd better throw my lot in with you. Um, can I ask, where are you taking him?"

The simple question triggered another paroxysm of mirth in O'Hara, and he began to choke, tears seeping from his eyes. I finally took pity on the American.

"As you said, we're arresting him—taking him to Delhi to answer for his crimes. If the Army has to come in after him, a lot of people will die unnecessarily." The original summons to Delhi, of course, the letter that had set off the maharaja's final madness, had concerned the disappearance of the neighbouring *nawab*'s daughter—a sin which seemed less and less likely to be laid to his account. But that summons had been sent before the contents of the *godown*s came to light; once

Nesbit's report reached his superiors, a stern letter would not be deemed sufficient. I was hit by a brief vision: serried ranks of Tommies marching up the road to Khanpur, while just over a rise lay a phalanx of those machine-guns I had seen, draped and oiled and waiting.

"Is this kind of arrest legal here?" Goodheart asked, then hurried to explain, "Not that I mind, if it's not. I'd just like to know."

"Probably not," Holmes said.

"Oh. Well, all right. How can I help?"

"You can take his legs for a while, since O'Hara seems to have lost his strength."

Goodheart and I took a turn lugging our royal prisoner, and conversation lapsed. When we switched over again, twenty minutes later, he caught his breath and then asked, "How do you plan on getting him out of Khanpur?"

"Carrying him." Holmes said it sharply.

"You could take some horses from the stables."

"There are a dozen or more *syces* living at the stables," I explained. "The way we came, cross-country, we may not be noticed until the first farmers rise."

"I see. And that goes against borrowing a car, as well."

"Doubly so, considering the terrain between here and the border."

"Of course." We went on for a while in silence, and then he said diffidently, "And I'd guess the aeroplanes are guarded, too."

"Probably. Plus there'd be the small problem of flying it."

"Why would that be a problem?"

We stopped again to stare at him, but none of us were laughing this time.

"Are you saying you could fly one of the maharaja's aeroplanes?" Holmes demanded.

"Pretty much any of them, I'd guess. If there was fuel," he added. We looked at one another, then picked up the maharaja and continued.

We made the lower door shortly after three A.M., arms stretched and shoulders aching, Goodheart's head bleeding from two or three encounters with the low roof, our bellies empty and our throats parched. I distributed leathery chapatis and we shared out a bottle of water, chewing and swallowing and feeling the cold seeping its way into our tired muscles. As we sat on our haunches, the man at our feet stirred, and Holmes bent to feel his pulse and look under his eyelids. Wordlessly, O'Hara handed him the needle and morphia bottle, and Holmes slid another injection into our captive's arm.

As the prince dropped more deeply into his sleep, I took a final swallow of water and asked, "What is our decision? Five miles to the border, or two to the air field?"

"With four backs to carry it, the load is eased," O'Hara said. "I would choose the silent way."

"I agree," I said, getting my vote in so as not to be the last voice. "There are too many variables the other way: Are the aeroplanes fuelled up; are they unguarded; can we get past the stables without waking the *syces*?" I also wondered, but did not ask aloud, Does this wealthy American dilettante actually know how to pilot the things? And more to the point, will he—or is he waiting for an opportunity to stab us in the back? Yes, he distracted the guards back in the Fort, but . . .

Holmes nodded, albeit hesitantly. "The way we came is slower, but would appear to involve less risk."

The Buddhist member of our conspiracy summed up the decision, making it sound like a philosophical dictum: "The simple path is best."

I did not know how simple it was going to be, staggering across the countryside with a royal personage across our backs and the sun fast coming up to the horizon, but I had no wish to spend the day in this dark, cramped, and poorly provisioned place. I folded the last of the chapatis back into my rucksack, and we were ready.

The cold air that washed through the narrow doorway smelt of lions and greenery, alive and reassuring after our long passage through inert stone. We threaded our burden out, not bothering to lock the door, and when our eyes had adjusted from candlelight to moonlight, O'Hara squatted down and slung the maharaja easily over his shoulders. He followed me, with Goodheart behind him and Holmes bringing up the rear, as I picked my way forward, one hand brushing the wall of the lion house, until I saw the white gravel path.

Three more steps and I halted, sharply putting out one hand to keep O'Hara from treading on my heels. There seemed to be someone at the main junction of the paths some fifty feet ahead of us, just after the lion cage. I couldn't see in detail, but my heart sank at the figure's size: one of the zoo-keeping dwarfs. And that was the only way past the cage: He couldn't miss seeing us. I turned to whisper to my companions that we would have to retreat, when the short, sharp whistle of a night bird rang out from behind my shoulder. In a panic, I slapped my hand over the maharaja's mouth, but it was slack. Goodheart—? But then I looked back at the junction and saw the small figure running in our direction. Oddly silent, but for the quick patter of feet on the gravel.

A voice in my ear murmured, "My son."

Bindra it was, his black eyes sparkling even in the moonlight, his entire body wriggling like a puppy with his own cleverness.

"What did you do with the horses?" I hissed at him.

"Nesbit *sahib* loosed himself and came, and said he would watch them. Oah, he is so very angry at the three of you, he says to tell you that he will have you locked into the Umballa cantonment. My father, who is this man?"

"His name is Goodheart," O'Hara told him in English, then added in Hindi, "It remains to be seen if he lives up to his name."

"If he does not, I will beat him," the child declared. "But, my father, I do think we need to be gone from this place. A little time ago, four angry soldiers came running down the road, and three of them went back, then I heard some others on the big road that goes between the two hills. I think maybe they have found that you have carried away their master."

"Hell," I said. "That was quick. What now?"

"Which way did the others go on the road?" Holmes asked the boy.

"Down towards the valley, not the hills."

South, then, towards Khanpur city.

"It'll have to be the aeroplanes," Holmes said decisively.

"But we cannot go between the stables and the lake. The ground is open, and there are birds nesting all along the waterfront, just waiting to raise an alarm."

"Only one guard at the stables."

"Plus the *syce*s."

"Russell, we waste time. Goodheart, take the maharaja. And if he makes a sound, you have my permission to bash his royal head in."

Chapter Twenty-Nine

The white gravel guided us from the zoo to the steps leading up to the path encircling the hill. The soldiers Bindra had heard pass were nowhere to be seen, although we expected with every step to come across the one left behind at the stables. Tom Goodheart, accomplished as he might be in amateur dramatics, failed miserably at surreptitious passage, his boots finding every twig and patch of gravel. Well short of the entrance to the compound, O'Hara stopped us.

"Goodheart needs to remain here with the prince. My son and I will go ahead through the stables and locate the guard. Miss Russell ought to come with us, as she best knows the terrain. Mr Holmes, you perhaps should assist Goodheart, watching for the approach of trouble." "Trouble" being either the royal guards or treachery from Goodheart, but no need to state it aloud. I caught the flash of O'Hara's white grin. "Perhaps you can make the call of a bird if it comes?"

He did not wait for any of us to disagree, and indeed,

there was little reason: Holmes did not know the stables and I did; someone had to stay with the loud-footed Goodheart until the way was declared clear. I touched Holmes' sleeve in passing, for the reassuring solidity of the arm beneath, then led the two O'Hara men down the steps.

The domestic odours of hay and horse dung scrubbed the last reek of big cats from my nostrils as we descended towards the buildings. Before, I had followed the track through the grand archway and into the central yard, but I had also noticed a footway that wound around the back of the first block in the direction of the road. This was how we went, picking our way by the blue reflected light, pausing to look closely into each shadow that might hide a clever sentinel, lingering long before stepping across the narrow gap between two buildings. We found the path both clear and well illuminated by the huge moon moving down in the western sky, and walked its length all the way to the main road without seeing anyone.

Back at the stables, O'Hara leant towards us and whispered, "I shall remain here. My son, you stop at the break between the buildings to watch. Miss Russell, you bring the others. And—perhaps the American would make less of a hubbub were he to remove his boots."

Bindra and I turned back, moving more quickly now that we'd been over the path once. He scurried in front, clearing the gap between the buildings with scarcely a glance. It was a mistake. I, two steps behind him, paid the price the instant I came even with the dark hole between the walls.

"*Thahro! Kaun hain?*" split the night, followed closely by the terrifying sound of a round being chambered.

One did not need to speak the language to know the command to freeze: I froze.

And Bindra saved me, saved us all. Before I could do more than raise my hands in surrender, the child was at my side, mindless of the watchman's gun, brisk and sure and heaven-sent.

"*Tum kaun hain?*" he demanded in return, his voice a fraction lower than its usual youthful tones: *Who is that?*

I thought he'd gone mad, and made to grab at his shoulders and dive for shelter but he moved too swiftly for me, striding openly down the narrow alleyway, talking all the while as my brain slowly squeezed out a translation.

"Are you the guard here?" he was asking. "Why was there only one left behind? Where are the others?"

His assumption of authority gave the other pause, and I belatedly realised that a resident of The Forts would be more apt to believe in an officious dwarf than someone in the outer world. I couldn't see if the man's finger loosed on his trigger, but I could feel it, could hear the loud tension in his voice give way to argument and, in less than a minute, irritation. No, he was here alone, and no, he'd had no such order, to wake the *syces* and send them to the Old Fort. Bindra took another step in his direction, hands on hips now and voice taking on an edge of incredulity.

And then there came a dull crack, and the guard's tirade was cut short in the sound of a falling body.

"My son, that was done well," came the low voice. "Go now."

We went, fast. Just not fast enough.

The rumour of approaching turmoil reached me at the same instant a bird-call floated down from the road. Bindra whistled sharply in reply, and we met the others on the steps, Goodheart in his stocking feet and Holmes with the prisoner slung across his shoulders. Bindra led them down the path at a run, I brought up the rear, my shoulder blades crawling with the sounds of half a dozen heavy men trotting rapidly down the road: They would be upon us in minutes.

At the stables entrance, O'Hara waved Holmes and Goodheart towards the main road, but made no sign of joining us.

"What are you doing?" I demanded in a whisper.

"My son and I will make a distraction with the horses. You take your gun to make certain Goodheart does not forget the controls of the aeroplane."

"You can't stay here. They'll kill you."

"If they catch us, they may try. But they will not catch us."

"I can't leave you here. What would Nesbit say?"

"Nesbit would say you are wasting what little time you have been given," he answered, his voice calm.

He was right. Damn it, he was right. I glanced down the road at the two tall and rapidly disappearing figures, then back at my companions, and stepped forward to seize Kimball O'Hara's shoulders, kissing him on the cheek. To his son I offered my hand, and while shaking it, told him, "Bindra, it has been an experience. And just now, with the guard? That was phenomenal. Very fine work," I added, by way of translation. "Thank you."

Then I left them and ran.

When I reached the main road, I halted, listening to the loud neighs of horses and the slamming of stable-doors, followed by more whinnying and snorting and the clatter of escaping hooves coming towards me, quickly drowning out the shouts of running men. I knew without thinking that these horses would be riderless, that the O'Haras would have taken others and ridden west, leading at least some of the guards away from the air field. Somewhere out there, God willing, they would slip down from the animals and hunker into hiding, for an hour or a day; sometime, God willing, they would make for the hills, and leave Khanpur at last.

I waited just long enough to meet the stampeding horses. As they neared, I jumped from the northern edge of their path, waving my hands to frighten them into a mad gallop south, before I spun around to beat my own hasty retreat north.

The two miles to the air field seemed twenty, but at last my feet hit the smooth runway, and faint sounds led me to our intended escape vehicle. The corrugation of its sides suggested that it was a Junkers—not, thank God, the three-engined monstrosity I'd seen parked to one side. Rather, it seemed to be the same F13 we'd arrived here in, and indeed, a glance inside confirmed it. I helped Holmes bind our now-mumbling prisoner into a seat. Goodheart was seated at the controls, muttering and cursing under his breath.

"I hope to Hannah this crate's got enough gas to get us out of here," he said grimly. "No time to check. Where the hell's the starter, anyway? Hey, I need somebody to undo the ties and take the blocks out from the wheels. And for God's sake stay clear of the propeller."

I jumped down to loose the ropes and kick away the chocks, then climbed back onto the wing to await further instructions. Clearly, Goodheart knew what he was doing, and as far as I could see, he was not in any need of an encouraging revolver at the back of his neck. Holmes and I made sure that we were never both out of the aeroplane at the same time, but Goodheart seemed oblivious as he checked the instruments by the light of the aeroplane's torch, tapped their glass faces and swore at them and threw switches.

As I crouched near the door, my mind's eye visualised the panicked horses slowing and being rounded up; the guards finding that we were not on their backs; the guards returning to the stables, where some would follow the lake-shore west in the footsteps of the O'Haras, while others came north to find . . .

My brain snagged on some unrelated imagery, spitting up an alarm composed of: horses, running loose; cows, wandering loose; cows, being chased from the road in Hijarkot—

"How do we know the runway is clear of animals?" I asked.

"Oh God," Goodheart groaned, and pounded a dial with his fist. I took that as his answer.

"Holmes," I said into the dim interior. "If we are discovered, get the maharaja away. I'll make my way to Hijarkot." I slid down the wing to the macadamized ground before he could object.

The moon was brushing the western mountains, but I could see well enough to follow the smooth river of air strip that cut between the rough grassland on either side. I didn't know just how much distance the aeroplane needed before it took to the air, but with four people on board, I decided to be conservative, and checked for sleeping bullocks all the way to the end. I found no bullocks, no living thing at all, but halfway back, there appeared to be some dark, tall shape near the machine's left wing. I held up a hand to block the faint light from Goodheart's cockpit torch, and it was still there. Not moving, and just the one, but it was the shape of a man.

I pulled the revolver from my pocket and crept forward, wishing there was something I might hide behind: If the moonlight was sufficient to illuminate him, it would betray me as well.

The man did nothing until I was perhaps fifty feet away. And then he spoke.

"I say, is there something on?"

"Who is it?" I demanded.

"Jack Merriam. Er, the pilot?"

I straightened. "Ex-RAF?"

"Right-o. Is the maharaja on one of his stunts?"

"You might say that."

"You need me to turn on the runway lights?"

"That would be most excellent."

"Happy to. I do wish he'd tell me when he's planning one of these night jaunts of his. I wouldn't have to turn out when I heard noises."

"This was somewhat spur-of-the-moment. But I'll mention it to him."

"I don't mean to complain. I'll get the lights, won't be a tick."

When I tumbled back through the open door, I found Goodheart's torch off.

"Who the hell was that?" he hissed.

"The pilot. He's turning on the runway lights for us. Would that be helpful?"

"Helpful? I thought I'd be doing this by torchlight. Thank God for the Brits. Hope the fellow doesn't get into trouble."

"Too late to worry about that."

True to his word, the pilot illuminated our abduction of his employer. The bank of lights flared on, one block at a time, glaring onto the clean, smooth surface. Our engine caught, the propeller began to turn, and

Goodheart pointed its nose between the twin rows of spotlights and revved the engine. We began to move, then to bounce, and on one of the bounces we hesitated briefly, then rose.

But our escape did not go unrecognised by the men we left behind. The guards must have been near the air field even before the lights attracted their attention, because we'd only been airborne a few moments, and were about to bank around the high trees at the end of the runway, when the roar of noise within the machine changed in some indefinable way, and the air blew into our faces in a manner it had not before. I suddenly could see light from the runway, spilling in three clear circles punched through the floor.

"The fools—they're shooting!" Holmes cried.

My body tried to crawl into itself, although there could be no escape, either from being hit directly, or from going down in a ball of flame. But Goodheart banked hard then, and the change in our outline, or the increased distance from their guns, or even their belated realisation that they might also be shooting at their prince, meant the end of it: No more holes appeared in the thin metal skin. When the plane's wings had levelled out and we were aimed south, I uncurled to pat our waking prisoner from head to toe. It was a huge relief to find him unwounded: Explaining an abducted maharaja was going to be hard enough; a dead one might present real problems. The man himself appreciated neither concern. He glared at me over his gag, drugged and drunk still but angry; I checked his bindings and went back to Holmes.

"He's all right. Where are we heading?"

"I don't suppose you know if the British encampment has a parade grounds?"

"I should very much doubt it, in these mountains."

"Then it's Hijarkot."

I sighed, foreseeing the hell that would break loose the minute we set down with our kidnapped maharaja and no authority, no legal stance, no Geoffrey Nesbit to explain.

I leant forward to yell into Holmes' ear. "Mycroft is going to be absolutely mortified when he finds out that his sources misled him regarding Goodheart."

"These amateurs," Holmes bellowed back, wagging his head in mock disapproval. "They present a continuous obstacle to the smooth running of the world."

Holmes shifted, intending to head forward and help Goodheart navigate his strange aeroplane across an impossible route between a place where men were shooting at us and a place where we would be unable to set down, over seventy miles of invisible and terrifying mountainside, by nothing but the fading moonlight. As he stood, I caught at his elbow and pulled him back so he could hear me.

"The next time Mycroft asks us to do something," I shouted to my husband, "we really must tell him no."

Chapter Thirty

It took three days to fetch Nesbit out of his hiding place near the border of Khanpur, days we spent holed up in the nondescript villa amidst the corn while messages of outrage and command heated the telegraph cables between Delhi and London. More than once I thought we should have to make good our threat to use the variety of guns we had found in the house; more than once, the maharaja came near to escape. If nothing else, the period proved to our satisfaction that Thomas Goodheart was on the side of the angels. Or at any rate, on the same side as Sherlock Holmes and his wife.

But on the third day, a tired-looking Geoffrey Nesbit rode into the front garden on an even tireder horse, and the machinery of government began to mesh again. That evening, the maharaja of Khanpur was quietly taken into custody to await His Majesty's pleasure in the contemplation of crimes against the Crown and the people of Khanpur, and for the first time, we slept the night through, no patrols set, no rifles at our sides.

We did not, I am sorry to say, see Kimball O'Hara or his son again. But the following afternoon, as we prepared to leave Nesbit's villa, my eye was caught by a flash out of the hills to the east. I stood and watched, and it came again, and again.

Holmes had noticed it as well, and stood at my side, reading the flares long and short.

One long, three shorts: the letter B. Short, long, two shorts: L. Short: E. Three shorts: S.

Blessings of the Compassionate One, said the message.

And with that, Kimball O'Hara went home to his high mountains, with his son, and his rosary, and his secrets.

Author's Thanks

As this volume's opening dedication was meant to indicate, the Russell books would not exist without the passionate dedication of librarians. I am particularly grateful to the staff at the McHenry Library of the University of California, Santa Cruz, who with endless good cheer unearth for people like me all those glorious treasures that are checked out once every thirty years, such as Malcolm Darling's *Rusticus Loquitur*, a closely detailed account of his 1928 tour as Registrar for the Punjab Co-Operative Societies, or the 1924 treatise written by Sir Robert Baden-Powell (yes, the Boy Scout man) with that most evocative of titles, *Pig-Sticking or Hog Hunting*.

I also thank Gordon Werne, of the Hiller Aviation Institute, for his good-humored expertise regarding antique planes, and Sirdar Tarlochan Singh, Ph.D., for details of Punjabi life. And anyone who has read into the time and place will realize how much the present work owes to Peter Hopkirk, not only for his brilliant expositions of the Victorian cold war—"The Great Game"—but specifically for his identification of Kimball O'Hara's birth date in 1875. For Hopkirk's and other titles, see my website, *laurierking.com*.

(I ought perhaps to point out that none of my maps shows the precise location of the place Miss Russell calls "Khanpur." Nor have I found it possible, after all this time, to determine which of the northern princely states she might have meant. An editor's task is never easy.)

And as always, I thank my husband, Noel King, in this case for introducing me to his mad homeland, and for providing Russell with her Hindustani curses.

The Game may be read as a humble and profoundly felt homage to Rudyard Kipling's *Kim*, one of the great novels of the English language. If you, the reader, do not know the book, please do not delay that acquaintance. If you read it in childhood and remember it as a juvenile adventure, may I suggest another read? *Kim* is a book for any age.

And for those skeptics in the audience, yes, Kipling did indeed begin to formulate the idea of *Kim* during that precise period when Sherlock Holmes was in India.

ABOUT THE AUTHOR

LAURIE R. KING became the first novelist since Patricia Cornwell to win prizes for Best First Crime Novel on both sides of the Atlantic with the publication of her debut thriller, *A Grave Talent*. She is the *New York Times* bestselling author of four contemporary novels featuring Kate Martinelli, seven Mary Russell mysteries, and the bestselling novels *Keeping Watch*, *A Darker Place* and the Macavity award-winner *Folly*. She lives in northern California, where she is at work on her eighth Mary Russell mystery, *Locked Rooms*.

Don't miss the latest installment in the enthralling
Mary Russell and *Sherlock Holmes* series
from bestselling author Laurie R. King.

Read on for an early look at

LOCKED ROOMS

by

Laurie R. King

*in which Russell and Holmes head to
San Francisco to delve into Russell's perplexing past.*

Coming in hardcover from Bantam Books
in July 2005

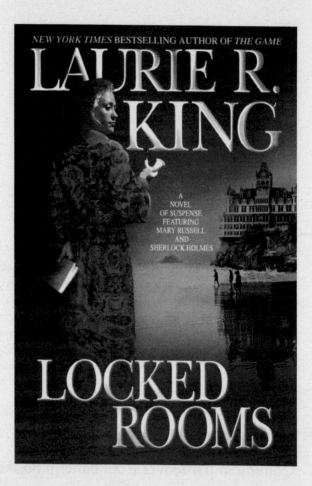

NEW YORK TIMES BESTSELLING AUTHOR OF *THE GAME*

LAURIE R. KING

A
NOVEL
OF SUSPENSE
FEATURING
MARY RUSSELL
AND
SHERLOCK HOLMES

LOCKED ROOMS

LOCKED ROOMS

On sale July 2005

We came at last to my childhood home, the West's biggest, youngest city that spread over the end of a peninsula between ocean and bay. Eighty years ago, a ship coming through the Golden Gate would have seen nothing but a handful of Indian shacks clustered around a crumbling mission. Then in 1848, John Marshall picked up a gleaming lump of yellow metal from a creek near Sutter's Mill, and the world came pouring in.

I had relatives in that first wave, victims of gold fever who worked claims, made fortunes, and lost them again. I had other relatives who joined the second wave of those who supplied and serviced miners; their fortunes were more slowly made, and not as quickly lost. But unlike the others who now reigned supreme in the state of California, my grandfather had clung to his East Coast roots: Although he had built a house in San Francisco, it had been on Pacific Heights, keeping its distance from the showy Nob Hill mansions of Hopkins and Stanford; and although he had kept his holdings and remained a financial power on the West Coast, he had also bowed to his wife's demands that they return to the civilised world of Boston to raise their children, and thus loosed his hold on Californian political authority.

Still, my restless iconoclast of a father had claimed San Francisco as his home, declaring his independence by settling his Jewish Englishwoman of a wife in the family house there, and taking control of the family's California business interests. My father loved California, that much I knew, and I remembered him speaking of San Francisco as The City, a phrase that from my mother's lips meant London. I remembered almost nothing about the place itself, but I looked forward to making The City's acquaintance before I turned my back on her for good.

Thus it was that on a morning in late April, seventy-five years after the gold rush began, I stood on the deck and saw the Gate that had welcomed my father's people, smooth hills bracketing the entrance to the bay—green now following the winter rains, but golden in summer's long drought. Stern gun placements protruded from the hills on our left, but as we entered the Golden Gate and followed the curve of the land to our right, the white-walled city that carpeted a dozen or more hills came into view, its myriad piers and docks stretching long fingers out into the bay.

Our pilot took us in to one gleaming set of buildings not far from the terminal where ferries bustled in and out. We eased slowly in, coming to rest with a barely perceptible judder; ropes were cast and tied, the crowds on board and on land pressed towards each other impatiently, behind them the stevedores with trucks and heavy wagons, rough men, smoking and making conversation. The first officials started up the board walkway; as if their uniforms made for a signal, the passengers turned and scurried for their cabins.

Holmes and I waited until the crowd had thinned, then went below to gather our hand-luggage and present ourselves for collection.

The only hitch was, no one appeared to be interested in our presence. We sat in the emptying dining room where the purser had told us we might wait, Holmes smoking cigarettes, both of us watching out the windows as the disembarking passengers went from a torrent to a stream to stragglers. I glanced at my watch for the twentieth time, and shook my head.

"It's been nearly an hour, Holmes. Shall we just make our own way?"

Wordlessly, he crushed his cigarette out in the overflowing tray, picked up his Gladstone bag, and paused, looking out the window.

"This may be your gentleman," he noted. I followed his gaze and saw a portly, tweed-clad, sandy-haired gentleman in his thirties working his way against the flow of porters down the gangway. Sure enough, he paused at the top to make frantic enquiries of the purser, who directed him towards our door. A moment later he burst into the room, red-faced and breathless, his hat clutched in his left hand as his right was extended in our direction.

"Miss Russell? Oh, I am so terribly sorry at the delay—the boy I sent to watch for the ship's docking appears to have a girl-friend in the vicinity, and he became distracted. Why didn't you have someone 'phone me? Have your bags been taken off? Hello," he inserted, his hand pumping mine, then moving to Holmes. "Good afternoon, Mr Holmes. So good to meet you. Henry Norbert, at your service. Welcome to San Francisco. And to you, Miss Russell, welcome back. Come, let's get you off the ship and to your hotel." He clapped his soft hat back onto his head, scooped up my bag, and urged us with his free hand in the direction of the doors.

"Why a hotel?" I asked. "Surely we can stay at the house?"

Norbert stopped and removed the hat from his head again. "Oh. Oh, no, no, I wouldn't think that's a good idea. No, you'd be much more comfortable at a hotel. I've made reservations for you at the St Francis. Right downtown, just around the corner from the of- fices."

"Is there something wrong with the house?"

The hat, which had been rising in the direction of the sandy head, descended again. "No, no, it's still standing strong, no trouble there. But of course, it's not terribly habitable after all these years."

I opened my mouth to protest that he'd been told to get it ready for us, then decided there was little point: Clearly, I should have to see for myself, and decide if the house was in fact uninhabitable, or simply uncomfort- able after ten years of standing empty. Probably hadn't had the dust-cloths cleared away. I closed my mouth again, Mr Norbert's hat resumed its head, and we al- lowed ourselves to be herded gently from the ship and into a gleaming saloon car that idled at the kerb.

Eighteen years ago, I reflected as we drove—almost exactly eighteen years ago—this city had been reduced literally to its very foundations. There was no sign of that catastrophe now. The busy docks gave way to a land of high buildings and black suits, then to the commercial centre. We passed between shop windows bright with spring frocks and alongside a square that had patches of spring flowers around a high pillar with some sort of winged statue at the top. Then the motor turned again, dodged the rumbling box of a cable car, and drifted to a halt before a dignified entranceway. Liveried men and boys relieved us of our burdens, and we followed Mr Norbert through the polished doors to the desk.

The equally polished gentleman behind the desk greeted us by name, with professional camaraderie, as if we were long-time guests instead of newcomers known only through our local escort. Another, even more dignified, man lingered in the background, casting a gimlet eye on the desk man's efficiency. While Holmes signed the register, I asked Mr Norbert if his office had received any messages for me.

"Hah!" he exclaimed, and dug into the breast pocket of his suit for a thick packet of letters. "Good thing you asked, I'd have had to come back across town with them when I got home."

I flipped through them—three from Mrs Hudson, Holmes' long-time housekeeper although more of an aunt to me, several from various friends that she had sent on for us, a post-card from Dr Watson showing Paris. Norbert noticed the disappointment on my face.

"Were you expecting something else?" he asked.

"I was, rather. It must have been delayed."

Back in Japan I had decided that the one person I wished to see in San Francisco was Dr Sylvia Ginzberg, the psychiatrist who had cared for me after the accident, in whose offices I had laboriously begun to piece together my life. I had written to tell her that I was going to be passing through the city, and asked her to write care of Mr Norbert.

Perhaps the mail from Japan was unreliable.

"Well, I'll certainly have my secretary check again," he said. "Perhaps it'll come in the afternoon delivery. Now, I'll have most of your paperwork together in the morning, if you'd like to come to the offices first thing we could have a look."

"I could come now, if that's convenient."

"Oh," Norbert said, "it's not, I'm afraid. There were some problems with the records of the water company shares, I had to send them back for clarification. But they promised to have them brought to me no later than nine in the morning. Shall we say nine-thirty?"

There did not seem to be much of a choice. I told him I'd see him at half past nine the following morning, and he shook our hands and hurried off.

Holmes had finished and was waiting for me, but before we could follow the boy with the keys, the dignified man who had been lingering in the background eased himself forward and held out his hand. "Miss Russell? My name is Auberon, I'm the manager of the St Francis. I just wanted to add my own personal welcome. I knew your father, not well, but enough to respect him deeply. I was sad to hear of the tragedy, and I am glad to see you here at last. If there's anything I can do, you need only ask."

"Why, thank you," I said in astonishment. Holmes had to touch my arm to get me moving in the direction of the lifts.

In our rooms, while Holmes threw himself onto the sofa and began ripping open letters, I stood and studied the neatly arranged bags and realized that, between the hasty packing of our January departure from

England and a most haphazard assortment of additions in the months since then, there was little in those bags that would impress a set of lawyers and business managers as to the solidity and competence of the heiress whose business they had maintained all these years. To say nothing of the long miles that lay between here and the final ship out of New York. I did have a couple of gorgeous kimonos and an assortment of dazzling Indian costumes, but my Western garments were suitable for English winters and two years out of date, which even here might be noticed. I wasn't even certain the trunk contained a pair of stockings that hadn't been mended twice.

"Oh, what I could do with that Simla tailor of Nesbit's," I muttered, interrupting my partner's sporadic recital of the news from home.

"Sorry?" said Holmes, looking up from his page.

"I was just thinking how nice it would be if women could get by with three suits and an evening wear. I'm going to have to go out to the shops."

"Sorry," he said again, this time intoned with sympathy rather than query.

I gathered my gloves and straw hat, then checked my wrist-watch. "I'll be back in a couple of hours, and we can have a cup of tea. Anything I can get you?"

"Those handkerchiefs I got in Japan were quite nice, but the socks are not really adequate. If you see any, I could use a half a dozen pair."

"Right you are."

Down at the concierge's desk, I asked about likely shops, receiving in response more details than I needed. I thanked the gentleman, then paused.

"May I have a piece of paper and an envelope?" I asked. "I ought to send a note."

I was led across the lobby to a shrine of the epistolary arts, where pen, stationery, and desk lay waiting for my attentions. I scribbled a brief message to Dr Ginzberg, explaining that an earlier letter appeared to have gone astray, but that I hoped very much to see her in the brief time I would be in San Francisco. I gave her both the hotel address and that of the law offices for her response, signed it "affectionately yours," then wrote on the envelope the address I still knew by heart and handed it to the desk for posting.

The doorman welcomed me out into a perfectly lovely spring afternoon. Far too nice to be spent wrangling with shopkeepers, but there was no help for it—no bespoke tailor could produce something by nine-thirty tomorrow morning. Grimly, I turned to the indicated set of display windows on the other side of the flowered square and entered the emporium.

An hour later, I was the richer by three dignified outfits with hats to match, two pair of shoes, ten of silk stockings, and six of men's woollen socks. I arranged to have everything delivered to the St Francis and left the shop, intending to continue down the street to another, more exclusive place mentioned by the concierge for dresses that did not come off a rack. But the sun was so delicious on my face, the gritty pavement so blessedly motionless underfoot, that I decided a brief walk through the flowered square wouldn't hurt any.

Union Square was full of other citizens enjoying the sunshine. The benches were well used, the paths busy with strolling shoppers and businessmen taking detours. Few children, I noted—and then a sound reached me, and my mind ceased to turn smoothly for a while.

A rhythmic clang, a rumble of heavy iron wheels,

the slap and whir of the underground cable: That most distinctive of San Francisco entities, a cable car, rumbled up Powell Street, its warning bell ringing merrily as it neared Post.

The combined noises acted like the trigger phrase of a hypnotist: I dropped into a sort of trance, staring at the bright, boxy vehicle as it passed. It paused to take on a passenger, then grabbed its ever-moving underground cable again to resume its implacable way down the centre of the street towards the heights. Before it had disappeared entirely, a passer-by brushed past me, waking me from the dream-world. I turned away from the tracks and began walking fast, head down, crossing the flower-bedecked square and fleeing up streets with whichever crowd carried me along.

I was dimly aware of changes: The standard odours of a downtown shopping district—petrol, perfume, perspiration—gave way to more exotic fragrances, chillies and sesame oil, roasting duck and incense. Then a splash of colour caught my eye. And I raised my head to look around me. A row of bright paper lamps danced in the spring breeze. The streets were discordant, both strongly remembered yet utterly foreign, as if I'd known the idea of the place, but not the reality. I walked on, but after a while the streets changed again. The air became redolent of garlic, tomato sauce, and coffee. In a short time, those smells faded beneath the air of a waterfront, and suddenly I had run out of land.

I stood on the edge of a wide, curving roadway fronting a row of piers bustling with machines and men, loading and unloading ships from a dozen countries. Heavy wagons and lorries came and went, few business suits appeared, and the air smelt only of sea and tar.

Reasuringly like London, in fact.

After a while I began to walk along the waterfront road, turning towards the western sun. It felt good on my face, as the unmoving ground felt good beneath my feet, and the muscles of my legs took pleasure in the fact that they could stride out without having to turn and retrace their steps every couple of minutes. The claustrophobic air of shipboard life slowly emptied from my lungs, and I thought, maybe it actually was some *"curious aversion to the ship itself"* that had inflicted the insomnia on me. That and lack of exercise.

I leant against the post to watch some fishermen at work, all high boots and loud voices, repairing holes in their nets while wearing sweaters more hole than wool. The fresh, powerful smell of fish and crab rose up all around me, to fade as I continued on. An Army post intruded between me and the water for a time, then allowed me back, and with the water before me, a dark round mountain rising from the northern shore and the island of Alcatraz before me, I stretched out my arms in the late sun, half inclined to shout my pleasure aloud, feeling a smile on my face. I turned to survey the rising city—and it was only then I noticed the length of the shadows the buildings were casting.

"Damn," I said aloud instead: I'd told Holmes I'd be back for tea.

I crossed the waterfront road to re-enter the city and in a couple of streets I spotted a sign announcing public telephones. At least three languages mingled in the small room, an appropriate accompaniment to the Indian, English, and Japanese coins I sorted through in my purse. At last I found some money the girl would accept and placed a call to the St Francis. Holmes did not answer, nor had he left a message for me, so I left one for him instead and walked out of the telephone office nursing a small glow of righteousness: Had I been at the hotel at the declared time, I told myself, I'd only have been cooling my heels waiting for him to return from heavens knows where.

I continued south, which I knew was the general direction of downtown—it is difficult to become seriously lost in a city with water on three sides. And I was beginning to take note of my surroundings again, raising my eyes from the pavement to look around me. This was a more heavily residential area, I noticed, the houses both older and larger than they had been in the area I had fled through, the residents less strikingly regional. As the ground rose, steeply now in a delicious challenge to my leg muscles, the houses began to retreat from the public gaze behind solid walls and gated drives. Street noises diminished with the loss of restaurants and shops, the trees grew taller and more thickly green, and the paving stones underfoot were more even although the number of pedestrians was markedly reduced.

The hilltop enclave might have had a moat around it and signs saying: *Important People Only.* From here, the bank manager's driver could take his employer to the financial district and easily return in time to run the man's wife to her luncheon date downtown. There was no risk of roving gangs of boisterous children here, or late-night revelers walking noisily past by way of a short-cut home.

Even the air smelt of money, I thought, crisp and clean.

I looked up smiling at the house opposite, an unassuming brick edifice of two tall stories, and nearly fell on my face over my suddenly unresponsive feet.

I saw: snippets of red-brick wall and once-white trim set well back from the street, now nearly obscured by a wildly overgrown vine and an equally undisciplined jungle of a garden; a grey stone garden wall separated jungle from pavement, in want of repointing and feeling shorter than it should; one set of ornate iron gates sagging across the drive and a smaller pedestrian entrance further along the wall, both gates looped through with heavy chains and solid padlocks; the chain on the walkway gate, which for lack of other fastening had been welded directly onto the strike-plate, the very strike-plate that had reached out to gash open my little brother's scalp when he had tripped while running through it.

There was no mistaking the shape of the house: My feet had led me home.

CHAPTER ONE

THE SWING DOORS were almost noiseless, but old George had been head porter at St Ethelburga's for so many years now that his ears were familiar with the faintest whisper of sound and identified it at once. He now put down his paper and peered through his cubbyhole window at the man who had just come in. A big man—a very big man; well over six and a half foot tall and broad with it; who strolled in leisurely fashion towards him. He was a handsome man too, with grey eyes, a straight nose and a wide firm mouth and dark hair, liberally sprinkled with grey. George was sure that he knew who he was; he beamed at him and said,

'Good morning, sir. Dr Van Beijen Doelsma, isn't it?' The big man, so addressed, winced slightly at the mutilation of his name by George's Cockney tongue, but smiled and nodded and said, 'Good morning,' in a pleasant voice. 'I believe I am early?'

George turned to his switchboard. 'If you'll wait a moment, sir, I'll ring Sir Charles, he told me to let him know when you arrived.'

Dr Doelsma nodded again, put vast hands into the pockets of his elegant suit, and leaned a shoulder against the wall. He appeared very relaxed—slumbrous, in fact, with eyes half closed. They flew open however as his attention was caught by a figure tearing across the hospital forecourt. It was a woman, and she ran well, and he wondered why a Ward Sister in all the dignity of navy blue and white uniform needed to race around in such an unheard-of fashion. In his experience, hospital Sisters moved calmly and with a self-confident authority, designed to gain respect both from the nurses under them and the doctors they themselves worked for. The swing doors burst open with a crash, and George, waiting for his connection, looked over his shoulder, tut-tutted loudly and put his old head through his little window.

'One day you'll get caught, Sister MacFergus, running like that; you ought to know better!'

The girl came to a halt in front of the cubbyhole, and Dr Doelsma, as yet unnoticed, looked her up and down in a leisurely fashion. She was a tall young woman, well built and nicely rounded; she reminded him of the women of his own native Friesland, save for her hair, which was a bright chestnut and inclined to curl, but tidily confined in a French pleat at the back. She put up a large shapely hand and gave her starched cap an impatient tweak, and he observed that despite her haste she was not in the least breathless. She bent her noble proportions to George's level.

'Am I late? Has he come, George? Nine o'clock for a lecture! The man ought to be shot!' She had a soft voice, with a lilt of the Highlands in it. 'There's Staff Nurse off sick, and four test meals, and do send a porter over, there's someone for X-ray.' She frowned heavily above magnificent dark eyes, and her splendid bosom heaved with exasperation.

'Why are you looking at me so strangely, George? I know I'm late; I'll just have to creep in unobserved.' She paused and looked down at herself. 'Well, not unobserved, perhaps—but he'll not notice. He'll be elderly and short-sighted and fat and bald, and I'll not understand a word the poor wee man says.' She caught the faint sound wrung from Dr Doelsma's lips, and glanced over her shoulder. She smiled at him kindly and said, 'Good morning. I didn't see you. Am I keeping you waiting?' She turned back to look at George's disconcerted face and added severely, 'Don't gobble, George,' and with a starched rustle swept away round the corner of the long corridor, and out of sight.

George pushed his old-fashioned steel spectacles down his nose and peered at Dr Doelsma, and was relieved to see that the doctor was laughing softly. The sight emboldened him to say:

'Sister MacFergus was a bit worried, sir; she'd be that upset if she knew who you were—you couldn't get a nicer young lady...' He broke off as an elderly man came rather vaguely towards them. Dr Doelsma straightened and went to meet him, and the older man shook hands, smiling delightedly.

'Paul, my dear boy, I'm delighted to see you again. How is your mother?' He didn't wait for a reply, but took the younger man's arm. 'Matron's got the hall full of nurses waiting for you; shall we go before they become restless?'

The elderly doctor and his former pupil, who had carved such a brilliant career for himself, set off down one of the interminable gloomy corridors so beloved of all old hos-pitals. Half way down it they encountered Matron—a handsome woman with a high-bridged nose, a formidable bust, and an unshakable air of authority acquired from years of seeing that nurses did the things she wanted them to do, without being too aware of the fact. Dr Doelsma re-membered her when he had been Casualty Officer at St

Ethelburga's—she didn't appear to have altered in the least. They greeted each other like old friends, and the three of them continued on their way to the lecture hall. It was familiar to them all, but even if they had been strangers to the hospital they would have found it just as easily—the subdued roar of a great many women talking could clearly be heard as they approached its doors. The sight of Matron entering, however, turned the tumult into a silence that could be felt, followed by the sound of several hundred well starched aprons crackling as their wearers rose to their feet. Matron reached the chair on the small platform and sat; the doctors followed suit, the wearers of the aprons, obedient to a nod from Matron, also sat, with a combined rustle which was deafening. The sisters were at the back of the hall; Dr Doelsma was immediately aware of the beautiful Amazon he had encountered in the entrance, sitting head and shoulders above her neighbours. Even at that distance he could see the consternation on her face—her mouth was slightly open—he wished he was near enough to see her eyes. A smile tugged at the corner of his mouth as he removed his gaze.

While Matron, followed by Sir Charles Warren, made the speeches usual to such an occasion, Dr Doelsma settled his vast bulk into his chair, and surveyed his audience. From where he was sitting most of them looked very pretty; those who were not were at least attractive, although his keen eye detected one or two really plain girls; he sighed—for the plain ones always asked questions. He had been lecturing for several years now; he knew what to expect. He supposed it was something to do with their egos. He rose to his feet, replied gracefully and briefly to the speeches and began his lecture. He was an excellent lecturer, and within a few minutes he had his audience's attention, and kept it. He made his subject, the malignant conditions of the stomach and their latest treatment, sound enthralling. He was a specialist in this field of medicine, and such was his interest and enthusiasm for his work that he had no difficulty in holding the attention of every girl there. Even the rebels, who hadn't wanted to go anyway, felt sorry for their colleagues who had been left on the wards.

Sir Charles, watching him from his side of the platform, thought what a first-rate man Paul had become. A pity he wasn't married, he mused, for he must be all of thirty-five. Too busy with his work, perhaps. It was nice for Henrietta to have such a son, though. He himself had known Paul's mother for years; his father too. Since the latter's death he had not lost contact with either of them. She would be coming over on a visit from Friesland in a few days. Behind the attentive façade of his nice elderly face, he began to make plans for her entertainment.

Matron, listening to the doctor's deep attractive voice discussing enzymes and their complex working, felt thankful that she no longer needed to know much about these new-fangled theories. In her day, a gastric ulcer was a gastric ulcer; you either recovered from it, or you died; nobody bothered with enzymes. So simple. Her massive bosom inflated on a sigh and she turned her full attention on to the nurses before her—rows of rapt attentive faces all looking at the lecturer. 'You'd think he would feel uncomfortable,' she mused, and transferred her gaze to the object of their attention, and studied him carefully. He was enough to catch the eye of any woman under eighty. He had a hawk-like distinction to crown his good looks, and as if that were not enough, his very massiveness made it impossible for him to go unnoticed. Her eyes swept the ranks of nurses before her, and she suppressed the chuckle which rose to her primly set mouth. No wonder they were all so attentive! No doubt they would all be dreaming of him tonight, and tomorrow there would be a queue of them outside her office, wanting to know if English-trained nurses were accepted in Dutch hospitals.

The applause at the end of the lecture was such that Dr Doelsma was surprised; it was, of course, more for him than for the lecture, but he was a man of little conceit, and that idea had never occurred to him. He was used to his size attracting stares, and although he had the self-confidence and assurance of a man of breeding and wealth, he was essentially modest. Now he waited patiently for the clapping to stop and then asked mildly.

'Has anyone any questions to ask?'

As he had foreseen, the plain nurses rose one by one and put their questions. They weren't particularly intelligent queries, either, but he was a kind man, and answered them in turn with a grave courtesy, leaving each of them in a rosy glow of satisfaction. He enjoyed answering the points raised by the more senior nurses and sisters; they showed a lively comprehension of his lecture and a shrewd knowledge of the subject. He had not looked at the back row since he had got to his feet; now he allowed his gaze to rest there for a moment. The Amazon of the entrance hall was in earnest conversation with her neighbour, who nodded and then got to her feet. The question she asked, 'What alternative is there to the use of vitamin $B12$ when both stomach and liver are diseased, making the storage of the vitamin an impossibility, and thus failing to check the anaemia?' had been well thought out. He had a shrewd suspicion as to the originator; he leaned back against the table in the middle of the platform, setting the water jug and glasses jangling, and looked over the rows of upturned pink faces, staring blandly at the big girl in the back row. Even at that distance he could see her blushing. He smiled gently and addressed himself to her.

'My answer would depend largely upon the patient. An elderly, ill patient would be best treated with palliative methods, as and when symptoms arose. But in the case of the younger person, and bearing in mind that the liver has six other functions than that of storing the anti-anaemic factor, it might be well worth attempting a liver transplant provided that the stomach condition could be controlled until such time as the resistance of the patient was sufficiently restored to warrant conservative surgery on the stomach. The hazards would be great, but in my opinion, worth while in suitable cases.' He paused, then added, 'I should like to add that this question showed a high rate of intelligence.' He didn't look at her any more after that, but after the closing speeches, followed Matron and Sir Charles out of the hall without a backward glance.

'Most successful,' breathed Matron. 'Coffee, I think, in my office.' She turned to Dr Doelsma. 'You're lunching with the consultants, I believe, but I hope I shall see you before you go.'

She led the way into her office, and they drank Nescafé, disguised in her best china. Dr Doelsma made himself very pleasant and asked a great many questions, so that after a few minutes he was able to discover that Sister MacFergus was in charge of Women's Medical. Over his second, unwanted cup, he blandly suggested that a quick tour round that particular ward would be highly interesting; there were doubtless several gastric cases there—he had remembered the four test meals. Sir Charles agreed readily enough, and politely invited Matron to accompany them. Rather to the doctors' surprise, she accepted with alacrity, and at once swept them out and away and up a series of staircases which eventually brought them on to the landing outside Women's Medical.

Their arrival was seen only by a small junior nurse, who looked at them in patent horror and scuttled, head down, to a door marked 'Sister's Office', where she knocked and entered. Dr Doelsma's lips twitched, but he avoided Sir Charles' amused look, and remarked politely upon the tasteful display of flowers on the window ledge. He turned from their contemplation in time to see Sister MacFergus emerge from her office. She looked cool and dignified, concealing the faint unease she was feeling. She addressed herself politely to Matron, and waited to hear what was wanted of her. She had smiled warmly at Sir Charles, who smiled back, but she carefully avoided the visiting doctor's eye.

'Sister MacFergus, this is Dr Doelsma. You were, of course, at his lecture. He would like to go round your ward—you have several gastrics. I believe?'

Sister MacFergus offered a hand, wordlessly, and raised her brown eyes to his grey ones in an unsmiling face, acknowledging his greeting with an inclination of her head. Of the fact that her heart was beating a tumultuous tattoo as his hand engulfed hers, she gave no sign. She turned to Matron.

'The ward's a wee bit untidy, Matron. Staff Nurse Williams is off sick with a raging toothache, the puir lass.'

'Oh, I forgot that, Sister. Perhaps it would be as well if we postponed our visit.' Matron glanced at Dr Doelsma, who flicked an infinitesimal speck off a beautifully tailored sleeve, remarking,

'Yes, of course—I must apologise for taking you unawares, Sister. I don't wish to add to your difficulties; doubtless you have more than you can cope with already.'

Sister MacFergus fancied that she detected derision in his voice. This had the immediate effect of causing her to say in a level voice,

'Thank you, sir, but I believe we will manage very well.' She turned her head and raised her voice slightly and called to the same little nurse whom they had first seen, and who now came trotting out of the office, listened to low-voiced instructions, cast her Ward Sister a look of devotion and made off.

They all heard the whispered warning, 'Don't run, Nurse!' But Sister MacFergus, aware of the strong views authority held regarding running nurses, caught Matron's eye and said before that lady could speak,

'Yon's a guid wee lass, and willing, Matron.' She stepped back so that Matron and Sir Charles could precede her through the door into the ward. There was a brief glimpse of bedpans being whisked into the sluice at the far end, and a nurse was coming at a brisk pace down the ward towards them. She bobbed her head at Matron and Sir Charles, and made eyes at Dr Doelsma before asking, 'Yes, Sister?' in a breathless whisper.

Sister MacFergus spoke unhurriedly. 'All the gastric X-rays, Nurse, and the notes, and make sure the patients are ready for examination. There's no time to get Mrs Burt ready, but you should have time to see to the others—be as quiet as you can.' She gave a smiling nod, and the nurse, with another look at Dr Doelsma, slipped away, leaving him standing with Sister MacFergus in the doorway.

'Allow me to compliment you on your ward, Sister; I see that you are indeed able to cope with any situation.' He paused, and when she looked at him, went on in a silky voice. 'Even the unexpected visit of a fat, elderly balding and near-sighted Dutchman.'

He smiled at her charmingly, and murmured. 'After you, Sister,' and she walked ahead of him into the ward, brown eyes flashing, head very high, and cheeks scarlet.

The round went smoothly. Dr Doelsma found himself with Matron, and when he at length contrived to get near the other two, it was to observe that they seemed on friendly terms—indeed. Sir Charles was calling Sister MacFergus Maggy without any objection on her part. With a little ingenuity, the doctor contrived to change places with Sir Charles, and conversed pleasantly enough between the beds.

'That was a very good question you put at the end of my lecture, Sister.'

Maggy MacFergus was taken completely off her guard. 'Thank you, Doctor. I have a patient with that very condition which you mentioned—Mrs Salt.' She stopped and looked at him enquiringly. 'Who told you it was my question?'

'No one. I have good eyesight, and I happened to be looking at the back row.'

They had reached Mrs Salt's bed; an old lady with black boot-button eyes and ill-fitting dentures. She had been in hospital for a long time and was regarded by the entire staff as a kind of ward mascot, whose elderly tantrums were to be cheerfully endured. She greeted Matron and Sir Charles in a piping voice and wasted no more time on them. Instead, she turned her gaze on Sister MacFergus.

'Ullo, dearie. Now that's what I like to see—a well-matched pair. And about time too; a nice girl like you going begging, Sister.'

Sister MacFergus, with great strength of mind, ignored this awful remark, merely saying in a repressive voice,

'Dr Doelsma would like to ask you a few questions. Mrs Salt.'

Mrs Salt turned her naughty old face up to his.

'And I'll answer 'em. Haven't seen such a 'andsome face for years. Just the right size for Sister too.' She grinned, well pleased with herself, and Dr Doelsma chuckled and sat down on the side of her bed and took one of her old hands in his; it felt quite weightless.

'I see that you are a great one for a joke, Mrs Salt.'

'I like a good larf—How come you speak English like us?' she queried.

'I went to school,' he answered gravely. 'And now, Mrs Salt, oblige me by putting out your tongue.'

She complied promptly, and answered his questions cheerfully enough, and when he had finished he got up, shook hands, and hoped that he would see her again the next time he came.

'Yer'd better 'urry up, then, Doctor. I'll be ninety in October.' She clutched his hand. 'And I bet it won't be me yer'll come to see.' She nodded and winked and jerked her thumb in the direction of Sister MacFergus, who, beyond going rather pink, and breathing loudly, ignored her. Mrs Salt looked disappointed at this poor response to her sally, and said resignedly,

'Now I suppose you're going to talk to old sour-face.' She jerked her head at the next bed, where a dark-haired woman with sallow skin and a sullen expression lay watching them. But Matron, who had looked at her watch, decreed otherwise. If the doctors were to go to their luncheon as arranged, they should leave the ward at once.

They all walked to the door, where farewells, gracious on Matron's part, friendly on Sir Charles' and casual on the part of Dr Doelsma, were said, and the visitors began their descent of the stairs. On the first half-landing, however, Dr Doelsma stopped, and said thoughtfully,

'I remember now, there was something I wished to say

to Sister—it quite slipped my mind on the ward. You will forgive me if I go back? I won't be above a minute or two.'

He went upstairs again, three steps at a time, to find the landing empty and Sister's door shut. He knocked without hesitation, and went in. Sister MacFergus was standing by her desk, doing nothing. The nurse who had eyed him in the ward was rattling cups and saucers on a tray. They both looked up, astonished, as he went in. The astonishment on Sister MacFergus's face, however, quickly turned to a heavy frown which she made no attempt to hide. The doctor, it seemed, was impervious to cross looks, for he merely held the door open, remarking,

'Perhaps Nurse could leave us for a moment? A small matter, purely between ourselves, Sister.'

The nurse smiled at him, and then looked at Sister MacFergus, who gave a brief nod of assent. As the girl slipped away through the door, she flashed beautiful green eyes at the doctor, and was rewarded by an appreciative stare as he shut the door behind her, and leaned against it with his hands in his pockets. Maggy MacFergus stood where she was, looking at him, her brows still drawn together in a thick line.

'What do you want?' she asked at length, quite forgetting to say 'sir'. He took a step into the little room, which brought him within inches of her. There was no space for her to step backwards; she couldn't very well push him aside. She stayed where she was.

'I want you to remember me.' He caught her by the shoulders and kissed her squarely on the mouth, and before she could think of anything to say he was at the door again, had opened it, and turned to say '*Tot ziens*, Maggy.' He sounded as though he was laughing. She went on standing there; her sensible, orderly mind a chaotic whirl of half-formed thoughts, most which she found bewildering and disturbing, especially as she would never see him again. At length she took off her cuffs and slowly rolled up her sleeves, pulled on her frills, and went into the ward to do some work.

CHAPTER TWO

FOR THE NEXT few days Maggy wasn't her usual cheerful, hard-working self. She was well aware of this, but took good care not to question herself as to the cause. She did a great deal of unnecessary work on the ward, as if the stacks of charts, laundry lists, off-duty rotas and all the other clutter accumulating on a Ward Sister's desk would make a pile sufficiently high under which to bury all thoughts of Dr Doelsma. After a time she did indeed manage to cram him into a remote corner of her mind. It was a pity that she had only just succeeded in doing this, when she was accosted by Sir Charles and asked her opinion of his erstwhile pupil. They were halfway round the ward at the time, and she had no chance to evade the question.

'He seemed a very nice wee man.' She was, idiotically, blushing.

Sir Charles gave her a look without appearing to do so.

'He's six foot four inches, Maggy, though being six foot yourself you'd not notice that. Don't you like him?'

She studied the path lab form in her hand as though she had never seen one before in her life. 'Aye. But every nurse in the hospital likes him, Sir Charles. He's a handsome man.'

Sir Charles scribbled his signature on an X-ray form before replying.

'Yes, he is. But not conceited with it. I've known him since he was a small boy—his parents were great friends of mine; his mother still is. He's clever, and he's made a successful career for himself.' He coughed. 'He knows exactly what he wants, and gets it too.' He looked so knowingly at Maggy that she went scarlet; surely Dr Doelsma hadn't told Sir Charles about the regrettable incident in her office? She realised that she hadn't forgotten it at all. Her brows drew together in so fierce a frown that Sir Charles allowed his vague manner to become even more vague, and pursued the topic in an even more ruthless fashion.

'Can't think why he's not married. Heaven knows the number of young women who have angled for him; still, as I said just now, he knows what he wants, and he has the patience to wait for it. But there, Sister, I mustn't waste your time boring on about someone you've no interest in.' He blinked rapidly and smiled disarmingly, while his elderly perceptive eye bored into hers. She met his gaze steadily.

'Aye, Sir Charles, I've no' the time to think about a man I'll not be seeing again.'

He nodded, and plunged into the highly technical details of the treatment he proposed for the patient whose bed they had reached. Mrs Salt greeted him as an old friend, gave him a colourful and most inaccurate account of her condition and asked what he'd done with the foreign doctor he'd had with him on his last visit.

'Nice, 'e was,' she reminisced. 'Now there's a man any girl could fall for.' She turned to peer at Maggy. "Ere's one 'ose just right for 'im, too, eh?' She cackled with mischievous mirth. 'Pity 'e ain't coming again—leastways, not until me birthday—that's if yer don't let me slip through yer fingers first.'

The remark was greeted with the derision she expected, and with a brief appeal from Sister MacFergus to be good, they left her bed, and passed on to her neighbour. This was a Belgian woman, Madame Riveau, she had been admitted ten days or so before with a suspected gastric ulcer. She was a silent morose woman who only answered Maggy's basic schoolgirl French when it was absolutely necessary. She was visited regularly by her husband and her son, two equally sour and dour men, who demanded at each visit that Madame Riveau should be sent home. So far Maggy had persuaded them to let her stay, but their demands were becoming so persistent that she realised that they would soon have their way—after all, no patient could be forced to remain against their wish, although she had noticed that the woman did not seem to share her menfolk's desire for her discharge—Maggy thought she seemed frightened of them; indeed, they gave her herself an uneasy feeling of menace, which was heightened by their secretiveness when asked even the simplest of questions.

She stood looking at Madame Riveau now as Sir Charles bent over the bed to examine her. She looked ill, and surely her face was swollen? Maggy waited until Sir Charles had finished and was conferring with his houseman before she asked in her rather halting French,

'Have you got the toothache, Madame Riveau?'

The result was electrifying. The sallow face on the pillow took on the greenish white of fear; the hate and terror in the dull black eyes sent Maggy back a pace.

'No. no! There's nothing wrong.' The woman's voice was a harsh whisper.

'There must be something wrong.' Maggy spoke gently;

the woman was so obviously terrified—of the dentist perhaps? 'Supposing we get you X-rayed just to make sure before you go home?'

She was rewarded by another look of venom. 'I refuse. My teeth are sound.'

Maggy ignored the look. 'I'll talk to your husband when he comes this evening; perhaps he can persuade you.'

Sir Charles had moved on, but stopped and listened to what Maggy had to say. When she had finished he nodded, and said,

'Dr Payne can sign an X-ray form, Sister. Probably she'll be better without her teeth—she's an unhealthy woman and I should suppose she'll need surgical treatment for that ulcer...'

They became immersed in the diabetic coma in the next bed, and in the ensuing calculations of insulin units, blood sugar tests, urine tests and a great many instructions concerning the intravenous drip, Madame Riveau's strange behaviour was forgotten, and when much later Maggy remembered it, she decided she must have imagined the woman's fear and anger.

She was due off duty at six o'clock. She gave the report to Staff Nurse and then waited for the visitors to arrive. She had two days off, and she wanted to see Monsieur Riveau, and get the question of his wife's teeth settled. She felt the usual thrill of distaste as she approached the bed. The two men were seated on either side of it; neither got up as she approached, but watched her with thinly veiled hostility. She wasted no time, but explained her errand and stood waiting for a reply. The men looked at her without speaking, their faces expressionless, and yet she had a prickle of fear so real that she put her hand up to the back of her neck to brush it away. At length the elder man said, 'No X-ray, no dentist for my wife. She refuses.'

'There's no pain involved,' Maggy replied doggedly. 'Her jaws are swollen; her teeth may be infected and it may make the ulcer worse.' He said 'No' in an ugly voice, and she damped down her temper and persevered in a reasonable way, struggling with her French.

'The teeth are probably decayed; she will be better without them.' She managed to smile at the unfriendly faces. 'It's very likely that in time they will make her condition worse.'

Their silence was worse than speech—chilling and unfriendly and completely uncooperative. She could feel their dislike of her pressing against her like a tangible thing. She gave herself a mental shake, asked them to reconsider their decision, and said goodnight. Her words fell into silence like stones, and as she walked away, she could feel their eyes on her back; it was a most unpleasant sensation.

Maggy spent her two days off with a former nurse who had trained with her and then left to get married. She came back to St Ethelburga's refreshed in mind if not in body, and with a strong desire to get married and have a husband and children of her own. She thought this unlikely. She had never met a man she wished to marry; but as if to give the lie to these thoughts, a picture of Dr Doelsma, very clear and accurate down to the last detail, came into her mind's eye. She shook her head, reducing his image to fragments and said something in the Gaelic tongue with such force that Sister Beecham, sitting opposite her in the sitting room, put down her knitting and looked at her.

'I don't know what it meant, Maggy MacFergus, but it sounded as though it was a good thing I didn't, and if you are going to make the tea—I'll not have milk; I'm dieting.'

Maggy got up obediently. Sister Beecham had been at St Ethelburga's for so long that her word was law to any Sister under forty, and Maggy was only twenty-four.

As she crossed the landing the next morning, she sensed an air of suppressed excitement, although there was no one to be seen. Staff was waiting for her in her office, standing by the well-polished desk, adorned by a vase of flowers. Funeral flowers, delivered at regular intervals to the wards and hailed as a mixed blessing by the unfortunate junior nurse whose lot it was to disentangle them from their wire supports and turn the anchors and wreaths into vases of normal-looking flowers. Maggy noted with relief that Nurse had achieved a very normal-looking bunch. She detested them, but had never had the heart to say so; she guessed that some nurse had taken a lot of trouble to please her. She exchanged good mornings with Staff Nurse Williams, and thought for the hundredth time what a pretty creature she was—small and blonde and blue-eyed—everything Maggy was not and wished to be. She had discovered long ago that there were few advantages in being six feet tall. It was, for a start, impossible to be fragile or clinging; it was taken for granted that she would undertake tasks that smaller women could be helpless about, and there was always the problem of dancing partners.

Staff's eyes were sparkling; she appeared to be labouring under some emotion. Maggy sat down, saying nothing. Whatever it was could come after the report. It took fifteen minutes or so, each patient discussed treatment checked, notes made. She came to the end of the page in the report book, and, she thought, the end of the report, but Staff said in a voice of suppressed excitement, 'There's another patient, Sister. Over the page—She's a Private; in Sep.'

Maggy turned the page and the name leapt out at her.

Mevrouw Van Beijen Doelsma: Coronary thrombosis. Her heart gave a lurch, but she turned no more than a faintly interested face to Williams.

'Sister, it's Dr Doelsma's mother—she's over here on holiday with Sir Charles.' Maggy nodded, remembering her conversation with him a few days ago. 'And he's been over to see her. He flew over...'

Maggy interrupted her firmly. 'When did the patient come in? Is she being specialled?'

'During the first night of your days off, Sister, and she's being specialled, though they're very short of nurses. Dr Doelsma...'

'How bad?' asked Maggy, forestalling what she felt sure was going to be a rhapsody with Dr Doelsma as the main theme.

Williams returned obediently to her report.

'Not too bad, Sister, and beginning to improve.' She went on to give a detailed account of treatment, drugs and nursing care, for she was devoted to Sister MacFergus, who was strict, kind, fair to the nurses, and had never been known to shirk the day's work; indeed, she could, if called upon, work for two—something she in fact frequently did. Williams finished her report; she had given it exactly as Sister liked it, and she hoped she was going to be asked about Dr Doelsma.

Maggy waved a capable well-kept hand at the chair. 'Sit down, Staff. Spare me two minutes and tell me all about it.'

Williams drew a long breath. 'Oh, Sister, he's smashing! He came ever so early, about eight o'clock—he flew over and stayed all day, and Sir Charles was here, of course, and they were in there hours, I was with them. He's got a gorgeous smile, and he's so tall. He went back last night. What a pity you missed him, Sister.'

Maggy smiled. 'It sounds to me, Staff, as if he had all

the help and attention he needed, I suppose you're the most envied girl in the hospital?'

Williams nodded with satisfaction. 'Yes, everyone's green with envy.' She gazed out of the window. 'He wore the loveliest waistcoat,' she said.

Maggy got up, telling herself that she had not the least desire to discuss the doctor's waistcoats. 'Williams, what about your faithful Jim?'

The other girl sighed. 'I know, Sister, but Dr Doelsma's like someone out of a dream—the sort of man you always want to meet, and never do. If he comes again, Sister, you'll see what I mean.'

Maggy saw exactly what she meant. 'I'm going to do my round,' she said firmly. She went to Sep last. Mevrouw Doelsma looked very small lying there in bed. Despite her grey pallor, Maggy could see that she was a most attractive woman, with white hair, excellently cut. Her eyes were closed, and Maggy stood with the charts, studying them, and listening to the nurse's report. Everything looked satisfactory. She sent the nurse to go and get her coffee, and turned back to the bed. Her patient's eyes were open and upon her. She smiled, but before she could say anything, Mevrouw Doelsma spoke.

'Maggy? I'm so glad. Charles said you would get me well.'

'Yes, of course, Mevrouw Doelsma, we'll have you well again very soon.'

The little lady smiled. 'Paul was cross because you weren't here. He had to go back.'

A faint colour stole into Maggy's cheeks at the mention of his name, but she told herself that he was probably annoyed because the Ward Sister wasn't on duty night and day. There were quite a few doctors who regarded nurses

as machines who could work twenty-four hours a day. The
door opened and Sir Charles Warren came in. He nodded
in the direction of the bed and said. 'Hullo, Henrietta.'
Then he turned to Maggy. 'There you are. Pity you weren't
here when Mevrouw Doelsma came in. Nice little staff
nurse you've got; you've trained her well, but she's not a
patch on you. Still, you're here now. I'll have a look at the
patient and we'll do an ECG and then we can have a chat.'

Half an hour later he followed Maggy into her office,
accepted a cup of coffee, drank it scalding hot and
demanded another. Maggy poured it out and put in his
usual four lumps of sugar.

'You'll get an ulcer, Sir Charles,' she said severely.

He agreed comfortably. 'Now, Mevrouw Doelsma. She
should do. I think. Had a nasty coronary, but it seems to be
settling. There's always the chance of another one, though.
Let me know at once, Maggy. You know what to do until I
arrive.' He got to his feet. 'I must go.' He gave a friendly
smile, and made for the door which Maggy was holding
open for him. 'Glad it's you looking after her, Sister.
Couldn't wish for anyone better. If anyone pulls her through
it'll be you.' He nodded in a satisfied way and went.

The rest of the day was busy. Maggy found to her annoyance that Madame Riveau had still refused to have her
X-rays. She would have liked to have seen her husband
during the evening visiting hours, but there was no nurse
available for specialling after six o'clock, so she left Staff
in charge of the ward, and went into Sep herself. It was ten
o'clock before she could be relieved by a night nurse.

Mevrouw Doelsma was an excellent patient, and had gone
quietly to sleep. Maggy thought she had a good chance
of recovery.

Williams wasn't on duty until one o'clock, so that Maggy had a very busy morning. She was glad to go off duty after dinner, although she knew she would have to come back early. There was a nurse off sick, and extra beds up and down the centre of the ward. But she didn't mind hard work. The ward was straight by seven o'clock, and she sent Williams and a junior nurse to supper. It was visiting time; the patients were occupied with their visitors. Maggy sat in Sep with the door open, so that she could see down the ward, and watch Mevrouw Doelsma at the same time; she was awake and lying quietly.

The restlessness came on suddenly. Maggy put down the report book and got to the bed as Mevrouw Doelsma gave a couple of painful gasps, went livid, and lapsed into unconsciousness. Maggy turned on the oxygen, and strapped the nasal catheter in position, then drew up and gave an injection of morphia. Only then did she press the button which would turn on the red light above the door of Sep. There was little hope of a nurse back from supper; there was a full five minutes to go, but someone might see it and come to investigate. She could feel no pulse under her steady fingers; she adjusted the BP armband on the flaccid arm, but could get no sound through the stethoscope; with it still swinging around her neck, she turned to draw the heparin and mephine.

She knew exactly what to do, and did it with calm speed, reflecting that it would have been easier with two. She had the syringe in hand when Dr Doelsma walked in. Without a word she handed it to him, and held the limp arm rigid so that he could inject the blood vessel in the elbow. 'Heparin,' she said. 'I gave morphia'—she glanced at the clock—'two minutes ago. The mephine is drawn up.'

He nodded, jabbed the needle in, took the mephine from her and gave that too.

She gave him the stethoscope and said quietly, 'I'll ring Sir Charles.' She sent her urgent message, and went back to find the doctor sitting on the edge of the bed, his mother's hand in his.

Mevrouw Doelsma still looked very ill, but they could see now that she wasn't going to die. Maggy wrote up the charts; Sir Charles would expect them accurate and ready for him. Dr Doelsma was using the stethoscope again; he took it off and handed it to Maggy. This time it recorded something—a poor something, but obviously the drugs were having effect. They agreed their reading, and smiled at each other; she could see how anxious his eyes were. They both stood looking down at the face on the pillow between them. It held some semblance of life again, and as they watched, the eyelids fluttered and his mother's eyes opened. She looked at her son and then at Maggy, and a tiny smile came and went, but as she was about to speak he gave her hand a warning squeeze.

'Don't talk, Mama, everything's all right. You shall have your say presently.'

She smiled again before she closed her eyes again. They stood on either side of her, patiently waiting. There was nothing very much to do now, except regular and frequent pulse and BP checks. By the time Sir Charles arrived, it was normal. He looked at the charts while he listened to Maggy's concise, brief report. He nodded at Dr Doelsma. 'Not much for me to do, eh, Paul? Lucky you turned up when you did.' He spent a little time examining his patient and said, 'She'll do, thanks to you, Paul.'

The other man shook his head. 'It is Sister MacFergus whom we must both thank. She did everything necessary in the most competent manner.'

Sir Charles smiled at Maggy. 'Yes, she always does. A most reliable girl.'

The two men stood looking at her; it was a relief to find Staff Nurse at her elbow.

'Shall I clear up here, Sister? Nurse Sims has got the ward straight—the night staff are on.'

Maggy thought a minute. 'Nurse Sims can go now; I'll give the report, then you can go. I'll stay here until they can send another nurse.'

Williams said eagerly, 'I'll stay…' but was interrupted by Sir Charles.

'Will you stay here for a while, Sister? Have you a good nurse for night duty here?'

Maggy shook her head. 'There's a shortage of nurses, Sir Charles, it's this gastric bug. There's no nurse at present, but Matron will arrange for one later on, I'm sure. I'll bide till she comes.' She looked at Williams and saw the disappointment on her face. 'When I come back, Staff, will you make coffee for all of us. I'm sure the doctors would like a cup.' She was rewarded by a grateful smile as she turned to Sir Charles.

'I'll give the report, sir, and be back. Staff Nurse will clear up and set the room ready.' She gave Williams the keys and slipped away, watched by the two doctors.

Paul said low-voiced, 'When Mother goes back home to Oudehof, I want Sister MacFergus to go with her.'

Sir Charles pursed his lips and looked doubtfully at his companion, who met his gaze with a cool determined look of his own.

'She's a ward sister, you know.'

'I know. Could she not have special leave for a couple of weeks or so? I'll pay whatever fee the hospital requires. I want someone I can trust to look after Mother.'

'Naturally. And you trust Sister MacFergus?'

'Yes, Uncle Charles, I do.'

The older man turned away and bent over his patient. There was a faint pink in her cheeks now; her pulse was regular and much stronger. He gave Williams some instructions, and went back to Paul. 'Very well, Paul, I'll do my best for you. Your mother will be here for a month—you know that. I daresay something can be arranged in the meantime. But I think we will say nothing of this for the time being. Do you agree?'

Paul nodded. 'I'd like to stay the night. I don't need to be back in Leiden until Monday morning.'

He broke off as Maggy came back into the room. She nodded to Williams, then took off her cuffs and rolled up her sleeves.

'Staff's making coffee. You'll have a cup, Sir Charles? And you, sir? It'll be ready in my office.'

'And you, Sister?' It was Dr Doelsma speaking.

'I'll be here, sir. I'll have mine later.' She didn't even look at him, but busied herself with the drip.

Williams was waiting for them, hovering over Sister's own coffee pot, very anxious to please. There were only two chairs, so Dr Doelsma sat on the desk and drank his coffee.

'Are you not off duty, Staff Nurse?'

Williams, the faithful Jim's image temporarily dimmed, fluttered her eyelashes and used a dimple devastatingly.

'Yes, sir. But the night staff haven't time to make coffee now.'

'And Sister?'

'She's off too. Oh…' she remembered… 'she's not been to supper, and she'll be on duty until two o'clock—there's no one to take over before then. I must make her some sandwiches.' She forgot all about charming the Dutch doctor in her anxiety for Sister MacFergus.

'Sister is fortunate to have a staff nurse who takes such

care of her.' He smiled down at the pretty little creature. Something in his face made her realise suddenly that behind his rather arrogant good looks there was strength of character, as well as kindness and a concern for others; it became of paramount importance to her to win his good opinion.

'No, we're the lucky ones. I mean the nurses on this ward. You see, sir, Sister's one of the nicest people any of us have ever met. Of course, we all call her Maggy behind her back, but that's because we like her—' She broke off and looked uncertainly at Sir Charles who called Sister MacFergus Maggy to her face.

'A good Scottish name,' he murmured, and got up. With a smile and a nod of thanks he went back to Sep where the ECG machine was ready by the bed. He said, 'Right, Sister,' and Maggy started fastening the straps very carefully and gently, leaving Dr Doelsma to connect up the leads, and then stood back, waiting for the doctors to make a recording. They had just finished when Williams came in, whispered to her, said a low goodnight, and went off duty. Maggy had hardly begun to disconnect the leads before Dr Doelsma was by her side.

'I'll do that, Sister. Go and have your coffee and sandwiches.' She glanced at Sir Charles. 'Yes, Maggy, go and sit down for ten minutes. I'll be over presently before I go. Dr Doelsma will be staying the night; he'll be on hand if you want anyone in a hurry.'

The night passed slowly. There wasn't a great deal to do. The doctor had refused the offer of a bed in the housemen's quarters, but had remained in the room, sitting relaxed and calm in an easy chair near the bed. He had opened the dispatch case he had brought with him, and was busily engaged writing. Maggy supposed it was another lecture.

Just after midnight Mevrouw Doelsma woke up, asked

for water in a thin voice and wanted to know the time. Maggy told her, and she frowned and whispered, 'You poor child, you must be worn out; you've been here all day.'

Maggy hastened to assure her that she wasn't in the least tired, but her patient only smiled and said, 'Stuff!' and then. 'But I'm glad you were here. I felt quite safe with you.' She turned her head to look at her son, standing beside her, his fingers on her pulse. 'I won't do it again. Don't go just yet, will you?'

'I can stay until tomorrow night, dear; you'll be feeling much better by then.' He gave the hand a squeeze and smiled, and she closed her eyes again, saying, 'You're both so enormous.'

Just before two o'clock, Maggy's relief arrived. She was a senior student and a very good nurse, and a very attractive one too. Maggy introduced the doctor, gave a report, said goodnight, and made for the door. The doctor, with the advantage of longer legs, got there first, opened it, and then filled the doorway with his bulk so that it was impossible for her to go through.

'I'm in your debt, Sister MacFergus,' he looked steadily into her weary face. 'You saved my mother's life. You have my gratitude and my thanks.'

'And I'll thank ye also, Doctor, for if ye hadna' come when ye did, I ken fine it might have gone ill with your mother.' She smiled, all six feet of her drooping with tiredness. 'Goodnight, sir.' She slipped past him and was gone.

Maggy was quite her usual self when she went on duty the next morning. She took the report and then went into Sep, Dr Doelsma rose from his chair and wished her a good morning. He looked immaculate, freshly shaven, and not a crease to be seen; his face was that of a man who had enjoyed an untroubled night's rest. The patient was sleeping, and according to the night nurse, entirely satisfactory. She picked up her report ready to give it, and was about to begin when Dr Doelsma coughed gently. 'Er—shall I go, Sister, or may I stay?' He sounded so meek that she shot him a suspicious glance before asking him politely to do as he wished. He settled back into his chair which creaked alarmingly under his weight, and opened out *The Times*, only lowering it briefly to wish the night nurse a warm farewell, coupled with a solicitous wish that she would sleep soundly, and all without a glance at Maggy, who had not failed to notice with an unusual flash of temper that he and the night nurse appeared to be on excellent terms. Despite herself, she gave an angry snort,

He lowered *The Times* for a second time. 'You spoke, Sister?'

'I did not,' she snapped, and added 'sir.'

He folded his paper carefully, glanced at his sleeping parent and asked.

'Must I be called sir?'

She charted the pulse carefully.

'Of course, Dr Doelsma. You are a consultant.'

'So, by the same token, I may call you Maggy?'

She took a deep breath and said deliberately, 'You are in a position to call me anything you wish, sir.' She realised her mistake as soon as she had spoken.

'My dear girl, how kind of you.' His voice was smooth. 'I wonder, what shall it be?'

She blushed under his mocking eye, and said with dignity, 'That's not what I meant, Doctor, and you know it.' She put down the chart and went on briskly, 'I doubt you'll be wanting your breakfast—I'll arrange that.'

'Don't bother—er—Sister. Now that you're here, I'll go

over and see Sir Charles and breakfast with him. I'll be back within the hour.'

'Very well, sir, I'll ring you if it should be necessary.'

She ignored him, and prepared to take Mevrouw Doelsma's blood pressure. Her patient opened her eyes at that moment, and said, 'Hullo, it's you again. I'm glad. A sweet girl, the night nurse, but so earnest, I felt as though I had one foot in the grave all night.'

Maggy smiled and said gently. 'Fiddlesticks, you were dreaming—and both feet are safe here in bed.'

She turned to find Dr Doelsma still there, looming over the end of the bed.

He said, 'Hullo, Mama. I'm going over to Uncle Charles. Be good.' He turned at the door, with his hand on the knob.

'You'll ring me, won't you, Sister?' He sounded casual, but she could see the worry in his eyes.

She smiled at him warmly. 'Of course.' She looked supremely confident and capable, standing there in her trim uniform.

There was still a shortage of nurses; if Williams was to get her half day. Maggy thought, she herself would have to go off duty that morning. She decided to do so as soon as Dr Doelsma returned. Williams could look after the ward, and Sibley, the third-year nurse, could come into Sep. Sir Charles came back with Dr Doelsma, they looked well fed and relaxed. Maggy, who had had a sketchy breakfast, thought longingly of coffee… She would never get off duty by ten o'clock. It was a quarter past the hour when Sir Charles finished examining his patient. He held a short discussion with Paul and called for another ECG.

Maggy was buckling the straps when Dr Doelsma came over to do his part.

'Are you not off duty, Sister?' She glanced up in surprise.

'How did you know?'

'That pretty little staff nurse of yours told me. Shall I get her in so that you can go?'

She tightened a buckle slowly. 'Why not?' she asked coolly. 'Though I'm afraid Staff won't be able to come for long. But Nurse Sibley shall relieve her; she's the pretty blonde with green eyes—I'm sure you will have noticed her.'

She didn't look up to see what effect her words had had, but finished what she was doing, sent for Williams to take her place, and went to the ward. By the time she had done a round it was almost eleven. She decided to have coffee in the Sisters' Home, but when she got there it didn't seem worth while. Dinner would be at twelve-thirty. She flounced into the sitting room, feeling pettish and more than a little sorry for herself, and buried herself in the papers for the next hour or so. There weren't any other Sisters off; she wished she had not bothered to go off duty at all, though that, she decided, would not have pleased Dr Doelsma, for then he would have had to have put up with her for the whole morning.

She returned on duty after lunch, her frame of mind by no means improved. The ward was fairly quiet. She sent Nurse Sibley to her dinner, and Williams to her afternoon with the faithful Jim. That left little Nurse Sims whom she sent into the ward to tidy it for visitors; she herself went into Sep until Sibley should return. Both doctors had gone to lunch; her patient was sleeping. She studied the charts and then started to pick up the papers littered around the doctor's chair. They were closely written in a foreign language—Dutch, she supposed; in any case, they would have been unintelligible in English. She made a tidy pile, then went to open the window wider. It was a lovely late

August day; she would have liked to have been home, tramping the hills with the dogs. The door opened, but she didn't turn round at once, but said,

'You should have taken your full hour, Nurse; I'll not need to go until two o'clock.'

She looked over her shoulder. Dr Doelsma was standing in the doorway.

'You're at lunch,' she said stupidly.

He ignored this piece of foolishness, but strolled into the room.

'Ah. I'm glad you're back on duty,' he said.

She frowned. Really, she thought, after his obvious anxiety to get rid of her that morning—'Did something go wrong?' she asked.

'No, no. Nurse Sibley was most competent, but I must admit that I prefer you here, Sister.' He stared at her. 'You needed to go off duty this morning, you were tired.'

She went pink; it was an unpleasant experience having her thoughts read so accurately. She asked, curiosity getting the better of discretion, 'Why do you prefer me here, Doctor?'

He considered his reply. 'I am a big man, Sister. People tend to stare at me as though I were something peculiar. You don't stare, presumably because you are such a big woman yourself. A purely selfish reason, you see.'

This truthful but unflattering description of herself did nothing to improve Maggy's mood, and the more so because she could think of nothing to say in reply. Nurse Sibley's return saved her from this difficulty, however. She handed over to her, and left the room with great dignity, feeling twelve feet tall, and very conscious of the largeness of her person.

The visitors, laden with flowers and fruit and unsuitable

food, began to straggle in, and Maggy was kept busy answering questions and making out certificates. Madame Riveau's husband and son hadn't arrived; she would have to see them that evening. She sat down at her desk and began the off-duty rota for the following week. It was an absorbing and irritating task, trying to fit in lectures, study days, and special requests for days off. She became immersed in it, then looked up to find the doctor standing by her. She stopped, pen poised.

'Did you want me, sir?'

He didn't answer her question, but said shortly, 'My mother's asleep.' He stretched out an arm and took the off duty book from her and studied it carefully. Maggy asked in an annoyed voice,

'Is there something you wish to know, Dr Doelsma?'

'Yes, there was,' he answered cheerfully, 'but I've seen all I want, thank you.' He gave the book back into a hand rendered nerveless with vexation, but made no effort to go.

Maggy filled in another name and then asked, 'Would you like tea, sir? It's early, I know, but perhaps in Holland you drink tea at a different time from us.'

'Probably. But I must point out to you that I am a Friesman, and not a Hollander, and proud of the fact—just as you, I imagine, are proud of being a Scotswoman. The Friesians and the Scots have mutual ancestors, you know.'

Maggy didn't know, and said so, adding, 'How interesting' in a cold voice which he ignored.

'How's Mrs Salt?' he enquired.

Maggy put down her pen in a deliberate manner. He seemed bent on engaging her in conversation, however unwilling on her part, so she said civilly, 'The path lab results came back yesterday—and the X-rays show an infiltration into the oesophagus—a blueprint of your lecture.'

'May I see her notes?' He was serious and rather remote now. She got the notes and X-rays and answered his questions sensibly. At length he handed them back to her, saying, 'A blueprint indeed, Sister, which bears out your question, does it not?'

She nodded. 'It's strange that a condition as rare as this one should coincide with your lecture.'

They discussed technicalities for a few minutes, and she surprised him with her sharp brain and knowledge used with so much intelligence.

'Could you spare time to come and see Mrs Salt?' he suggested. 'Not to examine her, just a social visit.'

They walked down the ward to the old lady's bed. She had no visitors—she had been a patient for so long that the novelty of coming to see her had worn off—and she hailed Dr Doelsma with delight.

'Cor, if it ain't Dr Dutch 'isself!' She extended a hand, which he observed had become more transparent, and if possible thinner than it had been a week ago. Her lively black eyes snapped at him, however.

'Don't feed me a lot of codswallop about getting better, doctor. I ain't a fool, no more I'm a cry-baby, though I'll be fair mad if I don't 'ave me birthday.' She turned her penetrating gaze on to Maggy. 'Goin' to 'ave a cake, ain't I, love?'

Sister MacFergus, replying to this endearing form of address, smiled and said, 'Yes, Mrs Salt, a cake with candles, so you'd better be good and do as you're asked so that you'll be able to blow them out. There'll be presents too.' she added.

The old lady brightened. "Oo from?'

Maggy smiled. 'That's a secret, but I can promise that you're going to get quite a lot of parcels.'

'Suppose I don't last, love?'

Maggy didn't hesitate. 'Mrs Salt, I promise you that you shall have a birthday party.'

The old lady nodded, satisfied. 'Right yer are. You're coming, young man?' She turned briskly to the doctor.

His eyes widened with laughter. 'No one's called me young man for years! How nice it sounds. For that I shall bring you a birthday present. Will you choose, or shall it be a surprise?'

'I'll 'ave a pink nightie with lots of lace,' she replied promptly. 'It'll cost yer a pretty penny; d'yer earn enough to buy one?'

He didn't smile, but answered gently, 'Yes, Mrs Salt, I do, and you shall have it—on condition that you wear it at the party.'

'O' course I shall! A bit of a waste on an old woman like me, ain't it? but I always wanted one—more sense ter give it ter Sister 'ere. She'd look nice in it, I reckon.'

Maggy kept her eyes on the counterpane, and concentrated on not blushing, but was well aware that Dr Doelsma was studying her with interest and taking his time about it.

'Yes, very nice, Mrs Salt,' he murmured, 'but she'll have to wait for her birthday, won't she?'

He said goodbye then, and they turned away. Madame Riveau, in the next bed, had visitors. Her husband and son sat one on each side of her; they looked, Maggy thought, as though they were guarding the woman in the bed. She wished them a good afternoon as she passed, and was surprised when they both got up and walked over to her. Subconsciously she recoiled and took an instinctive step towards the doctor, who looked faintly surprised but remained silent.

The older man spoke. 'I wish to take my wife home. You will arrange it?' It wasn't a request but a demand, couched in an insolent tone and awkward French.

Maggy stopped. 'I'm sorry, Monsieur Riveau; you must arrange that with the doctor. Your wife is almost better; please let her stay for another week.'

The younger man had joined his father. 'My mother is not to have her teeth X-rayed or drawn.' There was an ill-concealed dislike in his voice.

Maggy glanced at him briefly, refusing to be intimidated. Dr Doelsma had remained silent, but his presence gave her a good deal of courage.

'Your mother is in pain; surely she may decide herself?'

His small black eyes glared at her. She couldn't understand what he said, but evidently the doctor could. He stopped him and began to speak in a voice Maggy hadn't heard him use before; it was cold and hard and full of authority. He spoke in fluent French which she couldn't hope to follow, and she watched the two men cringe under it. When the doctor had finished, they made no reply but looked at Maggy with hate in their eyes, and went back to the bed.

Maggy stood irresolute, but Dr Doelsma tapped her on the shoulder in a peremptory fashion, and she found herself, rather to her own surprise, walking meekly beside him down the ward. By the time they had reached her office, however, she had begun to feel a slight indignation. He had had no right to interfere when she was discussing her own patients; the fact that she had been very glad to have him there while he talked with those two awful men had nothing to do with it. Standing by her desk, she said stiffly,

'Thank you for your help, although I am usually judged capable of dealing with matters concerning my patients.'

She was vexed to hear her voice shaking. She was enraged still further when he laughed.

'How pretty you are when you are angry! I'm sorry you are annoyed with me. Was I very high-handed? You didn't understand what that man was saying, did you? Shall I tell you, or will you take my word for it that he was crude and disgusting? If we had been anywhere else but a hospital ward, I should have knocked him down.'

She looked startled and contrite. 'I didn't understand him, you were kind to…to stop him. Thank you.'

'Why are you afraid of them?'

'Oh! How did you know—did they see…?'

'No, they did not. I don't blame you for disliking them. I found them most repulsive.' He smiled. 'Am I forgiven?'

'Yes, of course, sir. I'm sorry I was rude.' She looked at him anxiously. He was still smiling—she remembered that he had smiled on the day of the lecture and said quickly in a brisk fashion, 'Now I'll be helping Nurse with the teas. The visitors will be going…' She got as far as the door.

'My mother complains bitterly that she has hardly seen you all day. Could not the green-eyed blonde help with teas while you come into Sep? She has proved a poor substitute for you, Sister.'

She bristled. 'Nurse Sibley is a very competent nurse.'

Their eyes met; his were dancing with laughter.

'Indeed yes, Maggy. But that isn't what I meant.'

She found she had been ushered out of the office and across the landing into Sep and heard herself telling Nurse Sibley to go the ward and help with teas. She seemed to be doing exactly what the doctor wished her to do. She remembered Sir Charles' words, and made a resolve to be very much firmer in the future.

CHAPTER THREE

DR DOELSMA went back to Holland during Sunday night, and the ward seemed a very dull place without him. Maggy felt a thrill of excitement when Sir Charles mentioned in a casual manner that Paul would be visiting his mother at the end of the week. Nevertheless she felt constrained to change her off-duty so that she would be absent from the ward on that day. Staff Nurse Williams looked at her as if she was out of her mind.

'Sister! Dr Doelsma's coming—he'll get here about two o'clock and he's going again in the evening. You'll miss him.'

'Well, that can't be helped,' said Maggy reasonably. 'I promised I would go and see this friend of my mother's and it just so happens that she wants me to go on Friday.' She smiled at Williams. 'You can cope with anything that may crop up, and Mevrouw Doelsma is so much better now, I think she'll do. Besides, Dr Doelsma thinks you're a very pretty girl, and you know you're delighted to be seeing him.'

Williams giggled, 'Well, Sister, he is marvellous!'

So Maggy spent her day with elderly Miss MacIntyre, who hadn't seen her for a number of years and treated her like a schoolgirl; they went for a walk in the park, and changed the library books and discussed knitting patterns, and she went back to the hospital in the evening, wondering if she would be like Miss MacIntyre in forty years' time.

Rather to her surprise, the next morning, Williams gave her the report without mentioning Dr Doelsma, but as Maggy closed the report book her staff nurse opened a cupboard and produced an opulent box of Kersenbonbons, and laid it on the desk.

'He brought these,' she breathed. 'I said you weren't here, and he said how nice it was to see me again, and he gave me these and I told him I'd give them to you, and he said No, they're for the nurses, Sister will get something next time I come—but we thought we'd save them for you all the same.'

A small lump of hurt feelings settled in Maggy's throat, but she swallowed it resolutely.

'That was sweet of you all, but you take them and divide them up amongst you—Dr Doelsma might feel hurt in his feelings if ye didna' do as he asked.' She got up from her chair. 'Sit down now, Staff, and do it this minute.' She smiled at the other girl. 'I'm off on my round.'

As she went she told herself that it was her own fault anyway that she hadn't been on duty. Staff had said that he was coming again on the following Sunday—it was her free weekend in any case. The thought put her in mind of the amount of work she had to do, and she resolutely put all thoughts of the doctor out of her mind.

When she got to Mrs Salt's bed, she found that old lady in a gossiping mood.

'Yer missed 'im,' she informed Maggy. 'And now it's yer weekend, ain't it, love, so yer won't see 'im then either. But I 'eard 'im asking Staff if you was on duty next Thursday evening, and she said Yes, and 'e says Good, I'll be along then. So you'll see 'im then.'

Maggy straightened a pillow. 'Is that so, Mrs Salt? And I've just remembered that I'll have to change my off duty on Thursday. Isn't that a pity?'

She turned to the next bed, and found Madame Riveau sitting up in a chair. She would be going home very soon now, but she looked ill and spiritless. Maggy eyed her swollen jaws but remained silent. It was to be hoped that the woman would go to her own dentist as soon as she got home. She asked a few questions of her, but her answers were surly and unwilling, so she left her and went on down the ward and finally into Sep.

Mevrouw Doelsma smiled at her from her pillows, and Maggy thought how pretty she was now that she was better and had some colour in her cheeks, and a faint sparkle in her eyes.

'Maggy, Paul missed you yesterday. He expected you to be on duty.' Maggy went across the room and adjusted the blind, then said, with her back to her patient,

'I changed my off-duty at the last minute.' She smiled over her shoulder.

'And you won't be here tomorrow either?'

'No, it's my weekend, but Staff is very efficient...'

Mevrouw Doelsma looked at Maggy's rather nice back view. 'I wouldn't dream of asking you to lose a minute of your free time, but I'm selfish enough to like you here all the time. Oh well, he'll be over again on Thursday. You'll be here then, won't you?'

Maggy hesitated; she didn't like telling lies. 'Well, I usually am.' She achieved the half truth, feeling guilty.

She spent the weekend trying to think of a good excuse for changing her evening off. It was nothing short of a miracle that Williams should come to her during Monday and ask if she could possibly have Wednesday evening free. Maggy breathed a sigh of relief and, taking care not to appear too pleased, agreed.

Wednesday evening was fairly quiet. She did the medicine round and started the report before going to supper, and when she came back went to see Mevrouw Doelsma, who was sitting up in bed, ready for someone to talk to. She looked rather excited, Maggy thought, as she tidied her pillows, she supposed that she was pleased because she was making such good progress. Another two weeks and there would be talk of her going home. It was almost eight-thirty. She switched off the ceiling light, leaving the little bedside lamp burning, and went to the door and opened it, then turned round again to say,

'I'm going to give the report, Mevrouw Doelsma. Ring if you want anything; I'll be in to say goodnight later.' She stepped backwards on to a foot, and didn't need to hear the chuckle above her left ear to know whose it was. A very large gentle hand clipped her round the waist.

'And do you number me among your enemies that you trample me so ruthlessly under foot? At best a poor way of greeting me after almost two weeks!'

She stood within the circle of his arm, fighting to breathe normally.

'Ye ken well you're no enemy of mine, Dr Doelsma—and I didna' expect ye.'

He dropped his arm and she turned to face him with what dignity she could muster.

He smiled at her. 'No, you didn't, did you, Sister MacFergus? I should have warned you not to try the same trick twice.'

She opened her mouth to speak, but only succeeded in making a small choking sound.

'That's right,' he said kindly. 'I wouldn't say anything

you may regret later. And if you want to know how I found out, I have no intention of telling you.' He looked down at his well brushed shoes. 'Aren't you going to say you're sorry? I'm in great pain…'

Maggy laughed, 'Oh, Dr Doelsma, what's to be done with you?'

'I'm open to suggestions,' he murmured.

Maggy frowned. 'Yes, well,' she said briskly, 'I'll away to give the report.' She smiled at Mevrouw Doelsma and swept past him without a glance.

He went over to the bed then, kissed his mother, and tumbled a pile of books on to the bed-table. 'I've been to see Uncle Charles,' he said. 'He's very satisfied, Mother. If we can get Maggy to accompany you home, I should think you could go in a fortnight. You'll have to lead a quiet life for several weeks, you know.'

He drew up a chair, and they became immersed in plans.

There was a subdued hum of voices coming from behind the shut door of the office. Maggy opened the door and stood looking around her, too surprised to speak. The night nurses as well as Sibley and Sims were there, feverishly arranging a vast number of red roses into vases. Sibley looked up when the door opened, and said. 'Sister, Dr Doelsma asked us to put them in water—he brought them for you.'

Maggy closed her mouth, which had dropped open. 'But there are dozens. They can't all be for me, there must be some mistake.'

'No, Sister. He said, "These are all for Sister MacFergus." There's six dozen of them,' she added in an awed voice.

'How nice.' Maggy's voice sounded faint in her own ears. 'Thank you for arranging them.' She sent the day nurses off duty, and sitting in a bower of roses, gave the report. After she had done a round with the night nurse she went back to the office. The little room smelled delicious, she crossed the landing to Sep and went in. The doctor unfolded himself from his chair.

'I hear that my mother's progress is excellent, Sister.' He looked and sounded exactly like any other consultant—friendly, cool and remote.

She answered suitably, sedately, wished her patient a good night and went back to the door, feeling awkward. He opened it for her, and stood back politely, waiting for her to pass through. She stopped in the doorway, and raised her eyes to his, she sounded breathless.

'The roses are beautiful, thank you, Doctor. But I think the nurses mistook your message to me. They'll be for all of us and the ward too?'

'Your nurses made no mistake, Sister. The roses are for you.'

'But there are six dozen of them, Doctor; ye canna mean to give me seventy-two roses?' She looked at him, bewildered.

'Indeed I do mean it, Sister MacFergus.'

'I've never had such a lovely bouquet in my life before,' she said naïvely. 'I love red roses.'

'I'm glad. There's some charming poetry written about red roses,' he observed.

She was very conscious of him watching her while she thought. It didn't take her long to remember. She went pink and said,

'Aye, I expect so; I don't read poetry much—no time, that is.' She was becoming incoherent.

'Oh, come,' he said easily, 'everyone learns poetry at school. What about, "My love is like a red red rose"?'

'Well, yes, I'd—' She had been going to say that she had

forgotten it; but she hadn't. 'There must be any number…
such a lovely colour…and long stems…' She looked rather
wildly at him.

'Maggy, you're babbling.' He was laughing at her. She
didn't know whether to laugh with him or cry; she felt un-
accountably like doing both. He stopped laughing and said
quite seriously,

'I want to talk to you. Will you be here next Wednesday?'

She nodded and said goodnight in a low voice, then fled
through the door and over to her office, and stood amongst
the roses until she heard him shut the door. Then she picked
a bunch of roses from one of the vases and went over to
the Sisters' Home.

Maggy lay awake a long time trying to think sensibly.
But good sense had no chance against the wisps of wild
dreams floating in and out of her head. She wondered
what he wanted to see her about, and then caught the
tatters of her common sense about her, and told herself
sharply to stop behaving like a lovesick schoolgirl and
go to sleep.

In the morning the first thing she saw was the bunch of
roses, and she remembered what Sister Beecham had said
when they had met on the way to her room the night before.

'Red Roses, MacFergus? Who's in love with you?'

'In love with me?' She must have sounded stupid, for
the older woman had answered impatiently, 'Of course. You
must know that men send red roses to the girls they love.'
She had sniffed. 'Still, perhaps they don't do it nowadays.'

At the memory of her remark, Maggy said 'Nonsense'
very loudly and got out of bed, deliberately filling her
mind with thoughts as practical as the uniform she was
putting on.

* * *

She had little time for private thoughts during the next few days. Mrs Salt, prostrate after a sudden bout of pain and sickness, needed a great deal of encouragement and attention if she was to survive to celebrate her birthday. It took the combined skill and cunning of the nursing staff, coupled with pep talks from Sir Charles and the house physician, to get her sitting up against her pillows again.

Maggy had another problem on her hands too—Madame Riveau, due to go home in a couple of days, looked increasingly ill. Despite this, her husband and son asked sullenly each time they came if she could leave immediately. To her surprise, Madame Riveau had consented to have her teeth X-rayed on the morning of her discharge, but Maggy guessed that she had not told either her husband or her son. If she could persuade them to wait until the day the doctor had agreed upon for her discharge she could be seen before they called to fetch her home. The woman had been a lot of trouble and she would be glad to see her go.

Wednesday came at last. When she went into Sep, Maggy was greeted by Mevrouw Doelsma, whose manner was faintly tinged with excitement, but she chatted guilelessly while Maggy helped her out of her armchair and back into bed. When she was once more sitting back comfortably against the pillows she gave a contented sigh.

'It's wonderful to get up each day now, but bed is so delightful afterwards. I'm doing well, aren't I, Maggy?'

She was answered by a muffled voice from under her bed, where Maggy was lying, plugging in a second lamp. Sep, as Maggy had so often said, had been designed by a man with no imagination. The wall plugs were all ground level, behind the bed, and the nurses had long ago discovered that it was both quick and easy to reach them by getting under the bed rather than to pull the bed out from the wall, and then push it back again. Mrs Doelsma, having seen this operation performed countless times, thought nothing of the shapely pair of legs sticking out from under the side of her bed, but continued to address them.

'Do you suppose I shall be able to go home soon? I've been very happy here, but now I feel almost well again, and I should like to go back to Oudehof.'

Her voice tailed off. Her son was standing in the doorway; he gave a half smile in greeting and raised an eyebrow at the legs, but made no attempt to come into the room. There was a click, as the lamp was switched on.

'Of course you'll be going home soon, Mevrouw Doelsma.' Maggy spoke in a comforting voice. She had heard the slightly wistful note in the little lady's voice. She slid from under the bed and stood up. For all her size, she was a very graceful young woman; she gave herself a shake, twitched her apron bib straight, smiled at Mevrouw Doelsma, and turned in a leisurely fashion to the door. The sight of the doctor brought her up short. She blushed, to her own annoyance, and said in a rather weak voice. 'Oh! Have you been there long?' She looked at him anxiously, but there was nothing to read from his face. Perhaps he had just that minute arrived.

He smiled briefly and said, 'I'm early, I believe, Sister. I hope it is not inconvenient?' He sounded brisk and rather aloof. Just as though, thought Maggy, he had never seen red roses in his life. Well, she could be brisk too.

'No, sir, it's not inconvenient. Mevrouw Doelsma is quite ready to see you.'

She smiled at her patient and slipped through the door, determined to be very busy in the ward for the rest of the day; there were only a couple of hours to go before the night staff came on. She did the medicine round, and was writing her report at her desk when the doctor knocked and came in.

He spoke without preamble. 'Will you spare me five minutes of your time—there is something I want to ask you.' He pulled up a chair and sat down and smiled at her to make her heart turn over.

'Mother will be going home to Friesland in ten days or so.' He paused. 'Maggy, I'm not giving you much time to make up your mind about this—I want you to come too.' His voice was urgent.

Maggy, sitting very upright with her hands folded on her apron, kept her eyes on the desk. She was deafened by the thudding of her heart; her mind a jumble of thoughts and dreams. Before she had time to reply he went on,

'It will be just for a few weeks; you're an excellent nurse, and my mother is fond of you. I can trust her to your care, I know. I must confess that we thought of this some time ago, but I was doubtful if you would come.'

He sat back, looking at her smilingly. Maggy smiled back, pride keeping her mouth steady and her eyes dry. There would be plenty of time later on to call herself the silly romantic fool she undoubtedly was. She thought fleetingly of the red roses—all part of the softening process perhaps, deliberately planned so that she would fall in with his suggestion? When she spoke, her voice was quite steady.

'I'm flattered by your good opinion of me, sir, but I think that Matron will not allow it.'

He said with a trace of arrogance, 'I saw Matron some time ago about this. We—that is, Sir Charles and I— managed to persuade her to agree to you going. Provided you have no objection.' He looked at her sharply. 'But you haven't, of course.' Again the touch of arrogance.

She gave him a level glance. 'Dr Doelsma, I ken fine

that there's many a good nurse here in this hospital, better than I, who would nurse your mother devotedly.'

He looked at her in amazement. 'Are you refusing, Maggy?'

'Aye, sir, I'm refusing.'

He said in a kind of wonder, 'Do you not like us?'

It was her turn to look amazed. 'Gracious goodness, Doctor, I like you fine—the both of you.'

'So it is personal reasons which make you refuse?'

She considered a minute. 'Yes, I suppose you might say that.'

He said sharply, 'Selfish reasons?'

Maggy sat quite still, looking at the frowning face, then got up slowly. 'Ye've no right to speak to me like that, sir. Now if ye'll excuse me, I'll away to my supper.'

Without a word he stood up, opened the door for her, and stood watching while she spoke to Nurse Sims and then went downstairs.

Her gay and animated manner at supper caused her friends to look askance. Maggy, for all her size, perhaps because of it, was known to be rather shy and retiring. Those who knew her well realised that she was in a dreadful temper. She did indeed go back to the ward with little sparks of rage in her eyes, and pink cheeks; most of the rage was against herself. She opened her office door and stood staring. The little room seemed full of people— Sir Charles Warren, Matron and Dr Doelsma. She looked at him down her beautiful nose and then turned her back, waiting for someone to speak.

Matron began: 'Er—Sister MacFergus, we won't keep you from your work, but I am sure that this little matter can be cleared up in a few moments. I am certain that your reasons for not going to Holland are given from the highest of motives, but I can assure you that you need have no qualms about leaving the ward. It is unusual, I admit, for a Ward Sister to take over a private case; but Sir Charles wishes it, and it can be arranged quite simply.' She inflated her bosom and nodded briskly, signifying that it was now Maggy's turn to speak.

They were all three looking at her, Matron with the certain air of a woman who had stated her case and expected no argument. Sir Charles with a shrewd twinkle, and Dr Doelsma with a smile. How dared he? Maggy gave him a baleful stare and turned a shoulder to him again.

'I should be glad if you would take on Mevrouw Doelsma, Maggy.' It was Sir Charles, at his most wheedling. 'She is a lifelong friend of mine; I want her to have the best attention there is, and I consider you are the one to give it. As a personal favour, Maggy.'

She liked and admired Sir Charles; she could not refuse him. He was also senior consultant of the hospital, and she a Ward Sister, there to do her work under his guidance and carry out his orders.

'If you wish it, Sir Charles, I'll be glad to go with Mevrouw Doelsma.'

He beamed at her. 'Splendid! I'm sure that Matron will see you later and fix up all the details. I think you should go in about ten days' time, don't you. Paul?'

Maggy didn't look round when Dr Doelsma answered, nor when he said,

'May I have a few words with Sister, Matron? I promise I won't keep her for more than a minute.'

He ushered her and Sir Charles out of the little room and stood in the open doorway, contemplating Maggy's very straight back.

'You needn't be afraid,' he said blandly. 'I've left the door open this time.'

This remark had the effect of making her turn round to face him. She said with great hauteur and a rising colour,

'I do not wish to be reminded of that regrettable incident.'

He was instantly contrite. 'I'm sorry, indeed I am; not because I kissed you, but because I've made you angry. Forgive me, and for taking such shameful advantage of you just now. It was unfair, I know. But I want you to nurse Mother. I should have warned you that I like my own way, and go to any lengths to get it.' He waited a moment, but she did not speak. 'My mother is normally a bright and happy woman, but now she had been badly frightened. She hides her fear, but only when you or I are with her does she lose it. She is a sensible woman; in time she will overcome it, and forget. Until then, she needs help. She likes you, Maggy, and trusts you—as I do. Thank you for consenting to come.'

Maggy was still looking out of the window, facing a fact which could no longer be ignored. She was hopelessly in love with Dr Doelsma; and while her good sense counselled her to take the prudent action to withdrawing her consent and never seeing him again, the delightful prospect of being with him, perhaps frequently, for the next few weeks was impossible to ignore. Before she could change her mind, she turned round and said quietly,

'I'll be glad to go with your mother, Dr Doelsma, and stay with her until she is well again.'

He had been looking rather stern; now his whole face lighted up.

'You can't know how pleased I am that you will be at Oudehof with my mother. Come and tell her yourself, won't you?'

She was glad of her decision when she saw Mevrouw Doelsma, who took her hand and said, 'I'll never be able to thank you, my dear. I thought perhaps you wouldn't want to come—it will a dull life for you after the rush and bustle here.'

Maggy assured her that that was just what she would like, and went away to give the report to the night nurse. Before she went off duty she told a bewildered junior nurse to take all the roses from the office and carry them to the geriatric ward, and waited until the little room was once more bare. In her room, she took the remaining flowers over to the front lodge to George, whose wife was ill. She wasn't to know that Dr Doelsma would see them on his way out, and such were her feelings that she wouldn't have cared.

She cried slow bitter tears for a long time before she went to sleep that night.

CHAPTER FOUR

MAGGY SENSED that there was something amiss as soon as she got to her office the next morning. The night nurse looked nervous, even Williams looked worried. Maggy sat down at her desk. 'I'll have the report first, Nurse, shall I? Then you can tell me what's gone wrong.' She gave her an encouraging smile and opened the book. The report duly given and commented upon, the bad news came tumbling out. Madame Riveau had gone. It had happened during the busy period between six and seven, when the nurses were fully occupied with teas, bedpans, washing patients, giving medicines, changing beds... Madame Riveau had got up and dressed, unseen, what with screens being pulled and patients who were well enough walking up and down the ward to the bathroom. The first the nurses had known of it was the commotion caused by the two Riveau men, who, it seemed, had come into the ward via the fire escape. They had walked off with Madame Riveau before anything could be done. By the time the nurse had rung through to the porter, they had already gone, using the Casualty entrance. The nurse there, busy herself, had thought they were relatives who had spent the night with one of the ill patients.

'I'll have to let the Office know, and Matron,' said

Maggy. 'Write a statement, Nurse, and I'll sign it too, and take it along to Matron. It was no fault of yours. She's been a difficult patient and her husband has been wanting her home for a long time now. She was due out tomorrow morning anyway.' She sighed with relief at the thought that she would not have to meet those awful men again.

The days slipped by. Matron had told her that she would probably be in Holland for four weeks, perhaps a little longer; a relief Sister would run the ward until her return. Maggy wrote to her parents in Scotland, got herself a passport and looked through her clothes, openly envied by every nurse in the hospital.

It was arranged that they should travel on a morning plane. An ambulance took Mevrouw Doelsma and Maggy, very neat in her uniform and little cape, to the airport, where they were met by Sir Charles who had elected to see them off. Maggy had been surprised to see Dr Doelsma waiting with him when they arrived, but beyond a brief good morning he said nothing, but went away to see to the luggage. She had not anticipated that he would be travelling with them, indeed she had not known that he was in England. There was, she admitted to herself, no reason why he should have informed her of his plans. She spent the next ten minutes or so installing her patient and herself on the KLM plane. In this she had the good offices of the stewardess and between them Mevrouw Doelsma was made comfortable, reassured and generally made much of. Maggy was surprised to find Sir Charles at her elbow; in answer to her enquiring look, he said,

'No. I'm not coming with you—but Paul will be. I was allowed to make sure that everything was all right before take-off.' He stayed a few minutes, and then took his leave, saying,

'You'll do, Henrietta. I'll be over to see you as soon as

I can spare time for a holiday. Have a good trip—you too, Maggy, and I hope you enjoy your stay in Friesland.' He waved cheerfully from the door.

Mevrouw Doelsma watched Maggy fixing the portable oxygen cylinder so that it could be got at quickly and easily if it was wanted. She caught her eye and smiled and said,

'What a nuisance I'm being to everyone.' The smile flickered and went out. Her voice faltered. 'I hope you don't have to use it, Maggy.'

'Och, no,' Maggy said comfortably. 'It's like taking an umbrella with you to keep off the rain.'

Her patient giggled, and Paul, who had just entered the plane, decided that Maggy was indeed a blessing, with her calm efficient ways and her soothing Highland voice. He stowed away his medical bag and took the seat by his mother, leaving the window seat for Maggy. Having adjusted their seat belts, he talked gently about nothing in particular until they were airborne, when he opened *The Times* and a Dutch magazine called *Elsevier,* and became immersed in reading them. However, from time to time his eye strayed to Maggy, guarding her patient like a hawk, but finding time to glance out of the porthole with wide eyes.

'Have you not flown before, Sister?' he asked casually.

She looked across at him, her eyes alight with excitement.

'No, never. I've never left England before.' As she said it she realised how amusing she must be to the much-travelled doctor. She looked at him again to see if he was laughing at her, but he wasn't.

'We must make certain that you see as much of Holland as possible before you go back home.'

He became immersed in his papers again, but presently, when his mother went to sleep, he folded them carefully and crossed over to the seat beside Maggy. The coast of Holland was visible; he leant across her, and started to point out landmarks. Their heads were very close together. Maggy kept her gaze on the view below her, not hearing a word of what he was saying, but thinking of the weeks ahead.

The plane touched down at Schiphol, and with a minimum of delay and a maximum of efficiency Madame Doelsma was transferred to a small smart ambulance with rakish lines. Maggy was too occupied with her patient to do more than give a hasty look round. There was no sign of the doctor; she supposed he was seeing about their luggage. The white-coated ambulance driver prepared to shut them in, and said something to Maggy, who looked blank. Madame Doelsma murmured something and he laughed and looked at Maggy and nodded and gave the thumbs-up sign, the friendly little gesture warmed her heart.

As soon as the door was shut, she began a systematic search of the ambulance, so that she would be familiar with the equipment if she should need it. When she had made a thorough inspection she sat herself down on the collapsible seat by her patient. It was a very small seat; she wriggled experimentally, reflecting on the long journey ahead of them, Mevrouw Doelsma was lying with her eyes closed, so Maggy allowed her attention to wander out of the window in the door of the ambulance. Drawn up within a few yards of their own vehicle was an ink-blue Rolls-Royce convertible. Dr Doelsma, hands in pockets, was leaning against its well-bred bonnet, talking to an elderly man by the boot, who was supervising the stowing away of the luggage. When this had been done to his entire satisfaction, the elderly man tipped the porter and went round to the doctor. Maggy watched with interest while they carried on another short conversation, at the end of which the elderly man sketched a vague salute and disappeared round the corner of the airport building, while the doctor strolled over to the ambulance and opened the door. He nodded briefly at Maggy, and addressed himself to his mother, who had opened her eyes at the sound of the door opening.

'Another hour or two, and we'll be home, dear. Pratt sends his regards; he and Mrs Pratt hope to see you soon.' He transferred his gaze to Maggy, who looked tranquilly back at him. 'It's roughly a hundred and forty miles.' he said. 'The ambulance will take about four hours to do the journey. I believe there is everything you require here; there's a flask of coffee…' He stopped as she nodded. 'Of course, you would have discovered that for yourself. I'll travel behind you. If you want anything, anything at all, wave through the back window.' He added dryly. 'Wave to me first, won't you, before you ask the driver to stop, otherwise I might run into you.'

Maggy nodded meekly, hiding a slight scorn. Presumably he thought that, outside nursing, she was a fool.

'What word do I use to stop the driver?' she asked sensibly.

He smiled. 'Stop. It's the same word; but in any case I've warned him to pull up if you appear worried.' He looked her up and down, and said with some amusement,

'The seat is too small for you, isn't it? I'm afraid they don't cater for Amazons. Shall I find you a cushion?'

His solicitude met with a cold reception. She drew her black brows together and said tartly,

'I thank you, no, sir. I'm well able to look after myself.'

His eyes widened with laughter. 'But of course, Sister, I apologise if I implied otherwise.'

She felt her cheeks redden as he turned away to speak to his mother before shutting the door and going back to his car.

The journey seemed endless. Mevrouw Doelsma possessed herself of one of Maggy's hands, sighed contentedly and went to sleep. Maggy looked out of the window, trying to see the names of the towns and villages which they went through—not always successfully. The Rolls kept at a discreet distance behind them, and she felt a pang of sympathy for the doctor compelled as he was to travel at such a moderate speed.

The country was charming—bright with autumn colours, flat as a plate and incredibly tidy. As they slowed down through the towns she was able to glimpse the small gabled houses, living proofs of a long-dead age, and seemingly too diminutive to house a normal family; whereas the churches were so vast that she could only assume that they stood forlorn and half empty each Sunday.

It had been explained to her that they would be taking the eastern road to Oudehof. Maggy had looked up the route carefully beforehand, but as much of it led along the main motorways, which skirted the towns, her carefully acquired knowledge was not of much use to her. However, after a little time they entered country reminiscent of the New Forest and she at last knew where she was. The *Veluwe*—the road was bordered by charming thatched houses, quite small, but modern and enclosed in large gardens so perfect that she guessed that they must be occupied by the wealthy. The road widened again, and they emerged into rolling meadowlands with tantalising glimpses of small towns. She looked at her watch—there was, she reckoned, less than an hour of the journey to go. Mevrouw Doelsma woke up and asked where they were, and shortly after Maggy caught sight of a fast disappearing signpost.

'Heerenveen,' said Maggy. 'That's not far from Oudehof, is it?'

'No, we're nearly home, Maggy. We turn off on the

road to Balk; Oudehof is a mile or two this side of the village.' She smiled faintly. 'You know, dear, I thought, once or twice in the hospital, that I should never see Oudehof again. I do hope you are going to be happy there—it is very quiet, and you are so young and pretty, you should be having fun.'

Maggy laughed rather wistfully. 'Dinna worry, Mevrouw Doelsma, I'll not miss what I seldom had.'

Her patient raised her eyebrows. 'But, Maggy... I've not liked to ask you before, but surely you must have boyfriends, or one special one?'

Maggy chuckled. 'Nay, where will I find a wee man to top my size?' Her gaze fell on the sleek car loitering behind the ambulance and she looked away quickly with pink cheeks. 'I'll be very happy, Mevrouw Doelsma; I've never been in a foreign land, and everything is strange and exciting to me.'

She broke off as the ambulance turned off at right angles from the main road. Her patient became quite animated.

'Maggy, tell me anything you see, so that I know where we are.'

They travelled several kilometres thus, with Maggy describing windmills, canals, and houses as they passed them, until they turned off the narrow road through a pair of magnificent wrought iron gates and bowled along a semi-circular drive—Maggy could just see its other end sweeping back to the road again via another pair of gates. She twisted round and craned her neck to see through the tiny window behind the driver, and caught her first glimpse of Oudehof. It was red brick, square, and so symmetrical that it appeared to have been cut out of cardboard, and then stuck on to the surrounding countryside. There was an imposing door, approached by double steps, and flanked by large flat windows—the same windows crossed the face of the house in two neat rows above the door, capped by a steep roof. The house had the air of having been there a long time, and had every intention of remaining just as it was for a comfortable forever.

The ambulance drew up in front of the entrance, and before the driver was out of his seat, the Rolls had slid to a halt a couple of feet behind them, and it was the doctor who opened the door. His eyes went at once to his mother.

'All right, Mama? I'll carry you up to your room.' He slid the stretcher partly out on its runners, picked her up in his arms, and strode off to the door, where a small group of people had gathered.

Maggy, collecting the odds and ends of their journey, thought how much nicer it would have been if he had at least suggested that she should go with them. She eyed the figures in the doorway, feeling shy. Doubtless Dr Doelsma expected her to follow him. She walked across the broad sweep of the drive towards the door, and as she did so one of the people standing detached himself and came to meet her. He was grey-haired and pleasant-faced, and when he spoke she realised he was English. 'I'm Pratt, the butler, Sister.' He took her case and her cloak; he didn't smile, but she sensed his friendliness towards her. 'I'll take you to Madam's rooms, and later on, if you will ring, Mrs Pratt will take you to your room.'

She gave him a grateful glance and followed him into the hall. It was square and rather dim, and the black and white tiled floor gleamed richly underfoot. The walls were panelled and hung with portraits. There were doors leading off on either side, and a broad staircase, elaborately carved, rose from the back of the hall to a half-landing, and then branched off on either side to the floor above. Maggy found herself gently ushered past the handful of men and women gathered near the door and led upstairs to a broad corridor. He crossed this and knocked on a door decorated with swags of fruit and flowers, delicately carved in the wood. The doctor's voice answered and Pratt opened the door and ushered her in. Mevrouw Doelsma was lying on a fourposter bed; the doctor was in the act of covering her with a rug and looked over his shoulder at Maggy. He spoke rather testily. 'Why have you been so long?'

Maggy went over to the bed and eyed him coldly across it.

'Because, unlike you, sir, I didn't ken the way around the house.'

There was a faint giggle from the bed. 'You deserved that, Paul.'

A reluctant smile tugged at the corner of his mouth. 'I'm sorry, Sister MacFergus. I had no intention of giving you such a poor welcome to Oudehof. If you would be kind enough to settle my mother in bed, I'll find Mrs Pratt and tell her to bring up tea.'

He disappeared, and Maggy lost no time in getting Mevrouw Doelsma comfortable, thinking as she did so that it must be very pleasant to sleep between such fine linen sheets, monogrammed and embroidered; each of the square pillows was embellished with lace, and the counterpane of peach and silver brocade seemed to her eye to be old but still magnificent. Tea came just as she was finished, and, rather to her surprise, the doctor as well. He introduced Mrs Pratt after she had greeted her mistress with every sign of delight, and when she had puffed her good-natured person away, said,

'Will you pour out, Maggy?' He pulled up a chair to the small drum table where the tea tray had been set, and waved her to it. She hesitated. 'Will ye no' like to have tea together, sir? I have to unpack.'

'Certainly you must unpack, but only after we've had some tea. Do please pour out.'

She found herself yielding to his compelling charm, and took her place at the table, pouring tea from a magnificent silver tea-pot into paper-thin china cups. The small meal was a lighthearted affair, and Maggy relaxed despite herself after a few minutes of the doctor's easy conversation, forgetting to be shy of her rather grand surroundings, so that an hour slipped away before he suggested that she might like to see her room and unpack.

Mrs Pratt, summoned once more, led her through a door leading from her patient's room into another similar one, equally beautifully furnished. From here they went into the corridor, where Mrs Pratt opened another door, revealing a luxurious bathroom.

'This will be for your own use while you are here, Sister, and please ask me or Pratt for anything you may require.' The housekeeper nodded and smiled, and puffed back into the bedroom; she was a stout little woman, but very light and active on her feet. Expressing the hope that Maggy would be very happy while she was at Oudehof, she went away, leaving her to unpack and put her clothes away in the vast drawers and closets, where they were immediately lost in a luxurious vastness. When Maggy had tidied herself she went back to Mevrouw Doelsma's room, where the doctor was lounging in a very large chair by the window; he got up and she went in, saying,

'Ah, Sister, there are one or two things to discuss, are there not?' There was no trace of the charming friendly man with whom she had had tea; rather he was the bland consultant, giving instructions to his nurse—which, she supposed, in all fairness, was their correct relationship. They walked over to the window and she listened composedly to his directions. 'My mother's own doctor will call tomorrow morning; if he suggests any changes you will of course follow his wishes. Now I expect you wish to get my mother ready for the night—I suggest that she has a really long sleep. Order anything you may require from Mrs Pratt.' He smiled briefly at her, went over to bed and kissed his mother and wished her goodnight, and left the room.

Mevrouw Doelsma was tired but happy. Maggy dallied over the preparations for bed and stayed with her while she ate her supper, then, leaving a bedside lamp burning and one or two books within reach, prepared to take the tray downstairs. Her patient, looking extremely comfortable against her pillows, said,

'Now go down and have dinner, Maggy. I shall be all right. I'll ring if I want you.'

Maggy went downstairs with the tray to be met with a rather shocked Pratt, who assured her that there was no need for her to be carrying trays and that she had only to ring when she needed anything done. He put the tray down on a marble-topped wall table in the hall, and opened a pair of double doors and showed her into the dining room, led her to the vast table and pulled out her chair.

'Master Paul has gone back to Leiden, Sister. He wished you good night and hopes that you will be comfortable.'

Maggy ate the delicious meal, barely noticing what was on her plate. The room was large and of a rich unobtrusive splendour; she felt lost and very lonely in it. Why had she imagined that the doctor would stay—at least to dine? She was, after all, only the nurse. She sat at the gleaming mahogany table, drinking her coffee and wishing she had never come. She must have been mad to have consented to the doctor's wishes, she should have had nothing more to do with him, and then forgotten him completely. Upon reflection, she admitted to herself that this would have been very difficult indeed. She got up and strolled over to the window; it was a lovely moonlit evening, she could see quite clearly across the gardens to the country beyond. She closed her eyes and thought of her own lonely beautiful Highlands; she longed to be there, walking the dogs, with her home in the valley below; a small safe refuge where she could shut out the rest of the world—she opened her eyes—only she wouldn't be able to shut out Paul.

Maggy got up the next morning after a night of dreams and bouts of heavy sleep, and went to the window. It was a lovely morning; the country around was calm and peaceful, she could see a great distance in every direction. She dressed and went to see how her patient did.

Mevrouw Doelsma, after a sound night's sleep, was in the best of spirits. The day passed happily enough, as did the next two days. Maggy found that she had a fair amount of time to herself while her patient rested. Mrs Pratt took her on a tour of the house, which, she learned, was more than two hundred years old. A great deal of the furniture was almost as old too, and very beautiful. Maggy spent a long time studying the portraits on the walls. Several of them were very obvious ancestors of the doctor. She was surprised to find that there was an extensive park behind the house, and a sizeable stable block, which she made up her mind she would explore one day. She had already made friends with the gardeners and Piet, the groom, who spoke no English, but made things surprisingly clear by means of nods and smiles.

Mevrouw Doelsma was proving herself to be an excellent patient and progressing well, but Maggy took care not to stray too far from the house. They spent a long time in each other's company, and Maggy listened enthralled to her patient recounting the history of the house and the family. Of the doctor there was no sign. His mother spoke of him frequently, but gave no clue as to his whereabouts.

Maggy went to bed at the end of her fourth day there resigned to the possibility of not seeing him again. She presumed that he would come to see his mother, but it would be unlikely that he would seek her out other than to give her his instructions, and enquire as to his mother's condition. She told herself not to cry for the moon, and resolved to enjoy herself as far as possible while she was in Holland.

CHAPTER FIVE

MAGGY SUPPOSED IT was the wind that wakened her—it was sighing and rustling around the old house; she supposed that she would get used to it in a day or so. She lay listening to it, and gradually became aware of another sound. She sat up in bed and looked at her watch. Who would be walking about at half past one in the morning? She strained her ears and was sure that she heard voices. She got out of bed, pulled on her dressing gown and slippers, and went to the door and peered into the corridor. There was a dim light at the head of the stairs, and nothing to be seen, but the sounds, faint as a whisper, were still playing a duet with the wind. Maggy left the door open and padded across her room and into that of her patient. Mevrouw Doelsma was sleeping quietly. Maggy slid into the corridor and down the stairs; the dining room door was slightly open and there was a thin ribbon of light gleaming palely from it. She crossed the hall, thoughtfully picking up a poker as she passed the massive stove against one wall. The dining room was in darkness, but the kitchen beyond was brightly lit. She went steadily towards the partly open door, swallowing fear with a throat gone dry, and pushed it open. There were two people in the kitchen; one of them was Dr Doelsma. He and a very pretty girl were sitting side by side on the kitchen table in the middle of the room. He looked over his shoulder as Maggy went in, put down the mug he was holding, and got to his feet.

'Sister MacFergus, were we making so much noise?' He caught sight of the poker and came forward and took it from her. 'An Amazon, and armed!' he murmured with a twinkle, then turned to the girl still sitting on the table and said casually,

'Stien, this is Sister MacFergus, of whom I told you.' He smiled at Maggy, standing pokerless and awkward between the door and the kitchen table. 'May I introduce Juffrouw Stien van der Duren from Utrecht hospital?'

The girl got off the table and came over to Maggy, holding out her hand. She was small, barely up to Maggy's shoulder, and slim and very pretty with fair hair hanging in a shining curtain to her shoulders. Maggy shook hands, aware of her own junoesque proportions enveloped rather bunchily in a sensible dressing gown.

'How do you do,' she said rather stiffly. 'I'm sorry I disturbed you. I heard noises and thought I should see who it was. I'll wish you both a good night.'

She turned to the door, the dignified exit she had planned quite spoiled by a chair which she hadn't noticed and which she now tripped over. The doctor's large hand prevented her from falling, but she didn't look at him as she brushed past him with a muttered, 'My thanks to the doctor.'

As she went up the stairs she heard the girl's soft laughter.

Maggy awoke early and dressed, made her patient comfortable with her morning tea, and went down to get her own breakfast. Picking up her second cup of coffee, she took it to the window and stood looking out across the park. Presently she became aware of two people cantering towards the house, and had no difficulty in recognising them. The doctor, on a raw-boned bay worthy of his size, was slightly ahead, but drew in his mount so that his companion could catch up with him. Stien, Maggy noted sourly, looked as attractive on horseback as she did on her two feet. She watched them turn the corner of the house, talking animatedly, before going back to the table, banging her cup and saucer down on it, and going to the door. She had her hand on its big brass handle when she heard her name. Dr Doelsma had come in through the french window.

'Good morning—I saw you at the window. Have you breakfasted?' He scanned the table. 'I hadn't expected you up so early.'

She stood very straight, her voice as crisp and severe as her uniform.

'Your mother likes her breakfast about this time. It's easier if I have mine first. I'm used to early rising, Dr Doelsma.'

He surveyed her coolly. 'I hope you were not too badly frightened last night, Maggy?'

The unfairness of this remark brought a vexed flush to her cheeks, but she answered in a level voice 'If I had been badly frightened, sir, I should not have left my bedroom.'

He raised his eyebrows and grinned at her and seemed about to say something further, but turned instead to the window where Stien had appeared. Maggy wished her a quick good morning and made her escape. As she went up the stairs she wondered, as she had wondered many times in the night, just who Stien was.

Mevrouw Doelsma didn't need much done for her, but she loved company. She talked happily about Paul, and spoke of Stien as though she had known her intimately for a long time. Maggy wanted very much to ask if they were engaged, but could not quite bring herself to do so.

The morning passed with only a brief visit from the doctor, who, as he entered the room, suggested that she might like to take advantage of his visit to have her coffee or go for a turn in the gardens, so that when she returned shortly, their conversation was limited to questions and answers of a purely professional nature.

Maggy had a solitary lunch, waited upon by Pratt, and then returned upstairs to settle her patient for her afternoon nap. That lady, thoroughly rested from her journey, and delighted at the prospect of getting up and going downstairs on the following day, was disposed to talk, and it was almost two o'clock before Maggy left her, changed into a kilt and sweater and went downstairs. As she passed through the hall, she heard voices and laughter from the dining room, and supposed Dr Doelsma and Stien were having a late lunch. Perhaps they hadn't cared to lunch with the nurse. Maggy wondered if she should have asked to have her meals in her room. She had done no private nursing, and that aspect of it had not struck her. She should have found out more about it before leaving the hospital. However, it was too late now, so she smiled at Pratt who had appeared to open the door for her, and walked briskly down the drive towards the road. The doctor was home; she felt that she could safely go further afield for an hour or so.

The village was small—a cluster of houses, a few small shops and a large church, which she found to be locked. She bought some stamps, posted letters, and purchased some local views. There were some of Oudehof, so Maggy sent one to the nurses on her ward, and one to Mrs Salt. The people she met were pleasant and friendly, and though they spoke no English, were very helpful when it came to paying for her purchases. She walked back feeling much happier and less lonely.

She changed back into uniform and went to see how Mevrouw Doelsma was feeling; she found her awake and reading letters, which she put down as Maggy went in.

'Did you have a good walk? Paul and Stien have just gone—some play or other Stien wanted to see in Amsterdam. They asked me to say goodbye to you. Paul says that I may go for a check-up next week. He suggests that we stay for a day or two in Leiden—he has a house there—so that you can have a look round. You'll want to see Amsterdam, and Leiden and Delft, and perhaps the Hague.'

She chattered on, while Maggy helped her to the chair by the small open fire.

'Shall we have tea, and discuss what we can do tomorrow? Paul thought that if it is fine, I might go out for an hour in the car. Do you drive, Maggy?'

Maggy nodded, 'Aye, I do.'

Her patient's eyes sparkled. 'Would you be all right here, do you think?'

Maggy considered. 'Aye, I think so.' She had driven her father's old Landrover over some shocking bad roads in Scotland in snow and ice and fog. It should be easy in Holland, with never a hill to see. The signs might present a problem, but she thought that they were international to a large extent, and driving on the other side of the road, although strange, should present no difficulties.

'I'd like fine to drive,' she said.

'And so you shall, my dear, but perhaps we had better let Pratt drive tomorrow, and then you can take the wheel for a time. He's rather fussy, I'm afraid—he prefers horses.'

Maggy poured second cups. 'That was a fine beast the doctor was riding this morning.'

'Cobber? Yes, though he takes a bit of riding, Paul tells me. Do you ride, Maggy?'

'Since I was a wee girl; but there's not much chance in London, so when I'm home, I often spend the day riding in the hills.'

'But, Maggy, you must ride here—there are three or four horses in the stables. Ride every morning before breakfast. Pratt shall tell the groom.'

So it was settled, and early next morning Maggy spent a magic hour exploring the country. Her mount was not quite to her liking, however. Biddy was a well-mannered roan with a middle-aged disposition, and a dislike of any exercise harder than a canter. There was a wide sweep of parkland behind the house. Maggy longed to gallop over it, and Cobber, she felt sure, would share her views.

The drive to Sneek after lunch was a great success. The lakes sparkled in the autumn sunshine; they drove slowly through the little town, and then turned into the direction of Heerenveen. Pratt turned the car just below the town into Oranjewoud, where the roads were quiet, and changed places with Maggy. The car was a Daimler Sovereign, and she drove it through the wooded lanes before turning and going back the way they had come. Pratt sat silently beside her, but when she drew up before the door at Oudehof, gave his opinion that her driving was as good as his own, and he for his part felt quite happy about her taking the car whenever she wanted it. This was indeed high praise and she thanked him gratefully. While he was having his tea later, he informed his wife that Sister MacFergus was a well set up, sensible young lady, and pretty too, if you liked your women big.

The next few days passed happily enough. Maggy rode every morning and drove her patient, with Pratt in attendance, round the countryside each afternoon. There was no sign of Dr Doelsma; if his mother had heard from him, she said nothing. Friends began to call, and Maggy, with time on her hands, spent some time in the stables, making friends with Cobber. He rolled a wicked eye at her, but took her sugar lumps and listened while she talked to him. She had every intention of riding him when she had the opportunity. It came sooner than she had expected, a couple of mornings later when she slipped out of the side door. There was a grey sky with a hint of rain and more than a hint of wind, and no one about in the stables. Without hesitation she went to Cobber's stall, saddled him and led him out into the back drive.

Half an hour later, horse and rider turned for home, girl and beast both happy and satisfied. Some way from the house, Maggy turned off the track they had been following, and once on the grass gave Cobber his head. He needed no urging, but broke into a gallop across the parkland. With easy skill Maggy pulled him back into a canter as they neared the house, and turned the corner of the house at a gentle walk.

Dr Doelsma was standing on the side door steps. He was dressed for riding and white with well-controlled rage. Maggy stopped Cobber in front of him, leaned forward and patted the horse's neck, and said in a small voice. 'Good morning, Dr Doelsma.' She had gone rather white too, but met his furious gaze bravely. He stood at his ease, looking her up and down. It had been raining for some time, and her hair hung in a damp pony-tail, and small mist-spangled curls framed her face. She was only too aware of the bedraggled appearance of her sweater and slacks, and her lack of make-up. She sat quite still, waiting for him to speak.

'How dare you take my horse?' His voice was very soft. 'No one rides Cobber but myself.'

'Aye, I know, Doctor. But he was in need of a good gallop, and I've done him no harm.' She lapsed into broad

Scots: 'Dinna' fash yersel', sir, I ken well hoo to ride, and have done since I was a wee bairn.'

'So I am able to see for myself, but that is no excuse, I think.' His eyes were grey steel. 'I should like to shake you!' he added furiously. Maggy dismounted, and threw the bridle over one arm, and prepared to lead Cobber back to the stables.

'I'm sorry ye're disappointed at not getting your ride, Doctor, but it's as well. I'm thinking, for ye're in an awful rage. A good walk, now, is fine for the bad temper. I was not to know that ye'd be wanting Cobber, and please don't blame Pratt. I was earlier than usual this morning, and he knew nothing of this.'

She didn't wait for an answer, but led Cobber away without a backward glance.

She didn't see him again until after lunch—she had been taking her meals with Mevrouw Doelsma, but suggested that today it would be a good idea if she had hers in her room. Her patient agreed that she had a great deal to talk about with her son, mostly business, which could perhaps be better discussed if they were alone.

Accordingly, mother and son sat down to luncheon without Maggy. It wasn't until Paul looked up from his soup and enquired carelessly as to Maggy's whereabouts that Mevrouw Doelsma asked the question she had been pondering for most of the morning.

'What have you said to Maggy, Paul?'

He looked faintly annoyed. 'Nothing of consequence, Mama.'

'She's displeased you?'

'If you mean am I displeased with the nursing treatment she gives you, Mother—on the contrary, she is a splendid nurse. I am all admiration for her skill.'

His mother caught his eye. 'Please don't blame her, Paul. It was I who suggested she should drive in the first place, and Pratt says she handles the car to the manner born.'

Paul choked on his soup. 'The Daimler?' he enquired.

She nodded, then frowned. 'Wasn't that it?' She sounded worried. 'Is there something else?'

He said in an interested voice, 'I wasn't aware that Sister MacFergus had been driving the car. We can discuss that later. She was out riding this morning…' His mother interrupted eagerly.

'Yes, dear. She goes out every morning; she rides well, I believe. Did you join her?'

Her son smiled reluctantly. 'I had no opportunity, Mama, to do so. Maggy was riding Cobber.'

Mevrouw Doelsma gasped, 'Good heavens, Paul! Cobber's far too strong for her. Was she all right?'

The doctor inspected the roast partridge on his plate before replying.

'You are alarmed for Sister MacFergus, my dear mother, whereas I was alarmed for Cobber.'

His mother looked indignant.

'Paul, sometimes I have no patience with you! I hope that one day, when you do fall in love, it will be with a woman who refuses to be ignored for a horse!'

This remark made her son laugh and restored his good humour, so that the rest of the meal was spent cheerfully enough making plans for her forthcoming trip to Leiden.

After their coffee, Mevrouw Doelsma declared her intention of going to the kitchen and having a word with Mrs Pratt. Paul lighted his pipe and strolled across to his study. Maggy was coming down the stairs with her tray as he crossed the hall. She reddened when she saw him, but said nothing when he took the tray from her and said quite gently,

'You have no need to carry trays, Maggy.' He put it down, and went on, 'Will you come into the study for a moment?'

He opened the door for her, and she went in, still saying nothing. She had not been in the room before. It was lofty, with large windows overlooking the garden at the side of the house. The walls were panelled, and besides the enormous desk it was furnished with a selection of comfortable leather armchairs, piled untidily with books and papers which the shelves around the walls could no longer accommodate.

'Sit down, Sister,' he said quietly.

Maggy sat, her large capable hands folded in her white starched lap, her serene manner hiding her chaotic thoughts.

He came and stood in front of her, his hands in his pockets, and she studied his shoes—nice hand-made ones, not too new. She had no doubt that he was looking at her, and very crossly too, she was certain. She had no intention of meeting his gaze.

When he spoke, his voice was still quiet, but it sounded friendly.

'Maggy, I must beg your pardon.'

Her intention not to look at him was forgotten in her astonishment. Her head jerked back so that her eyes could verify what her ears had heard. Her mouth hung very slightly open.

'I had no right to speak to you as I did this morning; it was most uncivil of me—' he paused. She smiled warmly at him, but he chose to ignore this, looking severely over her head. 'Nevertheless, I must ask you not to ride Cobber unless I give my permission.'

Maggy stiffened slightly. 'I should not have ridden him; I have said I was sorry, sir...but I can manage him.' She encountered his furious glance, and stopped.

'Are you suggesting that you should ride Cobber whenever you wish? Indeed, Sister MacFergus, I hope that I am not an unreasonable man, but you must at least allow me my own horse!' He sounded as angry as he looked. 'My mother tells me that you have been driving the Daimler. You have your driving licence with you. I hope? I must take Pratt's word for it that you are competent, I suppose.' He spoke with an icy politeness; he had quite forgotten that only a few minutes before he had been begging her pardon.

Maggy rose to her feet, brows a rigid line above blazing eyes. It was obvious that she had inherited the temper of the more belligerent of her Highland forebears.

'Ye're an angry wee man, Doctor, and not worth the answering, and I'm none so mild mesel' at the present.'

He watched while she crossed to the door and went out, closing it very quietly behind her, and presently began to laugh.

Maggy tucked her patient up for her afternoon nap, and went to her room to write letters; she thought that the less she saw of the doctor, for a time at least, the better. She was feeling ashamed of herself. She had behaved badly, and now she would have to apologise; he might even ask her to return to England. She stopped writing, aghast at the idea, until common sense told her that he was unlikely to take such a step. He had only to tell Pratt and the groom that he didn't wish her to drive the car or ride. Maggy fancied that he was a man who expected and got his wishes obeyed. She would have to walk. She looked out of the window at the pleasant, placid scenery, stretching away flatly to the horizon, and suddenly wanted hills and heather; she struggled with a strong desire to burst into tears, and presently sat down and wrote several long and slightly mendacious letters.

She had tea with Mevrouw Doelsma and then helped her downstairs to the front door, where Pratt was waiting to take them for a drive. Maggy settled her patient in the back seat and got in beside her, saying: 'I'd like to sit beside you today, I can't enjoy the scenery if I'm driving.'

Mevrouw Doelsma agreed that this was a good idea, and the first part of the journey was passed pleasantly discussing the various landmarks they passed. Presently Maggy brought the conversation round to the proposed trip to Leiden, which interesting topic kept them engrossed until their return to Oudehof.

When they went down to dinner, the doctor was waiting for them in the drawing room. He greeted them pleasantly, and enquired after his mother's day. During dinner he included Maggy meticulously in the conversation, treating her with a frosty politeness which chilled her to the bone. When she had settled Mevrouw Doelsma by the fire once more, she excused herself on the pretext of writing letters, and escaped to her room. When she returned an hour later, she found them playing bézique and laughing a great deal; it was impossible not to notice how different the doctor looked when he laughed. Maggy thought wistfully that it would be fun to laugh with him; the possibility seemed unlikely.

Mevrouw Doelsma took a long time to put to bed—pills and blood pressure, TPR and checking carefully that her ankles hadn't swollen. At last she was lying comfortably against her pillows, with the bedside lamp adjusted, and book, glasses and bell all within reach. They wished each other a friendly goodnight, and Maggy went to her own room and to bed. She didn't think Dr Doelsma was expecting her downstairs again.

The bell woke her at once; she was out of bed, scuffing her feet into her slippers and putting on her dressing gown as she went. Mevrouw Doelsma looked small and white in the big bed, and there were beads of sweat on her forehead; her eyes implored Maggy, who took one all-embracing, understanding look and fetched a basin. She lifted Mevrouw Doelsma with one strong young arm and held her comfortably in its circle.

'That delicious lobster ye had for dinner,' she said practically. 'Ye'll feel better in a wee moment, and when ye are, I'll fetch the doctor…'

'I'm here.' His voice came from behind her.

She didn't turn round, but said in a sensible voice,

'If you'll go to the other side of the bed and hold Mevrouw Doelsma while I change the bowl…?'

He complied, and she heard him talking low-voiced to his mother. When she returned to the bedside, he had his mother's wrist in his fingers. Maggy fetched the BP box and wound the cuff on to Mevrouw Doelsma's arm, saying comfortably,

'You don't need to worry; the doctor'll tell you it's bilious ye've been.'

She handed the stethoscope across the bed to him, and tossed her hair, hanging loose around her shoulders and down her back; she was completely unself-conscious, intent only on her patient.

Dr Doelsma examined his mother, then handed the stethoscope back to Maggy without looking at her.

'Maggy's right, Mama. You've no need to worry; it's not a heart attack, it's lobster! You feel better already, don't you?'

His mother nodded. 'How silly of me! I'm so sorry to have got you both out of bed for nothing.'

'I'm not minding,' said Maggy calmly, 'and I doubt the doctor's minding either.' She looked across the bed. 'Will you be kind enough to support your mother, sir, while I

shake up the pillows?' She pushed up her dressing gown
sleeves the better to work. The cord of her dressing gown
had worked loose too, she undid it and wrapped the
garment closely around her, pulling the cord tightly around
her neat waist. The simple action, guilelessly done, made
her seem very young and childlike despite her size. She
shook the pillows with a vigorous grace, and having rear-
ranged them to her satisfaction waited while the doctor laid
his mother back amongst them.

'There,' she said cheerfully, 'I'll sponge your face and
hands, and make you a cup of tea, and you'll be asleep
again in ten minutes or so.'

She padded noiselessly around the big room collecting
what she needed, and went back to the bed to find the
doctor sitting on its edge, his mother's hand in his large
one. He looked quite different; his rather tousled hair made
him look very young, despite the elegant silk dressing
gown he was wearing. They smiled at each other in a comfortable friendly fashion and he got up.

'I'll go and put the kettle on. I'll be back in ten minutes,
will that be all right?'

Half an hour later Mevrouw Doelsma, now pleasantly
sleepy, said goodnight for the second time. Her son had
brought a cup of tea, and told her bracingly that there was
nothing for her to worry about, and she could now go to
sleep. He kissed her cheek gently, said goodnight and went
away, leaving Maggy to switch on the small night lamp
before she too went to her room.

It had become quite chilly. She looked at her watch, it
was almost three o'clock. She got the cooling bottle from
her bed and crept downstairs to fill it. There was a lamp
burning in the hall, but the dining room was in darkness.
Maggy made her away through it to the kitchen door and

opened it. It looked very cosy. There was a brown earthenware tea-pot on the table, with cups and saucers, and a milk jug and sugar bowl. Dr Doelsma was making toast. He looked up.

'Ah, there you are! I was going to bring it up to your room.' He saw the hot water bottle she was clutching, took the toast from toaster and said, 'Butter these, will you, while I fill your water bottle.' He didn't seem to expect an answer, so she obediently took the toast and buttered it, while he filled the hot water bottle and took it up to her room.

'I could have taken it,' Maggy said rather weakly when he came back.

'I'm sure you could.' He poured the tea. 'You are, I think, able to do most things very well.'

He handed her a cup, then fetched one of the old-fashioned ladderback chairs and set it behind her. 'Sit down.' He pulled up a second chair opposite to her, and handed her a slice of toast. They drank and munched in restful silence until he asked suddenly,

'Maggy do you like me?'

She put down her cup carefully. Her cheeks were pink, but she looked at him honestly.

'Aye, Doctor.'

'Even when I'm a wee evil-tempered man?'

The pinkness spread, but she replied steadily, 'Yes, even then.'

He went on conversationally, 'I like you—and admire your capabilities. Do you think we could be friends?' He held out a firm, well kept hand. 'I apologise again, Maggy.'

Maggy took the hand, and her own was immediately engulfed in its clasp; it felt very comforting. She said rather timidly, 'I was very rude; I'm sorry too. I thought you would send me back to England.'

He raised dark eyebrows at this, and then burst out laughing.

'My dear girl, surely you know that we would be lost without you? It's only because you are here that I am able to spend so much time in Leiden, and go to Utrecht whenever I wish.'

Stien lived in Utrecht. Of course, he would want to go there whenever he could. The thought hurt Maggy like a physical blow. She took a drink of hot strong tea and nearly choked at his next words.

'Will you ride with me tomorrow, Maggy?'

She didn't trust herself to look up, but said shyly, 'Thank you, I'd like to.'

'Er—I'll ride Cobber this time.' She did look up then, to find him smiling at her. He went on: 'But I'll tell Piet that you are to exercise him when I'm not here.' He took no notice of her attempt to thank him, but continued, 'I'm heaping coals of fire, aren't I? We'll take Mother for a run in the car tomorrow, and you shall drive; and don't think that I said that because I don't trust you to handle a car.'

He smiled again, and this time Maggy smiled back. She might not have his love, but to have his friendship would be worth a great deal to her. She wondered if Stien knew how lucky she was. She got up, collected the cups and saucers and stacked them neatly in the sink.

'I think I'll go to bed. Thank you for the tea, Dr Doelsma.' She stood, drooping with sleep, her hair hanging unheeded around her shoulders, her eyes enormous in a face devoid of make-up.

He looked at her briefly, then away again. 'Shall we say seven-thirty tomorrow?'

'Yes—that's provided Mevrouw Doelsma is all right.'

He opened the door for her, and Maggy said good-night and walked sleepily across the dining room and out into the hall, and up the stairs. Long before Paul turned out the lights and went to his own room, she was fast asleep.

They rode for almost an hour before breakfast, the doctor immaculate in riding kit, Maggy in her old slacks and thick sweater. She wasted a few moments wishing that she had other clothes to wear, then forgot about them as she swung herself easily on to Biddy's friendly back. If she envied the doctor Cobber, she gave no sign. As they turned for home, they broke into a brief gallop, and he held Cobber in, so that they raced neck and neck, until he allowed her to win by a short head. They pulled up outside the stables, and Maggy slid out of the saddle to make much of Biddy and give her the sugar lumps she loved. Her hair, which she had tied back in a ponytail, had come loose from its ribbon and her face glowed with happiness. She had been chattering to the doctor like an old friend. They left the horses with Piet, the groom, and went back to the house. At the door she paused.

'That was lovely,' she said. 'Thank you.'

He stood aside to let her pass, looking down at her. 'A delightful ride,' he said. 'We must do it again.'

They parted at the foot of the stairs, she to go to her room and change, and he to his breakfast. Maggy saw little of him that morning and he wasn't at lunch, but later that afternoon, when she and Mevrouw Doelsma went downstairs for their promised drive, they found him waiting for them beside the Rolls. He opened the door and helped his mother in, saying, 'Sit in front, Maggy, we'll change seats presently.'

She slid into the seat beside his. 'You don't mean that

I'm to drive this car?' She was astounded. 'But it's a Rolls-Royce!'

'Don't you want to drive it?'

'Yes, very much; but I might be a shocking bad driver.'

'In which case I shall tell you so, and drive myself.'

He took the same route that Pratt had taken on their first drive, and once they had entered the comparative quiet of the Oranjewoud, he stopped, got out, and waited while Maggy took his place. Having made sure that she indeed knew what she was about, he suggested that she should keep on the road they were already upon, and that he would take over again when it joined the main Assen-Meppel road. Having given this piece of sound advice he half turned in his seat and engaged his mother in conversation. Maggy was thankful for his tack; she knew quite a lot about cars but found the Rolls a little awe-inspiring. She need not have worried, though, for the Rolls was a lady, and behaved like one. She relaxed. The doctor saw it and asked,

'Have you driven a Rolls before?'

'No. It's like wearing a model dress when you're used to Marks and Spencers—though I've not worn a model dress,' she added, incurably truthful.

'How long have you been driving?'

'Five—no, six years.'

'In the Highlands, I expect?'

'Yes, mostly. The roads are surprisingly good, excepting in the winter.' She eased the car past a farm wagon, and put her foot down gently; the road was straight and nothing in sight. He watched the needle creep round the speedometer and said,

'I gather that you have your advanced driver's certificate.' It was more of a statement than a question. She said.

'Yes, Doctor,' in a meek voice and he chuckled. 'No wonder you were annoyed with me!'

Maggy made no answer to this, but smiled, then slowed down to pass through a very small village straddling a canal, and obedient to his direction, turned into a right-handed fork towards the main road. Presently, when it was within sight, she drew in to the side of the road, stopped the car and looked at him enquiringly.

'Very nice, Maggy; you drive as well as I do.' He said it without conceit. He turned to his mother. 'If I didn't know better, I'd say that Maggy was wasted as a nurse, wouldn't you, Mama?'

Mevrouw Doelsma wouldn't agree to this. 'Maggy's a born nurse, but it would be nice for her,' she went on pensively, 'if she married a man with a Rolls-Royce.'

Maggy turned her head and looked intently at a view which hardly merited her prolonged scrutiny, and Dr Doelsma eyed her back with a slight smile and decided twinkle in his eyes. He said briskly, 'That shouldn't be too difficult.'

He got out of the car, and Maggy slid back to her own seat as he got in. 'Shall I get in beside Mevrouw Doelsma?' she asked, giving him a very fleeting look. But her patient declared that she was perfectly happy as she was, and Maggy was to stay where she was. She settled her length into the comfortable seat. 'Thank you, Doctor. It was wonderful.' He answered her with some trivial remark about the car, and by the time the car was on the main road they had entered into a lively discussion concerning various aspects of motoring, so that she forgot to be shy.

Once on the high road, clear of traffic, the doctor gathered speed. There was no limit on the motorway; the needle hovered on a hundred and sixty kilometers, and he asked. 'Nervous?'

'Not in the least,' Maggy retorted, 'but what about Mevrouw Doelsma?'

The little lady in the back seat laughed. 'I enjoy it. Pratt disapproves of me when I tell him to travel faster, but Paul knows how I like it.'

They flashed past a signpost and Dr Doelsma slowed down and turned into a narrow road.

'We'll go back to Heerenveen across country,' he said. 'The country's nothing like your Highlands, Maggy, but it's very pleasant.'

'That burst of speed was most enjoyable, Doctor.' Maggy sounded sedate. 'You'll be holding the same certificate as myself, I think.'

'*Hemel!*' He was half laughing. 'I've been guilty of showing off.'

'I was showing off too,' said Maggy, 'but it's plain that you're a better driver than I am.'

They all returned to Oudehof in excellent spirits, and later at dinner the doctor made himself so pleasant that as Maggy went upstairs, leaving him and his mother together, she reflected that she hadn't enjoyed herself so much for a long time.

Mother and son settled down to their usual game of cards, and after a few minutes Mevrouw Doelsma remarked, 'Maggy drives very well, Paul.'

Paul took a trick. 'Yes, Mother. I noticed that you were sufficiently impressed to suggest that she should find a husband with a Rolls-Royce.'

His mother looked at her cards, wondering if she dared cheat. 'Yes, dear, such a good idea.' She cheated, and took the next trick, and he tried not to laugh.

'Mama, I have a Rolls-Royce.'

She looked up smilingly. 'Yes, dear, that's what I meant,' she said.

Paul stared at her. 'Mother dear, it has taken a whole evening of bright conversation to convince Maggy that that was not what you meant.'

His mother cheated again. 'The poor child! I only wanted to put an idea into your head, Paul.'

Paul took a trick and said, 'My dear, you surely know by now that the only ideas I act upon my own?' He smiled at her. 'If you cheat cleverly enough, you'll win this game!'

Maggy came back presently, and sat in a nice old Friesian chair, painted all over with small flowers. Her uniform looked very severe against it, but she suited the chair very well; it had been made for big men and women.

The doctor stacked the cards neatly.

'I must leave at six tomorrow morning, so we had better settle the arrangements for next week. I'll get an appointment for you, Mother, and Pratt can drive you both down. Stay for three or four days, and Maggy can have a couple of days off and go sightseeing. I'll be too busy to bring you back, but Pratt can fetch you whenever you want.'

His mother nodded. 'It will be nice to come to Leiden for a few days, even if it is to go to the hospital. And nice for Maggy too.'

He opened the door for them. 'It will be pleasant having you, Mother, and you too, Maggy. You'll exercise Cobber, won't you? I've spoken to Piet.' He kissed his mother, then took Maggy's hand and smiled down at her. 'I shall enjoy showing you my house in Leiden, Maggy.'

She felt suddenly shy, and murmured something incoherent. She wouldn't see him for a week, but then she would see him every day while she was in Leiden. She resolved, then and there, not to think about it.

They arrived in Leiden just in time for tea. The doctor wasn't home, but a housekeeper ushered them into the sitting room and went off to fetch their tea.

Maggy took a long look at the sitting room, and said, 'Please may I walk round?' Her patient laughed and said of course; so Maggy made Mevrouw Doelsma comfortable by the window, and started on an eager inspection of the room. It was large, stretching from front to back of the house, with folding doors dividing its length half way. The walls were panelled and the plaster ceiling festooned with swags of fruit and flowers. She could see that it had been furnished with care and an eye for detail. She wondered who had done this, and said so, out loud.

Mevrouw Doelsma smiled at her. 'I think you are feeling as I did the first time I saw this room. It's like walking into a Dutch interior, isn't it? All the furniture is antique and more or less as it was when the house was first built, and each generation has taken care to keep it that way. Paul loves every inch of it. He'll take you round, I expect, and tell you the history of everything, down to the last spoon.' She broke off as the housekeeper came in with the tea tray.

When she had gone, Maggy handed Mevrouw Doelsma her tea and sat herself down on the velvet covered window seat and drank her own out of a cup of very old Delft china of a delicate pinkish-mauve colour. She guessed that it was priceless, as was the silver tea tray, plain and solid, though the sugar bowl and cream jug were in the baroque style, very like those used at Oudehof. She struggled to remember who had made them, and was pleased when she recollected that it was Lely. They ate paper-thin sandwiches and little biscuits, richly covered in almonds, and there was a rich plum cake which reminded her of her mother's cooking.

They had almost finished when she saw the Rolls draw up outside, and the doctor mount the small flight of steps to his front door. He shut it firmly, as though he had come into his own little world, snug and secure. The thought crossed her mind that there should be small children running to meet him, and a wife waiting. She wished with all her heart that she could be that wife, and turned a face full of dreams to the door as he entered the room, so that he stood, staring. By the time he had greeted his mother, however, and walked over to the window, Maggy was her usual self, calmly friendly, neat as a new pin in her uniform, ready to pour the fresh tea the housekeeper brought in, and answer readily the questions Paul put to her about their journey.

He turned to his mother. 'I'm sorry I couldn't be here when you arrived, Mama.'

'Yes, dear, so was I. I should have liked you to have seen Maggy when we came into this room.' She paused. 'It sounds absurd; it had the same effect on her as it did on me, Paul. She—gathered it to her. That sounds silly, but you know what I mean, I think?'

'Indeed I do.' He sat down in a beautiful carved chair with blue damask cushions, looking exactly like his ancestors on the wall behind him. But beyond this brief remark, he said no more about it, but entertained his mother with the kind of gossip she liked to hear, at the same time eating his way steadily through the plum cake. After a while he put his plate down.

'Have you been up to your rooms yet?'

Mevrouw Doelsma shook her head. 'No, dear. I thought I'd wait a while.'

'Then I'll show Maggy the house, and by the time we're done, I daresay you'll feel like going up.'

Maggy sat quietly in the window, taking little part in their conversation, but now she looked up as the doctor came towards her.

He held out a hand wordlessly, and she stood up and took it, and he led her through the door into the hall. It was dim and cool, but not dreary. The black and white tiles glowed underfoot with the patina of age, as did the panelling, which stretched to the heavily ornamental ceiling. A carved staircase rose from the back of the hall, which narrowed to a passage leading to the back of the house, through a graceful archway.

They crossed the hall, and entered a much smaller room, with a similar panelling and ceiling, furnished with a heavy oaken table and chairs. There was a massive buffet against one wall, and in one corner, a large circular stove, with a tile surround, rising to the ceiling. Maggy lingered over the display of silver on the buffet, fingering the flat serving dishes and tureens with a loving hand, and only leaving them when the doctor invited her to inspect the engraved goblets in a corner cupboard. She held one, and marvelled at the beauty of its cupids and roses. The doctor put it back with its fellows and said,

'It was made by David Wolff for my great-great-grand-father. He loved beautiful things. He was a doctor too.'

'Have there always been doctors in your family?' Maggy wanted to know.

'For the last two hundred years or so, yes,' he answered. 'Before that we had land and ships and a great many sheep. We still have the land, but no ships and only the sheep we own on the farms.'

Maggy found this remark rather daunting; he seemed

even more removed from her world than before. She said hesitantly, 'I thought Friesland was famous for its cows.'

'So it is; I must take you to Leeuwarden one day and show you the statue of Mother Cow in the Zuiderplein. We have two farms in the Achterhoek—quite small ones run by cousins of mine. They find sheep pay better.'

He had opened a door as he was speaking and they entered the library. It was at the back of the house, and had ground-length windows opening out on to a small balcony overlooking a very small, beautifully kept garden which ran down to the edge of a small canal. Maggy walked round the shelves, looking at the books, and said over her shoulder, 'Would you not like to shut yourself in here for years and read all these books?'

He laughed. 'Well, I've read a great number of them. I daresay when I am a very old man, I shall take your advice and read the remainder.' He stood by the window, watching her browsing. 'Please feel free to come here whenever you wish, Maggy, and borrow anything you want.'

Maggy thanked him and followed him back into the hall, from whence they mounted the staircase which opened on to a square landing, lighted by the high window over the front door. He led the way down a small passage leading to the back of the house and opened a door.

'This will be your room. I hope you will be comfortable; anything you want my housekeeper, Anny, will gladly get for you.'

It overlooked the canal and the garden and was furnished charmingly in mahogany and chintz. There was a small fourposter bed against one wall. It had a curved canopy and a coverlet of silk and lace. Maggy had thought Oudehof a very grand place, but this house on the edge of the Rapenburg canal, although much smaller, was even more richly furnished.

The doctor showed her several more rooms, all equally beautiful. On the opposite side of the landing he passed a door, commenting that it was his room, and led her past an elaborately carved double door, remarking briefly that it was naturally not in use, as it was the master bedroom, thence to a small narrow staircase, carved with as much skill as the one they had already ascended. At the top of the stairs was a very small sitting room with painted walls, a replica of one of the rooms at Oudehof which an ancestor had had copied, so that he should be reminded of Friesland while he lived in Leiden. The remaining rooms were intercommunicating, with wooden bars fixed across the narrow windows. In the first room there was a rocking horse pushed into a corner. The furniture was simple, rather old-fashioned and very cosy. They stood close together in the doorway, looking at it.

'The nurseries,' said the doctor. 'There's room for six children and two nursemaids up here. There were only three of us, so we had plenty of room.'

Maggy nodded. She was looking at a magnificent doll's house and a row of dolls on a shelf. She said regretfully, 'They look so lonely.'

He smiled. 'I don't come up here very often, I'm afraid; but when I marry and have children, I expect I shall be up here a great deal.'

Maggy swallowed. 'Yes, of course,' she said in a colour-less voice.

'There's another floor above this one,' he continued. 'Would you like to see that as well?'

He led the way up to the small rooms under the steep roof. They were as charming as the larger rooms on the floors below.

'What do you use them for?' Maggy enquired.

He shrugged. 'An overflow of guests. At one time the servants slept here, but Anny has a small flat downstairs; and the other servants don't sleep in the house.'

They went downstairs slowly, stopping to look at portraits and paintings as they went. On the first floor Maggy stopped before the painting of a girl with eyes and hair done in the style of the mid-eighteenth century.

'She's not Dutch, I think?'

'No—she was the bride of the Doelsma who built this house; she came from Scotland to marry him and because she hadn't been to Holland before he had the furniture in her bedroom sent from England, so that she shouldn't feel strange. There's a family tradition that no bride may see the room until she comes to this house after her marriage.'

Maggy studied the pretty face in the portrait. 'He must have loved her very much,' she said at last.

He smiled. 'Yes, indeed, as she loved him. They had nine children, all of whom survived—a miracle for those days, was it not?' He turned down a short passage and switched on a light. 'Here they are—the whole family.' He pointed to a small canvas.

'You look exactly like him,' Maggy cried—as indeed he did.

'Yes, I know, but whether I follow his excellent example and have nine children is still a matter for conjecture.' He was laughing as he switched off the light and led the way downstairs.

As they entered the drawing room, Mevrouw Doelsma looked up.

'Well, my dear, what do you think of the house?'

'It's beautiful, Mevrouw Doelsma. I haven't any words to say how beautiful. Thank you for waiting so patiently

for me. I expect you would like to go upstairs and rest for
an hour. I'll read to you if you like—you'll enjoy the
evening more if you lie down for a wee while.'

Dinner was a pleasant meal. Maggy still found a secret
delight in the delicious food, even more delicious when
eaten off Meissen plates with silver knives and forks.

The hospital appointment was for ten o'clock the following morning and was thoroughly discussed. They were
to be driven to the nearby hospital by Pratt, who would then
return to Oudehof.

'I shall go to bed early,' declared Mevrouw Doelsma,
'for I have no intention of anybody finding anything wrong
with me tomorrow.' Accordingly, soon after dinner, she said
goodnight to Paul, but when Maggy wished him goodnight too, he said,

'Come downstairs again, Maggy, when Mother is safely
in bed, and I'll take you on a tour of the salon.'

His mother paused on her way upstairs. 'What a good
idea, Paul! Maggy, it's only just after nine, you can't
possibly go to bed yet.'

Maggy agreed; indeed, it would have been difficult for
her to do otherwise, and her inclination to spend an hour
in Paul's company was very strong.

It was an hour or more before she went quietly into the
drawing room. As the doctor got up from his chair she said
rather breathlessly,

'I'm sorry I have been so long. Your mother is excited,
I couldna' leave her. She's douce the noo'. I've kept ye
out of bed.'

The doctor looked astonished. 'I seldom go upstairs
before midnight and very often later; being solitary, I'm
afraid I have acquired bad habits.' His grey eyes twinkled at
her, and she smiled shyly, supposing he thought her foolish,

but there was no mockery in his gaze; he was looking at her kindly with no trace of his usual slightly arrogant expression. He crossed the room and stood beside her.

'Shall we start on this side first?' he queried mildly.

They lingered a long time over the china and silver and the numerous paintings on the walls. Some of them, he told her, had been in the family for many years. They pored over a small Cornelis Troost and a skating scene by Avercamp, and at length came back to the big stove where he pulled the bell rope. When Anny came, Paul said, 'You'd like a cup of coffee, wouldn't you, Maggy?'

She was absorbed in the tiles around the stove. 'Aye, Doctor, coffee will suit me fine. I canna' understand this wee tile.' She pointed to it, set high in the wall behind the stove. It had a design of ships and sheep and a disembodied hand holding a sword aloft, the whole encircled by an inscription impossible for her to read.

He came and stood beside her. 'That's the family crest; the ships and the sheep from which we made our living—the sword is a polite indication that we are prepared to fight for what we have.' He traced the writing with a long forefinger, and spelled it out in the Friesian tongue. 'I honour God, and love that which is mine.'

Maggy turned to look at him. 'And you do, don't you?' she asked.

His grey eyes smiled down into her brown ones.

'Yes, Maggy, I do.' He bent his head and kissed her on one soft cheek.

'Oh!' said Maggy, and said no more, for Anny had opened the door and was coming in with the coffee tray. The doctor laughed softly and said, 'Do pour out, Maggy.'

She did so, with commendable calm, and even maintained her share of conversation while they drank it, and then wished the doctor a quiet goodnight before going upstairs to her pretty bedroom, to lie awake in the canopied bed, her usual good sense wholly at war with her unbidden thoughts.

CHAPTER SIX

THERE WAS NO SIGN of Dr Doelsma when Maggy and Mevrouw Doelsma arrived at the hospital the following morning. Instead they were met by a comfortable middle-aged Sister, who bore them off to the X-ray department. Maggy looked around her with professional interest, oblivious of the equally interested glances she received as they walked through the corridors. The cubicle they were shown into was small and white-painted, and smelled, inevitably, of hospital. It looked exactly the same as those in her own hospital. She helped her patient to undress, and persuaded her to put on the shapeless white cotton garment, tied with tapes at the back. Dr Doelsma had told them that an ECG would be done first, before the X-ray examination, and Maggy made her patient as comfortable as possible on the narrow couch, keeping up a calming flow of small talk meanwhile. Mevrouw Doelsma was nervous, but Maggy knew that they wouldn't have to wait. There were, she thought dryly, many advantages in being a relative of a hospital consultant. The ECG technician proved to be a white-overalled girl, pretty and competent. Between them she and Maggy made tight work of the tiresome straps and buckles criss-crossed over Mevrouw Doelsma's unwilling body. Ten minutes later she was sitting up once more, asking rather querulously how much longer she had to wear the shapeless white garment.

'A wee while, yet, Mevrouw Doelsma,' said Maggy soothingly. 'I've your dressing gown and slippers here.' This act of thoughtfulness had quite a cheering effect as they were conducted to the consultant's room. Maggy had expected to remain outside while Dr Bennink examined Mevrouw Doelsma, but was bidden to stay by Dr Bennink, who was obviously good friends with his patient. He was a short, rather stout man, with grey hair receding from a high forehead; he wore very thick glasses and peered at Maggy through them rather like an earnest little boy looking through the end of a bottle. He beamed at her, lowered the glasses to have a better look, and then shook hands, and such was his personality that she was unaware that she towered over him by more than eight inches.

'*Kijk maar*—the Scottish Sister. I know of you, naturally. I am now happy to be acquainted.' He waved her to a seat by Mevrouw Doelsma and took his own chair again.

Dr Bennink had undoubtedly earned his reputation as a leading heart consultant. His questions were searching and he was very thorough. Maggy came in for her fair share and answered him with an unflurried accuracy which pleased him mightily. He liked the way she did everything necessary during the ensuing examination too. She appeared to read his wishes before they were voiced and acted upon them before he uttered them. After half an hour, he sat back. 'You're as good as new, Henrietta, due doubtless to your stubbornness and this young woman. I'll see Paul after your barium meal. With a regular check-up and sensible living, you'll outlive the lot of us.'

His myopic eyes twinkled as they all shook hands, and

a cheerful buxom little nurse with a round face and bright blue eyes took charge of them once more. Back in the cubicle, she produced a tumbler of thick white fluid and gave it to Maggy. Maggy in her turn proffered it to her patient, who obediently took a sip, and immediately declared her intention of not drinking any more of it.

'It's revolting!' she said indignantly.

'Yes, I know,' said Maggy, 'but it will be impossible to carry out the tests unless you drink it,' she added reasonably.

'Then I won't have the tests,' said Mevrouw Doelsma testily.

'Paul wanted you to have them.' Maggy no sooner uttered the words than she blushed; she always thought of the doctor as Paul, but that was no excuse. She could have bitten her thoughtless tongue. Fortunately Mevrouw Doelsma hadn't seemed to have noticed her words, but was busy pulling a loose thread on her despised gown. Maggy proffered the glass once more, and was surprised when the nauseating liquid was swallowed without further fuss, and she was able to lead a surprisingly docile patient into the X-ray room.

Excepting for a dim red light, the place was in darkness. Mevrouw Doelsma clutched Maggy's hand and jumped when a vague figure loomed before them. It spoke in a re-assuringly human voice, albeit in Dutch; However, it sounded soothing and friendly, and Mevrouw Doelsma answered it with every sign of pleasure. The voice changed to a pedantic and nearly perfect English.

'How do you do, Sister. Paul has told me of you, and I am happy to see you.'

Maggy said politely. 'How do you do?' wondering if the figure could see her any better than she could see him. He went on to give a few brisk instructions, which Maggy carried out before stepping backwards against the wall, out of the way. A slight sound and a draught behind her made her realise that she was standing in front of a door. Before she could move, a vast arm was dropped lightly about her shoulders.

'Hallo, Maggy,' said the doctor very softly; she felt his breath on her cheek, and fought to keep her own breath steady, trying to ignore the rush of feeling at his touch. He remained where he was for a long minute, then gave her shoulder a friendly squeeze and went silently through the gloom to the radiographer. They murmured together until Paul said, 'Hallo, Mother. We shan't be long now.'

His mother's voice sounded faintly querulous. 'It's so dark, Paul, and I don't know where Maggy is.'

'She's quite close, dear, but she must keep out of the way for a moment. She'll stand by you presently while we screen your tummy. Now do what Dirk says, Mama.'

The lights went on again, Mevrouw Doelsma was arranged as comfortably as possible on the table, and Maggy, protected by a lead apron, stood beside her, holding her hand. The dark was intense this time, with only the greenish, dim flicker of the screen. Maggy listened to the two men making their observations in low voices, and gave the small clutching hand she was holding a reassuring squeeze. It seemed a long time before the lights went on again and she led her patient back to the cubicle and helped her dress. Both doctors were waiting for them; it was the radiologist who spoke.

'Mevrouw Doelsma, as far as I can see there's nothing at all for you to worry about. I'll have to check the X-rays, of course, but neither Paul nor I could see anything amiss. So you need have no fear of complications. Dr Bennink will be seeing you shortly again, I expect. I must congratulate you on an excellent recovery.'

There was delicious hot coffee waiting for them in the doctor's office, where they were joined by Dr Bennick. Maggy sat quietly, saying almost nothing, and feeling uncomfortable. Her presence meant that the other three must speak English. She was sure that they must have a great deal to talk about—the intimate gossip of old friends, perhaps; family matters in which she had no part. She struggled to think of an excuse so that she could leave them. She put her coffee cup down on the desk beside her, and as though it were a signal, the doctor got up and came over to her.

'I'd like to take you round part of the hospital. Are you ready, Maggy?'

He didn't wait for an answer, but opened the door, calling a casual *'dag'* over his shoulder at his mother and Dr Bennink as he stood waiting for Maggy to join him.

They walked along a number of rather bleak corridors, and she, feeling that anything was better than silence, plunged into a series of questions which the doctor answered patiently, pausing only to acknowledge gravely any greetings he received from passing doctors and students. They went first, and inevitably, to the women's medical ward. Maggy was surprised and faintly amused to see that the nurses held the doctor in some awe. Even the Ward Sister, a gaunt, elderly woman with a sweet face, seemed stiff and formal with him. They walked round the ward, the two women comparing notes with the doctor acting as interpreter, and then sat in Sister's office drinking another cup of coffee, telling each other about salaries and off-duty and lack of nurses, and stopped reluctantly when the doctor remarked mildly that he thought it a good idea if they went to see the children's ward. Here everything was noise and bustle and small children shouting and crying and laughing, according to how they felt. The doctor seemed to know them all as they wandered through the ward to the balcony, accompanied by Sister, a pretty young creature who quite obviously loved her work.

'There's a child I want you to see, Maggy. She's making a remarkable recovery after eating coal, safety-pins, a few small coins and a large lump of Plasticine. She's Sister's pet, isn't she, Sister?' He turned to the Ward Sister and said something in Dutch to make her laugh; she was still laughing when she went back into the ward, leaving them looking at the small blonde angel playing with a doll on the floor. She eyed them for a moment, then threw the doll away and got on to rather spindly little legs and toddled over to Maggy, who bent and swung her up to be cuddled.

'You clever girl,' said Maggy, dropping a kiss on the straight hair. She looked at Paul. 'Isn't she beautiful, Doctor?'

'The most beautiful girl in the world.' But he wasn't looking at his small patient. He bent forward, and Maggy felt his lips on hers. She stood quite still, looking at him, her cheeks very pink, but her brown eyes met his grey ones squarely.

'I don't intend to apologise, Maggy,' he said, almost lazily.

Maggy forced her voice to normality. 'There is no need, Doctor. I doubt ye've kissed many a girl before me, and will kiss many more. I ken well it means nothing to ye.' She gave the toddler a reassuring hug, and put her back on the rug on the floor.

'Just a minute, Maggy. Are you so sure of that?'

She looked over her shoulder at him; he was standing with his hands in his pockets, looking at her with a faint mocking smile on his face.

'Aye,' she said slowly. 'I'm sure. A kiss can mean everything in this world to two people, and it can be just an empty gesture, like saying "How do you do" and not wanting to know.' She bent down and gave the little girl her doll, then went on, 'Ye must be proud of the bairn, in a few weeks she'll be a bonny wee lassie.'

She blew kisses to the small creature, and went back into the ward without looking at him. They said goodbye to the Sister and started on their way back to his office. Maggy kept up a steady flow of small talk, scarcely waiting for his replies before plunging into a fresh topic; walking just ahead of him, so that she didn't need to look at him. When they reached the office door, she put her hand on the knob and faced him. She had forced a cheerful expression on to her face, but her eyes looked like a small girl's when she'd been hurt.

'Thank you for showing me round, Dr Doelsma. It was most interesting.'

He put a large hand over hers, so that she was unable to turn the knob.

'My poor Maggy,' he said. 'You may be six feet tall, but you've not grown up yet.'

He opened the door then, and Maggy went inside, and waited while Mevrouw Doelsma made her farewells, then said goodbye quietly herself, before going out to the car and back to the Rapoenburg and the doctor's house. As they entered the hall, Mevrouw Doelsma said, 'Paul will be home for lunch. I expect. What a pity the weather is so bad, Maggy—it's no day for sightseeing.' She started up the stairs, with Maggy beside her. 'Never mind, I daresay it will be better tomorrow. We're staying a few days, anyway, and you shall have two or three days quite free to go sightseeing. We'll talk about it later, shall we?' She paused as the phone rang, and waited while Anny answered it.

'It's Mr Paul, madam, he asks me to tell you that he will

be going to Utrecht almost immediately, and will lunch there. He expects to be home for dinner.'

Mevrouw Doelsma said nothing, but that evening, when she and Maggy went downstairs to the salon and found Paul waiting, she remarked rather tartly,

'Paul, I know the love of your life is in Utrecht, but did you really have to go this morning? I know you like to go as often as possible, but surely, when we are here…?'

He was pouring drinks at a side table and turned a suddenly forbidding face to her.

'I'm sorry, Mother, but it is important to me, and there is no point in discussing it, is there?' He walked across the room and gave her the small glass of sherry she was allowed, then bent his great height and kissed her cheek. He was smiling again. 'I had no idea that I would be going to Utrecht until I rang up, Mama. Am I forgiven?'

He turned away to get a drink for Maggy, and drew her into a conversation he deliberately made light.

Maggy had spent a wretched afternoon; it seemed obvious to her that Paul, however good his opinion was of her as a nurse, had none at all of her as a woman. She sipped some sherry. How could she have thought even for one moment that he had any interest in her whatsoever? He was quite right, she hadn't grown up. But now, she told herself firmly, she had very positive proof; Stien lived in Utrecht—the love of his life. Mevrouw Doelsma had said.

Her good Scottish pride came to her rescue. She drank the rest of her sherry in time to answer a question from the doctor in a perfectly natural and friendly voice.

Dinner was a gay meal; they drank champagne to celebrate Mevrouw Doelsma's recovery, and sat round the table talking long after the meal was finished.

'Maggy's having a day off in a couple of days' time,' said Mevrouw Doelsma.

Paul glanced briefly at the serene profile; Maggy had contrived not to look at him, save for a fleeting glance when she spoke to him. She didn't look now.

'Where are you going?'

'Amsterdam,' she replied promptly. 'I want to see the museums and churches first, and the Dam Palace, and tour the canals, and look at the shops…'

Her companions laughed. 'Why, Maggy,' said Mevrouw Doelsma, 'you'll be worn out. You must have another day…'

'Then I shall go again and just walk around, looking.'

The doctor leaned back in his chair. 'There is a great deal to see, but may I suggest that you keep to the main streets—it's easy to get lost unless you know the city, especially if you intend to roam. I've a map you shall have—there are one or two areas I should avoid if I were you. The Jordaan, picturesque and harmless enough, but if you got lost there I doubt if they would understand you, and you certainly wouldn't understand them.' He paused. 'There are one or two other districts you should avoid.'

Maggy looked at him with brows raised. 'But, Doctor,' she said mildly, 'I'm six feet tall, but for a quarter of an inch, and well used to managing for myself.'

A corner of the doctor's mouth twitched. 'The particular district I have in mind is behind the Oude Kerk, which I imagine is one of the churches you wish to see. We call it the Rossebuurt. The—er—ladies of the town ply their trade there.' He added gently, 'They'd do you no harm, but you would be out of your element, wouldn't you?'

Maggy could think of nothing to say in answer to this, but sat, staring at him, and going slowly very red. Mevrouw Doelsma came to her rescue. 'Paul, you're making Maggy blush; be quiet! Give the child your map and mark off the less inviting areas and then she'll know what to avoid.' She got up. 'Now I'm going up to bed; I've had an exciting day.'

Accompanied by Maggy, she crossed the lovely room and the hall and started up the stairs. The doctor had come with them; now he kissed his mother and turned to Maggy.

'When Mother is safely in bed, will you come down again and I will give you the map.'

Maggy took a step up the stairs, away from him. 'Perhaps you would leave it somewhere?' She glanced around her. 'On one of the tables here perhaps?' She took another step. 'I'm rather tired, Doctor. I think I shall go to my room when I've put Mevrouw Doelsma to bed.'

'It would be better if I showed you the map—if you are too tired to come down, I'll come up to your room presently, shall I?' He looked at his watch. 'Half an hour—forty minutes?' He was laughing at her.

Maggy quelled him with a severe glance. 'I'll be down in half an hour or so, Doctor,' she said soberly, and went upstairs without another word.

It was almost an hour later when she knocked on the library door and went inside. The doctor got up from his desk and came over to her, for she had made no effort to go into the room. He held the map in his hand. 'You'll have to come over to the desk, I think, so that I can spread it out.'

She went rather reluctantly to stand beside him while he pointed out the areas he had ringed and the neat list of train and bus times he had written in one corner.

'I don't like you going alone, Maggy, but I have no right or reason to ask you not to. Will you ring up either the hospital or here if you want to be fetched. The phone numbers are here.'

Maggy took the map from him. 'It's a great trouble ye've taken, Doctor, and I'm grateful.'

'I am, after all, responsible for you while you are under my roof, my dear girl, and it's very little I'm doing.'

She turned to the door, and he made no attempt to stop her.

'Thank you. Doctor, I'll away to my bed.'

She was at the door when he spoke. 'Still friends, Maggy?'

She turned and gave him a steady look. 'Aye, Doctor, still friends.'

Maggy went down to her breakfast the next morning, wondering if she would see the doctor. There was no sign of him, however, although when she returned to her patient, who had breakfasted in bed, it was to hear that he had been in to see his mother while Maggy was at her own breakfast. There was very little nursing treatment to be done, and later, when Mevrouw Doelsma was dressed and she was standing looking out of the window, she said suddenly,

'We will go for a little run in the car—Paul has arranged for Pratt to stay on for a few days.' She seemed delighted with the idea, and Maggy agreed readily—it was a pleasant enough day, and it would be nice to see something of the country around Leiden. Pratt installed them both comfortably in the back of the car, and asked, 'A little drive to the villa, perhaps, madam?'

'An excellent idea, Pratt, and keep off the main roads, won't you?' Pratt agreed gravely to this request, and took them through the peaceful, quiet countryside; he drove at considerably less speed than did the doctor, and it took them an hour or more to reach the village of Loenen, where, it seemed, Mevrouw Doelsma wished to go. It was an enchanting spot, on the banks of the River Vecht. They left the village and travelled along the road running beside the river; on both banks there were charming, rather ornate villas. Maggy found them rather too elaborate—they reminded her of birthday cakes—but there was no denying their charm, or the beauty of their surroundings.

Pratt slowed down and turned into an unpretentious gateway leading to one of the smaller and less ornate of the houses. Maggy caught a glimpse of the river at the back of the garden as he drew up before its solid front door. They got out, assisted in a fatherly fashion by Pratt. 'We'll have coffee here,' said Mevrouw Doelsma, as he rang the bell. The door was opened by a short, stout, elderly woman in a blue striped dress and white apron, who broke immediately into speech.

'Madam dear! Come in—I said to myself today, Madam will be here any day now; and so I told Mijnheer.' She paused for breath and embraced Mevrouw Doelsma, then stood back and looked at her. 'You look wonderful, madam, and how's my boy? I haven't seen him for weeks.'

Mevrouw Doelsma took this torrent of speech calmly. 'Mr Paul is a busy man, as you know, Nanny.' She turned to Maggy, standing patiently beside her. 'Maggy, you must meet Nanny. She looked after Paul and Saskia and Wiebecka, and now she lives here and looks after my brother-in-law.'

Maggy proffered a hand, and shook the small plump one offered to her carefully, taking care not to squeeze the elderly fingers with her own strong large ones. Nanny looked her up and down, and she stood quietly waiting for the sharp blue eyes to have their fill.

'There's a big girl now,' said Nanny comfortably. 'Not far short of Master Paul, I daresay.'

She led the way indoors through an elegant small hall into the living room, and went to fetch the master of the house.

He was, even at seventy, very like Paul. He had the same grey eyes and straight nose, and the same air of arrogance. He greeted them with delight, and openly looked Maggy over as they drank their coffee.

'You're a fine girl,' he said with the outspokenness of the elderly. 'I like an Amazon myself—just as Paul does—or perhaps he hasn't told you that,' he added slyly.

Maggy blushed, but answered coolly enough, 'No, I don't believe he has.'

'You can colour up too,' he went on relentlessly. 'Haven't seen a girl blush for years—didn't know they could any more.' He put on a pair of old-fashioned spectacles and peered at her. 'Has Paul seen you blush?'

Maggy put down her coffee cup carefully.

'Very probably—it's an unfortunate habit I haven't been able to stop.'

She was scarlet by now, and decided that he was quite the most impossible old gentleman she had met. She was horrified when he answered her unspoken thought.

'I'm a rude old man, aren't I?' He spoke with satisfaction in his careful English. He added obscurely, 'I'm fond of Paul.'

Maggy replied politely that she supposed he was, and he smiled at her, looking so like Paul that she smiled back. 'Delightful,' he murmured, and then out loud. 'Go and have a look at the garden, you'll be glad of a breath of air. You're too young to be cooped up indoors.'

Maggy got up obediently and went outside and walked around the small paths between the flower beds, and down to the river, where she sat down to admire the view on a seat thoughtfully provided for just that purpose. She supposed she could stay for half an hour or so. Mevrouw Doelsma would want to talk for a little while. She decided that she liked Paul's uncle despite his forthright manner;

she wished she knew more about him. Her thoughts were interrupted by Nanny, who had appeared silently beside her and offered to keep her company. Maggy made room for her on the seat, and spent the next ten minutes asking questions about the river and the fairy-tale houses bordering it. Nanny replied to her questions at some length, so that Maggy not only heard about the houses but the people who lived in them as well.

When she at length paused to draw breath, Maggy asked. 'Have you lived here long, and may I know your name? I don't feel that I should call you Nanny.'

'The name's Coffin—a good West Country name, miss. I came to Holland with Madam when she married and I've been here ever since. The master sent us to England, but Master Paul, he wouldn't go—stayed with his father. Not eight he wasn't, but very determined. He was a fine boy, and grown to a fine man. Very naughty he was when he was a little boy.'

It was obvious to her listener that Nanny adored him. 'That makes two of us,' thought Maggy wistfully. She listened to the old lady reliving her busy, happy past, until, in the middle of an involved story about Paul's eventful childhood, she broke off.

'There, miss, you won't want to hear all this...?'

Maggy answered without thinking. 'Oh, but I do! Please go on—I'm so very interested.' She was watching the river as she spoke, and didn't see Nanny's beady eyes studying her face. Nanny said nothing, but finished her story, and then said surprisingly,

'I'd be happy for you to call me Nanny, miss.'

Maggy realised that Nanny was bestowing a favour, not lightly given. She answered gravely, 'Thank you, Miss Coffin. I should like to call you Nanny.'

Nanny nodded her head. 'I have the second sight,' she said obscurely, and plunged back into the past, sure of her audience.

Mevrouw Doelsma and Maggy, being driven back to Leiden by the sedate Pratt, had plenty to talk about; at least, Mevrouw Doelsma chattered happily about the visit.

'Did you like Mijnheer Doelsma, Maggy?' she asked.

'Aye. Mevrouw Doelsma, I did—he and the doctor are very like.'

'Yes, indeed. They're fond of each other too. It's Paul's house, you know, but he gave it to his uncle to live in until his death, and it's so convenient that Nanny is there to keep house for him—Isn't Nanny wonderful?'

Maggy agreed. 'I didn't know there were nannies like her—I mean outside books.'

'She's never changed since she first came to me; that's—let me see. Paul's thirty-six—it must be all of thirty-seven years. She went and looked after Saskia's and Wiebecka's babies when they were born, but she wouldn't stay with them—said she had to be free to look after Paul's children when he marries.'

That was the second time in twenty-four hours that Paul's marriage had been mentioned. Maggy watched the half-formed wisps of her dreams dissolve into a bleak future, then turned her attention to the countryside, asking sensible, observant questions of her patient which kept that lady fully occupied until they reached the doctor's house once more.

They ate a leisurely lunch, and having seen Mevrouw Doelsma tucked up for her afternoon nap, Maggy donned a raincoat, tied a scarf under her chin against the threatening rain, and set off to explore. Pratt, appearing in a silent, magic sort of way, opened the front door and hoped that she would enjoy her walk. She smiled at him, went down the double steps to the pavement, and started walking along the Rapenburg. The houses which lined the canal were beautiful, some very old, some not so old, but all making a harmonious whole. She didn't hurry, but looked at each house as she passed it. She turned back from the contemplation of a particularly fine fanlight, to find the Rolls loitering to a gentle halt beside her; the top was down, and Dr Doelsma, apparently impervious to the chilly wind blowing along the canal, was sitting at the wheel. He waved a languid hand, elegantly gloved.

'Good afternoon, Maggy. Off duty?'

She nodded, looking cross because she was blushing for no reason at all, and because she was wearing her serviceable raincoat and had her hair tied up anyhow in the first scarf she could find. His glance flickered over her, and he said,

'Don't worry, Maggy, you look delightful.'

Her brows met in a thunderous frown, and an explosive, 'Och!' burst from her lips, but before she could answer, he had waved again and slid quietly away. By concentrating hard on the houses she was passing, she managed not to think of him at all, as she made her way to Noordeind, where she turned back and started to walk back on the other side of the canal. There was a nice old house on the corner which had been turned into a restaurant, and she stopped to look at it. The interior was discreetly veiled from the vulgar eye of the passer-by, but it looked expensive. She stood in front of the door, wondering what it would be like inside, and heard nothing at all until the doctor spoke just behind her.

'Ah! As usual, Sister MacFergus is in the right place at the right time.'

Before she could turn her head, she was guided by an inescapable hand on her elbow through the door. It was another Dutch interior—very old, very quaint and quiet. She sat down, speechlessly obedient, at the small table to which he had guided her, while he ordered tea. He sat down opposite her, the frail chair creaking alarmingly under his weight.

'And what have you done today, Maggy?'

She undid her head-scarf with fingers which shook slightly, willing her voice to normality.

'Mevrouw Doelsma took me to visit your uncle at Loenen.'

'Uncle Cornelis?' He laughed softly. 'Was he outrageous? I'm sure he made you blush, Maggy—' he watched her across the table. 'Yes, I see he did.'

She looked down her exquisite nose at him.

'Your uncle is—is very nice. I like him.'

'I'm sure he liked you too. He has a passion for large women.'

She went scarlet under his amused gaze, and said haughtily,

'I'm aware, Doctor. He told me so—' She remembered what else he had said, and looked down at her plate, so that her black lashes lay on her cheeks, wishing to be anywhere but where she was.

'Did he tell you that I have a passion for big women too?'

She refused to look up, and after a moment he said with a laugh in his voice, 'Poor Maggy, I mustn't tease.'

The tea came, and with it the return of her composure. The doctor maintained an easy flow of small talk, and as always in his company, she found herself responding to his friendliness.

She passed him his tea, and watched while he helped

himself lavishly to sugar, then turned to choose a monumental confection of chocolate and whipped cream and pineapple from the proffered tray. She eyed it with healthy pleasure, and attacked it with the endearing enthusiasm of a small girl having an unexpected treat. The doctor chose *boterkoek* and asked,

'Did you see Nanny?'

'Yes, she came and sat with me in the garden and told me tales of when you were a little boy. You were naughty, weren't you?' she added severely.

'Oh dear! Not the one about the Ambassador's wig?'

She nodded. 'Yes, Dr Doelsma, and the frog in your Great-Aunt Wilhelmina's bed, and skating instead of going to school…'

He held up a large hand. 'Enough! Maggy, I'm on my knees. Nanny has been devastatingly plain-spoken, as always.' He passed his tea cup for more tea. 'Did you like the villa?'

'Aye, Doctor, such a dear wee place, and the beautiful garden and the river close by.'

He nodded. 'Yes, it's pretty enough—just right for my uncle. Nanny finds it quiet; she has an insatiable passion for babies and small children.'

Just for a moment Maggy glimpsed a lovely impossible dream, then said in a bright voice,

'She looks just as a nanny should look. She's very fond of you, isn't she?'

'I believe so, though I can't think why. I must have been a great trial to her. She seems to have—er—unburdened herself to you.'

Maggy looked surprised. 'Did she? She asked me to call her Nanny,' she added.

He raised his eyebrows. 'Did she indeed? That's

unusual. She's more fiercely family than we are, you know. I've never known her do that before.'

Maggy agreed. 'I realised that. I felt honoured. She told me about her second sight too.'

The doctor gave her a long stare across the table, and said nothing, watching Maggy tie on her scarf again.

'Thank you for my tea, Doctor, and I'll be on my way.'

Outside it was raining in earnest and the wind was coming and going in spiteful little gusts. The doctor took her arm and said,

'It won't take any longer to walk this way—I'll show you the University. We can cross the bridge there and walk back on the other side.'

They stepped out briskly, not saying much until they reached the old building. 'Did you study here, Doctor?' Maggy asked.

'Yes—it's the oldest university in Holland, you know, and we're all rather proud of it. I was at Cambridge too, and Edinburgh Royal, but I came back here.'

They walked on, more slowly.

'Do you like Leiden?' he asked.

'Very much, so far. The Rapenburg is beautiful. Do you prefer it to Oudehof?'

They crossed the bridge, she could see his home now, and the Rolls-Royce standing outside.

'What a difficult question to answer. I think I like them both equally.'

They reached the house, and he went up the steps with her, pulled the old-fashioned bell, and waited until Anny opened the door. He didn't go in, but said,

'Goodbye, Maggy. Will you make my excuses to my mother? I'm going over to Utrecht and shan't be back until late. Have a good day in Amsterdam if I don't see you again.'

He sounded casual. Maggy answered him quietly and went through the door and up the stairs to her room, where she stood before the mirror looking at herself. He had said 'You look delightful,' but he hadn't meant it, of course. Slow tears started to trickle down her cheeks. He would be on his way to Utrecht now—on his way to Stien. She tore off her coat and scarf and washed her face and changed into uniform again, and went, with a cheerful face, to deliver Paul's message to his mother.

CHAPTER SEVEN

MAGGY LEFT the house quite early the next morning making sure before she went that Mevrouw Doelsma's gently patterned day should run smoothly. She sat in the train, wondering whether she should make the suggestion that there was really no further need of her services. She got out at Amsterdam with the question still unsolved, and then forgot all about it in the excitement of being in a strange city in a strange land, and with all day before her to explore it.

It seemed logic to take a canal trip straight away—there was a launch standing beside its own small pier just across the street. Maggy crossed cautiously, bought her ticket and spent the next hour or so looking at Amsterdam from the water. She didn't listen to the guide, saying everything three times in three languages; she didn't care about the names of the old buildings they passed, or who owned them, but just sat quietly, looking about her; she would go for a second time on her next free day, and behave like a tourist.

Back on the Damrak, she took out her map and studied it carefully, then made her way to the Palace and the War Memorial in the Dam Square; she studied them both at length, then strolled down the Kalverstraat, looking at the shops—they were inviting and expensive. Maggy studied the gay autumn colours. It would be nice to buy anything one fancied without having to worry if it would wear well or look fashionable in a year's time. She glanced down at her own dress, a navy blue and white checked tricot, well cut but not, she realised, spectacular. There was a vivid coral pink jersey dress in one window, very plain, very well cut. It had no price tag. Maggy went inside, and speaking good clear Scots, asked to see it. The price was high, but as the saleswoman assured her, it was exactly the right dress for her. Looking at herself in the long, elegant mirror in the small fitting room, Maggy had to agree. It was a beautiful dress. She paid for it quickly before her practical mind told her that she was being extravagant, and left the shop happily.

She lunched at the Formosa Café, because the doctor had told her to do so, and ate her way through a *twaalf*, studying her map. The Rijksmuseum was easy to find, but after half an hour she decided that she was doing the magnificent paintings less than justice by offering them the glance that was all the time she had for them. She wanted to sit and look at them in her own good time. She would most certainly have to return on the second free day Mevrouw Doelsma had promised her.

She walked back towards the centre of the city, getting happily lost, and spending far too long peering into the antique shops in the narrow streets lining the canals. Eventually she found her way back to the Kalverstraat, and because she couldn't find a tea-shop, ventured rather shyly into the Hotel Polen, where a fatherly waiter gave her tea, straw-coloured and very weak, and dish of delightful cakes. The day had passed very quickly. Maggy looked at her watch and decided that she would just have time to visit the Scottish Church before she went back to the station. It was easy enough to find, and surprisingly peaceful, standing in the little square of old houses, with the bustle of the city all round it. She left it reluctantly, and found her way back to the Dam Square; and because she had a little time to spare plunged into the Nieuwendijk. According to the map, the station would be at the other end, and it looked interesting, with a great many shops each side of a very narrow street, there was a strip of pavement on either side of the cobblestones, and Maggy walked briskly, resisting the temptation to stop and look in the shop windows; she wasn't sure how far away the station was.

There were a great many people about; she was pushed and jostled and bumped into, but all with the greatest good humour, and after a time she hardly noticed it until a small woman, darting out of a narrow alley, knocked against her and would have fallen if Maggy hadn't caught her by the shoulder. Their surprise was mutual—it was Madame Riveau. Maggy recognised her at once, and Madame Riveau knew her too. She was very pale, her black eyes blank with what might have been pain. Maggy blinked with astonishment. The woman looked far worse than she had ever looked at St Ethelburga's. She said gently, remembering to speak French,

'Are you hurt, Madame Riveau? You are so white.'

The woman shook her head, staring at Maggy as though she could not believe her eyes.

'You're not well?' Maggy went on. This time Madame Riveau mumbled, 'Yes, yes, Sister.' Maggy, puzzled at her strange behaviour, tried again.

'Do you live near here?'

Her companion nodded again, and this time nodded reluctantly, displaying toothless gums.

'So you've had your teeth out,' said Maggy, glad of something to talk about to this awkward woman. 'Do you remember that I said you should do so?' She remembered how unpleasant the men had been about it. 'Was your husband angry?' She saw fear flicker in the woman's eyes. 'Does he take you to the doctor?'

Madame Riveau went even whiter. So that was it! She said, 'Sister, come again, I must see you. Why are you here?'

'I came to Holland to work,' Maggy said briefly. She saw no reason to tell the woman more—besides, her vocabulary was being stretched to its limits. She held out her hand, but surprisingly Madame Riveau became all of a sudden quite friendly.

'Do you often come to Amsterdam, Sister?'

'No, I don't,' said Maggy, 'but I shall be here again tomorrow or the next day.'

Madame Riveau was still holding her hand. 'I should like to see you and talk—I am not well, you saw that, did you not? I live near here. Perhaps if you come again, about this time—just for a few minutes.'

Maggy gently withdrew her hand; the woman certainly looked ill, and after all she wasn't a stranger. She nodded reluctantly. 'I may come, but I can't promise,' she said.

Madame Riveau smiled her horrible toothless smile. 'Good, good, I shall count on you. *Au revoir,* Sister.'

She disappeared into the crowd of people milling around them on the narrow pavement, and Maggy, mindful of her train, quickened her steps to the station.

When she got back to the doctor's house, she was fully occupied with Mevrouw Doelsma until dinner time. The doctor joined them in the dining room, but it wasn't until half way through the meal that he asked Maggy casually if she had enjoyed her day. She answered briefly, afraid that it would bore him to have a detailed account of her comings and goings. He listened courteously, but didn't press her for details, and presently began to talk about plans for his mother's proposed holiday later on—it seemed that he owned a villa in the south of France as well. She supposed he was quite rich, and the thought depressed her.

Maggy turned to answer a question from Mevrouw Doelsma; she wasn't wearing uniform but had put on a sleeveless dress in a pink patterned silky material; its simple lines accentuated her delightful figure, the colour suited her clear skin and brown hair. She felt the doctor's eyes on her and looked at him and smiled pleasantly and entirely without coquetry, and turned her attention back to his mother. Paul sat deep in thought, remembering what Nanny had said to him earlier that day. He became aware of Maggy's lilting voice saying something about meeting a woman she knew; he caught the name and asked,

'Do you mean that peculiar French woman with the gastric ulcer in your ward at St Ethelburga's?'

She half turned her head. 'Yes, Doctor, only she is a Belgian. Do you remember her too? She had a horrid husband and an ugly wee brute of a son—she ran out of an alley today and almost knocked me down. She looked so frightened at first, and then became quite friendly. I expect she was as surprised as I was.'

He was on the point of asking her where she had met the woman when Anny came in to tell him that he was wanted on the telephone, and presently he came back to say that he had to go out to a patient and they didn't see him again that evening.

The next day was cold and blustery. Mevrouw Doelsma's hairdresser came in the morning, and after lunch they drove to the Hague where Maggy accompanied

her patient from shop to shop. Mevrouw Doelsma had a
nice taste in dress and bought several things that caught her
fancy, never once, to Maggy's astonishment, enquiring
their price. There was no sign of the doctor when they got
back at tea time, nor did he appear at dinner. Anny volun-
teered the information that her master had gone to Utrecht
again, and didn't know when he would be back.

'He's always in Utrecht,' grumbled Mevrouw Doelsma,
'but really I haven't the heart to say anything to him; after
all, it is what he wants.'

Maggy murmured non-committally and looked at the
trifle on her plate, something to which she was very partial,
then found that she had no appetite for it. She would have
to go back to London as soon as possible; she seemed in-
capable of controlling her feelings any more. If she never
saw Paul again, perhaps she would be able to forget him;
the unlikelihood of this was of no comfort to her. She swallowed the lump in her throat, and before she could change
her treacherous mind, said, 'Mevrouw Doelsma, you'll not
be needing me much longer. I'll be sorry to go, but I should
return to hospital, you know.'

The little lady blinked at her across the beautifully ap-
pointed table.

'Maggy! Go? But I shall miss you terribly. I know I don't
need you, but couldn't you stay another week or so?' She
looked at Maggy's face, and sighed. 'No, I see you couldn't.
But what will Paul say? Has he mentioned it to you?'

Maggy shook her head without speaking. 'Well,' said
Mevrouw Doelsma, 'you can't go until the doctor says so.'

'Doctor Bennink said that you were ready to return to
normal life, didn't he? And you are his patient.'

'Maggy, you sound as though you wanted to go.'

Maggy made haste to deny this and said hastily, 'No

indeed, I've enjoyed every moment of my stay in Holland—and Friesland,' she added, mindful of the doctor's strong views, even though he wasn't there. 'There's a shortage of staff at St Ethelburga's, and I ought to go.'

Mevrouw Doelsma sighed for a second time. 'Yes, my dear. I understand, but I shall be very sorry to see you go. We'll tell Paul tomorrow. We shall be going back to Oudehof in a few days' time; you can return from there, can't you?'

Maggy thanked her gravely. 'I'll write to Matron…' she began, to be interrupted by Mevrouw Doelsma.

'And, Maggy, you must go to Amsterdam again tomorrow as you planned. Mijnheer Doelsma will be coming to lunch, and will be very cross to miss you—but you may not have another chance. Oh dear! I can't bear the thought of you going.'

Maggy smiled at her. She had become very fond of Paul's mother while she had been nursing her.

'Now that you can lead a usual life again, you won't miss me for long,' she consoled her. 'You'll be going on holiday soon, and visiting your daughters, and seeing all your friends again.'

She led the conversation back to more cheerful topics, and succeeded so well that by bedtime Mevrouw Doelsma was happy again.

Maggy went to her own room, determined not to think about the doctor. She got out her map and began to plan her visit for the next day. She must remember to go down the Nieuwendijk again, in case Madame Riveau was looking for her. Maggy hoped that she wouldn't be there, but she had promised to look out for her, and her dislike of the woman was no reason for breaking her word.

She put the map aside and got up from the little chintz-covered chair by the window, and started to walk restlessly about the charming room, her thoughts a muddle of bitter regret at leaving and the certainty that she was doing the only thing possible.

Her eye lighted on the cardboard box containing her new dress. What a terrible waste of money! Paul was unlikely to see her in it now—that, she was honest to admit to herself, was why she had bought it. She shook it out of its tissue paper wrappings, and tried it on, then stood looking at her reflection in the long mirror hanging on one wall. She wasn't a vain girl, but she could see that it was very becoming to her. She decided to wear it in the morning, and took it off and hung it carefully in the vast wardrobe, thinking how nice it would be if Paul were to come back from Utrecht before they left for Oudehof, but it was unlikely that he would return from Utrecht just to wish her goodbye.

It was still early when she finally got to bed, and she wasn't in the least sleepy. She had been down to the library earlier in the evening, and spent a little while choosing a book, and when she came across *The Wind in the Willows* with Paul's name written on the fly-leaf, in a careful large hand, with the date, she had taken it. She liked the story, but she had chosen it because it had belonged to him when he was a small boy. She lay in bed, turning the pages, and wondering what he had been like all those years ago, and after a little while she fell asleep.

The persistent, gentle tapping on the door roused her, she sat up in bed and looked at her watch—it was past one o'clock. Maggy reached for her dressing gown, ran bare-footed to the door, and flung it open, the only thought in her mind the one that Mevrouw Doelsma had been taken ill. The doctor looked enormous in the dim light of the passage.

She clutched at an elegant coat sleeve. 'Your mother?' she asked breathlessly.

He answered coolly, 'Sleeping soundly. I'm sorry if I wakened you; your light was on—it's rather late, I wondered if there was anything wrong.'

Maggy became aware of her hand, still on his arm. She whipped it away as though the fine cloth had burned it.

'Wrong? With me? No; I fell asleep with the lamp still on. It was careless of me. I'm sorry, Doctor.' She sounded very polite. The doctor didn't move, and Maggy, aware of bare feet and a dressing gown bundled around her like a sack, put a tentative hand up to her hair, certain that she looked terrible. She would have liked to shut the door; the longing to put out her hand again and touch him was so great that she put her hands behind her back like a small girl, and stood looking at him wordlessly.

He stared down at her without expression, and said in the same cool voice, 'You'd better get some sleep, hadn't you? Goodnight.'

He turned on his heel and went quietly down the passage to the front of the house, where his own room was, leaving her to go back to bed, to lie awake. He had wanted to be friends; Maggy wondered what had happened to change him; she went to sleep at last, still puzzling about it.

The weather was glorious when she set out the next morning, and she wore the new dress. There was the possibility of rain—there always was in Holland—so at the last minute she tucked the scarf she had worn when she had had tea with Paul into her handbag. The wind could be worse than the rain.

She spent the morning walking about the Singels, wishing she could see inside the lovely old houses which lined them, and then did some shopping for presents and had a leisurely lunch at the Formosa again. By the time she had paid a visit to Rembrandt's house and had a second trip around the canals, it was almost teatime. She strolled up the Kalverstraat once more, enjoying the shops. It was quite by chance that she came upon the small church, tucked away between two doorways; its own door stood open, and Maggy went in. It wasn't until she was inside that she realised that it was that enemy of her Calvinist forebears—a Popish church—but it was old and tranquil; she didn't think that the dominie at home would mind her being there.

She wandered around, looking at the windows and plaques, and then sat quietly, soothed by its peace and quiet, and thinking about England. She imagined herself back on the ward again, and was even able to convince herself that she would enjoy working hard once more. She would write to Matron when she got back to the Rapenburg, and within a week she would be back at St Ethelburga's, her visit to Holland a fast-fading dream. She stared at the beautiful altar through tears, fiercely wiped away. 'Fool,' she whispered, 'greeting like a bairn; ye need yer tea, lass.' She caught the gentle eye of Mary, poised beside her in her niche. 'I shouldn't be here, but there's no harm in telling ye.' She studied the calm sweet face. 'I should have liked fine to be his wife and raised his bairns.' She blew her nose, powdered it and smiled at the little statue. And Mary smiled back, or so it seemed, so that Maggy left the church quite comforted.

She had tea in the Bijenkorf—it was crowded and noisy and gave her no chance to think; she felt better after it, and crossed the Damrak to skirt the Dam Square and walk down Nieuwendijk with plenty of time for her train.

She was surprised to find Madame Riveau waiting for

her; she hadn't really expected her to take the trouble to meet her again. She looked just as frightened as before, but this time there was another look in the beady black eyes which Maggy couldn't understand. She stopped, listening with half-comprehending ears to the woman's torrent of words.

'I hoped you'd come, Sister. I haven't been well, but I had to do the shopping today, and I hoped that I should see you, so I waited, and now I feel faint.' She put a hand to her head. Certainly her face was white.

Maggy said with real sympathy, 'I'm sorry ye're not well. Why don't ye go home to rest? It was nice to see you again.' She moved away from her companion, who caught hold of her arm.

'Sister, don't go! I feel dreadful: I live close by—please help me to my home, it's but two minutes' walk.'

Maggy hesitated. Madame Riveau did indeed look ghastly; she had time enough if she walked quickly—she didn't want to go with the woman, but in common humanity she couldn't leave her. The woman leaned heavily on her arm as they turned down the little alley; there was barely room for two to walk abreast. At the end of it they crossed a dreary little square and turned into a cul-de-sac lined on one side by a row of hideous little houses, fallen into dreadful decay, and facing a window-less length of grimy brick shed. Maggy hadn't seen anything so unlike Holland since she had arrived there. Halfway along the row, Madame Riveau stopped at what was surely the most dilapidated house of them all. The door stood half open, but the dirty windows, shrouded by even dirtier curtains, were shut. She leaned with her full weight against Maggy and said in a faint whining voice,

'Please come inside for a moment and help me to chair—and if I could have a little water…'

Maggy looked around. There was no one about, and she couldn't leave Madame Riveau to fend for herself; she would have to go in. She pushed the door wide open, and with her companion clinging to one arm, went inside.

The little house was horrid inside; small and dark and meanly furnished. It smelled of dirt and damp washing and badly cooked meals, and, Maggy suspected, a lack of decent sanitation. Madame Riveau, still clutching her arm, drew her into what appeared to be the living room, and Maggy's nostrils flared at the increasing strength of the smells. She gently disengaged herself, sat the woman down on a chair and turned to the disgraceful sink, where she found a cup. She cleaned it as best she could, filled it with water and gave Madame Riveau one or two sips. To Maggy's kindly and professional eye, she looked really ill—she looked at her watch; if she left now she would be able to catch her train. On the other hand, it would be nothing short of callous to leave Madame Riveau alone. She stared at the silent figure on the chair, and then gazed with distaste around the room and made up her mind. She would make Madame Riveau comfortable and then go and telephone a doctor; by then either her husband or son might have returned, and she need not leave her alone.

Bed seemed the best thing. Maggy rotated slowly, looking for a staircase and failing to find one—the narrow passage led only to a cluttered little room with a sink and tap in one corner. It smelled of mice, and Maggy retreated to the living room to investigate the doors in its walls. The first one was a cupboard, but the double doors beside the stove revealed a large alcove with a bed built into it like a bunk—Maggy had seen something very like it that morning in a museum, only that one had been spotlessly clean, with gaily painted walls and bedlinen to shame the whitest snow... She pulled back the blankets with a tentative hand and wrinkled her nose and looked over her shoulder at Madame Riveau. 'Sheets?' she asked without much hope, and obeyed the feeble nod towards an old chest pushed against the wall. There were sheets inside, and pillowcases, even a nightgown of sorts, all of a uniform dingy grey, but better than nothing.

Maggy stripped and made up the bed, eased Madame Riveau out of her clothes and into the nightgown, and helped her into the comparative comfort of the stuffy little alcove, then looked once more at her watch. It had all taken much longer than she had expected. She had not only missed her train, she had missed the next one as well. As soon as one of the men came home—and that must surely be soon—they would have to telephone Leiden as well as the doctor. It wasn't very likely that she would be missed, at least, not for an hour or so.

She picked up the pile of discarded sheets, smiled reassuringly at Madame Riveau and went to the kitchen, where, being of a practical turn of mind, she set about finding a kettle, filling it and setting it on the gas ring to boil before setting out on a tour of inspection. The cupboard held a variety of food, all of it quite unsuitable for Madame Riveau's stomach. However, there was a bottle of milk which looked fresh. Maggy uttered a cry of triumph and looked round for something to boil it in. The saucepan she found, even after she had scoured it, fell far short of her standards of cleanliness, but it would have to do. She warmed some milk and took a little of it back to the bed. Madame Riveau drank it with an eagerness which made Maggy wonder when she had last had any, and asked for more.

'No,' said Maggy, 'for I don't know what's wrong with

you.' She leaned down and tucked her in with a swift gentleness. 'Go to sleep. I'll stay until someone comes home.'

She collected a pile of dirty cups and plates on the table and went back to the kitchen; she might as well wash up while she was waiting. There was an apron hanging behind the door. She put it on, thinking ruefully that her new dress no longer looked new… She left the clean crocks to drain and eyed the furniture. There was another kettle of water on the boil; it would be a pity to sit and do nothing while she was waiting. The back door opened on to a small yard, damp and dark and sour-smelling. Maggy dumped the meagre furniture into it and set to with a will. Half an hour later, a bit grubby and dishevelled, she stood back and gave a satisfied nod. The kitchen was by no means spotless, but at least she could look at it now without feeling sick. She washed her hands and went to look at Madame Riveau, who, secure in her cupboard, had fallen asleep. She looked no better, indeed, her face was as grey as the sheets, but her pulse was stronger. Maggy opened the front door quietly and looked up and down the alley. There was no one to be seen and nothing to be heard except the subdued hum of the city all around her. She knocked at the doors on either side of her with no result, and then, rather desperately, tried each door in the row. The last three were boarded up anyway, ready for demolition, and there didn't seem to be anyone in any of the other houses. She went back indoors and found Madame Riveau awake. She fixed Maggy with a lustreless eye and muttered, 'Don't go.'

'Of course I won't,' said Maggy cheerfully, and when the woman's eyes had closed again, looked at her watch. She would be very late getting back to Leiden; she wondered if they had noticed her absence yet, and if they would be annoyed. They had a right to be—she was after all, Mevrouw Doelsma's nurse. Dr Doelsma would probably be icily, politely disapproving; yet what else could she do? She decided not to think about it; needless worry wouldn't help. With a gentle stealth and an economy of movement unexpected in so large a young woman, she started to put the odds and ends of furniture outside the front door, to attack them presently with renewed energy and a great deal of hot soapy water. Satisfied at length, she left them to dry and went back inside and started on the buffet. She had almost finished when both men arrived together. They stood in the doorway, staring at her, suspicious and unfriendly.

'Why are you here?' Monsieur Riveau asked surlily.

Maggy decided that it would take too long to explain in her slow-thinking French. 'Your wife's ill. Will you fetch a doctor quickly?'

He stood, not heeding her at all, looking across the room at his wife.

Maggy gave an impatient snort. 'Go on,' she said, 'hurry!' and was surprised when he turned and started walking rapidly away. Before the younger man had a chance to speak she turned to him.

'Will you get me another bucket of hot water, please, and then take the table outside.'

He muttered something and scowled at her to send a shiver down her back, but did as he was bid, and after watching her from the doorway for a minute he went into the kitchen. Maggy hitched the apron more securely around her waist and set to work on the floor. It was almost finished when she heard footsteps. There must have been a doctor living close by, or perhaps there was a hospital nearby. She wrung out the cloth, and with it in her hand, and still on her knees, turned round to see who Monsieur Riveau had brought with him.

He was, of course, the last man she had expected to see. It was a pity that just the sight of him should take her breath so that her voice, when she found it, was unsteady. Nevertheless, she contrived to say in her usual practical way,

'I'm so glad to see you, though I can't think how you came to be here.'

She smiled with relief and a delight she had forgotten to conceal, then saw that he had no intention of smiling back. His face was full of a thunderous anger which he hadn't troubled to conceal. He stood in the doorway staring at her, so that she was all at once very aware of the deplorable apron and the wisps of hair which had come loose. She put up an instinctive hand to tidy them away, then caught sight of its grubbiness and put it quickly behind her back.

He said with icy silkiness, 'It is only too obvious that you can't think. In your zeal—to—er—springclean this deplorable house, you appear to have overlooked that fact that you had a train to catch—and a patient expecting you back round about six o'clock.' He looked at his watch. 'It is now almost half past seven.'

Maggy dropped the cloth still in her hand into the bucket beside her, and wiped her grimy hand on the grimy apron. Her heart was beating unpleasantly fast, but she kept her voice calm.

'I didn't overlook anything,' she said quietly. 'I met Madame Riveau and she was ill and asked me to help her home. I couldn't leave her, so I started to tidy up a little.' She stopped, flushing, while he looked at the bucket of filthy water with raised eyebrows and a half smile which seemed to make nonsense of her words. Maggy felt rage bubble within her, and said in a shaking voice,

'If you think that I was neglectful of your mother, then I am sorry, though I must point out to you that your opinion could have no effect upon my actions as a nurse when I'm needed.'

It was disconcerting when he laughed at this neat speech. He was being hateful! She fixed her eyes on a level with his chin and said, 'Perhaps you will be good enough to look at Madame Riveau.' She took off the apron and tossed it on to the buffet, trying not to see the spots of dirty water on the new dress. Paul shouldered his way past her without a word and bent his length to look at the ill woman, and she, forgetful of their quarrelling, made haste to help him. He was quick and gentle and when he spoke his voice was calmly reassuringly, so that Madame Riveau answered his questions willingly. When he at length straightened up, he turned at once to the door.

'I'm going to ring the hospital and get an ambulance. She'll probably perforate—so the quicker they look at her the better.' He paused, and looked over his shoulder. 'If you have finished your scrubbing by the time I come back, I can give you a lift to Leiden.'

Maggy didn't answer. She would have to go back with him, anyway; it would be quicker. She handed the bucket to Monsieur Riveau with a request for more water; she might as well finish the floor.

She was ready and waiting when she heard the ambulance arrive and stop at the top of the alley. She had scrubbed her hands and arms clean and dried them on the hem of her slip and had tidied her hair; the dress would have to wait until she got back. Paul came in with the ambulance men and she just had time to shake her patient's hand before she was carried away on the stretcher.

Paul stood at the door while she was being stowed away, talking to the Riveau men, and presently they too got into the ambulance. Neither of them had spoken to Maggy; she hadn't expected them to, anyway, and turned away to tidy the bed and lock the back door and turn off the gas. Paul followed her into the little kitchen, and stood watching her hang the apron on the door.

'What about the front door key?' she asked.

'I have it—it goes under a stone in the guttering. Are you ready?' She turned, to find him staring at her. 'That's a pretty dress,' he said equably.

Maggy took a long shuddering breath. 'Are you being beastly?' she asked in a hollow voice. 'It's new and this is the first time I've worn it, and now it's filthy and not pretty at all.'

She turned her back. She thought that she would probably burst into tears at any moment; the desire to do so was overwhelming. So she clamped her nice white teeth together and swallowed down the sobs crowding into her throat. She was succeeding very nicely when he said mildly,

'I'm not being—what was it?—beastly. You must surely know that a potato sack would look—nice—on you.'

Maggy gave a noisy gulp; his voice had sounded gentle and kind.

'Now you've made me cry!' she wailed, and burst into tears after all. Paul turned her round to face him and she made no effort to resist him. 'In that case, have my shoulder to cry on,' he said soothingly. His arm clamped her close while she sniffed and sobbed. She could feel his hand stroking the awful bird's nest of her hair, and presently it calmed her.

'Why were you so angry?' she asked in a watery voice, muffled by the cloth of his jacket.

Paul caught her by the shoulders, so that he could look intently into her damp, blotchy face.

'Is that why you are crying?'

Something in his voice made her heart beat faster. She blinked her puffy lids and stared steadily back at him.

'I'm sorry I was silly—it was because my dress was spoilt.' It was, after all, partly true.

He went on looking at her, and she fidgeted uneasily until he said, 'Of course,' in a dry voice, and went on, 'Here, take my handkerchief.'

He took a hand from her shoulder to search for one, and then stood, still holding her firmly while she dried her tears.

'We were all rather worried when you didn't arrive home—you see, you are always so punctual—and anything might have happened to you. I came into Amsterdam in case you...' he paused, 'no matter. I remembered that you had said that you might see Madame Riveau again, and I felt sure, from what you had said, that you had met her in the Nieuwendijk, so I left the car near the station and walked down on the chance of seeing you. I found Monsieur Riveau instead—I imagine that he shared my doubtful pleasure in renewing our acquaintance.'

Maggy was folding the handkerchief into a neat, sodden square. She said in a small resolute voice, 'I'm sorry if I've caused a bother; I didn't mean to, you know.' She gave the handkerchief a final pat and looked gravely at Paul. 'But I should do the same again...'

He took the handkerchief from her and stowed it in a pocket.

'Yes, I know you would; and you would be quite right, Maggy.' He bent his head and kissed her on the mouth, then stood back and said with a little smile, 'You'd better do something to that hair before we go, or people will think I've been ill-treating you!'

Maggy was glad of something to do. The kiss hadn't meant anything—not for Paul; but it had to her. She turned away and got a comb from her bag, then went into the little front room and did the best she could with her hair. It annoyed her that her hands were shaking so that the pins kept falling out again. She powdered her nose and lipsticked her mouth and felt better. She didn't look too bad in the miserable light of the gas jet. She turned it out and went back to the kitchen and said in a matter-of-fact voice,

'I'm ready, Dr Doelsma.'

It was quite chilly outside, she shivered as she waited for Paul to put the key in its hiding place. He caught her by the arm and started to walk briskly through the dark little cul-de-sac and across the small square to the alley leading to the Nieuwendijk. It was still full of people, most of them walking with the air of those on pleasure bent. Paul took the crown of the narrow street, Maggy's arm still firmly tucked in his. They had only gone a little way when he stopped and pulled her round to face him, ignoring the frustrated, good-natured cyclists weaving around them.

'You're shivering.'

'It's my own fault,' said Maggy soberly. 'It wasn't really warm enough to wear this dress, but I—I wanted to…' Her voice died away uncertainly; she had remembered why she had wanted to wear the dress in the first place. Well, Paul had seen her in it, and a fine sight she had looked!

Paul had let go of her and was taking off his jacket. The comforting warmth of it was already around her shoulders when she started to protest.

'Paul, no! You can't walk through Amsterdam in shirtsleeves and a waistcoat!'

'You called me Paul,' he said quietly.

Maggy felt her face getting hot, and was glad of the dark. 'I wasna' thinking—I didna' guard my tongue…will you take your jacket back?'

He caught her by the arm again, and started to walk her along at a great rate.

'Don't be silly,' was all he said.

Maggy was glad of her long legs to keep up with his. She peeped sideways at him and saw that he was frowning fiercely.

'I'm sorry if I've been tiresome.'

'I've already told you not to be silly.'

There seemed no point in continuing even so meagre a conversation as theirs was. Maggy held her tongue, and continued to do so, sitting quietly in the car beside Paul and saying, 'Yes, Dr Doelsma. No, Dr Doelsma' in appropriate context to the few remarks he made on their homeward journey. When they reached his house, she jumped out quickly, thankful to find the door open. Anny was hovering in the hall. She gave her Paul's jacket, and started up the stairs. She was out of sight by the time he appeared in the doorway.

Mevrouw Doelsma was in her room, lying comfortably on a chaise-longue. She put down her book when she saw Maggy and said in a relieved voice,

'Maggy, there you are! We have all been so worried about you. Fortunately Paul came home early and went at once to Amsterdam. Sit down and tell me all about it; dinner can wait.'

It was during that meal, half an hour later, that it was decided that they should return the following day to Oudehof. Maggy sat listening to the discussion. She wouldn't see much more of Paul—she would be returning to England very soon now; probably before he paid another visit to his mother. She sighed at the sadness of her thoughts, and Paul said,

'Will you be sorry to leave Leiden, Maggy?'

She assumed a determinedly cheerful face. 'Yes, Doctor, but Oudehof is lovely too.'

He nodded. 'A pity you won't be here for the skating.'

It was a nice safe topic, and lasted them until the meal was finished and she was able to slip upstairs and leave Mevrouw Doelsma and Paul to their nightly game. When she went down later to suggest that her patient went to bed, he gave her a cursory glance, wished her goodnight and remarked in casual tones that he would see her in the morning. She waited until she had shepherded Mevrouw Doelsma to the door before replying in a colourless voice,

'Very well, Dr Doelsma—and thank you for bringing me back this evening, and for being so…so…'

He stood looking at her, his mouth faintly curved in a smile.

'Magnanimous?' he suggested.

There were sparks in Maggy's eyes; she drew a deep breath.

'Whatever you say, Doctor,' she said. It was amusing to him, she supposed, to tease her. She started to shut the door.

'You haven't said goodnight, Maggy.'

She paused and looked over her shoulder. 'Goodnight, Doctor.'

'Paul,' he interrupted. He was smiling, and her heart gave a lurch.

'Goodnight, Paul,' she said obediently, and shut the door.

There was no sign of Paul when she went down to breakfast the following morning—Anny offered the information that the doctor had gone out early and would be back later. Maggy ate without appetite and went upstairs to get Mevrouw Doelsma ready for her journey. It was ten o'clock before they were ready and made their way down to the hall. Dr Doelsma was sitting on one of the carved chairs ranged against the wall, reading a newspaper. He looked up unhurriedly as they approached and got up, bidding them a cheerful good morning. His mother turned to make her farewells to Anny, and Maggy found herself a little apart, under a leisurely scrutiny from Paul. She drew her brows together and looked haughtily away, the hateful colour, creeping up her cheeks. She had dressed with care in a blue-green tweed suit, its velvet collar exactly matching the beret which went with it. Her shoes and handbag weren't new, but they were good and beautifully polished. With female logic she had wanted to look her best for this, their probable last meeting. Even if he saw her again, she would most likely be in uniform.

It was a pity that her gaze had settled on a portrait of a Doelsma ancestor—it might have been Paul gazing down at her from the canvas, with the same dark eyebrows and smile.

Paul said softly in her ear, 'Poor Maggy, we're all round you, aren't we?'

She had lost her breath and made do with a dignified nod, only to be plunged into further confusion by his remarking,

'You look delightful. Without retracting anything I may have said about potato sacks, I must admit that your obvious charms are greatly enhanced. Why have I not seen it before? It seems to me that whenever we have met you have been entrenched behind your uniform—you look delightful in that too, but intimidating.'

Maggy raised astonished eyes to his. She asked uncertainly, 'Me? Intimidating?'

'Oh, yes. I was quite terrified of you at St Ethelburga's when we went round your ward.' He went on gravely, his eyes twinkling, 'As stiff as a poker—I longed to pinch you to see if you were real. I kissed you instead, if you remember.' Maggy blushed, and he stood and watched her. 'It was a great relief to find that you were.'

Maggy cast around for an answer to this and failed to find one; it was fortunate that Mevrouw Doelsma was on the point of rejoining them, she would get her goodbyes said quickly. She raised her lovely eyes to Paul and opened her mouth and was on the point of uttering when he said, reading her thoughts, 'My dear good girl, don't say goodbye. I'm driving you back to Oudehof.' He grinned and took his mother's arm, leaving her to take her leave of Anny. When she got outside, Mevrouw Doelsma was already sitting in the back of the car, and Paul was waiting by the open door. 'Get in front,' he said, in a voice which brooked no argument.

Maggy got in without a word and sat passive while he fastened her seat-belt. Her thanks, uttered in a meek voice, caused him to look at her with suspicion.

'You're remarkably humble,' he remarked. She ignored both the tone and the look, and instead looked over her shoulder to where his mother was sitting in the back of the car.

'Mevrouw Doelsma, would you not prefer me to sit with you?'

Her patient barely glanced up from the pile of letters in her lap.

'No, dear. You see I have all these letters to read, and a shopping list to make out for Mrs Pratt—such a good idea of Paul's that I should save myself the trouble of doing it once we get back to Oudehof.' She opened an envelope, smiled vaguely in Maggy's direction, and became at once immersed in its contents.

Paul started the car. 'Never mind,' he said in a maddeningly sympathetic voice, 'It's only for a couple of hours.'

Maggy caught his smile and found herself smiling back and decided, with her usual good sense, to enjoy the present. The future, bleak though it was going to be, could take care of itself, so she sat back composedly, giving no sign of her thumping heart, and was glad when Paul did not appear to notice her pink cheeks and breathless voice.

Once out of Leyden and on to the broad motorway, he started a gentle flow of inconsequential talk which put her so much at her ease that she forgot to be shy, and was soon chattering away with an enjoyment which she refrained from reminding herself would be but short-lived. After fifteen minutes or so, Paul turned off the Amsterdam road. 'We'll go through Haarlem,' he said, 'and Alkmaar. You might as well see as much of Holland as you can before you go back.'

Maggy turned her head to look out of the window; she hadn't wanted to be reminded. She said in a carefully cheerful voice. 'How kind of you. I shall have such a lot to remember…'

She watched the green meadows bordering the road—each with its complement of cows, neatly coated against the chill of autumn. 'I mustn't remember,' she thought. 'I must forget as quickly as possible—perhaps if I'm very busy.' She became aware that he had spoken. 'I'm sorry,' she said. 'I was thinking.'

He smiled slowly; she couldn't see his eyes beneath their drooping lids.

'Madame Riveau asked me to thank you for your help yesterday.' He gentled the Rolls to a smooth standstill, while the road ahead of them lifted itself on a giant hinge to allow a barge of incredible length to ooze its way beneath it on the canal bisecting the road.

Maggy felt contrite. 'Madame Riveau! How awful of me to forget her. Did you telephone the hospital—is she all right?'

The bridge started to swing down. Paul, with his eyes on the traffic lights, said, 'I went to see her this morning—they operated last night. She should do well now—no thanks to those graceless menfolk of hers.'

The Rolls surged ahead again. Maggy took a quick look behind her, to see Mevrouw Doelsma still happily reading her letters. 'I'm glad she'll be well again—she worried me when I had her on my ward at St Ethelburga's.'

'You take your work very seriously, don't you?' Paul asked.

Maggy raised her eyes to his. 'Don't you, too, Doctor?'

His eyes were on the road ahead. They were approaching Haarlem, and he slowed down. 'I? Of course, but I have the advantage over you, have I not? For when I marry, I shall have a wife and children to fill my life, as well as my work.'

The pain in her heart seemed physical. 'You mean that I have only my job? But that keeps me very busy.'

'Don't you want to marry, Maggy?' he asked casually.

'I'm quite happy, Doctor,' she said, and gasped as he said, 'You're a poor liar, my girl,' and before she could think of a reply, 'Mama, shall we stop in Alkmaar for coffee and show Maggy the cheese market?'

The conversation became three-cornered and stayed so until they entered Alkmaar, when Paul slowed the car so that Maggy might admire the grass-encircled water before they entered its narrow streets. It was getting on for midday, and the streets were pleasantly bustling.

'What a cosy place!' Maggy cried.

Paul agreed. 'Though it wasn't always so—the Spaniards laid siege to it in the sixteenth century, you know. I imagine it was far from cosy then.'

They had reached the end of the main street, and he turned the car into a very narrow street, lined with small shops. It opened rather unexpectedly on to a cobbled area, with a canal on one side and a row of houses and shops on the other. In its centre stood the Weigh-House, its delightful step gables climbing upwards, to culminate in a weather vane. Paul parked the Rolls just beyond this fairy-tale edifice and looked at his watch.

'We're just in time to see the clock. Jump out, Maggy.' He leaned across her and undid her belt and opened the door. 'We'll be back in a moment, Mama.'

Maggy found herself being hustled over the cobbles, just in time to watch the quaint little figures appear as the clock chimed. She stood gazing upwards, her eyes alight with interest, her lovely mouth slightly open. Paul stood beside her, an arm flung carelessly around her shoulders. When it was finished she said, 'I think the bells and chimes are the things I'll remember most. They're so beautiful.'

They started back towards the car, walking slowly, his arm still around her while he told her of the town. They collected Mevrouw Doelsma and crossed the cobbles to a small unpretentious café facing them. It was warm and very clean and smelled appetisingly of soup with a distinct whiff of brandy. They sat at a table covered with what Maggy thought was a run, and drank delicious coffee, while the proprietor stood chatting to them. She had to admire the way Paul contrived to translate for her, without interrupting the flow of the conversation.

The weather had clouded over by the time they left the café. There was a cold wind blowing; it ruffled the canal water and made the trees rustle dryly. They got back into the car and Paul drove out of the little town on to the Den Helder road; it ran alongside a canal, running as straight as a ruler through the flat bare country. Maggy didn't care for it, and said so. Paul agreed. 'But I came this way so that you could see as much of Holland as possible. It isn't all as beautiful as the country around Oudehof.'

The road was empty ahead of them. The Rolls flashed along without hindrance. The tall blocks of flats on the outskirts of Den Helder appeared on the skyline. Maggy looked at them with a critical eye and offered the opinion that it appeared to be an ugly place.

'Very ugly,' said Mevrouw Doelsma. 'Fortunately you aren't likely to come this way again; I shall close my eyes,' she added, 'and you can tell me when we get to Hippolytushoef, for there it is much prettier.'

This she did, leaving Paul to point out the meagre attractions of the town and then to explain the far more interesting details of the dyke they were about to cross. They went sedately through the great sluices and on to the road under the great sea dyke wall. Maggy thought it was a pity that it hid the sea from their sight, but the Ijlselmeer on their other side held sufficient of interest to keep her busy asking questions for the first few miles. Paul answered her carefully and with no sign of impatience, until she paused and asked, 'Am I boring you? It must be tedious for you to tell me all this…'

They were approaching the café half way along the Afsluitdijk. The car leapt ahead, eating up distance with effortless ease, as the needle crept up and up. Paul looked at her, and said, unsmiling,

'You never bore me, Maggy, and never will. I thought you knew that.'

'No. I didn't know,' said Maggy. Happiness swelled up inside her; it wouldn't last, but it would be something to treasure—something she wouldn't forget. She fidgeted like an awkward child, knowing that he was looking at her.

'All right, you want to change the subject, don't you?'

He scarcely waited for her nod. 'That's Friesland ahead—once we're on the mainland, we turn off for Bolsward.'

She watched the coastline rushing to meet them, grey against a grey sky, and presently they passed through a tongue of land, standing forlornly with a single row of small houses and a tiny lock, abandoned by the mainland. There was a woman hanging washing on a line in one of the back gardens, and no one else to be seen.

'Do people really live there?' Maggy wanted to know, 'What do they do?'

'Work on the *dijk*, fish...' Paul answered carelessly. 'It's called Kornwerderzand.'

They laughed at her attempts to pronounce it, but after half a dozen attempts she thought she did it rather well—it was another word to add to her small vocabulary.

The mainland was reached and with it the Friesian farmsteads, standing solidly, backed by their enormous barns and surrounded by their acres of rolling meadows. Mevrouw Doelsma gave a satisfied sigh.

'Oh, how nice to be back! I love Leiden, but this is my home.'

'Mother's a dyed-in-the-wool Friesian in everything but size,' Paul teased gently. 'Fortunately for her self-esteem, the girls and I managed to achieve the height and size she had set her heart on.'

He had pulled into the side of the road while a high, wide farm cart, drawn by a magnificent Flemish horse, rolled slowly past.

'Yes, I have been so glad about that,' murmured his mother, 'and now all the children are shooting up so satisfactorily,' she sighed. 'I hope yours will be true Friesians, Paul.'

They were moving again, and on the outskirts of Bolsward.

'We shall have to wait and see, shan't we, Mother?' Paul

answered blandly, and then, 'Look on your left, Maggy, here's the Gemeentehuis you so much admired.'

She looked obediently, glad to have her thoughts diverted, and asked intelligent questions which kept the conversation safely impersonal, if slightly dull. It was a relief to leave Sneek behind and know that the journey was almost over. Probably Paul would go straight back after a late lunch. She fell silent, weighed down by the possibility that she would probably not see him again and that there was nothing that she could do about it. It was with feelings of relief that she saw that they were approaching Oudehof. They swept through the gates, and as Paul stopped the car, the front door opened to reveal Pratt, who had gone back several days earlier, his elderly sombre face wreathed in rare smiles. Mrs Pratt came bustling across the hall as they went in and in a surprisingly short time had them sitting down to the excellent luncheon she had prepared for them.

They had eaten their smoked filleted eel on its hot buttered toast, and were half way through the *Rolpens met Rodekool*—spiced and pickled minced beef and tripe and apples and red cabbage—when Mevrouw Doelsma, who had been talking about nothing in particular, asked,

'Paul, do you have to go back at once?'

He put down his knife and fork and sat back in his high-backed chair so that he could watch Maggy.

'No, Mama. If I may, I'll stay until tomorrow morning.'

Maggy's hands tightened on her own knife and fork, but she didn't look up when his mother said,

'Of course you may stay, Paul. What nonsense to ask when it's your house! I felt sure you would want to go to Utrecht.' He made no answer and she went on airily, 'I suppose I shall have to rest until teatime. May I not lie down on the sofa in the drawing room—just for once?' She looked enquiringly at Maggy, who smiled and said comfortably that she didn't see why not—just for once, and then relapsed into silence while Paul and his mother discussed the visits she was planning to make to her daughters.

It was as they were leaving the dining room that Mevrouw Doelsma said,

'Why don't you take Maggy for a walk, Paul? I'm sure you would both enjoy the exercise.'

Maggy watched the dark brows gather in a frown before he answered shortly. His, 'Yes, of course,' was uninviting. 'Would you like that, Maggy?' He barely glanced at her.

Maggy gave him a cool stare. She loved him with her whole heart, but he could annoy her very much too! 'I think not, thank you, Dr Doelsma, there are several things I should like to do before tea.'

She might have saved her breath. As he opened the door for them to pass through, he said coolly,

'I have some telephone calls to make. I'll be in the study…about ten minutes, if that suits you?'

She made no answer; what was the use? She wasn't going to stand there wrangling about a walk, but she had no intention of going with him, not after that frown. Besides, she told herself for the hundredth time, the less she saw of him before she went back to England, the better.

She followed Mevrouw Doelsma into the drawing room and unhurriedly set about making her comfortable on the large velvet-covered sofa before the log fire, and lingered about her small tasks in the beautiful room, until, lying back against high-piled cushions, glasses and book within reach, her patient said, 'There, Maggy, there's not another thing I want. Go and enjoy your walk.'

But Maggy lingered. 'Would you not like me to read to you, Mevrouw Doelsma?'

'Not today, my dear. I shall go to sleep at once.'

She closed her eyes in proof of her statement, and Maggy walked reluctantly to the door. It was a large double one, but it opened noiselessly under her hand; she closed it quietly behind her. The walls of the old house were very thick, but she didn't think anyone—Paul—would hear her. The study door was across the hall to her left, and she kept her eyes on it as she took off her shoes. If she could get upstairs to her room he would probably forget about the wretched walk. There was a vast expanse of black and white tiles between her and the staircase. Maggy started to cross it, her eyes on the door.

She had almost reached the stairs when she froze at Paul's voice. Without turning round she knew where he was. There was a great chair by one of the console tables on the right of the drawing room door...she hadn't even glanced that way.

'Were you thinking of changing your shoes? There's no need, you know. It isn't wet underfoot.' He was gently mocking; she knew that if she looked at him, he would be smiling. She sat down deliberately on the bottom stair and put on her shoes.

'I did say that I would prefer not to go for a walk, Doctor,' she said in a reasonable voice. 'I meant it.' She ventured to look at him. Yes, he was smiling—she looked away quickly, and reiterated, 'There are some things I wish to do.'

He had got up from his chair. 'Something very secret,' he remarked affably, 'since it requires you to creep about the house in your stockings.' He walked over to where she was standing on the lowest stair, and despite her own six feet, he still looked down at her. 'And now tell me the real reason. Maggy.'

She said, very calm and composed. 'You frowned...

you looked quite—quite saturnine. I have no intention of going for a walk with someone who finds the prospect so unwelcome.'

She turned on her heel and started up the stairs, to be caught round the waist and swung round and put gently on her feet beside him.

He released her at once. 'Maggy, I'm sorry. What an ill-mannered boor you must think me.' His grey eyes looked very bright; she wanted to look away and found she couldn't. 'Will it be enough if I say that I should very much like to go walking with you?'

It was impossible to say no when he was looking at her like that. She went over to the table where she had put hat and gloves, and he followed her over and opened a drawer, pulled out a scarf and tossed it to her.

'Here,' he said lightly, 'tie your hair up in this—there's a wind blowing.'

They went out of the door together and started down the short drive.

'Let's go to the village—have you seen the church?'

'No,' said Maggy. 'It's always shut, and I didn't know how to ask for the key.'

He gave her a brief look. 'Poor girl, we've treated you very badly. You've been left a great deal to your own devices, haven't you?'

Maggy looked surprised. 'I'm not on holiday, Doctor.'

Paul looked as though he was about to say something else, but he remained silent, striding along the pleasant road. Maggy for once was glad to match him for size; anyone smaller would have been running by now… Stien, for instance. She squashed the thought— she would enjoy herself; had Paul not said that he had wanted to take her walking? She looked at him and met the same bright gaze she had found so disturbing in the hall. He blinked rapidly and his eyes were their usual cool grey once more.

'We're on a dead dyke,' he explained. Maggy stood still and looked around her. They were indeed walking above the level of the fields all around them. But the sea was several miles away.

'It's not needed any more,' she hazarded. 'You reclaimed the land, and so another dyke was built…'

'Clever girl!' He sounded pleased at her interest. By the time they reached the village, he had told her all about Sleepers and Dreamers and Watchers.

'Such lovely names,' she said. 'They sound like sentinels on duty.'

Paul smiled. 'But that's just what they are,' he said.

They were in the village by now and he slowed his pace a little. The few people about greeted him with smiles and nods and incomprehensible words.

'We like to speak our own language,' he explained briefly as he knocked on the door of a very small house indeed; the end one in a similar row. 'You were disgusted with Madame Riveau's house, weren't you? Now you shall see how a Friesian housewife keeps house.'

The woman who answered the door was big and tall—as tall as Maggy herself—but no longer young. When she saw Paul she beamed and shook hands, and when he introduced Maggy, wrung her hand too.

'We're to go inside and have tea—Mevrouw Stijlma is the sexton's wife; we can get the keys of the church from her.'

The three of them almost filled the tiny room. Maggy, pushed gently into a chair by Paul, looked around her with interest.

'May I stare?' she enquired of him. 'I know it's rude, but there's so much to see.'

The room sparkled and shone with a perfection of cleanliness Maggy had seldom seen. The walls were almost covered with enlarged photos, some of them a dingy brown with age, and all framed in dark wood. They jostled some of the most beautiful plates; worthy of a museum. The mantelpiece was shrouded in plum-coloured chenille with an important bobble fringe; it held brass candlesticks of as fine a workmanship as could be found. She guessed that they were probably two hundred years old. The furniture was solid and Victorian in style and draped in snowy antimacassars, but the wooden chairs round the table were painted in the traditional bright colours of Hindeloopen and were a great deal older than the rest of the furniture.

Paul left her to gaze her fill, and then asked, 'Well?'

'It's so clean. I mean everything—and some of the things are beautiful.'

Her startled eye lighted on a large woollen square hung on the wall, woven into a startling picture of unlikely kittens and a ball of very pink wool. Next to it hung a sampler, exquisitely stitched and almost colourless with age.

'Things get handed down from one generation to another.' Paul's eyes were twinkling. 'There's quite a variety.'

They drank their tea, milkless and in paper-thin cups, while he and the sexton's wife talked with little pauses while the conversation was translated for Maggy's benefit. After a little while they took their leave, the church keys swinging from Paul's hand.

It was a large church, old and rather austere, with a thin spire crowned by its weathercock. Paul opened the low wide door and it creaked ajar to let them pass through. It was quiet and cool inside, with plain white-washed walls and no stained glass windows or ornaments, and no flowers. Maggy found it very much to her taste, for it reminded her of the bare little church near her own home. It seemed natural for Paul to take her hand and lead her down the centre aisle between the high wooden pews with their carved ends, each with its card, neatly inserted in its brass holder, bearing the names of its occupants. He stopped by the front pew and she stooped down to see his name, Van Beijen Doelsma, and his mother's name beneath it, and when she looked at the stone flags they were standing upon, his name was there too. The letters were impossible to understand but the name was clear and the date: 1649.

She said quietly, 'It makes you feel small, doesn't it?' and then, 'You really belong here, don't you?'

They were peering up at a wall plaque, a riot of carved plumes, elaborate scrolls and cherubim arranged around the stone profile of a haughty-looking gentleman with a determined chin and a Napoleonic hairstyle.

'Great-great-Grandfather,' said Paul. 'He didn't take kindly to being occupied by the French troops under Napoleon. He spent a lot of time in prison, leaving his wife to bring up six children—they're all here—each generation follows the same pattern of life as the previous one. We are christened and married and buried here.' He looked down at her. 'And I shall follow that pattern.'

Maggy had a sudden blindingly vivid picture of Stien standing in the aged church, a vision in white satin and tulle. She said hastily, to forget it, 'Won't that be rather difficult for you? You work in Leiden and you are often in Utrecht.'

They moved slowly side by side down the aisle and contemplated the magnificent sounding-board above the pulpit.

'I shan't need to go to Utrecht so often,'—Maggy silently agreed; he would have Stien with him always, wouldn't he?—'We'll spend the week in Leiden and come up here for weekends, and my wife and children will do the same.'

'Naturally,' murmured Maggy. She supposed Stien wouldn't mind—after all, she would have the best of both worlds and Paul for a husband; what more could any girl want?

They wandered slowly to the door and so out into the late afternoon and back down the road to return the keys to Mevrouw Stijlma, and when they turned to leave, Maggy, rather shyly, said, '*Dag,* Mevrouw,' which released a flood of kindly praise, not one word of which she could understand.

'Very nice,' said Paul. 'Have you managed to acquire any Dutch while you've been in Holland?' He sounded really interested, and Maggy was emboldened to recite her vocabulary—a hotch-potch of words she had heard and remembered to look up in her dictionary. He laughed a good deal at some of them, and spent the whole of the walk back to Oudehof explaining the complications of Dutch grammar to her. Maggy listened attentively and thought wistfully that there were more interesting things to talk of other than the pitfalls to be found in the Dutch language.

The afternoon had become unpleasantly chilly by the time they had reached the house. Great clouds billowed over the wide sky, the wind tore at Maggy's headscarf and whipped her hair around her face. The hall was warm and welcoming. Maggy stood at the foot of the staircase, taking off her gloves. Her face glowed with the chill; her eyes sparkled. She refused Paul's offer of tea and in reply to his enquiry as to whether she had enjoyed her walk, said soberly,

'Aye, it was a grand wee walk, Dr Doelsma. Thank you for showing me the kirk…'

He interrupted her rather impatiently.

'There's no question of thanks, Maggy. I don't know when I have enjoyed a walk so much, perhaps because I seldom have the chance of airing my knowledge to such a good listener as yourself.'

'Och, aye,' Maggy said shortly. Her brows knitted into a frown; she was suddenly out of temper with her world. If it had been Stien with Paul, it wouldn't have mattered what sort of a listener he had…

'I'm away to Mevrouw Doelsma.' She didn't look at him, but went upstairs at a great rate, her long legs taking two steps at a time.

By the time she had left Mevrouw Doelsma there wasn't more than half an hour to dinner. She changed rapidly into the pink dress and pinned her hair neatly. It was still damp from her bath and she brushed the curly tendrils tidily aside, and then, when they sprang loose again, threw down her brush with an unwonted impatience, and with barely a second glance in the mirror went down to the drawing room to find Mevrouw Doelsma and the doctor already there.

Dinner passed pleasantly enough. The talk was of the kind that needed very little thought, the food and pleasant surroundings had their effect on her. Maggy rose from the table quite cheerful and went as usual to her room while Paul and his mother had their hour or so together. It was almost ten o'clock when she returned to the drawing room. Mevrouw Doelsma was more than ready for bed and got up at once and kissed her son. 'Goodnight, Paul. I'll see you before you go in the morning.'

'Of course.' He looked at Maggy standing quietly near the door. She said goodnight, too, but he didn't answer at once, and she turned to go. He said, at his most persuasive, 'Come riding in the morning, Maggy? Is seven o'clock too early for you?'

She hadn't meant to say yes. She was half way up the

stairs, still trying to decide why she had been so weak-willed, and at the same time bubbling over with happiness.

It was a wild grey morning, but dry, Maggy was at the stables well before the hour, to find the doctor gentling Cobber and Biddy ready for her. They swung into the saddles and started off across the park and out into the little lane at its back, not hurrying, but talking idly. She was completely taken by surprise when Paul said casually,

'I should like to take you out, Maggy. Perhaps we could have dinner and dance somewhere, if you would like that.'

She took so long to reply that he turned to look at her.

'Of course, if you don't want to, my dear girl, don't hesitate to say so.'

'Of course I want to come!' Maggy burst out, and stopped. She did, but was it rather unwise? She squashed her more prudent thoughts, and said, 'You see, I haven't a dress.'

He chuckled. 'That's the first time I've heard that used as an excuse for not going on a date! Usually it's the other way round; surely an invitation is a good reason for buying a new dress?'

They turned the horses and started for home.

'Mother shall go with you to Leeuwarden. You may have discovered already that she loves to shop. There's bound to be something to fit you there. They cater for big women here, you know.'

Maggy said indignantly, 'I wish you wouldn't call me a big woman!'

He gave her a sideways glance; there was a gleam in his eye. 'Certainly I won't call you a big woman if you don't like it. I can think of several alternatives—shall I try out a few?'

Maggy frowned. 'No,' she said severely.

He said. 'Just as you like, Maggy,' in a deceptively meek

voice, so that she had to laugh. 'That's better,' he said. 'Now about this evening…'

He left soon after breakfast, and his mother came down to see him off.

'You'll be in Leiden for lunch,' she remarked.

'I'm going to Utrecht, Mother.' He was stuffing papers into a briefcase.

'I can't think why you don't live there!' his mother declared rather pettishly.

'Yes, you can, dearest. You know how much I am attached to my home in Leiden, I could never give it up. Besides, my son must inherit it in his turn, must he not?'

Maggy, standing rather uncertainly close by, not sure if she was wanted, heard him. He looked very handsome and more arrogant than ever. She thought of him in his house on the Rapenburg, with a very large family and a devoted and well-loved wife. She couldn't bear it and turned to slip quietly upstairs, but he had seen her move and put out a long arm and swung her round to walk with them to the door, where he kissed his mother, then turned and dropped a light kiss on the tip of her own nose and got into his car and drove away.

He had said that he was coming back in two days' time to take her out. Maggy had plenty of time to think about it meanwhile. She supposed that the evening out was a kind of thank-you from a grateful employer. She would be going back to England in a few days, just as soon as she heard from Matron. Paul, she thought without conceit, had grown to like her as a friend, and there was no reason why two friends shouldn't have a pleasant evening together. She hadn't expected to see him again; she would make the most of what would most certainly be their last meeting.

CHAPTER EIGHT

MAGGY STOOD in front of the mirror in her bedroom at Grotehof, and looked at herself. She supposed she was all right—it was a pity that there was so much of her—but the dress was certainly rather nice, cream guipure lace over a matching slip with a narrow blue velvet ribbon at the waist. It just skimmed her knees, showing off her long legs to advantage; it was sleeveless too. She had been rather doubtful about so much bosom showing, but Mevrouw Doelsma had told her that a low décolleté was quite a proper thing.

Maggy gave her hair a final pat, picked up her little evening purse and went downstairs. Paul and his mother were sitting by the fire in the hall. He saw her first and got up and came towards her, looking elegant and immensely tall. She stood shyly on the bottom step while he looked her frankly up and down.

'Delightful, Maggy. I can see that you will turn all the men's heads this evening.'

But not yours, Paul, she thought, and added out loud, 'Och, who'd want to look at a great lass like me?'

She went over to the fire to show herself to Mevrouw Doelsma, who pronounced herself more than satisfied with Maggy's appearance.

'I'll get my coat,' said Maggy, but before she could take more than a couple of steps, Paul stopped her.

'It will be quite chilly later on—it's a long drive.' He took no notice of her look of surprise, but went on, 'I wondered if you would like to borrow Cousin Marthe's coat—it's only gathering dust in a closet upstairs.' He lifted an armful of superb cashmere coat from the back of one of the chairs, and stood holding it out.

Maggy put out a hand and touched it. 'It's beautiful!' she breathed. 'It looks like cashmere.'

'It is cashmere,' he answered.

'But I can't wear it; what would your cousin say?'

The doctor looked at her, his head a little on one side.

'Nothing at all,' he said, with perfect truth. He strode forward and wrapped it around Maggy. 'It fits you very well, too,' he said, avoiding his mother's eye.

Maggy walked slowly over to the large gilt-framed mirror on one wall, and stood in front of it, stroking the coat gently. 'I've never had a cashmere coat,' she murmured. She looked anxiously at the doctor over one shoulder. 'Is it not impertinent to wear something so costly? I mean—' she sought for words—'I would never be able to buy a coat like this one in my whole life.'

Paul was getting into his own coat and replied easily,

'Well, if it were an old coat, you'd not think twice about it, would you? But we haven't an old tweed coat to fit you, so you'll have to do with this one.' He didn't give Maggy time to think too deeply about this, but he had spoken in such a matter-of-fact voice that her face cleared and she walked over to Mevrouw Doelsma with her doubt dispelled, and said goodnight before going out to the car with the doctor.

It was barely half-past six. Paul allowed the Rolls to idle

along the narrow road to Heerenveen, but once on the main road to the south he allowed the needle to creep up to the hundred mark and steady itself there. He settled himself so that he could watch her face, and said,

'Do you like travelling fast, Maggy?'

'Aye, I like it fine, Doctor.' She gave him a fleeting smile. 'Though I'd not dare myself,' she added truthfully. 'I'd not feel safe.'

'I trust you feel safe with me?'

She laughed. 'You know I do, Doctor.'

He sighed loudly. 'Maggy, must we have this formality? If my memory serves me aright, you've called me Paul on previous occasions.'

She said, with rather a heightened colour, 'Well, I was a wee bit fashed…'

'Is it only when you're fashed that you forget to guard your tongue, Maggy?'

She made a fierce little sound; the weak ghostling of some old Gaelic word. 'I shall not say, Doc…'

'Paul,' he said.

'Paul,' she finished.

He chuckled and gentled the Rolls back to a ladylike pace as they went through Amersfoort, so that he could point out some of the more interesting aspects of the pleasant town. 'We're almost there,' he said.

Maggy gave him a questioning look. 'It's a long way to come for dinner,' she said. 'Wasn't there anything nearer Oudehof?'

The doctor's lips twitched as he thought of the numbers of young ladies who had been only too glad to travel for an hour in his company.

'Is my company so irksome?' he asked. 'I thought you would like the ride; I'm sorry if you have found it boring.'

He kept his attention on the road as they passed an articulated lorry, travelling hell-for-leather from Germany to the coast; he was trying not to laugh.

Maggy gave a gasp, and put a hand on his knee, 'I didn't mean that,' she uttered. 'You must know I didn't, I wanted to go out with you.' She took a sharp breath—she hadn't meant to say quite that—and made haste to modify it. 'I mean,' she said carefully, 'you've gone to so much trouble to arrange the evening, even finding a coat for me—and there must be any number of hotels near Leeuwarden where we could have gone, and you need not have spent the entire evening…' She stopped. He had steered the car into the slow traffic lane, and now he took a hand off the wheel and covered hers with it. He wasn't laughing any more.

'Maggy, stop! Why do you suppose I asked you out this evening?'

'Well, Doc… Paul,' she explained, 'I think it's a…a kind of treat because my job is finished and I'll be leaving…'

'A sweet after the medicine?' he asked quietly.

'Aye, that's it.'

He pulled into the side of the motorway and stopped the car, then turned deliberately in his seat so that he could see her.

'I asked you out because I wanted to spend an evening with you, Maggy—I enjoy your company. I am not giving you a treat—I am the one who is having that. You could have easily refused to come.'

She looked back at him steadily. 'I never thought to do that,' she replied honestly.

He switched on the engine again. 'Having cleared up that knotty little problem, let's dine. I hope you're hungry, for I'm famished. Years ago, I took a girl out to dinner at this same place. She was very small and dainty and had an appetite to match. She refused almost all solid food, and I spent a dreadful evening, dancing on an empty stomach.' They laughed together and fell into a comfortable discussion about food, until he drew up outside the imposing doors of the Hotel Kasteel Hooge Vuursche. Maggy found its splendid magnificence rather overpowering, but she suffered the cashmere coat to be taken from her, and followed the waiter to a table on the edge of the dance floor. Paul following her, nodded to several acquaintances, and watched the interested glances cast at Maggy. She didn't seem to notice them, but sat down with charming dignity, as though she were in the habit of dining there every evening. She studied the menu card, and Paul picked up his own and waited, not sure if her schoolgirl French could cope with it. Presently he said, 'Is there anything particular you would like, or will you leave it to me?'

She gave him a grateful glance. 'Please will you choose? Though I would very much like to try the *caneton à la Rouennaise*'—she pronounced it beautifully.

The doctor wondered where she had got her knowledge of the famous dish, but was far too well-mannered to ask; but she seemed to think that an explanation was due to him.

'I've never eaten it—I've never been to a restaurant grand enough to serve it—but the laird—my father is his factor—used to walk with me sometimes and talk about food, and it was one of the dishes he told me I must try if ever I had the opportunity.'

'It's an excellent choice, Maggy. Shall we have *consommé* first and then *Sole Normande*, and finish with a *bombe bouché aux fruits?*'

'It sounds lovely.' She looked around her while he conferred with the waiter. This done, he sat back in his chair and said,

'And now I'll answer the questions I can see trembling on your lips. You want to know what the place is and how old it is and who lived here, don't you?'

Maggy looked surprised. 'Yes, I do, but how did you know?'

'You have an expressive face; besides, I can read your thoughts.' He spoke lightly and plunged into the hotel's history until he was interrupted by the wine waiter. Maggy allowed her gaze to wander once more—it really was delightful, and very smart. She had never been to anything quite like it before, and, she reminded herself soberly, was very unlikely to do so again. She was glad she had on a pretty dress. Would they dance? she wondered. The band seemed good. She turned back to Paul, to find him watching her.

'We'll have a drink, then perhaps you would like to dance?'

The drinks were brought, and she wasn't quite sure what they were.

The doctor raised his glass. 'Champagne cocktail,' he explained, 'to put wings on our feet.'

Maggy didn't need wings. She was a good dancer and as light as a feather despite her size. They were well matched, and circled the floor, not speaking; it didn't seem necessary.

They went back to their table and started a leisurely dinner, and when the waiter removed the remains of the *Sole Normande,* Paul stretched out a hand. 'Let's dance again, shall we?'

Maggy got up at once, her eyes sparkling and her cheeks pink with excitement and the excellent champagne he had chosen. The band was playing a Viennese waltz and they drifted around, scarcely talking. His arm tightened around her and she raised her face to his, smiling, and said, 'I could dance for hours—it's wonderful!'

'You're a beautiful dancer, Maggy.' He was staring down at her.

'And you're a beautiful woman too.' He spoke quietly, without smiling.

Her eyes widened. 'Thank you,' she stammered a little. 'I've never been called beautiful before, it makes a wonderful evening even more wonderful.'

'Don't you believe me?'

She smiled and shook her head. 'No, not really, but it's nice all the same.'

The duckling was everything it should have been, so that it seemed sacrilege to follow it with anything else, but the *bombe bouché aux fruits* was perfection of its kind. When she had eaten the last morsel, Maggy said, 'I'll never forget this dinner, or any moment of this evening.'

'Nor I,' he replied. 'I have seldom enjoyed myself so much. What shall we do, talk or dance?'

'Both,' she answered promptly. 'I should like to know more about the hospital at Leiden.'

He obliged her with a great many interesting details, and she listened absorbed, until he said suddenly,

'You know, it's a great waste of time to talk about work when we could be dancing.' They danced for an hour or more, and if they talked Maggy had no idea what the conversation was about. They were standing waiting for the band to play an encore, when she asked,

'I wonder what the time is?'

Paul looked at his watch. 'Almost twelve.'

'It can't be! We must go home; you have to be in Utrecht by ten tomorrow—you said so.'

The band started up again. He scooped her up neatly, and they were half way round the room before he answered her.

'Plenty of time if I leave Oudehof by eight o'clock.'

'But we're not there yet.'

'What a fearful bully you are, Maggy! We'll go after this dance, provided you promise not to say another word.'

They finished their dance in a companionable silence, and went outside to the car. The night air was cool, and there was plenty of wind, but the sky was clear. Maggy was glad of the soft warmth of the sable coat, despite the warmth of the car. She sat quietly beside Paul, and he didn't speak until they were clear of Baarn.

'Tired?' he asked.

'No, not a bit. It's just so restful sitting here while you drive; and my head's buzzing with the wonderful evening I've had.'

He said he was delighted to hear it, and led the conversation round to her family and home, but while she answered his apparently guileless questions readily enough, she gave him no clue as to where her home actually was. She had told him that it was in the Highlands; but that was a vast, sparsely populated area. He tried again now, but she changed the subject gently but firmly enough for him to be unable to continue with his questions without being guilty of bad manners. He followed her lead, and Maggy sighed with relief. She had made up her mind that when she left Oudehof it would be with no trace of herself left behind.

There was a light in the hall when they returned, Paul got out of the car and opened the big door for her, then said, 'There'll be hot coffee in the kitchen. I'll put the car away while you fill the mugs.'

Maggy waited for the doctor, sitting on the kitchen table, swinging her long shapely legs. She was in a dream-like state of happiness which she was well aware was only temporary; but the future seemed a long way off at that moment. Paul came in and closed the door quietly behind him, and Maggy slid off the table and poured the coffee, then went and sat sedately in the comfortable old Windsor chair near the stove. The doctor, mug in hand, leaned against the table, watching her. Presently he spoke. 'Shall we go riding before breakfast, Maggy?'

Maggy looked at the old wall clock; it was already three—she didn't feel in the least tired. She agreed happily.

'About seven? Just a quick gallop before you go? I'd like that fine.'

Their eyes met and held and she felt the pink creeping into her cheeks, and hoped he wouldn't see it by the single light she had switched on; she found it impossible to look away.

'Why do you stare so?' she asked at length.

'I'm sorry,' he said quietly. 'I was remembering the night you came down here armed with the poker...'

'Stien was here.' Maggy spoke before she had thought, and then went on, deliberately giving herself the hurt. 'She is the loveliest girl I have ever seen.'

A look of faint surprise crossed the doctor's face as he answered coolly. 'Yes, she is, isn't she? She will make a most decorative wife.'

Maggy stared down at her mug, the pretty colour fading from her cheeks. She had read a number of novels in which the heroine fell in love with an unresponsive hero, and she now knew exactly how the poor girl felt—only, unlike the girl in the novel, she saw little chance of falling into his arms on the last page.

'You're not listening,' his voice interrupted her unhappy thoughts, and she looked up and said in a bright little voice, unlike hers.

'I'm so sorry.' The change was so sudden that his

eyebrows rose in surprise, but before he could comment upon it she stood up.

'I think I'll go to bed. Thank you again for a lovely evening.' Even in her own ears this sounded rather bald, and she cast around for something else to say. 'I expect you go there quite often.'

The doctor was looking at her with narrowed eyes, and answered slowly.

'I think I'll must have taken every girl I ever knew there at some time or other.'

Maggy said, 'Oh!' and scrutinised her nails with care. 'It's a wonderful way to spend an evening.' Her voice was still dreadfully bright.

He agreed, lounging on the table, his eyes on her face. 'Does it surprise you to know that I cannot remember a single girl I took there?'

'Not even Stien?' she asked.

Paul looked puzzled. 'Stien?' He stood up. 'Yes, of course—she being the last of a long line of girls.' He started walking towards Maggy. 'It's strange how, when you meet the woman of your dreams, no one and nothing else matters.'

Maggy listened to his deep voice; he was telling her, very tactfully, that he was going to marry Stien. She would have to go quickly, before she made a fool of herself. She swept the mugs into the sink with the briskness of an early morning east wind, and turned a determinedly cheerful face to him.

'Now I really am going to bed—and I don't think I'll ride in the morning after all. It's so very late, isn't it?' She smiled woodenly and said goodnight and thank you like a well-brought-up child, then went to the door.

Paul was there before her, standing in front of it, searching her face. He looked more arrogant than ever and rather angry as well.

'Ah!' he said softly. 'Maggy is annoyed, and I wonder why, I know of no reason, but I can provide you with one…'

He bent his head, and his mouth came down on hers. His kiss was hard, and without tenderness. She saw the half mocking smile on his lips and ran from the room without a word, scarlet with mortification, trying not to cry.

She didn't sleep. At six o'clock she heard his steps on the drive outside, and a little later, the sound of Cobber's hooves. She got up and dressed, waited until she heard the Rolls stealing away, and then went downstairs to her break-fast. She wondered if there would be a note…then decided that Paul wasn't the sort of man to leave notes. All the same she looked carefully in all the most likely places, before going sadly upstairs again to re-do her face and put on a bright smile, before going along to Mevrouw Doelsma's room to regale her with a detailed account of her evening out.

CHAPTER NINE

MATRON'S LETTER arrived the next morning, like an answer to Maggy's rather muddled prayers.

It was kind, to the point and brief. Matron wrote to say that if Sister MacFergus could return to duty as soon as possible it would be most convenient, as a number of the nursing staff were off sick... She was hers sincerely, Agatha Humble.

Maggy, that strictly reared member of the Scottish Kirk, was also a true daughter of the Highlands; she could see that Matron's letter was an omen. Without allowing herself more than a few moments' thought of Paul, she sat down at the charming writing desk in her room and answered the letter, assuring Matron that she would return at the earliest time convenient to her patient. Then she went in search of Mevrouw Doelsma and showed her Matron's missive.

Mevrouw Doelsma read it through, dabbed her eyes, and said tearfully,

'Of course you must go, Maggy. I know it's selfish of me to keep you, though I don't know how I'll get on without you; you are so kind and sweet. And what will Paul say?' she went on.

Maggy was half turned away from her, looking out of

the windows, across the pleasant gardens. 'I think the doctor knows that I will be returning to England soon.'

'Yes, of course, dear; but surely not as soon as this? When do you suppose you should go?' She looked at her watch. 'Not today, surely? Oh, dear! He will be vexed—he went to Munich to lecture for two days.'

Maggy tried to feel pleased at this news. She need not see him again.

'Then the doctor mustn't be bothered,' she said firmly. 'We...we more or less said goodbye last night. Perhaps I could get a flight tomorrow?'

Mevrouw Doelsma looked at her, began to say something, thought better of it and said, 'Yes, Maggy, of course. Pratt shall ring through to Schiphol and see if they can get you on to a flight. He'll take you down in the car.' She raised a sudden authoritative hand as Maggy started to protest. 'No, I insist. If Paul were here, he would have driven you himself. Now ring for Pratt, please, dear.'

There was a seat on a KLM plane the following evening, Maggy agreed with Mevrouw Doelsma in a rather hollow voice that everything was most satisfactory.

As it was Maggy's last day, her patient insisted that they should go out for a last ride. Maggy drove to Franeker and they visited the Solarium and then went on to Sneek and dawdled between the lakes. The weather was chilly and overcast; the Dutch countryside looked sad—probably at the thought of the cold winter ahead. They arrived back in time for tea, a meal which Mevrouw Doelsma had kept essentially English, abetted by Mrs Pratt, who had a strong belief that tea was not tea without scones and fruit cake and muffins in their season.

Maggy, pouring tea from the lovely silver pot into the delicate cups, wondered if she would ever enjoy hospital tea again. She packed before dinner, and went to Mevrouw Doelsma's room as was her custom. The little lady pressed a fair-sized box in her hands, and begged her to accept it as a small parting gift. Maggy, who had retained a childish delight in receiving presents, sat down at once and undid the wrappings.

The box contained a soft kid leather handbag; its magnificence rendered her speechless for a moment. She stammered her thanks and Mevrouw Doelsma reached up and kissed her and said, 'There, Maggy, it will last you all your life, and every time you use it, you'll remember me,' and she burst into tears.

Maggy hugged her gently. 'I'll remember you even without your lovely present to remind me.'

'And Paul—will you remember Paul too?'

Maggy managed a smile, and said quite naturally, 'Yes, I shall remember Paul too.'

They played bezique after dinner, until Mevrouw Doelsma declared that she was tired and said goodnight and went up to bed. Once there, however, she went straight to the telephone and dialled her son's home in Leiden. Anny answered and she wasted no words before asking,

'Did Mr Paul leave a telephone number with you, Anny?'

'No, madam. He usually does, but this was only a short trip; but I think I can get a message to the University early tomorrow—he has a lecture there at nine, but he might be able to telephone you before then.'

Mevrouw Doelsma considered this advice and said, 'Yes, do that, Anny. Please tell him that Sister MacFergus is leaving tomorrow evening from Schipol. He could telephone here if he wishes.' She paused. 'You are sure you can get him, aren't you, Anny?'

Anny was sure. 'I can contact the head porter, madam,

and he will see that Master Paul gets your message when he arrives.' Mevrouw Doelsma rang off, satisfied.

The doctor arrived in good time to give his lecture. He had, during the course of a wakeful night, decided to leave Munich as soon as was decently possible. There was a dinner that evening which he should attend. He would take an early morning flight to Schipol, telephone Pratt to bring the car to the airport, and go straight to Oudehof. He had to see Maggy.

He went thoughtfully through the imposing doors and looked up, vaguely irritated, as the porter called him by name, and then ran out from his little lodge in the entrance hall. Paul listened to Anny's message without comment, grey eyes staring at the man from a white face. He thanked him politely, asked him to dial a number at Oudehof, just after ten o'clock, when his first lecture would be over, and strode on to the lecture hall, where, with an iron self-control which did not allow of his thoughts straying to Maggy, he delivered one of the best lectures he had ever given.

He was in the consultants' room, talking quietly with a group of doctors, when his call came through. He took it in a quiet corner of the room, away from the others.

Pratt's voice came, clear and rather thin, over the wire. 'Mr Paul? I'll fetch Madam at once.'

The doctor said quietly, 'Wait, Pratt. Please find Sister MacFergus, and ask her to speak to me, and send someone to ask my mother to come to the telephone meanwhile. Hurry, will you? I have only a few minutes.'

He sat patiently until he heard his mother's voice.

'Paul? They're looking for Maggy. She's leaving just after lunch, and catching the eight o'clock plane. I—I tried to stop her, dear.'

'Don't worry, Mother; I'm sure you did all you could.'

'Yes, I did, Paul. But when Maggy told me that you'd already said goodbye and that you would understand why she was going, there wasn't much I could say.'

'No, of course not, dearest.' He spoke slowly, looking at the wall in front of him, remembering Maggy's soft lips under his.

'Pratt's here,' his mother told him. 'No one can find Maggy. Perhaps she is out.' She sounded doubtful.

The doctor looked at the clock on the wall before him. He had less than three minutes before the next lecture; the room was emptying already. He spoke unhurriedly.

'Mother, will you tell Maggy to wait in the reception hall at Schipol. I'll try and get a seat on the early evening plane from here. I believe it gets in thirty minutes before her flight leaves—No, that's not enough time; ask her to transfer to the ten o'clock flight.'

He said goodbye, hung up and went back to the lecture hall; pausing at the lodge to tell the porter to get him a seat on the plane leaving Munich just before five o'clock that afternoon.

Maggy hated saying goodbye; it was with a feeling almost of relief that she saw the last of Oudehof as Pratt drove through the gates on to the main road and turned the car towards the Afsluitdijk. It was, he declared, the quickest way to the airport, even if not the prettiest. It was a sad, grey day, and Maggy's face reflected the sadness. Pratt, a kindly man, did his best to maintain a cheerful conversation, and Maggy realising it, answered him civilly in an unhappy voice, telling herself that none of it was true, and that presently she would wake up and find herself back in her bedroom at Oudehof.

They got to Schiphol with almost an hour to spare. Pratt shepherded her past authority, found her a seat in the reception hall, and wished her a reluctant farewell, adding the fervent hope that they would all be seeing her again before very long. She shook his hand and laughed a little and said,

'I think that is most unlikely, Pratt, but I shall remember these few weeks all my life, and Mrs Pratt's and your kind help to me.'

She watched his elderly back disappearing through the door, and felt suddenly very lonely. He was her last link with Paul. She looked at her watch; she had almost half an hour before her plane left; the doctor's flight was due in fifteen minutes. Not very long for her to decide how to avoid him. When Mevrouw Doelsma had given her his message, she had realised at once that she must not see him again. She had heard Pratt and Mrs Pratt calling to her that morning because the doctor was on the phone and wanted to speak to her, and she had stayed quiet in the stable with Cobber, longing to go. She had no idea what he would or what he could want to say to her; only she wanted to hear his voice, just once more.

Now she looked around her. There were a great many people milling around—late holidaymakers; business men; a small group of nuns, even a party of uniformed schoolgirls in charge of a harassed teacher. Maggy walked slowly towards them, wishing that it was time to board the plane. The temptation to go to the desk and get a transfer to the later plane was very strong, but she fought it back; there was no point in seeing Paul again. She looked nervously at the clock, then at her watch, and saw with a kind of despair that it wanted a minute to the half-hour. There was a plane circling to land—it touched down as she watched from the window; that would be Paul's plane. She would be gone by the time he had cleared Customs and reached the departure hall.

In sudden panic she visualised him finding her before she could get away, and turned to see the long straggling queue, already spilling back into the hall from the pier leading to her gate. The hall seemed very empty. If she took her place at the back of the queue now, he would be sure to see her; she had her wretched size to thank for that certainty. She looked at the clock again; ten minutes had gone by, but the obedient crocodile was still standing patiently, waiting for the gate to open. There had been a delay perhaps, some small hitch; just enough to spoil her careful, unhappy planning. She wasted precious seconds, imagining Paul coming through the doors at the far end of the hall, and seeing her—and saying what? She only had to stay where she was to find out...

Maggy turned with a resolution she was far from feeling. She had to get to the head of the queue; she could see the gate at the far end of the pier. It was still shut, almost obscured by a bevy of navy blue school hats. She began to weave her way through the waiting passengers—a slow business with frequent pauses while she explained that she was travelling with the school party in front. She reached her goal at last, and smiled with such friendliness and relief at the schoolteacher that the worried little woman imagined that she must be someone she had met at some time, and smiled back and even made a remark about the delay, so that those in the queue behind who suspected Maggy of jumping the line decided that they had been mistaken after all. The man at the gate shared their views too, and told Maggy cheerfully that the girls would soon be safely on board—the delay wouldn't last more than another ten minutes or so.

Maggy stood very still, not daring to turn around, realising sickeningly that by some stroke of fate she stood head and shoulders above her immediate neighbours. It was five past eight when the gate opened, and the first reluctant schoolgirl went through. Maggy looked back. Paul was approaching the pier; he looked immense and confident, and rather arrogant, even at that distance. He looked at her over the heads of the people between them. Their eyes met for a long moment before she turned quickly, showed her ticket, and walked as fast as possible to the waiting plane.

Paul watched the big KLM plane glide down the runway and waited until it was a speck in the grey, darkening sky, before he made his way to a telephone booth and rang Pratt. Having done this, he went and sat down, outwardly composed and patient, waiting for him to bring the Rolls back to the airport.

He replied to Pratt's greeting with a brief grunt, then took the wheel himself and drove the short distance to Leiden at a speed which left his faithful friend and servant speechless. His house reached, Paul left Pratt to put the car away and went indoors, throwing his coat and gloves on to a chair as he strode through the hall to his study. A few minutes later, Pratt, on his way to the kitchen, was arrested by his master's imperative voice demanding his presence, and made haste to answer the summons. The doctor was at his desk, unlocking a drawer.

'Pratt, I shall want the car to take to England on tomorrow night's Hoek boat. See about tickets and all the necessary papers, will you? Telephone Mijnheer Felman at his house and ask him to arrange it, and get that man—what was his name—to see to the insurance.'

'The name is Mulder, sir. Shall I collect them for you tomorrow?'

Pratt was already dialling a number. Dr Doelsma put his passport in his pocket and walked across to the wall safe concealed behind a small picture on it. He selected a key from the bunch in his hand, and opened the safe door, felt around inside and withdrew a small leather bag, which he transferred to a pocket; it took him a little longer to find a small leather-covered case. He opened it, and stood looking at the magnificent sapphire and diamond ring, before closing it, and transferring it likewise to the same pocket. He stood deep in thought until Pratt had finished telephoning, then said,

'Will you get hold of the Customs people first thing in the morning? I want to take the Van Beijnen pearls and a ring to England. They will be brought back within a few days. Arrange it, will you, Pratt? I'll let you have their description, and leave you a blank cheque.'

Pratt inclined his head. 'I'll see to it, sir. Mijnheer Mulder will have everything ready by about three o'clock tomorrow afternoon.'

The doctor had seated himself at his desk, and was checking his appointments book. 'I shall want Anny to pack a few things, too,' he said.

'For how long will you be gone, sir?'

The doctor met Pratt's fatherly eye with his own grey ones, and said blandly, 'That depends entirely upon Miss MacFergus. I daresay I shall telephone you within a day or so.'

Pratt allowed his elderly features to break into a smile. 'Just so, sir,' he said in a satisfied voice. Paul looked up from his desk again.

'Don't go, Pratt. Do I not have an uncle who has a slight acquaintance with the Archbishop of Canterbury?'

Pratt, who knew the doctor's family history as well as he did himself, had only to think for a moment.

'Indeed you have, sir. Your Great-Uncle Bartholomew on your mother's side. He is, if you remember, a Bishop, and must, I feel sure, carry some weight in ecclesiastical circles. I gather it is a special marriage licence you have in mind, sir?'

Dr Doelsma leaned back and surveyed the older man with twinkling eyes. His earlier rage had entirely disappeared.

'You gather correctly, Pratt, as always. How long will it take?'

'I suggest you telephone the Bishop now, sir. He should be able to expedite the matter.'

The doctor got up. 'Get him for me, will you, Pratt? I shall be in the kitchen; I want a word with Anny.'

Anny was sitting in her easy chair by the Aga, reading a magazine. She put it down as Paul entered the room, and started to get up, but he pushed her back with a gentle hand, helped himself to a slice of cake from the kitchen table, and drew up a chair to sit by her.

The housekeeper looked at him severely. 'What about your dinner, Mr Paul? Done to a turn when you got in, and you went straight to the study.'

He looked rather blankly at her. 'I forgot, Anny.' He munched his cake.

'So you missed Miss Maggy, sir.'

He reached for another piece of cake. 'Yes, Anny, I did. But not, I fancy, through any fault of mine. I shall be going over to England tomorrow. Can I leave you to see that the master bedroom is prepared for our return?'

Anny settled her glasses more firmly on her nose, 'It'll be a real pleasure, Master Paul…'

She was interrupted by the telephone and Paul went to

answer it. It was Uncle Bartholomew, who wasted several minutes discussing his arthritis, but once Paul had explained what he wanted became extremely businesslike. Paul put down the receiver at length, to encounter Anny's eyes, round with excitement.

'Do you know where Sister MacFergus is, sir?' she asked.

He stood up. 'No, Anny. I don't, but if I have the licence, we can marry wherever we meet.' He waved an airy hand, and disappeared, leaving her with her unopened magazine on her lap; her thoughts were far more interesting.

It took most of the evening to arrange for clinics and lectures to be taken by colleagues—his own patients he persuaded Dr Bennink to take over for a few days. He would have to make time to go to the hospital in the morning, before he went to Oudehof to see his mother. It was quite late when he sat down to a supper insisted upon by Anny; he sat over it a long time, thinking about Maggy.

St Ethelburga's looked grey and rather grim as Paul drew up on the courtyard the following afternoon. He got out of the car and went inside, and old George, recognising him at once, said, 'There's a letter for you, sir. Is it Sir Charles Warren you wanted to see?'

Paul asked if he might have a few minutes of the Matron's time, and while George was ringing her office, examined the entirely satisfactory contents of the envelope. Great-Uncle Bartholomew had certainly lost no time.

If Matron was surprised to see the doctor, she showed no sign of it, and it was only after a few minutes of polite conversation that she enquired if she could do anything for him. Paul shifted his bulk cautiously on the small chair. 'I should like to see Sister MacFergus, if that is possible, Matron.'

She looked faintly surprised. 'But Sister only returned from Holland the day before yesterday.'

Her tone implied that he had had ample opportunity to see her there should he have wished. 'She was due some leave, and she didn't look at all her usual self. I need her badly here, but I advised her to go to her home for a week or two.'

'May I have her address?' he asked abruptly.

Matron hesitated. 'I suppose so. Sister MacFergus made no mention of you coming...'

'I don't suppose she did,' he answered easily. 'She didn't know.'

'If I don't give it to you, Dr Doelsma, I suppose you will find someone who will—'

'Most certainly I shall, Matron.' He smiled charmingly at her.

'Very well. Her parents live in the factor's house on Aultostish estate in Inverness-shire—her father is factor to the laird.' She added dryly, 'It's about six hundred miles from here.'

He stood up. 'Fortunately I brought the car over with me. Thank you for your help, Matron. Before I go, might I visit Mrs Salt for a moment? There is something I must tell her.'

Matron nodded dumbly, wondering what on earth he could have to say to old Mrs Salt on Women's Medical. 'Can you find the way, or shall I get a porter?'

Paul held out his hand. 'I'll find my own way; and thank you again.'

Mrs Salt didn't seem very surprised to see him. She waited until he was standing by the bed and then said, "Ullo. I thought yer'd be 'ere. Sister came to see me. Wot yer done to 'er? She don't look 'erself no more.' She frowned fiercely at him.

He sat down beside her and said gently, 'I'm not quite

sure, Mrs Salt, but whatever it was it wasn't intentional. I'm on my way to see her now.'

'Ho, are yer?' The old lady spoke belligerently.

Paul ignored her cross tone, but went on, 'We shall both be here for your birthday.'

'Are yer goin' ter marry 'er?' Mrs Salt smiled for the first time.

He got up. 'Yes, Mrs Salt, before your birthday. Goodbye.' He enchanted her by lifting one of her bony hands and kissing it.

He left the car where it was and took a taxi to Simpson's, and over lunch mapped out his route. By three o'clock he was threading his way through London's suburbia, the Rolls' elegant nose pointing north. He eased the car through Welwyn, confident of making up time on the motorway ahead. He was however doomed to disappointment; an accident some way ahead had closed the road before him for some miles. Paul sat calmly at the wheel showing no sign of his raging impatience. When at last the road was clear again, he had lost almost an hour.

He drove on steadily, barely noticing the towns through which he passed—St Neots; Stamford; Grantham—and skimmed up the motorway beyond Doncaster. He had done almost a quarter of his journey, and it was seven o'clock, and he was hungry. But he didn't stop for another hour, when he pulled in for petrol at Scotch Corner and had a quick meal at the hotel, poring over his maps, committing the road to his excellent memory. With luck on his side, he should be at Maggy's home soon after breakfast. He wasn't tired; the whole of his strength and energy was concentrated on reaching her at the earliest possible moment.

It was almost nine o'clock when he set off again; four hours later he was going through Edinburgh, still with two hundred miles to go. Probably the last part of the journey would be over difficult country. He crossed the Forth Bridge, and took the A9 to Perth. It was a brilliant night, with a small slice of moon dangling amongst the stars. The road started to climb steadily; he was on the fringe of the Highlands, and there was almost no traffic. The Rolls tore ahead with effortless speed. Paul touched a switch, and the hood sank back, leaving the cold night air to rush at him; he welcomed its tonic chill, and began to whistle softly.

Paul made his way through a sleeping Perth, and on to Inverness. It was six o'clock and growing light. He stopped for petrol and found a hotel open nearby, where he shaved and washed and drank several cups of coffee while he listened to the careful instruction of the night porter. He went on out of the town, the man's directions ringing in his ears. The porter had been right; the road was a good one as far as Garve, but after that he was forced to slow his pace as he crossed the river and turned up the small hilly road to Aultdearg. He was going very slowly now, so that he would not miss the narrow dirt road which would lead him to the factor's house.

There was a wall marching with the road now, and rounding a corner Paul saw the house, tucked into the side of the lane, with its back to the hills. It looked square and solid and welcoming in the early morning sun. Paul stopped the car at its gate and looked at his watch; it was nine o'clock. He got out of the car and walked slowly up the flag-stone path to the front door. The knocker was large and old-fashioned and highly polished. It echoed through the quietness around and was finally answered by the brisk opening of a window above the doctor's head. A woman, with Maggy's eyes and Maggy's hair, looked down at him and then at the Rolls, travel-stained but still magnificent, standing at the gate.

Dr Doelsma smiled, 'Mrs MacFergus? I've come to see Maggy.'

'Aye, and a long way, by the look of ye, Doctor. I'll be down to let ye in.' She returned his smile, and disappeared, to stand before him a moment later, holding the door open.

'Maggy's out with the dogs,' she said. 'Will ye have breakfast now, and wait here?'

The doctor smiled again. 'I'll own I'm hungry, but if you would tell me where I can find her—?'

Maggy's mother twinkled at him. 'She's gone up the hill path at the back of the house—it'll stretch your legs nicely for you after the long sit ye've had in that car.'

She led him through the house and out into the garden beyond, where there was a gate opening on to a field of rough grass leading up to the wooded hills beyond. He could see the rough path winding up between the trees before it disappeared around the brow of the nearest hill, misty with threatening rain.

Maggy came over the crest of the hill, walking slowly, the dogs weaving to and fro before her, trying to attract her attention. There had been a singular lack of sticks thrown, to be caught and brought back. Maggy did not care about sticks; occasionally she said 'Good dog' or 'Go, seek,' in an absent-minded fashion, but her heart wasn't in it, and the dogs knew this. She was suffering from the bitter after-taste of something done which, however right, was against personal inclination.

She plodded on in her elderly kilt and thick sweater. The drizzle had covered her in a fine spangle of silvery drops, and the wind had whipped her hair into feathery curls. She was contemplating a day stretching emptily ahead of her, followed by other days, all equally empty. For the hundredth time she thought of Paul. The dogs gave tongue, and

Maggy abandoned her hopeless dreams to stand and look around her. Coming towards her down the other side of the glen was the doctor, covering the ground rapidly with long easy strides.

Maggy closed her eyes, and then looked again. He was still there. She stood, stunned by the fact that her dreams had all at once become reality. It was extraordinary how the mist-covered hills around her had suddenly become Paradise. She started to run down the narrow path, her heart racing in time with her feet, the dogs running on either side. The doctor had stopped and stood watching her headlong flight, to open his arms and catch her close as she reached him, apparently unshaken by the onslaught of six feet of well-rounded girl.

Maggy said into his shoulder, 'Paul! Oh, Paul! I wanted you to come so much, and you came.'

Paul tightened an arm around her, and if he found this remark, in the light of recent events, rather puzzling, he made no comment. Instead he said, 'My dear girl, naturally I came.' There was a ghost of a laugh in his voice.

'How did you find me?' She looked up at him, suddenly feeling shy. He didn't answer, but kissed her mouth with a sudden fierceness that left her breathless. When she could speak again, she said,

'I didn't mean you to find me, Paul.'

His eyes twinkled. 'My dearest goose, did you really think that a mere seven or eight hundred miles would keep me from following you?' He kissed her again, gently. 'My delightful Maggy, you have no idea what a nuisance you have been to me; do you know that I have left patients and lectures and clinics in the unwilling laps of half the medical profession in Leiden?'

'I'm sorry, Paul...do you find me very silly?'

He kissed her again in a reassuring fashion. 'No, darling. Only I don't know why you needed to run away. You're not afraid of me?'

Maggy raised an astonished face. 'Afraid of you? Paul, how could I be afraid of you when I love you?'

Paul looked at her tenderly. 'Then why, my dearest?'

'I—I didn't think you loved me…at least, once or twice I thought perhaps you did, a little, and then that night when we went out and we were talking in the kitchen and you told me about the girls you had taken out and you said that Stien would make a decorative wife…'

'So I did,' Paul agreed, 'but I don't remember saying that she was going to be my wife.'

Maggy said rather crossly, 'No, of course you didn't; but she's in Utrecht, and you practically live there.'

The grey eyes opened wide and stared down at her. 'My love, my bad-tempered little love! I have set eyes on Stien just once since she was at Oudehof, and that was when she asked me to give her a lift to a party in Utrecht because her car had broken down. I go to Utrecht because I have a home for old people there. You see, Maggy, I have a great deal of money…I bought an old house and converted it…it has taken up much of my time. But not,' he added softly, 'as much as you.' He kissed her again. 'Is that why you couldn't be found when I telephoned Oudehof from Munich?' Maggy nodded into his shoulder. 'And avoided me so cleverly at Schiphol?' he went on. Maggy nodded again.

'Will you marry me, my darling? Very soon, before you get any more ideas into your head. There is, I know, a lot of explaining to do, but I think I prefer to do it at my leisure, in the comfort of our own home.'

They smiled at each other. 'It will be very nice to come home in the evening,' said Paul, 'and find you waiting.'

He kissed her again, with an urgency that left her pink-cheeked and shaking, so that he held her gently while he said the things she had longed to hear him say. Neither of them noticed the thickening drizzle. After a time the patient dogs, at last grown impatient, got up and shook themselves, and trotted off into the trees, their tongues lolling. They looked back once as they went, but neither Paul nor Maggy had seen them go.

* * * * *